Robert Harris

ARCHANGEL

FATHERLAND

This edition published in 2000 by Cresset Editions,
an imprint of The Random House Group Ltd,
20 Vauxhall Bridge Road, London SW1V 2SA

Copyright © Robert Harris 2000
Archangel first published in 1998 by Hutchinson
Fatherland first published in 1992 by Hutchinson

Printed and bound in Germany

ISBN 0 09187 209 X

ROBERT HARRIS

Archangel

Prologue

Rapava's story

'Death solves all problems – no man, no problem.'

J. V. Stalin, 1918

LATE ONE NIGHT a long time ago – before you were even born, boy – a bodyguard stood on the verandah at the back of a big house in Moscow, smoking a cigarette. It was a cold night, without stars or moon, and he smoked for the warmth of it as much as anything else, his big, farm lad's hands cupped around the burning cardboard tube of a Georgian *papirosa*.

This bodyguard's name was Papu Rapava. He was twenty-five years old, a Mingrelian, from the north-eastern shoreland of the Black Sea. And as for the house – well, *fortress* would have been a better word. It was a tsarist mansion, half a block long, in the diplomatic sector, not far from the river. Somewhere in the frosty darkness at the bottom of the walled garden was a cherry orchard, and beyond it a wide street – Sadovaya-Kudrinskaya – and beyond that the grounds of the Moscow Zoo.

There was no traffic. Very faintly in the distance, when it was quiet, like now, and the wind was in the right direction, you could hear the howling of caged wolves.

By this time the girl had stopped screaming, which was a mercy, for it had got on Rapava's nerves. She couldn't have been more than fifteen, not much older than his own kid sister, and when he had picked her up and delivered her, she had looked at him – looked at him – well, to be honest, boy, he preferred not to talk of it, even now, nearly fifty years later.

Anyway, the girl had finally shut up and he was enjoying his cigarette when the telephone rang. This must have been about two a.m. He would never forget it. Two o'clock in the morning on the second of March, 1953. In the cold stillness of the night the bell sounded as loud as a fire alarm.

Now, normally – you have to understand this – there were four guards on duty during an evening shift: two in the house and two in the street. But when there was a girl, the Boss liked his security kept to a minimum, at least indoors, so on this particular night Rapava was alone. He threw down his cigarette, sprinted through the guard room, past the kitchen and into the hall. The phone was old-fashioned, pre-war, fastened to the wall – Holy Mother, it was making a racket! – and he grabbed the receiver mid-ring.

A man said: 'Lavrenty?'

'He's not here, comrade.'

'Get him. It's Malenkov.' The normally ponderous voice was hoarse with panic.

'Comrade –'

'Get him. Tell him something's happened. Something's happened at Blizhny.'

'KNOW what I mean by Blizhny, boy?' asked the old man.

There were two of them in the tiny bedroom, on the twenty-third floor of the Ukraina Hotel, slumped in a pair of cheap foam armchairs, so close their knees were almost touching. A bedside lamp threw their dim shadows on to the curtained window – one profile bony, picked bare by time, the other still fleshy, middle-aged.

'Yes,' said the middle-aged man, whose name was Fluke Kelso. 'Yes, I know what Blizhny means.' (*Of course I bloody know*, he felt like saying, *I did teach Soviet history at Oxford for ten bloody years –*)

Blizhny is the Russian word for 'near'. 'Near', in the Kremlin of the forties and fifties, was shorthand for the 'Near

Dacha'. And the Near Dacha was at Kuntsevo, just outside Moscow – double-perimeter fence, three hundred NKVD special troops and eight camouflaged 30-millimetre anti-aircraft guns, all hidden in the birch forest to protect the dacha's solitary, elderly resident.

Kelso waited for the old man to carry on, but Rapava was suddenly preoccupied, trying to light a cigarette from a book of matches. He couldn't manage it. His fingers couldn't grasp the flimsy sticks. He had no fingernails.

'So what did you do?' Kelso leaned across and lit Rapava's cigarette for him, hoping to mask the question with the gesture, trying to keep the excitement out of his voice. On the little table between them, hidden among the empty bottles and the dirty glasses and the ashtray and the crumpled packs of Marlboro, was a miniature cassette recorder which Kelso had put there when he thought Rapava wasn't looking. The old man sucked hard on the cigarette and then contemplated the tip with gratitude. He tossed the matches on to the floor.

'You know about Blizhny?' he said at last, settling back in his chair. 'Then you know what I did.'

Thirty seconds after answering the telephone, young Papu Rapava was knocking on Beria's door.

POLITBURO member Lavrenty Pavlovich Beria, draped in a loose red silk kimono through which his belly sloped like a great white sack of sand, called Rapava a cunt in Mingrelian, and gave him a shove in the chest that sent him stumbling backwards into the corridor. Then he pushed past him and padded off towards the stairs, his sweaty white feet leaving prints of moisture on the parquet flooring.

Through the open door, Rapava could see into the bedroom – the big wooden bed, a heavy brass lampstand in the form of a dragon, the crimson sheets, the white limbs of the girl, sprawled like a sacrifice. Her eyes were wide open, dark and vacant. She made no effort to cover herself. On the bedside table was a jug of water and an array of medicine bottles. A scattering of large white pills had fallen across the pale yellow Aubusson carpet.

He couldn't remember anything else, or exactly how long he had stood there before Beria came panting back up the stairs, all fired up by his conversation with Malenkov, throwing the girl's clothes at her, shouting at her to *get out, get out,* ordering Rapava to bring round the car.

Rapava asked who else he wanted. (He had in mind Nadaraya, the head of the bodyguard, who normally went everywhere with the Boss. And maybe Sarsikov, who at that moment was deep in a vodka stupor, snoring in the guard house at the side of the building.) At this, Beria, who had his back to Rapava and was beginning to shrug off his dressing gown, stopped for a moment, and glanced over his fleshy shoulder – thinking, thinking – you could see his little eyes flickering behind their rimless pince-nez.

'No,' he said at last. 'Just you.'

The car was American – a Packard, twelve cylinders, dark green bodywork, running-board a half-metre wide – a beauty. Rapava backed it out of the garage and reversed it down Vspolnyi Street until he was directly outside the front entrance. He left the engine running to try to get the heater going, jumped out and took up the standard NKVD position beside the rear passenger door: left hand on hip, coat and jacket pulled slightly open, shoulder holster exposed, right hand on the butt of his Makarov pistol, checking the street up and down. Beso Dumbadze, another of the Mingrelian boys, came running round the corner to see what

was going on, just as the Boss stepped out of the house and
on to the pavement.

'WHAT was he wearing?'

'What the hell do I know what he was wearing, boy?' said
the old man, irritably. 'What the hell does it matter what he
was wearing?'

ACTUALLY, now he stopped to think of it, the Boss was
wearing grey – grey coat, grey suit, grey pullover, no tie – and
what with this, and his pince-nez, and his sloping shoulders,
and his big, domed head, he looked like nothing so much as
an owl – an old, malevolent grey owl. Rapava opened the
door and Beria got in the back, and Dumbadze – who was
about ten yards away – made a little *what the fuck do I do?*
gesture with his hands, to which Rapava gave a shrug – what
the fuck did *he* know? He ran round the car to the driver's
seat, slid behind the wheel, jammed the gear stick in to first,
and they were off.

He had driven the fifteen miles out to Kuntsevo a dozen
times before, always at night and always as part of the
General Secretary's convoy – and *that* was some performance, boy, I can tell you. Fifteen cars with curtained rear
windows, half the Politburo – Beria, Malenkov, Molotov,
Bulganin, Khrushchev – plus bodyguards: out of the
Kremlin, through the Borovitskiy Gate, down the ramp,
accelerating to 75 miles an hour, the militia holding back the
traffic at every intersection, two thousand plainclothes
NKVD men lining the government route. And you never
knew which car the GenSec was in until, at the last minute,
just as they turned off the highway into the woods, one of the
big ZiLs would pull out and accelerate to the front of the

cortège, and the rest of them would all slow down to let the Rightful Heir of Lenin go in first.

But there was nothing like that tonight. The wide road was empty and once they were across the river Rapava was able to let the big Yankee car have its head, the speedo flickering up to nearly 90, while Beria sat in the back as still as a rock. After twelve minutes, the city was behind them. After fifteen, at the end of the highway from Poklonnaya Gora, they slowed for the hidden turning. The tall white strips of the silver birches strobed in the headlights.

How quiet the forest was, how dark, how limitless – like a gently rustling sea. Rapava felt that it might stretch all the way to the Ukraine. A half-mile of track took them to the first perimeter fence where a red-and-white pole lay waist-high across the road. Two NKVD specials in capes and caps carrying sub-machine guns strolled out of the sentry box, saw Beria's stone face, saluted smartly and raised the barrier. The road curved for another hundred yards, past the hunched shadows of big shrubs, and then the Packard's powerful lights picked out the second fence, a fifteen foot high wall with gun-slits. Iron gates were swung open from the inside by unseen hands.

And then the dacha.

Rapava had been expecting something unusual – he wasn't sure what – cars, men, uniforms, the bustle of a crisis. But the two-storey house was in darkness, save for one yellow lantern above the entrance. In this light, a figure waited – the unmistakable plump and dark-haired form of the Deputy Chairman of the Council of Ministers, Georgiy Maksimilanovich Malenkov. And here was an odd thing, boy: he had taken off his shiny new shoes and had them wedged under one fat arm.

8

Beria was out of the car almost before it had stopped and in a flash he had Malenkov by the elbow and was listening to him, nodding, talking quietly, looking this way and that. Rapava heard him say, 'Moved him? Have you moved him?' And then Beria snapped his fingers in Rapava's direction, and Rapava realised he was being summoned to follow them inside.

Always before on his visits to the dacha he had either waited in the car for the Boss to emerge, or had gone to the guardhouse for a drink and a smoke with the other drivers. You have to understand that *inside* was forbidden territory. Nobody except the GenSec's staff and invited guests ever went *inside*. Now, moving into the hall, Rapava suddenly felt almost suffocated by panic – physically choked, as if someone had their hands around his windpipe.

Malenkov was walking ahead in his stockinged feet and even the Boss was on tiptoe, so Rapava played follow-my-leader and tried not to make a sound. Nobody else was about. The house seemed empty. The three of them crept down a passage, past an upright piano, and into a dining room with chairs for eight. The light was on. The curtains were drawn. There were some papers on the table, and a rack of Dunhill pipes. A wind-up gramophone was in one corner. Above the fireplace was a blown up black and white photograph in a cheap wooden frame: the GenSec as a younger man, sitting in a garden somewhere on a sunny day with Comrade Lenin. At the far end of the room was a door. Malenkov turned to them and put a pudgy finger to his lips, then opened it very slowly.

THE old man closed his eyes and held out his empty glass for a refill. He sighed.

'You know, boy, people criticise Stalin, but you've got to say this for him: he lived like a worker. Not like Beria – *he* thought he was a prince. But Comrade Stalin's room was a plain man's room. You've got to say that for Stalin. He was always one of us.'

CAUGHT in the draught of the opening door, a red candle flickered in the corner beneath a small icon of Lenin. The only other source of light was a shaded reading lamp on a desk. In the centre of the room was a large sofa that had been made up as a bed. A coarse brown army blanket trailed off it on to a tiger-skin rug. On the rug, on his back, breathing heavily and apparently asleep, was a short, fat, elderly, ruddy-faced man in a dirty white vest and long woollen underpants. He had soiled himself. The room was hot and stank of human waste.

Malenkov put his podgy hand to his mouth and stayed close to the door. Beria went quickly over to the rug, unbuttoned his overcoat and fell to his knees. He put his hands on Stalin's forehead and pulled back both eyelids with his thumbs, revealing sightless, bloodshot yolks.

'Josef Vissarionovich,' he said softly, 'it's Lavrenty. Dear comrade, if you can hear me, move your eyes. Comrade?' Then to Malenkov, but all the while looking at Stalin: 'And you say he could have been like this for *twenty hours?*'

Behind his palm, Malenkov made a gagging sound. There were tears on his smooth cheeks.

'Dear comrade, move your eyes . . . Your eyes, dear comrade . . . Comrade? Ah, fuck it.' Beria pulled his hands away and stood up, wiping his fingers on his coat. 'It's a stroke right enough. He's meat. Where are Starostin and the boys? And Butusova?'

Malenkov was blubbing by now and Beria had to stand between him and the body – literally had to block his view to get his attention. He grasped Malenkov by the shoulders and began talking very quietly and very fast to him, as one would to a child – told him to forget Stalin, that Stalin was history, Stalin was meat, that the important thing was what they did next, that they had to stand together. Now: where were the boys? Were they still in the guard room?

Malenkov nodded and wiped his nose on his sleeve.

'All right,' said Beria. 'This is what you do.'

Malenkov was to put on his shoes and go tell the guards that Comrade Stalin was sleeping, that he was drunk and why the fuck had he and Comrade Beria been dragged out of their beds for nothing? He was to tell them not to touch the telephone, and not to call any doctors. ('You listening, Georgiy?') Especially no doctors, because the GenSec thought all doctors were Jewish poisoners – remember? Now, what was the time? Three? All right. At eight – no, better, seven-thirty – Malenkov was to start calling the leadership. He was to say that he and Beria wanted a full Politburo meeting here, at Blizhny, at nine. He was to say they were worried about Josef Vissarionovich's health and that a collective decision on treatment was necessary.

Beria rubbed his hands. 'That should start them shitting themselves. Now let's get him up on the couch. You,' he said to Rapava. 'Get hold of his legs.'

THE old man had been sinking deeper into his chair as he talked, his feet sprawled, his eyes shut, his voice a monotone. Suddenly he let out a long breath and hauled himself upright again. He looked around the hotel bedroom in a panic. 'Need to have a piss, boy. Gotta piss.'

'In there.'

He rose with a drunk's careful dignity. Through the flimsy wall, Kelso heard the sound of his urine drilling into the back of the toilet bowl. Fair enough, he thought. There was a lot to unload. He had been lubricating Rapava's memory for the best part of four hours by now: Baltika beer first, in the Ukraina's lobby bar, then Zubrovka in a café across the street, and finally single-malt Scotch in the cramped intimacy of his room. It was like playing a fish: playing a fish through a river of booze. He noticed the book of matches lying on the floor where Rapava had thrown it and he reached down and picked it up. On the back flap was the name of a bar or a nightclub – ROBOTNIK – and an address near the Dinamo Stadium. The lavatory flushed and Kelso quickly slipped the matches into his pocket, then Rapava reappeared, leaning against the door jamb, buttoning his flies.

'What's the time, boy?'

'Nearly one.'

'Gotta go. They'll think I'm your fucking boyfriend.' Rapava made an obscene gesture with his hand.

Kelso pretended to laugh. Sure, he'd call down for a taxi in a minute. Sure. But let's just finish this bottle first – he reached over for the Scotch and surreptitiously checked that the tape was still running – finish the bottle, comrade, *and finish the story.*

The old man scowled and looked at the floor. The story was finished already. There was nothing more to say. They got Stalin up on to the couch – so, what of it? Malenkov went off to talk to the guards. Rapava drove Beria home. Everyone knows the rest. A day or two later, Stalin was dead. And not long after that, Beria was dead. Malenkov – well, Malenkov hung around for years after his disgrace (Rapava saw him once, in the seventies, shuffling through the Arbat) but now even Malenkov was dead. Nadaraya, Sarsikov, Dumbadze, Starostin, Butusova – dead, dead. The Party was dead. The whole fucking country was dead, come to that.

'But there's more to your story, surely,' said Kelso. 'Please sit down Papu Gerasimovich, and let us finish the bottle.'

He spoke politely and hesitantly, for he sensed that the anaesthetic of alcohol and vanity might be wearing off, and that Rapava, on coming round, might suddenly realise he was talking far too much. He felt another spasm of irritation. Christ, they were always so bloody *difficult*, these old NKVD men – difficult and maybe even still *dangerous*. Kelso was a historian, in his middle forties, thirty years younger than Papu Rapava. But he was out of condition – to be truthful, he had never really been *in* condition – and he wouldn't have fancied his chances if the old man turned rough. Rapava, after all, was a survivor of the Arctic Circle camps. He wouldn't have forgotten how to hurt someone – hurt someone very quickly, guessed Kelso, and probably very badly.

He filled Rapava's glass, topped up his own, and forced himself to keep on talking.

'I mean, here you are, twenty-five years old, in the General Secretary's bedroom. You couldn't get any closer to the centre than that – that was the inner sanctum, that was *sacred*. So what was Beria up to, taking you in there?'

'You deaf, boy? I said. He needed me to move the body.'

'But why you? Why not one of Stalin's regular guards? It was they who'd found him, after all, and alerted Malenkov in the first place. Or why didn't Beria take one of his more senior boys out to Blizhny? Why did he specifically take *you*?'

Rapava was swaying, staring now at the glass of Scotch,

and afterwards Kelso decided that the whole night really turned upon this one thing: that Rapava needed another drink, and he needed it at that precise instant, and he needed these two things in combination more than he needed to leave. He came back and sat down heavily, drained the glass in one, then held it out to be filled again.

'Papu Rapava,' continued Kelso, pouring another three fingers of scotch. 'Nephew of Avksenty Rapava, Beria's oldest crony in the Georgian NKVD. Younger than the others on the staff. A new boy in the city. Maybe a little more naïve than the rest? Am I right? Precisely the sort of eager young fellow the Boss might have looked at and thought: *yes, I could use him, I could use Rapava's boy, he would keep a secret.'*

The silence lengthened and deepened until it was almost tangible, as if someone had come into the room and joined them. Rapava's head began to rock from side to side, then he leaned forward and clasped the back of his scrawny neck with his hands, staring at the worn carpet. His grey hair was cropped close to his skull. An old, puckered scar ran from his crown almost to his temple. It looked as if it had been stitched up by a blind man using string. And those fingers: blackened yellow tips and not a nail on one of them.

'Turn off your machine, boy,' he said, quietly. He nodded towards the table. 'Turn it off. Now take out the tape – that's it – and leave it where I can see it.'

COMRADE Stalin was only a short man – five foot four – but he was heavy. Holy Mother, he was heavy! It was as if he wasn't made of fat and bone, but of some denser stuff. They dragged him across the wooden floor, his head lolling and banging on the polished blocks, and then they had to lever him up, legs first. Rapava noticed – couldn't help noticing, as they were almost in his face – that the second and third toes of the GenSec's left foot were webbed – the Devil's mark – and when the others weren't looking, he crossed himself.

'Now, young comrade,' said Beria, when Malenkov had gone, 'do you like standing on the ground, or would you prefer to be under it?'

At first, Rapava couldn't believe he had heard properly. That was when he knew his life would never be the same again, and that he'd be lucky to survive this night. He whispered, 'I like standing on it, Boss.'

'Good lad.' Beria made a pincer of his thumb and forefinger. 'We need to find a key. About so big. Looks like the sort of key you might use to wind a clock. He keeps it on a brass ring with a piece of string attached. Check his clothes.'

The familiar grey tunic was hanging off the back of a chair. Grey pants were neatly folded over it. Beside them was a pair of high black cavalry boots, their heels built up an inch or so. Rapava's limbs moved jerkily. What kind of dream was this? The Father and Teacher of the Soviet People, the Inspirer and Organiser of the Victory of Communism, the Leader of All Progressive Humanity, with half his iron brain destroyed, lying filthy on the sofa, while the two of them went through his room like a pair of thieves? Nevertheless, he did as he was ordered and started on the tunic while Beria attacked the desk with an old Chekist's skill – pulling out drawers, upending them, scavenging through their contents, sweeping back the detritus and replacing them on their runners.

There was nothing in the tunic and nothing in the trousers, either, apart from a soiled handkerchief, brittle with dried phlegm. By now, Rapava's eyes had grown used to the gloom, and he was better able to see his surroundings. On one wall was a large Chinese print of a tiger. On another – and this was the strangest thing of all – Stalin had stuck up photographs of children. Toddlers, mostly. Not proper prints, but pictures roughly torn out of magazines and newspapers. There must have been a couple of dozen of them.

'Anything?'

'No, Boss.'

'Try the couch.'

They had put Stalin on his back, with his hands folded on his paunch, and you'd have thought the old fellow was merely asleep. His breathing was heavy. He was almost snoring. Close up, he didn't look much like his pictures. His face was mottled red and fleshy, pitted with shallow cratered scars. His moustache and eyebrows were whitish grey. You could see his scalp through his thin hair. Rapava leaned over him – ah! the smell: it was as if he were already rotting – and slid his hand down into the gap between the cushions and the sofa's back. He worked his fingers all the way down, leaning left towards the GenSec's feet then moving right again, up towards the head until, at last, the tip of his forefinger touched something hard and he had to stretch to retrieve it, his arm pressing gently against Stalin's chest.

And then – an awful thing: the most horrible, terrible thing. As he withdrew the key and called in a whisper to the Boss, the GenSec gave a grunt and his eyes jerked open – an animal's yellow eyes, full of rage and fear. Even Beria faltered when he saw them. No other part of the body moved, but a kind of straining growl came from the throat. Hesitantly, Beria came closer and peered down at him, then passed his hand in front of Stalin's eyes. That seemed to give him an idea. He took the key from Rapava and let it dangle at the end of its cord a few inches above Stalin's face. The yellow eyes locked on to it at once, and followed it, never left it, through all the points of the compass. Beria, smiling now, let it circle slowly for at least half a minute, then abruptly snatched it away and caught it in his palm. He closed his fingers around it and offered his clenched fist to Stalin.

Such a sound, boy! More animal than human! It pursued Rapava out of that room and along the passage and down all the years, from that night to this.

THE bottle of Scotch was drained and Kelso was on his knees now before the mini-bar like a priest before his altar. He wondered how his hosts at the historical symposium would feel when they got the bar bill, but that was less important right now than the task of keeping the old man fuelled and talking. He pulled out handfuls of miniatures – vodka, more Scotch, gin, brandy, something German made of cherries – and cradled them across the room to the table. As he sat down and released them a couple of bottles rolled on to the floor but Rapava paid them no heed. He wasn't an old man in the Ukraina any more; he was back in fifty-three – a frightened twenty-five-year-old at the wheel of a dark green Packard, the highway to Moscow shining white in the headlights before him, Lavrenty Beria rocklike in the rear.

THE big car flew along the Kutuzovskiy Prospekt and through the silent sweep of the western suburbs. At three-thirty it crossed the Moskva at the Borodinskiy Bridge and headed at speed towards the Kremlin, entering through the south-western gate on the opposite side to Red Square.

Once they had been waved inside, Beria leaned forward

and gave Rapava directions – left past the Armoury, then sharp right through a narrow entrance into an inner courtyard. There were no windows, just half a dozen small doors. The icy cobbles in the darkness glowed crimson like wet blood. Looking up, Rapava saw they were beneath a giant red neon star.

Beria was quickly through one of the doors and Rapava had to scramble to follow him. A little flagstoned passage took them to a cage-lift that was older than the Revolution. A rattle of iron and the drone of an engine accompanied their slow ascent through two silent, unlit floors. They jolted to a stop and Beria wrenched back the gate. Then he was off again, down the corridor, walking fast, swinging the key on the end of its length of string.

Don't ask me where we went, boy, because I can't tell you. There was a long, carpeted corridor lined with fancy busts on marble pedestals, then an iron spiral staircase which had to be climbed down, and then a huge ballroom, as vast as an ocean liner, with giant mirrors ten yards high, and fancy gilt chairs set around the walls. Finally, not long after the ballroom, came a wide corridor with lime-green, shiny plaster, a floor that smelt of wood-polish and a big, heavy door that Beria unlocked with a key he kept in a bunch on a chain.

Rapava followed him in. The door, on an old imperial pneumatic hinge, closed slowly behind them.

It wasn't much of an office. Eight yards by six. It might have done for some factory director at the arse-end of Vologda or Magnitogorsk – a desk with a couple of telephones, a bit of carpet on the floor, a table and a few chairs, a heavily-curtained window. On the wall was one of those big, pink, roll-up maps of the USSR – this was back in

the days when there *was* a USSR – and next to the map was
another, smaller door, to which Beria immediately headed.
Again, he had a key. The door opened into a kind of walk-in
cupboard in which there was a blackened samovar, a bottle of
Armenian brandy and some stuff for making herbal teas.
There was also a wall-safe, with a sturdy brass front on which
was a manufacturer's label – not in Russian Cyrillic but in
some western language. The safe wasn't very big – a foot
across, if that. Square. Well fashioned. Straight handle, also
brass.

Beria noticed Rapava staring at it and told him roughly to
clear off back outside.

NEARLY an hour passed.

Standing in the corridor, Rapava tried to keep himself
alert, practising drawing his pistol, imagining every little
creak of the great building was a footstep, every moan of
wind a voice. He tried to picture the GenSec striding down
this wide, polished corridor in his cavalry boots, and then he
tried to reconcile that image with the ruined figure lying
imprisoned in his own rancid flesh out at Blizhny.

And you know something, boy? I cried. I might have cried
a bit for myself as well – I can't deny it, I was scared – I was
shitless – but really I cried for Comrade Stalin. I cried more
over Stalin than I did when my own father died. And that
goes for most of the boys I knew.

A distant bell chimed four.

At around half-past, Beria at last emerged. He was
carrying a small leather satchel stuffed with something –
papers, certainly, but there might have been other objects:
Rapava couldn't tell. The contents, presumably, had come
from the safe, and the satchel might have come from there,

too. Or it might have come from the office. Or it might –
Rapava couldn't swear to this, but it was possible – it might
have been in Beria's hand right from the moment he got out
of the car. At any rate, he had what he wanted, and he was
smiling.

Smiling?

Like I say, boy. Yes – smiling. Not a smile of pleasure, mark
you. More a kind of –

Rueful?

– That's it, a rueful kind of smile. A would-you-fucking-
believe-it? kind of a smile. Like he'd just been beaten at cards.

They went back the way they had come, only this time in
the bust-lined passage they ran into a guard. He practically
dropped to his knees when he saw the Boss. But Beria just
dead-eyed the man and kept on walking – the coolest piece
of thievery you ever saw. In the car he said, 'Vspolnyi Street.'

By now it was nearly five, still dark, but the trams had
started running and there were people on the streets –
babushkas, mostly, who had cleaned the government offices
under the Tsar and under Lenin, and who, after tomorrow,
would be cleaning them under somebody else. Outside the
Lenin Library a vast poster of Stalin, in red, white and black,
gazed down upon a line of workers queuing outside the
metro station. Beria had the satchel open on his lap. His head
was bent. The interior light was on. He was reading
something, tapping his fingers with anxiety.

'Is there a shovel in the back?' he asked, suddenly.

Rapava said there was. For snowdrifts.

'And a toolbox?'

'Yes, Boss.' A big one: car jack, wheel wrench, wheel nuts,
spare starting handle, spark plugs . . .

Beria grunted and returned his attention to his reading.

*

BACK at the house, the surface of the ground was diamond-hard, set with glittering points of ice, much too hard for the shovel, and Rapava had to hunt around the outbuildings at the bottom of the garden for a pick-axe. He took off his coat and wielded the axe like he used to when he worked his father's patch of Georgian dirt, bringing it down in a great smooth arc over his head, letting the weight and the velocity of the tool do the job, the edge of the blade burying itself in the frozen earth almost to the shaft. He wrestled it back and forth and pulled it free, adjusted his stance, then brought it down again.

He worked in the little cherry orchard by the light of a hurricane lamp suspended from a nearby branch, and he worked at a frantic pace, conscious that in the darkness behind him, invisible on the far side of the light, Beria was sitting on a stone bench watching him. Soon he was sweating so heavily that despite the March cold he had to stop and take off his jacket and roll up his sleeves. A large patch of his shirt was stuck to his back and he had an involuntary memory of other men doing this while he nursed his rifle and watched – other men on a much hotter day, hacking away at the ground in a forest, then lying obediently on their faces in the freshly dug earth. He remembered the smell of moist soil and the hot drowsy silence of the wood and he wondered how cold it would be if Beria made him lie down now.

A voice came out of the darkness. 'Don't make it so wide. It's not a grave. You're making work for yourself.'

After a while, he began alternating between the axe and the shovel, hacking off chunks of earth and jumping into the hole to clear the debris. At first the ground came up to his knees, and then it lapped his waist, and finally it was at his chest – at which point Beria's moon face appeared above him and told him to stop, that he had done well, it was enough. The Boss was actually smiling and held out his hand to pull Rapava from the hole, and Rapava at that moment, as he grasped that soft palm, was filled with such love – such a surge of gratitude and devotion: he would never feel anything like it again.

It was as comrades, in Rapava's memory, that they each took hold of one end of the long metal toolbox and lowered it into the ground. They kicked the earth in after it, stamped it tight, and then Rapava hammered the mound flat with the back of the shovel and scattered dead leaves over the site. By the time they turned to walk across the lawn to the house, the faintest gleams of grey were beginning to infiltrate the eastern sky.

BETWEEN them, Kelso and Rapava had drained the miniatures and had moved on to a kind of home-made pepper vodka, which the old man had produced from a battered tin flask. God alone knew what he had made it from. It could have been shampoo. He sniffed it, sneezed, then winked and poured a brimming, oily glass for Kelso. It was the colour of a pigeon's breast and Kelso felt his stomach lurch.

'And Stalin died,' he said, trying to avoid taking a sip. His words slurred into one another. His jaw was numb.

'And Stalin died.' Rapava shook his head in sorrow. He suddenly leaned forward and clinked glasses. 'To Comrade Stalin!'

'To Comrade Stalin!'

They drank.

AND Stalin died. And everyone went mad with grief. Everyone, that is, except Comrade Beria, who delivered his eulogy to the thousands of hysterical mourners in Red Square like he was reading a railway announcement, and had a good laugh about it afterwards with the boys.

Word of this got around.

Now Beria was a clever man, much cleverer even than you are, boy – he'd have eaten you for breakfast. But clever people all make one mistake. They all think everyone else is stupid. And everyone isn't stupid. They just take a bit more time, that's all.

The Boss thought he was going to be in power for twenty years. He lasted three months.

It was late one morning in June and Rapava was on duty with the usual team – Nadaraya, Sarsikov, Dumbadze – when word came through that there was a special meeting of the Presidium in Malenkov's office in the Kremlin. And because it was at Malenkov's place, the Boss thought nothing of it. Who was fat Malenkov? Fat Malenkov was nothing. He was just a dumb brown bear. The Boss had Malenkov on the end of a rope.

So when he got in to the car to go to the meeting, he wasn't even wearing a tie, just an open-necked shirt and a worn-out old suit. Why should he wear a tie? It was a hot day and Stalin was dead and Moscow was full of girls and he was going to be in power for twenty years.

The cherry orchard at the bottom of the garden had not long finished flowering.

They arrived at Malenkov's building and the Boss went upstairs to see him, while the rest of them sat around in the ante-room by the entrance. And one by one the big guys arrived, all the comrades Beria used to laugh about behind their backs – old 'Stone Arse' Molotov and that fat peasant Khrushchev and the ninny Voroshilov, and finally Marshal Zhukov, the puffed-up peacock, with his boards of tin and ribbon. They all went upstairs and Nadaraya rubbed his hands and said to Rapava: 'Now then, Papu Gerasimovich, why don't you go to the canteen and get us some coffee?'

The day passed and from time to time Nadaraya would wander upstairs to see what was happening, and always he came back with the same message: meeting still in progress. And again: so what? It wasn't unusual for the Presidium to sit for hours. But by eight o'clock, the chief of the bodyguard was starting to look worried and, at ten, with the summer darkness gathering, he told them all to follow him upstairs.

They crashed straight past Malenkov's protesting secretaries and into the big room. It was empty. Sarsikov tried the phones and they were dead. One of the chairs had been tipped back and on the floor around it were some folded scraps of paper, on each of which, in red ink, in Beria's writing, was the single word 'Alarm!'

THEY could have made a fight of it, perhaps, but what would have been the point? The whole thing was an ambush, a Red Army operation. Zhukov had even brought up tanks – stationed twenty T34s at the back of the Boss's house (Rapava heard this later). There were armoured cars inside the Kremlin. It was hopeless. They wouldn't have lasted five minutes.

The boys were split up there and then. Rapava was taken to a military prison in the northern suburbs where they proceeded to beat ten kinds of shit out of him, accused him of procuring little girls, showed him witness statements and photographs of the victims and finally a list of thirty names that Sarsikov (great big swaggering Sarsikov – some tough guy *he* turned out to be) had written down for them on the second day.

Rapava said nothing. The whole thing made him sick.

And then, one night, about ten days after the coup – for a coup was how Rapava would always think of it – he was patched up and given a wash and a clean prison uniform and taken up in handcuffs to the director's office to meet some big shot from the Ministry of State Security. He was a tough-looking, miserable bastard, aged between forty and fifty – said he was a Deputy Minister – and he wanted to talk about Comrade Stalin's private papers.

Rapava was handcuffed to the chair. The guards were sent out of the room. The Deputy Minister sat behind the director's desk. There was a picture of Stalin on the wall behind him.

It seems, said the Deputy Minister – after looking at Rapava for a while – that Comrade Stalin, in recent years, to assist him in his mighty tasks, had got into the habit of making notes. Sometimes these notes were confided to ordinary sheets of writing paper and sometimes to an exercise book with a black oilskin cover. The existence of these notes was known only to certain members of the Presidium, and to Comrade Poskrebyshev, Comrade Stalin's long-standing secretary, whom the traitor Beria recently had falsely imprisoned on fraudulent charges. All witnesses agree that Comrade Stalin kept these papers in a personal safe in his private office, to which he alone had the key.

The Deputy Minister leaned forwards. His dark eyes searched Rapava's face.

Following Comrade Stalin's tragic death, attempts were made to locate this key. It could not be found. It was therefore agreed by the Presidium to have this safe broken into, in the presence of them all, to see if Comrade Stalin had left behind material that might be of historical value, or which might assist the Central Committee in its stupendous responsibility of appointing Comrade Stalin's successor.

The safe was duly broken open, under the supervision of the Presidium, and found to be empty, apart from a few minor items, such as Comrade Stalin's party card.

'And now,' said the Deputy Minister, getting slowly to his feet, 'we come to the crux of the matter.'

He walked around and sat on the edge of the desk directly in front of Rapava. Oh, he was a big bastard, boy, a fleshy tank.

We know, he said, from Comrade Malenkov that in the early hours of the second of March, you went to the Kuntsevo dacha in the company of the traitor, Beria, and that you were both left alone with Comrade Stalin for several minutes. Was anything removed from the room?

No, comrade.

Nothing at all?

No, comrade.

And where did you go when you left Kuntsevo?

I drove Comrade Beria back to his house, comrade.

Directly back to his house?

Yes, comrade.

You are lying.

No, comrade.

You are lying. We have a witness who saw you both inside the Kremlin shortly before dawn. A sentry who met you in a corridor.

Yes, comrade. I remember now. Comrade Beria said he needed to collect something from his office –

Something from Comrade Stalin's office!

No, comrade.

You are lying! You are a traitor! You and the English spy Beria broke into Stalin's office and stole his papers! Where are those papers?

No, comrade –

Traitor! Thief! Spy!

Each word accompanied by a punch in the face.

And so on.

I'LL tell you something, boy. Nobody knows the full truth of what happened to the Boss, even now – even after Gorbachev and Yeltsin have sold off our whole fucking birthright to the capitalists and let the CIA go picnicking in our files. The papers on the Boss are still closed. They smuggled him out of the Kremlin on the floor of a car, rolled up in a carpet, and some say Zhukov shot him that very night. Others say they shot him the following week. Most say they kept him alive for five months – *five months!* – sweated him in a bunker underneath the Moscow Military District – and shot him after a secret trial.

Either way, they shot him. He was dead by Christmas Day.

And this is what they did to me.

Rapava held up his mutilated fingers and wiggled them. Then he clumsily unbuttoned his shirt, pulled it from the waistband of his pants, and twisted his scrawny torso to show his back. His vertebrae were criss-crossed with shiny roughened panes of scar-tissue – translucent windows on to the flesh beneath. His stomach and chest were whorls of blue-black tattoos.

Kelso didn't speak. Rapava sat back leaving his shirt unbuttoned. His scars and his tattoos were the medals of his lifetime. He was proud to wear them.

NOT a word, boy. You listening? They did not get. One. Single. Word.

Throughout it all, he didn't know if the Boss was still alive, or if the Boss was talking. But it didn't matter: Papu Gerasimovich Rapava, at least, would hold his silence.

Why? Was it loyalty? A bit, perhaps – the memory of that reprieving hand. But he wasn't such a young fool that he didn't also realise that silence was his only hope. How long do you think they'd have let him live if he'd led them to that place? It was his own death warrant he'd buried under that tree. So, softly, softly: not a word.

He lay shivering on the floor of his unheated cell as the winter came and dreamed of cherry trees, the leaves dying and falling now, the branches dark against the sky, the howling of the wolves.

And then, around Christmas, like bored children, they suddenly seemed to lose interest in the whole business. The beating went on for a while – by now it was a matter of honour on both sides, you must understand – but the questions stopped, and finally, after one prolonged and imaginative session, the beating stopped as well. The Deputy Minister never came again and Rapava guessed that Beria must be dead. He also guessed that someone had decided that Stalin's papers, if they did exist, were better left unread.

Rapava expected to get his seven grams of lead at any moment. It never occurred to him that he wouldn't, not after Beria had been liquidated. So of his journey, in a snowstorm, to the Red Army building on Kommissariat Street, and of the makeshift courtroom, with its high, barred windows and its troika of judges, he remembered nothing. He blanked his mind with snow. He watched it through the window, advancing in waves up the Moskva and along the embankment, smothering the afternoon lights on the opposite side of the river – high white columns of snow on a death march from the east. Voices droned around him. Later, when it was dark and he was being taken outside, he assumed to be shot, he asked if he could stop for a minute on the steps and bury his hands in the drifts. A guard asked why, and Rapava said: 'To feel snow between my fingers one last time, comrade.'

They laughed a lot at that. But when they found out he was serious they laughed a whole lot more. 'If there's one thing you'll never go hungry for, Georgian,' they told him, as they pushed him into the back of the van, 'it's snow.' That was how he learned he had been sentenced to fifteen years' hard labour in the Kolyma territory.

KHRUSHCHEV amnestied a whole bunch of Gulag prisoners in fifty-six, but nobody amnestied Papu Rapava. Papu Rapava was forgotten. Papu Rapava alternately rotted and froze in the forests of Siberia for the next decade and a half – rotted in the short summer, when each man worked in his own private fever-cloud of mosquitoes, and froze in the long winter when the ice made rock of the swamps.

They say that people who survive the camps all look alike because, once a man's skeleton has been exposed, it doesn't matter how well-padded his flesh subsequently becomes, or how carefully he dresses – the bones will always poke through. Kelso had interviewed enough Gulag survivors in his time to recognise the camp skeleton in Rapava's face even now, as he talked, in the sockets of his eyes and in the crack of his jaw. He could see it in the hinges of his wrists and ankles, and the flat blade of his sternum.

He wasn't amnestied, Rapava was saying, because he killed

a man, a Chechen, who tried to sodomise him – gutted him with a shank he'd made from a piece of saw.

And what happened to your head? said Kelso.

Rapava fingered the scar. He couldn't remember. Sometimes, when it was especially cold, the scar ached and gave him dreams.

What kind of dreams?

Rapava showed the dark glint of his mouth. He wouldn't say.

Fifteen years . . .

They returned him to Moscow in the summer of sixty-nine, on the day the Yankees put a man on the moon. Rapava left the ex-prisoners' hostel and wandered round the hot and crowded streets and couldn't make sense of anything. Where was Stalin? That was what amazed him. Where were the statues and the pictures? Where was the respect? The boys all looked like girls and the girls all looked like whores. Clearly, the country was already halfway in the shit. But still – you have to say – at least in those days there were jobs for everyone, even for old *zeki* like him. They sent him to the engine sheds at the Leningrad Station, to work as a labourer. He was only forty-one and as strong as a bear. Everything he had in the world was in a cardboard suitcase.

Did he ever marry?

Rapava shrugged. Sure, he married. That was the way you got an apartment. He married and got himself fixed up with a place.

And what happened? Where was she?

She died. It was a decent block in those days, boy, before the drugs and the crime.

Where was his place?

Fucking criminals . . .

And children?

A son. He died as well. In Afghanistan. And a daughter.

His daughter was dead?

No. She was a whore.

And Stalin's papers?

Drunk as he was, there was no way Kelso could make *that* question casual and the old man shot him a crafty look; a peasant's look.

Rapava said softly, 'Go on, boy. Yes? And Stalin's papers? What about Stalin's papers?'

Kelso hesitated.

'Only that if they still existed – if there was a chance – a possibility –'

'You'd want to see them?'

'Of course.'

Rapava laughed.

'And why should I help you, boy? Fifteen years in Kolyma, and for what? To help you spin more lies? For love?'

'No. Not for love. For history.'

'For history? Do me a favour, boy!'

'All right – for money, then.'

'What?'

'For money. A share in the profits. A lot of money.'

The peasant Rapava stroked the side of his nose.

'How much money?'

'A lot. If this is true. If we could find them. Believe me: a lot of money.'

THE momentary silence was broken by the sound of voices in the corridor, voices talking in English, and Kelso guessed who this would be: his fellow historians – Adelman, Duberstein and the rest – coming back late from dinner, wondering where he'd got to. It suddenly seemed overwhelmingly important to him that no one else – least of all his colleagues – should know anything at all about Papu Rapava.

Someone tapped softly on the door and he held up a warning hand to the old man. Very quietly he reached over and turned off the bedside lamp.

They sat together and listened to the whispers, magnified by the darkness but still muffled and indistinct. There was another knock, and then a splutter of laughter, hushed by the others. Maybe they had seen the light go out. Perhaps they thought he was with a woman – such was his reputation.

After a few more seconds, the voices faded and the corridor was silent again. Kelso turned on the light. He smiled and patted his heart. The old man's face was a mask, but then he smiled and began to sing – he had a quavering, unexpectedly melodious voice –

> *Kolyma, Kolyma,*
> *What a wonderful place!*
> *Twelve months of winter*
> *Summer all the rest . . .*

AFTER his release, he was this and no more: Papu Rapava, railway worker, who had done a spell in the camps, and if anyone wanted to take it further – well? yes? come on, then, comrade! – he was always ready with his fists or an iron spike.

Two men watched him from the start. Antipin, who was a foreman in the Lenin No. 1 shed, and a cripple in the downstairs flat called Senka. And they were as pretty a pair of canaries as you could ever hope to meet. You could practically hear them singing to the KGB before you were out of the room. The others came and went – the men on foot, the men in parked cars, the men asking 'routine questions, comrade' – but Antipin and Senka were the faithful watchers, though they never got a thing, neither of them. Rapava had buried his past in a hole far deeper than the one he'd dug for Beria.

Senka died five years ago. He never knew what became of Antipin. The Lenin No. 1 shed was now the property of a private collective, importing French wine.

Stalin's papers, boy? Who gives a shit? He wasn't afraid of anything any more.

A lot of money, you say? Well, well –

He leaned over and spat into the ashtray, then seemed to fall asleep. After a while, he muttered, My lad died. Did I tell you that?

Yes.

He died in a night ambush on the road to Mazar-i-Sharif. One of the last to be sent. Killed by stone-age devils with blackened faces and Yankee missiles. Could anyone imagine Stalin letting the country be humiliated by such savages? Think of it! He'd have crushed them into dust and scattered the powder in Siberia! After the lad was gone, Rapava took to walking. Great long hikes that could last a day and a night. He criss-crossed the city, from Perovo to the lakes, from Bittsevskiy Park to the Television Tower. And on one of these walks – it must have been six or seven years ago, around the time of the coup – he found himself walking into one of his own dreams. Couldn't figure it out at first. Then he realised he was on Vspolnyi Street. He got out of there fast. His lad was a radio man in a tank unit. Liked fiddling with radios. No fighter.

And the house? said Kelso. Was the house still standing?

He was nineteen.

And the house? What had happened to the house?

Rapava's head drooped.

The *house,* comrade –

There was a red sickle moon, and a single red star. And the place was guarded by devils with blackened faces –

KELSO could get no more sense out of him after that. The old man's eyelids fluttered and closed. His mouth slackened. Yellow saliva leaked across his cheek.

Kelso watched him for a minute or two, feeling the pressure build in his stomach, then rose suddenly from his chair and moved as quickly as he could to the lavatory, where he was violently and copiously sick. He rested his hot forehead against the cold enamel bowl and licked his lips. His tongue felt huge to him, and bitter, like a swollen piece of black fruit. There was something stuck in his throat. He tried to clear it by coughing but that didn't work so he tried swallowing and was promptly sick again. When he pulled his head back, the bathroom fixtures seemed to have detached themselves from their moorings and to be revolving around him in a slow tribal dance. A line of silver mucus extended in a shimmering arc from his nose to the toilet seat.

Endure, he told himself. This, too, will pass.

He clutched again at the cool white bowl, a drowning man, as the horizon tilted and the room darkened, slid –

A RUSTLE in the blackness of his dreams. A pair of yellow eyes.

'Who are you,' said Stalin, 'to steal my private papers?'

He sprang from his couch like a wolf.

KELSO jerked awake and cracked his head on the protruding lip of the bath. He groaned and rolled on to his back, dabbing at his skull for signs of blood. He was sure he felt some tacky liquid, but when he brought his fingers up close to his eyes and squinted at them they were clean.

As always, even now, even as he lay sprawled on the floor of a Moscow bathroom, there was a part of him that remained mercilessly sober, like the wounded captain on the bridge of a stricken ship, calling calmly through the smoke of battle for damage assessments. This was the part of him which concluded that, bad as he felt, he had – amazingly – sometimes felt worse. And this was the part of him that also heard, beyond the dusty thump of his pulse, the creak of a footstep and the click of a door being quietly closed.

Kelso set his jaw and rose, by force of will, through all the stages of human evolution – from the slime of the floor, to his hands and knees, to a kind of shuffling, simian crouch – and propelled himself into the empty bedroom. Grey light seeped through thin orange curtains and lit the detritus of the night. The sour reek of spilled booze and stale smoke made his stomach coil. Still – and there was heroism as well as desperation in the effort – he headed for the door.

'Papu Gerasimovich! Wait!'

The corridor was dim and deserted. From the end of it, around the corner, came the ping of an arriving elevator. Wincing, Kelso loped towards it, arriving just in time to see the doors close. He tried to prise them open with his fingers, shouting into the crevice for Rapava to come back. He punched the call button with the heel of his hand a few times, but nothing happened so he took the stairs. He got as far as the twenty-first floor before he acknowledged he was beaten. He stopped on the landing and summoned the express elevator, and stood there waiting for it, leaning against the wall, breathless, nauseous, with a knife behind his eyes. The car was a long time coming and when, at last, it did arrive, it promptly took him back up the two floors he had just run down. The doors slid open mockingly on to the empty passage.

By the time Kelso reached ground level, his ears popping from the speed of his descent, Rapava was gone. In the marble vault of the Ukraina's reception there was nobody about except for a babushka, hoovering ash from the red carpet, and a platinum-blonde hooker with a fake sable curled over her shoulders, arguing with a security man. As he made for the entrance he was aware that all three had stopped what they were doing and were staring at him. He put his hand to his forehead. He was dripping with sweat.

It was cold outside and barely light. A sharp October morning. A damp chill rising off the river. Yet already the rush-hour traffic was beginning to build along the Kutuzovskiy Prospekt, backing up from the Kalininskiy Bridge. He walked on for a while until he came to the main road, and there he stood for a minute or two, shivering in his shirtsleeves. There was no sign of Rapava. Along the sidewalk to his right, an old grey dog, big and half-starved, went slouching past the heavy buildings, heading east, towards the waking city.

Part One

Moscow

'To choose one's victims, to prepare one's plans minutely,
to slake an implacable vengeance, and then to go to bed . . .
there is nothing sweeter in the world.'

J. V. Stalin
in conversation with Kamenev and Dzerzhinsky

Chapter One

OLGA KOMAROVA OF the Russian Archive Service, Rosarkhiv, wielding a collapsible pink umbrella, prodded and shooed her distinguished charges across the Ukraina's lobby towards the revolving door. It was an old door, of heavy wood and glass, too narrow to cope with more than one body at a time, so the scholars formed a line in the dim light, like parachutists over a target zone, and as they passed her, Olga touched each one lightly on the shoulder with her umbrella, counting them off one by one as they were propelled into the freezing Moscow air.

Franklin Adelman of Yale went first, as befitted his age and status, then Moldenhauer of the Bundesarchiv in Koblenz, with his absurd double-doctorate – Doctor Doctor Karl-bloody-Moldenhauer – then the neo-Marxists, Enrico Banfi of Milan and Eric Chambers of the LSE, then the great cold warrior, Phil Duberstein of NYU, then Ivo Godelier of the Ecole Normale Superieure, followed by glum Dave Richards of St Antony's, Oxford – another Sovietologist whose world was rubble – then Velma Byrd of the US National Archive, then Alastair Findlay of Edinburgh's Department of War Studies, who still thought the sun shone out of Comrade Stalin's arse, then Arthur Saunders of Stanford, and finally – the man whose lateness had kept them waiting in the lobby for an extra five minutes – Dr C. R. A. Kelso, commonly known as Fluke.

The door banged hard against his heels. Outside the weather had worsened. It was trying to snow. Tiny flakes, as hard as grit, came whipping across the wide grey concourse and spattered his face and hair. At the bottom of the flight of steps, shuddering in a cloud of its own white fumes, was a dilapidated bus, waiting to take them to the symposium. Kelso stopped to light a cigarette.

'Jesus, Fluke,' called Adelman, cheerfully, 'you look just *awful.*'

Kelso raised a fragile hand in acknowledgement. He could see a huddle of taxi drivers in quilted jackets stamping their feet against the cold. Workmen were struggling to lift a roll of tin off the back of a lorry. One Korean businessman in a fur hat was photographing a group of twenty others, similarly dressed. But of Papu Rapava: no sign.

'Doctor Kelso, please, we are waiting again.' The umbrella wagged at him in reproof. He transferred the cigarette to the corner of his mouth, hitched his bag up on to his shoulder and moved towards the bus.

'A battered Byron' was how one Sunday newspaper had described him when he had resigned his Oxford lectureship and moved to New York, and the description wasn't a bad one – curly black hair too long and thick for neatness, a moist, expressive mouth, pale cheeks and the glow of a certain reputation – if Byron hadn't died on Missolonghi but had spent the next ten years drinking whisky, smoking, staying indoors and resolutely avoiding all exercise, he, too, might have come to look a little like Fluke Kelso.

He was wearing what he always wore: a faded dark blue shirt of heavy cotton with the top button undone, a loosely knotted and vaguely stained dark tie, a black corduroy suit with a black leather belt over which his stomach bulged slightly, red cotton handkerchief in his breast pocket, scuffed boots of brown suede, an old blue raincoat. This was Kelso's uniform, unvaried for twenty years.

'Boy,' Rapava had called him, and the word was both absurd for a middle-aged man and yet oddly accurate. *Boy.*

The heater was going full blast. Nobody was saying much. He sat on his own near the back of the bus and rubbed at the wet glass as they jolted up the slip-road to join the traffic on the bridge. Across the aisle, Saunders made an ostentatious display of batting Kelso's smoke away. Beneath them, in the filthy waters of the Moskva, a dredger with a crane mounted on its aft deck beat sluggishly upstream.

He nearly hadn't come to Russia. That was the joke of it. He knew well enough what it would be like: the bad food, the stale gossip, the sheer bloody tedium of academic life – of more and more being said about less and less – that was one reason why he had chucked in Oxford and gone to live in New York. But somehow the books he was supposed to write had not quite materialised. And besides, he never could resist the lure of Moscow. Even now, sitting on a stale bus in the Wednesday rush-hour, he could feel the charge of history beyond the muddy glass: in the dark and renamed streets, the vast apartment blocks, the toppled statues. It was stronger here than anywhere he knew; stronger even than in Berlin. That was what always drew him back to Moscow – the way history hung in the air between the blackened buildings like sulphur after a lightning-strike.

'You think you know it all about Comrade Stalin, don't you boy? Well, let me tell you: you don't know fuck.'

Kelso had already delivered his short paper, on Stalin and the archives, at the end of the previous day: delivered it in his trademark style – without notes, with one hand in his pocket, extempore, provocative. His Russian hosts had looked gratifyingly shifty. A couple of people had even walked out. So, all in all, a triumph.

Afterwards, finding himself predictably alone, he had decided to walk back to the Ukraina. It was a long walk, and it was getting dark, but he needed the air. And at some point – he couldn't remember where: maybe it was in one of the back streets behind the Institute, or maybe it was later, along the Noviy Arbat – but at some point he had realised he was being followed. It was nothing tangible, just a fleeting impression of something seen too often – the flash of a coat, perhaps, or the shape of a head – but Kelso had been in Moscow often enough in the bad old days to know that you were seldom wrong about these things. You always knew if a film was out of synch, however fractionally; you always knew if someone fancied you, however improbably; and you always knew when someone was on your tail.

He had just stepped into his hotel room and was contemplating some primary research in the mini-bar when the front desk had called up to say there was a man in the lobby who wanted to see him. Who? He wouldn't give his name, sir. But he was most insistent and he wouldn't leave. So Kelso had gone down, reluctantly, and found Papu Rapava sitting on one of the Ukraina's imitation leather sofas, staring straight ahead, in his papery blue suit, his wrists and ankles sticking out as thin as broomsticks.

'*You think you know it all about Comrade Stalin, don't you, boy . . . ?*' Those had been his opening words.

And that was the moment that Kelso had realised where he had first seen the old man: at the symposium, in the front row of the public seats, listening intently to the simultaneous translation over his headphones, muttering in violent disagreement at any hostile mention of J. V. Stalin.

Who are you? thought Kelso, staring out of the grimy window. Fantasist? Con man? The answer to a prayer?

*

THE symposium was only scheduled to last one more day – for which relief, in Kelso's view, much thanks. It was being held in the Institute of Marxism–Leninism, an orthodox temple of grey concrete, consecrated in the Brezhnev years, with Marx, Engels and Lenin in gigantic bas-relief above the pillared entrance. The ground floor had been leased to a private bank, since gone bust, which added to the air of dereliction.

On the opposite side of the street, watched by a couple of bored-looking militia men, a small demonstration was in progress – maybe a hundred people, mostly elderly, but with a few youths in black berets and leather jackets. It was the usual mixture of fanatics and grudge-holders – Marxists, nationalists, anti-semites. Crimson flags bearing the hammer and sickle hung beside black flags embroidered with the tsarist eagle. One old lady carried a picture of Stalin; another sold cassettes of SS marching songs. An elderly man with an umbrella held over him was addressing the crowd through a bullhorn, his voice a distorted, metallic rant. Stewards were handing out a free newspaper called *Aurora*.

'Take no notice,' instructed Olga Komarova, standing up beside the driver. She tapped the side of her head. 'These are crazy people. Red fascists.'

'What's he saying?' demanded Duberstein, who was considered a world authority on Soviet communism even though he had never quite got round to learning Russian.

'He's talking about how the Hoover Institution tried to buy the Party archive for five million bucks,' said Adelman. 'He says we're trying to steal their history.'

Duberstein sniggered. 'Who'd want to steal *their* goddamned history?' He tapped on the window with his signet ring. 'Say, isn't that a TV crew?'

The sight of a camera caused a predictable, wistful stir among the academics.

'I believe so . . .'

'How very flattering . . .'

'What's the name,' said Adelman, 'of the fellow who runs *Aurora*? Is it still the same one?' He twisted round in his seat and called up the aisle. 'Fluke – you should know. What's his name? Old KGB –'

'Mamantov,' said Kelso. The driver braked hard and he had to swallow to stop himself being sick. 'Vladimir Mamantov.'

'Crazy people,' repeated Olga, bracing herself as they came to a stop. 'I apologise on behalf of Rosarkhiv. They are not representative. Follow me, please. Ignore them.'

They filed off the bus and a television cameraman filmed them as they trudged across the asphalt forecourt, past a couple of drooping, silvery fir trees, pursued by jeers.

Fluke Kelso moved delicately at the rear of the column, nursing his hangover, holding his head at a careful angle, as if he was balancing a pitcher of water. A pimply youth in wire spectacles thrust a copy of *Aurora* at him and Kelso got a quick glimpse of the front page – a cartoon caricature of Zionist conspirators and a weird cabalistic symbol that was something between a swastika and a red cross – before he rammed it back in the young man's chest. The demonstrators jeered.

A thermometer on the wall outside the entrance read minus one. The old nameplate had been taken down and a new one had been screwed in its place, but it didn't quite fit so you could tell that the building had been renamed. It now proclaimed itself 'The Russian Centre for the Preservation and Study of Documents Relating to Modern History'.

Once again, Kelso lingered behind after the others had gone in, squinting at the hate-filled faces across the street. There were a lot of old men of a similar age, pinched and raw-cheeked in the cold, but Rapava wasn't among them. He turned away and moved inside, into the shadowy lobby, where he gave his coat and bag to the cloakroom attendant, before passing beneath the familiar statue of Lenin towards the lecture hall.

Another day began.

There were ninety-one delegates at the symposium and almost all of them seemed to be crowded into the small ante-room where coffee was being served. He collected his cup and lit another cigarette.

'Who's up first?' said a voice behind him. It was Adelman.

'Askenov, I think. On the microfilm project.'

Adelman groaned. He was a Bostonian, in his seventies, at that twilight stage in his career when most of life seemed to be spent in airplanes or foreign hotels: symposia, conferences, honorary degrees – Duberstein maintained that Adelman had given up pursuing history in favour of collecting air miles. But Kelso didn't begrudge him his honours. He was good. And brave. It had taken courage to write his kind of books, thirty years ago, on the Famine and the Terror, when every other useful idiot in academia was screeching for détente.

'Listen, Frank,' he said, 'I'm sorry about dinner.'

'Forget it. You got a better offer?'

'Kind of.'

The refreshment room was at the back of the Institute and looked out on to an inner courtyard, in the centre of which, dumped on their sides amid the weeds, were a pair of statues, of Marx and Engels – a couple of Victorian gentlemen taking time off from the long march of history for a morning doze.

'They don't mind taking down those two,' said Adelman. 'That's easy. They're foreigners. And one of them's a Jew. It's when they take down Lenin – that's when you'll know the place has really changed.'

Kelso took another sip of coffee. 'A man came to see me last night.'

'A man? I'm disappointed.'

'Could I ask your advice, Frank?'

Adelman shrugged. 'Go ahead.'

'In private?'

ADELMAN stroked his chin. 'You got his name, this guy?'

'Of course I got his name.'

'His real name?'

'How do I know if it's his real name?'

'His address, then? You got his address?'

'No, Frank, I didn't get his address. But he did leave these.'

Adelman took off his glasses and peered closely at the book of matches. 'It's a set-up,' he said at last, handing them back. 'I wouldn't touch it. Whoever heard of a bar called "Robotnik", anyhow? "Worker"? Sounds phoney to me.'

'But if it was a set-up,' said Kelso, weighing the match-book in his palm, 'why would he run away?'

'Obviously, because he doesn't want it to *look* like a set-up. He wants you to have to work at it – track him down, persuade him to help you. That's the psychology of a clever fraud – the victims wind up doing so much chasing around, they start *wanting* to believe it's true. Remember the Hitler diaries. Either that or he's a lunatic.'

'He was very convincing.'

'Lunatics often are. Or it's a practical joke. Someone wants to make you look a fool. Have you thought of that? You're not exactly the most popular kid in the school.'

Kelso glanced up the corridor towards the lecture hall. It wasn't a bad theory. There were plenty in there who didn't like him. He had appeared on too many television programmes, knocked out too many newspaper columns, reviewed too many of their useless books. Saunders was loitering at the corner, pretending to talk to Moldenhauer, both men obviously straining to overhear what he was saying to Adelman. (Saunders had complained bitterly after Kelso's paper about his 'subjectivity': 'Why was he even invited, that's what one wants to know. One had been given to understand this was a symposium for *serious* scholars . . .')

'They don't have the wit,' he said. He gave them a wave and was pleased to see them duck out of sight. 'Or the imagination.'

'You sure have a genius for making enemies.'

'Ah well. You know what they say: more enemies, more honour.'

Adelman smiled and opened his mouth to say something, but then seemed to think better of it. 'How's Margaret, dare one ask?'

'Who? Oh, you mean *poor* Margaret? She's fine, thank you. Fine and feisty. According to the lawyers.'

'And the boys?'

'Entering the springtime of their adolescence.'

'And the book? That's been a while. How much of this new book have you actually written?'

'I'm writing it.'

'Two hundred pages? A hundred?'

'What is this, Frank?'

'How many pages?'

'I don't know.' Kelso licked his dry lips. Almost unbelievably, he realised he could do with a drink. 'A hundred maybe.' He had a vision of a blank grey screen, a cursor flashing weakly, like a pulse on a life-support machine begging to be switched off. He hadn't written a word. 'Listen, Frank, there *could* be something in this, couldn't there? Stalin was a hoarder, don't forget. Didn't Khrushchev find some letter in a secret compartment in the old man's desk after he died?' He rubbed his aching head. 'That letter from Lenin, complaining about Stalin's treatment of his wife? And then there was that list of the Politburo, with crosses against everyone he was planning to purge. And his library – remember his library? He made notes in almost every book.'

'So what are you saying?'

'I'm just saying it's possible, that's all. That Stalin wasn't Hitler. That he wrote things down.'

'*Quod volimus credimus libenter,*' intoned Adelman. 'Which means –'

'I know what it means –'

' – which *means*, my dear Fluke, we always believe what we want to believe.' Adelman patted Kelso's arm. 'You don't want to hear this, do you? I'm sorry. I'll lie if you prefer it. I'll tell you he's the one guy in a million with a story like this who turns out not to be full of shit. I'll tell you he's going to lead you to Stalin's unpublished memoirs, that you'll rewrite history, millions of dollars will be yours, women will lie at your feet, Duberstein and Saunders will form a choir to sing your praises in the middle of Harvard Yard . . .'

'All right, Frank.' Kelso leaned the back of his head against the wall. 'You've made your point. I don't know. It's just – Maybe you had to be there with him –' He pressed on, reluctant to admit defeat. 'It's just it rings a bell with me somewhere. Does it ring a bell with you?'

'Oh sure. It rings a bell, okay. An alarm bell.' Adelman pulled out an old pocket watch. 'We ought to be getting back. D'you mind? Olga will be frantic.' He put his arm round Kelso's shoulders and led him down the corridor. 'In any case, there's nothing you can do. We're flying back to New York tomorrow. Let's talk when we get back. See if there's anything for you in the faculty. You were a great teacher.'

'I was a lousy teacher.'

'You were a great teacher, until you were lured from the path of scholarship and rectitude by the cheap sirens of journalism and publicity. Hello, Olga.'

'So here you are! The session is almost starting. Oh, Doctor Kelso – now this is not so good – no smoking, thank you.' She leaned over and removed the cigarette from his lips. She had a shiny face with plucked eyebrows and a very fine moustache, bleached white. She dropped the stub into the dregs of his coffee and took away his cup.

'Olga, Olga, why so bright?' groaned Kelso, putting his hand to his brow. The lecture hall exuded a tungsten glare.

'Television,' said Olga, with pride. 'They are making a programme of us.'

'Local?' Adelman was straightening his bow tie. 'Network?'

'Satellite, professor. *International.*'

'Say, now, where are our seats?' whispered Adelman, shielding his eyes from the lights.

'Doctor Kelso? Any chance of a word, sir?' An American accent. Kelso turned to find a large young man he vaguely recognised.

'I'm sorry?'

'R. J. O'Brian,' said the young man, holding out his hand. 'Moscow correspondent, Satellite News System. We're making a special report on the controversy –'

'I don't think so,' said Kelso. 'But Professor Adelman, here – I'm sure he'd be delighted –'

At the prospect of a television interview, Adelman seemed physically to swell in size, like an inflating doll. 'Well, as long as it's not in any *official* capacity . . .'

O'Brian ignored him. 'You sure I can't tempt you?' he said to Kelso. 'Nothing you want to say to the world? I read your book on the fall of communism. When was that? Three years ago?'

'Four,' said Kelso.

'Actually, I believe it was five,' said Adelman.

Actually, thought Kelso, it was nearer six: dear God, where were all the years going? 'No,' he said, 'thanks all the same, but I'm keeping off television these days.' He looked at Adelman. 'It's a cheap siren, apparently.'

'Later, please,' hissed Olga. 'Interviews are later. The director is talking. Please.' Kelso felt her umbrella in his back again as she steered him into the hall. 'Please. *Please* –'

By the time the Russian delegates were added in, plus a few diplomatic observers, the press, and maybe fifty members of the public, the hall was impressively full. Kelso sank heavily into his place in the second row. Up on the platform, Professor Valentin Askenov of the Russian State Archives had launched into a long explanation of the microfilming of the Party records. O'Brian's cameraman walked backwards down the central aisle, filming the audience. The sharp amplification of Askenov's sonorous voice seemed to pierce some painful chamber of Kelso's inner ear. Already, a kind of metallic, neon torpor had descended over the hall. The day stretched ahead. He covered his face with his hands.

Twenty-five million sheets . . . recited Askenov, *twenty-five thousand reels of microfilm . . . seven million dollars . . .*

Kelso slid his hands down his cheeks until his fingers converged and covered his mouth. *Frauds!* he wanted to shout. *Liars!* Why were they all just sitting here? They knew as well as he did that nine-tenths of the best material was still locked up, and to see most of the rest required a bribe. He'd heard that the going rate for a captured Nazi file was $1,000 and a bottle of Scotch.

He whispered to Adelman, 'I'm getting out of here.'

'You can't.'

'Why not?'

'It's discourteous. Just sit there, for pete's sake, and pretend to be interested like everyone else.' Adelman said all this out of the side of his mouth, without taking his eyes off the platform. Kelso stuck it for another half minute.

'Tell them I'm ill.'

'I shall not.'

'Let me by, Frank. I'm going to be sick.'

'Jesus . . .'

Adelman swung his legs to one side and pressed himself back in his seat. Hunched in a vain effort to make himself less conspicuous, Kelso stumbled over the feet of his colleagues, kicking in the process the elegant black shin of Ms Velma Byrd.

'Aw, fuck, Kelso,' said Velma.

Professor Askenov looked up from his notes and paused in mid-drone. Kelso was conscious of an amplified, humming silence, and of a kind of collective movement in the audience, as if some great beast had turned in its field to watch his progress. This seemed to last a long time, for at least as long as it took him to walk to the back of the hall. Not until he had passed beneath the marble gaze of Lenin and into the deserted corridor did the droning begin again.

KELSO sat behind the bolted door of a lavatory cubicle on the ground floor of the former Institute of Marxism–Leninism and opened his canvas bag. Here were the tools of his trade: a yellow legal pad, pencils, an eraser, a small Swiss army knife, a welcome pack from the organisers of the symposium, a dictionary, a street map of Moscow, his cassette recorder, and a Filofax that was a palimpsest of ancient numbers, lost contacts, old girlfriends, former lives.

There *was* something about the old man's story that was familiar to him, but he couldn't remember what it was. He picked up the cassette recorder, pressed REWIND, let it spool back for a while, then pressed PLAY. He held it to his ear and listened to the tinny ghost of Rapava's voice.

'. . . *Comrade Stalin's room was a plain man's room. You've got to say that for Stalin. He was always one of us . . .* '

REWIND. PLAY.

'. . . *and here was an odd thing, boy – he had taken off his shiny new shoes and had them wedged under one fat arm . . .*'

REWIND. PLAY.

'. . . *Know what I mean by Blizhny, boy? . . .*'

'. . . *by Blizhny, boy? . . .*'

'. . . *by Blizhny . . .* '

Chapter Two

THE MOSCOW AIR tasted of Asia – of dust and soot and eastern spices, cheap petrol, black tobacco, sweat. Kelso came out of the Institute and turned up the collar of his raincoat. He walked across the rutted concourse, skirting the frozen puddles, resisting the temptation to wave at the sullen crowd – that would have been 'a western provocation'.

The street sloped southwards, down towards the centre of the city. Every other building was encased in scaffolding. Beside him, debris hurtled down a metal chute and exploded into a fountain of dust. He passed a shady casino, anonymous except for a sign showing a pair of rolling dice. A fur boutique. A shop selling nothing but Italian shoes. A single pair of handmade loafers would have cost any one of the demonstrators a whole month's wages and he felt a stab of sympathy. He remembered a line of Evelyn Waugh's he had used before about Russia: 'The foundations of Empire are often occasions of woe; their dismemberment, always.'

At the bottom of the hill he turned right, into the wind. The snow had stopped but the cold blast was hard and unyielding. He could see tiny figures bent into it, across the road, beneath the red rock-face of the Kremlin wall, while the golden domes of the churches rose above the parapet like the globes of some vast meteorological machine.

His destination lay straight ahead. Like the Institute of Marxism–Leninism, the Lenin Library had been renamed. It was now the Central Library of the Russian Federation, but everyone still called it the Lenin. He stepped through the familiar triple doors, gave his bag and coat to the babushka behind the cloakroom counter, then showed his old reader's ticket to an armed guard in a glass booth.

He signed his name in the register and added the time. It was eleven minutes past ten.

They had yet to get around to computerising the Lenin, which meant forty million titles were still on index cards. At the top of a wide flight of stone steps, beneath the vaulted ceiling, was a sea of wooden cabinets, and Kelso moved among them as he had done years ago, sliding open one drawer after another, riffling through the familiar titles. Radzinsky he would need, and the second volume of Volkogonov, and Khrushchev and Alliluyeva. The cards for these last two were marked with the Cyrillic symbol '¢' which meant they had been held in the secret index until 1991. How many titles was he allowed? Five, wasn't it? Finally, he decided on Chuyev's series of interviews with the ancient Molotov. Then he took his request slips to the issuing desk and watched as they were fitted into a metal canister and fired down the pneumatic tube into the Lenin's lower depths.

'What's the wait today?'

The assistant shrugged. Who was she to say?

'An hour?'

She shrugged again.

He thought: nothing changes.

He wandered back across the landing into Reading Room No. 3, and trod softly down the path of worn green carpet that led to his old seat. And nothing had changed here, either – not the rich brownness of the wood-panelled, galleried hall, nor the dry smell of it, nor its sacrilegious hush. At one end was a statue of Lenin reading a book, at the other an astrological clock. Maybe two hundred people were bent over their desks. Through the window to his left he could see the dome and spire of St Nicholas's. He might never have left; the past eighteen years might have been a dream.

He sat down and laid out his things and in that instant he was a student of twenty-six again, living in a single room in Corpus V of Moscow University, paying 260 roubles a month for a desk, a bed, a chair and a cupboard, taking meals in the basement canteen that was overrun by cockroaches, spending his days in the Lenin and his nights with a girlfriend – with Nadya, or Katya, or Margarita, or Irina. *Irina.* Now there was a woman. He ran his hand over the scratched surface of the desk and wondered what had become of Irina. Perhaps he should have stuck with her – serious, beautiful Irina, with her *samizdat* magazines and her basement meetings, making love to the accompaniment of a rattling Gestetner duplicator and afterwards vowing that they would be different, that they would change the world.

Irina. He wondered what she would make of the new Russia. The last he had heard she was a dental assistant in South Wales.

He glanced around the reading room and closed his eyes, trying to keep hold of the past for a minute longer, a fattening and hungover middle-aged historian in a black corduroy suit.

HIS books arrived at the issuing stack just after eleven, or at any rate four of them did: they had fetched up volume one of Volkogonov rather than volume two and he had to send it back. Still, he had enough. He carried the books back to his desk and gradually he became absorbed in his task, reading, noting and cross-referencing the various eyewitness accounts of Stalin's death. He found, as usual, an aesthetic pleasure in the sheer detective work of research. Secondhand sources and speculation he discarded. He was only interested in those people who had actually been in the same room as the GenSec and had left behind a description he could match against Rapava's.

By his reckoning there were seven: the Politburo members, Khrushchev and Molotov; Stalin's daughter, Svetlana Alliluyeva; two of Stalin's bodyguards, Rybin and Lozgachev; and two of his medical staff: the physician, Myasnikov, and the recuscitator, a woman named Chesnokova. The other eyewitnesses had either killed themselves (like the bodyguard, Khrustalev, who drank himself to death after watching the autopsy), or had died soon afterwards, or had disappeared.

The accounts all differed in detail but were in essence the same. Stalin had suffered a catastrophic haemorrhage in the left cerebral hemisphere some time when he was alone in his room between 4 a.m. and 10 p.m. on Sunday March 1 1953. Academician Vinogradov, who examined the brain after death, found serious hardening of the cerebral arteries which suggested Stalin had probably been half-crazy for a long while, maybe even years. Nobody could tell what time the stroke had hit. His door had stayed closed all day and his staff had been too scared to enter his room. The bodyguard Lozgachev told the writer Radzinsky that he had been the first to pluck up the courage:

I opened the door . . . and there was the Boss lying on the floor holding up his right hand like this. I was petrified. My hands and legs wouldn't obey me. He had probably not yet lost consciousness but he couldn't speak. He had good hearing, he'd obviously heard me coming, and probably raised his hand slightly to call me in to help him. I hurried up to him and said 'Comrade Stalin, what's wrong?' He'd – you know – wet himself while he was lying there, and was trying to straighten something with his left hand. I said, 'Shall I call the doctor, maybe?' He made some incoherent noise – like 'Dz – dz . . . ,' all he could do was keep on 'dz'-ing.

It was immediately after this that the guards had called in Malenkov. Malenkov had called in Beria. And Beria's order, tantamount to murder by negligence, had been that Stalin was drunk and should be left to sleep it off.

Kelso made a careful note of the passage. Nothing here contradicted Rapava. That didn't prove Rapava was telling the truth, of course – he could have got hold of Lozgachev's testimony for himself, and tailored his story to fit. But it didn't suggest he was lying, either, and certainly the details tallied – the time frame, the order not to call for medical help, the way Stalin had wet himself, the way he would regain consciousness but be unable to speak. This happened at least twice over the three days it took Stalin to die. Once, according to Khrushchev, when the doctors at last brought in by the Politburo were spoon-feeding him soup and weak tea, he had raised his hand and pointed at one of the pictures of children on the wall. The second return to consciousness occurred just before the end and was noted by everyone, especially his daughter, Svetlana:

At what seemed like the very last moment he suddenly opened his eyes and cast a glance over everyone in the room. It was a terrible glance, insane or perhaps angry and full of fear of death and the unfamiliar faces of the doctors bent over him. The glance swept over everyone in a second. Then something incomprehensible and terrible happened that to this day I can't forget and don't understand. He suddenly lifted his left hand as though he were pointing to something up above and bringing down a curse on us all. The gesture was incomprehensible and full of menace, and no one could say to whom or what it might be directed. The next moment, after a final effort, the spirit wrenched itself free of the flesh.

That had been written in 1967. After his heart had stopped, the doctors had ordered the resuscitator, Chesnokova – a strong young woman – to pound at Stalin's chest and blow into his mouth, until Khrushchev had heard the old man's ribs snap and had told her to pack it in. '... *no one could say to whom or what it might be directed* ...' Kelso underlined the words lightly with his pencil. If Rapava was telling the truth, it was fairly obvious whom Stalin must have been cursing: the man who had stolen the key to his private safe – Lavrenty Beria. Why he should have pointed at a picture of a child was less clear.

Kelso tapped the pencil against his teeth. It was all very circumstantial. He could imagine Adelman's reaction if he tried to offer it as any sort of supporting evidence. The thought of Adelman made him look at his watch. If he set off now he could be back at the symposium comfortably in time for lunch and there was a good chance they wouldn't even have missed him. He gathered up the books and took them back to the issuing desk, where the second volume of Volkogonov had just arrived.

'Well,' said the librarian, her thin lips crimped with irritation, 'do you want it or not?'

Kelso hesitated, almost said no, then decided he might as well finish what he'd started. He handed over the other books and carried the Volkogonov back into the reading room.

It lay before him on his desk like a dull brown brick. *Triyumf i Tragediya: politicheskii portret I. V. Stalina,* Novosti publishers, Moscow 1989. He had read it when it first came out and hadn't felt the need to look at it since. He regarded it now without enthusiasm, then flicked the cover open with his finger. Volkogonov was a three-star Red Army general with powerful contacts inside the Kremlin, granted special access to the archives under Gorbachev and Yeltsin which he had used to produce a trio of tombstone lives – Stalin, Trotsky, Lenin – each one more revisionist than the last. Kelso picked it up and leafed through it to the index, looked up the relevant entries for Stalin's death – and a moment later there it was, the memory that had been niggling at the back of his mind ever since Papu Rapava disappeared into the Moscow dawn:

A. A. Yepishev, who was at one time deputy Minister of State Security, told me that Stalin kept a black oilskin exercise book in which he would make occasional notes, and that for some time Stalin kept letters from Zinoviev, Kamenev, Bukharin and even Trotsky. All efforts to discover either the notebook or these letters have failed, and Yepishev did not reveal his source.

Yepishev did not reveal his source but he did, according to Volkogonov, have a theory. He believed that Stalin's private papers had been removed from his Kremlin safe by Lavrenty Beria, while the General Secretary lay paralysed by his stroke.

Beria made a dash for the Kremlin where it is reasonable to assume he cleaned out the safe, removing the Boss's personal papers and with them, one assumes, the black notebook ... Having destroyed Stalin's notebook, if indeed it was there, Beria would have cleared the path to his own ascendancy. Perhaps the truth will never be known, but Yepishev was convinced that Beria cleaned out the safe before the others could get to it.

*

Now calm yourself, and don't get excited, because this proves nothing, you understand? Nothing whatever.

But it does make it a thousand times more likely.

Back outside the entrance to the reading room, Kelso yanked open the narrow wooden drawer and searched through it quickly until he found the index cards to Yepishev, A. A. (1908–85). The old man had written a score of books, of uniform dullness and hackery: *History Teaches: The Lessons of the Twentieth Anniversary of Victory in the Great Patriotic War* (1965), *Ideological Warfare and Military Problems* (1974), *We Are True to the Ideas of the Party* (1981) ...

Kelso's hangover had gone, to be replaced by that familiar phase of post-alcoholic euphoria – always, in the past, his most productive time of day – a feeling that alone was enough to make getting drunk worthwhile. He ran down the flight of steps and along the wide and gloomy corridor that led to the Lenin's military section. This was a small and self-contained area, neon-lit, with a subterranean feel to it. A young man in a grey pullover was leaning against the counter, reading a 1970s *MAD* comic.

'What do you have on an army man named Yepishev?' asked Kelso. 'A. A. Yepishev?'

'Who wants to know?'

Kelso handed over his reader's card and the young man examined it with interest.

'Hey, are you the Kelso who wrote that book a few years back on the end of the Party?'

Kelso hesitated – this could go either way – but finally he admitted he was. The young man put down the comic and shook his hand. 'Andrei Efanov. Great book. You really stuffed the bastards. I'll see what we have.'

THERE were two reference books with entries for Yepishev: the *Military Encyclopaedia of the USSR* and the *Directory of Heroes of the Soviet Union*, and both told pretty much the same story, if you knew how to read between the lines, which was that Aleksey Alekseevich Yepishev had been an armour-plated, ocean-going Stalinist of the old school: Komsomol and Party instructor in the twenties and thirties; Red Army Military Academy, 1938; Commissar of the Komintern Factory in Kharkov, 1942; Military Council of the Thirty-Eighth Army of the 1st Ukrainian Front, 1943; Deputy People's Commissar for Medium Machine Building, also 1943 –

'What's a "medium machine",' asked Efanov, who was peering at the books over Kelso's shoulder. Efanov turned out to have done his military service in Lithuania – two years of hell – and to have been refused admittance to Moscow University in the communist time on the grounds he was a Jew. Now he was taking a huge delight in poking over the dust and ashes of Yepishev's career.

'Cover-name for the Soviet atomic bomb programme,' said Kelso. 'Beria's pet project.' *Beria*. He made a note.

– Secretary of the Central Committee of the Ukrainian Communist Party, 1946 –

'That was when they purged the Ukraine of collaborators, after the war,' said Efanov. 'A bloody time.'

– First Secretary of the Odessa Regional Party Committee, 1950; Deputy Minister of State Security, 1951 –

Deputy Minister . . .

Each entry was illustrated with the same official photograph of Yepishev. Kelso looked again at the the square jaw, the thick brow, the grim face set above the boxer's neck.

'Oh, he was a big bastard, boy. A fleshy tank . . . '

'Gotcha,' whispered Kelso to himself.

After Stalin's death, Yepishev's career had taken a dive. First he had been sent back to Odessa, then he had been packed off abroad. Ambassador to Romania, 1955-61. Ambassador to Yugoslavia, 1961-62. And then, at last, the long-awaited summons back to Moscow, as Head of the Central Political Department of the Soviet Armed Forces – its ideological commissar – a position he held for the next twenty-three years. And who had served as his deputy? None other than Dmitri Volkogonov, three-star general and future biographer of Josef Stalin.

To extract these small plums of information it was necessary to dig through a great pudding of cliché and jargon, praising Yepishev for his 'important role in shaping the necessary political attitudes and enforcing Marxist–Leninist orthodoxy in the Armed Forces, in strengthening military discipline and fostering ideological readiness'. He had died aged seventy-seven. Volkogonov, Kelso knew, had died ten years later.

The list of Yepishev's honours and medals took up the rest of his entry: Hero of the Soviet Union, winner of the Lenin Prize, holder of four Orders of Lenin, the October Revolution Order, four Orders of the Red Banner, two

Orders of the Great Patriotic War (1ˢᵗ class), the Order of the Red Banner, three Orders of the Red Star, the Order of Service to the Motherland . . .

'It's a wonder he could stand up.'

'And I'll bet you he never shot anyone,' sneered Efanov, 'except on his own side. So what's so interesting about Yepishev, if you don't mind me asking?'

'What's this?' said Kelso suddenly. He pointed to a line at the foot of the column: 'V. P. Mamantov.'

'He's the author of the entry.'

'Yepishev's entry was written by Mamantov? *Vladimir* Mamantov? The KGB man?'

'That's him. So what? The entries are usually written by friends. Why? D'you know him?'

'I don't *know* him. I've *met* him.' He frowned at the name. 'His people were demonstrating – this morning –'

'Oh, them? They're always demonstrating. When did you meet Mamantov?'

Kelso reached for his notebook and began skimming back through the pages. 'About five years ago, I suppose. When I was researching my book on the Party.'

Vladimir Mamantov. My God, he hadn't thought about Vladimir Mamantov in half a decade, and suddenly here he was, crossing his path twice in a morning. The years fluttered through his fingers – *ninety-five, ninety-four* . . . Some details of the meeting were starting to come back to him now: a morning in late spring, a dead dog revealed in the thawing snow outside an apartment block in the suburbs, a gorgon of a wife. Mamantov had just finished serving fourteen months in Lefortovo for his part in the attempted coup against Gorbachev, and Kelso had been the first to interview him when he came out of jail. It had taken an age to fix the appointment and then it had proved, as so often in these cases, not worth the effort. Mamantov had refused point-blank to talk about himself, or the coup, and had simply spouted Party slogans straight out of the pages of *Pravda*.

He found Mamantov's home telephone number from 1991, next to an office address for a lowly Party functionary, Gennady Zyuganov.

'You're going to try to see him?' asked Efanov, anxiously. 'You know he hates all Westerners? Almost as much as he hates the Jews.'

'You're right,' said Kelso, staring at the seven digits. Mamantov had been a formidable man even in defeat, his Soviet suit hanging loose off his wide shoulders, the grey pallor of prison still dull on his cheeks, murder in his eyes. Kelso's book had not been flattering about Vladimir Mamantov, to put it mildly. And it had been translated into Russian – Mamantov must have seen it.

'You're right,' he repeated. 'It would be stupid even to try.'

FLUKE Kelso walked out of the Lenin Library a little after two that afternoon, pausing briefly at a stall in the lobby to buy a couple of bread rolls and a bottle of warm and salty mineral water.

He remembered passing a row of public telephones opposite the Kremlin, close to the Intourist office, and he ate his lunch as he walked – first down into the gloom of the metro station to buy some plastic tokens for the phone, and then back along Mokhavaya Street towards the high red wall and the golden domes.

He was not alone, it seemed to him. His younger self was ambling alongside him now – floppy-haired, chain-smoking, forever in a hurry, forever optimistic, a writer on the rise.

('Dr Kelso brings to the study of contemporary Soviet history the skills of a first-rate scholar and the energy of a good reporter' – *The New York Times*.) This younger Kelso wouldn't have hesitated to call up Vladimir Mamantov, that was for sure – by God, he would have battered his bloody door down by now if necessary.

Think about it: if Yepishev had told Volkogonov about Stalin's notebook, might he not also have told Mamantov? Might he not have left behind papers? Might he not have a family?

It had to be worth a try.

He wiped his mouth and fingers on the little paper napkin and as he picked up the receiver and inserted the tokens he felt a familiar tightening of his stomach muscles, a butteriness around his heart. Was this sensible? No. But who cared about that? Adelman – he was sensible. And Saunders – he was *very* sensible.

Go for it.

He dialled the number.

The first call was an anti-climax. The Mamantovs had moved and the man who now lived at their old address was reluctant to give out their new number. Only after he had held a whispered consultation with someone at his end did he pass it on. Kelso hung up and dialled again. This time the phone rang for a long time before it was answered. The tokens dropped and an old woman with a trembling voice said, 'Who is this?'

He gave his name. 'Could I speak with Comrade Mamantov?' He was careful to say 'comrade': 'mister' would never do.

'Yes? Who is this?'

Kelso was patient. 'As I said, my name is Kelso. I'm using a public telephone. It's urgent.'

'Yes, but who is this?'

He was about to repeat his name for a third time when he heard what sounded like a scuffle at the other end of the line and a harsh male voice cut in. 'All right. This is Mamantov. Who are you?'

'It's Kelso.' There was a silence. 'Doctor Kelso? You may remember me?'

'I remember you. What do you want?'

'To see you.'

'Why should I see you after that shit you wrote?'

'I wanted to ask you some questions.'

'About?'

'A black oilskin notebook that used to belong to Josef Stalin.'

'Shut up,' said Mamantov.

'What?' Kelso frowned at the receiver.

'I said shut up. I'm thinking it over. Where are you?'

'Near the Intourist building, on Mokhavaya Street.'

There was another silence.

Mamantov said, 'You're close.'

And then he said, 'You'd better come.'

He gave his address. The line went dead.

THE line went dead and Major Feliks Suvorin of the Russian intelligence service, the SVR, sitting in his office in the south-eastern suburb of Yasenevo, carefully slipped off his headphones and wiped his neat pink ears with a clean white handkerchief. On the notepad in front of him he had written: *A black oilskin notebook that used to belong to Josef Stalin . . . '*

Chapter Three

'Confronting the Past'
An International Symposium on the
Archives of the Russian Federation

Tuesday 27 October,
final afternoon session

DR KELSO: *Ladies and gentlemen, whenever I think of Josef Stalin, I find myself thinking of one image in particular. I think of Stalin, as an old man, standing beside his gramophone.*

He would finish working late, usually at nine or ten, and then he would go to the Kremlin movie theatre to watch a film. Often, it was one of the Tarzan series – for some reason Stalin loved the idea of a young man growing up and living among wild animals – then he and his cronies in the Politburo would drive out to his dacha at Kuntsevo for dinner, and, after dinner, he would go over to his gramophone and put on a record. His particular favourite, according to Milovan Djilas, was a song in which howling dogs replaced the sound of human voices. And then Stalin would make the Politburo dance.

Some of them were quite good dancers. Mikoyan, for example: he was a lovely dancer. And Bulganin wasn't bad; he could follow a beat. Khrushchev, though, was a lousy dancer – 'like a cow on ice' – and so was Malenkov and so was Kaganovich, for that matter.

Anyway, one evening – drawn, we might speculate, by the peculiar noise of grown men dancing to the baying of hounds – Stalin's daughter, Svetlana, put her head round the door, and

Stalin made her start dancing, too. Well, after a time, she grew tired, and her feet were hardly moving, and this made Stalin angry. He shouted at her, 'Dance!' And she said, 'But I've already danced, papa, I'm tired.' At which Stalin – and here I quote Khrushchev's description – 'grabbed her like this, by the hair, a whole fistful, I mean by her forelock, as it were, and pulled, you understand, very hard . . . pulled, jerked and jerked.'

Now keep that image in your mind for a moment, and let us consider the fate of Stalin's family. His first wife died. His oldest son, Yakov, tried to shoot himself when he was twenty-one, but only succeeded in inflicting severe wounds. (When Stalin saw him, according to Svetlana, he laughed. 'Ha!' he said. 'Missed! Couldn't even shoot straight!') Yakov was captured by the Germans during the war and, after Stalin refused a prisoner exchange, he tried suicide again – successfully this time, by hurling himself at the electrified fence of his prison camp.

Stalin had one other child, a son, Vasily, an alcoholic, who died aged forty-one.

Stalin's second wife, Nadezhda, refused to bear her husband any more children – according to Svetlana, she had a couple of abortions – and late one night, aged thirty-one, she shot herself through the heart. (Or perhaps it would be more accurate to say that someone *shot her: no suicide note has ever been found.)*

Nadezhda was one of four children. Her older brother, Pavel, was murdered by Stalin during the purges; the death certificate recorded a heart attack. Her younger brother, Fyodor, was driven insane when a friend of Stalin's, an Armenian bank robber named Kamo, handed him a gouged-out human heart. Her sister, Anna, was arrested on Stalin's orders and sentenced to ten years in solitary confinement. By the time she came out she was no longer capable of recognising her own children. So that was one set of Stalin's relatives.

And what of the other set? Well, there was Aleksandr Svanidze, the brother of Stalin's first wife – he was arrested in thirty-seven and shot in forty-one. And there was Svanidze's wife, Maria, who was also arrested; she was shot in forty-two. Their surviving child, Ivan – Stalin's nephew – was sent into exile, to a ghastly state orphanage for the children of 'enemies of the state', and when he emerged, nearly twenty years later, he was profoundly psychologically damaged. And finally there was Stalin's sister-in-law, Maria – she was also arrested in thirty-seven and died mysteriously in prison.

Now let us go back to that image of Svetlana. Her mother is dead. Her half-brother is dead. Her other brother is an alcoholic. Two uncles are dead and one is insane. Two aunts are dead and one is in prison. She is being dragged around by her hair, by her father, in front of a roomful of the most powerful men in Russia, all of whom are being forced to dance, maybe to the sound of howling dogs.

Colleagues, whenever I sit in an archive or, more rarely these days, attend a symposium like this one, I always try to remember that scene, because it reminds me to be wary of imposing a rational structure on the past. There is nothing in the archives here to show us that the Deputy Chairman of the Council of Ministers, or the Commissar for Foreign Affairs, when they made their decisions, were shattered by exhaustion, and very probably terrified – that they had been up until three a.m. dancing for their lives, and knew they might well be dancing again that evening.

Not that I am saying that Stalin was crazy. On the contrary. One could argue that the man who worked the gramophone was the sanest person in the room. When Svetlana asked him why her Aunt Anna was being held in solitary confinement, he answered, 'Because she talks too much.' With Stalin, there was usually a logic to his actions. He didn't need a sixteenth-century English philosopher to tell him that 'knowledge is power'. That realisation is the absolute essence of Stalinism. Among other things, it explains why Stalin murdered so many of his own family and close colleagues – he wanted to destroy anyone who had any first-hand knowledge of him.

And this policy, we must concede, was remarkably successful. Here we are, gathered in Moscow, forty-five years after Stalin's death, to discuss the newly-opened archives of the Soviet era. Above our heads, in fire-proofed strong-rooms, maintained at a constant temperature of eighteen degrees celsius and sixty per cent humidity, are one and a half million files – the entire archive of the Central Committee of the Communist Party of the Soviet Union.

Yet how much does this archive really tell us about Stalin? What can we see today that we couldn't see when the communists were in power? Stalin's letters to Molotov – we can see those – and they are not without interest. But clearly they have been heavily censored. And not just that: they end in thirty-six, at precisely the point when the real killing started.

We can also see the death lists that Stalin signed. And we have his appointments book. So we know that on the eighth of December, nineteen thirty-eight, Stalin signed thirty death lists containing five thousand names, many of them of his so-called friends. And we also know, thanks to his appointments book, that on that very same evening he went to the Kremlin movie theatre and watched, not Tarzan this time, but a comedy called Happy Guys.

But between these two events, between the killing and the laughter, there lies – what? who? We do not know. And why? Because Stalin made it his business to murder almost everyone who might have been in a position to tell us what he was like . . .

Chapter Four

MAMANTOV'S NEW PLACE turned out to be just across the river, in the big apartment complex on Serafimovich Street known as the House on the Embankment. This was the building to which Comrade Stalin, with typical generosity, had insisted that leading Party members go to live with their families. There were ten floors with twenty-five different entrances at ground level, at each of which the GenSec had thoughtfully posted an NKVD guard – purely for your security, comrades.

By the time the purges were finished, six hundred of the building's tenants had been liquidated. Now the flats were privately owned and the good ones, with a view across the Moskva to the Kremlin, sold for upwards of half a million dollars. Kelso wondered how Mamantov could afford it.

He came down the steps from the bridge and crossed the road. Parked outside the entrance to Mamantov's staircase was a boxy white Lada, its windows open, two men in the front seat, chewing gum. One had a livid scar running almost from the corner of his eye to the edge of his mouth. They watched Kelso with undisguised interest as he walked past them towards the entrance.

Inside the apartment block, next to the elevator, someone had written, neatly, in English, in capitals and lower case, 'Fuck Off'. A tribute to the Russian education system, thought Kelso. He whistled nervously, a made-up tune. The lift rose smoothly and he got out at the ninth floor to be met by the distant thump of western rock music.

Mamantov's apartment had an outer door of steel plate. A

red aerosol swastika had been sprayed on to the metal. The paint was old and faded but no attempt had been made to clean it off. Set in the wall above it was a small remote TV camera.

There was already plenty about this set-up that Kelso didn't like – the heavy security, the guys in the car downstairs – and for a moment he could almost smell the terror from sixty years ago, as if the sweat had seeped into the brickwork: the clattering footsteps, the heavy knocking, the hurried goodbyes, the sobs, silence. His hand paused over the buzzer. What a place to choose to live.

He pressed the button.

After a long wait, the door was opened by an elderly woman. Madame Mamantov was as he remembered her – tall and broad, not fat, but heavily built. She was draped in a shapeless, flowery smock and looked as though she had just finished crying. Her red eyes rested on him briefly, distractedly, but before he could even open his mouth she had wandered off and suddenly there was Vladimir Mamantov, looming down the dark passage, dressed as if he still had an office to go to – white shirt, blue tie, black suit with a small red star pinned in his lapel.

He didn't say anything, but he offered his hand. He had a crushing handshake, perfected, it was said, by squeezing balls of vulcanized rubber during KGB meetings. (A lot of things were said about Mamantov: for example – and Kelso had put it in his book – that at the famous meeting in the Lubyanka on the night of 20 August 1991, when the plotters of the coup had realised the game was up, Mamantov had offered to fly down to Gorbachev's dacha at Foros on the Black Sea and shoot the Soviet President personally; Mamantov had dismissed the story as 'a provocation'.)

A young man in a black shirt with a shoulder holster appeared in the gloom behind Mamantov, and Mamantov said, without looking round, 'It's all right, Viktor. I'm dealing with the situation.' Mamantov had a bureaucrat's face – steel-coloured hair, steel-framed glasses and pouched cheeks, like a suspicious hound's. You could pass it in the street a hundred times and never notice it. But his eyes were bright: a fanatic's eyes, thought Kelso; he could imagine Eichmann or some other Nazi desk-murderer having eyes like these. The old woman had started making a curious howling noise from the other end of the flat, and Mamantov told Viktor to go and sort her out.

'So you're part of the gathering of thieves,' he said to Kelso.

'What?'

'The symposium. *Pravda* published a list of the foreign historians they invited to speak. Your name was on it.'

'Historians are hardly thieves, Comrade Mamantov. Even foreign historians.'

'No? Nothing is more important to a nation than its history. It is the earth upon which any society stands. Ours has been stolen from us – gouged and blackened by the libels of our enemies until the people have become lost.'

Kelso smiled. Mamantov hadn't changed at all. 'You can't seriously believe that.'

'You're not Russian. Imagine if your country offered to sell its national archive to a foreign power for a miserable few million dollars.'

'You're not selling your archive. The plan is to microfilm the records and make them available to scholars.'

'To scholars *in California*,' said Mamantov, as if this settled the argument. 'But this is tedious. I have an urgent appointment.' He looked at his watch. 'I can only give you five minutes, so get to the point. What's all this about Stalin's notebook?'

'It comes into some research I'm doing.'

'Research? Research into what?'

Kelso hesitated. 'The events surrounding Stalin's death.'

'Go on.'

'If I could just ask you a couple of questions, then perhaps I could explain the relevance –'

'No,' said Mamantov. 'Let us do this the other way round. You tell me about this notebook and then I might answer your questions.'

'You *might* answer my questions?'

Mamantov consulted his watch again. 'Four minutes.'

'All right,' said Kelso, quickly. 'You remember the official biography of Stalin, by Dmitri Volkogonov?'

'The traitor Volkogonov? You're wasting my time. That book is a piece of shit.'

'You've read it?'

'Of course not. There's enough filth in this world without my volunteering to go jump in it.'

'Volkogonov claimed that Stalin kept certain papers – private papers, including a black oilskin exercise book – in his safe at the Kremlin, and that these papers were stolen by Beria. His source for this story was a man you're familiar with, I think. Aleksey Alekseevich Yepishev.'

There was a slight movement – a flicker, no more – in Mamantov's hard grey eyes. He's heard of it, thought Kelso, he knows about the notebook –

'And?'

'And I wondered if you'd come across this story while you were writing your entry on Yepishev for the biographical guide. He was a friend of yours, I assume?'

'What's it to you?' Mamantov glanced at Kelso's bag. 'Have you found the notebook?'

'No.'

'But you know someone who may know where it is?'

'Someone came to see me,' began Kelso, then stopped. The apartment was very quiet now. The old woman had finished wailing, but the bodyguard hadn't reappeared. On the hall table was a copy of *Aurora*.

Nobody in Moscow knew where he was, he realised. He had dropped off the map.

'I'm wasting your time,' he said. 'Perhaps I might come back when I've –'

'That's unnecessary,' said Mamantov, softening his tone. His sharp eyes were checking Kelso up and down – flickering across his face, his hands, gauging the potential strength of his arms and chest, darting up to his face again. His conversational technique was pure Leninism, thought Kelso: *'Push out a bayonet. If it strikes fat, push deeper. If it strikes iron, pull back for another day.'*

'I'll tell you what, Doctor Kelso,' said Mamantov. 'I'll show you something. It will interest you. And then I'll tell you something. And then you'll tell me something.' He waved his fingers back and forth between them. 'We'll trade. Is it a deal?'

AFTERWARDS, Kelso tried to make a list of it all, but there was too much of it for him to remember: the immense oil painting, by Gerasimov, of Stalin on the ramparts of the Kremlin, and the neon-lit glass cabinet with its miniatures of Stalin – its Stalin dishes and its Stalin boxes, its Stalin stamps and Stalin medals – and the case of books by Stalin, and the books about Stalin, and the photographs of Stalin – signed and unsigned – and the scrap of Stalin's handwriting – blue pencil, lined paper, quarto-sized and framed – that hung above the bust of Stalin by Vuchetich ('. . . don't spare individuals, no matter what position they occupy, spare only the cause, the interests of the cause . . .').

He moved among the collection while Mamantov watched him closely.

The handwriting sample, said Kelso – that . . . that was a note for a speech, was it not? Correct, said Mamantov: October 1920, address to the Worker–Peasant Inspection. And the Gerasimov? Wasn't it similar to the artist's 1938 study of Stalin and Voroshilov on the Kremlin Wall? Mamantov nodded again, apparently pleased to share these moments with a fellow connoisseur: yes, the GenSec had ordered Gerasimov to paint a second version, leaving out Voroshilov – it was Stalin's way of reminding Voroshilov that life (how to put it?) could always be *rearranged* to imitate art. A collector in Maryland and another in Dusseldorf had each offered Mamantov $100,000 for the picture but he would never permit it to leave Russian soil. Never. One day, he hoped to exhibit it in Moscow, along with the rest of his collection – 'when the political situation is more favourable'.

'And you think one day the situation will be favourable?'

'Oh yes. Objectively, history will record that Stalin was right. That is how it is with Stalin. From the subjective perspective, he may seem cruel, even wicked. But the glory of the man is to be found in the objective perspective. There he is a towering figure. It is my unshakeable belief that when the proper perspective is restored, statues will be raised again to Stalin.'

'Goering said the same of Hitler during the Nuremberg trial. I don't see any statues –'

'Hitler lost.'

'But surely Stalin lost? In the end? From the "objective perspective"?'

'Stalin inherited a nation with wooden ploughs and bequeathed us an empire armed with atomic weapons. How can you say he lost? The men who came after him – they lost. Not Stalin. Stalin foresaw what would happen, of course. Khrushchev, Molotov, Beria, Malenkov – they thought they were hard, but he saw through them. "After I've gone, the capitalists will drown you like blind kittens." His analysis was correct, as always.'

'So you think that if Stalin had lived –'

'We would still be a superpower? Absolutely. But men of Stalin's genius are only given to a country perhaps once in a century. And even Stalin could not devise a strategy to defeat death. Tell me, did you see the survey of opinion to mark the forty-fifth anniversary of his passing?'

'I did.'

'And what did you think of the results?'

'I thought they were –' Kelso tried to find a neutral word ' – remarkable.'

(Remarkable? Christ. They were horrifying. One third of Russians said they thought Stalin was a great war leader. One in six thought he was the greatest ruler the country had ever had. Stalin was seven times more popular than Boris Yeltsin, while poor old Gorbachev hadn't even scored enough votes to register. This was in March. Kelso had been so appalled he had tried to sell an op-ed piece to the *New York Times* but they weren't interested.)

'Remarkable,' agreed Mamantov. 'I should even say astounding, considering his vilification by so-called "historians".'

There was an awkward silence.

'Such a collection,' said Kelso, 'it must have taken years to assemble.' And cost a fortune, he almost added.

'I have a few business interests,' said Mamantov, dismissively. 'And a considerable amount of spare time, since my retirement.' He put out his hand to touch the bust, but then hesitated and drew it back. 'The difficulty, of course, for any collector, is that he left so little behind in the way of personal possessions. He had no interest in private property, not like these corrupt swine we have in the Kremlin nowadays. A few sticks of government-issue furniture was all he had. That and the clothes he stood up in. And his private notebook, of course.' He gave Kelso a crafty look. 'Now that would be something. Something – what is the American phrase? – *to die for?*'

'So you have heard of it?'

Mamantov smiled – an unheard-of occurrence – a narrow, thin, rapid smile, like a sudden crack in ice. 'You're interested in Yepishev?'

'Anything you can tell me.'

Mamantov crossed the room to the bookshelf and pulled down a large, leather-bound album. On a higher shelf Kelso could see the two volumes of Volkogonov – of course Mamantov had read them.

'I first met Aleksey Alekseevich,' he said, 'in fifty-seven, when he was ambassador in Bucharest. I was on my way back from Hungary, after we'd sorted things out there. Nine months work, without a break. I needed a rest, I can tell you. We went shooting together in the Azuga region.'

He carefully peeled back a layer of tissue paper and offered the heavy album to Kelso. It was open at a small photograph, taken by an amateur camera, and Kelso had to stare at it closely to make out what was happening. In the background, a forest. In the foreground, two men in leather hunting caps with fleece-lined jackets, smiling, holding rifles, dead birds piled at their booted feet. Yepishev was on the left, Mamantov next to him – still hard-faced but leaner then, a cold war caricature of a KGB man.

'And somewhere there's another.' Mamantov leaned over Kelso's shoulder and turned a couple of pages. Close up, he smelled elderly, of mothballs and carbolic, and he had shaved badly, as old men do, leaving grey stubble in the shadow of his nose and in the cleft of his broad chin. 'There.'

This was a much bigger, professional picture, showing maybe two hundred men, arranged in four ranks, as if at a graduation. Some were in uniform, some in civilian suits. A caption underneath said 'Sverdlovsk, 1980'.

'This was an ideological collegium, organised by the Central Committee Secretariat. On the final day, Comrade Suslov himself addressed us. This is me.' He pointed to a grim face in the third row, then moved his finger to the front, to a relaxed, uniformed figure sitting cross-legged on the ground. 'And this – would you believe? – is Volkogonov. And here again is Aleksey Alekseevich.'

It was like looking at a picture of Imperial officers in the tsarist time, thought Kelso – such confidence, such order, such masculine arrogance! Yet within ten years, their world had been atomised: Yepishev was dead, Volkogonov had renounced the Party, Mamantov was in jail.

Yepishev had died in 1985, said Mamantov. He had passed on just as Gorbachev came to power. And that was a good time for a decent communist to die, in Mamantov's opinion: Aleksey Alekseevich had been *spared*. Here was a man whose whole life had been devoted to Marxism–Leninism, who had helped plan the fraternal assistance to Czechoslovakia and Afghanistan. What a mercy he hadn't lived to see the whole lot thrown away. Writing Yepishev's entry for the *Book of Heroes* had been a privilege, and if nobody ever read it nowadays – well, that was what he meant. The country had been robbed of its history.

'And did Yepishev tell you the same story about Stalin's papers as he told Volkogonov?'

'He did. He talked more freely towards the end. He was often ill. I visited him in the leadership clinic. Brezhnev and he were treated together by the parapsychic healer, Davitashvili.'

'I don't suppose he left any papers.'

'Papers? Men like Yepishev didn't keep papers.'

'Any relatives?'

'None that I knew of. We never discussed *families*.' Mamantov pronounced the word as if it was absurd. 'Did you know that one of the things Aleksey had to do was interrogate Beria? Night after night. Can you imagine what that must have been like? But Beria never cracked, not once in nearly half a year, until right at the very end, after his trial, when they were strapping him to the board to shoot him. He hadn't believed they'd dare to kill him.'

'How do you mean, he cracked?'

'He was squealing like a pig – that's what Yepishev said. Shouting something about Stalin and something about an archangel. Can you imagine that? Beria, of all people, getting religious! But then they put a scarf in his mouth and shot him. I don't know any more.' Mamantov closed the albums tenderly and placed them back on the shelf. 'So,' he said, turning to face Kelso with a look of menacing innocence, 'someone came to see you. When was this?'

Kelso was on his guard at once. 'I'd prefer not to say.'

'And he told you about Stalin's papers? He *was* a man, I assume? An eyewitness, from that time?'

Kelso hesitated.

'Named?'

Kelso smiled and shook his head. Mamantov seemed to think he was back in the Lubyanka.

'His profession, then?'

'I can't tell you that, either.'

'Does he know where these papers are?'

'Perhaps.'

'He offered to show you?'

'No.'

'But you *asked* him to show you?'

'No.'

'You're a very disappointing historian, Dr Kelso. I thought you were famous for your diligence –'

'If you must know, he disappeared before I had the chance.'

He regretted the words the instant they were out of his mouth.

'What do you mean, he "disappeared"?'

'We were drinking,' muttered Kelso. 'I left him alone for a minute. When I came back he'd run away.'

It sounded implausible, even to his own ears.

'Run away?' Mamantov's eyes were as grey as winter. 'I don't believe you.'

'Vladimir Pavlovich,' said Kelso, meeting his gaze and holding it, 'I can assure you this is the truth.'

'You're lying. Why? *Why?*' Mamantov rubbed his chin. 'I think it must be because you have the notebook.'

'If I had the notebook, ask yourself: Would I be here?

Wouldn't I be on the first flight back to New York? Isn't that what thieves are supposed to do?'

Mamantov continued to stare at him for a few more seconds, then looked away. 'Clearly we need to find this man.'

We . . .

'I don't think he wants to be found.'

'He will contact you again.'

'I doubt it.' Kelso badly wanted to get out of here now. He felt compromised, somehow; complicit. 'Besides, I'm flying back to America tomorrow. Which, now I come to think of it, really means I ought –'

He made a move towards the door but Mamantov barred it. 'Are you excited, Dr Kelso? Do you feel the force of Comrade Stalin, even from the grave?'

Kelso laughed unhappily. 'I don't think I quite share your . . . obsession.'

'Go fuck your mother! I've read your work. Does that surprise you? I'll pass no comment on its quality. But I'll tell you this: you're as obsessed as I am.'

'Perhaps. But in a different way.'

'Power,' said Mamantov, savouring the word in his mouth like wine, 'the absolute mastery and understanding of *power*. No man ever matched him for it. Do this, do that. Think this, think that. Now I say you live, and now I say you die, and all you say is, "Thank you for your kindness, Comrade Stalin." *That's* the obsession.'

'Yes, but then there's the difference, if you'll permit me, which is you want him back.'

'And you just like to watch, is that it? I like fucking and you like pornography?' Mamantov jerked his thumb at the room. 'You should have seen yourself just now. "Isn't this a note for a speech?" "Isn't that a copy of an earlier painting?" Eyes wide, tongue out – the western liberal, getting his safe thrill. Of course, *he* understood that, too. And now you tell me you're going to give up trying to find his private notebook and just run away back to America?'

'May I get by?'

Kelso stepped to his left but Mamantov moved smartly to block him.

'This could be one of the greatest historical discoveries of the age. And you want to run away? It *must* be found. We must find it *together*. And then you must present it to the world. I want no credit – I promise you: I prefer the shadows – the honour will be yours alone.'

'So, what's all this then, Comrade Mamantov?' said Kelso, with forced cheerfulness. 'Am I a prisoner?'

Between him and the outside world there were, he calculated, one fit and obviously crazy ex-KGB man, one armed bodyguard, and two doors, one of them armour-plated. And for a moment, he thought that Mamantov might indeed be intending to keep him: that he had everything else connected with Stalin, so why not a Stalin historian, pickled in formaldehyde and laid out in a glass case, like V. I. Lenin? But then Madame Mamantov shouted from the passage – 'What's going on in there?' – and the spell was broken.

'Nothing,' called Mamantov. 'Stop listening. Go back to your room. Viktor!'

'But who is everyone?' wailed the woman. 'That's what I want to know. And why is it always so dark?' She started to cry. They heard the shuffle of her feet and the sound of a door closing.

'I'm sorry,' said Kelso.

'Keep your pity,' said Mamantov. He stood aside. 'Go on,

then. Get out of here. Go.' But when Kelso was halfway down the passage he shouted after him: 'We'll talk again about this matter. One way or another.'

THERE were three men now in the car downstairs, although Kelso was too preoccupied to pay them much attention. He paused in the gloomy portal of the House on the Embankment, to hoist his canvas bag more firmly on to his shoulder, then set off in the direction of the Bolshoy Kamenniy bridge.

'That's him, major,' said the man with the scar, and Feliks Suvorin leaned forward in his seat to get a better look. Suvorin was young to be a full major in the SVR – he was only in his thirties – a dapper figure, with blond hair and cornflower blue eyes. And he wore a western aftershave, that was the other thing that was very noticeable at this moment: the little car was fragrant with the smell of Eau Sauvage.

'He had that bag with him when he went in?'

'Yes, major.'

Suvorin glanced up at the Mamantovs' ninth-floor apartment. What was needed here was better coverage. The SVR had managed to get a bug into the flat at the start of the operation, but it had lasted just three hours before Mamantov's people had found it and ripped it out.

Kelso had begun climbing the flight of stairs that led up to the bridge.

'Off you go, Bunin,' said Suvorin, tapping the man in front of him lightly on the shoulder. 'Nothing too obvious, mind you. Just try to keep him in view. We don't want a diplomatic protest.'

Grumbling under his breath, Bunin levered himself out of the car.

Kelso was moving rapidly now, had almost reached road-level, and the Russian had to jog across to the bottom of the steps to make up part of the distance.

Well, well, thought Suvorin, he's certainly in a hurry to get somewhere. Or is it just that he wants to get away from here?

He watched the blurred pink faces of the two men above the stone parapet as they headed north across the river into the grey afternoon and then were lost from view.

Chapter Five

KELSO PAID HIS two-rouble fare at the Borovitskaya metro station, collected his plastic token, and descended gratefully into the Moscow earth. At the entrance to the northbound platform something made him glance back up the moving staircase to see if Mamantov was following, but there was no sign of him among the tiers of exhausted faces.

It was a stupid thought – he tried to smile at himself for his paranoia – and he turned away, towards the welcoming dimness and the warm gusts of oil and electricity. Almost at once, a yellow headlight danced around a bend in the track and the rush of the train sucked him forwards. Kelso let the crowd jostle him into a carriage. There was an odd comfort in this dowdy, silent multitude. He hung on to the metal handrail and pitched and swayed with the rest as they plunged back into the tunnel.

They hadn't gone far when the train suddenly slowed and stopped – a bomb scare, it turned out, at the next station: the militia had to check it out – and so they sat there in the semi-darkness, nobody speaking, just the occasional cough, the tension rising by imperceptible degrees.

Kelso stared at his reflection in the dark glass. He was jumpy, he had to admit it. He couldn't help feeling he had just put himself into some kind of danger, that telling Mamantov about the notebook had been a reckless mistake. What had the Russian called it? Something *to die for?*

It was a relief to his nerves when the lights eventually flickered back on and the train jolted forwards. The soothing rhythm of normality resumed.

By the time Kelso emerged above ground it was after four. Low in the western sky, barely clearing the tops of the dark trees that fringed the Zoopark, was a lemony crack in the clouds. A winter sunset was little more than an hour away. He would have to hurry. He folded the map into a small square and twisted it so that the metro station was to his right. Across the road was the entrance to the zoo – red rocks, a waterfall, a fairy tower – and, a little further along, a beer garden, closed for the season, its plastic tables stacked, its striped umbrellas down and flapping. He could hear the roar of the traffic on the Garden Ring road, about two hundred yards straight ahead. Across that, sharp left, then right, and there it ought to be. He stuffed the map into his pocket, picked up his bag and climbed the cobbled slope that led to the big intersection.

Ten lanes of traffic formed an immense, slow-moving river of light and steel. He crossed it in a dog-leg and suddenly he was into diplomatic Moscow: wide streets, grand houses, old birch trees weeping dead leaves on to sleek black cars. There wasn't much life. He passed a silvery-headed man walking a poodle and a woman in green rubber boots that poked incongruously from beneath her Muslim robe. Behind the thick gauze of the curtained windows, he could see the occasional yellow constellation of a chandelier. He stopped at the corner of Vspolnyi Street and peered along it. A militia car drove towards him very slowly and passed away to his right. The road was deserted.

He located the house at once, but he wanted to get his bearings and to check if anyone was about, so he made himself walk past it, right to the end of the street before returning along the opposite side. *There was a red sickle moon, and a single red star. And the place was guarded by devils with blackened faces . . .'* Suddenly he saw what the old man must have meant. A red sickle moon and a single red star – that would be a flag: a Muslim flag. And black faces? The place must have been an embassy – it was too big for anything else – an embassy of a Muslim country, perhaps in North Africa. He was certain he was right. It was a big building, that was for sure, forbidding and ugly, built of sandy-coloured stone which made it look like a bunker. It ran for at least forty yards along the western side of the road. He counted thirteen sets of windows. Above the massive entrance was an iron balcony with double doors leading on to it. There was no nameplate and no flag. If it had been an embassy it was abandoned now; it was lifeless.

He crossed the street and went up close to it, patting the coarse stone with his palm. He stood on tiptoe and tried to see through the windows. But they were set too high and besides were blanked off by the ubiquitous grey netting. He gave up and followed the façade around the corner. The house went on down this street, too. Thirteen windows again, no door, thirty or forty yards of heavy masonry – immense, impregnable. Where this elevation of the house eventually ended there was a wall made of the same stone, about eight feet high, with a locked, iron-studded wooden door set into it. The wall ran on – down this street, along the side of the ring-road, and finally back up the narrow alley which formed the fourth side of the property. Walking round it, Kelso could see why Beria had chosen it, and why his rivals had decided the only place to capture him was inside the Kremlin. Holed up in this fortress he could have withstood a siege.

In the neighbouring houses, the lights were becoming sharper as the afternoon faded into dusk. But Beria's place remained a square of darkness. It seemed to be gathering the shadows into itself. He heard a car door slam and he walked back up to the corner of Vspolnyi Street. While he had been at the back of the property, a small van had arrived at the front.

He hesitated, then began to move towards it.

The van was a Russian model – white, unmarked, unoccupied. Its engine had just been switched off and it was making a slight ticking noise as it cooled. As he came level with it, he glanced towards the door of the house and saw that it was slightly open. Again he hesitated, looking up and down the quiet street. He went over and put his head into the gap and shouted a greeting.

His words echoed in the empty hall. The light inside was weak and bluish, but even without taking another step he could see that the floor was of black and white tiles. To his left was the start of a wide staircase. The house smelled strongly of sour dust and old carpets, and there was an immense stillness to it, as though it had been shut up for months. He pushed the door wide open and took a step inside.

He called out again.

He had two options now. He could stay by the door, or he could go further inside. He went further inside and immediately, like a laboratory rat in a maze, he found his options multiplied. He could stay where he was, or he could take the door to his left, or the stairs, or the passage that led off into the darkness beyond the stairs, or one of the three doors to his right. For a moment, the weight of choice paralysed him. But the stairs were straight ahead and seemed the obvious course – and perhaps, subconsciously, he also wanted to get the advantage of height, to get above whoever might be on the ground floor, or at least to get on equal terms with them if they were already above.

The stairs were stone. He was wearing brown suede boots with leather soles he'd bought in Oxford years ago and no matter how quietly he tried to walk his steps seemed to ring like gunshots. But that was good. He wasn't a thief, and to emphasise the point he called out again. *Pree-vyet! Kto tam?* Hello? Is anybody there? The stairs curled round to his right and he had a good, high view now, looking down into the dark blue well of the hall, pierced by the softer shaft of blue that shone from the open door. He reached the top of the stairs and came out into a wide corridor that stretched to right and left, vanishing at either end into Rembrandt gloom. Ahead of him was a door. He tried to take his bearings. That must lead to the room above the front entrance, the one with the iron balcony. What was it? A ballroom? The master bedroom? The corridor floor was parquet and he remembered Rapava's description of Beria's damp footprints on the polished wood as he hurried off to take the call from Malenkov.

Kelso opened the heavy door and the stale air hit him like a wall. He had to clamp a hand to his mouth and nose to keep from gagging. The smell that pervaded the whole house seemed to have its source in here. It was a big room, bare, lit from the opposite wall by three tall, net-curtained windows, high oblongs of translucent grey. He moved towards them. The floor seemed to be strewn with pools of tiny black husks. His idea was that if he pulled back the curtain, he could throw light on the room, and see what he was treading on. But as his hand touched the rough nylon net, the material seemed to split and ripple downwards and a shower of black granules went pattering across his hand and brushed the back of his neck. He twitched the curtain again and the shower became a cascade, a waterfall of dead, winged insects. Millions of them must have hatched and died in here over the summer, trapped in the airless room. They had a papery, acid smell. They were in his hair. He could feel them rustling under his feet. He stepped backwards, furiously brushing at himself and shaking his head.

Down in the lobby, a man shouted. *Kto idyot?* Is somebody up there?

Kelso knew he should have shouted back. What greater proof could he have offered of his blameless intentions – of his innocence – than to have stepped at once out on to the landing, identified himself and apologised? He was very sorry. The door was open. This was an interesting old house. He was a historian. Curiosity had got the better of him. And obviously, there was nothing here to steal. Really, he was truly sorry –

That was Kelso's alternative history. He didn't take it. He didn't *choose* not to take it. He merely did nothing, which was a form of choice. He stood there, in Lavrenty Beria's old bedroom, frozen, half bent, as if the creaking of his bones might give him away, and listened. With each second that passed, his chances of talking his way out of the building dwindled. The man began to climb the staircase. He came up seven steps – Kelso counted them – then stopped and stayed very still for perhaps a minute.

Then he walked down again and crossed the lobby and the front door closed.

Kelso moved now. He went to the window. Without touching the curtain he found it was possible, by pressing his cheek to the wall, to peer around the edge of the dusty nylon mesh, down into the street. From this oblique angle, he could see a man in a black uniform, standing on the pavement next to the van, holding a flashlight. The man stepped off the kerb and into the gutter and squinted up at the house. He was squat and simian. His arms seemed too long for his thick trunk. Suddenly, he was looking directly at Kelso – a brutal, stupid face – and Kelso drew back. When he next dared to risk a look, the man was bending to open the door on the driver's side. He threw in the flashlight and climbed in after it. The engine started. The van drove off.

Kelso gave him thirty seconds then hurried downstairs. He was locked in. He couldn't believe it. The absurdity of his predicament almost made him smile. He was locked inside Beria's house! The front door was huge, with a big iron ball for a handle and a lock the size of a telephone directory. He tried it hopelessly, then looked around. What if there was an intruder alarm? In the gloom, he couldn't see anything attached to the walls, but maybe it was an old-fashioned system – that would be more likely, wouldn't it? – something triggered by pressure-pads rather than beams? The idea froze him.

What set him moving again was the gathering darkness and the realisation that if he didn't find an escape route now he might be trapped by his blindness all night. There was a light switch by the door but he didn't dare try it – the guard was obviously suspicious: he might drive by for a second look. In any case, something about the silence of the place, its utter deadness, made him sure all forms of life-support had been disconnected, that the house had been left to rot. He tried to recall Rapava's description of the lay-out when he came in to answer Malenkov's call. Something about coming in off a verandah, through a duty room, past a kitchen and into the hall.

He headed into the blackness of the passage beyond the stairs, feeling his way along the left-hand wall. The plaster was cool and smooth. The first door he encountered was locked. The second wasn't – he felt a draught of cold air, but sensed a drop, into a cellar, presumably – and closed it quickly. The third opened on to the dull blue gleam of metal surfaces and a faint smell of old food. The fourth was at the end, facing him, and revealed the room where he guessed that Beria's guards must once have sat.

Unlike the rest of the house, which seemed to have been stripped bare, there was furniture here – a plain wooden table and a chair, and an old sideboard – and some signs of life. A copy of *Pravda* – he could just make out the familiar masthead – a kitchen knife, an ashtray. He touched the table and felt crumbs. Pale light leaked through a pair of small windows. Between them was a door. It was locked. There was no key. He looked again at the windows. Too narrow for him to squeeze through. He took a breath. Some habits, surely, are international? He ran his hand along the sill to the right of the door and it was there and it turned easily in the lock.

When the door was opened he removed the key, and – a nice touch this, he remembered thinking – replaced it on the sill.

HE emerged on to a narrow verandah, about two yards wide, with weathered floorboards and a broken handrail. He could hear traffic at the bottom of the garden and the laborious whine of a big jet, dropping towards Sheremetevo Airport. The breeze was cold, scented by the smoke of a bonfire. There was a last pale flush of daylight in the sky.

He guessed the garden must have been abandoned at the same time as the house. Nobody could have worked in it for months. To his left was an ornate greenhouse with an iron chimney, partially overgrown by Russian vines. To his right, a ragged thicket of dark green shrubs. Ahead were trees. He stepped down off the verandah on to the carpet of leaves that covered the lawn. The wind stirred and lofted some of them, sent a detachment cartwheeling towards the house. He kicked through the drifts towards the orchard – a cherry orchard he could see now as he came closer: big old trees, maybe twenty feet high, at least a hundred of them, a Chekhovian scene. Suddenly he stopped. The ground beneath the trees was flat and level except in one place. At the base of one tree, close to a stone bench, was a patch of blackness, darker than the surrounding shadows. He frowned. Was he sure he wasn't imagining it?

He went over, knelt and slowly sank his hands into the leaves. On the surface they were dry but the lower levels were damp and mulchy. He brushed them back, releasing a rich smell of moist soil – the black and fragrant earth of Mother Russia.

'Don't make it so wide. It's not a grave. You're making work for yourself . . . '

He cleared away the leaves from an area about a yard square, and although he couldn't see much, he could see enough, and he could feel it. The grass had been removed and a hole had been dug. And then it had been filled in again and an attempt had been made to jam the turfs back into their original positions. But some parts had crumbled and others overlapped the lip of the hole and the result was a mess, like a broken, muddy jigsaw. It had been done in a hurry, thought Kelso, and it had been done recently, possibly even today. He stood and brushed the wet leaves from his coat.

'Do you feel the force of Comrade Stalin, even from the grave . . .?'

Beyond the high wall he could hear the traffic on the wide highway. Normality seemed close enough to touch. He used the side of his foot to scrape a covering of leaves back across the scarred surface, grabbed his bag and stumbled through the orchard towards the end of the garden, towards the sounds of life. He had to get out now. He didn't mind admitting it. He was rattled. The cherry trees stretched almost to the wall which rose up blank and sheer before him, like the perimeter of a Victorian gaol. There was no way he could scale it.

A narrow cinder path followed the line of the wall. He headed left. The path turned the corner and took him back in the direction of the house. About halfway along, he could see a darkened oblong – the garden door he had noticed from the street – but even this was overgrown and he had to pull back the trailing branches of a bush to get at it. It was locked, maybe even rusted shut. The big iron ring of the handle wouldn't turn. He flicked his cigarette lighter and held it close to get a better view. The door was solid but the frame looked weak. He stood back and aimed a kick at it, but nothing happened. He tried again. Hopeless.

He stepped back on to the path. He was now about thirty yards from the house. Its low roof was clearly silhouetted. He could see an aerial and the bulk of a tall chimney with a satellite dish attached to it. It was too big to be an ordinary domestic receiver.

It was while he was staring distractedly at the dish that his eye was caught by a glimmer of light in an upstairs window. It vanished so quickly he thought he might have imagined it and he told himself to keep his nerve, just find a tool, get out of here. But then it flashed again, like the beam of a lighthouse – pale, then bright, then pale again – as someone holding a powerful torch swivelled anti-clockwise towards the window then back towards the blackness of the room.

The suspicious security guard was back.

'God.' Kelso's lips were so tightly drawn he could barely shape his breath into the syllable. 'God, God, God.'

He ran up the path towards the greenhouse. A rickety door slid back just far enough for him to slip through. The vines made it darker inside than out. Trestle tables, an old trug, empty trays for seedlings, terracotta pots – nothing, nothing. He blundered down a narrow aisle, a frond of something brushed his face and then he collided with an object immense and metal. An old bulbous, cast-iron stove. And next to it, a heap of discarded implements – shovel, scuttle, riddling iron, poker. *Poker.*

He squeezed back on to the path, holding his prize, and jammed the poker into the gap between the garden door and the frame, just above the lock. He heaved and heard a crack. The poker came loose. He jammed it back and pulled again. Another crack. He worked it downwards. The frame was splintering.

He took a few paces back and ran at the door, rammed it with his shoulder, and some force that seemed to him beyond the physical – some fusion of will and fear and imagination – carried him through the door and out of the garden and into the quiet emptiness of the street.

Chapter Six

AT SIX O'CLOCK that evening, Major Feliks Suvorin, accompanied by his assistant, Lieutenant Vissari Netto, presented an account of the day's developments to their immediate boss, the chief of the RT Directorate, Colonel Yuri Arsenyev.

The atmosphere was informal, as usual. Arsenyev sprawled sleepily behind his desk, on which had been placed a map of Moscow and a cassette player. Suvorin reclined on the sofa next to the window, smoking his pipe. Netto worked the tape machine.

'The first voice you'll hear, colonel,' Netto was saying to Arsenyev, 'is that of Madame Mamantov.'

He pressed PLAY.

'Who is this?'

'Christopher Kelso. Could I speak with Comrade Mamantov?'

'Yes? Who is this?'

'As I said, my name is Kelso. I'm using a public telephone. It's urgent.'

'Yes, but who is this?'

Netto pressed PAUSE.

'Poor Ludmilla Fedorova,' said Arsenyev, sadly. 'Did you know her, Feliks? I knew her when she was at the Lubyanka. Oh, she was a piece of work! A body like a pagoda, a mind like a razor and a tongue to match.'

'Not any more,' said Suvorin. 'Not the mind, anyway.'

Netto said, 'The next voice will be even more familiar, colonel.'

PLAY.

'All right, this is Mamantov. Who are you?'

'It's Kelso. Doctor Kelso? You may remember me?'

'I remember you. What do you want?'

'To see you.'

'Why should I see you after that shit you wrote?'

'I wanted to ask you some questions.'

'About?'

'A black oilskin notebook that used to belong to Josef Stalin.'

'Shut up.'

'What?'

'I said shut up. I'm thinking it over. Where are you?'

'Near the Intourist building, on Mohavaja Street.'

'You're close. You'd better come.'

STOP.

'Play it again,' said Arsenyev. 'Not Ludmilla. The latter part.'

Through the armoured glass at Arsenyev's back Suvorin could see the ripple of the office lights reflected in Yasenevo's ornamental lake, and the massive floodlit head of Lenin, and beyond these, almost invisible now, the dark line of the forest, its edge serrated against the evening sky. A pair of headlights winked through the trees and disappeared. A security patrol, thought Suvorin, suppressing a yawn. He was happy to let Netto do the talking. Give the lad a chance.

'A black oilskin notebook that used to belong to Josef Stalin . . .'

'Fuck me,' said Arsenyev, softly, and his flabby face tautened.

'The call was initiated this afternoon, at fourteen-fourteen, by this man,' continued Netto, handing out two flimsy buff-coloured folders. 'Christopher Richard Andrew Kelso, commonly known as "Fluke".'

'Now this is nice,' said Suvorin, who hadn't seen the photograph before. It was still glistening from the darkroom, and reeked of sodium thiosulphate. 'Where are we?'

'Third floor, inner courtyard, opposite the entrance to Mamantov's staircase.'

'So now we can afford an apartment in the House on the Embankment?' grumbled Arsenyev.

'It's empty. Doesn't cost us a rouble.'

'How long did he stay?'

'Arrived at fourteen-thirty-two, colonel. Left at fifteen-seven. One of our operatives, Lieutenant Bunin, was then detailed to follow him. Kelso caught the metro at Borovitskaya, here, changed once, got out at Krasno-presnenskaya, and walked to a house here –' Netto again put his finger on the map ' – in Vspolnyi Street. A deserted property. He made an illegal entry and spent approximately forty-five minutes inside. He was last reported here, heading south on foot along the Garden Ring. That was ten minutes ago.'

'What does that mean exactly? "Fluke"?'

'"A lucky stroke", colonel,' said Netto, smartly. '"An unexpected success."'

'Sergo? Where's that damned coffee?' Arsenyev, immensely fat, had a habit of falling asleep if he didn't have caffeine every hour.

'It's coming, Yuri Semonovich,' said a voice from the intercom.

'Kelso's parents were both in their forties, sir, when he was born.'

Arsenyev turned a tiny and astonished eye towards Vissari Netto. 'Why do we care about his parents?'

'Well –' The young man wilted, stalled, appealed to Suvorin.

'Kelso was a fluke,' said Suvorin. 'The joke. It's a joke.'

'And that is funny?'

They were spared by the arrival of the coffee, borne in by Arsenyev's male assistant. The blue mug said 'I LOVE NEW YORK' and Arsenyev raised it towards them, as if drinking their health. 'So tell me,' he said, blinking through the steam over the rim, 'about Mister Fluke.'

'Born Wimbledon, England, nineteen fifty-four,' said Netto, reading from the file (he had done well, thought Suvorin, to get all this together in the space of an afternoon – the lad was keen, you couldn't fault him on ambition). 'Father, a typical petit-bourgeois, a clerk in legal chambers; three sisters, all older; standard education; nineteen seventy-three, scholarship to study history at the college of St John, Cambridge; starred first class honours degree, nineteen seventy-six –'

Suvorin had already skimmed through all of this – the personal file dredged up from the Registry, a few newspaper cuttings, the entry in *Who's Who* – and now he tried to reconcile the biography with this snatched picture of a figure in a raincoat leaving an apartment. The graininess of the picture had a pleasing, fifties feel: the man, glancing across the street, a cigarette in his mouth, had the appearance of a slightly seedy French actor playing a dodgy cop. *Fluke.* Does a name stick because it suits a man or does the man, unconsciously, evolve into his name? Fluke, the spoiled and lazy teenager, doted on by all these family women, who astonishes his teachers by winning a scholarship to Cambridge – the first in the history of his minor grammar school. Fluke, the carousing student who, after three years of no apparent effort, walks away with the best history degree of his year. Fluke, who just happens to turn up on the doorstep of one of the most dangerous men in Moscow – although, naturally, as a foreigner he would have felt invulnerable. Yes, one would have to be wary of this *Fluke* –

' – scholarship to Harvard, nineteen seventy-eight; admitted to Moscow University, under the "Students for Peace" scheme, nineteen eighty; dissident contacts – see annex "A" – led to recategorisation from "bourgeois-liberal" to "conservative and reactionary"; doctoral thesis published eighty-four, *Power in the Land: The Peasantry of the Volga Region, 1917–22*; lecturer in modern history, Oxford University, eighty-three to ninety-four; now resident in New York City; author of the *Oxford History of Eastern Europe, 1945–87; Vortex: The Collapse of the Soviet Empire*, published ninety-three; numerous articles –'

'All right, Netto,' said Arsenyev, holding up a hand. 'It's getting late. Did we ever make a pass at him?' This question was addressed to Suvorin.

'Twice,' said Suvorin. 'Once at the University, obviously, in nineteen eighty. Again in Moscow in ninety-one, when we tried to sell him on democracy and the New Russia.'

'And?'

'And? Looking at the reports? I should say he laughed in our faces.'

'He's a western asset, do we think?'

'Unlikely. He wrote an article in the *New Yorker* – it's in the file – describing how the Agency and SIS both tried to sign him. Rather a funny piece, in fact.'

Arsenyev frowned. He disapproved of publicity, on either side. 'Wife? Kids?'

Netto jumped in again: 'Married three times.' He glanced at Suvorin, and Suvorin made a little 'go ahead' gesture with his hand: he was happy to take a back seat. 'First, as a student, Katherine Jane Owen, marriage dissolved, seventy-nine. Second, Irina Mikhailovna Pugacheva, married eighty-one – '

'He married a Russian?'

'Ukrainian. Almost certainly a marriage of convenience. She was expelled from the University for anti-state activity. This is the beginning of Kelso's dissident contact. She was granted a visa in eighty-four.'

'So we blocked her entry into Britain for three years?'

'No, colonel, the British did. By the time they let her in, Kelso was living with one of his students, an American, a Rhodes Scholar. Marriage to Pugacheva dissolved in eighty-five. She is now married to an orthodontist in Glamorgan. There is a file but I'm afraid I haven't – '

'Forget it,' said Arsenyev. 'We'll drown in paper. And the third marriage?' He winked at Suvorin. 'A real romeo!'

'Margaret Madeline Lodge, an American student – '

'This is the Rhodes Scholar?'

'No, this is a different Rhodes Scholar. He married this one in eighty-six. The marriage was dissolved last year.'

'Kids?'

'Two sons. Resident with their mother in New York City.'

'One cannot help but admire this fellow,' said Arsenyev, who, despite his bulk, had a mistress of his own in Technical Support. He contemplated the photograph, the corners of his mouth turned down in admiration. 'What's he doing in Moscow?'

'Rosarkhiv are holding a conference,' said Netto, 'for foreign scholars.'

'Feliks?'

Major Suvorin had his right ankle swung up on to his left knee, his elbows resting casually on the sofa back, his sports jacket unbuttoned – easy, confident, Americanized: his style. He took a pull on his pipe before he spoke.

'The words used on the telephone are ambiguous, obviously. The implication could be that Mamantov has this notebook, and the historian wishes to see it. Or the historian himself has the notebook, or has heard of it, and wishes to check some detail with Mamantov. Whichever is the case, Mamantov is clearly aware of our surveillance, which is why he cuts the conversation short. When is Kelso due to leave the Federation, Vissari, do we know yet?'

'Tomorrow lunchtime,' said Netto. 'Delta flight to JFK, leaves Sheremetevo-2 at thirteen-thirty. Seat booked and confirmed.'

'I recommend we arrange for Kelso to be stopped and searched,' said Suvorin. 'Strip-searched, it had better be – delay the flight if necessary – on suspicion of exporting material of historical or cultural interest. If he's taken anything from this house in Vspolnyi Street, we can get it off him. In the meantime, we maintain our coverage of Mamantov.'

A buzzer sounded on Arsenyev's desk; Sergo's voice.

'There's a call for Vissari Petrovich.'

'All right, Netto,' said Arsenyev. 'Take it in the outer office.' When the door was closed, he scowled at Suvorin, 'Efficient little bastard, isn't he?'

'He's harmless enough, Yuri. He's just keen.'

Arsenyev grunted, took two long squirts from his inhaler, unhitched his belt a notch, let his flesh sag towards his desk. The colonel's fat was a kind of camouflage: a blubbery, dimpled netting thrown over an acute mind, so that while other, sleeker men had fallen, Arsenyev had safely waddled on – through the cold war (KGB chief resident in Canberra and Ottawa), through glasnost and the failed coup and the break-up of the service, on and on, beneath the armoured soft protective shell of his flesh, until now, at last, he was into the final stretch: retirement in one year, dacha, mistress, pension, and the rest of the world could go fuck its collective mother. Suvorin rather liked him.

'All right, Feliks. What do you think?'

'The purpose of the Mamantov operation,' said Suvorin, carefully, 'is to discover how five hundred million roubles were siphoned out of KGB funds, where Mamantov hid them, and how this money is being used to fund the anti-democratic opposition. We already know he bankrolls that red fascist mucksheet –'

'*Aurora* –'

' – *Aurora* – if it now turns out he's spending it on guns as well, I'm interested. If he's buying Stalin memorabilia, or selling it, for that matter – well, it's sick, but –'

'This isn't just *memorabilia*, Feliks. This – this is famous – there was a file on this notebook – it was one of "the legends of Lubyanka".'

Suvorin's first reaction was to laugh. The old man couldn't be serious, surely? Stalin's *notebook?* But then he saw the expression on Arsenyev's face and hastily turned his laughter into a cough. 'I'm sorry, Yuri Semonovich – forgive me – if you take it seriously, then, of course, I take it seriously.'

'Run the tape again, Feliks, would you be so good? I never could work these damned machines.'

He slid it across the desk with a hairy, pudgy forefinger. Suvorin came over from the sofa and they listened to it together, Arsenyev breathing heavily, tugging at the thick flesh of his fat neck, which was what he always did when he scented trouble.

'. . . *a black oilskin notebook that used to belong to Josef Stalin . . .*'

They were still bent over the tape when Netto crept back in, his complexion three shades paler than usual, to announce he had bad news.

FELIKS Stepanovich Suvorin, with Netto at his heels, walked back, grim-faced, to his office. It was a long trek from the leadership suites in the west of the building to the operational block in the east, and in the course of it at least a dozen people must have nodded and smiled at him, for in the Finnish-designed, wood and white-tile corridors of Yasenevo, the major was the golden boy, the coming man. He spoke English with an American accent, subscribed to the leading American magazines and had a collection of modern American jazz, which he listened to with his wife, the daughter of one of the President's most liberal economic advisers. Even Suvorin's clothes were American – the button-down shirt, the striped tie, the brown sports jacket – each one a legacy of his years as the KGB resident in Washington.

Look at Feliks Stepanovich!, you could see them thinking, as they struggled into their winter coats and hurried past to catch the buses home. Put in as number two to that fat old timer, Arsenyev, primed to take over an entire directorate at the age of thirty-eight. And not just any directorate, either, but RT – one of the most secret of them all! – licensed to conduct foreign intelligence operations on Russian soil. Look at him, the coming man, hurrying back to his office to work, while we go off home for the night . . .

'Good evening to you, Feliks Stepanovich!'
'So long, Feliks! Cheer up!'
'Working late again, I see, comrade major!'

Suvorin half-smiled, nodded, gestured vaguely with his pipe, preoccupied.

The details, as Netto had relayed them, were sparse but eloquent. Fluke Kelso had left the Mamantovs' apartment at fifteen-seven. Suvorin had also left the scene a few minutes later. At fifteen-twenty-two, Ludmilla Fedorova Mamantova, in the company of the bodyguard, Viktor Buḇka, was also observed to leave the apartment for her customary afternoon stroll to the Bolotnaya Park (given her confused condition, she had always to be accompanied). Since there was only one man on duty, they were not followed.

They did not return.

Shortly after seventeen hundred, a neighbour in the apartment beneath the Mamantovs' reported hearing prolonged, hysterical screams. The porter had been summoned, the apartment – with difficulty – opened and Madame Mamantov had been discovered alone, in her undergarments, locked inside a cupboard, through the door of which she had nevertheless managed to kick a hole using her bare feet. She had been taken to the Diplomatic Policlinic in a state of extreme distress. Both her ankles were broken.

'This must be an emergency escape plan,' said Suvorin, as they reached his office. 'He's clearly had this up his sleeve for quite a while, even down to establishing a routine for his wife. The question is: what's the emergency?'

He pressed the light switch. Neon panels stuttered into life. The leadership's side of the building had the view of the lake and the trees while Suvorin's office looked north, towards the Moscow ring road and the squat and crowded tower blocks of a housing estate. Suvorin threw himself into his chair, grabbed his tobacco pouch and swung his feet up on to the window sill. He saw Netto, reflected, coming in and closing the door. Arsenyev had given him a blasting, which wasn't really fair. If anyone was to blame, it was Suvorin, for sending Bunin after Kelso.

'How many men do we have at Mamantov's apartment right now?'

'Two, major.'

'Split them. One to the Policlinic to keep an eye on the wife, one to stay in place. Bunin's to stick with Kelso. What's his hotel?'

'The Ukraina.'

'Right. If he's heading south down the Garden Ring he's probably on his way back. Call Gromov at the Sixteenth and tell him we want a full communications intercept on Kelso. He'll tell you he hasn't the resources. Refer him to Arsenyev. Have the authorisation papers on my desk within fifteen minutes.'

'Yes, major.'

'Leave the Tenth to me.'

'The Tenth, major?' The Tenth was the archives branch.

'According to the colonel, there should be a file on this Stalin notebook.' Legend of the Lubyanka, indeed! 'I'll need to dream up some excuse to see it. Check on this place in Vspolnyi Street: what is it exactly? God, we need more men!' Suvorin banged his desk in frustration. 'Where's Kolosov?'

'He left for Switzerland yesterday.'

'Anybody else around? Barsukov?'

'Barsukov's in Ivanovo with his Germans.'

Suvorin groaned. This operation was running on paraffin and thin air, that was the trouble with it. It didn't have a name, a budget. Technically, it wasn't even legal.

Netto was writing rapidly. 'What do you want to do with Kelso?'

'Just continue to keep an eye on him.'

'Not pick him up?'

'For what exactly? And where do we take him? We have no cells. We have no legal basis to make arrests. How long's Mamantov been loose?'

'Three hours, major. I'm sorry, I –' Netto looked close to tears.

'Forget it, Vissi. It's not your fault.' He smiled at the young man's reflection. 'Mamantov was pulling stunts like that while we were in the womb. We'll find him,' he added, with a confidence he did not feel, 'sooner or later. Now off you go. I've got to call my wife.'

After Netto had gone, Suvorin removed the photograph of Kelso from its folder and pinned it to the noticeboard beside his desk. Here he was, with so much else to do, on issues which really mattered – economic intelligence, bio-technology, fibre optics – reduced to worrying about whether and why Vladimir Mamantov was after Stalin's notebook. It was absurd. It was worse than absurd. It was shaming. What kind of a country was this? Slowly, he tamped the tobacco in his pipe and lit it. And then he stood there for a full minute, his hands clasped behind his back, his pipe between his teeth, regarding the historian with an expression of pure loathing.

Chapter Seven

FLUKE KELSO LAY on his back, on his bed, in his room on the twenty-third floor of the Ukraina Hotel, smoking a cigarette and staring at the ceiling, the fingers of his left hand curled around the comforting and familiar shape of a quarter-bottle of Scotch.

He hadn't bothered to take off his coat, nor had he turned on the bedside lamp. Not that he needed to. The brilliant white floodlights that lit the Stalinist–Gothic skyscraper shone into his room and provided a feverish illumination. Through the closed window he could hear the sound of the early evening traffic on the wet road far below.

A melancholy hour this, he always thought, for a stranger in a foreign city – nightfall, the brittle lights, the temperature dropping, the office workers hurrying home, the businessmen trying to look cheerful in the hotel bars.

He took another swig of Scotch, then reached over for the ashtray and balanced it on his chest, tapping the end of his cigarette into it. The bowl hadn't been cleaned properly. Still stuck to its dusty bottom, like a small green egg, nested a gobbet of Papu Rapava's phlegm.

It had taken Kelso only a few minutes – the length of one short visit to the Ukraina's business centre and the time it took to flick through an old Moscow telephone directory – to establish that the house on Vspolnyi Street had indeed once been an African embassy. It was listed under the Republic of Tunisia.

And it had taken him only slightly longer to extract the rest of the information he needed – sitting on the edge of his hard and narrow bed, talking earnestly on the telephone to the press attaché at the new Tunisian Embassy, pretending an intense interest in the booming Moscow property market and the precise design of the Tunisian flag.

According to the press attaché, the Tunisians had been offered the mansion on Vspolnyi Street by the Soviet government in 1956, on a short-term lease, renewable every seven years. In January, the ambassador had been notified that the lease would not be extended when it came up for renegotiation, and in August they had moved out. And in truth, sir, they had not been too sorry to go, no indeed, not after that unfortunate business in 1993 when workmen had dug up twelve human skeletons, victims of the Stalinist repression, buried beneath the pavement outside. No explanation for the eviction had been offered, but, as everyone knew, great swathes of state property were now being privatised in central Moscow and sold on to foreign investors; fortunes were being made.

And the flag? The flag of the Tunisian Republic, honourable sir, was a red crescent and a red star in a white orb, all on a red ground.

'. . . *there was a red sickle moon and a single red star* . . . '

The blue shaving of cigarette smoke curled and broke against the dusty plaster.

Oh, he thought, how prettily it all hung together – Rapava's story and Yepishev's story and the convenient emptiness of the Beria mansion and the freshly turned earth and the bar named 'Robotnik'.

He finished the Scotch and stubbed out his cigarette and lay there for a while, turning the book of matches over and over, anti-clockwise in his fingers.

*

STILL unsure of what he should do, Kelso went down to the front desk and changed the last of his travellers' cheques into roubles. He would need to have cash, whatever happened. He would need ready money. His credit card was not entirely reliable these days – witness that unfortunate incident at the hotel shop, when he had tried to use it to buy his Scotch.

He thought he saw someone he recognised – from the symposium, presumably – and he raised his hand but they had already turned away.

On the counter of the reception was a sign – *Any guest requiring to make an international telephone call must please to leave a cash deposit* – and seeing it gave him a second stab of homesickness. So much happening, nobody to tell. On impulse he handed over $50 and made his way back through the crowded lobby towards the elevators.

Three marriages. He contemplated this extraordinary feat as the elevator shot him skywards. Three divorces in ascending order of bitterness.

Kate – well, Kate, that hardly counted, they were students, it was doomed from the start. She had even sent him Christmas cards until he moved to New York. And Irina – she at least had got her passport, which was always, he suspected, the main point of the exercise. But Margaret – poor Margaret – she was pregnant when he married her, which was why he married her, and no sooner had one boy arrived than the next was coming, and suddenly they were stuck in four cramped rooms off the Woodstock Road: the history teacher and the history student who between them had no history. It had lasted twelve years – 'as long as the Third Reich,' Fluke, drunk, had told an inquiring gossip columnist on the day that Margaret's petition for divorce had been published. He had never been forgiven.

Still, she was the mother of his children. Maggie. Margaret. He would call poor Margaret.

The line sounded strange from the moment the operator got on to the international circuit, and his first reaction was, *Russian phones!* He shook it hard as the New York number began to ring.

'Hello.' The familiar voice, sounding unfamiliarly bright.

'It's me.'

'Oh.' Flat, suddenly; dead. Not even hostile.

'Sorry to ruin your day.' It was meant to be a joke, but it came out badly, bitter and self-pitying. He tried again. 'I'm calling from Moscow.'

'Why?'

'Why am I calling or why am I calling from Moscow?'

'Are you drinking?'

He glanced at the empty bottle. He had forgotten her capacity to smell breath at four thousand miles. 'How are the boys? Can I talk to them?'

'It's eleven o'clock on a Tuesday morning. Where do you think they are?'

'School?'

'Well done, *dad*.' She laughed, despite herself.

'Listen,' he said, 'I'm sorry.'

'For what in particular?'

'For last month's money.'

'*Three* months' money.'

'It was some cock-up at the bank.'

'Get a job, Fluke.'

'Like you, you mean?'

'Fuck you.'

'All right. Withdrawn.' He tried again. 'I spoke to Adelman this morning. He might have something for me.'

'Because things can't go on like this, you know?'

'I know. Listen. I may be on to something here –'

'What's Adelman offering?'

'Adelman? Oh, teaching. But that's not what I mean. I'm on to something here. In Moscow. It could be nothing. It could be huge.'

'What is it?'

There was definitely something odd about the line. Kelso could hear his own voice playing back in his ear, too late to be an echo. *'It could be huge,'* he heard himself say.

'I don't want to talk about it on the phone.'

'You don't want to talk about it on the phone –'

'I don't want to talk about it on the phone.'

' – no, sure you don't. You know why? Because it's just more of the same old shit –'

'Hold on, Maggie. Are you hearing me twice?'

' – and here's Adelman offering you a proper job, but of course you don't want that, because that means facing up –'

'Are you hearing me twice?'

' – to your responsibilities –'

Quietly, Kelso replaced the receiver. He looked at it for a moment, and chewed his lip, then lay back on the bed and lit another cigarette.

STALIN, *as you know, was dismissive of women.*

Indeed, he believed the very notion of an intelligent woman was an oxymoron: he called them 'herrings with ideas'. Of Lenin's wife, Nadezhda Krupskaya, he once observed to Molotov: 'She may use the same lavatory as Lenin, but that doesn't mean she knows anything about Leninism.' After Lenin's death, Krupskaya believed her status as the great man's widow would protect her from Stalin's purges, but Stalin quickly disabused her. 'If you don't shut your mouth,' he told her, 'we'll get the Party a new Lenin's widow.'

However, this is not the whole story. And here we come to one of those strange reversals of the accepted wisdom which occasionally make our profession so rewarding. For while the common view of Stalin has always been that he was largely indifferent to sex – the classic case of the politician who channels all his carnal appetites into the pursuit of power – the truth appears to have been the opposite. Stalin was a womaniser.

The recognition of this facet of his character is recent. It was Molotov, in 1988, who coyly told Chuyev (Sto sorok besed s Molotovym, Moscow) *that Stalin had 'always been attractive to women'. In 1990, Khrushchev, with the posthumous publication of his last set of interviews* (The Glasnost Tapes, Boston) *lifted the curtain a little further. And now the archives have added still more valuable detail.*

Who were these women, whose favours Stalin enjoyed both before and after the suicide of his second wife? Some we know of. There was the wife of A. I. Yegorov, First Deputy People's Commissar of Defence, who was notorious in Party circles for her numerous affairs. And then there was the wife of another military man – Gusev – a lady who was allegedly in bed with Stalin on the night Nadezhda shot herself. There was Rosa Kaganovich, whom Stalin, as a widower, seems for a time to have thought of marrying. Most interesting of all, perhaps, there was Zhenya Alliluyeva, the wife of Stalin's brother-in-law, Pavel. Her relationship with Stalin is described in a diary which was kept by his sister-in-law, Maria. It was seized on Maria's arrest and only recently declassified (F45 O1 D1).

These, of course, are only the women we know something about. Others are mere shadows in history, like the young maidservant, Valechka Istomina, who joined Stalin's personal staff in 1935 ('whether or not she was Stalin's wife is nobody else's business,' Molotov told Chuyev), or the 'beautiful young woman with dark skin' Khrushchev once saw at Stalin's dacha. 'I was told later she was a tutor for Stalin's children,' he said, 'but she was not there for long. Later she vanished. She was there on Beria's recommendation. Beria knew how to pick tutors . . .'

'Later she vanished . . .'

Once again, the familiar pattern asserts itself: it was never very wise to know too much about Comrade Stalin's private life. One of the men he cuckolded, Yegorov, was shot; another, Pavel Alliluyev, was poisoned. And Zhenya herself, his mistress and his sister-in-law by marriage – 'the rose of the Novgorod fields' – was arrested on Stalin's orders and spent so long in solitary confinement that when eventually she was released, after his death, she could no longer talk – her vocal cords had atrophied . . .

HE must have fallen asleep because the next he knew the telephone was ringing.

The room was still in semi-darkness. He switched on the lamp and looked at his watch. Nearly eight.

He swung his legs off the bed and took a couple of stiff paces across the room to the little desk next to the window.

He hesitated, then picked up the receiver.

But it was only Adelman, wanting to know if he was coming down to dinner.

'Dinner?'

'My dear fellow, it's the great symposium farewell supper, not to be missed. Olga's going to come out of a cake.'

'Christ. Do I have a choice?'

'Nope. The story, by the way, is that you had a hangover of such epic proportions this morning you had to go back to your room and sleep it off.'

'Oh, that's lovely, Frank. Thank you.'

Adelman paused. 'So what happened? You find your man?'

'Of course not.'

'It's all balls?'

'Absolutely. Nothing in it.'

'Only – you know – you were gone all day –'

'I looked up an old friend.'

'Oh, I *get* you,' said Adelman, with heavy emphasis. 'Same old Fluke. Say, are you looking at this view?'

A glittering nightscape spread out at Kelso's feet, neon banners hoisted across the city like the standards of an invading army. Philips, Marlboro, Sony, Mercedes-Benz . . . There was a time when Moscow after sunset was as gloomy as any capital in Africa. Not any more.

There wasn't a Russian word in sight.

'Never thought I'd live to see this, did you?' Adelman's voice crackled down the receiver. 'This is victory we're looking at, my friend. You realise that? Total victory.'

'Is it really, Frank? It just looks like a lot of lights to me.'

'Oh no. It's more than that, believe me. They ain't coming back from this.'

'You'll be telling me next it's "the end of history".'

'Maybe it is. But not the end of historians, thank God.' Adelman laughed. 'Okay, I'll see you in the lobby. Say twenty minutes?' He hung up.

The searchlight on the opposite side of the Moskva, next to the White House, shone fiercely into the room. Kelso reached across and opened the wooden frame of the inner window and then of the outer, admitting a particulate breath of yellow mist and the white noise of the distant traffic. A few snowflakes fluttered across the sill and melted.

The end of history, my arse, he thought. This was

History's town. This was History's bloody *country*.

He stuck his head into the cold, leaning out to see as much of the city as he could across the river, before it was lost in the murk of the horizon.

If one Russian in six believed that Stalin was their greatest ruler, that meant he had about twenty million supporters. (The sainted Lenin, of course, had many more.) And even if you halved that figure, just to get down to the hard core, that still left ten million. Ten million Stalinists in the Russian Federation, after forty years of denigration?

Mamantov was right. It was an astounding figure. Christ, if one in six Germans had said they thought Hitler was the greatest leader they'd ever had, the *New York Times* wouldn't just have wanted an op-ed piece. They'd have put it on the front page.

He closed the window and began gathering together what he would need for the evening: his last two packets of duty free cigarettes, his passport and visa (in case he was picked up), his lighter, his bulging wallet, the book of matches with Robotnik's address.

It was no use pretending he was happy about this, especially after that business at the embassy, and if it hadn't been for Mamantov, he might have been tempted to leave matters as they stood – to play it safe, the Adelman way, and to come back to find Rapava in a week or two, perhaps after wangling a commission in New York from some sympathetic publisher (assuming such a mythical creature still existed).

But if Mamantov was on the trail, he couldn't afford to wait. That was his conclusion. Mamantov had resources at his disposal Kelso couldn't hope to beat. Mamantov was a collector, a fanatic.

And it was the thought of what Mamantov might do with

this notebook, if he found it first, that was also beginning to nag at him. Because the more Kelso turned matters over in his mind, the more obvious it became that whatever Stalin had written was important. It couldn't be some mere compendium of senile jottings, not if Beria wanted it enough to steal it and then, having stolen it, was willing to risk hiding it, rather than destroying it.

'He was squealing like a pig . . . shouting something about Stalin and something about an archangel . . . Then they put a scarf in his mouth and shot him . . .'

Kelso took a last look around the bedroom and turned out the light.

IT wasn't until he got down to the restaurant that he realised how hungry he was. He hadn't had a proper meal for a day and a half. He ate cabbage soup, then pickled fish, then mutton in a cream cheese sauce, with the Georgian red wine, Mukuzani, and sulphurous Narzan mineral water. The wine was dark and heavy and after a couple of glasses on top of the whisky he could feel himself becoming dangerously relaxed. There were more than a hundred diners at four big tables and the noise of the conversation and the clink and chime of glass and cutlery were soporific. Ukrainian folk music was being played over loudspeakers. He started to dilute his wine.

Someone – a Japanese historian, whose name he didn't know – leaned across and asked if this was Stalin's favourite drink and Kelso said no, that Stalin preferred the sweeter Georgian wines, Kindzmarauli and Hvanchkara. Stalin liked sweet wines and syrupy brandies, sugared herbal teas and strong tobacco –

'And Tarzan movies . . .' said someone.

'And the sound of dogs singing . . .'

Kelso joined in the laughter. What else could he do? He clinked glasses with the Japanese across the table, bowed and sat back, sipping his watery wine.

'Who's paying for all this?' someone asked.

'The sponsor who paid for the symposium, I guess.'

'Who's that?'

'American?'

'Swiss, I heard . . .'

The conversation resumed around him. After about an hour, when he thought no one was looking, he folded his napkin and pushed back his chair.

Adelman looked up and said, 'Not again? You can't run out on them again?'

'A call of nature,' said Kelso, and then, as he passed behind Adelman, he bent down and whispered, 'What's the plan for tomorrow?'

'The bus leaves for the airport after breakfast,' said Adelman. 'Check-in at Sheremetevo at eleven-fifteen.' He grabbed Kelso's arm. 'I thought you said this was all balls?'

'I did. I just want to find out what kind of balls.'

Adelman shook his head. 'This just isn't history, Fluke –'

Kelso gestured across the room. 'And this is?' Suddenly there was the sound of a knife being rapped against a glass, and Askenov pushed himself heavily to his feet. Hands banged the table in approval.

'Colleagues,' began Askenov.

'I'd sooner take my chances, Frank. I'll see you.'

He detached himself gently from Adelman's grip and headed towards the exit.

The cloakroom was by the toilets, next door to the dining room. He handed over his token, put down a tip and collected his coat, and he was just shrugging it on when he saw, at the end of the passage leading to the hotel lobby, a man. The man wasn't looking in his direction. He was pacing backwards and forwards across the corridor, talking into a mobile phone. If Kelso had seen him full-face he probably wouldn't have recognised him, and then everything would have turned out differently. But in profile the scar on the side of his face was unmistakable. He was one of the men who had been parked outside Mamantov's apartment.

Through the closed door behind him, Kelso could hear laughter and applause. He backed towards it, until he could feel the doorhandle – all this time keeping his eyes on the man – then he turned and quickly re-entered the restaurant.

Askenov was still on his feet and talking. He stopped when he saw Kelso. 'Doctor Kelso,' he said, 'seems to have a deep aversion to the sound of my voice.'

Saunders called out, 'He has an aversion to the sound of everyone's voice, except his own.'

There was more laughter. Kelso strode on.

Through the swing doors the kitchen was in pandemonium. He had an overpowering impression of heat and steam and of noise and the hot stink of cabbage and boiled fish. Waiters were lining up with trays of cups and coffee pots, being screamed at by a red-faced man in a stained tuxedo. Nobody paid Kelso any attention. He walked quickly across the huge room to the far end, where a woman in a green apron was unloading trays of dirty crockery off a trolley.

'The way out?' he said.

'*Tam,*' she said, gesturing with her chin. '*Tam.*' Over there.

The door had been wedged open to let in some cold air. He went down a dark flight of concrete steps and then he was outside, in the slushy snow, moving through a yard of overflowing trash bins and burst plastic sacks. A rat went scrabbling for safety in the shadows. It took him a minute or so to find his way out, and then he was in the big, enclosed courtyard at the rear of the hotel. Dark walls studded with lit windows rose on three sides of him. The low clouds above his head seemed to boil a yellowish-grey where they were struck by the beam of the searchlight.

He got out down a side-street on to Kutuzovskiy Prospekt and trudged through the wet snow beside the busy highway trying to find a taxi. A dirty, unmarked Volga swerved across two lanes of traffic and the driver tried to persuade him to get in, but Kelso waved him away and kept on walking until he came to the taxi rank at the front of the hotel. He couldn't be bothered to haggle. He climbed into the back of the first yellow cab in the queue and asked to be driven off, quickly.

Chapter Eight

THERE WAS A big football match in progress at the Dinamo stadium – an international, Russia playing someone-or-other, two-all, extra time. The taxi driver was listening to the commentary on the radio and as they came closer to the stadium, the cheers on the cheap plastic loudspeaker were subsumed into the roar of eighty thousand Muscovite throats less than two hundred yards away. The flurries of snow swelled and lifted like sails in the floodlights above the stands.

They had to go up Leningradskiy Prospekt, make a U-turn and come back down the other side to reach the stadium of the Young Pioneers. The taxi, an old Zhiguli that stank of sweat, turned off right, through a pair of iron gates, and bounced down a rutted track and into the sports ground. A few cars were drawn up in the snow in front of the grandstand, and there was a queue of people, mostly girls, outside an iron door with a peep-hole set into it. A sign above the entrance said 'Robotnik'.

Kelso paid the taxi driver a hundred roubles – a ludicrous amount, the price of not haggling before the journey started – and watched with some dismay as the red lights bucked across the rough surface, turned and disappeared. An immense noise, like a breaking wave, came from the phos-phorescent sky above the trees and rolled across the white sweep of the pitch. 'Three–two,' said a man with an Australian accent. 'It's over.' He pulled out a tiny black earpiece and stuffed it into his pocket. Kelso said to the nearest person, a girl, 'What time does it open?' and she turned to look at him. She was startlingly beautiful: wide dark eyes and wide cheekbones. She must have been about twenty. Snow flecked her black hair.

'Ten,' she said, and slipped her arm through his, pressing her breast against his elbow. 'Can I have a cigarette?'

He gave one to her and took one himself and their heads brushed as they bent to share the flame. He inhaled her perfume with the smoke. They straightened. 'One minute,' he said, smiling, and moved away, and she smiled back, waving the cigarette at him. He walked along the edge of the pitch, smoking, looking at the girls. Were they *all* hookers? They didn't seem like hookers. What were they, then? Most of the men were foreigners. The Russians looked rich. The cars were big and German, apart from one Bentley and one Rolls. He could see men in the back of them. In the Bentley, a red tip the size of a burning coal glowed and faded as someone smoked an immense cigar.

At five past ten, the door opened – a yellow light, the silhouettes of the girls, the steamy glow of their perfumed breath – a festive sight, thought Kelso, in the snow. And from the cars now came the serious money. You could tell the seriousness not just by the weight of the coats and the jewellery, but by the way their owners carried themselves, straight to the head of the queue, and by the amount of protection they left hanging around at the door. Clearly, the only guns allowed on the premises belonged to the management, which Kelso found reassuring. He went through a metal detector, then his pockets were checked for explosives by a goon with a wand. The admission fee was three hundred roubles – fifty dollars, the average weekly wage, payable in either currency – and in return for this he got an ultra-violet stamp on his wrist and a voucher for one free drink.

A spiral staircase led down to darkness, smoke and laser beams, a wall of techno-music pitched to make the stomach shake. Some of the girls were dancing listlessly together, the men were standing, drinking, watching. The idea of Papu Rapava showing his scowling face in here was a joke, and Kelso would have turned round there and then, but he felt in need of another drink, and fifty dollars was fifty dollars. He gave his voucher to the barman and took a bottle of beer. Almost as an afterthought, he beckoned the bartender towards him.

'Rapava,' he said. The barman frowned and cupped his ear, and Kelso bent closer. 'Rapava,' he shouted.

The barman nodded slowly, and said in English, 'I know.'

'You know?'

He nodded again. He was a young man, with a wispy blond beard and a gold earring. He began to turn away, to serve another customer so Kelso pulled out his wallet and put a one-hundred rouble note on the bar. That got his attention. 'I want to find Rapava,' he shouted.

The money was carefully folded and tucked into the barman's breast pocket. 'Later,' said the young man. 'Okay? I tell you.'

'When?'

But the young man smirked and moved further up the bar.

'Bribing bartenders?' said an American voice at Kelso's elbow. 'That's smart. Never thought of that. Get served first? Impress the ladies? Hello, Dr Kelso. Remember me?'

In the half-light, the handsome face was patched with colour and it took Kelso a couple of seconds to work out who he was. 'Mr O'Brian.' A television reporter. Wonderful. This was all he needed.

They shook hands. The young man's palm was moist and

fleshy. He was wearing his off-duty uniform – pressed blue jeans, white T-shirt, leather jacket – and Kelso registered broad shoulders, pectorals, thick hair glistening with some aromatic gel.

O'Brian gestured across the dance floor with his bottle. 'The new Russia,' he shouted. 'Whatever you want, you buy, and someone's always selling. Where're you staying?'

'The Ukraina.'

O'Brian made a face. 'Save your bribe for later's my advice. You'll need it. They're strict on the door at the old Ukraina. And those beds. Boy.' O'Brian shook his head and drained his bottle, and Kelso smiled and drank as well.

'Any other advice?' he yelled.

'Plenty, since you ask.' O'Brian beckoned him in close. 'The good ones'll ask for six hundred. Offer two. Settle on three. And we're talking all-night rates, remember, so keep some money back. As an incentive, let's say. And be careful of the real, *real* babes, 'cause they may be spoken for. If the other fellow's Russian, just walk away. It's safer, and there's plenty more – we're not talking life partners here. Oh, and they don't do triples. As a rule. These are respectable girls.'

'I'm sure.'

O'Brian looked at him. 'You don't get it, do you, professor? This ain't a whorehouse. Anna here –' he curled his arm around the waist of a blonde girl standing next to him and used his beer bottle as a microphone ' – Anna, tell the professor here what you do for a living.'

Anna spoke solemnly into the bottle. 'I lease property to Scandinavian businesses.'

O'Brian nuzzled her cheek and licked her ear and released her. 'Galina over there – the skinny one in the blue dress? – she works at the Moscow stock exchange. Who else? Damnit, they all look alike, after you've been here a time. Nataliya, the one you spoke to outside – oh, yes, I was watchin' you, professor, you sly old dog – Anna, darlin', what does Nataliya do?'

'Comstar, R.J.,' said Anna. 'Nataliya works for Comstar, remember?'

'Sure, sure. And what was the name of that cute kid at Moscow U? The psychologist, you know the one –'

'Alissa.'

'Alissa, right. Alissa – she in tonight?'

'She got shot, R.J.'

'Boy! Did she? *Really?*'

'Why were you watching me outside?' asked Kelso.

'That's commerce, I guess. You wanna make money, you gotta take risks. Three hundred a night. Let's say three nights a week. Nine hundred dollars. Give three hundred for protection. Still leaves six hundred clear. Twenty thousand dollars a year – that's not hard. What's that – seven times the average annual wage? And no tax? Gotta pay a price for that. Gotta take a risk. Like working on an oil rig. Let me get you a beer, professor. Why shouldn't I watch you? I'm a reporter, goddamnit. Everyone comes here watches everyone else. There's half a billion dollars worth of custom here tonight. And that's just the Russians.'

'Mafia?'

'No, just business. Same as any place else.'

The dance floor was packed now, the noise louder, the smoke denser. A new kind of lightshow had been switched on – lights that made everything that was white stand out dazzlingly bright. Teeth and eyes and nails and banknotes flashed in the gloom like knives. Kelso felt disorientated and vaguely drunk. But not, he thought, as drunk as O'Brian was pretending to be. There was something about the reporter that gave him the creeps. How old was he? Thirty? A young man in a hurry, if ever he'd seen one.

He said to Anna, 'What time does this finish?'

She held up five fingers. 'You want to dance, Mister Professor?'

'Later,' said Kelso. 'Maybe.'

'It's the Weimar Republic,' said O'Brian, coming back with two bottles of beer and a can of Diet Coke for Anna. 'Isn't that what you wrote? Look at it. Christ. All we need is Marlene Dietrich in a tuxedo and we might as well be in Berlin. I liked your book, professor, by the way. Did I say that already?'

'You did. Thanks. Cheers.'

'Cheers.' O'Brian raised his bottle and took a swig, then he leaned over and shouted in Kelso's ear. 'Weimar Republic, that's how I see it. Like you see it. Six things the same, okay? One: you have a big country, proud country, lost its empire, really lost a war, but can't figure out *how* – figures it must've been stabbed in the back, so there's a lot of resentment, right? Two: democracy in a country with no tradition of democracy – Russia doesn't know democracy from a fuckin' hole in the ground, frankly – people don't like it, sick of all the arguing, they want a strong line, *any* line. Three: border trouble – lots of your own ethnic nationals suddenly stuck in other countries, saying they're getting picked on. Four: anti-semitism – you can buy SS marchin' songs on the street corners, for Christ's sake. That leaves two.'

'All right.' It was disconcerting, hearing your own views so crudely parroted; like an Oxford tutorial –

'Economic crash, and that's coming, don't you think?'

'And?'

'Isn't it obvious? *Hitler.* They haven't found their Hitler yet. But when they do, it's watch out, world, I reckon.' O'Brian put his left forefinger under his nose and raised his right arm in a Nazi salute. Across the bar, a group of Russian businessmen whooped and cheered.

AFTER that, the evening accelerated. Kelso danced with Anna, O'Brian danced with Nataliya, they had more drinks – the American stuck to beer while Kelso tried the cocktails: B-52s, Kamikazes – they swapped girls, danced some more and then it was after midnight. Nataliya was in a tight red dress that was slippery, like plastic, and her flesh beneath it, despite the heat, felt cold and hard. She had taken something. Her eyes were wide and poorly focused. She asked if he wanted to go somewhere – she liked him a lot, she whispered, she'd do it for five hundred – but he just gave her fifty, for the pleasure of the dance, and went back to the bar.

Depression stalked him. He wasn't sure why. He could smell desperation, that was it: desperation stank as strongly as the perfume and the sweat. Desperation to buy. Desperation to sell. Desperation to pretend you were having a good time. A young man in a suit, so drunk he could barely walk, was being led away by his tie by a hard-faced girl with long blonde hair. Kelso decided he would have a smoke at the bar and then go – no, on second thoughts, forget the cigarette – he stuffed it back into the pack – he would go.

'Rapava,' yelled the barman.

'What?' Kelso cupped his hand to his ear.

'That's her. She's here.'

'What?'

Kelso looked to where the barman was pointing and saw her at once. *Her.* He let his gaze travel past her and then come back. She was older than the others: close-cropped black hair, black eyeshadow like bruises, black lipstick, a dead white face at once broad and thin, with cheekbones as sharp as a skull. Asiatic-looking. Mingrelian.

Papu Rapava: released from the camps in 1969. Married, say 1970, 1971. A son just old enough to fight in Afghanistan. And a daughter?

'My daughter's a whore . . . '

'Night night, professor –' O'Brian swept past with a wink over his shoulder, Nataliya on one arm, Anna on the other. The rest of his words were lost in the noise. Nataliya turned, giggled, blew Kelso a kiss. Kelso smiled vaguely, waved, put down his drink and moved along the bar.

A black cocktail dress – fabric shiny, knee-length, sleeveless – bare white throat and arms (not even a wrist watch), black stockings, black shoes. And something not quite right about her, some disturbance in the atmosphere around her, so that even at the crowded bar she was in a space, alone. No one was talking to her. She was drinking a bottle of mineral water without a glass and looking at nothing, her dark eyes were blank, and when he said hello she turned to face him, without interest. He asked if she wanted a drink.

No.

A dance, then?

She looked him over, thought about it, shrugged.

Okay.

She drained the bottle, set it on the bar, and pushed past him on to the dance floor, turned, waited for him. He followed her.

She didn't make much of a pretence and he rather liked her for that. The dance was merely a polite prelude to business, like a broker and a client spending ten seconds inquiring after each other's health. For about a minute she moved idly, at the edge of the pack, then she leaned over and said, 'Four hundred?'

No trace of perfume, just a vague scent of soap.

Kelso said, 'Two hundred.'

'Okay.'

She walked straight off the floor without looking back and he was so surprised by her failure to haggle that for a moment he was left alone. Then he went after her, up the spiral staircase. Her hips were full in the tight black dress, her waist thick, and it occurred to him that she didn't have long to go at this end of the game, that it was a mistake to invite immediate comparison with women eight, ten, maybe even twelve years her junior.

They collected their coats in silence. Hers was cheap, thin, too short for the season.

They went out into the cold. She took his arm. That was when he kissed her. He was slightly drunk and the situation was so surreal that he actually thought for a moment that he might combine business and pleasure. And he was curious, he had to admit it. She responded immediately, and with more passion than he'd expected. Her lips parted. His tongue touched her teeth. She tasted unexpectedly of something sweet and he remembered thinking that maybe her lipstick was flavoured with liquorice: was that possible?

She pulled away from him.

'What's your name?' he said.

'What name do you like?'

He had to smile at that. His luck: to find the first post-modern whore in Moscow. When she saw him smiling, she frowned.

'What's your wife's name?'

'I don't have a wife.'

'Girlfriend?'

'No girlfriend, either.'

She shivered and thrust her hands deep into her pockets. It had stopped snowing, and now that the metal door had closed behind them the night was silent.

She said, 'What's your hotel?'

'The Ukraina.'

She rolled her eyes.

'Listen,' he began, but he had no name to ease the conversation. 'Listen, I don't want to sleep with you. Or rather,' he corrected himself, 'I do, but that isn't what I had in mind.'

Was that clear?

'Ah,' she said, and looked knowing – looked like a whore for the first time, in fact. 'Whatever you want, it's still two hundred.'

'Do you have a car?'

'Yes.' She paused. 'Why?'

'The truth is,' he said, wincing at the lie, 'I'm a friend of your father's. I want you to take me to see him –'

That shocked her. She reeled back, laughing, panicky. 'You don't know my *father*.'

'Rapava. His name's Papu Rapava.'

She stared at him, slack mouthed, then slapped his face – hard, the heel of her hand connecting with the edge of his cheekbone – and started walking away, fast, stumbling a little: it couldn't have been easy in high heels on freezing snow. He let her go. He wiped his mouth with his fingers. They came away black with something. Not blood he realised: lipstick. Oh, but she packed a punch, though: he was hurting. Behind him, the door had opened. He was aware of people watching, and a murmur of disapproval. He could guess what they were thinking: rich westerner gets honest Russian girl outside, tries to renegotiate the terms, or suggests something so disgusting she can only turn and run – *bastard*. He set off after her.

She had veered on to the virgin snow of the pitch and had stopped, somewhere near the halfway line, staring into the dark sky. He trod along the path of her small footprints, came up behind her and waited, a couple of yards away.

After a while, he said, 'I don't know who you are. And I don't want to know who you are. And I won't tell your father how I found him. I won't tell anyone. I give you my word. I just want you to take me to where he lives. Take me to where he lives and I'll give you two hundred dollars.'

She didn't turn. He couldn't see her face.

'Four hundred,' she said.

Chapter Nine

FELIKS SUVORIN, IN a dark blue Crombie overcoat from Saks of Fifth Avenue, had arrived at the Lubyanka in the snow a little after eight that evening, sweeping up the slushy hill in the back of an official Volga.

His path had been eased by a call from Yuri Arsenyev to his old buddy, Nikolai Oborin – hunting crony, vodka partner and nowadays chief of the Tenth Directorate, or the Special Federal Archive Resource Bureau, or whatever the Squirrels had decided to call themselves that particular week.

'Now listen, Niki, I've got a young fellow in the office with me, name of Suvorin, and we've come up with a ploy . . . That's him . . . Now, listen, Niki, I can't say more than this: there's a foreign diplomat – western, highly placed – he's got a racket going, smuggling . . . No, not icons, this time, wait for it – documents – and we thought we'd lay a trap . . . That's it, that's it, you're way ahead of me, comrade – something big, something irresistible . . . Yes, that's an idea, but what about this: what about that notebook the old NKVDers used to go on about, what was it? . . . That's it, "Stalin's testament" . . . Well, this is why I'm calling now. We've got a problem. He's meeting the target tomorrow . . . *Tonight?* He can do tonight, Niki, I'm certain – I'm looking at him now, he's nodding – he can do tonight . . .'

Suvorin hadn't even had to repeat the tale, let alone elaborate upon it. Once inside the Lubyanka's marble hall, his papers checked, he'd followed his instructions and called a man named Blok, who was expecting him. He stood around the empty lobby, watched by the silent, uncurious

133

guards and contemplated the big white bust of Andropov, and presently there were footsteps. Blok – an ageless creature, stooped and dusty, with a bunch of keys on his belt – led him into the depths of the building, then out into a dark, wet courtyard and across it and into what looked like a small fortress. Up the stairs to the second floor: a small room, a desk, a chair, a wood-block floor, barred windows –

'How much do you want to see?'

'Everything.'

'That's your decision,' said Blok, and left.

Suvorin had always preferred to look ahead rather than to live in the past: something else he admired about the Americans. What was the alternative for a modern Russian? Paralysis! The end of history struck him as an excellent idea. History couldn't end soon enough, as far as Feliks Suvorin was concerned.

But even he could not escape the ghosts in this place. After a minute he got to his feet and prowled around. Craning his head at the high window he found he could see up to the narrow strip of night sky, and then down to the tiny windows, level with the earth, that marked the old Lubyanka cells. He thought of Isaak Babel, down there somewhere, tortured into betraying his friends, then frantically retracting, and of Bukharin, and his final letter to Stalin (*'I feel, toward you, toward the Party, toward the cause as a whole nothing but great and boundless love: I embrace you in my thoughts, farewell forever . . .'*) and of Zinoviev, disbelieving, being dragged away by his guard to be shot (*'Please comrade, please, for God's sake call Josef Vissarionovich . . .'*)

He pulled out his mobile phone, tapped in the familiar number and spoke to his wife.

'Hi, you'll never guess where I am . . . Who's to say?' He

felt better immediately for hearing her voice. 'I'm sorry about tonight. Hey, kiss the babies for me, will you . . .? And one for you, too, Serafima Suvorina . . .'

The secret police was beyond the reach of time and history. It was protean. *That* was its secret. The Cheka had become the GPU, and then the OGPU, and then the NKVD, and then the NKGB, and then the MGB, and then the MVD, and finally the KGB: the highest stage of evolution. And then, lo and behold!, the mighty KGB itself had been obliged by the failed coup to mutate into two entirely new sets of initials: the SVR – the spies – stationed out at Yasenevo, and the FSB – internal security – still here, in the Lubyanka, amid the bones.

And the view in the Kremlin's highest reaches was that the FSB, at least, was really nothing more than the latest in the long tradition of rearranged letters – that, in the immortal words of Boris Nikolaevich himself, delivered to Arsenyev in the course of a steam bath at the Presidential dacha, 'those motherfuckers in the Lubyanka are still the same old motherfuckers they always were'. Which was why, when the President decreed that Vladimir Mamantov had to be investigated, the task could not be entrusted to the FSB, but had to be farmed out to the SVR – and never mind if they hadn't the resources.

Suvorin had four men to cover the city. He called Vissari Netto for an update. The situation hadn't changed: the primary target – No. 1 – had still not returned to his apartment, the target's wife – No. 2 – was still under sedation, the historian – No. 3 – was still at his hotel and now having dinner.

'Lucky for some,' muttered Suvorin. There was a clatter in the corridor. 'Keep me informed,' he added firmly, and pressed END. He thought it sounded like the right kind of thing to say.

He had been expecting one file, maybe two. Instead, Blok threw open the door and wheeled in a steel trolley stacked with folders – twenty or thirty of them – some so old that when he lost control of the heavy contraption and collided with the wall, they sent up protesting clouds of dust.

'That's your decision,' he repeated.

'Is this the lot?'

'This goes up to sixty-one. You want the rest?'

'Of course.'

HE couldn't read them all. It would have taken him a month. He confined himself to untying the ribbon from each bundle, riffling through the torn and brittle pages to see if they contained anything of interest, then tying them up again. It was filthy work. His hands turned black. The spores invaded the membrane of his nose and made his head ache.

Highly confidential
28 June 1953
To Central Committee, Comrade Malenkov
I hereby enclose the deposition of the cross-examination of prisoner A. N. Poskrebyshev, former assistant to J. V. Stalin, concerning his work as an anti-Soviet spy.
The investigation is continuing.
USSR Deputy Minister of State Security,
A. A. Yepishev

This had been the start of it – a couple of pages, in the middle of Poskrebyshev's interrogation, underscored in red ink almost half a century ago, by an agitated hand:

Interrogator: Describe the demeanour of the General Secretary in the four years, 1949-53.

Poskrebyshev: The General Secretary became increasingly withdrawn and secretive. After 1951, he never left the Moscow district. His health deteriorated sharply, I should say from his 70th birthday. On several occasions I witnessed cerebral disturbances leading to blackouts, from which he quickly recovered. I told him: "Let me call the doctors, Comrade Stalin. You need a doctor." The General Secretary refused, stating that the 4th Main Administration of the Ministry of Health was under the control of Beria, and that while he would trust Beria to shoot a man, he would not trust him to cure one. Instead I prepared for the General Secretary herbal infusions.

Interrogator: Describe the effect of these health problems upon the General Secretary's conduct of his duties.

Poskrebyshev: Before the blackouts commenced, the General Secretary would sustain a workload of approximately two hundred documents each day. Afterwards, this number declined sharply and he ceased to see many of his colleagues. He made numerous writings of his own, to which I was not permitted access.

Interrogator: Describe the form of these private writings.

Poskreybshev: These private writings took various forms. In his final year, for example, he acquired a notebook.

Interrogator: Describe this notebook.

Poskrebyshev: This notebook was of an ordinary sort,

which might be bought in any stationers, with a black oilskin cover.

Interrogator: Which other persons knew of the existence of this notebook?

Poskrebyshev: The chief of his bodyguard, General Vlasik, knew of it. Beria also knew of it and asked me on several occasions to obtain a copy of it. This was not possible, even for me, as the General Secretary confined it to an office safe to which he alone possessed the key.

Interrogator: Speculate as to the contents of this notebook.

Poskrebyshev: I cannot speculate. I do not know.

Highly Confidential
30 June 1953
To USSR Deputy Minister of State Security, A. A. Yepishev

You are instructed to investigate the whereabouts of the personal writings of J. V. Stalin referred to by A. N. Poskrebyshev as a matter of supreme urgency and using all appropriate measures.

Central Committee,
Malenkov

Cross-examination of prisoner Lieutenant-General N. S. Vlasik
1 July 1953 [Extract]

Interrogator: Describe the black notebook belonging to J. V. Stalin.

Vlasik: I do not remember such a notebook.

Interrogator: Describe the black notebook belonging to J. V. Stalin.

Vlasik: I remember now. I first became aware of this in December 1952. One day I saw this notebook on Comrade Stalin's desk. I asked Poskrebyshev what it contained, but Poskrebyshev could not tell me. Comrade Stalin saw me looking at it and asked me what I was doing. I replied that I was doing nothing, that my eye had merely fallen upon this notebook, but that I had not touched it. Comrade Stalin said: "You as well, Vlasik, after more than thirty years?" I was arrested the following morning and brought to the Lubyanka.

Interrogator: Describe the circumstances of your arrest.

Vlasik: I was arrested by Beria, and subjected to numberless cruelties at his hands. Beria questioned me repeatedly about the notebook of Comrade Stalin. I was unable to tell him details. I know nothing further of this matter.

Statement of Lieutenant A. P. Titov, Kremlin Guard
6 July 1953 [Extract]
I was on duty in the leadership area of the Kremlin from 22:00 on 1 March 1953 until 06:00 the following day. At approximately 04:40, I encountered in the Passage of Heroes Comrade L. P. Beria and a second comrade whose identity is not known to me. Comrade Beria was carrying a small case or bag.

Interrogation of Lieutenant P. G. Rapava, NKVD
7 July 1953 [Extract]
Interrogator: Describe what happened following your departure from J. V. Stalin's dacha with the traitor Beria.

Rapava: I drove Comrade Beria to his home.

Interrogator: Describe what happened following your departure from J. V. Stalin's dacha with the traitor Beria.

Rapava: I remember now. I drove Comrade Beria to the Kremlin to enable him to collect material from his office.

Interrogator: Describe what happened following your departure from J. V. Stalin's dacha with the traitor Beria.

Rapava: I have nothing to add to my previous statement.

Interrogator: Describe what happened following your departure from J. V. Stalin's dacha with the traitor Beria.

Rapava: I have nothing to add to my previous statement.

Interrogation of L. P. Beria

8 July 1953 [Extract]

Interrogator: When did you first become aware of the personal notebook belonging to J. V. Stalin?

Beria: I refuse to answer any questions until I have been allowed to express myself before a full meeting of the Central Committee.

Interrogator: Both Vlasik and Poskrebyshev have confirmed your interest in this notebook.

Beria: The Central Committee is the proper forum in which all these matters should be addressed.

Interrogator: You do not deny your interest in this notebook.

Beria: The Central Committee is the proper forum.

Highly Confidential
30 November 1953
To USSR Deputy Minister of State Security, A. A. Yepishev
You are instructed to bring the investigation into the anti-Party criminal and traitor Beria to a rapid conclusion, and to move this matter to trial.
Central Committee,
Malenkov
Khrushchev

Interrogation of L. P. Beria
2 December 1953 [Extract]
Interrogator: We know that you took possession of the notebook of J. V. Stalin, yet you continue to deny this matter. What was your interest in this notebook?
Beria: End it.
Interrogator: What was your interest in this notebook?
Beria: [The accused indicated by gesture his refusal to co-operate]

Highly confidential
23 December 1953
To Central Committee, Comrades Malenkov, Khrushchev
I beg to report that the sentence of death by shooting imposed on L. P. Beria was carried out today at 01:50.
T. R. Falin,
Procurator General

27 December 1953
Judgement of the People's Special Court in the case of

Lieutenant P. G. Rapava: 15 years' penal servitude.

SUVORIN couldn't bear the filth of his hands any longer. He wandered the empty corridor until he found a toilet with a sink where he could wash himself down. He was still in there, trying to get the last of the dust out from under his fingernails, when his mobile phone rang. In the silence of the Lubyanka it made him jump.

'Suvorin.'

'It's Netto. We've lost him. No. 3.'

'Who? What're you talking about?'

'No. 3. The historian. He went in to eat with the others. He never came out. It looks as though he left through the kitchens.'

Suvorin groaned, turned, leaned against the wall. This whole business was spinning out of control.

'How long ago?'

'About an hour. In defence of Bunin, he has been on duty for eighteen hours.' A pause. 'Major?'

Suvorin had the phone wedged between his chin and shoulder. He was drying his hands, thinking. He didn't blame Bunin, actually. To mount a decent surveillance took at least four watchers; six for safety.

'I'm still here. Stand him down.'

'Do you want me to tell the chief?'

'I think not, don't you? Not twice in one day. He might begin to think we're incompetent.' He licked his lips, tasting dust. 'Why don't you go home yourself, Vissari? We'll meet in my office, eight tomorrow.'

'Have you discovered anything?'

'Only that when people go on about "the good old days" they're talking shit.'

He rinsed his mouth, spat, went back to work.

BERIA was shot, Poskrebyshev released, Vlasik got a sentence of ten years, Rapava was sent to Kolyma, Yepishev was taken off the case, the investigation meandered on.

Beria's house was searched from attic to cellar and yielded no further evidence, apart from some pieces of human remains (female) that had been partially dissolved by acid and bricked up. He had his own private network of cells in the basement. The property was sealed. In 1956, the Ministry for Foreign Affairs asked the KGB if it had any suitable premises which might be offered as an embassy to the new Republic of Tunisia, and, after a final brief investigation, Vspolnyi Street was handed over.

Vlasik was interrogated twice more about the notebook, but added nothing new. Poskrebyshev was watched, bugged, encouraged to write his memoirs and, when he had finished, the manuscript was seized 'for permanent retention'. An extract, a single page, had been clipped to the file:

What went through the mind of this incomparable genius in that final year, as he confronted the obvious fact of his own mortality, I do not know. Josef Vissarionovich may have confided his most private thoughts to a notebook, which rarely left his side during his final months of unstinting toil for his people and the cause of progressive humanity. Containing, as it may do, the distillation of his wisdom as the leading theoretician of Marxism–Leninism, it must be hoped that this remarkable document will one day be discovered and published for the benefit . . .

Suvorin yawned, closed the bundle and put it to one side, grabbed another. This turned out to be the weekly reports of a Gulag stool-pigeon named Abidov, assigned to keep an eye on the prisoner Rapava during his time at the Butugychag uranium mine. There was nothing of interest in the smudged carbons, which ended abruptly with a laconic note from the camp KGB officer, recording Abidov's death from a stab wound, and Rapava's transfer to a forestry labour detail.

More files, more stoolies, more of nothing. Papers authorising Rapava's release at the conclusion of his sentence, reviewed by a special commission of the Second Chief Directorate – passed, stamped, authorised. Appropriate work selected for the returning prisoner at the Leningrad Station engine sheds; KGB informer-in-place: Antipin, foreman. Appropriate housing selected for the returning prisoner at the newly built Victory of the Revolution complex; KGB informer-in-place: Senka, building supervisor. More reports. Nothing. Case reviewed and classified as 'diversion of resources', 1975. Nothing on file until 1983, when Rapava was briefly re-examined at the request of the deputy chief of the Fifth Directorate (Ideology and Dissidents).

Well, well . . .

Suvorin pulled out his pipe and sucked at it, scratched his forehead with the stem, then went searching back through the files. How old was this fellow? Rapava, Rapava, Rapava – here it was, Papu Gerasimovich Rapava, born 9.9.27.

Old, then – in his seventies. But not *that* old. Not so old that even in a country where the average male life expectancy was fifty-eight and falling – worse than it had been in Stalin's time – not so old that he need necessarily be *dead*.

He flipped back to the 1983 report, and scanned it. It told him nothing he didn't know already. Oh, he was a tight one, this Rapava – not a word in thirty years. Only when he reached the bottom, and saw the recommendation to take no further action, and the name of the officer accepting this recommendation did he jolt up in his chair.

He swore and fumbled for his mobile, tapped out the number of the SVR's night duty officer and asked to be patched through to the home of Vissari Netto.

Chapter Ten

THEY SETTLED ON three hundred, and for that he insisted on two things: first, that she drove him there herself and, secondly, that she waited an hour. An address on its own would be useless at this time of night, and if Rapava's neighbourhood was as rough as the old man had implied it was (*it was a decent block in those days, boy, before the drugs and the crime . . .*) then no foreigner in his right mind would go stumbling around there alone.

Her car was a battered, ancient Lada, sand-coloured, parked in the dark street that led to the stadium, and they walked to it in silence. She opened her door first and then reached across to let him in. There was a pile of books on the passenger seat – legal textbooks, he noticed – and she moved them quickly into the back.

He said, 'Are you a lawyer? Are you studying the law?'

'Three hundred dollars,' she said, and held out her hand. 'US.'

'Later.'

'Now.'

'Half now,' he said, cunningly, 'half later.'

'I can get another fuck, mister. Can you get another ride?'

It was her longest speech of the night.

'Okay, okay.' He pulled out his wallet. 'You'll make a good lawyer.' Jesus. Three hundred to her, after more than a hundred at the club – it just about cleaned him out. He had thought he might try offering the old man some cash, this evening, as a downpayment for the notebook, but that wouldn't be possible now.

She re-counted the notes, folded them carefully and put them away in her coat pocket. The little car rattled down to the Leningradskiy Prospekt. She made a right into the quiet traffic, then did a U-turn, and now they were heading out of the city, back past the deserted Dinamo stadium, north-west, towards the airport.

She drove fast. He guessed she wanted to be rid of him. Who was she? The Lada's interior offered him no clues. It was fastidiously clean, almost empty. He gave her profile a surreptitious look. Her face was tilted downwards slightly. She was scowling at the road. The black lips, the white cheeks, the small and delicately pointed ears below the lick of short black hair – she had a vampirish look: disturbing, he thought again. Disturbed. He still had the taste of her in his mouth and he couldn't help wondering what the sex would have been like – she was so utterly out of reach now, yet fifteen minutes earlier she would have done whatever he asked.

She glanced up at the mirror and caught him looking at her. 'Cut that out.'

He continued to stare anyway – more frankly now: he was making a point, he had paid for the ride – but then he felt cheap and turned away.

The streets beyond the glass had become much darker. He didn't know where they were. They had passed the Park of Friendship, he knew that, and passed a power station, a railway junction. Thick pipes carrying communal hot water ran beside the road, across the road, along the other side, steam leaking from their joints. Occasionally, in the patches of blackness, he could see the flames of bonfires and people moving around them. After another ten minutes, they turned off left into a street as wide and rough as a field, with scruffy birch trees on either side. They hit a pothole and the chassis cracked, scraped rock. She spun the wheel and they hit another. Orange lights beyond the trees dimly lit the gantries and stairwells of a giant housing complex.

She had slowed the car now almost to walking pace. She stopped beside a broken-down wooden bus shelter.

'That's his place,' she said. 'Block number nine.'

It was about a hundred yards away, across a snowy strip of waste ground.

'You'll wait here?'

'Entrance D. Fifth floor. Apartment twelve.'

'But you'll wait?'

'If you want.'

'We did agree.'

Kelso looked at his watch. It was twenty-five past one. Then he looked again at the apartment block, trying to think what he would say to Rapava, wondering what reception he would get.

'So this is where you grew up?'

She didn't answer. She switched off the engine and turned up her collar, put her hands in her pockets, stared ahead. He sighed and got out of the car, walked around it. The powdery snow creaked as it compacted under his feet. He shivered and began to pick his way over the rough ground.

He was about halfway across when he heard the grating of an ignition and an engine firing up. He swung round to see the Lada moving off slowly, lights doused. She hadn't even bothered to wait until he was out of sight. *Bitch*. He began running towards her. He shouted – not loudly, and not in anger really: it was more a groan at his own stupidity. The little car was shuddering, stalling, and for a moment he thought he might catch up with it, but then it coughed, lurched, the lights came on and it accelerated away from him. He stood and watched it helplessly as it vanished into the labyrinth of concrete.

He was alone. Not a soul in view.

He turned and began quickly retracing his steps, crunching across the snow towards the building. He felt vulnerable in the open and panic sharpened his senses. Somewhere to his left, he could hear the bark of a dog and a baby's cry, and ahead of him there was music – it was faint, there was scarcely more than a thread of it, but it was coming from Block Nine and it was getting louder with each step. His eyes were making out details now – the ribbed concrete, the shadowed doorways, the stacked balconies crammed with junk: bed frames, bike frames, old tyres, dead plants; three windows were lit, the rest in darkness.

At Entrance D something crunched beneath his foot and he bent to pick it up, then dropped it, fast. A hypodermic syringe.

The stairwell was a sump of piss and vomit, stained newsprint, limp condoms, dead leaves. He covered his nose with the back of his hand. There was an elevator, and it might have been working – a Moscow miracle that would have been – but he didn't propose to try. He climbed the stairs, and by the time he reached the third floor he could hear the music much more clearly. Someone was playing the old Soviet national anthem – the *old* old anthem, that was – the one they used to sing before Khrushchev had it censored. 'Party of Lenin!' shouted the chorus. 'Party of Stalin!' Kelso took the last two flights more quickly, with a sudden rush of hope. She hadn't entirely tricked him, then, for who else but Papu Rapava would be playing the greatest hits of Josef Stalin at half-past one in the morning?

He came out on to the fifth floor and followed the noise along the dingy passage to number twelve. The block was largely derelict. Most of the doors were boarded over, but not Rapava's. Oh no, boy. Rapava's door wasn't boarded over. Rapava's door was open and outside it, for reasons Kelso couldn't begin to fathom, there were feathers on the floor.

The music stopped.

COME on then, boy. What're you waiting for? What's up? Don't tell me you haven't the balls –

For several seconds, Kelso stood on the threshold, listening.

Suddenly there was a drumroll.

The anthem began again.

Cautiously, he pushed at the door. It was partially open, but it wouldn't go back any further. There was something behind it, blocking it.

He squeezed around the edge. The lights were on.

Dear God –

Thought you'd be impressed, boy! Thought you'd be surprised! If you're going to get fucked over, you might as well get fucked over by professionals, eh?

At Kelso's feet were more feathers, leaking from a cushion that had been disembowelled. These feathers could not be said to be on the floor, however, because there was no floor. The boards were all prised up and stacked around the edges of the room. Strewn across the rib-cage of the joists were the remains of Rapava's few possessions – books with splayed and shattered spines, punched-through pictures, the skeletons of chairs, an exploded television, a table with its legs in the air, bits of crockery, shards of glass, shredded fabric. The interior walls had been skinned to expose the cavities. The exterior walls were bruised and dented, apparently by a sledgehammer. Much of the ceiling was hanging down. Plaster dust frosted the room.

Balanced in the centre of this chaos, amid a black and jagged pool of broken records, was a bulky 1970s Telefunken record player, set to automatic replay.

Party of Lenin!

Party of Stalin!

Kelso stepped carefully from rib to rib and lifted the needle.

In the silence: the dripping of a broken tap.

The extent of the destruction was so overwhelming, so utterly beyond anything he had ever seen, that once he was satisfied the apartment was empty, it barely occurred to him that he ought to be scared. Not at first. He peered around him, baffled.

So where am I, boy? That's the question. What have they done with poor old Papu? Come on then, come and get me. Chop, chop, comrade – we haven't got all night!

Kelso, wobbling, tightrope-walked along a joist, into the kitchen alcove: slashed packets, upended ice-box, wrenched-down cupboards . . .

He edged backwards and round the corner into a little passage, scrabbling at the broken wall to stop himself from slipping.

Two doors here, boy – right and left. You take your pick.

He swayed, indecisive, then reached out a hand.

The first – a bedroom.

Now you're getting warm, boy. By the way: did you want to fuck my daughter?

Slashed mattress. Slashed pillow. Overturned bed. Empty drawers. Small and tatty nylon carpet, rolled and stacked. Clumps of plaster everywhere. Floor up. Ceiling down.

Kelso back in the passage, breathing hard, balanced on a rib, summoning the nerve.

The second door –

Very warm now, boy!

– the second door: the bathroom. Cistern lid off, propped against the toilet. Sink dragged away from the wall. A white plastic tub brimming with pinkish water that made Kelso think of diluted Georgian wine. He dipped his finger in and pulled it out sharply, shocked at the coldness, his fingertip sheathed in red.

Floating on the surface: a ring of hair still attached to a small flap of skin.

Let's go, boy.

Rib to rib, plaster dust in his hair, on his hands, all over his coat, his shoes –

He stumbled in his panic, lost his footing on the beam, and his left shoe punched a hole into the ceiling of the flat beneath. A piece of debris detached itself. He heard it fall into the darkness of the empty apartment. It took him half a minute and both hands to pull his foot free, and then he was out of there.

He squashed himself around the door and into the corridor and moved quickly back along the passage, past abandoned apartments, towards the stairs. He heard a thump.

He stopped and listened.

Thump.

Oh, you're hot, now, boy, you're very, very hot . . .

It was the elevator. It was someone inside the elevator.

Thump.

*

THE Lubyanka, the still of night, the long black car with the engine running, two agents in overcoats charging down the steps – *was there no escaping the past?* thought Suvorin, bitterly, as they accelerated away. He was surprised there were no tourists on hand to record this traditional scene of life in Mother Russia. *Why not put it in the album, darling, between St Basil's Cathedral and a troika in the snow?*

They thumped into a dip at the bottom of the hill near the Metropol Hotel, and his head connected with the cushioned roof. In the front seat, next to the driver, Netto was unfolding a large-scale map of the Moscow streets of a detail that no tourist would ever see because it was still officially secret. Suvorin snapped on the interior light and leaned forward for a better look. The apartment blocks of the Victory of the Revolution complex were scattered like postage stamps across the Tagansko–Krasno metro line, in the north-west outer suburb.

'How long do you reckon? Twenty minutes?'

'Fifteen,' said the driver, showing off. He gunned the engine, shot the lights, swung right, and Suvorin was pitched the other way, against the door. He had a brief impression of the Lenin Library flashing past.

'Relax,' he said, 'for pity's sake. We don't want to get a ticket.'

They sped on. Once they were clear of the centre, Netto unlocked the glove compartment and handed Suvorin a well-oiled Makarov and a clip of ammunition. Suvorin took it reluctantly, felt the unfamiliar weight in his hand, checked the mechanism and sighted briefly at a passing birch tree. He hadn't joined the service because he enjoyed this kind of thing. He had joined because his father was a diplomat who had taught him early on that the best thing to do if you lived in the Soviet Union was to get a posting abroad. Guns? Suvorin hadn't set foot on the Yasenevo range inside a year. He gave the weapon back to Netto who shrugged and stuffed it in his own pocket.

A blue dot grew noisily in the road behind them, swelled and flashed past like an angry fly – a patrol car of the Moscow militia. It dwindled into the distance.

'Asshole,' said their driver.

A few minutes later they turned off the main road and headed into the wilderness of concrete and wasteland that was the Victory of the Revolution. Fifteen years in Kolyma, thought Suvorin, then welcome home to this. And the joke was, it must have seemed like paradise.

Netto said, 'According to the map, Block Nine should be just round this corner.'

'Slow down,' ordered Suvorin, suddenly, putting his hand on the driver's shoulder. 'Can you hear something?'

He wound down his window. Another siren, off to the left. It faded for a moment, muffled by a building, then became very loud, and colours burst ahead – a blue and yellow light-show, rather pretty, moving fast. For a couple of seconds the patrol car seemed to be coming straight at them but then it swung off the road and bounced over the rough ground, and a moment later they were level with it and could see the entrance to the block themselves, lit up like a fairyland – three cars, an ambulance, people moving, shadowed tracks in the snow.

They cruised round the building a couple of times, a trio of ghouls, unnoticed, as the stretcher men brought out the body and then Kelso was driven away.

Chapter Eleven

SIMONOV TELLS THE following story.

At meetings of the Council of People's Commissars, it was Comrade Stalin's habit to rise from his place at the head of the long table and to pace behind the backs of the participants. Nobody dared to look round at him: they could establish where he was only by the soft squeak of his leather boots or by the passing fragrance of his Dunhill pipe. On this particular occasion, the conversation concerned the large number of recent plane crashes. The head of the air force, Rychagov, was drunk. 'There will continue to be a high level of accidents,' he blurted out, 'as long as we're compelled by you to go up in flying coffins.' There was a long silence, at the end of which Stalin murmured, 'You really shouldn't have said that.' A few days later, Rychagov was shot.

One could quote any number of such stories. His favourite technique, according to Khrushchev, was suddenly to look at a man and say: 'Why is your face so shifty today? Why can't you look Comrade Stalin directly in the eyes?' That was the moment when one's life hung in the balance.

Stalin's use of terror seems to have been partly instinctive (he was naturally physically violent: he sometimes struck his subordinates in the face) and partly calculated. 'The people,' he told Maria Svanidze, 'need a tsar.' And the tsar upon whom he modelled himself was Ivan the Terrible. We have written confirmation of that here in this archive, in Stalin's personal library, which contains a copy of A. M. Tolstoy's 1942 play, Ivan Grozny (F558 O3 D350). *Not only has Stalin corrected the speeches of Ivan to make them sound more clipped and laconic –*

to sound more like himself, in fact – but he has also scrawled repeatedly over the title page 'Teacher'.

Indeed, he had only one criticism of his role model: that he was too weak. As he told the director, Sergei Eisenstein: 'Ivan the Terrible would execute someone and then spend a long time repenting and praying. God got in his way in this matter. He ought to have been still more decisive!' (Moskovskie novosti, no. 32, 1988).

Stalin was nothing if not decisive.

Professor I. A. Kuganov estimates that some sixty-six million people were killed in the USSR between 1917 and 1953 – shot, tortured, starved mostly, frozen or worked to death. Others say the true figure is a mere forty-five million. Who knows?

Neither estimate, by the way, includes the thirty million now known to have been killed in the Second World War.

To put this loss in context: the Russian Federation today has a population of roughly 150 million. Assuming the ravages inflicted by communism had never occurred, and assuming normal demographic trends, the actual population should be about 300 million.

And yet – and this is surely one of the most astounding phenomena of the age – Stalin continues to enjoy a wide measure of popular support in this half-empty land. His statues have been taken down, true. The street names have been changed. But there have been no Nuremberg Trials, as there were in Germany. There has been no process here equivalent to de-Nazification. There has been no Truth Commission, of the sort established in South Africa.

And the opening of the archives? 'Confronting the past'? Come, ladies and gentlemen, let us say frankly what we all know to be the case. That the Russian government today is scared, and that it is actually harder to gain access to the archives now than it was six or seven years ago. You all know the facts as well as I do. Beria's files: closed. The Politburo's files: closed. Stalin's files – the real files, I mean, not the window dressing on offer here: closed.

I can see my remarks are not being well received by one or two colleagues –

All right, I shall draw them to a conclusion, with this observation: that there can now be no doubt that it is Stalin rather than Hitler who is the most alarming figure of the twentieth century.

I say this –

I say this not merely because Stalin killed more people than Hitler – although clearly he did – and not even because Stalin was more of a psychopath than Hitler – although clearly he was. I say it because Stalin, unlike Hitler, has not yet been exorcised. And also because Stalin was not a one-off like Hitler, an eruption from nowhere. Stalin stands in a historical tradition of rule by terror which existed before him, which he refined, and which could exist again. His, not Hitler's, is the spectre that should worry us.

Because, you know, you think about it. You hail a taxi in Munich – you don't find the driver displaying Hitler's portrait in his cab, do you? Hitler's birthplace isn't a shrine. Hitler's grave isn't piled with fresh flowers every day. You can't buy tapes of Hitler's speeches on the streets of Berlin. Hitler isn't routinely praised as 'a great patriot' by leading German politicians. Hitler's old party didn't receive more than forty per cent of the votes in the last German election –

But all these things are true of Stalin in Russia today, which is what makes the words of Yevtushenko, in 'The Heirs of Stalin', more relevant now than ever:

'So I ask our government
    To double
        To treble
            The guard
                Over this tomb.'

FLUKE Kelso was escorted into the headquarters of the central division of the Moscow City Militia shortly before three a.m. And there he was left, washed up with the rest of the night's detritus – half a dozen hookers, a Chechen pimp, two white-faced Belgian bankers, a troupe of transsexual dancers from Turkestan and the usual midnight chorus of outraged lunatics, tramps and bloodied addicts. High-corniced ceilings and half-blown chandeliers gave proceedings a Revolutionary epic look.

He sat alone on a hard wooden bench, his head leaning back on the peeling plaster, staring ahead, unseeing. So that – *that* was what it looked like? Oh, you could spend half a lifetime *writing* about it all, about the millions – about Marshal Tukhachevsky, say, beaten to a pulp by the NKVD: there was his confession in the archives, still sprinkled with his dried blood: you even held it in your hands – and you thought for a moment you had a sense of what it must have been like, but then you confronted the reality and you realised you hadn't understood it at all, you hadn't even *begun* to know what it was like.

After a while two militia men wandered up and stood at the metal drinking fountain next to him, discussing the case of the Uzbeki bandit, Tsexer, apparently machine-gunned earlier that evening in the cloakroom of the Babylon.

'Is anyone dealing with my case?' interrupted Kelso. 'It is a murder.'

'Ah, a murder!' One of the men rolled his eyes in mock surprise. The other laughed. They dropped their paper cones in the trash can and moved off.

'Wait!' shouted Kelso.

Across the corridor, an elderly woman with a bandaged hand started screaming.

He sank back on to the bench.

Presently, a third officer, powerfully built, with a Gorky moustache, came wearily downstairs and introduced himself as Investigator Belenky, a homicide detective. He was holding a piece of grubby paper.

'You're the witness in the business involving the old man, Rapazin?'

'Rapava,' corrected Kelso.

'Right. That's it.' Belenky squinted at the top and bottom of the paper. Perhaps it was the walrus moustache or maybe it was his watery eyes but he seemed immensely sad. He sighed. 'Okay. We'd better have a statement.'

Belenky led him up a grand staircase to the second floor, to a room with flaking green walls and an uneven, shiny woodblock floor. He gestured to Kelso to sit, and put a pad of lined forms in front of him.

'The old man had Stalin's papers,' began Kelso, lighting a cigarette. He exhaled quickly. 'You ought to know that. Almost certainly he had them hidden in his apartment. That's why –'

But Belenky wasn't listening. 'Everything you can remember.' He slapped a blue biro down on the table.

'But you hear what I'm saying? Stalin's papers –'

'Right, right.' The Russian still wasn't listening. 'We'll sort out the details later. Need a statement first.'

'All of it?'

'Of course. Who you are. How you met the old man. What you were doing at the apartment. The whole story. Write it down. I'll be back.'

After he had gone, Kelso stared at the blank paper for a couple of minutes. Mechanically, he wrote his full name, his date of birth and his address in neat Cyrillic script. His mind was a fog. '*I arrived,*' he wrote, and paused. The plastic pen felt as heavy between his fingers as a crowbar. '*I arrived in Moscow on –*' He couldn't even remember the date. He who was normally so good at dates! (25 October 1917, the battle-cruiser *Aurora* shells the Winter Palace and begins the Revolution; 17 January 1927, Leon Trotsky is expelled from the Politburo; 23 August 1939: the Molotov–Ribbentrop pact is signed . . .) He bent his head to the desk. ' *– I arrived in Moscow on the morning of Monday October 26 from New York at the invitation of the Russian Archive Service to deliver a short lecture on Josef Stalin . . .*'

He finished his statement in less than an hour. He did as he was told and left nothing out – the symposium, Rapava's visit, the Stalin notebook, the Lenin Library, Yepishev and the meeting with Mamantov, the house on Vspolnyi Street, the freshly dug earth, Robotnik and Rapava's daughter . . . He filled seven pages with his tiny scrawl, and took the final section even quicker, hurrying over the scene in the apartment, the discovery of the body, his desperate search for a working telephone in the next-door block, eventually rousing a young woman with a baby on her hip. It felt good to be writing again, to be imposing some kind of rational order on the chaos of the past.

Belenky put his head round the door just as Kelso added the final sentence.

'You can forget that now.'

'I've done.'

'No?' Belenky stared at the small pile of sheets and then at Kelso. There was a commotion in the corridor behind him. He frowned, then yelled over his shoulder, 'Tell him to wait.' He came into the room and closed the door.

Something had happened to Belenky, that much was obvious. His tunic was unbuttoned, his tie loose. Dark patches of sweat stained his khaki shirt. Without taking his eyes off Kelso's face, he held out his massive hand and Kelso gave him the statement. He sat down with a grunt on the opposite side of the table and took a plastic case from his breast pocket. From the case he withdrew a surprisingly delicate pair of gold-framed, half-moon glasses, shook them open, perched them on the end of his nose, and began to read.

His heavy chin jutted forwards. Occasionally, his eyes would flicker up from the page to Kelso, study him for a moment, then return to the text. He winced. His moustache sagged lower over his tightening lips. He chewed the knuckle of his right thumb.

When he laid the final page aside he gave a sigh.

'And this is true?'

'All of it.'

'Well, fuck your mother.' Belenky took off his glasses and rubbed his eyes with the side of his hand. 'Now what am I supposed to do?'

'Mamantov,' said Kelso. 'He must have been involved. I was careful not to give him any details but –'

The door opened and a small, thin man, a Laurel to Belenky's Hardy, said, in a frightened voice, 'Sima! Quick! They're here!'

Belenky gave Kelso a significant look, gathered the statement together and pushed back his chair. 'You'll have to go down to the cells for a bit. Don't be alarmed.'

At the mention of cells Kelso felt a spasm of panic. 'I'd like to speak to someone from the embassy.'

Belenky stood and slid his tie back up into a tight knot, fastened the buttons of his tunic, tugged the jacket down in a hopeless attempt to straighten it.

'Can I speak to someone from the embassy?' repeated Kelso. 'I'd like to know my rights.'

Belenky squared his shoulders and moved towards the door. 'Too late,' he said.

IN the cells beneath the headquarters of the Central Division of the Moscow City Militia, Kelso was roughly frisked and parted from his passport, wallet, watch, fountain pen, belt, tie and shoelaces. He watched them shovelled into a cardboard envelope, signed a form, was handed a receipt. Then, with his boots in one hand, his chit in the other and his coat over his arm, he followed the guard down a whitewashed passage lined on either side with steel doors. The guard was suffering from a plague of boils – his neck above his greasy brown collar looked like a plate of red dumplings – and at the sound of his footsteps, the inmates of some of the cells began a frantic shouting and banging. He took no notice.

The eighth cubicle on the left. Three yards by four. No window. A metal cot. No blanket. An enamel pail in the corner with a square of stained wood for a lid.

Kelso went slowly into the cell on his stockinged feet, threw his coat and boots down on the cot. Behind him, the door swung shut with a submarine clang.

Acceptance. That, he had learned in Russia many years ago, was the secret of survival. At the frontier, when your papers were being checked for the fifteenth time. At the road block, when you were pulled over for no reason and kept waiting for an hour and a half. At the ministry, when you went to get your visa stamped and no one had bothered to show up. Accept it. Wait. Let the system exhaust itself. Protest will only raise your blood pressure.

The spyhole in the centre of the door clicked open, stayed open for a moment, clicked shut. He listened to the guard's footsteps retreat.

He sat on the bed and closed his eyes and saw, at once, unbidden, like the after-image of a bright light imprinted on his retina, the white and naked body revolving in the down draught of the elevator shaft – shoulders, heels and trussed hands rebounding gently off the walls.

He sprang at the door and hammered on it with his empty boots and yelled for a while, until he'd got something out of himself. Then he turned and rested his back against the metal, confronting the narrow limits of his cell. Slowly he allowed himself to slide down until he was resting on his haunches, his arms clasped around his knees.

TIME. Now here is a peculiar commodity, boy. The measurement of time. Best accomplished, obviously, with a watch. But, lacking a watch, a man may use instead the ebb and flow of light and dark. Lacking, however, a window through which to see such movement, the reliance must be devolved upon some inner mechanism of the mind. But if the mind has received a shock, the mechanism is disturbed, and time becomes as the ground is to a drunkard, variable.

Thus Kelso, at some point indeterminate, transferred his body from the doorway to the cot and drew his coat across himself. His teeth were chattering.

His thoughts were random, disconnected. He thought of Mamantov, going back over their meeting again and again, trying to remember if he had said anything that could have led him to Rapava. And he thought about Rapava's daughter and the way he had broken his word in his statement. She had abandoned him. Now he had revealed her as a whore. So the world turns. Somewhere, presumably, the militia would have her address on file. Her name as well. The news about her father would be broken to her, and she would be – what? Dry-eyed, he was fairly sure. Yet vengeful.

In his dreams he moved to kiss her again but she evaded his embrace. She danced jerkily across the snow outside the apartment block while O'Brian paraded up and down pretending to be Hitler. Madame Mamantov raged against her madness. And behind a door somewhere, Papu Rapava went on knocking to be let out. In here, boy! Thump. Thump. *Thump.*

HE woke to find a cool blue eye regarding him through the spyhole. The metal eyelid drooped and closed, the lock rattled.

Behind the pustulous guard there stood a second man – blond-headed, well-dressed – and Kelso's first thought was a happy one: *The embassy, they've come to get me out.* But then blond-head said, in Russian, 'Dr Kelso, put your boots on, please,' and the guard shook the contents of the envelope out on to the cot.

Kelso bent to thread his laces. The stranger, he noticed, was wearing a smart pair of western brogues. He straightened and strapped on his watch and saw that it was only six-twenty. A mere two hours in the cells, but enough to last him a lifetime. He felt more human with his boots on. A man can face the world with something on his feet. They passed down the corridor, triggering the same desperate hammering and shouting.

He assumed he would be taken back upstairs for more questioning, but instead they came out into a rear courtyard where a car was waiting with two men in the front seats. Blond-head opened the rear passenger door for Kelso – 'Please,' he said, with cold politeness – then went round and got in the other side. The interior of the car was hot and fetid, as if at the end of a long journey, sweetened only by blond-head's delicate aftershave. They pulled away, out of militia headquarters and into the quiet street. Nobody spoke.

It was beginning to get light – light enough, at least, for Kelso to recognise roughly where they were heading. He had already marked this trio down as secret police, which meant the FSB, which meant the Lubyanka. But to his surprise he realised they were travelling east, not west. They came down the Noviy Arbat, past the deserted shops, and the Ukraina came into view. So they were taking him back to the hotel, he thought. But he was wrong again. Instead of crossing the bridge they turned right and followed the course of the Moskva. Dawn was coming on quickly now, like a chemical reaction, darkness dissolving across the river, first to grey and then to a dirty alkali blue. Streaks of smoke and steam from the factory chimneys on the opposite bank – a tannery, a brewery – turned a corrosive pink.

They drove on in silence for a few more minutes and then suddenly swung off the embankment and parked in a derelict patch of reclaimed land that jutted out into the water. A couple of big sea-birds flapped and rose, and span away, crying. Blond-head was out first and then, after a brief hesitation, Kelso followed him. It crossed his mind that they had brought him to the perfect spot for an accident: a simple push, a flurry of news reports, a long investigation for a London colour supplement, suspicions raised and then forgotten. But he put a brave face on it. What else could he do?

Blond-head was reading the statement Kelso had given to the militia. It flapped in the breeze that was coming off the river. Something about him was familiar.

'Your plane,' he said, without turning round, 'leaves Sheremetevo-2 at one-thirty. You will be on board it.'

'Who are you?'

'You'll be taken back to your hotel now, and then you'll catch the bus to the airport with your colleagues.'

'Why are you doing this?'

'You may try to re-enter the Russian Federation in the near future. In fact, I'm sure you will: you're a persistent fellow, anyone can see that. But I must tell you that your application for a visa will be rejected.'

'This is a bloody *outrage*.' It was stupid, of course, to lose his temper, but he was too tired and shaken-up to help himself. 'A complete bloody *disgrace*. Anyone would think that I was the killer.'

'But you *did* kill him.' The Russian turned round. 'You *are* the killer.'

'This is a joke, is it? I didn't have to come forward. I didn't have to call the militia. I could have run away.'

And don't think I didn't consider it –

'It's here in your own words.' Blond-head slapped the statement. 'You went to Mamantov yesterday afternoon and told him a "witness from the old time" had approached you with information about Stalin's papers. That was a death sentence.'

Kelso faltered. 'I never gave a name. I've been over that conversation in my mind a hundred times –'

'Mamantov didn't need a name. He already *had* the name.'

'You can't be certain –'

'Papu Rapava,' said the Russian, with exaggerated patience, 'was re-investigated by the KGB in nineteen eighty-three. The investigation was at the request of the deputy chief of the Fifth Directorate – Vladimir Pavlovich Mamantov. Do you see?'

Kelso closed his eyes.

'Mamantov knew precisely who you were talking about. There is no other "witness from the old time". Everyone else is dead. So: fifteen minutes after you left Mamantov's apartment, Mamantov also left. He even knew where the old man lived, from his file. He had seven, possibly eight hours to question Rapava. With the assistance of his friends. Believe me, a professional like Mamantov can do a lot of damage to a person in eight hours. Would you like me to give you some of the medical details? No? Then go back to New York, Dr Kelso, and play your games of history in somebody else's country, because this isn't England or America, the past isn't safely dead here. In Russia, the past carries razors and a pair of handcuffs. Ask Papu Rapava.'

A gust of wind swept the surface of the river, raised waves, set a nearby buoy clanking against its rusting chains.

'I can testify,' said Kelso after a while. 'To arrest Mamantov, you'll need my evidence.'

For the first time, the Russian smiled. 'How well do you know Mamantov?'

'Hardly at all.'

'You know him hardly at all. That is your good fortune. Some of us have come to know him well. And I can assure you that Comrade V. P. Mamantov will have no fewer than six witnesses – none of them below the rank of full colonel – who will swear that he spent the whole of last evening with them, discussing charity work, one hundred miles from Papu Rapava's apartment. So much for the value of your testimony.'

He tore Kelso's statement in half, then halved it again, and again – kept on until it couldn't be reduced further. He crumpled the pieces between his hands, cupped them and threw the fragments out across the water. The wind caught them. The seagulls swooped in the hope of food then wheeled away, shrieking with disappointment.

'Nothing is as it was,' he said. 'You ought to know that. The investigation begins again from scratch this morning. This statement was never taken. You were never detained by the militia. The officer who questioned you has been promoted and is being transferred, even as we speak, by military transport plane to Magadan.'

'Magadan?' Magadan was on the eastern rim of Siberia, four thousand miles away.

'Oh, we'll bring him back,' said the Russian, airily, 'when this is sorted out. What we don't want is the Moscow press corps trampling over everything. That really would be embarrassing. Now, I tell you all this, knowing there's nothing we can do to prevent you publishing your version of events abroad. But there will be no official corroboration from here, you understand? Rather the contrary. We reserve the right to make public *our* record of your day's activity, in which your motives will be made to look quite different. For example: you were arrested for indecent exposure to a couple of children in the Zoopark, the daughters of one of my men. Or you were picked up drunk on the Smolenskaya embankment, urinating into the river, and had to be locked up for violent and abusive behavior.'

'Nobody will believe it,' said Kelso, trying to summon a last vestige of outrage. But, of course, they would. He could make a list now of everyone who would believe it. He said, bitterly, 'So that's it then? Mamantov goes free? Or perhaps you'll try to find Stalin's papers yourselves, so you can bury them somewhere, like you people bury everything else that's "embarrassing"?'

'Oh, but you *irritate* me,' said the Russian, and now it was his turn to lose his temper. 'People like you. How much more is it you want of us? You've won, but is that enough? No, you have to rub our faces in it – Stalin, Lenin, Beria: I'm sick of hearing their damn names – make us turn out all our filthy closets, wallow in guilt, so you can feel superior –'

Kelso snorted, 'You sound like Mamantov.'

'I *despise* Mamantov,' said the Russian. 'Do you understand me? For the same reason I despise you. We want to put an end to Comrade Mamantov and his kind – what d'you suppose this is all about? But now you've come along – blundered into something much bigger – something you can't even begin to understand –'

He stopped – goaded, Kelso could tell, into saying more than he intended – and then Kelso realised where he must have seen him before.

'You were there, weren't you?' he said. 'When I went to see him. You were one of the men outside his apartment –'

But he was talking to himself. The Russian was striding back to the car.

'Take him to the Ukraina,' he said to the driver, 'then come back here and pick me up. I need some air.'

'Who *are* you?'

'Just go. And be grateful.'

Kelso hesitated but suddenly he was too tired to argue. He climbed, weary and defeated, into the back seat as the engine started. The Russian slammed the door on him, emphatically. He felt numb and shut his eyes again and there was Rapava's corpse swinging in the darkness. Thump. *Thump.* He opened his eyes and saw that it was the blond-headed man, knocking on the window. Kelso wound it down.

'A final thought.' He was making an effort to be polite again. He even smiled. 'We're working on the assumption, obviously, that Mamantov now has this notebook. But have you considered the alternative? Remember, Papu Rapava withstood six months of interrogation back in fifty-three, and then fifteen years in Kolyma. Suppose Mamantov and his friends didn't manage to break him in one evening. It's a possibility: it would explain the . . . ferocity of their behaviour: frustration. In that case, if you were Mamantov, who would you want to question next?' He banged on the roof. 'Sleep well in New York.'

SUVORIN watched the big car as it bounced over the rough ground and out of sight. He turned away, towards the river, and walked along the quayside, smoking his pipe, until he came to a big metal post set into the concrete, to which ships had moored in the communist time, before economics had accomplished what Hitler's bombers had never managed, and laid waste the docks. His performance had exhausted him. He wiped the surface with his handkerchief, sat down, and pulled out his photocopy of Kelso's statement. To have written so much – perhaps two thousand words – so quickly and with such clarity, after such an experience . . . Well, it proved his hunch: he was a clever one, this fellow, Fluke.

Troublesome. Persistent. *Clever.*

He went through the pages again with a gold propelling pencil and made a list of matters for Netto to check. They needed to visit the house on Vspolnyi Street – Beria's place, well, well. They ought to find this daughter of Rapava's. They should compile a list of every forensic document examiner in the Moscow region to whom Mamantov might take the notebook for authentication. And every handwriting expert. And they should find a couple of tame historians and ask them to make the best guess possible as to what this notebook might contain. *And and and . . .* He felt as though he was trying to stuff gas back into a cylinder with his hands.

He was still writing when Netto and the driver returned. He rose stiffly. To his dismay he found that the mooring-post had left a rust-coloured mark on the back of his beautiful coat, and he spent much of the journey to Yasenevo picking at it obsessively, trying to make it clean.

Chapter Twelve

KELSO'S HOTEL ROOM was in darkness, the curtains closed. He pulled aside the cheap nylon drapes. There was an odd smell of something – talcum powder? Aftershave? Someone had been in here. Blond-head, was it? Eau Sauvage? He lifted the telephone receiver. The line hummed. He felt breathless. His skin was crawling. He could have done with a whisky but the mini-bar was still empty after his night with Rapava; there was nothing in it apart from soda and orange juice. And he could have done with a bath but there wasn't a plug.

He guessed now who the blond-headed man was. He knew the species – smooth and sharply-dressed, westernised, *deracinated* – too sharp for the secret police. He had been meeting men like that at embassy receptions for more than twenty years, dodging their discreet invitations for lunch and drinks, listening to their carefully indiscreet jokes about life in Moscow. They used to be called the First Chief Directorate of the KGB. Now they called themselves the SVR. The name had changed but the job had not. Blond-head was a spy. And he was investigating Mamantov. They had set the spies on Mamantov, which was not much of a vote of confidence in the FSB.

At the thought of Mamantov, he stepped quickly over to the door and turned the heavy lock and set the chain. Through the spy-hole he took a fish-eyed squint down the empty corridor.

'But you did kill him . . . You are the killer.'

He was shaking now with delayed shock. He felt filthy,

somehow, defiled. The memory of the night was like grit against his skin.

He went into the little green-tiled bathroom, took off his clothes and turned on the shower, set the water as hot as he could bear, and soaped himself from head to foot. The suds turned grey with the Moscow grime. He stood under the steaming jet and let it scourge him for another ten minutes, thrashing his shoulders and his chest, then he stepped out of the tub, slopping water over the uneven lino. He lit a cigarette and smoked as he shaved, transferring it from one side of his mouth to the other, working his razor around it, standing in a puddle. Then he dried himself off, got into bed and pulled the cover up to his chin. But he didn't sleep.

A little after nine o'clock the telephone began to ring. The bell was shrill. It rang for a long while, stopped, then started again. This time, though, whoever it was hung up quickly.

A few minutes later, someone knocked softly on his bedroom door.

Kelso felt vulnerable now, naked. He waited ten minutes, threw off the sheet, dressed, packed – that didn't take long – then sat in one of the foam rubber chairs facing the door. The cover of the other chair was rucked, he noticed, the seat still slightly depressed from the imprint of poor Papu Rapava.

AT ten-fifteen, carrying his suitcase in one hand and with his raincoat over his arm, Kelso unlocked and unchained his door, checked the corridor and descended via the express elevator into the hubub of the ground floor.

He handed in his key at the reception desk and was in the act of turning away, towards the main entrance, when a man shouted 'Professor!'

It was O'Brian, hurrying over from the news-stand. He

was still wearing his clothes from the night before – jeans a little less pressed, T-shirt no longer as white – and he had a couple of newspapers tucked under his arm. He hadn't shaved. He seemed even bigger in the daylight. 'Morning, professor. So. What's new?'

Kelso made a groaning noise in the back of his throat but managed to hoist up a smile. 'Leaving, I'm afraid.' He displayed his suitcase, bag and coat.

'Now I'm sorry to hear that. Let me help you with those.'

'I'm fine.' He began to move around O'Brian. 'Really.'

'Aw, come on.' The reporter's arm flashed out, grabbing the handle, squeezing Kelso's fingers out of the way. In a second he had the suitcase. He quickly transferred it to his other hand, out of Kelso's reach. 'Where to, sir? Outside?'

'What the fuck are you playing at?' Kelso strode after him. People sitting in reception turned to watch. 'Give me back my case –'

'That was some night, though, wasn't it? That place? Those girls?' O'Brian shook his head and grinned as they walked. 'And then you go and find that body and all – must've been one hell of a shock. Look out, professor, here we go.'

He plunged through the revolving door and Kelso, after a hesitation, followed him. He came out the other side to find O'Brian looking serious.

'All right,' said O'Brian, 'don't let's embarrass one another. I know what's going on.'

'I will take my case now, thank you.'

'I decided to hang around outside Robotnik last night. Forgo the pleasures of the flesh.'

'My *case* –'

'Let's say I had a hunch. Saw you leave with the girl. Saw

you kiss her. Saw her *hit* you – what was that all about, by the way? Saw you get in her car. Saw you go into the apartment block. Saw you run out ten minutes later like all the hounds of hell were after you. And then I saw the cops arrive. Oh, professor, you are a character, you are a man of surprises.'

'And you're a creep.' Kelso began pulling on his raincoat, making an effort to seem unconcerned. 'What were you doing at Robotnik anyway? Don't tell me: it was a coincidence.'

'I go to Robotnik, sure,' said O'Brian. 'That's how I like my relationships: on a business footing. Why get a girl for free when you can pay for one, that's my philosophy.'

'God.' Kelso held out his hand. 'Just give me my case.'

'Okay, okay.' O'Brian glanced over his shoulder. The bus was in its usual place, waiting to ferry the historians to the airport. Moldenhauer was taking a picture of Saunders with the hotel in the background, Olga was watching them, fondly. 'If you want to know the truth, it was Adelman.'

Kelso drew his head back slowly. '*Adelman?*'

'Yeah, at the symposium yesterday, during the morning break, I asked Adelman where you were and he told me you were after some Stalin papers.'

'*Adelman* said that?'

'Oh, come on, don't tell me you trusted Adelman?' O'Brian grinned. 'One sniff of a scoop and you guys make the paparazzi look like choirboys. Adelman proposed a deal. Fifty-fifty. He said I should try to find the papers, see if there was anything in it, and if there was then he'd authenticate them. He told me everything you'd told him.'

'Including Robotnik?'

'Including Robotnik.'

'Bastard.'

Now Olga was taking a picture of Moldenhauer and Saunders. They stood shyly, side by side, and it struck Kelso for the first time that they were gay. Why hadn't he realised it before? This trip was nothing but surprises –

'Come on, professor. Don't get all shocked on me. And don't get shocked about Adelman, either. This is a story. This is a *hell* of a story. And it just keeps on getting better. Not only d'you find this poor bastard hanging in the elevator shaft with his pecker in his mouth, you also tell the militia that the guy who did it is none other than Vladimir Mamantov. And not only that – the whole investigation's now been canned on the orders of the Kremlin. Or so I hear. What's so funny?'

'Nothing.' Kelso couldn't help smiling, thinking of the blond-headed spy. ('*What we don't want is the Moscow press corps trampling over everything . . .*') 'Well, I'll say this for you, Mr O'Brian: you have good contacts.'

O'Brian made a dismissive gesture. 'There's not a secret in this town that can't be bought for a bottle of Scotch and fifty bucks. And man, I tell you, they're in a *rage* down there, you know? They're leaking like a *nuclear reactor*. They don't like being told what to do.'

The driver of the bus sounded his horn. Saunders was on board now. Moldenhauer had taken out his handkerchief to wave goodbye. Kelso could see the faces of the other historians through the glass, like pale fish in an aquarium.

He said, 'You really had better give me my case now. I've got to go.'

'You can't just run out, professor.' But there was a defeated tone to his appeal and this time he let Kelso take the handle. 'Come on, Fluke, just one little interview? One brief comment?' He followed at Kelso's heels, an importunate beggar. 'I need an interview, to stand this thing up.'

'It would be irresponsible.'

'Irresponsible? Balls! You won't talk because you want to keep it all for yourself! Well, you're crazy. The cover-up isn't working. This story's going to blow – if not today, tomorrow.'

'And you want it today, naturally, ahead of everyone else?'

'That's my job. Oh, come on, professor. Stop being so goddamn snooty. We're not so very different –'

Kelso was at the door of the bus. It opened with a pneumatic sigh. From the interior came a ragged, ironic cheer.

'Goodbye, Mr O'Brian.'

Still O'Brian wouldn't give up. He climbed up on to the first step. 'Take a look at what's happening here.' He jammed his roll of newspapers into Kelso's coat pocket. 'Take a look. That's Russia. Nothing here keeps until *tomorrow*. This place might not be here *tomorrow*. You're – oh, shit –'

He had to jump to avoid the closing door. He gave a last, despairing thump on the bodywork from outside.

'Dr Kelso,' said Olga, stonily.

'Olga,' said Kelso.

He pushed his way down the aisle. When he came level with Adelman he stopped, and Adelman, who must have watched his whole encounter with O'Brian, glanced away. Beyond the muddy glass the reporter was trudging towards the hotel, his hands in his pockets. Moldenhauer's white handkerchief fluttered in farewell.

The bus lurched. Kelso turned, half-walking, half-tumbling, towards his usual place, alone and at the back.

*

FOR five minutes he did nothing except stare out of the window. He knew he ought to write this down, prepare another record while it was still clear in his mind. But he couldn't, not yet. For now, all roads of thought seemed to lead back to the same image of the figure in the elevator-shaft.

Like a side of beef in a butcher's shop –

He patted his pockets to find his cigarettes and pulled out O'Brian's newspapers. He threw them on the seat beside him and tried to ignore them. But after a couple of minutes he found himself reading the headlines upside down, then reluctantly he picked them up.

They were nothing special, just a couple of English-language freesheets, given away in every hotel lobby.

The *Moscow Times*. Domestic news: the President was ill again, or drunk again, or both. A serial cannibal in the Kemerovo region was believed to have killed and eaten eighty people. Interfax reported that 60,000 children were sleeping on the streets each night in Moscow. Gorbachev was recording another television commercial for Pizza Hut. A bomb had been planted at the Nagornaya metro station by a group opposed to plans to remove Lenin's mummified body from public display in Red Square.

Foreign news: The IMF was threatening to withold $700 million in aid unless Moscow cut its budget deficit.

Business news: interest rates had tripled, stock market prices halved.

Religious news: A nineteen-year-old nun with ten thousand followers was predicting the end of the world on Hallowe'en. A statue of the Virgin Mother was trundling around the Black Earth region, weeping real blood. There was a holy man from Tarko-Sele who spoke in tongues.

There were fakirs and Pentecostalists, faith healers, shamans, workers of miracles, anchorites and marabouts and followers of the *skoptsy*, who believed themselves the Lords Incarnate . . . It was like Rasputin's time. The whole country was a tumult of bloody auguries and false prophets.

He picked up the other paper, *The eXile*, this one written for young westerners like O'Brian working in Moscow. No religion here, but a lot of crime:

> In the village of Kamenka, in the Smolenskaya Oblast, where the local collective farm is bankrupt and state employees haven't been paid all year, the big summer activity for kids is hanging around the Moscow–Minsk highway and sniffing gasoline, bought in half-litre jugs for a rouble. In August, two of the biggest gasoline addicts, Pavel Mikheenkov, 11, and Anton Malyarenko, 13, graduated from their favourite pastime – torturing cats – to tying a five year-old boy named Sasha Petrochenkov to a tree and burning him alive. Malyarenk was deported to his native Tashkent, but Mikheenkov has had to stay in Kamenka, unpunished: sending him to reform school would cost 15,000 roubles and the town doesn't have the money. The victim's mother, Svetlana Petrochenkova, has been told she can have her son's killer sent away if she digs up the money herself, but failing that must live with him in the village. According to police, Mikheenkov had been drinking vodka regularly with his parents since the age of four.

He turned the page quickly and found a guide to Moscow night life. Gay bars – Dyke, The Three Monkeys, Queer

Nation; strip clubs – Navada, Rasputin, The Intim Peep Show; nightclubs – the Buchenwald (where the staff wore Nazi uniforms), Bulgakov, Utopiya. He looked up Robotnik: *'No place could better exemplify the excesses of the New Russia than Robotnik: bitchin interior, ear-splitting techno, Babe-O-Litas and their flathead keepers, Die Hard security, black-eyed patrons sucking down Evians. Get laid and see someone get shot.'*

That sounded about right, he thought.

THE departure terminal at Sheremetevo-2 was crammed with people trying to get out of Russia. Queues formed like cells under a microscope – grew from nothing, wormed back on themselves, broke, re-formed, and merged into other queues: queues for customs, for tickets, for security, for passport controls. You finished one and joined the next. The hall was dark and cavernous, sour with the reek of aviation spirit and the thin acid of anxiety. Adelman, Duberstein, Byrd, Saunders and Kelso, plus a couple of Americans who had been staying at the Mir – Pete Maddox of Princeton and Vobster of Chicago – stood in a group at the end of the nearest line while Olga went off to see if she could speed things up.

After a couple of minutes, they still hadn't moved. Kelso ignored Adelman who sat on his suitcase reading a biography of Chekhov with extravagant intensity. Saunders sighed and flapped his arms with frustration. Maddox wandered away and came back to report that customs seemed to be opening every bag.

'Shit, and I bought an icon,' complained Duberstein. 'I knew I shouldn't've bought an icon. I'll never get it through.'

'Where'd you get it?'

'That big bookstore on the Noviy Arbat.'

'Give it to Olga. She'll get it out. How much d'you pay?'

'Five hundred bucks.'

'Five *hundred?*'

Kelso remembered he hadn't any money. There was a news-stand at the end of the terminal. He needed more cigarettes. If he asked for a seat in smoking he could keep clear of the others.

'Phil,' he said to Duberstein, 'you couldn't lend me ten dollars, could you?'

Duberstein started laughing. 'What're you going to do, Fluke? Buy Stalin's notebook?'

Saunders sniggered. Velma Byrd raised her hand to her mouth and looked away.

'You told them as well?' Kelso stared at Adelman in disbelief.

'And why not?' Adelman licked a finger and turned over a page without looking up. 'Is it a secret?'

'Tell you what,' said Duberstein, pulling out his wallet. 'Here's twenty. Buy one for me as well.'

They all laughed at that, and openly this time, watching Kelso to see what he would do. He took the money.

'All right, Phil,' he said, quietly. 'I'll tell you what. Let's make a deal. If Stalin's notebook turns up by the end of the year, I'll just keep this and then we're quits. But if it doesn't, I'll pay you back a thousand dollars.'

Maddox gave a low whistle.

'Fifty to one,' said Duberstein, swallowing. 'You're offering me fifty to one?'

'We've got a deal?'

'Well, you bet.' Duberstein laughed again, but nervously this time. He glanced around at the others. 'You hear that everyone?'

They'd heard. They were staring at Kelso. And for him, at that moment, it was worth a thousand dollars – worth it just for the way they looked: open-mouthed, stricken, panicked. Even Adelman had temporarily forgotten his book.

'Easiest twenty dollars I ever made,' said Kelso. He stuffed the bill into his pocket and picked up his suitcase. 'Save my place for me, will you?'

He moved off across the crowded terminal, quickly, quitting while he was still ahead, easing his way through the people and the piles of luggage. He felt a childish pleasure. A few fleeting victories here and there – what more could a man hope for in this life?

Over the loudspeaker, a woman with a harsh voice made a deafening announcement about the departure of an Aeroflot flight to Delhi.

At the news-stand he made a quick check to see if they had the paperback of his book. They did not. Naturally. He turned his attention to a rack of magazines. Last week's *Time* and *Newsweek*, and the current *Der Spiegel*. So. He would take *Der Spiegel*. It would do him good. It would certainly last him an eleven-hour plane ride. He fished in his pocket for Duberstein's $20 and turned towards the till. Through the plate glass window he could see the wet sweep of concrete, a jammed line of cars and taxis and buses, grey buildings, abandoned trolleys, a girl with cropped dark hair, a white face watching him. He looked away casually. Frowned. Checked himself.

He stuffed the magazine back into the rack and returned to the window. It was her, all right, standing alone, in jeans and a fleece-lined leather jacket. His breath misted on the cold glass. *Wait*, he mouthed at her. She stared at him blankly. He pointed at her feet. *Stay there.*

To get to her he had to walk away from her, following the line of the glass wall, trying to find an exit. The first set of doors was chained shut. The second opened. He came out into the cold and wet. She was standing about fifty yards away. He looked back at the crowded terminal – he couldn't see the others – and then at her, and now she was moving away from him, heading across a pedestrian crossing, heedless of the cars. He hesitated: what to do? A bus momentarily wiped her from view and that made his mind up for him. He hoisted his luggage and set off after her, breaking into a trot. She drew him on, always maintaining the same distance, until they were into the big outdoor car park, and then he lost her.

Grey light, snow and frozen slush. The stink of fuel much sharper here. Row upon row of boxy cars, some muffled white, others thinly wrapped in a film of mud and grit. He walked on. The air shook. A big old Tupolev jet swept directly over his head, so low he could see the lines of rust where the plates of the fuselage were welded together. Instinctively, he ducked, just as a sandy-coloured Lada emerged slowly from the end of the line and stopped, its engine running.

SHE didn't make it easy for him, even then. She didn't drive over to where he was; he had to walk to her. She didn't open the door; he had to do it. She didn't speak; it was left to him to break the silence. She didn't even tell him her name – not then, at least, although he discovered it later. She was called Zinaida. Zinaida Rapava.

She knew what had happened, that was obvious by the strain on her face, and he felt guiltily relieved at that, because at least he wouldn't have to break the news. He had always been a coward when it came to breaking bad news – that was one reason he'd been married three times. He sat in the front passenger seat, his suitcase wedged across his knees. The heater was running. The windscreen wiper flicked intermittently across the dirty glass. He knew he would have to say something soon. Delta to New York was the one event of the symposium he had no intention of missing.

'Tell me what I can do to help.'

'Who killed him?'

'A man named Vladimir Mamantov. Ex-KGB. He knew of your father from the old time.'

'The old time,' she said, bitterly.

Silence – long enough for the wiper to scrape back and forth, back and forth.

'How did you know where to find me?'

'Always, all my life: the *old time*.'

Another Tupolev rumbled low overhead.

'Listen,' he said, 'I've got to go in a minute. I've got to catch a plane to New York. When I get there, I'm going to write everything down – are you listening? I'll send you a copy. Tell me where to send it. You need anything, I'll help.'

It was hard to move with his case on his lap. He unbuttoned his coat and reached awkwardly into his inside pocket for his pen. She wasn't listening to him. She was staring straight ahead, talking almost to herself.

'It'd been years since I saw him. Why would I want to? I hadn't been near that dump in eight years till you asked me to take you.' She turned to him for the first time. She had washed off her makeup. She looked younger, more pretty. Her leather jacket was old, brown, zipped tight to the neck. 'After I left you, I went home. Then I went back to his place again. I had to find out – you know – what was going on.

Never saw so many cops in my life. You'd been taken away by then. I didn't say who I was. Not to the cops. I had to think things through. I –' She stopped. She seemed baffled, lost.

'What's your name?' he said. 'Where can I reach you?'

'Then, this morning, I went to the Ukraina. I rang you. Went up to your room. When they said you'd checked out I came here and waited.'

'Can't you just tell me your name?' He looked at his watch, hopelessly. 'Only I've got to catch this plane, you see.'

'I don't ask favours,' she said fiercely. 'I never ask favours.'

'Listen, don't worry. I want to help. I feel responsible.'

'Then help me. He said you'd help me'

'*He?*'

'The thing is, mister, he's left me something.' Her leather jacket creaked as she unzipped it. She felt around inside and brought out a scrap of paper. 'Something worth a lot? In a toolbox? He says that you can tell me what it is.'

Chapter Thirteen

THEY DROVE OUT of the airport perimeter onto the St Petersburg highway and turned south towards the city. A big truck overtook them, its wheels as high as their roof, rocking them in its wake, soaking them in a filthy spray.

Kelso had promised himself he wouldn't look back, but of course he did – looked back and saw the terminal building, like a great grey ocean liner, sink out of sight behind a line of birch trees until only a few watery lights were visible, and then they disappeared.

He winced and nearly asked the girl to take him back. He gave her a sideways glance. In her scuffed flying jacket she looked intrepid: an aviatrix at the controls of her battered plane.

He said, 'Who's Sergo?'

'My brother.' She glanced in the rear-view mirror. 'He's dead.'

He turned the note over and read it again. Rough paper. Pencil scrawl. Written quickly. Stuffed under the door of her apartment, or so she said: she had found it when she got back after dropping Kelso outside her father's block.

My little one, Greetings!
I have been a bad one, you're right. All you said was right. So don't think I don't know it! But here is a chance to do some good. You wouldn't let me tell you yesterday, so listen now. Remember that place I used to have, when Mama was alive? It's still there! And there's a toolbox with a present for you that's worth a lot.

Are you listening, Zinaida?
*Nothing will happen to me, but if it does – take the box
and hide it safe. But it could be dangerous, so mind
yourself. You'll see what I mean.*
Destroy this note.
I kiss my little one,
Papa.
*– There's a Britisher called Kelso, get him through the
Ukraina, he knows the story. Remember your papa!*
I kiss you again, Zinaida.
Remember Sergo!!

'So he came to see you – when was it? The day before
yesterday?'

She nodded, without looking round at him, concentrating
on the road. 'It was the first time I'd seen him in nearly ten
years.'

'You didn't get on, then?'

'Oh, you're a smart one.' Her laugh was brief, sarcastic: a
short expulsion of breath. 'No, we didn't get on.'

He ignored her aggression. She was entitled to it. 'What
was he like, the last time you saw him?'

'Like?'

'His mood.'

'A bastard. Same as always.' She frowned at the oncoming
traffic. 'He must have been waiting for me all night, outside
my place. I got back about six. I'd been at the club, you know,
been working. The moment he saw me he started shouting.
Saw my clothes. Called me a whore.' She shook her head at
the memory.

'Then what happened?'

'He followed me in. Into my place. I said to him, I said:

"You hit me, I'll take your fucking eye out, I'm not your little girl any more." That calmed him down.'

'What did he want?'

'To talk, he said. It was a shock after all that time. I didn't think he knew where I lived. I didn't even know he was still alive. Thought I'd got away from him for good. Oh, but he'd known, he said – known where I was for a long time. Said he used to come and watch me sometimes. He said, "You don't get away from the past that easily." Why did he come to see me?' She looked at Kelso for the first time since they'd left the airport. 'Can you tell me that?'

'What did he want to talk about?'

'I don't know. I wouldn't listen. I didn't want him in my place, looking at my things. I didn't want to hear his stories. He started going on about his time in the camps. I gave him some cigarettes to get rid of him and told him to go. I was tired and I'd got to go to work.'

'Work?'

'I work at GUM in the daytime. I learn law at college in the evenings. Some nights, I screw. Why? Is it a problem?'

'You lead a full life.'

'I have to.'

He tried to picture her behind the counter at GUM. 'What do you sell?'

'What?'

'At the store. What do you sell?'

'Nothing.' She checked the mirror again. 'I work the switchboard.'

Closer to the city, the road was clogged. They slowed to a crawl. There had been an accident up ahead. A rickety Skoda had run into the back of a big old Zhiguli. Broken glass and bits of metal were scattered across two lanes. The militia were on the scene. It looked as though one of the drivers had punched the other: he had splashes of blood on the front of his shirt. As they passed the policemen, Kelso turned his head away. The road cleared. They picked up speed.

He tried to fit all this together: Papu Rapava's last two days on earth. Tuesday 27 October: he goes to see his daughter for the first time in a decade, because, he says, he wants to talk. She throws him out, buys him off with a pack of cigarettes and a book of matches labelled 'Robotnik'. In the afternoon, he turns up, of all places, at the Institute of Marxism–Leninism and listens to Fluke Kelso deliver a paper on Josef Stalin. Then he follows Kelso back to the Ukraina and sits up all night drinking. And talking. He certainly talked. *Perhaps he told me what he would have told his daughter if she'd only listened.*

And then it's dawn and he leaves the Ukraina. This is now Wednesday 28 October. And what does he do after he's slipped away into the morning? Does he go to the deserted house on Vspolnyi Street and dig up the secret of his life? He must have done. And then he hides it, and he leaves a note for his daughter, telling her where to find it ('*remember that place I used to have when Mama was alive?*') and then, late in the afternoon, his killers come for him. And either he had told them everything, or he hadn't, and if he hadn't, then it must have been partly out of love, surely? To make certain that the only thing he had in the world that might be worth anything should go not to them but to his daughter.

God, thought Kelso, what an ending. What a way to leave a life – and how in keeping with the rest of it.

'He must have cared for you,' said Kelso. He wondered if she knew how the old man had died. If she didn't, he couldn't bring himself to tell her. 'He must have cared for you, to have come to find you.'

'I don't think so. He used to hit me. And my mother. And my brother.' She glared at the oncoming traffic. 'He used to hit me when I was little. What does a child know?' She shook her head. 'I don't think so.'

Kelso tried to imagine the four of them in the one-bedroom apartment. Where would her parents have slept? On a mattress in the sitting-room? And Rapava, after a decade and a half in Kolyma – violent, unstable, confined. It didn't bear contemplating.

'When did your mother die?'

'Do you ever stop asking questions, mister?'

They came off the highway and down a slip road. Half of it had never been completed. One lane curved like a water-chute, ending abruptly in a row of dripping metal rods and a ten-yard drop to waste ground.

'When I was eighteen, if that makes any difference.'

The ugliness around them was heroic. In Russia it could afford to be – could afford to take its time, stretch out a bit. Minor roads ran as wide as motorways, with flooded potholes the size of ponds. Each concrete stack of apartments, each belching industrial plant had an entire wilderness to itself to pollute. Kelso remembered the night before – the endless run from Block Nine to Block Eight to raise the alarm: it had gone on and on, like a journey in a nightmare.

Rapava's place in the daylight looked even more derelict than it had seemed in the darkness. Scorch marks shot up the wall from a set of windows on the second floor where an apartment had been torched. There was a crowd outside and Zinaida slowed so they could take a look.

O'Brian was right. The word was out. That much was obvious. A solitary militia man blocked the doorway, holding at bay a dozen cameramen and reporters, who were themselves being watched by a straggling semi-circle of apathetic neighbours. Some kids kicked a ball on the waste ground. Others hung around the media's fancy western cars.

'What was he to them?' Zinaida said suddenly. 'What was he to any of you? You're all vultures.'

She gave a grimace of disgust, and for the third time Kelso noticed her adjusting the rear-view mirror.

'Is someone behind us?' He turned round sharply.

'Maybe. A car from the airport. But not any more.'

'What sort of a car?' He tried to keep his voice calm.

'A BMW. Seven series.'

'You know about cars?'

'More questions?' She shot him another look. 'Cars were my father's interest. Cars and Comrade Stalin. He was a driver, wasn't he, for some big shot in the old days? You'll see.'

She put her foot down.

She knows nothing, thought Kelso. She has no idea of the risks. He began making promises to himself of what he would do: you take a quick look now to see if this toolbox is here (it wouldn't be) then ask her to take you back to the airport and see if you can talk your way on to the next flight out –

Two minutes from Rapava's apartment they turned off the main street and on to a muddy track that led through a scrappy copse of birch to a field that had been divided into small-holdings. A pig snuffled in the earth in an enclosure made of old car doors tied together with wire. There were a few scrawny chickens, some frost-blasted vegetables. Children had made a snowman out of yesterday's fall. It had melted in the light rain and looked grotesque in the dirt, like a lump of white fat.

Facing this rural scene was a row of lock-up garages. On the long flat roof sat the remains of half a dozen small cars – rusted red skeletons picked bare of windows, engines, tyres, upholstery. Zinaida switched off the engine and they climbed out into the mud. An old man leaned on his shovel and watched them. Zinaida stared him down, her hands on her hips. Eventually, he spat on the ground and returned to his digging.

She had a key. Kelso looked back along the deserted track. His hands felt numb. He stuffed them into his coat pockets. She was the calm one. She was wearing a pair of knee-length leather boots and to avoid getting them dirty she stepped carefully across the lumpy ground. He looked around again. He didn't like it: the encroaching trees, the derelict cars, this bewildering woman with her kaleidoscope of roles – GUM telephonist, would-be lawyer, part-time hooker and now griefless daughter.

He said, 'Where did you get the key?'

'It was with the note.'

'I don't understand why you didn't come here on your own straight away. Why do you need me?'

'Because I don't know what I'm looking for, do I? Are you coming or not?' She was fitting the key into a big padlock on the nearest lock-up. 'What are we looking for, anyway?'

'A notebook.'

'What?' She stopped fiddling with the key and stared at him.

'A black oilskin notebook that used to belong to Josef Stalin.' He repeated the familiar phrase. It was becoming his mantra. (It wouldn't be here, he told himself again. It was the Holy Grail. The quest was all that mattered. It wasn't supposed to be found.)

'Stalin's notebook? And what's that worth?'

'Worth?' He tried to make it sound as if the question had never occurred to him. 'Worth?' he repeated. 'It's hard to put an exact figure on it. There are some rich collectors. It depends what's in it.' He spread his hands. 'Half a million, maybe.'

'Roubles?'

'Dollars.'

'Dollars? Shit. *Shit*.' She resumed her efforts to undo the padlock, clumsy now with her eagerness.

And suddenly, watching her, he caught her mood and then of course he knew why he had come. Because it was everything, really, wasn't it? It was much more than mere money. It was vindication. Vindication for twenty years of freezing his arse off in basement archives, and dragging himself to lectures in the winter dark – first to listen, then to give them – twenty years of teaching and faculty politics and trying to write books that mostly didn't sell and all the while hoping that one day he would produce something worthwhile – something true and big and definitive – a piece of history that would explain *why things had happened as they did*.

'Here,' he said, almost pushing her out of the way, 'let me try.'

He jiggled the key in the lock. At last it turned and the arm sprang open. He pulled the chain through the heavy eye-bolts.

COLD, oily darkness. No window. No electricity. An ancient paraffin lamp hanging on a nail by the door.

He took down the lamp and shook it – it was full – and she said she knew how to light it. She knelt on the earth floor and struck a match, applied it to the wick. A blue flame, then yellow. She held it up while he dragged the door shut behind them.

The garage was a bone-yard of old spare parts, stacked around the walls. At the far end in the shadows was a row of car seats arranged to form a bed, with a sleeping bag and a blanket, neatly folded. Suspended from a beam in the roof was a block and tackle, a chain, a hook. Beneath the hook were floorboards forming a rectangle a yard and a half wide by two yards long.

She said, 'He's had this place for as long as I've been alive. He used to sleep here, when things were bad.'

'How bad did they get?'

'Bad.'

He took the lamp and walked around, shining it into the corners. There was nothing like a toolbox that he could see. On a work bench was a tin tray with a metal brush, some rods, a cylinder, a small coil of copper wire: what was all that? Fluke Kelso's ignorance of mechanics was deep and carefully maintained.

'Did he have a car of his own?'

'I don't know. He fixed them up for people. People gave him things.'

He stopped next to the makeshift bed. Something glinted above it. He called to her, 'Look at this,' and raised the light to the wall. Stalin's sombre face gazed down at them from an old poster. There were a dozen more pictures of the General Secretary, torn from magazines. Stalin looking thoughtful behind a desk. Stalin in a fur hat. Stalin shaking hands with a general. Stalin, dead, lying in state.

'And who's this? This is you?'

It was a photograph of Zinaida, aged about twelve, in

school uniform. She stepped closer to it, surprised.

'Who'd have thought it?' She laughed uneasily. 'Me up there with Stalin.'

She stared at it a while longer.

'Let's find this thing,' she said, turning away. 'I want to get out of here.'

Kelso was prodding one of the floorboards with his foot. It rested loosely on a wooden frame set into the earth. This was it, he thought. This had to be the place.

They worked together, watched by Stalin, stacking the short planks against the wall, uncovering a mechanic's pit. It was deep. In the weak light it looked like a grave. He held the lamp over it. The floor was sand, stamped smooth and hard, stained black with oil. The sides were shored up with old timber, into which Rapava had let alcoves for tools. He gave her the lamp and wiped his palms on his coat. Why was he so damned nervous? He sat on the edge for a moment, legs dangling, before cautiously lowering himself. He knelt on the floor of the pit, his bones cracking, and felt around in the damp gloom. His hands touched sacking.

He called up to her, 'Shine the light here.'

The rough cloth pulled away easily. Next came something solid, wrapped in newspaper. He passed it up to Zinaida. She set down the lamp and unwrapped a gun. She was surprisingly deft with it, he noticed, sliding out the clip of ammunition, checking it – eight rounds loaded – sliding it back again, pushing the safety catch down then up.

'You know how it works?'

'Of course. It's his. A Makarov. When we were little, he taught us how to strip it, clean it, fire it. He always kept it by him. He said he'd kill if he had to.'

'That's a nice memory.' He thought he heard a sound

outside. 'Did you hear that?'

But she shook her head, preoccupied with the gun.

He sank back down to his knees.

And here, jammed into the aperture, was the square end of a metal box, flaking with rust and dried mud. If you didn't know what you were looking for, you would never have bothered with it. Rapava had hidden well. He put his hands on either side of it and tugged.

Well, *something* was heavy. Either the box or what was in it. The handles had rusted flat. It was hard to get a grip. He dragged it into the centre of the pit and hoisted it up to the edge. His cheek was close to it. He could taste the smell of rusted steel, like blood in his mouth. Zinaida bent to help. And this was peculiar: for an instant he thought that the box was exuding an unearthly, blue-grey light. There was a rush of cold air. But then he saw that the garage door was open and that framed in it was the silhouette of a man, watching them.

AFTERWARDS, Kelso was to recognise this as the decisive moment: as the point at which he lost control of events. If he didn't see it at the time it was because his main concern was simply to stop her blowing a hole in R. J. O'Brian's chest.

The reporter stood against the garage wall, his hands above his head. Kelso could tell he didn't quite believe she would shoot. But a gun was a gun. They could go off accidentally. And this one was old.

'Professor, do me a favour, would you, and tell her to put that thing down?'

But Zinaida jabbed it again towards his chest and O'Brian, groaning, raised his hands still further.

Okay, okay, he said. He was sorry. He had followed them

from the airport. It hadn't been hard, for Christ's sake. He was only doing his job. *Sorry.*

His eyes flickered to the toolbox. 'Is that it?'

Kelso's immediate reaction on seeing the American had been relief: thank God it was only O'Brian who had followed them from Sheremetevo and not Mamantov. But Zinaida had grabbed the gun and had backed him against the wall.

She said, 'Shut up.'

'Look, professor, I've seen these suckers go off. And I have to tell you: they really make a mess.'

Kelso said to her, in Russian, 'Put it away, Zinaida.' It was the first time he had used her name. 'Put it away and let's sort this out.'

'I don't trust him.'

'Neither do I. But what can we do? Put it away.'

'Zinaida? Who is she? Don't I know her from someplace?'

'She goes to the Robotnik.' Kelso spoke through his teeth. 'Will you let me handle this?'

'Does she, by God?' O'Brian passed his tongue across his thick lips. In the yellow lamplight his broad and well-fed face looked like a Hallowe'en pumpkin. 'That's right. Of course she does. She's the babe you were with last night. I thought I knew her.'

'Shut up,' she said again.

O'Brian grinned. 'Listen, Zinaida, we don't have to be in competition. We can share, can't we? Split this three ways? I just want a story. Tell her, Fluke. Tell her I can keep her name out of it. She knows me. She'll understand. She's a business-minded kind of a girl, aren't you, darlin'?'

'What's he saying?'

He told her.

'*Nyet*,' she said. And then, in English, to O'Brian, 'No way.'

'You two,' said O'Brian. 'You make me laugh. The historian and the whore. Okay, tell her this. Tell her she can either deal with me or we can stand around like this for an hour or two and you'll have half the Moscow press pack on your back. And the militia. And maybe the guys who killed the old man. Tell her that.'

But Kelso didn't need to translate. She understood.

She stood there for another quarter of a minute, frowning, then clicked on the safety catch and slowly lowered the gun. O'Brian let out a breath.

'What's she doing in all this anyway?'

'She's Papu Rapava's daughter.'

'Ah.' O'Brian nodded. Now he got the picture.

THE toolbox lay on the earth floor. O'Brian wouldn't let them open it, not right away. He wanted to capture the great moment, he said – 'for posterity and the evening news'. He went off to get his camera.

Once he'd gone, Kelso shook a cigarette out of his half-empty pack and offered it to Zinaida. She took it and leaned towards him, looking at him steadily as he lit it for her, the flame reflected in her dark eyes. He thought: less than twelve hours ago you were going to go to bed with me for $200 – who the hell are you?

She said, 'What's on your mind?'

'Nothing. Are you all right?'

'I don't trust him,' she repeated. She threw back her head and blew smoke at the roof. 'What's he doing?'

'I'll tell him to hurry up.'

Outside, O'Brian was sitting in the front seat of a four-wheel drive Toyota Land Crusier, snapping a new battery on to the back of a tiny video camera. At the sight of the Toyota,

Kelso felt a fresh sweat of anxiety.

'You don't drive a BMW?'

'A BMW? I'm not a businessman. Why should I?'

The field was deserted. The old man who had been digging had gone.

'Zinaida thought we were followed from the airport by a BMW. Seven series.'

'Seven series? That's a mafia car.' O'Brian got out of the Toyota and put the camera to his eye. 'I wouldn't pay any attention to Zinaida. She's crazy.' The pig emerged from its sty and trotted over for a look at them, hopeful of some food. 'Here, piggy piggy.' He began filming it. 'Remember what the man said? "A dog looks up to you, a cat looks down on you, but a pig looks you straight in the eye"?' He swung round and pointed the camera at Kelso's face. 'Smile, professor. I'm going to make you famous.'

Kelso put his hand over the lens. 'Listen, Mr O'Brian –'

'R. J.'

'And what does that stand for?'

'Everybody calls me R. J.'

'All right, *R. J.* I'm going to do this. I'll let you film me. If you insist. But on three conditions.'

'Which are?'

'One, you stop calling me bloody *professor*. Two, you keep her name out of it. And three, none of this is shown – not a second, you hear? – until this notebook, or whatever it is, has been forensically verified.'

'Agreed.' O'Brian slipped the camera into his pocket. 'Actually, it may surprise you to hear this, but I've got a reputation of my own to consider. And from what I hear, *doctor*, it's one hell of a sight better than yours.'

He pointed a remote key at the Toyota. It bleeped and

locked. Kelso took a last look around and followed him into the garage.

O'BRIAN made Kelso put the toolbox back in its hiding place and drag it out again. He made him do this twice, filming him once from the front and then from the side. Zinaida watched them closely but was careful to keep out of shot. She smoked incessantly, one arm clasped defensively across her stomach. When O'Brian had what he needed, Kelso carried the box over to the workbench and brought the lamp up close to it. There wasn't a lock. There were two spring-loaded catches at either end of the lid. They had been cleaned up recently, and oiled. One was broken. The other opened.

Here we go, boy.

'What I want you to do,' said O'Brian, 'is describe what you see. Talk us through it.'

Kelso contemplated the box.

'D'you have any gloves?'

'Gloves?'

'If what's inside is genuine, Stalin's fingerprints should be on it. And Beria's. I don't want to contaminate the evidence.'

'Stalin's *fingerprints?*'

'Of course. Don't you know about Stalin's fingers? The Bolshevik poet, Demyan Bedny, once complained that he didn't like lending his books to Stalin because they always came back with such greasy finger marks on them. Osip Mandelstam – a much greater poet – got to hear about this, and put the image into a poem about Stalin: "His fingers are fat as grubs".'

'What did Stalin think of that?'

'Mandelstam died in a labour camp.'

'Right. I guess I should have figured that out.' O'Brian dug around in his pockets. 'Okay: gloves. There you go.'

Kelso pulled them on. They were dark blue leather, slightly too big, but they would do. He flexed his fingers – a surgeon before a transplant, a pianist before a concert. The thought made him smile. He glanced at Zinaida. Her face was clenched. O'Brian's expression was hidden by the camera.

'Okay. I'm running. In your own time.'

'Right. I'm opening the lid, which is . . . *stiff*, as you'd . . . *expect*.' Kelso winced with the effort. The top wrenched up a crack, just wide enough for him to jam his fingers into the gap, and then it took all his strength to break the two edges apart. It came open suddenly, like a broken jaw, with a scream of oxidised metal. 'There's only one object inside . . . a bag of some kind . . . leather, by the look of it . . . badly moulded.'

The satchel had grown a shroud of fungus – of different fungi – pale blues and greens and greys, vegetative filaments and white patches mottled black. It stank of decay. He lifted it clear of the box and turned it round in the light. He rubbed at the surface with his thumb. Very faintly, the ghost of an image began to appear. 'It's embossed here with the hammer and sickle . . . That suggests it's an official document pouch of some kind . . . Oil here on the buckle . . . Some of the rust has been cleaned off . . . ' He imagined Rapava's nail-less fingers, fumbling to discover what had cost him so much of his life.

The strap unthreaded through the pitted metal, leaving a floury residue. The satchel opened. The hyphae had spread inside, feeding off the dank skin, and as he lifted out the contents he knew, whatever else it was, that this was genuine, that no forger would have done all this, would have allowed so much damage to be inflicted on his work: it went against nature. What had once been a packet of papers had fused together, swollen, and was covered in the same destructive cancer of spores as the leather. The pages of the notebook had also warped, but less badly, protected as they were by a smooth outer layer of black oilskin.

The cover opened, the binding split.

On the first page: nothing.

On the second: a photograph, neatly cut out of a magazine, glued down in the centre of the page. A group of young women, in their late teens, dressed as athletes – shorts, singlets, sashes – marching in step, eyes right, carrying a picture of Stalin. Parading in Red Square by the look of it. Caption: *Komsomol Unit No. 2 from Archangel oblast display their paces! Front row, l. to r. I. Primakova, A. Safanova, D. Merkulova, K. Til, M. Arsenyeva* . . . Against the youthful face of A. Safanova there was a tiny red cross.

He picked up the notebook and blew, to separate the second page from the third. His hands were sweating inside the gloves. He felt absurdly clumsy, as if he were trying to thread a needle while wearing gauntlets.

On the third page: writing, in faint pencil.

O'Brian touched his shoulder, prompting him to say something.

'It's not Stalin's writing, I'm sure of that . . . It reads more like someone writing *about* Stalin . . .' He held it closer to the lamp. '"He stands apart from the others, high on the roof of Lenin's tomb. His hand is raised in greeting. He smiles. We pass beneath him. His glance falls across us like the rays of the sun. He looks directly into my eyes. I am pierced by his power. All around us, the crowd breaks into stormy applause." The next part is smudged. And then it's written, "Great Stalin lived! Great Stalin lives! Great Stalin will live for ever! . . .'"

Chapter Fourteen

> *. . . Great Stalin lived!*
> *Great Stalin lives!*
> *Great Stalin will live for ever!*

12.5.51 Our picture is in Ogonyok! Maria runs in at the end of the first class to show me. I am displeased with my appearance and M. chides me for my vanity. (She always says I think too much of being pretty: it is not fitting for a candidate-member of the Party. Fine for her to say, who always looks like a tank!) All morning comrades hurry up to us to offer their congratulations. The usual trouble of this time is forgotten for once. We are so happy . . .

5.6.51 The day is hot and sunny. The Dvina is gold. I return home from the Institute. Papa is there, much earlier than usual, looking grave. Mama is strong, as ever. With them is a stranger, a comrade from the organs of the Central Committee in Moscow! I am not afraid of him. I know I have done nothing wrong. And the stranger is smiling. A little man – I like him. Despite the heat he is carrying a hat and wears a leather coat. This stranger is named, I think, Mekhlis. He explains that after a thorough investigation, I have been selected for special tasks relating to the high Party leadership. He cannot say more for reasons of security. If I accept, I must travel to Moscow and stay for one year, perhaps for two. Then I may return to Archangel and resume my studies. He offers to come back the next morning for my answer, but I give it now, with all my heart: Yes! But because I am nineteen, he needs the permission of my parents. Oh, please papa! Please,

please! Papa is deeply moved by the scene. He goes with Comrade Mekhlis into the garden, and when he returns his face is solemn. If it is my wish, and if it is the will of the Party, he will not prevent me. Mama is so proud.

To Moscow, then, for the second time in my life!

I know His hand is behind this.

I am so happy, I could die . . .

10.6.51 Mama brings me to the station. Papa stays behind. I kiss her dear cheeks. Farewell to her, farewell to childhood. The carriages are crowded. The train moves off. Others run along the platform, but mama stays still and is quickly lost. We cross the river. I am alone. Poor Anna! And this is the worst of days to travel. But I have my clothes, some food, a book or two, and this journal, in which I shall record my thoughts – this will be my friend. We plunge south through the forest, the tundra. A great red sunset blazes like a fire through the trees. Isakogorka. Obozerskiy. And now I have written down everything that has happened until this time and I can no longer see to write.

11.6.51 Monday morning. The town of Vozhega appears with the dawn. Passengers alight to stretch their legs, but I stay where I am. From the corridor comes a smell of smoke. A man watches me write from the opposite seat, pretending to be asleep. He is curious about me. If only he knew! And still there are eleven hours to Moscow. How can one man rule such a nation? How could such a nation exist without such a man to rule it?

Konosha. Kharovsk. Names on a map become real to me.

Vologda. Danilov. Yaroslavl.

A fear has come upon me. I am so far from home. Last time there were twenty of us, silly laughing girls. O, papa!

Alexandrov.

And now we reach the outskirts of Moscow. A tremor of excitement runs through the train. The blocks and factories stretch as far and wide as the tundra. A hot haze of metal and smoke. The June sun is much warmer than at home. I am excited again.

4.30! Yaroslavskaya station! And now what?

LATER. *The train halts, the man opposite, who had been watching me all journey, leans forward. 'Anna Mikhailovna Safanova?' For a moment I am too amazed to speak. Yes? 'Welcome to Moscow. Come with me, please.' He wears a leather coat, like Comrade Mekhlis. He carries my case along the platform to the station entrance on Komsomolskaya Square. A car is waiting, with a driver. We drive for a long while. An hour at least. I don't know where. Right across the city it seems to me, and out again. Along a highway that leads to a birch forest. There is a high fence and soldiers who check our papers. We drive some more. Another fence. And then a house, in a large garden.*

(And Mama, yes, it is a modest house! Two storeys only. Your good Bolshevik heart would rejoice at its simplicity!)

I am taken around the side of the house to the back. A servants' wing, connected to the main quarters by a long passageway. Here in the kitchen a woman is waiting. She is grey-haired, almost old. And kindly. She calls me 'child'. Her name is Valechka Istomina. A simple meal has been prepared — cold meat and bread, pickled herring, kvas. She watches me. (Everyone here watches everyone else: it is strange to look up and find a pair of eyes regarding you.) From time to time, guards come by to take a look at me. They don't talk much but when they do they sound like Georgians. One asks, 'Well, now, Valechka, and what was the Boss's humour this morning?' but Valechka hushes him and nods to me.

I am not such a young fool as to ask any questions. Not yet.

Valechka says: 'Tomorrow we shall talk. Now rest.'

I have a room to myself. The girl who had it before has gone away. Two plain black blouses and skirts have been left behind for me.

I have a view of a corner of the lawn, a tiny summer house, the woods. The birds sing in the early summer evening. It seems so peaceful. Yet every couple of minutes a guard goes past the window.

I lie on my little bed in the heat and try to sleep. I think of Archangel in the winter: the coloured lanterns strung out across the frozen river, skating on the Dvina, the sound of ice cracking at night, hunting for mushrooms in the forest. I wish I was at home. But these are foolish thoughts.

I must sleep.

Why did that man watch me on the train for all that time?

LATER: In the darkness, the sound of cars.

He is home.

12.6.51 This is a day! I can hardly set it down. My hand shakes so. (It did not at the time but now it does!) At seven I go to the kitchen. Valechka is already up, sorting through a great mess of broken crockery, glass, spilled food, which lies in a heap in the centre of a big tablecloth. She explains how the table is cleared every night: two guards each take two corners of the cloth and carry everything out! So our first task every morning is to rescue all that isn't broken, and wash it. As we work, Valechka explains the routine of the house. He rises quite late and sometimes likes to work in the garden. Then he goes to the Kremlin and his quarters are cleaned. He never returns before nine or ten in the evening, and then there is a dinner. At two or three He goes to bed. This happens seven days a week. The rules: when one approaches Him, do so openly, He hates it when people creep up on Him. If a door has to be knocked on, knock upon it loudly. Don't stand around. Don't speak unless you are spoken to. And if you do have to speak, always look Him in the eyes.

She prepares a simple breakfast of coffee, bread and meat, and takes it out. Later, she asks me to collect the tray. Before I go, she makes me tie up my hair and turn around while she examines me. I will do, she says. She says He is working at a table at the edge of the lawn on the south side of the house. Or was. He moves restlessly, from place to place. It is His way. The guards will know where to look.

What can I write of this moment? I am calm. You would have been proud of me. I remember what to do. I walk around the edge of the lawn and approach Him in plain view. He's sitting on a bench, alone, bent over some papers. The tray is on a table beside Him. He glances up at my approach, then returns to His work. But as I walk away across the grass – then, I swear, I feel His eyes upon my back, all the way, until I'm out of sight. Valechka laughs at my white face.

I don't see Him again after that.

Just now (it is after ten): the sound of cars.

14.6.51 Last night. Late. I'm in the kitchen with Valechka when Lozgachev (a guard) comes rushing in, all steamed up, to say the Boss is out of Ararat. Valechka fetches a bottle, but instead of giving it to Lozgachev, she gives it to me: 'Let Anna take it in.' She wants to help me – dear Valechka! So Lozgachev takes me down the passage to the main part of the house. I can hear male voices. Laughter. He knocks hard on the door and stands aside. I go in. The room is hot, stuffy. Seven or eight men around a table – familiar faces, all of them. One – Comrade Khrushchev,

I think – is on his feet, proposing a toast. His face is flushed, sweating. He stops. There is food all over the place, as if they have been throwing it. All look at me. Comrade Stalin is at the head of the table. I set the brandy next to him. His voice is soft and kindly. He says, 'And what is your name, young comrade?' 'Anna Safanova, Comrade Stalin.' I remember to look into his eyes. They are very deep. The man next to him says, 'She's from Archangel, Boss.' And Comrade Khrushchev says, 'Trust Lavrenty to know where she's from!' More laughter. 'Ignore these rough fellows,' says Comrade Stalin. 'Thank you, Anna Safanova.' As I close the door, their talk resumes. Valechka is waiting for me at the end of the passage. She puts her arm around me and we go back in to the kitchen. I am shaking, it must be with joy.

16.6.51 Comrade Stalin has said that from now on I am to bring him breakfast.

21.6.51 He is in the garden as usual this morning. How I wish the people could see him here! He likes to listen to the birdsong, to prune the flowers. But his hands shake. As I am setting down the tray, I hear him curse. He has cut himself. I pick up the napkin and take it over to him. At first, he looks at me suspiciously. Then he holds out his hand. I wrap it in the white linen. Bright spots of blood soak through. 'You are not afraid of Comrade Stalin, Anna Safanova?' 'Why should I be afraid of you, Comrade Stalin?' 'The doctors are afraid of Comrade Stalin. When they come to change a dressing on Comrade Stalin, their hands shake so much, he has to do it himself. Ah, but if their hands didn't shake – well then, what would that mean? Thank you, Anna Safanova.'

O, mama and papa, he is so lonely! Your hearts would go out to him. He is only flesh and blood, after all, like us. And close-up he is old. Much older than he appears in his pictures. His moustache is grey, the underside stained yellow by his pipe smoke. His teeth are almost all gone. His chest rattles when he breathes. I fear for him. For all of us.

30.6.51 Three a.m. A knock at my door. Valechka is outside, in her nightdress, with a pocket torch. He has been in the garden, pruning by moonlight, and he has cut himself again! He is calling for me! I dress quickly and follow her along the passage. The night is warm. We pass through the dining room and in to his private quarters. He has three rooms and he moves between them, one night in this one, one night in another. Nobody is ever sure where. He sleeps beneath a blanket on a couch. Valechka leaves us. He is sitting on the couch, his hand outstretched. It is only a graze. It takes me half a minute to bind it with my handkerchief. 'The fearless Anna Safanova . . .'

I sense he wants me to stay. He asks me about my home and parents, my Party work, my plans for the future. I tell him of my interest in the law. He snorts: he doesn't think much of lawyers! He wants to know of life in Archangel in the winter. Have I seen the lights of the Northern Aurora? (Of course!) When do the first snows come? At the end of September, I tell him, and by the end of October, the city is snowbound and only the trains can get through. He is hungry for details. How the Dvina freezes and wooden tracks are laid across it and there is light for only four hours a day. How the temperature drops to 35 below and people go into the forests for ice-fishing . . .

He listens most intently. 'Comrade Stalin believes the soul of Russia lies in the ice and solitude of the far north. When Comrade Stalin was in exile – this was before the Revolution, in Kureika, within the Arctic Circle – it was his happiest time. It was here Comrade Stalin learned how to hunt and fish. That swine Trotsky maintained that Comrade Stalin used only traps. A filthy lie! Comrade Stalin set traps, yes, but he also set lines in the ice holes, and such was his success in the detection of fish that the local people credited him with supernatural powers. In one day, Comrade Stalin travelled forty-five versts on skis and killed twelve brace of partridge with twenty-four shots. Could Trotsky claim as much?'

I wish I could remember all he said. Perhaps this should be my destiny: to record his words for History?

By the time I leave him to return to my bed, it is light.

8.7.51 The same performance as last time. Valechka at my door at 3 a.m.: he has cut himself, he wants me. But when I get there, I can see no wound. He laughs at my face – his joke! – and tells me to bind his hand in any case. He strokes my cheek, then pinches it. 'You see, fearless Anna Safanova, how you make a prisoner of me?!'

He is in a different room from the last time. On the walls are pictures of children, torn from magazines. Children playing in a cherry orchard. A boy on skis. A girl drinking goat's milk from a horn. Many pictures. He notices me staring at them and this prompts him to talk frankly of his own children. One son dead. One a drunkard. His daughter married twice, the first time to a Jew: he never even allowed him in to the house! What has Comrade Stalin done to deserve this? Other men produce normal children. Was it bad blood or bad upbringing? Was there something wrong with the mothers? (He thinks so, to judge from their families, who have been a constant plague to him.) Or was it impossible for the children of Comrade Stalin ever to develop normally, given his high position in the State and Party? Here is the age-old conflict, older even than the struggle between the classes.

He asks if I have heard of Comrade Trofim Lysenko's 1948 speech to the Lenin All-Union Academy of Agricultural Sciences? I say that I have. My answer pleases him.

'But Comrade Stalin wrote this speech! It was Comrade Stalin's insight, after a lifetime of study and struggle, that acquired characteristics are inheritable. Though naturally these discoveries must be put into the mouths of others, just as it is for others to turn the principle into a practical science.'

'Remember Comrade Stalin's historic words to Gorky: "It is the task of the proletarian state to produce engineers of human souls."'

'Are you a good Bolshevik, Anna Safanova?'

I swear to him that I am.

'Will you prove it? Will you dance for Comrade Stalin?'

There is a gramophone in the corner of the room. He goes to it. I —

Chapter Fifteen

'AND THAT'S HOW it ends?' said O'Brian. His voice was heavy with disappointment. 'Just like that?'

'See for yourself.' Kelso turned the book round and showed it to the other two. 'The next twenty pages have been removed. And here – look – you can see the way it's been done. The torn edges attached to the spine are all different lengths.'

'What's so significant about that?'

'It means they weren't torn out all at once, but one by one. Methodically.' Kelso resumed his examination. 'There are some pages left at the back, about fifty, but they've not been written on. They've been drawn on – doodled on, I should say – in red pencil. The same image again and again, d'you see?'

'What are they?' O'Brian moved in closer with the camera running. 'They look like wolves.'

'They are wolves. The heads of wolves. Stalin often drew wolves in the margins of official documents when he was thinking.'

'Jesus. So it's genuine, you think?'

'Until it's been forensically tested, I'm not prepared to say. I'm sorry. Not officially.'

'Unofficially, then – not for attribution until later – what d'you think?'

'Oh, it's genuine,' said Kelso, without hesitation. 'I'd stake my life on it.'

O'Brian switched the camera off.

*

THEY had left the lock-up by this time and were sitting in the Moscow bureau of the Satellite News System which occupied the top floor of a ten-storey office block just south of the Olympic Stadium. A glass partition separated O'Brian's room from the main production office, where a secretary sat listlessly before a computer screen. Next to her, a mute television, tuned to SNS, was showing clips of the previous night's baseball games. Through a skylight Kelso could see a big satellite dish, raised like an offertory plate to the bulging Moscow clouds.

O'Brian said, 'And how long is it going to take us to get this stuff tested?'

'A couple of weeks, perhaps,' said Kelso. 'A month.'

'No way,' said O'Brian. 'No way can we wait that long.'

'Well, think about it. First of all this material technically belongs to the Russian government. Or Stalin's heirs. Or someone. Anyway, it isn't ours – Zinaida's, I mean.'

Zinaida was standing at the window, staring out through a gap she had made with her fingers in the slatted blinds. At the mention of her name she glanced briefly in Kelso's direction. She had barely said a word in the last hour – not when they were still in the garage, not even on their cautious drive across Moscow, following O'Brian.

'So it isn't safe to keep it here,' continued Kelso. 'We've got to get it out of the country. That's the first priority. God knows who's after it now. Just being in the same *room* is bloody dangerous as far as I'm concerned. The tests themselves – well, we can have those done anywhere. I know some people in Oxford who can check the ink and paper. There are document examiners in Germany, Switzerland –'

O'Brian didn't seem to be listening. He had his feet up on his desk, his long body lolling back in his chair, his hands clasped behind his head. 'You know what we've really got to do?' he mused. 'We've got to find the girl.'

Kelso stared at him for a moment. 'Find the girl? What are you talking about? There isn't going to be a girl. The girl's going to be dead.'

'You can't be sure of that. She'd only be – what? – sixty-something?'

'She'd be sixty-six. But that's hardly the point. It's not *old age* she'll have died of. Who d'you think she was getting mixed up with here? Prince Charming? She won't have lived happily ever after.'

'Maybe not, but we still need to find out what happened to her. What happened to her folks. Human interest. *That's* the story.'

The wall behind O'Brian's head was plastered with photographs: O'Brian with Yasser Arafat, O'Brian with Gerry Adams, O'Brian in a flak jacket next to a mass grave in the Balkans somewhere and another of him, in protective gear, stepping through a minefield with the Princess of Wales. O'Brian in a tuxedo, collecting an award – for the sheer genius of simply being O'Brian, perhaps? Citations for O'Brian. Reviews of O'Brian. A herogram from the Chief Executive of SNS, praising O'Brian for his 'relentless dedication to triumphing over our competitors'. For the first time, and far too late, Kelso began to get a measure of the man's ambition.

'Nothing,' said Kelso very deliberately, so there was no room for misunderstanding, '*nothing* is to be made public until this material is out of the country and has been forensically verified. Do you hear me? That's what we agreed.'

O'Brian clicked his fingers. 'Yeah, yeah, yeah. All right.

But in the meantime we should find out what happened to the girl. We've got to do that anyway. If we go on air with the notebook before we find out what happened to Anna, someone else'll come along and get the best part of the story.' He lifted his feet off the desk and spun around in his chair to a set of bookshelves beside his desk. 'Now where the hell is Archangel, anyway?'

IT happened with a kind of inexorable logic so that later, when Kelso had the time to review his actions, he still could never identify a precise moment when he could have stopped it, when he could have diverted events on to a different course –

"'Archangel,"' said O'Brian, reading aloud from a guidebook. "'Northern Russian port city. Population: four hundred thousand. Situated on the River Dvina, thirty miles upstream from the White Sea. Principal industries: timber, shipbuilding and fishing. From the end of October until the beginning of April, Archangel is snowbound." Shit. What's the date?'

'October the twenty-ninth.'

O'Brian picked up the telephone and jabbed out a number. From his position on the sofa Kelso watched through the thick glass wall as the secretary reached silently for the receiver.

'Sweetheart,' said O'Brian, 'do me a favour will you? Get on to the System's weather centre in Florida and get the latest weather prediction for Archangel.' He spelt it out for her. 'That's it. Quick as you can.'

Kelso closed his eyes.

The point was – he knew it in his heart – that O'Brian was right. The story *was* the girl. And the story couldn't be pursued in Moscow. If the trail could be picked up anywhere, it could only be in the north, on her home territory, where it was possible there might still be some family or friends who would remember her: remember the Komsomol girl of nineteen and the dramatic summons to Moscow in the summer of 1951 –

'"Archangel,"' resumed O'Brian, '"was founded by Peter the Great and named after Archangel Michael, the Warrior-Angel. See the Book of Revelation, chapter twelve, verses seven to eight: 'And there was war in heaven: Michael and his angels fought against the dragon; and the dragon fought and his angels,/And prevailed not.' In the nineteen-thirties – "'

'Do we really have to listen to this?'

But O'Brian held up his finger.

'" – in the nineteen-thirties, Stalin exiled two million Ukrainian kulaks into the Archangel oblast, a region of forest and tundra larger than the whole of France. After the war, this vast area was used for testing nuclear weapons. Archangel's outport is Severodvinsk, centre of Russia's nuclear submarine construction programme. Until the fall of communism, Archangel was a closed city, forbidden to all outside visitors.

'"Traveller's tip,"' concluded O'Brian. '"When arriving at the Archangel Railway Station, always be sure to check the digital radiation meter – if it shows 15 microRads per hour or below, it's safe."' He closed the book with a cheerful snap. 'Sounds like a fun place. What d'you think? You up for this?'

I am trapped, thought Kelso. *I am a victim of historical inevitability. Comrade Stalin would have approved.*

'You know I've no money – ?'

'I'll lend you money.'

'No winter clothes –'

'We've got clothes.'

'No *visa* –'

'A detail.'

'A *detail?*'

'Come on, Fluke. You're the Stalin expert. I need you.'

'Well that's touching. And if I say no, presumably you'll go anyway?'

O'Brian grinned. The telephone rang. He picked it up, listened, made a few notes. When he put it down, he was frowning and Kelso entertained a brief hope of reprieve. But no.

The weather in Archangel at 11:00 GMT that day (3 p.m. local time) was being reported as partly cloudy, minus four degrees, with light winds and snow flurries. However, a deep depression was rolling westwards from Siberia and that was promising snow heavy enough to close the city within a day or two.

In other words, said O'Brian, they would have to hurry.

HE fetched an atlas and opened it on his desk.

The fastest way into Archangel, obviously, was by air, but the Aeroflot flight didn't leave until the following morning and the airline would require Kelso to show his visa which would expire at midnight. So that was out. The train took more than twenty hours, and even O'Brian could see the risks in that – trapped on board a slow-moving sleeper for the best part of a day.

Which left the road – specifically, the M8 – which ran nearly 700 miles, more or less direct, according to the map, swerving slightly to take in the city of Yaroslavl, then following the river plateaux of the Vaga and the Dvina, across the taiga and the tundra and the great virgin forests of northern

Russia, directly into Archangel itself, where the road ended.

Kelso said, 'It's not a freeway, you know. There are no motels.'

'It's nothing, man. It'll be a breeze, I promise. What've we got now – let's see – couple of hours of daylight left? That should get us well clear of Moscow. You drive, don't you?'

'Yes.'

'There you go. We'll take turns. These journeys, I tell you, they always look worse on paper. Once we're in the groove, we'll eat those miles. You'll see.' He was making a calculation on a pad. 'I figure we could hit Archangel about nine or ten tomorrow morning.'

'So we drive through the night?'

'Sure. Or we can stop if you'd sooner. The thing is to quit talking and start moving. Quicker we hit the road, quicker we get there. We need to pack that book in something –'

He came round from behind his desk and headed towards the notebook that was lying on the coffee table, next to the congealed mass of papers. But before he could reach it, Zinaida grabbed it.

'This,' she said in English, 'mine.'

'What?'

'Mine.'

Kelso said, 'That's right. Her father left it for her.'

'I only want to borrow it.'

'*Nyet!*'

O'Brian appealed to Kelso. 'Is she crazy? Supposing we find Anna Safanova?'

'Supposing we do? What do you have in mind exactly? Stalin's grey-haired old lover in a rocking chair, reading aloud for the viewers?'

'Oh, funny guy. Listen: people are a whole lot more likely

to talk to us if we're carrying proof. I say that book should come with us. Why's it hers, anyhow? It's no more hers than mine. Or anybody else's.'

'Because that was the deal, remember?'

'Deal? Seems to me it's you two've got the only *deal* going round here.' He slipped back into his wheedling mode. 'Come on, Fluke, it's not safe for her in Moscow. Where's she gonna keep it? What if Mamantov comes after her?'

Kelso had to concede this point. 'Then why doesn't she come with us?' He turned to Zinaida, 'Come with us to Archangel –'

'With him?' she said in Russian. 'No way. He'll kill us all.'

Kelso was beginning to lose patience. 'Then let's postpone Archangel,' he said irritably to O'Brian, 'until we can get the material copied.'

'But you heard the forecast. In a day or two we won't be able to move up there. Besides, this is a story. Stories don't keep.' He raised his hands in disgust. 'Shit, I can't stand around here bitching all afternoon. Need to get some equipment together. Need supplies. Need to get going. Talk some sense into her, man, for God's sake.'

'I told you,' said Zinaida, after O'Brian had stamped out of the office, banging the glass door behind him. 'I told you we couldn't trust him.'

Kelso sank back into the sofa. He rubbed his face with both hands. This was starting to get dangerous, he thought. Not physically – in a curious way that was still unreal to him – but professionally. It was professional danger he scented now. Because Adelman was right: these big frauds did usually follow a pattern. And part of it involved being rushed to judgement. Here he was – a trained scholar, supposedly – and what had he done? He'd read through the notebook once. *Once.* He hadn't even done the most basic check to see whether the dates in the journal tallied with Stalin's known movements in the summer of 1951. He could just imagine the reaction of his former colleagues, probably leaving Russian airspace right now. If they could see how he was handling this –

The thought bothered him more than he cared to admit.

And then there was the other bundle of papers, lying on the table, mouldering and congealed. Those he hadn't even begun to look at.

He pulled on O'Brian's gloves and leaned forwards. He ran his forefinger experimentally through the grey spores on the top sheet. There was writing underneath. He rubbed again and the letters NKVD appeared.

'Zinaida,' he said.

She was sitting behind O'Brian's desk, turning the pages of the notebook, *her* notebook. At the sound of her name she looked up.

KELSO borrowed her tweezers to peel away the outer layer of paper. It came off like dead skin, flaking here and there, but cleanly enough for him to make out some of the words on the page underneath. It was a typed document, a surveillance report of some kind by the look of it, dated 24 May 1951, signed by Major I. T. Mekhlis of the NKVD.

'. . . *summary of finding to the 23rd instant . . . Anna Mikhailovna Safanova, born Archangel 27.2.32 . . . Maxim Gorky Academy . . . reputation (see attached). Health: good . . . diptheria, aged 8 yrs. 3 mths . . . Rubella, 10yrs. 1 mth . . . No family history of genetic disorder. Party work: outstanding . . . Pioneers . . . Komsomol . . .*'

Kelso peeled back more layers. Sometimes they came away

singly, sometimes fused in twos or threes. It was painstaking work. Through the glass partition he caught occasional glimpses of O'Brian, lugging suitcases across the outer office to the elevator doors, but he was too absorbed to pay much attention. What he was reading was as full a record of a nineteen-year-old girl's life as it was possible for a secret police force to compile. There was something almost pornographic about it. Here was an account of every childhood ailment, details of her blood group (O), the state of her teeth (excellent), her height and weight and hair-colour (light auburn), her physical aptitude ('in gymnastics she displays a particularly high aptitude ...'), mental abilities ('overall, in the 90th percentile ... '), ideological correctness ('the firmest grasp of Marxist theory ... '), interviews with her doctor, coach, teachers, Komsomol group leader, schoolfriends.

The worst that could be said about her was that she had, perhaps 'a slightly dreamy temperament' (Comrade Oborin) and 'a certain tendency to subjectivity and bourgeois sentimentalism rather than objectivity in all her personal relations' (Elena Satsanova). Against a further criticism from the same Comrade Satsanova, that she was 'naïve,' a marginal comment had been appended, in red pencil: 'Good!' and, later, 'Who is this old bitch?' There were numerous other underlinings, exclamation marks, queries and marginalia: 'Ha ha ha', 'And so?', 'Acceptable!'

Kelso had spent enough time in the archives to recognise this hand and style. The jagged scrawl was Stalin's. There was no question of it.

After half an hour he put the papers back in their original order and took off his gloves. His hands felt claw-like, raw and sweaty. He was suddenly overcome with self-disgust.

Zinaida was watching him.

'What do you think happened to her?'

'Nothing good.'

'He brought her down from the north to screw her?'

'That's one way of putting it.'

'Poor kid.'

'Poor kid,' he agreed.

'So why did he keep her book?'

'Obsession? Infatuation?' He shrugged. 'Who's to say. He was a sick man by then. He only had twenty months to live. Maybe she described what happened to her, then thought better of it, and tore out the pages. Or, more likely, he got hold of her book and ripped them out himself. He didn't like people knowing too much about him.'

'Well, I can tell you one thing: he didn't screw her that night.'

Kelso laughed. 'And how do you know that?'

'Easy. Look.' She opened the notebook. 'Here on the twelfth of May, she's got "the usual trouble of this time", right? On the tenth of June, on the train, it's "the worst of days to travel". Well, you can work it out for yourself, can't you? There's exactly twenty-eight days between the two. And twenty-eight days after the tenth of June is July the eighth. Which is the last entry.'

Kelso stood slowly and went over to the desk. He peered over her shoulder at the childish writing.

'What are you talking about?'

'She was a regular girl. A regular little Komsomol girl.'

Kelso absorbed this information, put the gloves back on, took the book from her, flicked between the two pages. Well, now, this was crazy, wasn't it? This was *sick*. He could barely bring himself to acknowledge the suspicion that was forming in the back of his mind. But why else would Stalin have been so interested in whether or not she had had *rubella*, of all things? Or whether her family had any history of congenital disorders?

'Tell me,' he said, quietly, 'when would she have been fertile?'

'Fourteen days later. On the twenty-second.'

AND suddenly she couldn't get out of there fast enough.

She pushed her chair back from the desk and stared at the notebook with revulsion.

'Take the damned thing,' she said. 'Take it. Keep it.'

She didn't want to touch it again. She didn't even want to *see* it.

It was *cursed*.

In a couple of seconds she had her bag over her shoulder and was flinging open the door and Kelso had to scramble to catch up with her as she strode across the office towards the elevators. O'Brian came out of an editing suite to see what was going on. He was in a heavy waterproof jacket with two pairs of binoculars slung around his thick neck. He started to follow them but Kelso waved him back.

'I'll handle this.'

She was standing in the corridor, her back to him.

'Listen Zinaida,' he said. The lift door opened and he stepped in after her. 'Listen. It's not safe for you out there –'

Almost immediately the car stopped and a man got in – heavy-set, middle-aged, black leather coat and a black leather cap. He stood between them, glanced at Zinaida, then at Kelso, sensing the edge to their silence. He looked straight ahead and stuck out his chin, smiling slightly. Kelso could tell what he was thinking: *a lovers' tiff – well, that was life, they'd get over it.*

When they reached the ground floor he stood back politely to let them out first and Zinaida clattered quickly across the marble in her knee-length boots. A security guard pressed a switch to unlock the doors.

'You,' she said, zipping up her jacket, 'should worry about yourself.'

It was just after four. People were beginning to leave from work. In the offices across the road Kelso could see the green glow of computer screens. A woman had shrunk herself into a doorway and was talking into a mobile phone. A motorcyclist went past, slowly.

'Zinaida, listen.' He grabbed her arm, stopping her from walking away. She wouldn't look at him. He pulled her close to the wall. 'Your father died badly, do you understand what I'm saying? The people who did it – Mamantov and his people – they're after this notebook. They know there's something important about it – don't ask me how. If they realise your father had a daughter – and they're bound to because Mamantov used to have access to his file – well, think about it. They're going to come after you.'

'And they killed him for *that?*'

'They killed him because he wouldn't tell them where it was. And he wouldn't tell them where it was because he wanted you to have it.'

'But it wasn't worth *dying* for. The stupid old fool.' She glared at him. Her eyes were wet for the first time that day. 'Stupid *stubborn* old fool.'

'Is there someone you can stay with? Family?'

'My family are dead.'

'A friend maybe?'

'Friend? I've got this, remember?' She lifted the flap of her bag, showing him her father's pistol.

Kelso said, as calmly as he could, 'At least give me your address, Zinaida. Your phone number –'

She looked at him suspiciously. 'Why?'

'Because I feel responsible.' He glanced around. This was madness, talking in the street. He felt in his pocket for a pen, couldn't find any paper, tore the side off a pack of cigarettes. 'Come on, write it for me. Quickly.'

He thought she wouldn't do it. She turned to go. But then, abruptly, she swung back and scribbled something down. She had a place near Izmaylovo Park, he saw, where the big flea market was.

She didn't say goodbye. She set off up the street, dodging the pedestrians, walking fast. He watched her, waiting to see if she might look back. But of course she didn't. He knew she wouldn't. She wasn't the looking-back kind.

Part Two

Archangel

'If you are afraid of wolves, keep out of the woods.'

J. V. Stalin, 1936

Chapter Sixteen

BEFORE THEY COULD get out of Moscow they had to take on fuel – because, as O'Brian said, you never knew what kind of rusty, watered-down *horse's piss* they might try to sell you once you got out of town. So they stopped at the new Nefto Agip on Prospekt Mira and O'Brian filled the Land Cruiser's tank and four big jerrycans with forty gallons of high-octane, lead-free gasoline. Then he checked the tyres and the oil, and by the time they were back on the road the evening rush was in full and sluggish spate.

It took them the best part of an hour to reach the outer ring, but there, at last, the traffic thinned, the monotonous apartment blocks and factory chimneys fell away, and suddenly they were out and free – into the flat open countryside, with its grey-green fields and giant pylons and a vast sky: a Kansas sky. It was more than ten years since Kelso had ventured north on the M8. Village churches, used as grain stores since the Revolution, were being restored, encased in webworks of wooden scaffolding. Near Dvoriki, a golden dome gathered the weak afternoon light and shone from the horizon like an autumn bonfire.

O'Brian was in his element. 'On the road,' he would say occasionally, 'and out of town – it's great, isn't it? Just great.' He drove at a steady sixty-five miles an hour, talking constantly, one hand on the wheel, the other beating time to a tape of thumping rock music.

'Just great . . .'

The satchel was on the back seat, wrapped in plastic. Heaped around it was an extravagant array of equipment and provisions: a couple of sleeping bags, thermal underwear ('Got any thermals, Fluke? Gotta have those thermals!'), two waterproof and fur-lined jackets, rubber boots and army boots, ordinary binoculars, binoculars with night-imaging, a shovel, a compass, water bottles, water purification tablets, two six-packs of Budweiser, a box of Hershey chocolate bars, two vacuum flasks filled with coffee, pot noodles, a torch, a short-wave transistor radio, spare batteries, a travelling kettle that could be plugged into the car's cigarette lighter – Kelso lost count after that.

In the rear section of the Toyota were the jerrycans and four rigid cases stamped SNS, whose contents O'Brian described with professional relish: a miniaturised, digital camcorder; an Inmarsat satellite telephone; a laptop-sized DVC-PRO video editing machine; and something he called a Toko Video Store and Forward Unit. Total value of these four items: $120,000.

'Ever hear of travelling light?' asked Kelso.

'Light?' O'Brian grinned. 'You can't get any lighter. Give me four suitcases and I can do what it used to take six guys and a truckful of equipment to do. If there's any excess baggage around here, my friend, it's you.'

'It wasn't my idea to come.'

But O'Brian wasn't listening. Thanks to these four cases, he said, his beat was the *world*. African famines. The genocide in Rwanda. The bomb in the village in Northern Ireland that he'd actually filmed go off (he'd won an award for that one). The mass graves in Bosnia. The cruise missiles in Baghdad, trundling down the streets at roof-top level – left, then right, then right again, and which way, please, for the presidential palace? And then of course there was Chechnya. Now, the trouble with Chechnya –

(You are a bird of ill-omen, thought Kelso. You circle the world and wherever you land there is famine and death and destruction: in an earlier and less credulous age, the local citizens would have gathered at the first sight of you and driven you off with stones –)

– the trouble with Chechnya, O'Brian was saying, was that the sucker had ended just as he arrived, so he had pitched up in Moscow for a while. Now *that* was a scary town: 'Give me Sarajevo any day.'

'How long are you planning to stay in Moscow?'

'Not long. Till the presidential elections. Should be fun, I reckon.'

Fun?

'And then where are you going?'

'Who knows? Why d'you ask?'

'I just want to make sure I'm nowhere around, that's all.'

O'Brian laughed and put his foot down. The speedometer flickered up towards seventy.

THEY maintained this pace as the afternoon turned to dusk, O'Brian still prattling on. (Jesus, did the man *never* shut up?) At Rostov the road ran beside a great lake. Boats, moored and tarpaulined for the winter, lined a jetty, close to a row of shuttered, timbered buildings. Far out on the water Kelso could see a lone sailboat with a light at its stern. He watched it swing about in the wind and tack for the shore and he felt again the familiar depression of nightfall starting to creep over him.

He could sense Stalin's papers behind him now almost as a physical presence, as if the GenSec were in the car with them. He worried about Zinaida. He would have liked a drink, or a cigarette, come to that, but O'Brian had declared the Toyota a smoke-free zone.

'You're jumpy,' said O'Brian, interrupting himself. 'I can tell.'

'Do you blame me?'

'Why? Because of Mamantov?' The reporter flicked his hand. 'He doesn't scare me.'

'You didn't see what he did to the old man.'

'Yeah, well he wouldn't do that to us. Not to a Brit and a Yank. He's not completely nuts.'

'Maybe not. But he might do it to Zinaida.'

'I wouldn't worry about Zinaida. Besides, she hasn't got the stuff any more. We have.'

'You're a nice man, you know that? And what if they don't believe her?'

'I'm just saying you should quit bothering about Mamantov, that's all. I've interviewed him a couple of times and I can tell you, he's a busted flash. The man lives in the past. Like you.'

'And you? You don't live in the past, I suppose?'

'Me? No way. Can't afford to, in my job.'

'Now let's just analyse that,' said Kelso, pleasantly. In his mind he was opening a drawer, selecting the sharpest knife he could find. 'So all these places you've been boasting about for the past two hours – Africa, Bosnia, the Middle East, Northern Ireland – the past isn't important there, is that what you're saying? You think they're all living in the present? They all just woke up one morning, saw you were there with your four little suitcases, and decided to have a war? It wasn't happening till you arrived? "Gee, hey, look everyone, I'm R. J. O'Brian and I just discovered the fucking *Balkans* – "'

'Okay,' muttered O'Brian, 'there's no need to be offensive about it.'

'Oh but there is.' Kelso was warming up. 'This is the great

myth, you see, of our age. The great western myth. The arrogance of our time, personified – if you'll excuse me for saying so – in *you*. That just because a place has a McDonalds and MTV and takes American Express it's exactly the same as everywhere else – it doesn't have a past any more, it's Year Zero. But it's not true.'

'You think you're better than me, don't you?'

'No.'

'Smarter then?'

'Not even that. Look. You say Moscow is a scary town. It is. Why? I'll tell you. Because there's no tradition of private property in Russia. First of all there were workers and peasants who had nothing and the nobility owned the country. Then there were workers and peasants with nothing and the Party owned the country. Now there are still workers and peasants with nothing and the country's owned, as it's always been owned, by whoever has the biggest fists. Unless you understand that, you can't begin to understand Russia. You can't make sense of the present unless a part of you lives in the past.' Kelso sat back in his seat. 'End of lecture.'

And for half an hour, as O'Brian pondered this, there was blessed peace.

THEY reached the big town of Yaroslavl just after nine and crossed the Volga. Kelso poured them each a cup of coffee. It slopped across his lap as they hit a rough patch of road. O'Brian drank as he drove. They ate chocolate. The headlights that had blazed towards them around the city gradually dwindled to the occasional flash.

Kelso said, 'Do you want me to take over?'

O'Brian shook his head. 'I'm fine. Let's change at midnight. You should get some sleep.'

They listened on the radio to the news at ten o'clock. The communists and the nationalists in the lower senate, the Duma, were using their majority to block the President's latest measures: another political crisis threatened. The Moscow stock exchange was continuing its plunge. A secret report from the Interior Ministry to the President, warning of a danger of armed rebellion, had been leaked and printed in *Aurora*.

Of Rapava, Mamantov or Stalin's papers there was no mention.

'Shouldn't you be in Moscow, covering all this?'

O'Brian snorted. 'What? "New Political Crisis in Russia"? Give me a break. R. J. O'Brian won't be on the hour every hour with *that*.'

'But he will with this?'

'"Stalin's Secret Lover, Mystery Girl Revealed"? What do you think?'

O'Brian switched off the radio.

Kelso reached over to the back seat and dragged one of the sleeping bags into the front. He opened it out and wrapped it around him like a blanket, then pressed a button and his seat slowly reclined.

He closed his eyes but he couldn't sleep. Images of Stalin gradually invaded his mind. Stalin as an old man. Stalin as glimpsed by Milovan Djilas after the war, leaning forward in his limousine while he was being driven back to Blizhny, turning on a little light in the panel in front of him to see the time on a pocket watch hanging there – 'and I observed directly in front of me his already hunched back and the bony grey nape of his neck with its wrinkled skin above the stiff marshal's collar . . .' (Djilas thought Stalin was senile that night: cramming his mouth with food, losing the thread of his stories, making jokes about the Jews.)

And Stalin, less than six months before he died, delivering his last, rambling speech to the Central Committee, describing how Lenin faced the crises of 1918 and repeating the same word over and over – 'he thundered away in an incredibly difficult situation, he thundered on, fearing nothing, he just thundered away . . .' – while the delegates sat stunned, transfixed.

And Stalin, alone in his bedroom, at night, tearing pictures of children out of magazines and plastering them around his walls. And then Stalin making Anna Safanova dance for him –

It was curious, but whenever Kelso tried to picture Anna Safanova dancing, the face he always gave her was that of Zinaida Rapava.

Chapter Seventeen

ZINAIDA RAPAVA WAS sitting in her parked car in Moscow in the darkness with her bag on her lap and her hands in that bag, feeling the outline of her father's Makarov pistol.

She had discovered that she could still strip and load it without looking at it – like riding a bicycle, it seemed: one of those childish accomplishments you never forgot. Release the spring at the bottom of the grip, pull out the magazine, squeeze in the bullets (six, seven, *eight* of them, smooth and cold to the touch), push the magazine back up, click, slide, then press the safety catch down to fire. *There.*

Papa would have been proud of her. But then she always had been better at this game than Sergo. Guns made Sergo nervous. Which was a joke, seeing as he was the one who had to do military service.

Thinking of Sergo made her cry again, but she wouldn't let herself give in to it for long. She pulled her hands out of her bag and wiped each eye irritably – so then so – on either sleeve of her jacket, then went back to her task.

Push. Click. Slide. Press . . .

SHE was scared. So scared, in fact, that when she had walked away from the westerner that afternoon she had wanted to look back at him standing outside the office block – had wanted to *go* back to him – but if she'd done that he would have known she was afraid, and fear, she had been taught, was something you must never show. Another of her father's lessons.

So she had hurried on to her car and had driven around

for a while without thinking until presently she had found herself heading in the direction of Red Square. She had parked in Bolshaya Lubyanka and had walked uphill to the little white Church of the Icon of the Virgin of Vladimir, where a service was in progress.

The place was packed. The churches were always packed now, not like in the old days. The music washed over her. She lit a candle. She wasn't sure why she did this because she had no faith; it was the sort of thing her mother used to do. *'And what has your god ever done for us?'* – her father's sneering voice. She thought of him, and of the girl who wrote the journal, Anna Safanova. Silly bitch, she thought. Poor silly bitch. And she lit a candle for her, too, and much good might it do her, wherever she was.

She wished her memories were better but they weren't and there was nothing to be done. She could remember him drunk, mostly, his eyes like worm holes, his fists flying. Or tired from work at the engine sheds, as rank as an old dog, too weary to rise from his chair to go to bed, sitting on a sheet of *Pravda* to keep the oil off the cover. Or paranoid, up half the night, staring out of the window, prowling the corridors – who was that looking at him? who was that talking about him? – spreading yet more sheets from *Pravda* down on the floor and obsessively cleaning his Makarov. (*'I'll kill them if I have to . . .'*)

But sometimes, when he wasn't drunk or exhausted or mad – in the mellow hour, between mere inebriation and oblivion – he'd talk about life in Kolyma: how you survived, traded favours and scraps of tobacco for food, wangled the easier jobs, learned to smell a stoolie – and then he'd take her on his lap and sing to her, some of the Kolyma songs, in his fine Mingrelian tenor.

That was a better memory.

At fifty he had seemed so *old* to her. He always had been an old man. His youth had gone when Stalin died. Maybe that was why he went on about him so much? He even had a picture of Stalin on the wall – remember that? – Stalin with his glossy moustaches, like great black slugs? Well, she could never take her friends back *there*, could she? Never let them see the pig state in which they lived. Two rooms, and her in the only bedroom, sharing first with Sergo and then, when he was too big and too embarrassed to look at her, with mama. And mama a wraith even before the cancer got her, then turning to gossamer and finally melting to nothing.

She'd died in eighty-nine when Zinaida was eighteen. And six months later they were back at the Troekurovo cemetery putting Sergo in the earth beside her. Zinaida closed her eyes and remembered papa, drunk, at the funeral, in the rain, and a couple of Sergo's army comrades, and a nervous young lieutenant, just a kid himself, who had been Sergo's commanding officer, talking about how Sergo had died for the motherland whilst rendering fraternal assistance to the progressive forces of the People's Republic of –

– oh, fuck it, what did it matter? The lieutenant had cleared off as soon as he decently could, after about ten minutes, and Zinaida had moved her things out of the ghost-filled apartment that night. He had tried to stop her, hitting her, sweating vodka through his open pores, stinking even more like an old dog from his soaking in the rain, and she had never seen him again. Never seen him again until last Tuesday morning when he had turned up on her doorstep and called her a whore. And she had thrown him out like a beggar, sent him away with a couple of packs of cigarettes, and now he was dead and she really would never see him again.

She bent her head, lips moving, and anyone watching might have thought she was praying, but actually she was reading his note and talking to herself.

'I have been a bad one, you're right. All you said was right. So don't think I don't know it –'

Oh, papa, you were, you know that? You really were.

'But here is a chance to do some good –'

Good? Is that what you call it? Good? That's a joke. They killed you for it and now they're going to kill me.

'Remember that place I used to have, when mama was alive?'

Yes, yes, I remember.

'And remember what I used to tell you? Are you listening to me, girl? Rule number one? What's rule number one?'

She folded away the note and glanced around. This was stupid.

'Speak up, girl!'

She bowed her head meekly.

Never show them you're afraid, papa.

'Again!'

'Never show them you're afraid.'

'And rule number two? What's rule number two?'

You've only got one friend in this world.

'And that friend is?'

Yourself.

'And what else?'

This.

'Show me.'

This, papa. This.

In the concealed darkness of the bag her fingers began to work her rosary, clumsily at first but with increasing dexterity –

Push. Click. Slide. Press –

*

239

SHE had left the church when the service ended and hurried down into Red Square, knowing what she had to do, much calmer now.

The westerner was right. She didn't dare risk her apartment. There wasn't a friend she knew well enough to ask if she could stay. And in a hotel she would have to register, and if Mamantov had friends in the FSB –

That only left one option.

It was nearly six and the shadows were beginning to collect and deepen around the base of Lenin's tomb. But across the cobbles the lights of the GUM department store blazed brighter by the minute – a line of yellow beacons, it seemed to her, in the gloom of the late October afternoon.

She made her purchases quickly, starting with a knee-length black cocktail dress of raw silk. She also bought herself sheer black tights, short black gloves, a black purse, a pair of black high-heeled shoes and make-up.

She paid for it all in cash, in dollars. She never went out with less than $1,000 in cash. She refused to use a credit card: they left too many traces. And she didn't trust the banks, either: thieving alchemists, the lot of them, who would take your precious dollars and conjure them into roubles, turn gold into base metal.

At the cosmetic counter one of the salesgirls recognised her – Hi, Zina! – and she had to turn and flee.

She went back into the boutique and took off her jeans and shirt and tugged herself into her new dress. It was hard to fasten the zip – she had to twist her left arm half way up her back and push her right hand down between her shoulder blades until her fingers touched, but it fastened eventually, pinching her flesh, and she stepped back a pace to look at herself – her hand on her hip, her chin tilted, her profile turned to the mirror.

Good.

Well: *good enough.*

The make-up took another ten minutes. She stuffed her old warm clothes into the GUM carrier bag, slipped on her leather jacket, and headed back into Red Square, tottering on her high heels over the big stones.

She was careful not to look at the Lenin mausoleum, nor at the Kremlin wall behind it, where her father used to take her when she was a girl to file past Stalin's tomb. Instead she walked quickly through the gate in the northern edge of the square, turned right and headed towards the Metropol. She wanted to have a drink at the hotel bar but the security men wouldn't let her through.

'No way, darling. Sorry.'

She could hear them laughing as she walked away.

'Starting early tonight?' one of them called after her.

It was dark by the time she reached her car.

WHICH was where she now sat.

Strange, she thought, looking back, the deaths of mama and Sergo – these two little deaths. *Strange.* They were like two small pebbles at the start of an avalanche. Because not long after they went, everything went – all the old, familiar world slid after them into the wet ground.

Not that Zinaida took much notice of the politics of it all. The first couple of years after leaving papa were a haze in her memory. She lived in a squat out in the Krasnogorsk district. Got pregnant twice. Had two abortions. (And not many days had gone by since when she hadn't wondered what they might have been like, those two – they'd be nearly nine and seven now – and whether they could have been any more clamorous than the spaces they'd left behind.)

Still: if she didn't notice the politics, she did notice the money that was now beginning to appear around the rich hotels – the Metropol, the Kempinski and the rest. And the money noticed her, like it noticed all the Moscow girls. Zinaida wasn't one of the most beautiful, maybe, but she was *good enough*: sufficiently Mingrelian to have an almost Oriental sharpness to her face, sufficiently Russian to have a padding of voluptuousness despite her skinny frame.

And as no girl in Moscow could earn in a month what a western businessman might spend in a night on a bottle of wine, you didn't have to be a genius at economics – you didn't have to be one of the hard-faced management consultants drinking at the bar – to see there was a market in the making here. Which was why one night in December 1992, at the age of twenty-one, in the hotel suite of a German engineer from Ludwigshafen am Rhein, Zinaida Rapava became a whore, tottering down the corridor after ninety sweaty minutes with $125 hidden in her bra, which was more money than she had ever even *seen*.

And shall I tell you something else, papa, now that we're talking at last? It was fine. *I* was fine. Because what was I doing, really, that ten million other girls don't do every night, only they don't have the sense to get paid for it? *That* was decadent. *This* was business – *kapitalism* – and it was fine, and it was like you said, I only had one friend: myself.

After a time, the trade moved out of the hotels and into the clubs, and that was easier. The clubs paid protection to the mafia, collecting a percentage from the girls, and in return the mafia kept the pimps out of it, so it all looked nice and respectable and everyone could pretend it was pleasure, not business.

Tonight, almost six years after that first encounter, hidden in her apartment – which was bought and paid for, by the way – Zinaida Rapava had nearly $30,000 in cash. And she had plans. She was studying law. She was going to be a lawyer. She was going to give up Robotnik, and Moscow with it, and move to St Petersburg and become a proper legal whore – a lawyer.

She was going to do all this until, on Tuesday morning, Papu Rapava had turned up out of nowhere, wanting to talk, calling her filthy names, bringing with him from the street the familiar, stinking dog's breath stench of *the past*.

SHE listened to the ten o'clock news, then switched on the ignition and drove slowly out of Bolshaya Lubyanka, heading north-west across Moscow to the Stadium of the Young Pioneers, where she parked in her usual spot, just off the darkened track.

The night was cold. The wind whipped the thin dress tight around her legs. She held on to her bag as she stumbled towards the lights. She would be safer inside.

Outside Robotnik there was a good crowd for a Thursday night, a nice line of rich western sheep all waiting to be fleeced. Normally her eyes would have flashed as sharp across them as a pair of shears, but not tonight, and she had to force herself forwards.

She went round to the back entrance, as normal, and the barman, Aleksey, let her in. She checked her jacket into the cloakroom and hesitated over her bag but then gave that to the old woman attendant as well: the floor of the Robotnik was not the wisest place in Moscow to be caught carrying a gun.

She could always pretend to be someone else when she

came to the club, and apart from the money that was the other good thing about it. (*'What's your name?'* they would say, trying to make some human contact. *'What name do you like?'* she would always reply.) She could leave her history at the door of the Robotnik, and hide behind this other Zinaida: sexy, self-possessed, hard. But not tonight. Tonight, as she stood in the ladies' toilet, freshening her make-up, the trick didn't seem to be working, and the face that stared back at her was indisputably her own: raw-eyed, frightened Zinaida Rapava.

SHE sat in one of the shadowy booths for an hour or more, watching. What she needed was someone who would take her for the whole night. Someone decent and respectable, with an apartment of his own. But how could you ever judge what men were really like? It was the young ones with the swaggering walks and the loud mouths who ended up bursting into tears and showing you pictures of their girlfriends. It was the bespectacled bankers and lawyers who liked to knock you around.

Just after half-past eleven, when the place was at its busiest, she made her move.

She circled the dance floor, smoking, holding a bottle of mineral water. Holy Mother, she thought, there were girls in here tonight who barely looked fifteen. She was practically old enough to have given them birth.

She was coming to the end of this life.

A man with dark curly hair poking through the straining buttons of his shirt came over to her but he reminded her of O'Brian and she side-stepped him through a cloud of aftershave, in favour of a big south-east Asian in an Armani suit.

He drained his drink – vodka, neat, no ice, she noticed: noticed it too late – and he got her on the dance floor. He quickly grabbed her backside, a cheek in either hand, and began digging his fingers into her, almost lifting her out of her new shoes. She told him to cut it out but he didn't seem to understand. She tried to press her arms against him, push him back, but he only increased his grip and something gave in her then, or rather joined – a kind of merging of the two Zinaidas –

'Are you a good Bolshevik, Anna Safanova? Will you prove it? Will you dance for Comrade Stalin?'

– and suddenly she raked the fingers of her right hand down his smooth cheek, so deep she was sure she could feel the glossy flesh clogging beneath her nails.

He released her then all right – roared and doubled over, shaking his head, spraying beads of blood around him in a series of perfect arcs, like a wet dog shaking off water. Someone screamed and people rippled away to give him space.

This was what they had come to see!

Zinaida ran – across the bar, up the spiral staircase, past the metal detectors and out into the cold. Her legs splayed like a cow's and gave way on the ice. She was sure he was coming after her. She dragged herself back up on to her feet and somehow made it to her car.

THE Victory of the Revolution apartment complex. Block Nine. In darkness. The cops had gone. The little crowd had gone. And soon the place itself would be gone – it had been jerrybuilt even by Soviet standards; it was going to be pulled down in a month or two.

She parked across the street, in the spot where she had

brought the westerner the night before, and stared at it across the roughened, freezing snow.

Block Nine.

Home.

She was so tired.

She grasped the top of the steering wheel with both hands and laid her forehead on her bare arms. She was done with crying by then. She had a very strong sense of her father's presence, and that stupid song he used to sing.

> *Kolyma, Kolyma,*
> *What a wonderful place!*
> *Twelve months of winter*
> *Summer all the rest . . .*

And wasn't there another verse? Something about twenty-four hours of work each day and sleeping all the rest? And so on and on? She knocked her head against her arms in time to the imagined beat, then rested her cheek against the wheel, and that was the moment that she remembered that she had left her bag with her gun in it back at the club.

She remembered it because a car, a big car, had drawn alongside her, very close, preventing her from pulling out, and a man's face was staring at her – a white blur distorted through two panes of dirty wet glass.

Chapter Eighteen

Silence woke him.

'What time is it?'

'Midnight.' O'Brian yawned noisily. 'Your shift.'

They were parked beside the deserted highway with the engine off. Kelso could see nothing, apart from a few faint stars up ahead. After the noise of the journey the stillness was almost physical, a pressure in the ears.

He pulled himself upright. 'Where are we?'

'About a hundred, maybe a hundred and twenty miles north of Vologda.' O'Brian snapped on the interior light, making Kelso flinch. 'Should be about here, I figure.'

He leaned over with the map, his big fingernail pressed to a spot that looked entirely blank, a white space split by the red line of the highway, with a few symbols for marshland dotted on either side of it. Further north the map turned green for the forest.

'I need a piss,' said O'Brian. 'You coming?'

It was much colder than in Moscow, the sky even bigger. A great fleet of vast clouds, pale-edged by the moonlight, moved slowly southwards, occasionally unveiling patches of stars. O'Brian had a torch. They scrambled down a short bank and stood urinating, companionably, side by side, for half a minute, steam rising from the ground before them, then O'Brian zipped up his flies and shone his torch around. The powerful beam stretched for a couple of hundred yards into the darkness, then dissipated; it lit nothing. A freezing mist hung low to the ground.

'Can you hear anything?' said O'Brian. His breath

flickered in the cold.

'No.'

'Neither can I.'

He switched off the torch and they stood there for a while.

'Oh, daddy,' whispered O'Brian, in a little boy's voice, 'I'm so *scared*.'

He turned the light back on and they climbed the bank to the Toyota. Kelso poured them both more coffee while O'Brian lifted up the rear door and dragged out a couple of the jerrycans. He found a funnel and began filling the tank.

Kelso, nursing his coffee, moved away from the gasoline fumes and lit a cigarette. In the darkness, in the cold, under the immense Eurasian sky, he felt disconnected from reality, frightened yet strangely exhilarated, his senses sharpened. He heard a rumble far away and a yellow dot appeared far back on the straight highway. He watched it grow slowly, saw the gleam divide and become two big headlights, and for a moment he thought they were coming directly at him, and then a big truck, a sixteen-wheeler, rushed past, the driver merrily sounding his horn. The noise of the engine was still faintly audible in the distance long after the red tail lights had vanished in the dark.

'Hey, Fluke! Give us a hand here, will you?'

Kelso took a last draw on his cigarette and flicked it away, spinning orange sparks across the road.

O'Brian wanted help lifting down one of his precious pieces of equipment, a white polycarbonate case, about two feet long and eighteen inches wide, with a small pair of black wheels mounted on one end. Once they'd pulled it out of the Toyota, O'Brian trundled it round to the front passenger door.

'Now what?' said Kelso.

'Don't tell me you've never seen one of these before?'

O'Brian opened the lid of the box and removed what looked like four white plastic trays, of the kind that fold out of aircraft seats. He slotted these together, creating a flat square about a yard across, which he then attached to the side of the case. Into the centre of the square he screwed a long, telescopic prong. He ran a cable from the side of the box to the Toyota's cigarette lighter, came back, flicked a switch and a variety of small lights blinked on.

'Impressed?' He produced a compass from his jacket pocket and shone his torch on it. 'Now where the hell is the Indian Ocean?'

'What?'

O'Brian glanced back along the M8. 'Right the way down there, by the look of it. Directly down there. A satellite in stationary orbit twenty thousand miles above the Indian Ocean. Think of that. Oh, but the world's a small place, is it not, Fluke? I swear I can almost hold it in my hand.' He grinned and knelt by the box, moving it around by degrees until the antenna was pointing directly south. At once the machine began to emit a whine. 'There you go. She's locked on to the bird.' He pressed a switch and the whining stopped. 'Now, we plug in the handset – so. We dial zero-four for the ground station at Eik in Norway – so. And now we dial the number. Easy as that.'

He stood and held out the handset and Kelso cautiously put his ear to it. He could hear a number ringing in America, and then a man said, 'Newsroom.'

KELSO lit another cigarette and walked away from the Toyota. O'Brian was in the front seat with the light on and even with the windows closed his voice carried in the cold silence.

'Yeah, yeah, we're on the road . . . About halfway I guess
. . . Yeah, he's with me . . . No, he's fine.' The door opened
and O'Brian shouted, 'You're fine, aren't you, professor?'

Kelso raised his hand.

'Yeah,' resumed O'Brian, 'he's fine.' The door slammed
and he must have lowered his voice because Kelso couldn't
catch much after that. 'Be there about nine . . . sure . . . good
stuff . . . looking good . . . '

Whatever it was, Kelso didn't like the sound of it. He
walked back to the car and flung open the door.

'Whoops. Gotta go, Joe. Bye.' O'Brian hung up quickly
and winked.

'What are you telling them exactly?'

'Nothing.' The reporter looked like a guilty boy.

'What d'you mean, nothing?'

'Come on, I had to give them the bones, Fluke. Give them
the gist –'

'The *gist*?' Kelso was shouting now. 'This was supposed to
be confidential –'

'Well, they're not going to tell anyone, are they? Come on,
I can't just take off without giving them an idea of what I'm
doing.'

'Christ.' Kelso slumped against the side of the Toyota and
appealed to the sky. 'What am I *doing*?'

'Want to make a call, Fluke?' O'Brian waved the handset
at him. 'Call a wife? On us?'

'No. There's no one I want to call right now. Thank you.'

'Zinaida?' said O'Brian craftily. 'Why don't you call
Zinaida?' He climbed out of the seat and pressed the telephone into Kelso's hand. 'Go ahead. I can tell you're worried.
It's *sweet*. Zero-four, then the number. Only don't take all
night about it. A fellow could freeze his balls off out here.'

He wandered away, flapping his arms against the cold, and Kelso, after a second's hesitation, hunted through his pockets for the scrap of paper with her address on it.

As he waited for the number to connect he tried to visualise her apartment, but he couldn't do it, he didn't know enough about her. He stared southwards down the M8 at the shadowy mass of departing clouds, fleeing as if from some calamity, and he imagined the route his call was taking – from the middle of nowhere to a satellite above the Indian Ocean, down to Scandinavia, across the earth to Moscow. O'Brian was right: you could stand in a great wilderness and the world still felt small enough to hold in your hand.

He let the number ring for a long time, alternately willing her to answer it so that he'd know she was safe, and hoping that she wouldn't, because her apartment was the least safe place of all.

She didn't answer and after a couple of minutes he hung up.

AND then it was Kelso's turn to drive while O'Brian slept, and even then the reporter couldn't be quiet. The sleeping bag was drawn tight up to his chin. His seat was tilted back almost to the horizontal. 'Yeah,' he'd mutter, and then, almost immediately, and with greater emphasis, '*yeah.*' He grunted. He curled up and flopped around like a landed fish. He snorted. He scratched his groin.

Kelso gripped the steering wheel hard. 'Can you shut up, O'Brian?' he said into the windscreen. 'I mean, just for once, could you possibly, as a favour to humanity, and more particularly to me, put a sock in your great fat mouth?'

There was nothing to see except the shifting patch of road in the headlights. Occasionally a car appeared in the opposite carriageway, lights full beam, blinding him. After about an hour he overtook the big truck that had passed them earlier. The driver hooted cheerfully again, and Kelso hooted back.

'Yeah,' said O'Brian, turning over at the sound of the horn, 'oh *yeah* –'

The drumming of the tyres was hypnotic and Kelso's thoughts were random, disconnected. He wondered what O'Brian would have been like in a *real* war, one in which he actually had to fight rather than just take pictures. Then he wondered what *he* would have been like. Most of the men he knew asked themselves that question, as if never having fought somehow made them incomplete – left a hole in their lives where a war should have been.

Was it possible that this *absence* of war – marvellous though it was and so forth: that went without saying – was it possible that it had actually *trivialised* people? Because everything was so bloody trivial now, wasn't it? This was The Trivial Age. Politics was trivial. What people worried about was trivial – mortgages and pensions and the dangers of passive smoking. Jesus! – he shot a look at O'Brian – is this what we've been reduced to, worrying about passive smoking, when our parents and our grandparents had to worry about being shot or bombed?

And then he began to feel guilty, because what was he implying here? That he wanted a war? Or a cold war, come to that? But it was true, he thought: he *did* miss the cold war. He was glad it was over, of course, in a way – glad the right side had won and all that – but at least while it was on people like him had known where they stood, could point to something and say: well, we may not know what we do believe in, but we don't believe in *that*.

The fact was, almost nothing had gone right for him since

the cold war ended. Here was a good joke. He and Mamantov: twin career victims of the end of the USSR! Both bemoaning the trivia of the modern world, both preoccupied with the past, and both in search of the mystery of Comrade Stalin –

He frowned, remembering something Mamantov had said.

'I'll tell you this, you're as obsessed as I am.'

He had laughed it off at the time. But now that he thought of it again, the line struck him as unexpectedly shrewd – unsettling, even, in the quality of its insight – and he found himself returning to it again and again as the temperature dropped and the road uncoiled endlessly from the freezing darkness.

HE drove for more than four hours, until his legs were numb and at one point he actually fell asleep, jerking awake to find the Toyota veering across the centre of the highway, the white lines flashing up at them like spears in the headlights.

A few minutes later they passed a kind of truckers' lay-by. He braked hard, stopped, and reversed back into it. Beside him, O'Brian struggled blearily into consciousness.

'Why're we stopping?'

'The tank's empty. And I've got to rest.' Kelso turned off the ignition and massaged the back of his neck. 'Why don't we stop here for a bit?'

'No. We need to keep moving. Fix us some coffee, will you? I'll fill her up.'

They went through the same ritual as before, O'Brian stumbling out into the cold and hoisting a pair of jerrycans from the back of the Toyota, while Kelso wandered away for a cigarette. The wind had a sharper edge to it this far north.

He could hear it slicing through trees he couldn't see. Running water splashed somewhere, softly.

When he got back into the car, O'Brian was in the driver's seat with the interior light on, running an electric shaver over his big chin, studying the map. It was an unnatural time to be awake, thought Kelso. It meant nothing good. He associated it with emergency, bereavement, conspiracy, flight; the sad skulk away at the end of a one-night affair.

Neither man spoke. O'Brian put away his shaver and stuffed the map into the pocket beside him.

The reclined seat was warm and so was the sleeping bag and within five minutes, despite his anxieties, Kelso was asleep – a dreamless, falling sleep – and when he awoke a few hours later it was as if they had crossed a barrier and entered another world.

Chapter Nineteen

A LITTLE TIME before this, when Kelso was still at the wheel, Major Feliks Suvorin had bent to kiss his wife, Serafima.

She offered him merely her cheek at first but then seemed to think the better of it. A warm, soft arm snaked up from beneath the duvet, a hand cupped the back of his head and drew him down. He kissed her mouth. She was wearing Chanel. Her father had brought it back from the last G8 meeting.

She whispered, 'You won't be back tonight.'

'I will.'

'You won't.'

'I'll try not to wake you.'

'Wake me.'

'Sleep.'

He put his finger to her lips and turned off the bedside lamp. The light from the passage showed him the way out of the bedroom. He could hear the sound of the boys' breathing. An ormolu clock announced it was one-thirty-five. He had been home two hours. *Hell.* He sat down on a gilt chair beside the door and put his shoes on, then collected his coat from its carved wooden hanger. The decor was copied from some glossy western magazine and it all cost far more than he earned as a major in the SVR; in fact, on his salary, they could barely afford the magazine. His father-in-law had paid.

On his way out, Suvorin glimpsed himself in the hall mirror, framed against a Jackson Pollock print. The lines and shadows of his exhausted face seemed to merge with those of the picture. He was getting too old for this kind of game, he thought: the golden boy no longer.

THE news that the Delta flight had taken off without Fluke Kelso had reached Yasenevo shortly after two in the afternoon. Colonel Arsenyev had expressed in various colourful colloquialisms – and had no doubt minuted elsewhere, for the record, more discreetly – his amazement that Suvorin had not arranged for the historian to be escorted on to the aircraft. Suvorin had choked back his response, which would have been to inquire, acidly, how he was supposed to locate Mamantov, control the militia, find the notebook *and* nursemaid an independent-minded western academic through Sheremetevo-2, all with the assistance of four men.

Besides, by then this was of less pressing importance than the discovery that the Interfax news agency was putting out a story on Papu Rapava's death, quoting unnamed 'militia sources' to the effect that the old man had been murdered while trying to sell some secret papers of Josef Stalin to a western author. Three outraged communist deputies had already attempted to raise the matter in the Duma. The Office of the President of the Federation had been on the line to Arsenyev, demanding to know (a direct quote from Boris Nikolaevich, apparently) *what the fuck was going on?* Ditto the FSB. Half a dozen reporters were camped outside Rapava's apartment block, more were besieging militia HQ, while the militia's official position was to hold up their hands and whistle.

For the first time, Suvorin had begun to see the merit of the old ways, when news was what Tass was pleased to announce and everything else was a state secret.

He had made one last attempt to play devil's advocate.

Weren't they in danger of getting this out of proportion? Weren't they playing Mamantov's game? What could Stalin's notebook possibly contain that would have any modern relevance?

Arsenyev had smiled: always a dangerous sign.

'When were you born, Feliks?' he had asked, pleasantly. 'Fifty-eight? Fifty-nine?'

'Sixty.'

'Sixty. You see, I was born in thirty-seven. My grandfather . . . he was shot. Two uncles went to the camps . . . never came back. My father died in some crazy business at the start of the war, trying to stop a German tank outside Poltava with a bit of rag and a bottle, and all because Comrade Stalin said that any soldier who surrendered would be considered a traitor. So I don't underestimate Comrade Stalin.'

'I'm sorry –'

But Arsenyev had waved him away. His voice was rising, his face red. 'If that bastard kept a notebook in his safe, he kept it for a reason, I can tell you that. And if Beria stole it, he had a reason. And if Mamantov is willing to risk torturing an old man to death, then he has a damned good reason for wanting to get his hands on it, too. So find it, Feliks Stepanovich, please, if you would be so good. *Find it.*'

And Suvorin had done his best. Every forensic document examiner in Moscow had been contacted. Kelso's description had been circulated, discreetly, to all the capital's militia posts, as well as to the traffic cops, the GAI. Technically, the SVR was now 'liaising' with the militia's murder inquiry, which meant at least he now had some resources to draw on: he had worked out a common line with the militia which they could spin to the media. He had spoken to a friend of his father-in-law's – the owner of the biggest chain of newspapers in the Federation – to plead for a little restraint. He had sent Netto to poke around Vspolnyi Street. He had arranged for a watch to be put on the apartment of Rapava's daughter, Zinaida, who had disappeared, and when she still hadn't turned up by nightfall he had sent Bunin to hang around the club she worked in, Robotnik.

Shortly after eleven o'clock, Suvorin had gone home.

And at one twenty-five he got the call that told him she had been found.

'WHERE was she?'

'Sitting in her car,' said Bunin. 'Outside her father's place. We followed her from the club. Waited to see if she was meeting anyone, but nobody else showed, so we picked her up. She's been in a fight, I reckon.'

'Why?'

'Well, you'll see when you go up. Take a look at her hand.'

They were standing, talking quietly, in the downstairs lobby of her apartment block, in the Zayauze district, a drab hinterland of eastern Moscow. She had a place close to the park – privatised, to judge by the neatness of its common parts; respectable. Suvorin wondered what the neighbours would think if they knew the girl on the third floor was a tart.

'Anything else?'

'The apartment's clean, and so's her car,' said Bunin. 'There's a bag of clothes in the back – jeans, T-shirt, pair of boots, knickers. But she's got a lot of money stashed up there. She doesn't know I found it yet.'

'How much?'

'Twenty, maybe thirty thousand dollars. Bound up tight in polythene and hidden in the lavatory cistern.'

'Where is it now?'

'I've got it.'

'Let's have it.'

Bunin hesitated, then handed it over: a thick bundle, all hundreds. He looked at it hungrily. It would take him four or five years to make that much and Suvorin guessed he had probably been on the point of helping himself to a percentage. Maybe he already had. He stuffed it into his pocket. 'What's she like?'

'A hard bitch, major. You won't get a lot out of her.' He tapped the side of his head. 'She's cracked, I reckon.'

'Thank you, lieutenant, for that valuable psychological insight. You can wait down here.'

Suvorin climbed the stairs. On the landing of the second floor, a middle-aged woman with her hair in curlers stuck her head round her door.

'What's going on?'

'Nothing, madam. Routine inquiries. You're perfectly safe.'

He carried on climbing. He had to make something of this, he thought. He must. It was the only lead he had. Outside the girl's apartment he squared his shoulders, knocked politely on the open door and went inside. A militia man got to his feet.

'Thank you,' said Suvorin. 'Why don't you go down and keep the lieutenant company?'

He waited until the door had closed before he took a proper look at her. She had a grey woollen cardigan on over her dress and she was sitting in the only chair, her legs crossed, smoking. In a dish on the little table next to her were the stubbed remains of five cigarettes. The apartment consisted of only this one room but it was neat and nicely done, with plenty of evidence of money spent: a western-made television with a satellite decoder, a video, a CD-player, a rack of dresses, all black. A little kitchen was off in one corner. A door led to the bathroom. There was a couch that presumably folded into a bed. Bunin was right about her hand, he noticed. The fingers that held the cigarette had blood crusted under the nails. She saw him looking.

'I fell,' she said, and uncrossed her legs, displaying a scraped knee, torn tights. 'All right?'

'I'll sit down.' She didn't reply, so he sat down anyway, on the edge of the couch, moving a couple of toys out of the way, a soldier and a ballerina. 'You have children?' he asked.

No answer.

'I have children. Two boys.' He searched the room for some other point of contact, some way of opening, but there was no evidence of any personality anywhere: no photographs, no books apart from legal manuals, no ornaments or knick-knacks. There was a row of CDs, all western and all by artists he'd never heard of. It reminded him of one Yasenevo's safe houses – a place to spend a night in and then move on.

She said, 'Are you a cop? You don't look like a cop.'

'No.'

'What are you, then?'

'I'm sorry about your father, Zinaida.'

'Thanks.'

'Tell me about your father.'

'What's to tell?'

'Did you get on with him?'

She looked away.

'Only I'm wondering, you see, why you didn't come forward when his body was discovered. You went to his apartment last night, didn't you, when the militia were there? And then you just drove away.'

'I was upset.'

'Naturally.' Suvorin smiled at her. 'Where's Fluke Kelso?'

'Who?'

Not bad, he thought: she didn't even flicker. But then she didn't know he had Kelso's statement.

'The man you drove to your father's apartment last night.'

'Kelso? Was that his name?'

'Oh you're a sharp one, Zinaida, aren't you? Sharp as a knife. So where have you been all day?'

'Driving around. Thinking.'

'Thinking about Stalin's notebook?'

'I don't know what you –'

'You've been with Kelso, haven't you?'

'No.'

'Where's Kelso? Where's the notebook?'

'Don't know what you're talking about. What d'you mean, anyway – you're not a cop? You got some papers that tell me who you are?'

'You spent the day with Kelso –'

'You've no right to be in my place without the proper papers. It says so in there.' She pointed to her legal books.

'Studying the law, Zinaida?' She was beginning to irritate him. 'You'll make a good lawyer.'

She seemed to find that funny: perhaps she had heard it before? He pulled out the bundle of dollars and that stopped her laughing. He thought she was going to faint.

'So what's the Federation statute on prostitution, Zinaida Rapava?' Her eyes on the money were like a mother's on her baby. 'You're the lawyer: you tell me. How many men in this little pile? A hundred? A hundred and fifty?' He flicked through the notes. 'Must be a hundred and fifty, surely – you're not getting any younger. But the others are, aren't they? They're getting younger every day. You know, I think you might never make this much back.'

'Bastard –'

He weighed the dollars from hand to hand. 'Think about it. A hundred and fifty men in return for telling me where I can find one? A hundred and fifty for one. That's not such a bad deal.'

'Bastard,' she said again, but with less conviction this time.

He leaned forward, soft-voiced, coaxing. 'Come on Zinaida: where's Fluke Kelso? It's important.'

And for a moment he thought she was going to tell him. But then her face hardened. '*You*,' she said. 'I don't care who *you* are. There's more honesty in whoring.'

'Now that may be true,' conceded Suvorin. Suddenly, he threw her the money. It bounced off her lap and on to the floor between her legs. She didn't even bend to pick it up, just looked at him. And he felt a great sadness then: sad for himself, that it should have come to this, sitting on a tart's bed in the Zayauze district, trying to bribe her with her own money. And sad for her, because Bunin was right, she *was* cracked, and now he would have to break her.

Chapter Twenty

IT NEVER SEEMED to get properly light, even two hours after dawn. It was as if the day had given up on itself before it even started. The sky stayed grey and the long concrete ribbon of road that ran straight ahead of them dwindled into a damp murk. On either side of the highway lay a wrinkled dead land of rust-coloured swamps and sickly, yellowish plains – the sub-Arctic tundra – that turned in the middle distance to dense, dark green forests of pine and fir.

It started to snow.

There was a lot of military traffic on the road. They passed a long column of armoured cars with watery headlights and soon afterwards began to see evidence of human settlement – shacks, barns, bits of agricultural machinery – even a collective farm with a broken hammer and sickle over the gate, and an old slogan: PRODUCTION IS VITAL FOR THE VICTORY OF SOCIALISM.

After a couple of miles the road crossed a railway line and a row of big chimneys appeared up ahead in the murk, gushing black soot into the snowy sky.

'That must be it,' said Kelso, looking up from the map. 'The M8 ends here, in the southern outskirts.'

'Shit,' said O'Brian.

'What?'

The reporter gestured with his chin. 'Road block.'

A hundred yards ahead a couple of GAI cops with lighted sticks and guns were waving down every vehicle to check the occupants' papers. O'Brian looked quickly in his mirror, but he couldn't reverse – there was too much traffic slowing behind them. And concrete sleepers laid across the centre of the road made it impossible to perform a U-turn and join the southbound carriageway. They were being forced into a single-lane queue.

'What did you call it?' said Kelso. 'My visa? A *detail?*'

O'Brian tapped his fingers on the top of the steering wheel.

'Is this check permanent, do you think, or just for us?'

Kelso could see a glass booth with a GAI man in it, reading a newspaper.

'I'd say permanent.'

'Well, that's something.' O'Brian began rummaging in the glove compartment. 'Pull your hood up,' he said, 'and get that sleeping bag up over your face. Pretend to be asleep. I'll tell 'em you're my cameraman.' He hauled out a crumpled set of papers. 'You're Vukov, okay? Foma Vukov.'

'Foma Vukov? What kind of a name is that?'

'You want to go straight back to Moscow? Well, do you? I'd say you've got two seconds to make up your mind.'

'And how old is this Foma Vukov?'

'Twentysomething.' O'Brian reached behind him and grabbed the leather satchel. 'You got a better idea? Stick this under your seat.'

Kelso hesitated, then wedged the satchel behind his legs. He lay back, drew up the sleeping bag and closed his eyes. Travelling without a visa was one crime. Travelling without a visa and using someone else's papers – that, he suspected, was quite another.

The car edged forwards, braked. He heard the engine switch off and then the hum of the driver's window being lowered. A blast of cold air. A gruff male voice said in Russian, 'Get out of the car please.'

The Toyota rocked as O'Brian clambered out.

With his heel, Kelso gently pushed at the satchel, jamming it further out of sight.

There was a second rush of cold as the rear door was lifted.

The sound of boxes being swung out, of catches snapping. Footsteps. A quiet conversation.

The door next to Kelso opened. He could hear the pattering of snowflakes, a man breathing. And then the door was closed – closed softly, with consideration, so as not to wake a sleeping passenger, and Kelso knew that he was safe.

He heard O'Brian load up the back and come round to the driver's seat. The engine started.

'It is surely most amazing,' said O'Brian, 'the effect of a hundred bucks on a cop who ain't been paid for six months.' He pulled the sleeping bag away from Kelso. 'This is your wake-up call, professor. Welcome to Archangel.'

THEY thumped across an iron bridge above the Northern Dvina. The river was wide, stained yellow by the tundra. Swollen currents rolled and flexed like muscles beneath its dirty skin. A couple of big black cargo barges, chained together, steamed north towards the White Sea. On the opposite bank, through the filter of snow and the spars of the bridge, they could see factory chimneys, cranes, apartment blocks, a big television tower with a winking red light.

As the vista broadened, even O'Brian's spirits seemed to fall. He called it a dump. He declared it a hole. He said it was the worst goddamn place he had ever seen.

A goods train clanked along the railroad track beside them. At the end of the bridge they turned left, towards what seemed to be the main part of the city. Everything had decayed. The façades of the buildings were pitted and peeling. Parts of the road had subsided. An ancient tram, in a brown and mustard livery, went rattling by, making a sound like a chain being dragged over cobbles. Pedestrians tilted drunkenly into the snow.

O'Brian drove slowly, shaking his head, and Kelso wondered what more he had been expecting. A press centre? A media hotel? They came out into the wide open space of a bus station. On the far side of it, on the waterfront, four giant Red Army men, cast in bronze, stood back to back, facing the four points of the compass, their rifles raised in triumph. At their feet, a pack of wild dogs scavenged among the trash. Nearby was a long, low building of white concrete and plate glass with a big sign: 'Harbour Master of Archangel'. If the city had a centre, this was probably it.

'Let's pull up over there,' suggested Kelso.

They cruised around the edge of the square and parked with their front bumper up close to the bent railings, looking directly out across the water. A husky watched them with detached interest, then brought its hind paw up to its neck and vigorously scratched its fleas. In the distance, through the snow, it was just possible to make out the flat shape of a tanker.

'You do realise,' said Kelso quietly, staring straight ahead across the water, 'that we are at the edge of the world? That at this point we are one hundred miles south of the Arctic Circle and there is nothing between us and the North Pole but sea and ice? You are aware of that?'

He started to laugh.

'What's funny?'

'Nothing.' He glanced at O'Brian and tried to stop himself, but it was no good, there was something about the reporter's utter dejection that set him off again. His vision was blurred by tears. 'I'm sorry,' he gasped. 'Sorry –'

'Oh, go ahead, enjoy yourself,' said O'Brian, bitterly. 'This is my idea of a perfect fucking Friday. Drive eight hundred miles to some dump that looks like Pittsburgh after a nuclear strike to try to find Stalin's fucking *girlfriend* –'

He snorted and started to laugh as well.

'You know what we haven't done?' O'Brian managed to say after a while.

Kelso took a breath and swallowed. 'What?'

'We haven't been to the railway station and checked the radiation meter . . . We're probably . . . being . . . fucking . . . *irradiated!*'

They roared. They cried. The Toyota rocked with it. The snow fell and the husky watched them, its head cocked in surprise.

O'BRIAN locked the car and they hurried through the snow, across the treacherous expanse of subsiding concrete, into the port authority building.

Kelso carried the satchel.

They were both still slightly shaky and the advertised ferry sailings – to Murmansk and the Groaning Islands – briefly set them off again.

The Groaning Islands?

'Oh come on, man. Stop it. We've got to do some work here.'

The building was bigger than it looked from the outside. On the ground floor there were shops – little kiosks selling clothes and toiletries – plus a café and a ticket booth. Downstairs, beneath banks of fluorescent lights, most of which had blown, was a gloomy underground market – stalls offering seeds, books, pirated cassettes, shoes, shampoo, sausages and some immense, sturdy Russian brassières in black and beige: miracles of cantilevered engineering.

O'Brian bought a couple of maps, one of the city and the other of the region, then they both went back upstairs to the ticket office where Kelso, in return for offering a dollar bill to a suspicious man in a greasy uniform, was permitted a brief look at the Archangel telephone directory. The book was small, red-bound, with hard covers and it took him less than thirty seconds to establish that no Safanov or Safanova was listed.

'Now what?' said O'Brian.

'Food,' said Kelso.

The café was an old-style *stolovaya*, a self-service workers' canteen, its floor wet and filthy with melted snow. There was a warm fug of strong tobacco. At the next door table a couple of German seamen were playing cards. Kelso had a big bowl of *shchi* – cabbage soup with a dollop of sour cream bobbing in its centre – black bread, a couple of hard-boiled eggs, and the effect of all this on his empty stomach was immediate. He began to feel almost euphoric. This was going to be all right, he thought. They were safe up here. Nobody could find them. And if they played it properly, they could be in and out in a day.

He tipped half a miniature of cognac into his instant coffee, looked at it, thought, *Sod it, why not?* and added the rest. He lit a cigarette and glanced around. The people up here appeared shabbier than they did in Moscow. They stared at foreign strangers. But when you attempted to meet their eyes they looked away.

O'Brian pushed his plate to one side. 'I've been thinking about this college, whatever it was – this "Maxim Gorky Academy". They'll have old records, right? And there was this girl she knew – what was her name, the ugly kid?'

'Maria.'

'Maria. Right. Let's find her class yearbook and find Maria.'

Class yearbook? thought Kelso. Who did O'Brian think she was? The Maxim Gorky prom queen, 1950? But he was too full of goodwill to pick a fight. 'Or,' he said, diplomatically, '*or* we could try the local Party. She was in Komsomol, remember. They might still have the old files.'

'Okay. You're the expert. How d'we find 'em?'

'Easy. Give me the town plan.'

O'Brian pulled the map from his inside pocket and scraped his chair round until he was sitting next to Kelso. They spread out the city plan.

The bulk of Archangel was crammed into a wide headland, about four miles across, with ribbons of development running out along either bank of the Dvina.

Kelso put his finger on the map. 'There,' he said. 'That's where they are. Or were. On the ploshchad Lenina, in the biggest building on the square. That's where the bastards always were.'

'And you think they'll help?'

'No. Not willingly. But if you can provide a little financial lubrication . . . It's worth a try, anyway.'

On the map it looked like a five-minute walk.

'You're really getting into this, aren't you?' said O'Brian. He gave Kelso's arm an affectionate pat. 'We make a good team, you know that? We'll show 'em.' He folded away the map and put five roubles under his plate as a tip.

Kelso finished his coffee. The cognac gave him a warm glow. O'Brian really wasn't such a bad fellow, he thought. Sooner him than Adelman and the rest of those waxworks, no doubt safely stowed in New York by now.

History wasn't made without taking risks, that much he knew. So maybe sometimes you had to take risks to write it, too?

O'Brian was right.

He would show them.

Chapter Twenty-one

THEY WENT BACK out into the snow, past the Toyota and past the shuttered front of a decaying hospital: the Northern Basin Seamen's Policlinic. The wind was driving the snow inshore across the water, whining through the steel rigging of the boats on the wooden jetty, bending the stumpy trees that had been planted along the promenade to protect the buildings. The two men had to struggle to keep their feet.

A couple of the boats had sunk, and so had the wooden hut at the end of the jetty. Benches had been heaved by vandals over the railings into the river. There was graffiti on the walls: a Star of David, dripping blood, with a swastika daubed across it; SS flashes; KKK.

One thing was sure: there wouldn't be any Italian shoe boutiques up here.

They turned inland.

Every Russian town still had its statue of Lenin. Archangel's portrayed the Leader, fifteen yards high, rising out of a block of granite, his face determined, his overcoat flapping, a roll of papers in his outstretched hand. He looked as if he were trying to hail a taxi. The square that still carried his name was huge, and smooth with snow, and deserted; in one corner, a couple of tethered goats nibbled at a bush. Fronting it were a big museum, the city's central post office, and a huge office block with the hammer and sickle still attached to the balcony.

Kelso led the way towards it and they had almost made it when a sandy-coloured jeep with a searchlight mounted on its hood came round the corner: Interior Ministry troops, the

MVD. That sobered him up. He could be stopped at any minute, he realised, and forced to show his visa. The pale faces of the soldiers stared at them. He bowed his head and trotted up the steps, O'Brian close behind him, as the jeep completed its cautious circuit of the square and passed out of sight.

THE communists had not been forced entirely from the building; they had merely moved round to the back. Here they maintained a small reception area presided over by a big, middle-aged woman with a froth of dyed yellow hair. Beside her, along the window sill, was a row of straggling spider plants in old tin cans; opposite her, a big colour poster of Gennady Zyuganov, the Party's pudding-faced candidate in the last presidential election.

She studied O'Brian's business card intently, turning it over, holding it to the light, as if she suspected forgery. Then she picked up the telephone and spoke quietly into the receiver.

Outside, through the double glass, the snow was beginning to pile in the courtyard. A clock ticked. Beside the door Kelso noticed a bundle of the latest issue of *Aurora*, tied up with string, awaiting distribution. The headline was a quote from the Interior Ministry's report to the president: 'VIOLENCE IS INEVITABLE'.

After a couple of minutes, a man appeared. He must have been about sixty – an odd-looking figure. His head was too small for his heavy torso, his features too small for his face. His name was Tsarev, he said, holding out a hand stained black with ink. *Professor* Tsarev. Deputy First Secretary of the Regional Committee.

Kelso asked if they could have a word.

Yes. Perhaps. That would be possible.

Now? In private?

Tsarev hesitated, then shrugged. 'Very well.'

He led them down a dark corridor and into his office, a little time warp from the Soviet days, with its pictures of Brezhnev and Andropov. Kelso reckoned he must have visited a score of offices like this over the years. Wood block flooring, thick water pipes, a heavy radiator, a desk calendar, a big green Bakelite telephone, like something out of a 1950s science fiction movie, the smell of polish and stale air – every detail was familiar, right down to the model Sputnik and the clock in the shape of Zimbabwe left behind by some visiting Marxist delegation. On the shelf behind Tsarev's head were six copies of Mamantov's memoirs, *I Still Believe*.

'I see you have Vladimir Mamantov's book.' It was a stupid thing to say but Kelso couldn't help himself.

Tsarev turned round, as if noticing them for the first time. 'Yes. Comrade Mamantov came to Archangel and campaigned for us, during the presidential elections. Why? Do you know him?'

'Yes. I know him.'

There was a silence. Kelso was aware of O'Brian looking at him, and of Tsarev waiting for him to speak. Hesitantly, he began his rehearsed speech. First of all, he said, he and Mr O'Brian would like to thank Professor Tsarev for seeing them at such short notice. They were in Archangel for one day only, making a film about the residual strength of the Communist Party. They were visiting various towns in Russia. He was sorry they had not been in contact earlier to make a proper appointment, but they were working quickly –

'And Comrade Mamantov sent you?' interrupted Tsarev.

'Comrade Mamantov sent you *here*?'

'I can truthfully say we would not be here without Vladimir Mamantov.'

Tsarev began nodding. Well, this was a most excellent subject. This was a subject *wilfully ignored* in the west. How many people in the west knew, for example, that in the Duma elections, the communists had taken thirty per cent of the votes, and then, in 1996, in the presidential elections, forty per cent? Yes, they would be in power again soon. Sharing power to begin with, perhaps, but afterwards – who could say?

He became more animated.

Take the situation here in Archangel. They had millionaires, of course. Wonderful! Unfortunately, they also had organised crime, unemployment, AIDS, prostitution, drug addiction. Were his visitors aware that life expectancy and child-mortality in Russia had now reached African levels? Such progress! Such freedoms! Tsarev had been a professor of Marxist theory in Archangel for twenty years – the post was now abolished, naturally – so he had taught Marxism in a Marxist state, but it was only now, as they were literally tearing down Marx's statues, that he had come to appreciate the genius of the man's insight: that money robs the whole world, both the human world and nature, of their own proper value –

'Ask him about the girl,' whispered O'Brian. 'We haven't got time for all this bullshit. Ask him about Anna.'

Tsarev had halted in mid-speech and was looking from one man to the other.

'Professor Tsarev,' said Kelso, 'to illustrate our film we need to look at particular human stories –'

That was good. Yes. He understood. The human element.

There were many such stories in Archangel.

'Yes, I'm sure. But we have in mind one in particular. A girl. Now a woman in her sixties. She would be about the same age as you. Her unmarried name was Safanova. Anna Mikhailovna Safanova. She was in the Komsomol.'

Tsarev stroked the end of his squat nose. The name, he said, after a moment's thought, was not familiar. This would have been some time ago, presumably?

'Almost fifty years.'

Fifty years? It was not possible! Please! He would find them other persons –

'But you must have records?'

– he would show them females who fought the fascists in the Great Patriotic War, Heroes of Socialist Labour, Holders of the Order of the Red Banner. Magnificent people –

'Ask him how much he wants,' said O'Brian, not even bothering to whisper now. He was pulling out his wallet. 'To look in his files. What's his price?'

'Your colleague,' said Tsarev, 'is not happy?'

'My colleague was wondering,' said Kelso, delicately, 'if it would be possible for you to undertake some research work for us. For which we would be happy to pay you – to pay the Party, that is – a fee . . .'

IT would not be easy, said Tsarev.

Kelso said he was sure it would not be.

The membership of the Communist Party in the last years of the Soviet Union comprised seven per cent of the adult population. Apply those figures to Archangel and what did you get? Maybe 20,000 members in the city alone, and perhaps the same number again in the oblast. And to those figures you had to add the membership of Komsomol and of all the other Party outfits. And then, if you included all the people who had been members over the past eighty years – the people who had died or dropped out, been shot, imprisoned, exiled, purged – you had to be looking at a really large number. A huge number. Still –

Two hundred dollars was the sum they agreed on. Tsarev insisted on providing a receipt. He locked the money into a battered cash box which he then locked in a drawer, and Kelso realised, with a curious sense of admiration, that Tsarev probably did intend to give the money to Party funds. He wouldn't keep it for himself: he was a true believer.

The Russian conducted them back along the passage and into reception. The woman with the dyed blonde hair was watering her tinned plants. *Aurora* still proclaimed that violence was inevitable. Zyuganov's fat smile remained in place. Tsarev collected a key from a metal cupboard and they followed him down two flights of stairs into the basement. A big, blast-proof iron door, studded with bolts, thickly painted a battleship grey, swung open to show a cellar, lined with wooden shelving, piled with files.

Tsarev put on a pair of heavy-framed spectacles and began pulling down dusty folders of documents while Kelso looked around with wonder. This was not a storeroom, he thought. This was a catacomb, a necropolis. Busts of Lenin, and of Marx and Engels, crowded the shelves like perfect clones. There were boxes of photographs of forgotten Party appa-ratchiks and stacked canvases of socialist realism, depicting bosomy peasant girls and worker-heroes with granite mus-cles. There were sacks of decorations, diplomas, membership cards, leaflets, pamphlets, books. And then there were the flags – little red flags for children to wave, and swirling crim-son banners for the likes of Anna Safanova to parade with.

It was as if a great world religion had been suddenly obliged to strip its temples and hide everything underground – to preserve its texts and icons out of sight, in the hope of better times, the Second Coming –

The Komsomol lists for 1950 and 1951 were missing.

'What?'

Kelso wheeled round to find Tsarev frowning over a pair of folders, one in either hand.

It was most curious, Tsarev was saying. This would need to be investigated further. They could see for themselves – he held out the files for their inspection – the lists were here for 1949 and here, also, for 1952. But in neither of those years was there an Anna Safanova listed.

'She was too young in forty-nine,' said Kelso, 'she wouldn't have qualified.' And by 1952 God alone knew what might have happened to her. 'When were they removed?'

'April, fifty-two,' said Tsarev, frowning. 'There's a note. "To be transferred to the archives of the Central Committee, Moscow."'

'Is there a signature?'

Tsarev showed it him: '"A. N. Poskrebyshev."'

O'Brian said, 'Who's Poskrebyshev?'

Kelso knew. And so, he could see, did Tsarev.

'General Poskrebyshev,' said Kelso, 'was Stalin's private secretary.'

'So,' said Tsarev, a little too quickly, 'a mystery.' He began putting the files back up on the shelf. Even after fifty years and all that had happened the signature of Stalin's secretary was still enough to unsettle a man of the right age. His hands shook. One of the folders slipped through his fingers and flopped to the floor. Pages spilled. 'Leave it, please. I'll attend to it.' But Kelso was already on his knees, gathering the loose sheets.

'There is one other thing you could do for us,' he said.

'I don't think so –'

'We believe that Anna Safanova's parents were probably both Party members.'

It was impossible, said Tsarev. He couldn't let them look. Those records were confidential.

'But you could look for us –'

No. He didn't think so.

He held out his inky hand for the missing pages and suddenly O'Brian was beside him, bending, and pressing into his outstretched palm another two hundred dollars.

'It really would help us very much,' said Kelso, desperately waving O'Brian away and nodding to emphasise each word, '*help us very much with our film*, if you could look them up.'

But Tsarev ignored him. He was staring at the two one-hundred dollar bills, and the face of Benjamin Franklin, shrewd and appraising, gazed back up at him.

'There isn't anything, is there,' he said slowly, 'that you people don't think you can buy with money?'

'No insult was intended,' said Kelso. He gave O'Brian a murderous look.

'Yeah,' muttered O'Brian, 'no offence.'

'You buy our industries. You buy our missiles. You try to buy our archives –'

His fingers contracted around the notes, screwing them tight, then he let the money fall.

'Keep your money. To hell with you and your money.'

He turned and bent his head, busied himself with putting all the records in the proper order. There was silence save for the rustling of dried paper.

Well done, mouthed Kelso at O'Brian. *Congratulations –*

A minute passed.

And then, unexpectedly, Tsarev spoke. 'What did you say their names were?' he said, without looking round. 'The parents?'

'Mikhail,' said Kelso quickly, 'and –' And, hell, what was the mother called? He tried to remember the NKVD report. Vera? Varushka? No, Vavara, that was it. 'Mikhail and Vavara Safanova.'

Tsarev hesitated. He turned to look at them, an expression on his narrow face that mingled dignity with contempt. 'Wait here,' he said. 'Don't touch anything.'

He disappeared to another part of the storeroom. They could hear him moving around.

O'Brian said, 'What's going on?'

'I think,' said Kelso, 'I *think* it's called making a point. He's gone to see if there are any records on Anna's parents. And no bloody thanks to you. Didn't I tell you: *leave the talking to me?*'

'Well, it worked didn't it?' O'Brian stooped and picked up the crumpled dollars, smoothed them out and replaced them in his wallet. 'Jesus, what a boneyard.' He picked up a nearby head of Lenin. 'Alas, poor Yorick . . .' He stopped. He couldn't remember the rest of the quotation. 'Here you go, professor. Have a souvenir.' He tossed the bust to Kelso, who caught it and quickly set it down.

'Don't,' he said. His good mood had gone. He was sick of O'Brian, but it wasn't only that. There was something else – something about the atmosphere down here. He couldn't define it exactly.

O'Brian sneered. 'What's up with you?'

'I don't know. "God is not mocked."'

'And neither is Comrade Lenin? Is that it? Poor old Fluke. You know what? I think you're beginning to lose it.'

Kelso would have told him to go to hell, but Tsarev was on his way back, carrying another file and now he was looking triumphant.

Here was a subject who would be suitable for their filming. Here was a woman who had never been bought – he glared at O'Brian – a person who was a lesson to them all. Vavara Safanova had joined the Communist Party in 1935 and had stayed with it, through good times and bad. She had a list of citations bestowed by the Archangel Central Committee that took up half a page. Oh yes: here was the indomitable spirit of socialism that could never be conquered!

Kelso smiled at him. 'When did she die?'

Ah! That was the thing. She hadn't died.

'Vavara Safanova?' repeated Kelso. He couldn't believe it. He exchanged a look with O'Brian. 'Anna Safanova's *mother*? Still *alive*?'

Still alive last month, said Tsarev. Still alive at eighty-five! It was written here. They could take a look. More than sixty years a faithful member – she had just paid her Party dues.

Chapter Twenty-two

IT WAS MORNING in Moscow.

Suvorin was in the back of the car with Zinaida Rapava. Militia liaison was sitting up front with the driver. The doors were locked. The Volga was wedged in the stream of sluggish traffic on the road heading south towards Lytkarino.

The militia man was complaining. They should have come in a different car – to force their way through this lot needed revolving lights and sound effects.

And who do you think you are? thought Suvorin. The President?

Zinaida's eyes looked bruised and puffy from lack of sleep. She wore a raincoat over her dress and her knees were turned towards the door, putting as much seat leather as she could between herself and Suvorin. He wondered if she knew where they were going. He doubted it. She seemed to have gone off somewhere into the heart of herself and barely to be aware of what was happening.

Where was Kelso? What was in the notebook? The same two questions, over and over, first at her place, then upstairs in the front office that the SVR maintained in downtown Moscow – the place where visiting western journalists were entertained by the Service's smiling, Americanized public relations officer. (See, gentlemen, how democratic we are! Now what can we do to help?) No coffee for her and no cigarettes, either, once she had smoked the last of her own. Write a statement, Zinaida, then we tear it up and we write it again, and again, as the clock drags on till nine, which is when Suvorin can play his ace.

She was as stubborn as her father.

In the old days, in the Lubyanka, they had operated a system called The Conveyer Belt: the suspect was passed between three investigators working eight-hour shifts in rotation. And after thirty-six hours without sleep most people would sign anything, incriminate anyone. But Suvorin didn't have back-up and he didn't have thirty-six hours. He yawned. His eyes seemed full of grit. He guessed he was as tired as she was.

His mobile telephone rang.

'Go ahead.'

It was Netto.

'Good morning, Vissari. What do you have?'

A couple of things, said Netto. One: the house in Vspolnyi Street. He had established that it belonged to a medium-sized property company called Moskprop, who were trying to let it for $15,000 a month. No takers so far.

'At that price? I'm not surprised.'

Two: it looked as though something *had* been dug up in the garden in the past couple of days. There was loose soil in one spot to a depth of five feet, and forensics reported traces of ferrous oxide in the earth. Something had been rusting away down there for years.

'Anything else?'

'No. Nothing on Mamantov. He's evaporated. And the colonel's agitated. He's been asking for you.'

'Did you tell him where I was?'

'No, lieutenant.'

'Good man.' Suvorin rang off. Zinaida was watching him.

'You know what I think?' said Suvorin, 'I think your old papa went and dug up that toolbox just before he died. And then I think he gave it to you. And then I reckon you gave it to Kelso.'

It was only a theory, but he thought he saw something flicker in her eyes before she turned away.

'You see,' he said, 'we *will* get there in the end. And we'll get there without you, if necessary. It's just going to take us more time, that's all.'

He settled back in his seat.

Wherever Kelso was, he thought, the notebook would be. And wherever the notebook was, Vladimir Mamantov would be as well – if not now, then very soon. So the answer to one question – where was Kelso? – would provide the solution to all three problems.

He glanced at Zinaida. Her eyes were closed.

And *she* knew it, he was sure of it.

It was so infuriatingly simple.

He wondered if Kelso had any idea how physically close Mamantov might be to him at that moment, and how much danger he was in. But of course he wouldn't, would he? He was a westerner. He would think he was immune.

The journey dragged on.

'THAT'S it,' said the militia man, pointing a thick forefinger. 'Up there, on the right.'

It looked a grim place in the rain, a warehouse of dull red brick, with small windows set behind the usual cobweb of iron bars. There was no nameplate beside the dingy entrance.

'Let's drive round the back,' suggested Suvorin. 'See if you can park.'

They swung right and right again, through open wooden gates, into an asphalt courtyard glistening in the wet. There was an old green ambulance with its windows painted out parked in one corner, next to a large black van. Big drums of corrugated metal were piled with white plastic sacks, tied with tape and stamped SURGICAL WASTE in red letters. Some had toppled off and split open, or been torn open by dogs, more like. Sodden, bloodied linen soaked up the rain.

The girl was sitting erect now, staring about her, beginning to guess where she was. The militia man levered his big frame out of the front seat and came round to open her door. She didn't move. It was Suvorin who had to take her gently by her arm and coax her out of the car.

'They've had to convert this place. And there's another warehouse out in Elektrostal, apparently. But there you are. That's the crime-wave for you. Even the dead are obliged to sleep rough. Come on, Zinaida. It's a formality. It has to be done. Besides, I'm told it often helps. We must always look our terrors in the eye.'

She shook her arm free of him and gathered her coat around herself and he realised that actually he was more nervous than she was. He had never seen a corpse before. Imagine it: a major of the former First Chief Directorate of the KGB and he had never seen a dead man. This whole case was proving an education.

They picked their way through the refuse, past a goods lift, and into the back of the warehouse – the militia man in the lead, then Zinaida, then Suvorin. It had been a cold store originally, for fish trucked north from the Black Sea, and there was still a slight tang of brine to the air, despite the smell of chemicals.

The policeman knew the drill. He put his head into a glassed-in office and shared a brief joke with whoever was inside, then another man appeared, shrugging on a white coat. He held back a high curtain of thick black rubber strips and they passed into a long corridor, wide enough to take a fork-lift truck, with heavy refrigerated doors off to either side.

In America – Suvorin had seen this on a video of a cops-and-robbers programme Serafima liked to watch – the bereaved could view their loved ones on a monitor, comfortably screened from the physical reality of death. In Russia, no such delicacy attended the extinct. But, there again, in fairness to the authorities, it had to be said that they had done their best with limited resources. The viewing room – if approached from the street entrance – was out of sight of the refrigerators. Also, a couple of bowls of plastic flowers had been placed on a covered table, on either side of a brass cross. The trolley was in front of these, the outline of the body clear beneath the white sheet. *Small*, thought Suvorin. He had expected a larger man.

He made sure he stood next to Zinaida. The militia man was beside his friend, the morgue technician. Suvorin nodded and the technician folded back the top part of the sheet.

Papu Rapava's mottled face, his thin grey hair combed back and neatly parted, stared through blackened eyelids at the peeling roof.

The militia man intoned the formal words in a bored voice, 'Witness, is this Papu Gerasimovich Rapava?'

Zinaida, her hand to her mouth, nodded.

'Speak please.'

'It is.' They could hardly hear her. And then, more loudly: 'Yes. It is.'

She glanced sideways at Suvorin, defiantly.

The technician began to replace the sheet.

'Wait,' said Suvorin.

He reached out for the edge of the sheet that was closest to him and pulled, hard. The thin nylon whisked away, billowed clear of the body and settled on the floor.

A silence, and then her scream split the room.

'And is *this* Papu Gerasimovich Rapava? Take a look, Zinaida.' He didn't look himself – he had only a vague impression, thankfully – his eyes were fixed on her. 'Take a look at what they did to him. This is what they'll do to you. And to your friend Kelso, if they catch him.'

The technician was shouting something. Zinaida, yelling, reeled away, towards the corner of the room, and Suvorin went after her – this was his moment, his only moment: he had to strike. 'Now, tell me where he is. I'm sorry, but you've got to tell me. Tell me where he is. I'm sorry. Now.'

She turned and her arm flailed out at him, but the militia man had her by her coat and was pulling her backwards. 'Eh, eh,' he said, 'enough of that,' and he spun her round and on to her knees.

Suvorin got on to his knees as well and shuffled after her. He cupped her face between his hands. 'I'm so sorry,' he said. Her face seemed to be dissolving beneath his fingers, her eyes were liquid, blackness was trickling down her cheeks, her mouth a black smear. 'It's all right. I'm sorry.'

She went still. He thought she might have fainted but her eyes were still open.

She wouldn't break. He knew it at that moment. She was her father's daughter.

After maybe half a minute, he released her and sat back on his heels, head bowed, breathing hard. Behind him, he heard the noise of the trolley being wheeled away.

'You're a madman,' said the technician, incredulously. 'You're fucking mad, you are.'

Suvorin raised his arm in weary acknowledgement. The door slammed shut. He rested his palms on the cold stone floor. He hated this case, he realised, not simply because it was so damned impossible and freighted with risk, but because it made him realise just how much he hated his own country: hated all those old-timers turning out on Sunday mornings with their pictures of Marx and Lenin, and the hard-faced fanatics like Mamantov who just wouldn't give up, who just didn't get it, couldn't see that the world had changed.

The dead weight of the past lay across him like a toppled statue.

It took an effort, pressing hard on the smooth stone, to push himself up on to his feet.

'Come on,' he said. He offered her his hand.

'Archangel.'

'What?' He looked down at her. She was watching him from the floor. There was a frightening calmness about her. He moved closer to her. 'What was that?'

She said it again.

'Archangel.'

HE held on to the tails of his overcoat and carefully lowered himself back to the floor and sat close to her. They both had their backs propped up against the wall, like a couple of survivors after an accident.

She was staring straight ahead and was talking in an odd monotone. He had his notebook open and his pen was working fast, tearing across the page, filling one sheet then flicking it over to start another. Because she might stop, he thought, stop talking as suddenly as she'd started –

He had gone to Archangel, she said. Driving. Gone up north, him and the reporter from the television.

Fine, Zinaida, take your time. And when was this?

Yesterday afternoon.

When exactly?

Four, maybe. Five. She couldn't remember. Did it matter?

What reporter?

O'Brian. An American. He was on the television. She didn't trust him.

And the notebook?

Gone. Gone with them. It was hers but she didn't want it. She wouldn't touch it. Not after she had worked out what it was about. It was cursed. The thing was cursed. It killed everyone who touched it.

She paused, staring at the spot where her father's body had been. She covered her eyes.

Suvorin waited, then said, Why Archangel?

Because that was where the girl had lived.

Girl? Suvorin stopped writing. What was she talking about? What *girl*?

'LISTEN,' he said, a few minutes later, when he had put his notebook away, 'you're going to be all right. I'm going to see to that, personally, do you understand me? The Russian government *guarantees* it.'

(What was he talking about? The Russian government couldn't guarantee a damned thing. The Russian government couldn't guarantee its president wouldn't drop his pants at a diplomatic reception and try to set light to one of his farts –)

'Now what I'm going to do is this. Here's my office number: it's a direct line. I'm going to get one of my men to take you back to your apartment, okay? And you can get some sleep. And I'll make sure there's a guard outside on the landing and one in the street. So no one's going to be able to get at you and harm you in any way. Right?'

He rushed on, making more promises he couldn't keep. I

should go into politics, he thought. I'm a natural.

'We're going to make sure Kelso is safe. And we're going to find the people – the man – who did this terrible thing to your father, and we're going to lock him up. Are you listening, Zinaida?'

He was on his feet again, surreptitiously looking at his watch.

'I've got to set things moving now. I've got to go. All right? I'm going to call Lieutenant Bunin – you remember Bunin, from last night? – and I'll get him to take you home.'

Halfway out the door he looked back at her.

'My name is Suvorin, by the way. Feliks Suvorin.'

THE militia man and the morgue assistant were waiting in the corridor. 'Leave her alone,' he said. 'She'll be fine.' They were looking at him strangely. Was it contempt, he wondered, or a wary respect? He wasn't sure which he deserved and he didn't have time to decide. He turned his back on them and called Arsenyev's number at Yasenevo.

'Sergo? I need to speak to the colonel . . . Yes, it's urgent. And I need you to fix some transport for me . . . Yes – are you ready? – I need you to fix me a *plane*.'

Chapter Twenty-three

ACCORDING TO HER Party record, Vavara Safanova had lived at the same address for more than sixty years, a place in the old part of Archangel, about ten minutes' drive from the waterfront, in a neighbourhood built of wood. Wooden houses were reached by wooden steps from wooden pavements – ancient timber, weathered grey, that must have been floated down the Dvina from the forests upstream long before the Revolution. It looked picturesque in the winter weather, if you could close your eyes to the concrete apartment blocks towering in the background. There were stacks of cordwood beside some of the houses and here and there a curl of smoke rose to lick the falling snow.

The roads were broad and empty, guarded on either side by sentinels of silver birch, and the surface in the snow was deceptively smooth. But the roads weren't made. The Toyota plunged into potholes as deep as a man's shin, jarring and bouncing down the wide track, until Kelso suggested they pull over and continue the search on foot.

He stood shivering on the duckboards as O'Brian rummaged around in the back. Across the street were a dozen railroad freight cars. Suddenly a homemade door in the side of one of them opened and a young woman climbed out, followed by two small children so thickly bundled against the cold they were almost spherical. She set off across the snowy field, the children dawdling behind her and staring at Kelso with solemn curiosity, until she turned and shouted sharply for them to follow her.

O'Brian locked the car. He was carrying one of the

aluminium cases. Kelso still had the satchel.

'Did you see that?' said Kelso. 'There are people actually living over there in those freight cars. Did you see that?'

O'Brian grunted and pulled up his hood.

They trudged down the side of the road, past a row of patched and tumbledown houses, each tilted at its own mad angle to the ground. Every summer the land must thaw, thought Kelso, and shift, and the houses with it. And then fresh boards would have to be nailed over the new cracks, so that some of the walls had skins of repairs that must date back to the Tsars. He had a sense of time frozen. It wasn't hard to imagine Anna Safanova, fifty years ago, walking where they walked, with a pair of ice skates slung around her shoulders.

It took them another ten minutes to find the old woman's street – an alley, really, no more, running off the main road, behind a clump of birch trees, and leading to the back of the house. In the yard were some animal coops: chickens, a pig, a couple of goats. And looming over it all, ghostly in the snow, a slab-sided fourteen-storey tower block, with a few yellow lights visible on the lower floors.

O'Brian unlocked his case, took out his video camera and started filming. Kelso watched him, unhappily.

'Shouldn't we check she's in first? Shouldn't you get her permission?'

'You ask her. Go ahead.'

Kelso glanced at the sky. The flakes seemed to be getting bigger – thick and soft as a baby's hand. He could feel a knot of tension in his stomach the size of his fist. He picked his way across the yard, past the hot stink of the goats, and started to climb the half-dozen loose wooden steps that led to the back porch. On the third step he paused. The door was partially open and in the narrow gap he could see an old woman, bent forwards, two hands resting on a stick, watching him.

He said, 'Vavara Safanova?'

She didn't say anything for a moment. Then she muttered, 'Who wants her?'

He took this as an invitation to climb the remaining steps. He wasn't a tall man but when he reached the rickety porch he soared above her. She had osteoporosis, he could see now. The tops of her shoulders were on a level with her ears and it gave her a watchful look.

He tugged down his hood and for the second time that morning he launched into his carefully prepared lie – they were in town to make a film about the communists; they were looking for people with interesting memories; they had been given her name and address by the local Party – and all the time he was appraising her, trying to reconcile this hunched figure with the matriarch who featured briefly in the girl's journal.

'Mama is strong, as ever . . . Mama brings me to the station . . . I kiss her dear cheeks . . .'

She had opened the door a crack wider to get a better look at him, and he could see more of her. Apart from her shawl the clothes she wore were masculine – old clothes: her dead husband's clothes, perhaps – with a man's thick socks and boots. Her face was still handsome. She might have been stunning once – the evidence was there, in the sharpness of her jaw and cheekbones, in the keenness of her one good blue-green eye; the other was milky with a cataract. It didn't take much effort to imagine her as a young communist in the 1930s, pioneer builder of a new civilisation, a socialist heroine to warm the hearts of Shaw or Wells. He bet she would have worshipped Stalin.

'*And Mama, yes, it is a modest house! Two storeys only. Your good Bolshevik heart would rejoice at its simplicity . . .* '

' – so if it would be possible,' he concluded, 'for us to take up some of your time, we would be very grateful.'

He transferred the satchel uneasily, from hand to hand. He was conscious of the snow settling in a cold clump on his back, of water trickling from his scalp, and of O'Brian at the foot of the steps, filming them.

Oh God, throw us out, he thought suddenly. Tell us to go to hell, and take our lies with us: I would if I were you. You must know why we're here.

But all she did was turn and shuffle back into the room, leaving the door wide open behind her.

KELSO went in first, and then O'Brian, who had to duck to get through the low entrance. It was dark. The solitary window was thickly glazed with snow.

If they wanted tea, she said, setting herself down heavily in a hard-backed wooden chair, then they would have to make it themselves.

'Tea?' said Kelso softly to O'Brian. 'She's offering to let us make her tea. I think yes, don't you?'

'Sure. I'll do it.'

She issued a stream of irritated instructions. Her voice, emanating from her buckled frame, was unexpectedly deep and masculine.

'Well, get the water from the pail, then – no, not *that* jug: *that* one, the *black* one – use the ladle, that's it – no, no *no* –' she banged her stick on the floor ' – not that much, *that* much. Now put it on the stove. And you can put some wood on the fire, too, while you're about it.' Another two bangs of the stick. '*Wood? Fire?*'

O'Brian appealed helplessly to Kelso for a translation.

'She wants you to put some wood on the fire.'

'Tea in that jar. No, no. Yes. *That* jar. Yes. *There.*'

Kelso couldn't get a handle on any of this – on the town, on her, on this place, on the speed with which everything seemed to be happening. It was like a dream. He thought he ought to start taking some notes, so he pulled out his yellow pad and began making a discreet inventory of the room. On the floor: a large square of grey linoleum. On the linoleum: one table, one chair and a bed covered with a woollen blanket. On the table: a pair of spectacles, a collection of pill-bottles and a copy of the northern edition of *Pravda*, open at the third page. On the walls: nothing, except in one corner, where a flickering red candle on a small sideboard punctuated the gloom, lighting a wood-framed photograph of V. I. Lenin. Hanging next to it were two medals for Socialist Labour and a certificate commemorating her fiftieth anniversary in the Party in 1984; by the time of her sixtieth, presumably, they couldn't run to such extravagance. The bones of communism and of Vavara Safanova had crumbled together.

The two men sat awkwardly on the bed. They drank their tea. It had a peculiar, herbal flavour, not unpleasant – cloudberries in it somewhere: a taste of the forest. She seemed to find nothing surprising in the fact of two foreigners arriving in her yard with a Japanese video camera, claiming to be making a film about the history of the Archangel Communist Party. It was as if she had been expecting them. Kelso guessed she would find no surprise in anything any more. She had the resigned indifference of extreme old age. Buildings and empires rose and fell. It snowed. It stopped snowing. People came and went. One day death would come for her, and she would not find that surprising, either, and she would not care – not so long as He trod in the proper places: 'No, not *there. There . . .'*

WELL, yes, she remembered the past, she said, settling back. Nobody in Archangel remembered the past better than she did. She remembered *everything.*

She could remember the Reds in 1917 coming out on to the street, and her uncle wheeling her up in the air, and kissing her and telling her the Tsar had gone and Paradise was on the way. She could remember her uncle and her father running away into the forest to hide when the British came to stop the Revolution in 1918 – a great grey battleship moored in the Dvina and runty little English soldiers swarming ashore. She *played* to the sound of gunfire. And then she remembered early one morning walking down to the harbour and the ship had gone. And that afternoon her uncle came back – but not her father: her father had been taken by the Whites and he never came back.

She remembered all these things.

And the kulaks?

Yes, she remembered the kulaks. She was seventeen. They arrived at the railway station, thousands of them, in their strange national dress. Ukrainians: you never saw so many people – covered in sores and carrying their bundles – they were locked in the churches and the townspeople were forbidden to approach them. Not that they wished to. The kulaks carried contamination, they all knew that.

Their sores were contagious?

No. The *kulaks* were contagious. Their *souls* were contagious. They carried the spores of counter-revolution. Bloodsuckers, spiders and vampires: that was what Lenin called them.

And so what happened to the kulaks?

It was like the English battleship. You went to bed at night and they were there, and you got up in the morning and they were gone. The churches were all closed after that. But now the churches were open again – she had seen it with her own eyes. The kulaks had come back. They were *everywhere*. It was a *tragedy*.

And the Great Patriotic War, she remembered that – the Allied ships moored out beyond the mouth of the river, and the docks working all day and all night, under the heroic direction of the Party, and the fascist planes dropping fire-bombs over the old wooden town and burning it, burning so much of it down. Those were the hardest times – her husband away fighting at the front, herself working as an auxiliary nurse at the Seamen's Policlinic, no food in the town and not much fuel, the black-out, the bombs and a daughter to bring up on her own . . .

ALL of this, of course, took much longer to extract than the printed record would suggest. There was a lot of banging of her stick and doubling-back and repitition and meandering, and Kelso was acutely aware of O'Brian fidgeting beside him and of the snow piling up and muffling the sounds outside. But he let her talk. Indeed, he kicked O'Brian twice on the ankle to warn him to be patient. He wanted to let her come to things in her own time.

Fluke Kelso was an expert at this. This was how the whole business had started, after all.

He sipped his cold tea.

So you had a daughter, Comrade Safanova? That's interesting. Tell us about your daughter.

Vavara prodded the linoleum with her stick. Her mouth turned down.

That was of no consequence to the history of the Archangel Regional Party.

'But it was of consequence to you?'

Well, naturally it was of consequence to *her*. She was the child's *mother*. But what was a child when set against the forces of history? It was a matter of *subjectivity* and *objectivity*. Of *who* and *whom*. And of various other slogans of the Party she could no longer fully remember, but which she knew to be true and which had been a comfort to her at the time.

She sat back, hunched in her chair.

Kelso reached for the satchel.

'Actually, I know something of what happened to your daughter,' he began. 'We have found a book, a journal, that Anna kept. That was her name, wasn't it? Anna? I wonder – can I show it you?'

Her eyes followed the movement of his hands, warily, as he began to unfasten the straps.

HER fingers were spotted with age, like the book itself, but they didn't tremble as she opened the cover. When she saw the picture of Anna, she touched it hesitantly, then her knuckle went to her mouth. She sucked on it. Slowly she brought the page up level with her face and held it close.

'I ought to be getting this on camera,' whispered O'Brian.

'Don't you dare even move,' hissed Kelso.

He couldn't see her expression, but he could hear her laboured breathing and again he had the odd sensation that she had been waiting for them – for years, maybe.

Eventually, she said, 'Where did you get this?'

'It was dug up. In a garden in Moscow. It was with some papers belonging to Stalin.'

When she lowered the book, her eyes were dry. She closed it and held it out to him.

'No. Read it,' he said. 'Please. It's hers.'

But she shook her head. She didn't want to.

'But that *is* her writing?'

'Yes, it's hers. Take it away.'

She waved the book at him and wouldn't rest until it was safely put back in the satchel. Then she sat back, leaning to her right, one hand covering her good eye, stabbing at the floor with her stick.

ANNA, she said, after a time.

Well. Anna.

Where to begin?

Truth to tell, she had been pregnant with Anna when she married. But people didn't care about such things in those times – the Party had done away with *priests*, thank God.

She was eighteen. Mikhail Safanov was five years older – a metallurgist in the shipyards and a member of the Party's factory committee.

A good-looking man. Their daughter took after him. Oh yes, Anna was a pretty thing. *That* was her tragedy.

'Tragedy?'

Clever, too. And growing up a good young communist. She was following her parents into the Party. She had served her time as a Pioneer. She was in the Komsomol: she looked like something out of a poster in her uniform. So much so that she had been picked for the Archangel Komsomol delegation to pass through Red Square – oh, a great honour, this – picked to pass beneath the eyes of the *Vozhd* himself, on May Day 1951.

Anna's picture had been in *Ogonyok* afterwards and

questions had been asked. That had been the start of it. Nothing had been the same after that.

Some comrades had come up from the Central Committee in Moscow the following week and had started asking around about her. And about the Safanovs.

And once word of this got out, some of their neighbours had started to avoid them. After all, though the arch-fiend Trotsky was dead at last, his spies and saboteurs might not be. Perhaps the Safanovs were wreckers or deviationists?

But of course nothing could have been further from the truth.

Mikhail had come home early from the shipyard one afternoon in the company of a comrade from Moscow – Comrade Mekhlis: she would never forget his name – and it was this comrade who had given them the good news. The Safanovs had been thoroughly checked and found to be loyal communists. Their daughter was a particular credit to them. So much so that she had been selected for special Party work in Moscow, attending to the needs of the senior leadership. Domestic service, but still: the work required intelligence and discretion, and afterwards the girl could resume her studies with good words on her file.

Anna – well, once Anna got to hear of it – there was no stopping her. And Vavara was in favour of it, too. Only Mikhail had been opposed. Something had happened to Mikhail. It pained her to say it. Something during the war. He had never spoken of it, except once, when Anna was talking, full of wonder, about the genius of Comrade Stalin. Mikhail said he had seen a lot of comrades die at the front: could she tell him, then, if Comrade Stalin was such a genius, why so many millions had had to die?

Vavara had made him rise from this very table – she struck

it with her hand – and go outside into the yard for his foolishness. No. He was not the man he had been before the war. He wouldn't even go to the railway station to see his daughter off.

She fell silent.

Kelso said quietly, 'And you never saw her again?'

Oh yes, said Vavara, surprised at the question. They saw her again.

She made a curving motion with her hands, outwards from her belly.

They saw her again when she came home to have the baby.

SILENCE.

O'Brian coughed and bent forwards, head down, his hands clasped tight in front of him, his elbows on his knees. 'Did she just say what I thought she said?'

Kelso ignored him. With great effort, he managed to keep his voice neutral.

'And when was this?'

Vavara thought for a while, tapping her stick against her boot.

The spring of 1952, she said eventually. That was it. She got through on the train in March 1952, when it was starting to thaw a bit. They had had no warning, she had just turned up, with no explanation. Not that she needed to explain anything. You only had to look at her. She was seven months gone by then.

'And the father . . . ? Did she say . . . ?'

No.

A vigorous shake of the head.

But you guessed, didn't you? thought Kelso.

No, she didn't say anything about the father, or about

what had happened in Moscow, and after a while they gave up asking. She just sat in the corner and waited for her term to come. She was very silent, this new girl, not like their old Anna. She wouldn't see her friends, or step outside. The truth was, she was scared.

'Scared? What was she scared of?'

Of giving birth, of course. And why not? Men! she said – and some of her old fire returned – what did men know of life? Naturally she was scared. Anyone with eyes in their head and a mind to think would be *scared*. And that baby didn't give her an easy time, either, the little devil. It sucked the goodness out of her. Oh, a proper little devil – what a kick it had! They would sit here in the evening and watch her belly heave.

Mekhlis came by sometimes to keep an eye on her. Most weeks there was a car at the bottom of the street with a couple of his men it.

No, they didn't ask who the father was.

She started to bleed at the beginning of April. They took her to the clinic. And that was the last time they saw her. She had a haemorrhage in the delivery room. The doctor told them everything about it afterwards. There was nothing to be done. She died on the operating table two days later. She was twenty.

'And the baby?'

The baby lived. A boy.

THE arrangements were all made by Comrade Mekhlis.

It was the least he could do, he told them. He felt responsible.

It was Mekhlis who provided the doctor – an academician, no less, the country's leading expert, flown up specially from

Moscow – and Mekhlis who arranged the adoption. The Safanovs would have reared the child themselves, willingly – they asked to do so: they begged – but Mekhlis had a paper, signed by Anna, in which she said that if anything happened to her, she wanted the baby to be adopted. She named some relatives of the father, a couple named Chizhikov.

'Chizhikov?' said Kelso. 'You're sure of that name?'

Certain.

They never even saw the baby. They weren't allowed inside the hospital.

Now she was willing to accept all this, because Vavara Safanova believed in the discipline of the Party. She still did. She would believe in it until the day she died. The Party was her god, and sometimes, like a god, the Party moved in a mysterious way.

But Mikhail Safanov no longer accepted the doctrine of infallibility. He was set on finding these Chizhikovs, whatever Mekhlis said, and he still had enough friends in the regional Party to help him do it. And that was how he discovered that the Chizhikovs were not fancy Moscow folk at all – which was what he had expected – but were northerners, like them, and had gone to live in a village in the forest outside Archangel. The whisper in the town was that Chizhikov was not their real name. That they were NKVD.

By this time it was winter and there was nothing Mikhail could do. And then one morning in early spring, while he was still looking out each day for the first signs of a thaw, they woke to solemn music on the radio and the news that Comrade Stalin was dead.

She had wept, and he had, too. Did that surprise him? Oh, they had howled and clutched at one another! They had cried in a way they never had before, not even for Anna. The whole of Archangel was in grief. She could still remember the day of the funeral. The long silence, broken by a thirty-gun salute. The echo of the gunfire had rolled across the Dvina like a distant storm in the forest.

Two months later, in May, when the ice had gone, Mikhail had filled a backpack and had set off to find his grandson.

She had known nothing good could come of it.

One day passed, then two, then three. He was a fit man, strong and healthy – he was only forty-five.

On the fifth day some fishermen had found his body, about thirty *versts* upstream, rushing along in the yellow meltwater that was pouring out of the forest, not far from Novodvinsk.

KELSO unfolded O'Brian's map and laid it out on the table. She put on her spectacles and hunted up and down the blue line of the Dvina, her good eye held very close.

There, she said, after a while, and pointed. That was the place where her husband's body had been found. A wild spot! There were wolves here in the forest, and lynx and bear. In some places the trees were too dense for a man to move. In others, there were swamps that could eat you in a minute. And here and there the grey weathered bones of the old kulak settlements. Almost all of the kulaks had perished, of course. There was not much of a living to be scratched in such a place.

Mikhail knew the forest as well as any man. He had been roaming the taiga since he was a child.

It had been a heart attack, according to the militia. That was what they said. Maybe he had been trying to fill his water bottle? He had fallen into the cold yellow water and the shock had stopped his heart.

She had buried him in the Kuznecheskoye Cemetery, next to Anna.

'And what,' said Kelso, conscious again of O'Brian just behind them, filming them now with his wretched miniature camera, 'what was the name of the village where your husband said the Chizhikovs lived?'

Ah! This was crazy! How could she be expected to remember that? It was so long ago – nearly fifty years . . .

She brought her face down close to the map again.

Here somewhere – she placed a wavering finger on a spot just north of the river – somewhere around here: a place too small to be worth recording. Too small to have a name, even.

She had never tried to find it herself?

Oh no.

She looked at Kelso in horror.

Nothing good could come of it. Not then. And not now.

Chapter Twenty-four

THE BIG CAR braked hard and swerved off the south Moscow highway into the Zhukovsky military airbase shortly before noon, Feliks Suvorin hanging grimly to the strap in the rear. Beyond the checkpoint, a jeep waited. It pulled away as the barrier rose, its tail lights flashing, and they followed it around the side of the terminal building, through a wire fence and on to the concrete apron.

A small grey aircraft, as requested – six-seater, prop-driven – was being fuelled by a tanker. Beyond the plane was a line of dark green army helicopters with drooping rotors; parked next to it, a big ZiL limousine.

Well, well, thought Suvorin. Some things still work round here.

He stuffed his notes into his briefcase and darted through the wind and rain towards the limousine where Arsenyev's driver was already opening the rear door.

'And?' said Arsenyev from the warmth of the interior.

'And,' said Suvorin, sliding along the seat to join him, 'it's not what we thought it was. And thank you for fixing the plane.'

'Wait in the other car,' said Arsenyev to his chauffeur.

'Yes, colonel.'

'What's not as who thought it was?' said Arsenyev, when the door was shut. 'Good morning, by the way.'

'Good morning, Yuri Semonovich. The notebook. Everybody's always believed it was Stalin's. Actually it turns out to have been a journal kept by a girl servant of Stalin's, Anna Mikhailovna Safanova. He had her brought down from Archangel to work for him in the summer of '51, about eighteen months before he died.'

Arsenyev blinked at him.

'And that's it? That's what Beria stole?'

'That's it. That and some papers about her, apparently.'

Arsenyev stared at Suvorin for a second or two, then started laughing. He shook his head with relief. 'Go fuck your mother! The old bastard was screwing his maid? Is that what he was up to?'

'Apparently.'

'That is priceless. That is brilliant!' Arsenyev punched the seat in front of him. 'Oh, let me be there! Let me be there to see Mamantov's face when he finds out his great Stalin testament is nothing more than a maid's account of getting screwed by the mighty *Vozhd!*' He glanced at Suvorin, his fat cheeks flushed with mirth, diamonds glistening in his eyes. 'What's the matter, Feliks? Don't tell me you can't see the funny side?' He stopped laughing. 'What's the matter? You are sure this is true, aren't you?'

'Pretty well sure, colonel, yes. This is all according to the woman we picked up last night, Zinaida Rapava. She read the notebook yesterday afternoon – her father left it hidden for her. I can't think that she would invent such a story. It defies imagination.'

'Right, right. So cheer up, eh? And where's this notebook now?'

'Well, that's the first complication.' Suvorin spoke hesitantly. It seemed such a shame to spoil the old fellow's mood. 'That's why I needed to talk to you. It seems she showed it to the historian, Kelso. According to her, he's taken it with him.'

'With him?'

'To Archangel. He's trying to find the woman who wrote it, this Anna Safanova.'

Arsenyev tugged nervously at his thick neck. 'When did he leave?'

'Yesterday afternoon. Four or five. She can't remember exactly.'

'How?'

'Driving.'

'Driving? That's all right. You'll catch him easily. By the time you land, you'll only be a few hours behind him. He's a rat in a trap up there.'

'Unfortunately, it's not just him. He's got a journalist with him. O'Brian. You know him? That correspondent with the satellite television station.'

'Ah.' Arsenyev stuck out his lower lip and pulled at his neck some more. After a while he said, 'But even so, the chances of this woman still being alive are small. And if she is – well, so, so, it's no disaster. Let them write their books and make their fucking news reports. I can't see Stalin entrusting his *maid* with a message for future generations. Can you?'

'Well, this is my worry –'

'His *maid?* Come on, Feliks! He was a Georgian, after all, and an old one at that. Women were good for only three things, as far as Comrade Stalin was concerned. Cooking, cleaning and having kids. He –' Arsenyev stopped. 'No –'

'It's insane,' said Suvorin, holding up his hand. 'I know that. I've been telling myself all the way over that it's crazy. But then, he *was* crazy. And he was a Georgian. Think about it. Why would he go to so much trouble to check out one girl? He had her medical records, apparently. And he wanted her checked for congenital abnormalities. Also, why would he keep her diary in his safe? And then there's more, you see –'

'More?' Arsenyev was no longer punching the front seat. He was clutching it for support.

'According to Zinaida, there are references in the girl's journal to Trofim Lysenko. You know: "the inheritability of acquired characteristics" and all that rubbish. And apparently he also goes on about how useless his own children are, and how "the soul of Russia is in the north".'

'Stop it, Feliks. This is too much.'

'And then there's Mamantov. I've never understood why Mamantov should have taken such an insane risk – to murder Rapava, and in such a way. Why? This is what I tried to say to you yesterday: what could Stalin possibly have written that could have any effect upon Russia nearly fifty years later? But if Mamantov knew – had heard some rumour years ago, maybe, from some of the old timers at the Lubyanka – that Stalin might deliberately have left behind an heir –'

'An *heir?*'

' – well, that would explain everything, wouldn't it? He'd take the risk for that. Let's face it, Yuri, Mamantov's just about sick enough to – oh, I don't know –' he tried to think of something utterly absurd ' – to run Stalin's son for the Presidency, or something. He does have half a billion roubles, after all . . .'

'Wait a minute,' said Arsenyev. 'Let me think about this.' He looked across the airfield to the line of helicopters. Suvorin could see a muscle like a fish hook twitching deep in his fleshy jaw. 'And we still have no idea where Mamantov is?'

'He could be anywhere.'

'Archangel?'

'It's a possibility. It must be. If Zinaida Rapava had the brains to find Kelso at the airport, why not Mamantov? He could have been tailing them for twenty-four hours. They're not professionals; he is. I'm worried, Yuri. They'd never know a thing until he made his hit.'

Arsenyev groaned.

'You got a phone?'

'Sure.' Suvorin dug in his pocket and produced it.

'Secure?'

'Supposedly.'

'Call my office for me, will you?'

Suvorin began punching in the number. Arsenyev said, 'Where's the Rapava girl?'

'I got Bunin to take her back home. I've fixed up a guard, for her own protection. She's not in a good state.'

'You saw this, I suppose?' Arsenyev pulled a copy of the latest *Aurora* out of the seat pocket. Suvorin saw the headline: 'VIOLENCE IS INEVITABLE'.

'I heard it on the news.'

'Well, you can imagine how pleasantly *that's* gone down –'

'Here,' said Suvorin, giving him the phone. 'It's ringing.'

'Sergo?' said Arsenyev. 'It's me. Listen. Can you patch me through to the President's office . . . ? That's it. Use the second number.' He put his hand over the mouthpiece. 'You'd better go. No. Wait. Tell me what you need.'

Suvorin spread his hands. He barely knew where to begin. 'I could do with the militia or someone up in Archangel to check out every Safanov or Safanova and have the job finished by the time I arrive. That would be a start. I'll need a couple of men to meet me at the airfield. Transport I'll need. And some place to stay.'

'It's done. Go carefully, Feliks. I hope –' But Suvorin never did discover what the colonel hoped, because Arsenyev suddenly held up a warning finger. 'Yes . . . Yes, I'm ready.' He took a breath and forced a smile; if he could have stood up and saluted, he would have done so. 'And good day to you, Boris Nikolaevich –'

Suvorin climbed quietly out of the car.

The tanker had been unhooked from the little aircraft and the hose was being wound up. There were rainbows of oil in the puddles beneath the wings. Close up, the dented, rust-streaked Tupolev looked even older than he expected. Forty, at least. Older than he was, in fact. Holy Mother, what a bucket!

A couple of ground crew watched him without curiosity.

'Where's the pilot?'

One of the men gestured with his head to the plane. Suvorin pulled himself up the steps and into the fuselage. It was cold inside and smelled like an old bus that hadn't been driven for years. The door to the cockpit was open. He could see the pilot idly pressing switches on and off. He ducked his head and went forward and tapped him on the shoulder. The airman had a pouchy face, with the sandy, dull-eyed, bloodshot look of a heavy drinker. Great, thought Suvorin. They shook hands.

'What's the weather like in Archangel?'

The pilot laughed. Suvorin could smell the booze: it was not only on his breath – he was sweating it. 'I'll risk it if you will.'

'Shouldn't you have a navigator or someone?'

'There's nobody about.'

'Great. Terrific.'

Suvorin went aft and took his seat. One engine coughed and started with a spurt of black smoke, and then the other.

Arsenyev's limousine had already gone, he noticed. The Tupolev turned and taxied across the deserted apron, out towards the runway. They turned again, the sawing whine of the propellers falling then rising, rising, rising. The wind whipped the rain like dirty laundry, in horizontal sheets across the concrete. He could see the narrow trunks of silver birches on the airfield perimeter, grown close together like a white palisade. He closed his eyes – it was stupid to be scared of flying, but there it was: he always had been – and they were off, scuttling and swaying down the runway, the pressure pushing him back in his seat, and then there was a lurch and they were airborne.

He opened his eyes. The plane rose beyond the edge of the airfield and banked across the city. Objects seemed to rush into his field of vision, only to dwindle and tilt away – yellow headlights reflecting on the wet streets, flat grey roofs and the dark green patches of trees. So many trees! It always surprised him. He thought of all the people he knew down there – Serafima at home in the apartment they couldn't quite afford and the boys at school and Arsenyev trembling after his call to the President and Zinaida Rapava and her silence when he left her in the morgue –

They hit the sudden underside of the low cloud and he was permitted one, two, three last glimpses through the shreds of thickening gauze before Moscow was blanked from view.

Chapter Twenty-five

R. J. O'Brian stood on the street corner at the end of the alleyway leading to Vavara Safanova's yard, his metal case on the ground between his legs, his head bent over the map.

'How long d'you figure it'll take us to get there? A couple of hours?'

Kelso looked back at the tiny wooden house. The old woman was still standing at her open door, leaning on her stick, watching them. He raised his hand to wave goodbye and the door slowly closed.

'Get where?'

'The Chizhikov place,' said O'Brian. 'How long d'you figure?'

'In this?' Kelso raised his eyes to the heavy sky. 'You want to try to find it now?'

'There's only one road. See for yourself. She said it was a village, right? If it's a village, it'll be on the road.' He brushed a dusting of snowflakes off the map and gave it to Kelso. 'I'd say two hours.'

'That's not a road,' said Kelso. 'That's a dotted line. That's a track.' It wandered eastwards through the forest, parallel with the Dvina for perhaps fifty miles, then struck north and ended nowhere – just stopped in the middle of the taiga after about two hundred miles. 'Take a look around you, man. They haven't even made most of the roads in the city. What d'you think they'll be like out there?'

He thrust the map back at O'Brian and began walking in the direction of the Toyota. O'Brian came after him. 'We got four-wheel drive, Fluke. We got snow chains.'

'And what if we break down?'

'We got food. We got fuel for a fire and a whole damn forest to burn. We can always drink the snow. We've got the satellite phone.' He clapped Kelso on the shoulder. 'Tell you what, how about this: you get scared, you can call your mommy. How's that?'

'My mommy's dead.'

'Zinaida then. You can call Zinaida.'

'Tell me, *did* you screw her, O'Brian? As a matter of interest?'

'What's that got to do with anything?'

'I just want to know why she doesn't trust you. Whether she's right. Is it sex or is it something personal?'

'Oh-ho. Is that what all this is about?' O'Brian smirked. 'Come on, Fluke. You know the rules. A gentleman never talks.'

Kelso huddled further into his jacket and increased his pace.

'It's not a question of being scared.'

'Oh really?'

They were within sight of the car now. Kelso stopped and turned to face him. 'All right, I admit it. I am scared. And you know what scares me most? The fact you're *not* scared. That *really* scares me.'

'Bullshit. A bit of snow –'

'Forget the snow. I'm not bothered about the snow.' Kelso glanced around at the tumbling houses. The scene was entirely brown and white and grey. And silent, like an old movie. 'You just don't get it, do you?' he said. 'You don't understand. You've no history, that's your problem. It's like this name "Chizhikov". What's that to you?'

'Nothing. It's just a name.'

'But it's not, you see. "Chizhikov" was one of Stalin's aliases before the Revolution. Stalin was issued with a passport in the name of P. A. Chizhikov in 1911.'

(*Are you excited, Dr Kelso? Do you feel the force of Comrade Stalin, even from the grave?* And he did. He did feel it. He felt as if a hand had reached out from the snow and touched his shoulder.)

O'Brian was quiet for a few seconds, but then he gave a dismissive sweep of his metal case. 'Well, you can stand here and *commune* with history if you want. I'm going to go and *find* it.' He set off across the street, turning as he walked. 'You coming or not? The train to Moscow leaves at ten past eight tonight. Or you can come with me. Make your choice.'

Kelso hesitated. He looked up again at the tumbling sky. It wasn't like any snowfall he had ever known in England or the States. It was as if something was disintegrating up there – flaking to pieces and crashing around them.

Choice? he thought. For a man with no visa and no money, no job, no book? For a man who had come this far? And what *choice* would that be, exactly?

Slowly, reluctantly, he began to walk towards the car.

THEY headed back out of the city, along a minor road, and northwards, so at least there was no GAI checkpoint to negotiate.

By now it must have been about one o'clock.

The road ran alongside an overgrown railroad track lined with ancient freight cars, and to start with it wasn't too bad. It could almost have been romantic, in the right company.

They overtook a gaily painted cart being pulled by a pony, its head down into the wind, and soon there were more wooden houses, also bright with paint – blue, green, red –

leaning in a picturesque way out in the marshland at the end of wooden jettys. In the snow it wasn't possible to tell where the solid ground ended and water began. Boats, cars, sheds, chicken coops and tethered goats were jumbled together. Even the big wood pulp mill across the wide Dvina, on the southern headland, had a kind of epic beauty, its cranes and smoking chimneys silhouetted against the concrete sky.

But then, abruptly, the houses disappeared and so did their view of the river. At the same time the hard surface gave way beneath their wheels and they began jolting along a rutted track. Birch and pine trees closed around them. In less than fifteen minutes they might have been a thousand miles from Archangel rather than a mere ten. The road wound on through the muffled forest. Sometimes the trees grew high and fine. But occasionally the woodland would thin and they would find themselves in a wilderness of blackened, blighted stumps, like a battlefield after heavy shelling. Or – and this was oddly more disconcerting – they would suddenly come across a small plantation of tall radio antennae.

Listening posts, O'Brian said, eavesdropping on Northern NATO.

He started to sing. *Walking in a Winter Wonderland.*

Kelso stood it for a couple of verses. 'Do you have to?'

O'Brian stopped.

'Gloomy sonofabitch,' he muttered under his breath.

The snow was still falling steadily. Occasional gunshots cracked and echoed in the distance – hunters in the woods – sending panicky birds flapping and crying across the track.

They went through several small villages, each smaller and more dilapidated than the last – a barracks in one with graffiti on its walls, and a satellite dish: a little chunk of Archangel dropped in the middle of nowhere. There was no one to be seen except a couple of gawping children and an old woman dressed entirely in black who stood at the roadside and tried to wave them down. When O'Brian didn't slow she shook her fist and cursed them.

'Hag.' O'Brian looked back at her in the mirror. 'What's eating her? Where are all the men, anyway? Drunk?' He meant it as a joke.

'Probably.'

'No? What? *All* of them?'

'Most of them, I should think. Home-made vodka. What else is there to do?'

'Jesus, what a country.'

After a while O'Brian began to sing again, but under his breath now and less confidently than before.

'We're walking in a winter wonderland . . .'

ONE hour passed, then another.

A couple of times the river came back briefly into view, and that, as O'Brian said, was a sight and a half – the swampy land, the wide and sluggish mass of water and, far beyond it, the flat, dark mass of trees picking up again, only to dissolve into the waves of snow. It was a primordial landscape. Kelso could imagine a dinosaur moving slowly across it.

From the map it was hard to tell exactly where they were. No habitations were recorded, no landmarks. He suggested they stop at the next village and try to regain their bearings.

'Whatever you want.'

But the next village was a long time coming, it never came, and Kelso noticed that the snow on the track was virgin: there hadn't been any traffic this far out for hours. They hit a drift for the first time – a pothole disguised by snow – and the Toyota slewed, its rear tyres flailing, until they bit on something solid. The car lurched. O'Brian spun the wheel and brought them back on course. He laughed – 'Whoa, that was fun!' – but Kelso could tell that even he was starting to feel unsettled now. The reporter slowed the engine, switched on the headlights and shifted forwards in his seat, peering into the swirling flakes.

'Fuel's low. I'd say we've got about fifteen minutes.'

'Then what?'

'Either we head back to Archangel, or we go on and try to find some place to stay the night.'

'Oh, what? You mean a Holiday Inn?'

'Fluke, Fluke –'

'Listen, if we try to stay the night here, we'll end up staying the winter.'

'Oh, come on, man, they have to send a snow plough, don't they? Surely? At some point?'

'*At some point?*' repeated Kelso. He shook his head. And there would have been another row if, just then, they hadn't rounded a curve and seen, above the snow-topped trees, a smudge of smoke.

O'BRIAN stood in the doorway of the Toyota, leaning on the roof, staring ahead through his binoculars. It looked as if there might be a settlement of some sort, he said, about half a mile off the road, along a rough track.

He slipped back behind the wheel. 'Let's take a look.'

The passage through the trees was like a tunnel, barely wide enough for a single vehicle, and O'Brian drove down it slowly. The branches clawed at them, slapping the windscreen, raking the sides of the car. The track worsened. They rocked sharply – hard left, hard right – and suddenly the Toyota plunged forwards and Kelso was thrown at the windscreen; only the seat belt saved him. The engine revved helplessly for a second, then stalled.

O'Brian turned the ignition, put the car into reverse and cautiously pressed the accelerator. The back wheels whined in the loose snow. He tried it again, harder. A howl like an animal trapped.

'Get out, could you, Fluke? Take a look.' He couldn't quite keep the edge of panic out of his voice.

Kelso had to push hard even to open the door. He jumped out and immediately sank up to his knees. The drift was axle-deep.

He banged on the back door and gestured to O'Brian to switch off the engine.

In the silence he could hear the snowflakes pattering in the trees. His knees were wet and cold. He trod awkwardly, bow-legged, through the deep drift round to the driver's door and had to dig away the snow with his gloved hands before he could drag it open. The Toyota was tilted forwards at an angle of at least twenty degrees. O'Brian struggled out.

'What'd we hit?' he demanded. He waded round to the front of the car. 'Jesus, it's like someone's dug a tank-trap. Will you look at this?'

It was indeed as if a trench had been laid across the track. A few paces further on the snow became more solid again.

'Maybe they were laying a cable or something,' said Kelso. But a cable for what? He cupped his hands above his eyes and stared through the snow towards the huddle of wooden huts about three hundred yards ahead. They didn't look as though they were connected to electricity, or to anything else. He noticed that the smoke had disappeared.

'Someone's put that fire out.'

'We're gonna need a tow.' O'Brian gave the side of the

Toyota a gloomy kick. 'Heap of junk.'

He held on to the car for support and edged round to the back, opened it up and pulled out a couple of pairs of boots, one of green rubber, the other of leather, high-sided, army-issue. He threw the rubber boots to Kelso. 'Get these on,' he said. 'Let's go parley with the natives.'

Five minutes later, their hoods up, the car locked, and each with a pair of binoculars hung round his neck, they set off down the track.

The settlement had been abandoned for at least a couple of years. The handful of wooden shacks had been ransacked. Rubbish poked through the snow – rusting sheets of corrugated tin roofing, shattered window frames, rotting planks, a torn fishing net, bottles, tin cans, a holed rowing boat, bits of machinery, ripped sacking and, bizarrely, a row of cinema seats. A timber-framed greenhouse fitted with polythene instead of glass had blown over on to its side.

Kelso ducked his head into one of the derelict buildings. It was roofless, freezing. It stank of animal excreta.

As he came out O'Brian caught his eye and shrugged.

Kelso stared towards the edge of the clearing. 'What's that over there?'

Both men raised their binoculars and trained them on what appeared to be a row of wooden crosses, half-hidden by the trees – Russian crosses, with three pairs of arms: short at the top, longer in the centre, and slanted downwards, left to right, at the bottom.

'Oh, that's marvellous,' said Kelso, trying to laugh. 'A cemetery. That's bloody perfect.'

'Let's take a look,' said O'Brian.

He set off eagerly with long, determined strides. Kelso, more reluctant, followed as best he could. Twenty years of cigarettes and Scotch seemed to have convened a protest meeting in his heart and lungs. He was sweating with the effort of moving through the snow. He had a pain in his side.

It was a cemetery right enough, sheltered by the trees, and as they came closer he could see six – or was it eight? – graves, arranged in twos, with a little wooden fence around each pair. The crosses were home-made but well done, with white enamel name-plates and small photographs covered in glass, in the traditional Russian manner. *A. I. Sumbatov*, read the first one, *22.1.20 – 9.8.81*. The picture showed a man, in middle age, in uniform. Next to him was *P. J. Sumbatova, 6.12.26 – 14.11.92*. She, too, was in uniform: a heavy-faced woman with a severe central parting. Next to them were the Yezhovs. And next to the Yezhovs, the Golubs. They were married couples, all about the same age. They were all in uniform. T. Y. Golub had been the first to die, in 1961. It was impossible to see his face. It had been scratched out.

'This must be the place,' said O'Brian, quietly. 'No question. This is it. Who are they all, Fluke? Army?'

'No.' Kelso shook his head slowly. 'The uniform is NKVD, I think. And here, look. Look at this.'

It was the final pair of graves, the ones furthest from the clearing, set slightly apart from the others. They had been the last survivors. *B. D. Chizhikov* – a major, by the look of his insignia – *19.2.19 – 9.3.96*. And next to him *M. G. Chizhikova, 16.4.24 – 16.3.96*. She had outlasted her husband by exactly one week. Her face was also obliterated.

They stood like mourners for a while: silent, their heads bowed.

'And then there were none,' murmured O'Brian.

'Or one.'

'I don't think so. No way. This place has been empty quite

a while. Shit,' he said suddenly, and took a kick at the snow, 'would you believe it, after all that? We *missed* him?'

The trees were thick here. It was impossible to see beyond a few dozen yards.

O'Brian said, 'I'd better get a shot of this while it's light. You wait here. I'll go back to the car.'

'Oh, great,' said Kelso. 'Thank you.'

'Scared, Fluke?'

'What do you think?'

'Whoo,' said O'Brian. He raised his arms and fluttered his fingers above his head.

'If you try playing any jokes, O'Brian, I'm warning you, I'll kill you.'

'Ho ho ho,' said O'Brian, moving away towards the track. 'Ho ho ho.' He disappeared beyond the trees. Kelso heard his stupid laugh for a few more seconds and then there was silence – just the rustle of the snow and the sound of his own breathing.

My God, what a set-up *this* was, just look at these dates: they were a story in themselves. He walked back to the first grave, pulled off his gloves, took out his notebook. Then he went down on one knee and began to copy the details from the crosses. An entire troop of bodyguards had been dispatched into the forest more than forty years earlier to protect one solitary baby boy, and all of them had stuck it out, had stayed at their posts, out of loyalty or habit or fear, until eventually they had dropped down dead, one after another. They were like those Japanese soldiers who stayed hidden in the jungle, unaware that the war was over.

He began to wonder how close Mikhail Safanov might have managed to get in the spring of 1953, and then he consciously abandoned this line of thought. It didn't bear contemplating – not yet; not *here*.

It was hard to hold the pencil between his cold fingers, and difficult to write as the snowflakes settled across the page. Still, he worked his way along to the final crosses.

'*B. D. Chizhikov,*' he wrote. '*Tough-looking, brutal face. Dark-skinned. A Georgian?? Died aged 77 . . .*'

He wondered what Comrades Golub and Chizhikova might have looked like, and who had blacked out their faces, and why. There was something infinitely sinister about their featureless silhouettes. He found himself writing, '*Could they have been purged?*'

Oh, where the hell was O'Brian?

His back was aching. His knees were wet. He stood and another thought occurred to him. He brushed the page clear of snow again and licked the end of his pencil.

'*The graves are all well kept,*' he wrote, '*plots appear to be weeded. If this place is abandoned, like the buildings, shouldn't they have grown over?*'

'O'Brian?' he called. 'R. J.?'

The snow deadened his shout.

He put away the notebook and began walking quickly away from the cemetery, pulling on his gloves. The wind stirred in the abandoned buildings ahead of him, catching the snow and lifting it here and there like the corner of a curtain. He picked his way across the ground, following O'Brian's large footprints until he came to the start of the track. The prints led off clearly in the direction of the Toyota. He raised the binoculars to his eyes and twisted the focus. The stricken car filled his vision, so still and distant it seemed unreal. There was no sign of anyone around it.

Odd.

He turned round very slowly, a complete 360 degrees,

scanning through the binoculars. Forest. Tumbled walls and wreckage. Forest. Graves. Forest. Track. Toyota. Forest again.

He lowered the binoculars, frowning, then began walking towards the car, still following O'Brian's trail. It took him a couple of minutes. Nobody else had been this way in the snow, that much was obvious: there were two pairs of tracks heading up to the clearing and one pair heading back. He approached the car and, by lengthening his stride and planting his feet in the prints of the bigger man, he was able to retrace O'Brian's movements exactly: so and so . . . and . . . *so* . . .

Kelso stopped, arms outstretched, wobbling. The American had definitely come this way, round to the back of the Toyota, had taken out the metal camera case – it was missing, he could see – and then it looked as though something had distracted him, because instead of heading back up the track to the settlement his footprints turned sharply and led directly away from the vehicle, at a right angle, straight into the forest.

He called O'Brian's name, softly. And then, in a spasm of panic, he cupped his hands and bellowed it as loud as he could.

Again, that same curious deadening effect, as if the trees were swallowing his words.

Cautiously, he stepped into the undergrowth.

Oh, but he had always hated forests, hadn't he? Hated even the woodland around Oxford, with its poetic shafts of dusty bloody sunlight, and its mossy vegetation, and the way things suddenly flew up at you or rustled away! And branches slapping back into your face . . . *Sorry, sorry* . . . Oh yes, give him a wide open space any day. Give him a hill. Give him a cliff-top. Give him the sparkling sea!

'R. J.?' What a damned silly name to have to yell, but he yelled it louder anyway: 'R. J.!'

There were no footprints visible here. The ground was rough. He could smell the decay of a swamp somewhere, as rank as dog's breath, and it was dark, too. He would have to watch himself, he thought, keep his back firmly to the road, because if he went too far, he would lose his bearings, and maybe end up walking further and further away from the car, until there would be nothing left to do but lie down in the darkness and freeze.

There was a sudden heavy crash off to his left, and then a succession of smaller bursts, like echoes. It sounded at first like someone running but then he realised it was only snow dislodging from the tops of some branches and plunging to the earth.

He cupped his hands.

'R. J . . . !'

And then he heard a human sound. A moan, was that it? A sob?

He tried to place where it was coming from. And then he heard it again. Nearer, and behind him now, it seemed to be. He pushed through a gap between a couple of close-growing trees into a tiny clearing, and there was O'Brian's camera case lying open on the ground and there, beyond it, was O'Brian himself, upside down and swinging gently, his fingertips barely brushing the surface of the snow, suspended by his left leg from a length of oily rope.

Chapter Twenty-six

THE ROPE WAS attached to the top of a tall birch sapling, bent almost double by O'Brian's weight. The reporter was groaning. He was barely conscious.

Kelso knelt by his head. At the sight of him, O'Brian began struggling feebly. He didn't seem able to form a sentence.

'It's all right,' said Kelso. He tried to sound calm. 'Don't worry. I'll get you down.'

Get him down. Kelso took off his gloves. Get him down. Right. Using what? He had a knife for sharpening pencils, but it was in the car. He patted his pockets and found his lighter. He flicked it on, showed the flame to O'Brian.

'We'll get you down. Look. You'll be all right.'

He stood and reached up, grabbing O'Brian by his booted ankle. A noose of thin rope had dug deep into the leather. It took all Kelso's weight to drag him down far enough for him to apply the flame to the taut rope just above his sole. O'Brian's shoulders rested in the snow.

'Asornim,' he was saying. 'Asornim.'

The rope was wet. It seemed to take an age for the lighter to have any effect. Kelso had to stop and shake it. The flame was beginning to turn blue and die before the first strands started to smoulder. But then under the strain they parted fast. The last of them snapped and the sapling whipped back and Kelso tried to support the legs with his free hand but he couldn't manage it and O'Brian's body crashed heavily into the snow.

The reporter struggled to sit up, managed to prop himself

on his elbows, then slumped back again. He was still mumbling something. Kelso knelt beside him.

'You're okay. You'll be fine. We'll get you out of here.'

'Asornim.'

I sore nim?

I saw him.

'Saw who? Who did you see?'

'Oh, Jesus. Oh, fuck.'

'Can you bend your leg? Is it broken?' Kelso shuffled on his knees through the snow and began digging with his fingernails at the knot of the noose, embedded in the side of O'Brian's boot.

'Fluke –' O'Brian held up his arm, desperately flexing his fingers. 'Give me a lift here, will you?'

Kelso took his hand and pulled until O'Brian was sitting upright. Then he put his arm round the reporter's broad chest and together they managed to get him up on to his feet. O'Brian stood, leaning heavily against Kelso, putting his weight on his right leg.

'Can you walk?'

'Not sure. Think so.' He hobbled a few steps. 'Just give me a minute.'

He stayed where he was, with his back to Kelso, staring into the trees. When he seemed to be breathing more normally, Kelso said, 'Saw *who?*'

SAW *him,* said O'Brian, turning round. His eyes were wild and fearful now, searching the forest behind Kelso's head. Saw *the man.* Saw him staring out of the fucking trees next to the car. *Jesus.* Just about jumped out of my fucking *skin.*

'What do you mean? What man?'

Took one step towards him – hands up, let's be friends,

white-man-he-come-in-peace – and presto! he was *gone*. I mean, he *vanished*. Never saw him properly again after that. Heard him, though, and kind of glimpsed him once – moving fast through the forest up ahead, away to the right – sort of a sawn-off figure, like a quarterback, built low to the ground. And *quick*. So quick you wouldn't believe it. Man, he seemed to move like an *ape*. Next thing I know, the world's turned upside down.

'He led me on, Fluke, you know that, don't you? Led me right into his fucking *trap*. He's probably out there now, *watching us*.'

He was getting his strength back, his recovery speeded by fear.

He hobbled a few steps. When he tried to put his left leg down properly he winced. But he could move it, that was something. It definitely wasn't broken.

'We gotta go. We gotta get out of here.' He bent awkwardly and closed the catches on the camera case.

Kelso needed no persuading. But they would have to go carefully, he said. They had to *think*. They had blundered into two of his traps already – one on the track and one here – and who could guess how many more there might be. In this snow it was so damned hard to see.

'Maybe,' said Kelso, 'if we try to follow my footprints –'

But his tracks were already beginning to be lost beneath the ceaseless soft downpour.

'Who is he, Fluke?' whispered O'Brian, as they went back into the trees. 'I mean, *what* is he? What is he so goddamned scared of?'

He's his father's son, thought Kelso, that's who he is. He's a forty-five-year-old paranoid psychopath, if such a thing is possible.

'Oh man,' said O'Brian, 'what was *that?*'

Kelso stopped.

It wasn't another avalanche of snow from the treetops, that was for sure. It went on too long. A heavy, sustained rustling, somewhere in front of them.

'It's him,' said O'Brian. 'He's moving again. He's trying to head us off.' The noise stopped abruptly and they stood, listening. 'Now what's he doing?'

'Watching us, at a guess.'

Again, Kelso strained his eyes into the gloom, but it was hopeless. Dense undergrowth, great patches of shadow, occasionally broken by torrents of snow – he couldn't get a fix on anything, it was so unlike any place he had ever seen. He was really sweating now, despite the cold. His skin was prickling.

That was when the howling started – a deafening, inhuman wail. It took Kelso a couple of seconds to realise it was the car alarm.

Then came two loud gunshots in rapid succession, a pause, and then a third.

Then silence.

AFTERWARDS, Kelso was never sure how long they stood there. He remembered only the immobilising sense of terror: the paralysis of thought and action that came from the realisation there was nothing they could do. He – whoever *he* was – knew where they were. He had shot up their car. He had booby-trapped the forest. He could come for them whenever he wanted. Or he could leave them where they were. There was no prospect of rescue from the outside world. He was their absolute master. Unseen. All-seeing. Omnipotent. *Mad.*

After a minute or two they risked a whispered conference. The telephone, said O'Brian, what if he had damaged the Inmarsat telephone? It was their only hope and it was in the back of the Toyota.

Maybe he wouldn't know what a satellite telephone looked like, said Kelso. Maybe if they stayed where they were until dark and then went to retrieve it –

Suddenly O'Brian grabbed him hard by the elbow.

A face was looking at them through the trees.

Kelso didn't see it at first, it was so perfectly still – so unnaturally, perfectly immobile, it took a moment for his mind to register it, to separate the pieces from the shapes of the forest, to assemble them and declare the composite human:

Dark impassive eyes that didn't blink. Black, arched brows. Coarse black hair hanging loose across a leathery forehead. A beard.

There was also a hood made of some kind of brown animal fur.

The apparition coughed. It grunted.

'Com-rades,' it said. The word was slurred, the voice harsh, like a tape being played at too slow a speed.

Kelso could feel the hair stirring on his scalp.

'Aw, Jesus,' said O'Brian, 'Jesusjesusjesus –'

There was another cough and a great gathering of phlegm. A gobbet of yellow spit was ejected into the undergrowth. 'Com-rades, I am a rude fell-ow. I cannot deny it. And I have been out of the way of hu-man com-pany. But there it is. Well then? D'yer want me to shoot yer? Yes?'

He stepped out in front of them – quickly, sharply: he barely disturbed a twig. He was wearing an old army greatcoat – patched, hacked off above the knees and belted with a length of rope – and cavalry boots into which his baggy trousers were stuffed. His hands were bare and huge. In one he carried an old rifle. In the other was the satchel with Anna Safanova's notebook and the papers.

Kelso felt O'Brian's grip tighten on his arm.

'This is the book of which it is spok-en? Yes? And the papers prove it!' The figure leaned towards them, rocking his head this way and that, studying them intently. 'You are the ones, then? You are truly the ones?'

He came closer, peering at them with his dark eyes, and Kelso could smell the stench of his body, sour with stale sweat.

'Or are you, perhaps, *spiders?*'

He took a pace back and swiftly raised the rifle, aiming it from his waist, his finger on the trigger.

'We are the ones,' said Kelso, quickly.

The man cocked an eyebrow in surprise. 'Imperialists?'

'I am an English comrade. The comrade here is American.'

'Well, well! England and America! And Engels was a Jew!' He laughed, showing black teeth, then spat. 'And yet you have not asked me for proof. Why so?'

'We trust you.'

'"We trust you."' He laughed again. 'Imperialists! Always sweet words. Sweet words and then they kill you for a kopek. For a kopek! If you *were* the ones, you would *demand* proof.'

'We demand proof.'

'I have *proof,*' he said defiantly. He glanced from one man to the other, then lowered the rifle, turned and began moving quickly back towards the trees.

'Now what?' whispered O'Brian.

'God knows.'

'Can we get that rifle off him? Two of us, one of him?'

Kelso stared at him in astonishment. 'Don't even *think* it.'

'Boy, but he's quick, though, isn't he? And completely fucking crazy.' O'Brian gave a nervous giggle. 'Look at him. Now what's he doing?'

But he was doing nothing, merely standing impassively at the edge of the trees, waiting.

THERE didn't seem to be much else for them to do except follow him, which wasn't easy, given his speed across the ground, the roughness of the forest floor, the handicap of O'Brian's injured leg. Kelso carried the camera case. Once or twice they seemed to lose him, but never for long. He must have kept stopping to let them catch up.

After a few minutes they came back out on to the track, but further up, roughly midway between the abandoned Toyota and the empty settlement.

He didn't pause. He led them straight across the snowy track and into the trees on the other side.

This was not good, thought Kelso, as they passed out of the grey light and back into the shadows. Surreptitiously, without slackening pace, he put his hand into his pocket and tore a page out of his yellow notebook, screwed it into a ball and dropped it behind him. He did this every fifty yards or so – hare and hounds: an old school game – only now he was hare *and* hound.

O'Brian, panting at his back, whispered, 'Nice work.'

They emerged into a small clearing, with a wooden cabin in the centre. He had built this well – and recently, by the look of it – cannibalising the old encampment for his materials. Why he had done this, Kelso never discovered. Perhaps the other place was too full of ghosts. Or, maybe he wanted a spot even more secluded, and more easily defensible. In the silence, Kelso thought he could hear running water and he guessed they must be near the river.

The cabin was made of the familiar grey timber, with one small window and a door to suit his height, set a yard above the ground and approached by four wooden steps. At the base of these he picked up a branch and prodded deep into the snow. There was a spurt of white powder as something jumped and snapped. He withdrew the branch. Clamped around the end was a large animal trap, the rusty metal teeth stuck deep into the wood.

He laid this carefully to one side, climbed the steps to his door, unfastened the padlock and went inside. After a brief exchange of looks with O'Brian, Kelso followed, ducking his head to pass through the low entrance, emerging into the one small room. It was dark and cold and he could smell the insanity – he inhaled the lonely madness, as sharp and sour as the lingering stink of unwashed flesh. He put his hand to his mouth. Behind him he heard O'Brian suck in his breath.

Their host had lit a kerosene lamp. The whitened skulls of a bear and a wolf shone from the shadows. He put the notebook on the table, next to a half-eaten plate of some dark and bony fish, put a pot of water on the hob and bent to rekindle the old iron stove, keeping his rifle close to hand.

Kelso could imagine him an hour ago: hearing the distant sound of their car on the track, abandoning his meal, grabbing his gun and heading for the forest, his fire doused, his trap set –

There wasn't a bed, merely a thin mattress, leaking stuffing, rolled and tied with string. Beside it was an ancient Soviet-made transistor radio, the size of a packing case, and next to that a wind-up gramophone with a tarnished brass horn.

The Russian unfastened the satchel and took out the notebook. He opened it at the picture of the girl gymnasts in Red Square and held it up for them: there, you see? They nodded. He set it down on the table. Then he pulled on a length of greasy leather hanging round his neck and kept on pulling until he hauled from somewhere deep in the fetid folds of his clothes a small piece of clear plastic. He offered it to Kelso. It was warm from the heat of his body: the same picture, but folded very small, so that only Anna Safanova's face was visible.

'You are the ones,' he said. 'I am the one you seek. And now: the proof.'

He kissed the home-made locket and lowered it back into his clothes. Then, from the belt of his greatcoat, he drew out a short, wide-bladed knife with a leather hilt. He turned it, showing them the sharpness of the edge. He grinned at them. He kicked back the bit of carpet at his feet, dropped to his knees and prised up a crude trapdoor.

He reached down and pulled out a large and shabby suitcase.

HE unpacked his reliquary like a priest, reverently placing each object on the crude wooden table as if it were an altar.

The holy texts came out first: the thirteen volumes of Stalin's collected works and thoughts, the *Sochineniya*, published in Moscow after the war. He showed the title page of each book to Kelso and then to O'Brian. All of them were signed in the same way – 'To the future, J. V. Stalin' – and all, clearly, had been read and re-read endlessly. On some of the volumes, the spines were badly cracked or hanging off. The pages were swollen by markers and bent corners.

Then came the uniform, each part carefully wrapped in

yellowing tissue paper. A pressed grey tunic with red epaulets. A pair of black trousers, also pressed. A greatcoat. A pair of black leather boots, gleaming like polished anthracite. A marshal's cap. A gold star in a crimson leather case embossed with the hammer and sickle, which Kelso recognised as the Order of Hero of the Soviet Union.

And then came the mementoes. A photograph (in a wooden frame, glazed) of Stalin standing behind a desk: signed, like the books, 'To the future, J. V. Stalin'. A Dunhill pipe. An envelope containing a lock of coarse grey hair. And finally a stack of gramophone records, old 78s, as thick as dinner plates, each still in its original paper sleeve: 'Mother, the Fields are Dusty', 'I'm Waiting For You', 'Nightingale of the Taiga,' 'J. V. Stalin: Speech to the First All-Union Congress of Collective Farm Shock Workers, February 19 1933', 'J. V. Stalin: Report to the Eighteenth Congress of the Communist Party of the Soviet Union, March 10 1939' . . .

Kelso couldn't move. He couldn't speak. It was O'Brian who took the first step. He glanced at the Russian, touched himself on his chest, gestured at the table, and received in return a nod of approval. Tentatively, he reached out to pick up the photograph. Kelso could see what he was thinking: the likeness was indeed striking. Not exact, of course – no man ever looks exactly like his father – but there was *something* there, no doubt about it, even with the younger man's beard and straggling hair. Something in the cast of the eyes and the bone structure, perhaps, or in the play of the expression: a kind of ponderous agility, a genetic shadow that was beyond the skills of any actor.

The Russian grinned again at O'Brian. He picked up his knife and pointed at the photograph, then mimed hacking at his beard. Yes?

For a moment, Kelso wasn't sure what he meant, but O'Brian did. O'Brian knew at once.

Yes. He nodded vigorously. Oh, yes. Yes, please.

The Russian promptly scythed away a great swathe of coarse black facial hair and held it out, with childish pleasure, for their inspection. He repeated the stroke, again and again, and there was something shocking about the way he did this, in the casual manipulation of the razor-edged knife – this side, that, and then the throat – in the careless self-mutilation of it. *There is nothing*, thought Kelso, with a flash of certainty, *there is no act of violence this man is not capable of.* The Russian reached behind his head and grabbed his hair into a thick ponytail and sliced it off as close to the roots as he could. Then he crossed the cabin in a couple of strides, opened the door of the iron stove, and flung the mass of hair on to the burning wood where it flared for an instant before shriveling to dust and smoke.

'Bloody hell,' whispered Kelso. He watched, disbelieving, as O'Brian began opening the camera case. 'Oh no. Not that. You can't be serious.'

'I can.'

'But he's mad.'

'So are half the people we put on television.' O'Brian pushed a new cassette into the side of the camera and smiled as it clicked home. 'Showtime.'

Behind him, the Russian had his head bent over the bowl of hot water steaming on the stove. He had stripped to a dirty yellow vest and had lathered his face with something. The rasp of the knife-blade on his bristle made Kelso's own flesh ache.

'Look at him,' said Kelso. 'He probably doesn't even know what television *is*.'

'Fine by me.'

'God.' Kelso closed his eyes.

The Russian turned towards them, wiping himself on his shirt. His face was blotchy, beaded with pinheads of blood, but he had left himself a heavy moustache, as black and oily as a crow's wings, and the transformation was stunning. Here stood the Stalin of the 1920s: Stalin in his prime, an animal force. What was it Lenin had predicted? *'This Georgian will serve us a peppery stew.'*

He tucked his hair under the marshal's cap. He slipped on the tunic. A little loose around the front, perhaps, but otherwise a perfect fit. He buttoned it and strutted up and down the room a couple of times, his right hand circling modestly in an imperial wave.

He picked up a volume of the *Collected Works,* opened it at random, glanced at the page and handed it to Kelso.

Then he smiled, held up a finger, coughed into his hand, cleared his throat and began to speak. And he was good. Kelso could tell that straight away. He was not merely word perfect. He was better than that. He must have studied the recordings, hour after hour, year after year since childhood. He had the familiar, flat, remorseless delivery; the brutal, incantatory beat. He had the expression of heavy sarcasm, the dark humour, the strength, the *hate*.

'This Trotsky–Bukharin bunch of spies, murderers and wreckers,' he began slowly, 'who kow-towed to the foreign world, who were possessed by a slavish instinct to grovel before every foreign bigwig, and who were ready to enter his employ as a spy –' his voice began to rise ' – this handful of people who did not understand that the *humblest* Soviet citizen, being free from the fetters of capital, stands head and shoulders above any high-placed foreign *bigwig* whose neck wears the yoke of capitalist slavery –' and now he was shouting ' – who needs this *miserable* band of venal *slaves,* of what value can they be to the people, and whom can they demoralise?'

He glared around, defying any of them – Kelso with the open book, O'Brian with the camera to his eye, the table, the stove, the skulls – any one of them to dare to answer him back.

He straightened, thrusting out his chin.

'In 1937 Tukhachevsky, Yakir, Uborevich and other fiends were sentenced to be shot. After that, the elections to the Supreme Soviet of the U.S.S.R. were held. In these elections, 98.6 per cent of the total vote was cast for the Soviet power!

'At the beginning of 1938 Rosengoltz, Rykov, Bukharin and other fiends were sentenced to be shot. After that, the elections to the Supreme Soviets of the Union Republics were held. In these elections 99.4 per cent of the total vote was cast for the Soviet power! Where are the symptoms of demoralisation, we would like to know?'

He placed his fist on his heart.

'Such was the *inglorious* end of the opponents of the line of our Party, who finished up as *enemies of the people!'*

'*Stormy applause,*' read Kelso. '*All the delegates rise and cheer the speaker. Shouts of "Hurrah for Comrade Stalin!" "Long live Comrade Stalin!" "Hurrah for the Central Committee of our Party!"*'

The Russian swayed before the rhythm of the dead crowd. He could hear the roars, the stamping feet, the cheers. He nodded modestly. He smiled. He applauded in return. The imaginary tumult rang around the narrow cabin and rolled out across the snowy clearing to split the silent trees.

Chapter Twenty-seven

FELIKS SUVORIN'S AIRCRAFT dropped through the base of low cloud and banked to starboard, following the line of the White Sea coast.

A stain of rust appeared in the snowy wilderness and spread, and he began to make out details. Drooping cranes, empty submarine pens, derelict construction sheds ... Severodvinsk, it must be – Brezhnev's big nuclear junkyard, just along the coast from Archangel, where they built the subs in the 1970s that were supposed to bring the imperialists to their knees.

He stared down at it as he fastened his seatbelt. Some mafia middlemen had been sniffing around up here, about a year ago, trying to buy a warhead for the Iraqis. He remembered the case. Chechens in the taiga! Unbelievable! And yet they would manage it one day, he thought. There was too much spare hardware, too little supervision, too much money chasing it. The law of supply and demand would mate with the law of averages and they would get something, sometime.

The wingflaps shuddered. There was a whine of cables. They descended further, yawing and pitching through the snowstorm. Severodvinsk slid away. He could see grey discs of freezing water, flat blank swampland, white-capped trees and more trees, running away for ever. What could live down there? Nothing, surely? No one. They were at the edge of the earth.

The old plane trundled on for another ten minutes, barely fifty yards above the forest ceiling, and then ahead Suvorin saw a pattern of lights in the snow.

It was a military airfield, secluded in the trees, with a snow plough parked at the edge of the apron. The runway had just been cleared but already a thin white skin was beginning to form again. They came in low to take a look then lifted once more, the engine straining, and turned to make a final approach. As they did so, Suvorin had a tilting glimpse of Archangel – of distant, shadowy tower blocks and filthy chimneys – and then in they came, bouncing off the runway, once, twice, before settling, turning, the propellers conjuring miniature blizzards from the snow.

When the pilot switched off the engine there was a quality of silence that Suvorin had never experienced before. Always in Moscow there was something to hear, even in the so-called still of night – a bit of traffic, maybe, a neighbour's quarrel. But not here. Here the quiet was absolute, and he loathed it. He found himself talking just to fill it.

'Good work,' he called up to the pilot. 'We made it.'

'You're welcome. By the way, there's a message for you from Moscow. You're to call the colonel before you go. Make any sense?'

'Before I go?'

'That's it.'

Before I go where?

There wasn't enough room to stand upright. Suvorin had to crouch. Drawn up beside a big hangar he could see a line of bi-planes painted in arctic camouflage.

The door at the back of the plane swung open. The temperature dropped about five degrees. Snowflakes billowed up the fuselage. Suvorin grabbed his attaché case and jumped down to the concrete. A technician in a fur hat pointed him towards the hangar. Its heavy sliding door was pulled a quarter open. Waiting in the shadows, next to a couple of jeeps, sheltering from the snow, was a reception committee: three men in MVD uniforms with AK-74 assault rifles, a guy from the militia and, most bizarrely, an elderly lady in thick male clothing, hunched like a vulture, leaning on a stick.

SOMETHING had happened, Suvorin could tell that right away, and whatever it was, it was not good. He knew it when he offered his hand to the senior Interior Ministry soldier – a surly-lipped, bull-necked young man named Major Kretov – and received in reply a salute of just sufficient idleness to imply an insult. And as for Kretov's two men, they never even bothered to acknowledge his arrival. They were too busy unloading a small armoury from the back of one of the jeeps – extra magazines for their AK-74s, pistols, flares and a big old RP46 machine gun with cannisters of belt-fed ammunition and a metal bipod.

'So, what are we expecting here, major?' Suvorin said, in an effort to be friendly. 'A small war?'

'We can discuss it on the way.'

'I'd prefer to discuss it now.'

Kretov hesitated. Clearly he would have liked to tell Suvorin to go to hell, but they had the same rank, and besides he hadn't quite got the measure yet of this civilian-soldier in his expensive western clothes. 'Well, quickly then.' He clicked his fingers irritably in the direction of the gangly young militia man. 'Tell him what's happened.'

'And you are?' said Suvorin.

The militia man came to attention. 'Lieutenant Korf, major.'

'So, Korf?'

The lieutenant delivered his report quickly, nervously.

Shortly after midday, the Archangel militia had been notified by Moscow central headquarters that two foreigners were believed to be in the vicinity of the city, possibly seeking to make contact with a person or persons named Safanov or Safanova. He had undertaken the inquiry himself. Only one such citizen had been located: the witness Vavara Safanova – he indicated the old woman – who had been picked up within ninety minutes of receipt of the telex from Moscow. She had confirmed that two foreigners had been to see her and had left her barely an hour earlier.

Suvorin smiled in a kindly way at Vavara Safanova. 'And what were you able to tell them, Comrade Safanova?'

She looked at the ground.

'She told them her daughter was dead,' cut in Kretov, impatiently. 'Died in childbirth, forty-five years ago, having a kid. A boy. Now: can we go? I've got all this out of her already.'

A boy, thought Suvorin. It had to be. A girl wouldn't have mattered. But a boy. An heir –

'And the boy lives?'

'Reared in the forest, she says. Like a wolf.'

Suvorin turned reluctantly from the silent old woman to the major. 'And Kelso and O'Brian have gone into the forest to find this "wolf", presumably?'

'They're about three hours ahead of us.' Kretov had a large-scale map spread over the hood of the nearest jeep. 'This is the road,' he said. 'There's no way out except back the way they went, and the snow will hold them up. Don't worry. We'll have them by nightfall.'

'And how do we reach them? Can we use a helicopter?'

Kretov winked at one of his men. 'I fear the major from

Moscow has not adequately studied our terrain. The taiga is not well supplied with *helicopter pads.*'

Suvorin tried to stay calm. 'Then we reach them how?'

'By snow plough,' said Kretov, as if it was obvious. 'Four of us can just fit in the cab. Or three, if you prefer not to wet your fancy footwear.'

Again, and with difficulty, Suvorin controlled his temper. 'So what's the plan? We clear a way for them to drive back into town behind us, is that it?'

'If that proves necessary.'

'If that proves necessary,' repeated Suvorin, slowly. Now he was beginning to understand. He gazed into the major's cold grey eyes, then looked at the two MVD men who had finished unloading the jeep. 'So what are you people running nowadays? Death squads, is that it? It's a little bit of South America you've got going up here?'

Kretov began folding up the map. 'We must move out immediately.'

'I need to speak to Moscow.'

'We've already spoken to Moscow.'

'*I* need to speak to Moscow, major, and if you attempt to leave without me, I can assure you that you will spend the next few years *building* helicopter pads.'

'I don't think so.'

'If it comes to a trial of strength between the SVR and the MVD, be aware of this: the SVR will win every time.' Suvorin turned and bowed to Vavara Safanova. 'Thank you for your assistance.' And then, to Korf, who was watching all this, goggle-eyed: 'Take her home, please. You did well.'

'I told them,' said the old woman suddenly. 'I told them nothing good could come of it.'

'That may be true,' said Suvorin. 'All right, lieutenant, off you go. Now,' he said to Kretov, 'where's that fucking telephone?'

O'BRIAN had insisted on shooting another twenty minutes of footage. By sign language he had persuaded the Russian to pack up his relics and then to unpack them again, holding each object up to the camera and explaining what it was. ('His book.' 'His picture.' 'His hair.' Each was dutifully kissed and arranged on the altar.) Then O'Brian showed him how he wanted him to sit at the table smoking his pipe and to read from Anna Safanova's journal, (*'Remember Comrade Stalin's historic words to Gorky: "It is the task of the proletarian state to produce the engineers of human souls . . ."'*)

'Great,' said O'Brian, moving around him with the camera. 'Fantastic. Isn't this fantastic, Fluke?'

'No,' said Kelso, 'it's a bloody circus.'

'Ask him a couple of questions, Fluke.'

'I shall not.'

'Go on. Just a couple. Ask him what he thinks of the new Russia.'

'No.'

'Two questions and we're out of here. I promise.'

Kelso hesitated. The Russian stared at him, stroking his moustache with the stem of his pipe. His teeth were yellowish and stumpy. The underside of his moustache was wet with saliva.

'My colleague would like to know,' Kelso said, 'if you have heard of the great changes that have taken place in Russia and what you think of them.'

For a moment, he was silent. Then he turned from Kelso and stared directly into the lens.

'One feature of the history of the old Russia,' he began,

'was the continual beatings she suffered. All beat her for her backwardness. She was beaten because to do so was profitable and could be done with impunity. Such is the law of the exploiters – to beat the backward and the weak. It is the jungle law of capitalism. You are backward, you are weak – therefore you are wrong; hence, you can be beaten and enslaved.'

He sat back, sucking on his pipe, his eyes half closed. O'Brian was standing directly behind Kelso, holding the camera, and Kelso felt the pressure of his hand on his shoulder, urging him to ask another question.

'I don't understand,' Kelso said. 'What are you saying? That the new Russia is beaten and enslaved? But surely most people would say the opposite: that however hard life might be, at least they now have freedom?'

A slow smile, directly into the camera. The Russian removed his pipe from his mouth and leaned forwards, jabbing it at Kelso's chest.

'That is very good. But, unfortunately, freedom alone is not enough, by far. If there is a shortage of bread, a shortage of butter and fats, a shortage of textiles, and if housing conditions are bad, freedom will not carry you very far. It is very difficult, comrades, to live on freedom alone.'

O'Brian whispered, 'What's he saying? Does it make sense?'

'It makes a kind of sense. But it's odd.'

O'Brian persuaded Kelso to ask a couple more questions, each of which drew similar, stilted replies, and then, when Kelso refused to translate any more, he insisted on taking the Russian outside for a final shot.

Kelso watched them for a minute through the narrow, dirty window: O'Brian making a mark in the snow and then walking towards the cabin, returning, pointing to the line, trying to make the Russian understand what he wanted him to do. It was almost as if he had been expecting them, Kelso thought. *'You are the ones,'* he had said. *'You are truly the ones . . .'*

'This is the book of which it is spoken . . .'

He had been educated, obviously – indoctrinated, perhaps, a better word. He could read. He seemed to have been brought up with a sense of destiny: a messianic certainty that one day strangers would appear in the forest, bearing a book, and that they, whoever they were – even if they were a couple of imperialists – *they would be the ones . . .*

The Russian was apparently in a great good humour, bringing his index finger up close to his eye and wiggling it at the camera, grinning, stooping and making a snowball, tossing it playfully at O'Brian's back.

Homo Sovieticus, thought Kelso. Soviet man.

He tried to remember something, a passage in Volkogonov's biography, quoting Sverdlov, who had been exiled with Stalin to Siberia in 1914. Stalin wouldn't associate with the other Bolsheviks, that was what had struck Sverdlov. Here he was: unknown, almost forty, had never done a day's work in his life, had no skills, no profession, yet he would simply go off on his own to hunt or fish, and 'gave the impression that he was waiting for something to happen'.

Hunting. Fishing. *Waiting*.

Kelso turned from the window and quickly slipped the notebook back into the satchel, stuffed the satchel into his jacket. He checked the window again, then stepped over to the table and began leafing through Stalin's *Collected Works*.

It took him a couple of minutes to find what he was looking for: a pair of dog-eared pages in different volumes, both passages heavily underlined with black pencil. And it was as he thought: the Russian's first answer was a direct quotation from a Stalin speech – to the All-Union Conference of Managers of Socialist Industry, February 4 1931, to be exact – while the second was lifted from an address to three thousand Stakhanovites, November 17 1935.

The son was speaking the words of the Father.

He heard the sound of Stalin's boots on the wooden steps and hastily replaced the books.

SUVORIN followed one of the MVD men out of the hangar and across the runway towards a single-storey block next to the control tower. The wind tore through his coat. Snow leaked through the tops of his shoes. By the time they reached the office he was freezing. A young corporal looked up as they came in, without interest. Suvorin was beginning to feel thoroughly sick of this tin pot, backwoods town, this *Archangel*. He slammed the door.

'Salute, man, damn you, when an officer comes into the room!'

The corporal leapt up so quickly he knocked over his chair.

'Get me a line to Moscow. Now. Then wait outside. Both of you wait outside.'

Suvorin didn't start to dial until they had gone. He picked up the chair and righted it and sat down heavily. The corporal had been reading a German pornographic magazine. A stockinged foot poked out glossily from beneath a pile of flight logs. He could hear the number ringing faintly. There was heavy static on the line.

'Sergo? It's Suvorin. Give me the chief.'

A moment later, Arsenyev came through. 'Feliks, listen.' His tone was strained. 'I've been trying to reach you. You've heard the news?'

'I've heard the news.'

'Unbelievable! You've talked to the others? You must move quickly.'

'Yes, I've talked to them, and I mean to say, what is this, colonel?' Suvorin had to put his finger into his other ear and shout into the receiver. 'What's going on? I've landed in the middle of nowhere and I'm looking out of the window here at three cut-throats loading a snow plough with enough firepower to take out a battalion of NATO –'

'Feliks,' said Arsenyev, 'it's out of our hands.'

'So what is this? Now we are supposed to take our orders from the MVD?'

'They're not MVD,' said Arsenyev quietly. 'They're Special Forces in MVD uniforms.'

'Spetsnaz?' Suvorin put his hand to his head. Spetsnaz. Commandos. Alpha Brigade. *Killers.* 'Who decided to turn them loose?'

As if he didn't know.

Arsenyev said, 'Guess.'

'And was His Excellency drunk as usual? Or was this a rare interlude of sobriety?'

'Have a care, major!' Arsenyev's voice was sharp.

The snow plough's heavy diesel cracked into life. The revving engine shook the double glass, briefly obliterating Arsenyev's voice. Big yellow headlights turned and flashed through the snow then began moving ponderously across the runway towards Suvorin.

'So what are my orders exactly?'

'To proceed as you think fit, using all force necessary.'

'All force necessary to achieve what?'

'Whatever you think fit.'

'Which is what?'

'That's for you to decide. I'm relying on you, major. I'm allowing you complete operational freedom –'

Oh but he was a wily one, wasn't he? The wiliest. A real survivor. Suvorin lost his temper.

'So how many are we supposed to kill then, colonel? One man is it? Two? *Three?*'

Arsenyev was shocked. He was profoundly disturbed. If the tape of the call was ever played back – which it would be, the following day – his expression would be obvious for all to hear. 'Nobody said anything about killing, major! Has anyone there said such a thing? Have I?'

'No, you haven't,' said Suvorin, finding within himself a depth of sarcasm and bitterness he didn't know he possessed, 'so obviously whatever happens is my responsibility alone. I haven't been guided by my superior officers in any way. And neither, I am sure, has the exemplary Major Kretov!'

Arsenyev started to say something but his voice was drowned out by the roar of the engine being revved again. The snow plough was nearly up against the window now. Its blade rose and fell like a guillotine. Suvorin could see Kretov in the driver's seat, passing his finger across his throat. The horn sounded. Suvorin waved at him irritably and turned his back.

'Say again, colonel.'

But the line was dead and all attempts to reconnect it failed. And that was the sound that Suvorin afterwards could never quite get out of his ears, as he sat squashed in the jumpseat of the snow plough, bouncing into the forest: the cold, implacable buzz of a number unobtainable.

Chapter Twenty-eight

THE SNOW HAD eased and it was much colder – it must have been minus three or four. Kelso pulled up his hood and set off as fast as he could towards the edge of the clearing. Ahead of him through the trees his paper trail of yellow markers blossomed every fifty yards in the snowy undergrowth like winter flowers.

Getting out of the cabin had not been easy. When he had told the Russian they needed to go back to their car – 'only to collect some more equipment, comrade,' he had added, quickly – he had received a look of such glinting suspicion he had almost quailed. But somehow he held the other man's gaze and eventually, after a final, searching glance, he was given a brief nod of permission. And even then O'Brian had lingered – 'you know, we could do with one more shot from over here . . .' – until Kelso had grabbed him hard by the elbow and steered him towards the door. The Russian watched them go, puffing on his pipe.

Kelso could hear O'Brian, breathing hard, stumbling after him, but he didn't stop to let him catch up until they were out of sight of the hut.

O'Brian said, 'You got the notebook?'

Kelso patted the front of his jacket. 'In here.'

'Oh, nice work,' said O'Brian. He performed a little victory shuffle in the snow. 'Jesus, this is a story, isn't it? This is a hell of a story.'

'A hell of a story,' repeated Kelso, but all he wanted was to get away. He resumed his walk, but more urgently now, his legs aching with the effort of pushing through the snow.

They came out on to the track and there was the Toyota, a hundred yards away, wrapped in a wet, white layer more than an inch deep, thicker towards the rear where the wind was blowing from, and as they came closer they could see that the surface was beginning to crystalise to ice. It was still tilting forwards, its back tyres almost clear of the snow, and it took them a while to locate all the damage. The Russian had fired three bullets into the car. One had blown off the lock on the back door. Another had opened up the driver's side. A third had gone through the hood into the engine, presumably to silence the alarm.

'That crazy sonofabitch,' said O'Brian, staring at the ugly holes. 'This is a forty-thousand-dollar vehicle –'

He squeezed behind the steering wheel, put the key in the ignition and turned it. Nothing. Not even a click.

'No wonder he didn't mind if we came back to the car,' said Kelso, quietly. 'He knew we weren't going anywhere.'

O'Brian had started looking worried again. He struggled out of the front seat and sank deep into the drift. He waded round to the back, lifted the rear door and blew out a long sigh of relief, his breath condensing in the cold air.

'Well, it doesn't look as though he's damaged the Inmarsat, thank Christ. That's something.' He glanced around, frowning.

Kelso said, 'Now what?'

O'Brian muttered, 'Trees.'

'*Trees?*'

'Yeah. The satellite's not straight above our heads, remember? She's over the equator. This far north, that means you need to keep the dish at a real low angle to send a signal. Trees, if they're close up – they, ah, well, they kind of *get in the way.*' He turned to Kelso, and Kelso could have murdered him then: killed him just for the nervous, sheepish grin on his big, handsome, stupid face. 'We're gonna need a space, Fluke. Sorry.'

A space?

Yeah. A space. They would have to return to the clearing.

O'Brian insisted they took the rest of the equipment back with them. That, after all, was what Kelso had told the Russian they were going to do, and they didn't want to make him suspicious, did they? Besides, no way was O'Brian going to leave over a hundred-grand's-worth of electronic gear sitting in a shot-up Toyota in the middle of nowhere. He wasn't going to let it out of his *sight*.

And so they struggled back along the track, O'Brian in the lead carrying the Inmarsat and the heavier of the big cases, with the Toyota's battery, wrapped in a black plastic sheet, jammed under his arm. Kelso had the camera case and the lap-top editing machine and he did his best to keep up, but it was heavy going. His arms ached. The snow sucked at him. Soon, O'Brian had turned into the forest and was out of sight, while Kelso had to keep stopping to transfer the damned bloody swine of an edit case from one hand to the other. He sweated and cursed. On his way back through the trees he stumbled over a hidden root and dropped to his knees.

By the time he reached the clearing, O'Brian already had the satellite dish connected to the battery and was trying to twist it into the right direction. The trajectory of the antenna pointed directly at the snowy tops of some big firs, about fifty yards away, and he was hunched over it, his jaw working with anxiety, holding the compass in one hand, pressing switches with the other. The snow had almost stopped and there was a faint blueness to the freezing air. Behind him, framed against the shadows of the trees, was the grey wooden cabin – utterly still, deserted apparently, apart from the thread of smoke rising from its narrow iron chimney.

Kelso let the cases drop and leaned forwards, his hands on his knees, trying to recover his breath.

'Anything?' he said.

'Nope.'

Kelso groaned.

A bloody circus –

'If that thing doesn't work,' he said, 'we're here for the duration, you realise that? We'll be stuck here till next April with nothing to do except listen to extracts from Stalin's *Complete Works*.'

It was such an appalling prospect, he actually found himself laughing, and for the second time that day, O'Brian joined in.

'Oh man,' he said, 'the things we do for glory.'

But he didn't laugh for long, and the machine stayed silent.

AND it was in this silence, about thirty seconds later, that Kelso thought he heard again the faint sound of rushing water.

He held up his hand.

'What?' said O'Brian.

'The river.' He closed his eyes and raised his face to the sky, straining to hear. 'The river, I *think –*'

It was hard to separate it from the noise of the wind in the trees. But it was more sustained than wind, and deeper, and it seemed to be coming from somewhere on the other side of the cabin.

'Let's go for it,' said O'Brian. He snatched the pair of crocodile clips off the battery terminals and began rapidly rolling up the cable. 'Makes sense, if you think of it. Must be how he gets about. A boat.'

Kelso hoisted the two cases and O'Brian called out, 'Watch yourself, Fluke.'

'What?'

'Traps. Remember? He's got this whole wood wired.'

Kelso stood, looking at the ground, uncertain, remembering the spurt of snow, the snap of the metal jaws. But it was hopeless to worry about that, he thought, just as there was no way they could avoid passing directly by the door of the cabin. He waited for O'Brian to finish packing up the Inmarsat, and then they started walking together, treading warily. And Kelso could sense the Russian everywhere now: at the window of his squalid hut, in the crawlspace underneath it, behind the stack of cordwood piled against the back wall, in the dank and mossy water barrel and in the darkness of the nearby trees. He could imagine the rifle trained on his back and he was acutely aware of the softness of his own skin, of its babyish vulnerability.

They reached the edge of the clearing and followed the perimeter of the forest. Dense undergrowth. Fallen, rotted logs. Strange white fungoid growths like melted faces. And occasionally, in the distance, crashes, as the wind shifted and brought down falls of frozen snow. It was impossible to see much further than a hand's reach. They couldn't find a path. There was nothing to do but plunge between the trees.

O'Brian went first and had the worst of it, lugging the two heavy cases and the big battery, having to twist his bulky body sideways to edge through the narrow gaps, sometimes left, sometimes right, ducking abruptly, no free hand to protect his face from the low branches. Kelso tried to follow in his footsteps and after half a dozen paces he was conscious of the forest swinging shut behind them like a solid door.

They stumbled on for a few minutes in the semi-darkness. Kelso wanted to stop and transfer the edit machine to his other hand but he didn't dare lose sight of O'Brian's back and soon he had forgotten about everything except the pain in his right shoulder and the acid in his lungs. Trickles of sweat and melted snow were running into his eyes, blurring his vision, and he was trying to bring his arm up to wipe his forehead on his wet sleeve when O'Brian gave a shout and lurched forwards, and suddenly – it was like passing through a wall – the trees parted and they were in the light again, standing on the ridge of a steep bank that fell away at their feet to a tumbling plain of yellowish-grey water a clear quarter-mile across.

IT was an awesome sight – God's work, truly – like finding a cathedral in the middle of a jungle – and for a while neither man spoke. Then O'Brian set down his cases and the battery and took out his compass. He showed it to Kelso. They were on the northern bank of the Dvina facing almost exactly due south.

Ten yards below them, and a hundred yards to their left, dragged clear of the water and covered in a dark green tarpaulin, was a small boat. It looked as though it had been taken out for the winter, and that would make sense, thought Kelso, because already ice was beginning to extend out into the river – a shelf maybe ten or fifteen yards across that seemed to be widening even as he watched.

On the opposite bank there was a similar strip of whiteness, and then the dark line of the trees began again.

Kelso raised his binoculars and inspected the far shore for signs of habitation but there was none. It looked utterly forbidding and gloomy. A wilderness.

He lowered the binoculars. 'Who're you going to call?'

'America. Get them to call the bureau in Moscow.' O'Brian already had the case of the Inmarsat open and was slotting together the plastic dish. He had taken off his gloves. In the extreme cold his hands looked raw. 'When's it gonna be dark?'

Kelso looked at his watch. 'It's nearly five now,' he said. 'An hour perhaps.'

'Okay, let's face it, even if the battery holds on this thing and I get through to the States and they fix us a rescue party – we're stuck here for the night. Unless we take some pretty dramatic action.'

'Meaning?'

'We take his boat.'

'You'd steal his boat?'

'I'd borrow it, sure.' He sat on his haunches, unwrapping the battery, refusing to meet Kelso's eyes. 'Oh, come on, man, don't look at me like that. Where's the harm? He's not going to need it till the spring anyhow – not if the temperature keeps on dropping like this – that river'll be iced over in a day or two. Besides, he shot up our car, didn't he? We'll use his boat – that's fair.'

'And you can work a boat, can you?'

'I can work a boat, I can work a camera, I can make pictures fly through the air – I'm fucking superman. Yeah, I can sail. Let's do it.'

'And what about him? He'll just stand there, will he, while we do it? He'll wave us off?' Kelso glanced back the way they had come. 'You realise he's probably watching us right now?'

'Okay. So you go keep him talking while I get everything ready.'

'Oh, thank you,' said Kelso. 'Thank you very much indeed.'

'Well, at least I've had a fucking idea. What's yours?'

A fair point, Kelso had to concede.

He hesitated, then focused his binoculars on the boat.

So this was how the Russian survived – how he made his occasional forays into the outside world. This was how he acquired the fuel for his lamp, the tobacco for his pipe, the ammunition for his guns, the battery for his transistor radio. What did he use for money? Did he barter what he caught or trapped. Or had the encampment been set up in the 1950s with a treasury of some sort – NKVD gold – which they had been eking out ever since?

The boat was concealed in a small depression, protected from the river by a low screen of trees: to anyone drifting by, she would be invisible. She was resting on her keel, propped up to port and starboard by logs – a sturdy-looking vessel, not big, room for four people, at a pinch. A bulge at her stern suggested an outboard motor, and if that was the case, and if O'Brian could make it work, they might reach Archangel in a couple of hours – less, probably, with the current flowing so fast through its narrowing channel.

He thought of the crosses in the cemetery, the dates, the obliterated faces.

It did not look as though many people had ever left this place.

It was worth a try.

'All right,' he said, reluctantly, 'let's do it.'

'That's my boy.'

When he stepped back into the trees, he left O'Brian

aiming the antenna across the river, and he had not gone far when he heard behind him the blissful, rising note of the Inmarsat locking on to the satellite.

THE snow plough was coming on fast now, thirty, forty miles an hour, rushing down the track, throwing up a great white bow wave of freezing surf that went smashing into the trees on either side. Kretov was driving. His men were jammed together next to him, nursing their guns. Suvorin was hanging on to the metal moorings of the jump seat at the back of the cab, the barrel of the RP46 poking into his thigh, feeling sick from the vibration and the diesel fumes. He marvelled at the complexities that had overwhelmed his life in so short a time, and pondered nervously the wisdom of the old Russian proverb: 'We are born in a clear field and die in a dark forest.'

He had plenty of time for his thoughts because none of the other three had addressed a word to him since they left the airfield. They passed chewing gum to one another and TU-144 cigarettes and talked quietly so he couldn't hear what they were saying above the racket of the engine. An intimate trio, he thought: clearly a partnership with some history. Where had they been last? Grozny, maybe, taking Moscow's peace to the Chechen rebels? (*'The terrorist gunmen all died at the scene . . .'*) In which case this would be a holiday for them. A picnic in the woods. And who was giving them their orders? *Guess . . .*

Arsenyev's joke.

It was hot in the cab. The single windscreen wiper batted away the pawprints of snow with a soporific beat.

He tried to shift his leg away from the machine gun.

Serafima had been on at him for months to get out of the

service and make some money – her father knew a man on the board of a big privatised energy consortium and, well, let's just say, my dear Feliks, that – how should we put this? – a number of *favours* are owed. So what would that be worth, papa, exactly? Ten times his official salary and a tenth of the work? To hell with Yasenevo. Perhaps it was time.

A heavy male voice started grunting from the radio. Suvorin leaned forwards. He couldn't make out exactly what was being said. It sounded like co-ordinates. Kretov was holding the microphone in one hand, steering with the other, craning his neck to study the map on the knee of the man sitting next to him, watching the road. 'Sure, sure. No problem.' He hung up.

Suvorin said, 'What was that?'

'Ah,' said Kretov, in mock-surprise, 'you're still here? You got it, Aleksey?' This was to the man with the map, and then, to Suvorin, 'That was the listening post at Onega. They just intercepted a satellite transmission.'

'Fifteen miles, major. It's right on the river.'

'You see?' said Kretov, grinning at Suvorin in the mirror. 'What did I tell you? Home by nightfall.'

Chapter Twenty-nine

KELSO CAME OUT of the trees and walked towards the wooden cabin. The surface of the snow had frozen to a thin crust and the wind had picked up slightly, sending little twisters of powder dancing across the clearing. Rising from the iron chimney the thin brown coil of smoke jerked and snagged in the breeze.

'When one approaches Him, do so openly.' That was the advice of the maidservant, Valechka. *'He hates it when people creep up on Him. If a door has to be knocked upon, knock upon it loudly . . .'*

Kelso tried his best to make his rubber boots thump on the wooden steps, and he hammered on the door with his gloved fist. There was no reply.

Now what?

He knocked again, waited, then raised the latch and pushed open the door, and immediately, the now-familiar smell – cold, close, *animal*, with an underlay of stale pipe tobacco – rose to overwhelm him.

The cabin was empty. The rifle was gone. It looked as though the Russian had been working at his table: papers were laid out, and a couple of stubby pencils.

Kelso stood just inside the doorway, eyeing the papers, trying to decide what to do. He checked over his shoulder. There was no sign of movement in the clearing. The Russian was probably down at the river's edge, spying on O'Brian. This was their only tactical advantage, he thought: the fact that there were two of them and only one of him and he couldn't watch them both at once. Hesitantly, he stepped over to the table.

He only meant to look for a minute, and probably that was all he did – just long enough to run his fingers through it all:

A pair of passports – red, stiff-backed, six inches by four, lion-crested, marked 'PASS' and 'NORGE', issued in Bergen, 1968 – a young couple, identical-looking: long hair, blond, hippyish, the girl quite pretty in a washed-out kind of way; he didn't register their names; entered the USSR via Leningrad, June 1969 –

Identity papers – old-style, Soviet Union, three different men: the first, a youngish, jug-eared fellow in spectacles, a student by the look of him; the second, old, in his sixties, weathered, self-reliant, a sailor perhaps; the third, bug-eyed, unkempt, a gypsy or a drifter; the names a blur –

And, finally, a stack of sheets, which, as he fanned them out, he saw were six sets of documents, of five or six pages each, pinned together and written in pencil or ink, in various hands – this one neat, that one hesitant, another a wild and desperate scrawl – but always, at the top of the first sheet, in neat Cyrillic capitals, the same word: *'Confession'*.

Kelso could feel the freezing draught from the open door shifting the hairs on the back of his scalp.

He replaced the pages carefully and backed away from them, his hands raised slightly as if to ward them off, and at the doorway he turned and stumbled out on to the steps. He sat down on the weathered planking and when he raised the binoculars and scanned the rim of the clearing he found that he was shaking.

He stayed there for a couple of minutes, recovering his nerve. It occurred to him that what he ought to do – the calm, rational, sensible thing: the not-leaping-to-any-hysterical-conclusions kind of thing, that a serious scholar would do – was to return and briefly make a note of the names for checking later.

So when he had satisfied himself for the twentieth time that not a soul was moving in the trees, he stood and ducked back through the low door, and the first thing he saw on re-entry was the rifle propped against the wall, and the second was the Russian, sitting at the table, perfectly still, watching him.

'He possessed in a high degree the gift for silence,' according to his secretary, *'and in this respect he was unique in a country where everybody talks far too much . . .'*

He was still in full uniform, still in his greatcoat and cap. The gold star of the Order of Hero of the Soviet Union was pinned to his lapel and shone in the dull light of the kerosene lamp.

How had he done that?

Kelso started gabbling into the silence. 'Comrade – you – I'm startled – I – came to find you – I wanted –' He fumbled with the zipper on the front of his jacket and held out the satchel. 'I wanted to return to you the papers of your mother, Anna Mikhailovna Safanova –'

Time stretched. Half a minute passed, a minute, and then the Russian said, softly, 'Good, comrade,' and made a note on the sheet of paper beside him. He indicated the table and Kelso took a pace towards it and laid the satchel down, like an offering placed to appease some unreliable and vengeful god.

Another endless silence followed.

'Capitalism,' said the Russian eventually, putting down his stub of pencil and reaching for his pipe, 'is thievery. And imperialism is the highest form of capitalism. Thus it follows that the imperialist is the greatest thief of all mankind. Steal a man's papers, he will. Oh, easily! Pick the last kopek from yer pocket! Or steal a man's boat, eh, comrade?'

He winked at Kelso and continued staring at him as he struck a match, sucking the fire into the bowl of his pipe, producing great spurts of smoke and flame.

'Close the door would you, comrade?'

It was beginning to get dark.

If we have to stay here the night, thought Kelso, we shall never leave.

Where the hell was O'Brian?

'Now,' the Russian continued, 'and this is the decisive question, comrade: how do we protect ourselves from these capitalists, these imperialists, these thieves? And we say the answer to this decisive question must be equally decisive.' He extinguished the match with one shake and leaned forwards. 'We protect ourselves from these capitalists, these imperialists, and these stinking, crawling thieves of all mankind only by the most ferocious vigilance. Take, for example, the Norway couple, with their serpenty smiles – crawling on their maggoty bellies through the undergrowth to ask for "directions, comrade," if you please! On a "walking holiday" if you please!'

He waved their open passports in Kelso's face and Kelso had a second glimpse of the two young people, the man in a psychedelic headband –

'Are we such *fools*,' he demanded, 'such backward *primitives*, not to recognise the capitalist–imperialist thief–spy when it worms its way among us? No, comrade, we are not such backward primitives! To such people we administer a hard lesson in socialist realities – I have their confessions here before me, they denied it at first but they admitted it all in the end – and we need say no more of them. They are as Lenin predicted they would be: dust on the dunghill of history. Nor need we say anything of him!' He waved a set of identity papers – the older man. 'And nor of him! Nor him!' The faces of the victims flashed briefly. '*That*,' said the Russian, 'is our decisive answer to the decisive question posed by all capitalists, imperialists and stinking thieves!'

He sat back with his arms folded, smiling grimly.

The rifle was almost within Kelso's reach but he didn't move. It might not be loaded. And even if it was loaded he wouldn't know how to fire it. And even if he fired it he knew he could never injure the Russian: he was a supernatural force. One minute he was ahead of you, one minute behind; now he was in the trees and now he was here, sitting at his table, poring over his collection of confessions, making the occasional note.

'Worse by far however,' said the Russian after a while, 'is the canker of the right-deviationism.' He relit his pipe, sucking noisily on the stem. 'And here Golub was the first.'

'Golub was the first,' repeated Kelso, numbly.

He was remembering the row of crosses: T. Y. Golub, his face blacked out, died November-the-something, 1961.

The essence of Stalin's success was really very simple, he thought, built around an insight that could be reduced to a mere three words: *people fear death*.

'Golub was the first to succumb to the classic conciliationist tendencies of the right-deviationism. Of course, I was merely a child at the time, but his whining still clamours in my ears: "Oh, comrades, they are saying in the villages that Comrade Stalin's body has been removed from his rightful place next to Lenin! Oh, comrades, what are we going to do? It is hopeless, comrades! They will come and they will kill us all! It's time for us to give up!"

'Have you ever seen fishermen when a storm is brewing on a great river? I have seen them many a time. In the face of a storm one group of fishermen will muster all their forces, encourage their fellows and boldly put out to meet the storm: "Cheer up, lads, hold tight to the tiller, cut the waves, we'll pull her through!" But there is another type of fishermen – those who, on sensing a storm, lose heart, begin to snivel and demoralise their own ranks: "What a misfortune, a storm is brewing; lie down, boys, in the bottom of the boat, shut your eyes; let's hope she'll make the shore somehow."'

The Russian spat on the floor.

'Chizhikov took him out into the dark part of the forest that very night and in the morning there was a cross and that was the end of Golub and that put an end to the bleatings of the right-deviationists – even that old hag his widow put a sock in her mouth after that. And for a few years more, the steady work went on, under our four-fold slogans: the slogan of *the fight against defeatism and complacency*, the slogan of *the struggle for self-sufficiency*, the slogan of *constructive self-criticism is the foundation of our Party*, and the slogan of *out of the fire comes steel*. And then the sabotage began.'

'Ah,' said Kelso. 'The sabotage. Of course.'

'It began with the poisoning of the sturgeon. This was soon after the trial of the foreign spies. Late in the summer this was. We came out one morning and there they were – white bellies floating in the river. And time without number we discovered that food had been taken from the traps and yet no animals were caught. The mushrooms were shrivelled, useless things – scarcely a *pood* to be had all year – and that had never happened before, either. Even the berries on the two-*verst* track were gone before we could pick them. I discussed the crisis confidentially with Comrade Chizhikov – I was older now, you understand, and able to take a hand – and his analysis was identical to mine: that this was a classic outbreak of Trotskyite wreckerism. And when Yezhov was discovered with a flashlight – out walking, after curfew: the *swine* – the case was made. And this,' he held up a thick pile of barely legible scrawl and slapped it against the table, 'this is his confession – you can see it, here, in his own hand – how he received his signals by torch-transmission from some spiderish associates he had made contact with while out fishing.'

'And Yezhov – ?'

'His widow hanged herself. They had a child.' He looked away. 'I don't know what became of it. They're all dead now, of course. Even Chizhikov.'

More silence. Kelso felt like Scheherazade: as long as he could keep talking, there was a chance. Death lay in the silences.

'Comrade Chizhikov,' he said. 'He must have been a –' he nearly said *'a monster''* – a formidable man?'

'A shock-worker,' said the Russian, 'a Stakhanovite, a soldier and a hunter, a red expert and a theoretician of the highest calibre.' His eyes were almost closed. His voice fell to a whisper. 'Oh, and he *beat* me, comrade. He beat me and he beat me, until I was *weeping* blood! On instructions that were given to him, as to the manner of my upbringing, by the highest organs: "You are to give him a good shaking every now and again!" All that I am, he made me.'

'When did Comrade Chizhikov die?'

'Two winters ago. He was clumsy and half-blind by then. He stepped into one of his own traps. The wound turned black. His leg turned black and stank like maggoty meat.

There was delirium. He raged. In the end, he begged us to leave him outside overnight, in the snow. A dog's death.'

'And his wife – she died soon afterwards?'

'Within the week.'

'She must have been like a mother to you?'

'She was. But she was old. She couldn't work. It was a hard thing to have to do – but it was for the best.'

'He never ever loved a human being,' said his schoolfriend, Iremashvili. *'He was incapable of feeling pity for man or beast, and I never knew him cry . . .'*

A hard thing –

For the best –

He opened one yellow eye.

'You are shifty, comrade. I can tell.'

Kelso's throat was dry. He looked at his watch. 'I was wondering what had become of my colleague –'

It was now more than half an hour since he had left O'Brian by the river.

'The Yankee? Take my tip there, comrade. Don't trust him. You'll see.'

He winked again, put his finger to his lips and stood. And then he moved across the cabin with an extraordinary speed and agility – it was grace, really: one, two, three steps, yet the soles of his boots barely seemed to connect with the boards – and he flung open the door and there was O'Brian.

And later Kelso was to wonder what might have happened next. Would it all have been treated as some terrific joke? (*'Your ears must be flapping like boards in this cold, comrade!'*) Or would O'Brian have been the next interloper in the miniature Stalinist state required to sign a confession?

But it was impossible to say what might have happened, because what did happen was that the Russian suddenly pulled O'Brian roughly into the cabin. Then he stood alone at the open door, his head tilted to one side, nostrils dilated, sniffing the air, listening.

SUVORIN never even saw the smoke. It was Major Kretov who spotted it.

He braked and pointed to it, put the snow plough into first gear, and they crawled forwards for a couple of hundred yards until they drew level with the entrance to the track. Halfway along it, the sharp white outline of the Toyota's roof showed up clear against the shadows of the trees.

Kretov stopped, reversed a short distance, and left the engine idling as he scanned the way ahead. Then he swung the wheel hard and the big vehicle lurched forwards again, off the road and down the track, clearing a path to within a few paces of the empty car. He turned the engine off and for a few moments Suvorin heard again that unnatural silence.

He said, 'Major, what *are* your orders, exactly?'

Kretov was opening the door. 'My orders are plain Russian good sense. "To stuff the cork back in to the bottle at the narrowest point."' He jumped down easily into the snow and reached back for his AK-74. He stuffed an extra magazine into his jacket. He checked his pistol.

'And this is the narrowest point?'

'Stay here and keep your backside warm, why don't you? This won't take us long.'

'I won't be a party to anything illegal,' said Suvorin. The words sounded absurdly prim and official, even to his ears, and Kretov took no notice. He was already beginning to move off with his men. 'The westerners, at least,' Suvorin called after them, 'are not to be harmed!'

He sat there for a few more seconds, watching the backs of

the soldiers as they fanned out across the track. Then, cursing, he shoved the front seat forwards and squeezed himself into the open door. The cab was unexpectedly high off the ground. He leapt and felt himself jerked backwards, heard a tearing sound. The lining of his coat had snagged on a bit of metal. He swore again and detached himself.

It was hard to keep up with the other three. They were fit and he was not. They had army boots and he had leather-soled brogues. It was difficult to maintain his footing in the snow and he wouldn't have caught them at all if they hadn't stopped to inspect something on the ground beside the track.

Kretov smoothed out the screwed-up yellow paper and turned it this way and that. It was blank. He balled it up again and dropped it. He inserted a small, flesh-coloured miniature receiver, like a hearing-aid, into his right ear. From his pocket he took out a black ski-mask and pulled it over his head. The others did the same. Kretov made a chopping motion with his gloved hand towards the forest and they set off again: Kretov first with his assault rifle held before him, turning as he walked, ducking this way and that, ready to rake the trees with bullets; then one soldier, then another, both keeping up the same wary surveillance, their faces like skulls in the masks; and finally Suvorin in his civilian clothes – stumbling, slipping, in every way absurd.

CALMLY the Russian closed the door and collected his rifle. He pulled out a wooden box from beneath the table and filled his pockets with bullets. In the same unhurried manner, he rolled back the carpet, lifted the trapdoor and leapt, cat-like, into the space.

'We stand for peace and champion the cause of peace,' he said. 'But we are not afraid of threats and are prepared to answer the instigators of war blow for blow. Those who try to attack us will receive a crushing repulse to teach them not to poke their pig snouts into our Soviet garden. Replace the carpet, comrade.'

He disappeared, closing the trapdoor after him.

O'Brian gaped at the floorboards and then at Kelso.

'What the fuck – ?'

'And where the hell have *you* been?' Kelso grabbed the satchel and quickly stuffed it back into his jacket. 'Never mind him,' he said, rolling back the carpet. 'Let's just get out of here.'

But before either of them could move a skull appeared at the cabin windows – two round eyes and a slit for a mouth. A boot kicked wood. The door splintered.

THEY were made to stand against the wall – shoved against the rough planked wall – and Kelso felt cold metal jabbed into the nape of his neck. O'Brian was a bit too slow on the uptake so he had his forehead banged against the planking, just to mend his manners and teach him a little Russian.

Their wrists were trussed tightly behind their backs with thin plastic.

A man said roughly, 'Where's the other?' He raised the butt of his rifle.

'Under the floorboards!' shouted O'Brian. 'Tell 'em, Fluke, he's under the fucking floorboards!'

'He's under the floorboards,' said a well-educated voice in Russian that Kelso thought he recognised.

Heavy boots clumped on the wooden floor. Turning his head, Kelso saw one of the masked men walk to the end of the cabin, point his gun at the ground and casually begin firing. He flinched at the deafening noise in the confined space and when he looked again the man was walking backwards, spraying bullets into the floor in neat rows, his weapon leaping in his hands like a pneumatic drill. Wood chips sprouted, ricocheted, and Kelso felt something strike the side of his head, just below his ear. Blood started trickling down his neck. He turned the other way and pressed his cheek to the wall. The noise stopped, there was a rattle of a fresh magazine being fitted, then it started again, then stopped. Something crashed to the floor. There was a stink of cordite. Acrid smoke made him clench his eyes and when he opened them again he could see the blond-headed spy from Moscow. The spy shook his head in disgust.

The man who had been firing kicked aside the shredded carpet and lifted the trapdoor. He shone a flashlight down through the rising dust, then clambered into the hole and disappeared. They could hear him moving around beneath their feet. After thirty seconds he reappeared at the door of the cabin, pulling off his mask.

'There's a tunnel. He's got out.'

He produced a pistol and gave it to the blond man.

'Watch them.'

Then he gestured to the other two and they clattered out into the snow.

Chapter Thirty

SUVORIN FELT WET. He glanced down and saw that he was standing in a puddle of melted snow. His trousers were sodden. So was the bottom of his overcoat. A piece of frayed silk lining trailed on the floor. And his shoes – his shoes were leaking and scuffed – they were *ruined.*

One of the two bound men – the reporter: O'Brian, wasn't that his name? – started to turn and say something.

'Shut up!' said Suvorin, furiously. He clicked off the safety catch and waved the gun. 'Shut up and face the wall!'

He sat down at the table and wiped his damp sleeve across his face.

Absolutely *ruined . . .*

He noticed Stalin glowering at him. He picked up the framed photograph with his free hand and tilted it to the light. It was signed. And what was all this other stuff? Passports, identity papers, a pipe, old gramophone records, an envelope with a piece of hair in it . . . It looked as though someone had been trying to perform a conjuring trick. He sprinkled the hair into his palm and rubbed it between his thumb and forefinger. The fibres were dry, grey, coarse, like a clump of bristles. He let them fall and wiped his hands on his coat. Then he laid the pistol on the table and massaged his eyes.

'Sit down,' he said, wearily, 'why don't you?'

Outside in the forest there was a long jabbering burst of gunfire.

'You know, he said sadly to Kelso, 'you really should have caught that plane.'

*

'WHAT happens next?' said the Englishman. It was obviously difficult for them to sit properly. They were on their knees, next to the wall. The stove had gone out. It was getting very cold. Suvorin had slid one of the records out of its paper sleeve and put it on the turntable of the ancient gramophone.

'It's a surprise,' he said.

'I am an accredited member of the foreign press corps –' began O'Brian.

The crack-crack of a high velocity rifle was answered by a heavier bang.

'The American ambassador –' said O'Brian.

Suvorin wound the handle of the gramophone very fast – anything to block out the noise from outside – and placed the needle on the record. Through a hailstorm of crackles, a tinny orchestra struck up a wavering tune.

More gunfire. Someone was screaming, far away, through the trees. Two shots followed in rapid succession. The screaming stopped and O'Brian started whining, 'They're going to shoot us. They'll shoot us, too!' He struggled against the plastic wire and tried to rise, but Suvorin put his wet shoe on O'Brian's chest and gently pushed him down again.

'Let us,' he said, in English, 'at least try to act like civilised men.'

This was not what I dreamed for myself, either, he wanted to say. It formed no part of my life's dreams, I do assure you, to arrive in some stinking madman's hovel and hunt him down like an animal. Honestly, I believe you would find me an amusing fellow, if only circumstances were different.

He made an effort to follow the beat of the music, conducting with his forefinger, but he couldn't find any rhythm, there seemed to be no sense to it.

'You'd better have brought an army,' said the Englishman,

'because if it's just three against one out there, they don't stand a chance.'

'Nonsense,' said Suvorin, patriotically. 'They're our special forces. They'll get him. And yes, if necessary, they *will* send an army.'

'Why?'

'Because I work for frightened men, Dr Kelso, some of whom are just about old enough to have been touched by Comrade Stalin.' He frowned at the gramophone. What a racket. It sounded like howling dogs. 'Do you know what Lenin called the Tsarovich, when the Bolsheviks were deciding the fate of the Imperial Family? He called the boy "the living banner". And there's only one way, Lenin said, to deal with a living banner.'

Kelso shook his head. 'You don't understand this man. Believe me – you should see him – he is criminally insane. He's probably killed half a dozen people over the past thirty years. He's nobody's banner. He's crazy.'

'Everyone said Zhirinovsky was crazy, remember? His foreign policy towards the Baltic States was to bury nuclear waste along the Lithuanian border and blow it into Vilnius every night using giant fans. He still got twenty-three per cent of the vote in the ninety-three election.'

Suvorin couldn't stand this unearthly, bestial music a moment more. He lifted the needle.

They heard a solitary shot.

Suvorin held his breath for an answering salvo.

'Perhaps,' he said doubtfully, after waiting a long while, 'I should think about calling up that army –'

'THERE are traps,' said Kelso.

'What?'

Suvorin was at the doorway, peering tentatively into the twilight. He looked back into the cabin. He had looped some rope around their wrists and attached it to the cold stove.

'He's put down traps. Be careful where you tread.'

'Thank you.' Suvorin planted his foot on the top step. 'I'll be back.'

His plan – and that was a good word, he thought, that had a certain ring to it: his *plan* – was to get back to the snow plough and use the radio to summon reinforcements. So he headed towards the entrance to the clearing, the only fixed point he had. There were good footprints to follow here, although it was getting dark, and he must have been midway along the rough path when he felt the explosion and a second later he heard it, a great rush of snow marking the passage of the shock wave as it travelled through the forest. Cascades of crystal pattered down from the higher branches and bounced off into space, leaving tiny clouds of particles hanging in the air like puffs of breath.

He spun around, the gun held out in a double grip, pointing uselessly in the direction of the blast.

He panicked then and began to run – a comic figure, a jerking marionette – trying to bring his knees up as high as they would go to avoid the sucking, clinging snow. His breath was coming in sobs.

He was so intent on keeping going he almost tripped over the first body.

It was one of the soldiers. He had been caught in a trap – a huge trap: a bear trap, maybe – so big and powerfully sprung, the jaws of it had actually clamped into the bone above his knee. There was a lot of blood smeared around in the flattened snow, blood from the shattered leg and blood from a big head wound that gaped through the back of the knitted ski-mask like a second mouth.

The corpse of the other soldier was a few paces further on. Unlike the first man, he was lying on his back, his arms outstretched, his legs arranged in a perfect figure 4. There was a puddle of blood on his chest.

Suvorin put down his gun, took off his gloves and checked the pulses of both men – although he knew it was useless – pulling aside the layers of clothing to feel their warm, dead wrists.

How had he ambushed them *both?*

He looked around.

Like this, probably: he had laid the trap on the path, buried in the snow, and had lured them over it; the man in the lead had missed it, somehow, the man in the rear had been caught – that was the screaming – and the lead man had turned to help only to find their quarry behind them – that was what was cunning: they wouldn't have expected that. And so he had been shot full in the front, and then the second man had been taken out at leisure, executioner-style, with a bullet at point-blank range in the back of the head.

And then he had taken their AK-74s.

What kind of creature *was* this?

Suvorin knelt by the head of the first soldier and pulled off his ski-mask. He took out his ear-piece and pressed it to his own ear. He thought he could hear something. A rushing sound. He found the little microphone attached to the inside cuff of the dead man's left hand.

'Kretov?' he whispered. 'Kretov?' But the only voice he could hear was his own.

Then the gunfire started up again.

*

THE fire was like a red dawn through the trees, and when Suvorin stepped out on to the track he could feel the heat of the burning snow plough, even at a range of a hundred yards. The fuel tank must have exploded and the inferno had melted the winter all around it. The vehicle stood blazing in the centre of its own scorched spring.

The gunfire was continuing sporadically, but that wasn't Kretov returning fire. That was boxes of ammunition, exploding in the cab. Kretov himself was sitting down, doubled over in the centre of the track, beside the RP46, as dead as his comrades. He looked as though he had been shot while trying to set up the machine gun. He had got as far as mounting it on to the bipod but he hadn't had time to open the cannister of ammunition.

Suvorin went up to him and touched his arm and Kretov toppled over, his grey eyes open, a look of astonishment on his broad, pink face. Suvorin couldn't see a wound, not at first, anyway. Perhaps the heroic major of the Spetsnaz had simply died of fright?

Another loud bang from the direction of the fire made him look up, to find himself being watched by Comrade Stalin, in his generalissimo's uniform and cap.

The GenSec was some way up the track, standing before the fire, his left hand on his hip, his right holding a rifle almost casually across his shoulder. His shadow was long in proportion to his squat torso. It danced and flickered on the churned snow.

Suvorin thought he would choke on his own heart. They looked at one another. Then Stalin started marching towards him. And *marching* – that was the word for the way he walked: quickly, but without hurrying, swinging his arms up across his barrel chest, left-right, left-right: look lively there, comrade, here I come!

Suvorin fumbled in his pocket for his pistol and realised he had left it in the trees, beside the first two corpses.

Left-right, left-right – the living banner, kicking up the snow –

Suvorin didn't dare look at him an instant longer. He knew that if he did he would never move.

'Why is your face so shifty, comrade?' called the advancing figure. 'Why can't you look Comrade Stalin directly in the eyes?'

Suvorin swung the barrel of the RP46, his memory toiling back twenty years, to his compulsory army training, shivering on some godforsaken range on the outskirts of Vitebsk. *'Cock gun by pulling operating handle to the rear. Pull rear sight base to the rear and lift cover. Lay belt, open side up, on the feed plate so that the leading round contacts the cartridge stop and close cover. Pull trigger and gun will fire . . .'*

He closed his eyes and squeezed the trigger and the machine gun jumped in his hands, sending a couple of dozen bullets sawing into a birch tree at a range of twenty yards.

When he dared to check the track again Comrade Stalin had disappeared.

IF Suvorin's memory served him right, the ammunition belt of the RP46 carried 250 rounds, which the gun would dispatch at a rate of, say, 600 rounds per minute. So, given he'd already used a few, he probably had something less than thirty seconds of firepower with which to cover 360 degrees of track and forest, with night coming on and the temperature plunging to a level that would kill him in a couple of hours.

He had to get out of the open, that was for sure. He couldn't keep on like this, scrambling round and round like a tethered goat in a tiger shoot, trying to see through the gloom of the trees.

He seemed to remember some abandoned wooden huts at the far end of the track. They might provide a bit of cover. He needed to get his back against a wall somewhere, needed time to *think*.

A wolf howled in the forest.

He disconnected the machine gun from the bipod and hoisted the long barrel up on to his shoulder, the ammunition belt heavy on his arm, his knees almost buckling under the weight, his feet sinking deeper into the snow.

The full-throated howling came again. It was not a wolf at all, he thought. It was a man – a man's exultant shout: a blood cry.

He started wading up the track, away from the burning snow plough, and he sensed that there was someone walking parallel with him through the trees, keeping an easy pace, laughing at his ponderous attempt at flight. He was being played with, that was all. He would be allowed to get within a few paces of his destination, then he would be shot.

He came out of the neck of the track and into the abandoned settlement and headed for the nearest wooden building. The windows were out, the door had gone, half the roof was missing, it stank. He put down the gun and crawled into the corner, then turned and dragged the weapon after him. He wedged himself against the wall and pointed the barrel at the door, his finger on the trigger.

KELSO heard the big explosion, gunfire, a long pause, and then the short and heavy clatter of a much bigger weapon opening up. He and O'Brian were on their feet by now, frantically trying to find some way of cutting the rope that bound them to the stove chimney. Each sound from the forest drove them to more desperate efforts. The thin plastic was digging into his wrists, his fingers were slippery with blood.

There was blood on the Russian, too, when he appeared in the doorway. Kelso saw it as he came towards them, unsheathing his knife – smeared across his face, on his forehead and on either cheek, like a hunter who had dipped himself in his kill.

'Comrades,' he reported, 'we are dizzy with success. Three are dead. Only one still lives. Are there more?'

'More coming.'

'How many more?'

'Fifty,' said Kelso. 'A hundred.' He tugged against the rope. 'Comrade, we must get clear of this place, or they will kill us all. Even you cannot stop so many. They are going to send an army.'

ACCORDING to Suvorin's watch, about fifteen minutes had elapsed.

The temperature was plunging as the light faded. His body began to vibrate with the cold – a steady, violent shaking he couldn't stop.

'Come on,' he whispered. 'Come on and finish the job.'

But nobody came.

Comrade Stalin's capacity for springing surprises was truly endless.

THE next thing Suvorin heard was a distant click, followed by a whirr.

Click-whirr. Click-whirr.

Now what was he doing?

Suvorin found it hard to move at first. The frost had locked his joints and starched his wet clothes to board. Still, he was on his feet in time to hear the mysterious click-whirr turn suddenly into a cough and then a roar as an engine started.

No, no, not an engine exactly: a motor – an outboard motor –

He was baffled for a moment, but then he realised.

'Fifteen miles, major. It's right on the river . . . '

WELL, the RP46 didn't get any lighter, nor the snow any easier, and now he had the oncoming darkness to contend with, but he tried. He made a valiant effort.

'Bastard, bastard, bastard,' he chanted as he ran, following the pulse of the revving outboard as it led him through the fifty yards or so of trees that screened the deserted fishing settlement from the river.

He crashed through the last barrier of undergrowth and came out on to the crest of a bank that sloped down steeply to the water's edge. He stumbled along the ridge, heading upstream. Some pieces of electronic equipment lay spread out in the snow. Grey ice extended for a little distance and the black water rushed beyond his reach – an immensity of it: he couldn't see the trees on the opposite shore. And already the little boat was heading towards the centre, and turning now, carving a great white sickle of spray in the darkness. He could just make out three crouched figures. One seemed to be trying to struggle to his feet, but another pulled him down.

Suvorin dropped to his knees and unshouldered the machine gun, fumbling to close the cover on the ammunition belt, which promptly jammed. By the time he had it free and ready to fire the boat had rounded the curve of the river – and then he couldn't see it any more, he could only hear it.

He put down the gun and bent his head.

Beside him, like a space probe landed on some hostile planet, the antenna of a satellite dish pointed low across the Dvina to the dissolving horizon. One set of cables connected the dish to a car battery. Another was linked to a small grey box labelled 'Transportable Video & Audio Transmission Terminal'. Even as he watched, a row of ten red zeros in a digital display winked at him briefly, faded and died.

He had an overwhelming sense of emptiness, squatting there, as if some malevolent force had erupted from this place and escaped for ever, a comet trailing darkness.

For perhaps half a minute he listened to the sound of the outboard motor and then that too was gone and he was left alone in the utter silence.

Chapter Thirty-one

THE FIGURE SUVORIN had seen trying to rise in the boat was O'Brian – *my gear!*, he shouted, *the tapes!* – and the figure who had pulled him down was Kelso – *forget the bloody gear, forget the tapes*. For a moment the boat rocked dangerously, and the Russian cursed them both, and then O'Brian moaned and sat down quickly and put his head in his hands.

Kelso couldn't make out anyone on the shore as they roared away from it. All he could see was the sky pulsing red above the tips of the darkening firs where something big was burning fiercely, and then very quickly a bend in the river obliterated even that and he was conscious only of speed – of the racket of the outboard motor and the rushing current hurtling them downstream through the forest.

He was thinking with great clarity now, everything else in his life irrelevant, everything narrowed to this one single point: survival. And it seemed to him that all that counted was to put as much distance as possible between themselves and this spot. He didn't know how many men were left alive behind them, but the best he reckoned they could hope for was that a search party wouldn't set out till the morning. The worst scenario was that the blond-headed man had radioed for help and Archangel would already be sealed.

There was no food or water in the boat, just a couple of oars, a boathook, the Russian's suitcase, his rifle, and a small tank that smelled as though it was leaking cheap fuel. In the darkness he had to hold his watch up very close to his eyes. It was just after half-past six. He leaned over and said to O'Brian, 'What time did you say the Moscow train left Archangel?'

O'Brian lifted his head long enough from his despair to mutter, 'Ten past eight.'

Kelso twisted round and shouted above the engine and the wind, 'Comrade, could we get to Archangel?' There was no reply. He tapped his watch. 'Could we get to the centre of Archangel in an hour?'

The Russian didn't seem to have heard. His hand was on the tiller and he was staring straight ahead. With his collar turned up and his cap pulled down, it was impossible to make out his expression. Kelso tried shouting again and then gave up. It was a new kind of horror, he thought, to realise that they probably owed their lives to him – that he was now their ally – and that their futures were at the mercy of his unfathomable mind.

THEY were heading roughly north-west and the cold was being hammered into them from all sides – a Siberian wind at their backs, the freezing water beneath their feet, the rushing air on their faces. O'Brian remained monosyllabic, inconsolable. There was a light in the prow, and Kelso found himself concentrating on that – on the shifting yellow path and the roiling water, black and viscous as it began to solidify.

After half an hour the snow resumed, the flakes huge and luminous in the dark, like falling ash. Occasionally something knocked against the hull and Kelso spotted lumps of ice drifting in the current. It was as if winter was clutching at them, determined not to let them go, and Kelso wondered if fear was the reason for the Russian's silence. Killers could be frightened, like anyone else, perhaps more than anyone else. Stalin lived half his life in a state of terror – scared of aeroplanes, scared of visiting the front, never eating food unless it had been tasted for poison, changing his guards, his routes, his beds – when you had murdered so many, you knew how easily death could come. And it could come for them here very easily, he thought. They would run into an ice barrier, the water would freeze behind them, they would be trapped; the ice-crust would be too thin to risk crawling across, and here they would die, covered for decency under a shroud of snow.

He wondered what people would make of it. Margaret – what would she say when she learned her ex-husband's body had been found in a forest nearly a thousand miles from Moscow. And his boys? He cared what they would think: he wouldn't miss much, but he would miss his sons. Perhaps he should try to scrawl them a heroic final note, like Captain Scott in Antarctica: 'These rough notes and our dead bodies must tell the tale –'

He thought that perhaps he didn't fear dying as much as he had expected he would, which surprised him as he had little physical courage and no religious faith. But a man would have to be a rare fool – wouldn't he? – to spend a lifetime studying history without acquiring at least some sense of perspective on his own mortality. Perhaps that was why he'd done it – devoted so many years to writing about the dead. He'd never thought of it that way.

He tried to imagine his obituaries: *'never quite fulfilled his early promise . . . never published the major work of scholarship of which he was once judged capable . . . the bizarre circumstances of his premature death may never be fully explained . . . '* The memorialising articles would all be the same and he would know every one of their grudging, time-serving authors.

The Russian opened the throttle wider and Kelso could hear him, muttering to himself.

*

ANOTHER half hour passed.

Kelso had his eyes closed and it was O'Brian who saw the lights first. He nudged Kelso and pointed, and after a second or two, Kelso saw them as well – high gantry lights on the chimneys and cranes of the big wood pulp factory on the headland outside the city. Presently more lights began to appear in the darkness on either bank and the night sky ahead became fractionally paler. Perhaps they would make it after all?

His face was frozen. It was hard to speak.

He said, 'Got the Archangel map?'

O'Brian turned stiffly. He looked like a white marble statue coming to life and as he moved small slabs of frozen snow cracked and slid off his jacket into the bottom of the boat. He dragged the city plan out of his inside pocket and Kelso shifted forwards off the thin plank that served as a seat, fell on to his hands and knees, and crawled awkwardly to the prow. He held the map to the light. The Dvina bulged as it came into the city, and a pair of islands split it into three channels. They needed to keep to the northern one.

It was a quarter to eight.

He moved back to the stern and managed to shout, 'Comrade!' He made a chopping motion with his hand to starboard. The Russian gave no sign of having understood but a minute later, as the dark mass of the island emerged out of the snow, he steered to the north of it and soon afterwards Kelso made out a rusty buoy and beyond that a line of lights in the sky.

He cupped his hand to O'Brian's ear. 'The bridge,' he said. O'Brian pulled down his hood and squinted at him. 'The bridge,' repeated Kelso. 'The one we came over this morning.'

He pointed and very quickly they were passing beneath it – a double-bridge, half-rail, half-road: heavy ironwork dangling stalactites of ice, a strong smell of sewage and chemicals, the drumming of vehicles overhead – and when he looked back he could see the headlights of traffic moving slowly through the snow.

The familiar shape of the Harbour Master's building appeared ahead of them on the starboard side, with a jetty stretching out and boats moored to it. They hit an invisible sheet of thick ice and Kelso and O'Brian were bounced forwards. The engine cut out. The Russian restarted it and reversed, then found a channel which must have been cut by a bigger boat earlier in the evening. There was still ice but it was thinner and it splintered as their prow sliced into it. Kelso looked back at the Russian. He was standing now, peering intently at the dark corridor, his hand on the tiller, taking them in. They came alongside the jetty and he put the outboard into reverse again, slowing them, stopping. He cut the motor and leapt nimbly on to the wooden planking, holding a length of rope.

O'BRIAN was out of the boat first, with Kelso after him. They stamped and brushed the snow off themselves and tried to stretch some life back into their frozen limbs. O'Brian started to say something about finding a hotel, maybe, calling the office, but Kelso cut him off.

'No hotel. Are you listening to me? No office. And no bloody story. We're getting out of here.'

They had thirteen minutes to catch the train.

'And him?'

O'Brian nodded to the Russian who was standing quietly, holding his suitcase, watching them. He looked oddly forlorn – vulnerable, even, now that he was out of his home territory. He was obviously expecting to come with them.

'Christ almighty,' muttered Kelso. He had the map open. He didn't know what to do. 'Let's just go.' He set off along the jetty towards the shore. O'Brian hurried after him.

'You still got the notebook?'

Kelso patted the front of his jacket.

'D'you think he's got a gun?' said O'Brian. He glanced back. 'Shit. He's following us.'

The Russian was trotting about a dozen paces behind them, wary and fearful, like a stray dog. It looked as though he had left his rifle behind in the boat. So what would he be armed with, wondered Kelso? His knife? He pushed his stiff legs forwards as hard as he could.

'But we can't just leave him –'

'Oh yes we bloody can,' said Kelso. He realised O'Brian didn't know about the Norwegian couple, or any of the others. 'I'll explain later. Just believe me – we don't want him anywhere near us.'

They almost ran off the jetty and came into the big bus park in front of the Harbour Master's building – a bleak expanse of snow, a few sorrowful orange sodium lights catching the whirling flakes, nobody else about. Kelso struck north, slithering on the ice, holding on to the map. The station was at least a mile away and they were never going to make it in time, not on foot. He looked around. A ubiquitous, boxy, sand-coloured Lada, spattered with mud and grit, was emerging slowly from the street to their right, and Kelso ran towards it, flapping his arms.

In the Russian provinces, every car is a potential taxi, most drivers willing to hire themselves out on the spur of the moment, and this one was no exception. He swerved towards them, throwing up a fountain of dirty snow, and even as he pulled up he was winding down his window. He looked respectable enough, muffled against the cold – a school-teacher, maybe, a clerk. Weak eyes blinked at them through thick-framed spectacles. 'Going to the concert hall?'

'Do us a favour, citizen, and take us to the railway station,' said Kelso. 'Ten dollars US if we catch the Moscow train.' He opened the passenger door without waiting for an answer and tipped forward the seat, shoving O'Brian into the back, and suddenly he saw that this was their chance, because the Russian, caught by surprise, had fallen behind slightly, and was making heavy progress through the snow with his case.

'Comrade!' he shouted.

Kelso didn't hesitate. He rammed back the seat and got in, slamming the door.

'Don't you want –' began the driver, looking in his mirror.

'No,' said Kelso. 'Go.'

The Lada skidded away and he turned to look back. The Russian had set down his case and was staring after them, seemingly bewildered, a lost figure in the widening vista of the alien city. He dwindled and disappeared into the night and snow.

'Can't help but feel sorry for the poor bastard,' said O'Brian, but Kelso's only emotion was relief.

'"Gratitude,"' he said, quoting Stalin, '"is a dog's disease."'

THE Archangel railway station was at the northern edge of a big square, directly opposite a huddle of apartment blocks and wind-blasted birch trees. O'Brian threw a $10 bill in the direction of the driver and they sprinted into the gloomy terminal. Seven wood-fronted ticket kiosks with net curtains, five of them closed, a long queue outside the two that were open, a baby crying. Students, backpackers, soldiers, people of all ages and races, families with their home-made luggage – huge cardboard boxes trussed with string – children running everywhere, sliding on the dirty, melted snow.

O'Brian pushed his way to the front of the nearest line, spraying dollars, playing the westerner: 'Sorry, lady. Excuse me. There you go. Sorry. Gotta catch this train –'

Kelso had an impression of a fortune changing hands – three hundred, four hundred dollars, murmurs from the people standing round – and then, a minute later, O'Brian was striding back through the crowd, waving a pair of tickets, and they ran up the stairs to the platform.

If they were going to be stopped then this would be the place. At least a dozen militia men were standing around, all of them young, all with their caps pushed back like Imperial Army privates off to war in 1914. They stared at Kelso and O'Brian as they hurried through the terminal, but it was no more than the frank stare that all foreigners received up here. They made no move to detain them.

No alert had been issued. *Whoever is running this show,* thought Kelso, as they came back out into the open air, *must be convinced we're already dead –*

Doors were being closed all the way along the great train; it must have been a quarter of a mile long. Low yellow lighting, snow falling, lovers embracing, army officers hurrying up and down with their cheap briefcases – he felt they had stepped back seventy years into some revolutionary tableau. Even the giant locomotive still had the hammer and sickle welded to its side. They found their carriage, three cars back from the engine, and Kelso held the door open while O'Brian darted across the platform to one of the babushkas selling food for the journey. She had a wart on her cheek the size of a walnut. He was still stuffing his pockets as the whistle blew.

The train pulled away so slowly it was hard at first to tell it was moving. People walked alongside it down the platform, heads bent into the snow, waving handkerchiefs. Others were holding hands through the open windows. Kelso had a sudden image of Anna Safanova here, almost fifty years ago – *'I kiss mama's dear cheeks, farewell to her, farewell to childhood'* – and the full sadness and the pity of it came home to him for the first time. The people ambling along the platform began to jog and then to run. He stretched out his hand and pulled O'Brian aboard. The train lurched forwards. The station disappeared.

Chapter Thirty-two

THEY SWAYED ALONG the narrow, blue-carpeted corridor until they found their compartment – one of eight, about halfway down the carriage. O'Brian pulled back the sliding wooden door and they lurched inside.

It was not too bad. A thousand roubles per head in 'soft' class bought two dusty, crimson banquettes facing one another, a white nylon sheet, a rolled mattress and a pillow neatly folded on each; a lot of laminated, imitation-wood panelling; green-shaded reading lamps; a little fold-up table; privacy.

Through the window they could see the spars of the iron bridge clicking past but once they were across the river there was nothing visible in the snowstorm except their own reflections staring back at them – haggard, soaking, unshaven. O'Brian drew the yellow curtains, unfastened the table and laid out their food – a grubby loaf, some kind of dried fish, a sausage, tea-bags – while Kelso went in search of hot water.

A blackened samovar stood at the far end of the corridor, opposite the cubicle of the carriage's female attendant, their *provodnik*: a hefty, unsmiling woman, like a camp guard in her grey-blue uniform. She had rigged up a little mirror so she could keep an eye on everyone without stirring from her stool. He could see her watching him as he stopped to study the timetable that was fixed to the wall. They had a journey of more than twenty hours ahead of them, and thirteen stops, not counting Moscow, which they would reach just after four in the afternoon.

Twenty hours.

What were their chances of lasting that long? He tried to calculate. By mid-morning at the latest, Moscow would know that the operation in the forest had been bungled. Then they would be bound to stop the only train out of Archangel and search it. Perhaps he and O'Brian would be wiser to get off at one of these earlier stops – Sokol, maybe, which they would reach at 7 a.m., or, better still, Vologda (Vologda was a big town) – get off the train at Vologda, get to a hotel, call the American Embassy –

He heard a sliding door open behind him and a businessman in a smartly cut blue suit came out of his compartment and went in to the lavatory. His neatness made Kelso aware of his own bizarre appearance – heavy waterproof jacket, rubber boots – and he hurried on down the corridor. It would be best to stay out of sight as much as possible. He begged a couple of plastic cups off the grim-faced guard, filled them with scalding water, and made his way unsteadily back to their sleeping-berth.

THEY sat opposite one another, chewing steadily on the dry, stale food.

Kelso said he thought they should get off the train early.

'Why?'

'Because I don't think we should risk being picked up. Not before people know where we are.'

O'Brian bit off a piece of bread and considered this.

'So you really think – back there in the forest – they'd've shot us?'

'Yes I do.'

O'Brian had apparently forgotten his earlier panic. He began to argue but Kelso cut him off impatiently. 'Think about it for a minute. Think how easy it could have been. All the Russians would have had to say is that some maniac took us hostage in the woods and they sent in the special forces to rescue us. They could have made it look as though he'd murdered us.'

'But nobody would've believed that –'

'Of course they would. He was a psychopath.'

'What?'

'A psychopath. This is why I didn't want to bring him with us. Half the people in that cemetery, he put there. And there were others.'

'Others?' O'Brian had stopped eating.

'At least five. A young Norwegian couple, and three other poor bastards, Russians who just happened to take a wrong turning. I found their papers while you were down at the river. They'd all been made to confess to spying, and then they were shot. I tell you, he's a sick piece of work. I only hope to God I never have to see him again. So should you.'

O'Brian seemed to be having difficulty swallowing. There were bits of fish stuck between his teeth. He said quietly, 'What d'you think's going to happen to him?'

'They'll get him in the end, I imagine. They'll close down Archangel until they find him. And I don't blame them, to be honest. Can you imagine what Mamantov and his people would do if they got hold of a man who looks like Stalin, talks like Stalin and comes with a written guarantee that he's Stalin's son? Wouldn't they have had some fun with that?'

O'Brian had slumped back in his seat, his eyes shut, his face stricken, and Kelso, watching him, felt a sudden twinge of unease. In the rush of events he had entirely forgotten Mamantov. His gaze shifted from O'Brian to the wire luggage rack where the satchel was still carefully wrapped inside his jacket.

He tried to think, but he couldn't. His mind was shutting down on him. It was three days since he'd had a proper sleep – the first night he'd sat up with Rapava, the second he'd ended in the cells beneath Moscow militia HQ, the third had been spent on the road travelling north to Archangel. He ached with exhaustion. It was all he could do to kick off his boots and begin making up his meagre bed.

'I'm all in,' he said. 'Let's work something out in the morning.'

O'Brian didn't answer.

As a flimsy precaution, Kelso locked the door.

IT must have been another twenty minutes before O'Brian finally moved. Kelso had his face to the wall by then and was drifting in the hinterland between sleep and wakefulness. He heard him unlace his boots, sigh and stretch out on the banquette. His reading lamp clicked off and the compartment was in darkness save for the blue neon night light that fizzed above the door.

The immense train rocked slowly southwards through the snow and Kelso slept, but not well. Hours passed and the sounds of the journey mingled with his uneasy dreams – the urgent whisperings from the compartments on either side; the *slop slop slop* of some babushka's slippers as she shuffled past in the corridor; the distant, tinny sound of a woman's voice over a loudspeaker as they stopped at the remote stations throughout the night – Nyandoma, Konosha, Yertsevo, Vozhega, Kharovsk – and people clumping on and off the train; the harsh white arc lights of the platforms shining through the thin curtains; O'Brian restless at some point, moving around.

He didn't hear the door open. All he knew was that

something rustled in the compartment for a fraction of a second, and then a hard pad of flesh clamped down over his mouth. His eyes jerked open as the point of a knife began to be inserted into his throat, at that point where the flesh of the under-jaw meets the ridged tube of the windpipe. He struggled to sit up but the hand pressed him down. His arms were somehow pinned beneath the twisted sheet. He couldn't see anyone but a voice whispered close to his ear – so close he could feel the hot wetness of the man's breath – 'A comrade who deserts a comrade is a cowardly dog, and all such dogs should die a dog's death, *comrade* –'

The knife slid deeper.

KELSO was awake in an instant – a cry rising in his throat, his eyes wide, the thin sheet balled and clenched between his sweating hands. The gently swaying compartment was empty above him, the blue-edged darkness faintly tinged by grey. For a moment he didn't move. He could hear O'Brian breathing heavily and when eventually he turned he could see him – head lolling, mouth open, one arm flung down almost to the floor, the other crooked across his forehead.

It took another couple of minutes for his panic to subside. He reached over his shoulder and lifted a corner of the curtain to check his watch. He thought it must be still the middle of the night, but to his surprise it was just after seven. He had slept for the best part of nine hours.

He raised himself up on to his elbow and pushed the curtain a fraction higher and saw at once the head of Stalin floating towards him, disconnected in the pale dawn beside the railway track. It drew level with the window and passed away very quickly.

He stayed at the window but saw nobody else, just the

scrubby land beyond the rails and the faint gleam of the electricity lines strung between the pylons seeming to swoop and rise, swoop and rise as the train trundled on. It wasn't snowing here, but there was a cold, bleached emptiness to the emerging sky.

Someone must have been holding up a picture, he realised. Holding up a picture of Stalin.

He let the curtain drop and swung his legs to the floor. Quietly, so as not to wake O'Brian, he tugged on his rubber boots and cautiously opened the door to the empty corridor. He peered both ways. Nobody about. He closed the latch behind him and began walking towards the rear of the train.

He passed through an empty carriage identical to the one he had just left, all the while glancing at the passing landscape, and then 'soft' class gave way to 'hard'. The accommodation here was much more crowded – two tiers of berths in open compartments down one side of the corridor, a single row arranged lengthwise on the other. Sixty people to a car. Luggage crammed everywhere. Some passengers sitting up, yawning, raw-eyed. Others still snoring, impervious to the waking carriage. People queuing for the stinking toilet. A mother changing a baby's filthy nappy (he caught the sour reek of milky faeces as he pushed past). The smokers huddled at the open windows at the far end of the carriage. The scent of their untipped tobacco. The sweet coldness of the rushing air.

He went through four 'hard' carriages and was on the threshold of the fifth, and had decided this would be the last – had concluded he was worrying about nothing: he must have dreamt it, the countryside was empty – when he saw another picture. Or, rather, he realised it was a pair of pictures coming towards him, one of Stalin, the other of

Lenin, being held aloft by an elderly couple, the man wearing medals, standing on a slight embankment. The train was slowing for a station and he could see them clearly as he passed – creased and leathery faces, almost brown, exhausted. And a couple of seconds later he saw them turn, suddenly years younger, smiling and waving at someone they had just seen in the carriage Kelso was about to enter.

Time seemed to decelerate, dreamily, along with the train. A line of railway workers in quilted jackets, leaning on their pick-axes and shovels, raised their gloved fists in salute. The carriage darkened as it drew alongside a platform. He could hear music, faintly, above the metallic scrape of the brakes – the old Soviet national anthem again –

Party of Lenin!
Party of Stalin!

– and a small band in pale blue uniforms slid past the window.

The train stopped with a sigh of pneumatics and he saw a sign: VOLOGDA. People were cheering on the platform. People were running. He opened the door to the carriage and there facing him was the Russian, still in his father's uniform, asleep, sitting no more than a dozen paces away, his suitcase wedged in the rack above his head, a clear space all around him, passengers standing back, respectful, watching.

The Russian was beginning to wake. His head stirred. He batted something away from his face with his hand and his eyes flickered open. He saw that he was being observed and carefully, warily, he straightened his back. Someone in the carriage started to clap and the applause was taken up by the others, spreading outside to the platform where people had crammed up against the window to watch. The Russian stared around him, the fear in his eyes giving way to bewilderment. A man nodded encouragingly at him, smiling, clapping, and he slowly nodded back, as if gradually beginning to understand some strange foreign ritual, and then he started to applaud softly in return, which only increased the volume of adulation. He nodded modestly and Kelso imagined he must have spent thirty years dreaming of this moment. *Really, comrades,* his expression seemed to say, *I am only one of you – a plain man, rough in my ways – but if venerating me in some way gives you pleasure –*

He wasn't aware of Kelso watching him – the historian was just another face in the crowd – and after a few seconds Kelso turned and began fighting his way back through the jostling throng.

His mind was in a turmoil.

The Russian must have got on board the train in Archangel, a minute or so after them – that was conceivable, if he had copied what they'd done and flagged down a car. That he could understand.

But this?

He knocked into a woman who was pushing her way roughly along the corridor, struggling with a pair of carrier bags, a red flag and an old camera.

He said to her, 'What's happening?'

'Haven't you heard? Stalin's son is with us! It's a miracle!' She couldn't stop smiling. Some of her teeth were metal.

'But how do you know?'

'It's been on the television,' she said, as if this settled matters. 'All night! And when I woke, his picture was still there and they were saying he'd been seen on the Moscow train!'

Someone pushed into her from behind and she was pitched into him. His face was very close to hers. He tried to disentangle himself but she clutched on to him, staring hard into his eyes.

'But you,' she said, 'you know all this! You were on the television, saying it was true!' She threw her heavy arms around him. Her bags jabbed into his back. 'Thank you. Thank you. It's a miracle!'

He could see a bright, white light moving along the platform behind her head and he scrambled past her. A television light. Television cameras. Big grey microphones. Technicians walking backwards, stumbling over one another. And in the middle of this mêlée, striding ahead towards his destiny, talking confidently, surrounded by a phalanx of black-jacketed bodyguards, was Vladimir Mamantov.

It took Kelso several minutes to claw and squeeze his way back through the crowds. When he opened the door to their compartment O'Brian had his back to him and was staring through the window. At the sound of Kelso entering, he wheeled round quickly, his hands up, his palms outwards – pre-emptive, guilty, apologetic.

'Now, I didn't know this was going to happen, Fluke, I swear to you –'

'What have you done?'

'Nothing –'

'What have you *done?*'

O'Brian flinched and muttered, 'I filed the story.'

'You *what?*'

'I filed the story,' he said, sounding more defiant now. 'Yesterday, from the river bank, while you were talking to him in the hut. I cut the pictures to three minutes forty, laid a commentary, converted them to digital and sent them over the satellite. I nearly told you last night, but I didn't want to upset you –'

'*Upset me?*'

'Come on, Fluke, for all I knew the story might not have gone through. Battery could've failed or something. Gear could've been shot up –'

Kelso was struggling to keep pace with all that was happening – the Russian on the train, the excitement, Mamantov. They still hadn't left Vologda, he noticed.

'These pictures – what time would they have been seen here?'

'Maybe nine o'clock last night.'

'And they would have run – what? Often? "On the hour, every hour"?'

'I guess so.'

'For *eleven hours?* And on other channels, too? Would they have sold them to the Russian networks?'

'They'd've *given* them to the Russians, as long as they were credited. It's good advertising, you know? CNN probably took them. Sky. BBC World –'

He couldn't help looking pleased.

'And you also used the interview with me, about the notebook?'

The hands came back up, defensively.

'Now, I don't know anything about that. I mean, okay, they *had* it, sure. I cut that and sent it back from Moscow before we left.'

'You irresponsible bastard,' said Kelso, slowly. 'You do know Mamantov's on the train?'

'Yeah. I saw him just now.' He glanced nervously at the window. 'Wonder what he's doing here?'

And there was something in the way he said this – a slight

falseness of tone: a pretence at being offhand – that made Kelso freeze. After a long pause he said, quietly, 'Did Mamantov put you up to this?'

O'Brian hesitated and Kelso was conscious of swaying slightly, like a boxer about to go down for the final time, or a drunk.

'Christ almighty, you've set me up –'

'No,' said O'Brian, 'that's not true. Okay, I admit Mamantov called me up once – I told you we'd met a few times. But all of this – finding the notebook, coming up here – no: that was all us, I swear. You and me. I knew nothing about what we'd find.'

Kelso closed his eyes. It was a nightmare.

'When did he call?'

'At the very beginning. It was just a tip. He didn't mention Stalin or anything else.'

'The very beginning?'

'The night before I showed up at the symposium. He said: "Go to the Institute of Marxism-Leninism with your camera, Mr O'Brian" – you know the way he talks – "find Dr Kelso, ask him if there is an announcement he wants to make." That was all he said. He put the phone down on me. Anyway, his tips are always good, so I went. Jesus –' he laughed ' – why else d'you think I was there? To film a bunch of historians talking about the archives? Do me a favour!'

'You irresponsible, duplicitous bloody *bastard* –'

Kelso took a step across the compartment and O'Brian backed away. But Kelso ignored him. He'd had a better idea. He dragged down his jacket from the luggage rack.

O'Brian said, 'What're you doing?'

'What I would have done at the beginning, if I'd known the truth. I'm going to destroy that bloody notebook.'

He pulled the satchel out of the inside pocket.

'But then you'll ruin the whole thing,' protested O'Brian. 'No notebook – no proof – no story. We'll look like complete assholes.'

'Good.'

'I'm not sure I can let you do that –'

'Just try and bloody stop me –'

It was the shock of the blow as much as the force of it that felled him. The compartment turned upside down and he was lying on his back.

'Don't make me hit you again,' begged O'Brian, looming over him. 'Please, Fluke. I like you too much for that.'

He held out his hand, but Kelso rolled away. He couldn't get his breath. His face was in the dust. Beneath his hands he could feel the heavy vibrations of the locomotive. He brought his fingers up to his mouth and touched his lip. It was bleeding slightly. He could taste salt. The big engine revved again, as if the driver was bored of waiting, but still the train didn't move.

Chapter Thirty-three

IN MOSCOW, COLONEL Yuri Arsenyev, clumsily juggling technologies, had a telephone receiver wedged between his shoulder and his ear, and a television remote control in his plump hands. He pointed it at the big television screen in the corner of his office and tried hopelessly to raise the volume, boosting first the brightness and then the contrast before he was at last able to hear what Mamantov was saying.

'. . . *flew up here from Moscow the moment I heard the news. I am therefore boarding this train to offer my protection, and that of the Aurora movement, to this historic figure, and we defy the great fascist usurper in the Kremlin to try to prevent us from reaching together the once and future seat of Soviet power . . .*'

The past twelve hours had already delivered a succession of unpleasant shocks to the chief of the RT Directorate, but this was the greatest. First, at eight o'clock the previous evening, there had been the anxious call reporting that Spetsnaz HQ had lost all communication with Suvorin and his unit in the forest. Then, an hour later, the first television pictures of the lunatic raving in his hut had begun to be broadcast (*'Such is the law of capitalism – to beat the backward and the weak. It is the jungle law of capitalism . . .'*) Reports that the man had been seen on the Moscow sleeper had reached Yasenevo just before dawn and a scratch force of militia units and MVD had been assembled at Vologda to stop the train. And now this!

Well, to take a man off under cover of darkness in some piddling little halt like Konosha or Yertsevo – that was one thing. But to storm a train in daylight, in full view of the media, in a city as big as Vologda, with V. P. Mamantov and his Aurora thugs on hand to put up a fight – that was something else entirely.

Arsenyev had called the Kremlin.

He was therefore hearing Mamantov's ponderous tones twice – once via the television in his own office and then again, a fraction later, coming down the telephone, filtered through the sound of an ailing man's laboured breathing. In the background at the other end of the line someone was shouting, there were general sounds of panic and commotion. He heard the clink of a glass and a liquid being poured.

Oh, please, he thought. *Not vodka, surely. Please. Not even him. Not this early in the morning –*

On the screen, Mamantov had turned and was boarding the train. He waved at the cameras. The band was playing. People were applauding.

Holy mother –

Arsenyev could feel the lurching of his heart, the clenching of his bronchial tubes. Getting air into his lungs was like sucking mud through a straw.

He took a couple of squirts on his inhaler.

'No,' grunted the familiar voice in Arsenyev's ear, and the line went dead.

'No,' wheezed Arsenyev, quickly, pointing at Vissari Netto.

'No,' said Netto, who was sitting on the sofa, also holding a telephone, patched through on a secure military circuit to the MVD commander in Vologda. 'I repeat: no move to be made. Stand your men down. Let the train go.'

'The right decision,' said Arsenyev, replacing the receiver. 'There could have been shooting. It wouldn't have looked good.'

Looking good was all that mattered now.

For a while Arsenyev said nothing as he contemplated, with increasing unease, this final fork in his life's road. One route, it seemed to him, took him to retirement, pension and a dacha; the other to almost certain dismissal, an official inquiry into illegal assassination attempts and, quite possibly, jail.

'Abandon the whole operation,' he said.

Netto's pen began to move across his pad. Deep in their fleshy sockets, like a pair of berries in dough, Arsenyev's little eyes blinked in alarm.

'No, no, no, man! Don't write any of this down! Just do it. Pull the surveillance off Mamantov's apartment. Remove the protection from the girl. Abort the whole thing.'

'And Archangel, colonel? We've still got a plane waiting up there for Major Suvorin.'

Arsenyev tugged at his thick neck for a few seconds. In his perennially fertile mind, the form of an unattributable briefing for the foreign media was already beginning to take shape: *'reports of shooting in the Archangel forest . . . regrettable incident . . . rogue officer took matters into his own hands . . . disobeyed strict orders . . . tragic outcome . . . profound apologies . . .'*

Poor Feliks, he thought.

'Order it back to Moscow.'

IT was as if the train had been held in check too long, so that when the brakes were finally released it lunged forwards and then stopped abruptly, and O'Brian, like the clapper of a bell, was slammed into the front and back of the compartment. The satchel flew out of his hands.

Very slowly, creaking and protesting, and with the same

infinitesimal speed as when they left Archangel, the locomotive began to haul them out of Vologda.

Kelso was still on the floor.

'No notebook – no proof – no story –'

He dived for the satchel and scooped it in one hand, got the fingertips of his other up on to the door handle, and was attempting to rise when he felt O'Brian grab his legs and try to drag him back. The handle tipped, the door slid open and he flopped out on to the carpeted corridor, kicking backwards frantically with his heels at O'Brian's head. He felt a satisfying contact of hard rubber on flesh and bone. There was a howl of pain. The boot came off and he left it behind like a lizard losing the tip of its tail. He limped away down the corridor on his stockinged foot.

The narrow passage was clogged with anxious 'soft' class passengers – *'Did you hear?' 'Is it true?'* – and it was impossible to make quick progress. O'Brian was coming after him. He could hear his shouts. At the end of the carriage the window of the door was open and he briefly considered hurling the satchel out on to the tracks. But the train hadn't cleared Vologda, was travelling much too slowly – the notebook was bound to land intact, he thought: was certain to be found –

'Fluke!'

He ran into the next carriage and realised too late that he was heading back towards 'hard' again, which was a mistake because 'hard' was where Mamantov and his thugs had boarded – and here, indeed was one of Mamantov's men, hastening down the corridor towards him, pushing people out of his way.

Kelso grabbed the door handle nearest him. It was locked. But the second handle turned and he almost fell into the empty compartment, locking the door after him. Inside it was shaded, the curtains closed, the berths unmade, a stale smell of cold, male sweat – whoever had occupied it must have got off at Vologda. He tried to open the window but it was stuck. The Aurora man was battering at the door, shouting at him to open up. The handle rattled furiously. Kelso unfastened the satchel and tipped out the contents and had his lighter in his hand as the lock gave way.

THE blinds of Zinaida Rapava's apartment were drawn. The lights were off. The television screen flickered in the corner of her tiny flat like a cold blue hearth.

There had been a plainclothes guard outside on the landing all night – Bunin to start with, and then a different man – and a militia car parked ostentatiously opposite the entrance to the apartment block. It was Bunin who had told her to keep the blinds closed and not to go out. She didn't like Bunin and she could tell he didn't like her. When she asked him how long she would have to stay like this, he had shrugged. Was she a prisoner, then? He had shrugged again.

She had lain in a foetal curl on her bed for the best part of twenty hours, listening to her neighbours coming home from work, then some of them going out for the evening. Later, she heard them preparing for bed. And she had discovered, lying in the darkness, that as long as something occupied her eye, she could prevent herself seeing her father: she could block out the image of the broken figure on the trolley. So she had watched television all night. And at one point, hopping between a game show and a black-and-white American movie, she had lighted on the pictures from the forest.

' . . . *freedom alone is not enough, by far . . . It is very difficult, comrades, to live on freedom alone . . .*'

407

She had watched, hypnotised, as the night went on, how the story had spread like a stain across the networks, until she could recite it by heart. There was her father's lock-up, and the notebook, and Kelso turning the pages (*'it's genuine – I'd stake my life on it'*). There was the old woman pointing at a map. There was the strange man walking across the forest clearing and staring into the camera as he spoke. He ranted part of a hate-filled speech and that had nagged at her memory for a while in the early hours, until she remembered that her father had sometimes played a record of it when she was a child.

(*'You should listen to this, girl – you might learn something.'*)

He was frightening, this man, comic and sinister – like Zhirinovsky, or Hitler – and when it was reported that he had been seen on the Moscow train, heading south, she felt almost as if he were coming for *her*. She could imagine him stamping down the halls of the big hotels, his boots hammering on the marble, his coat flying behind him, smashing the windows of the expensive boutiques, hurling the foreigners out on to the pavements, looking for her. She could see him in Robotnik, overturning the bar, calling the girls whores and shouting at them to cover themselves. He would paint out the western signs, shatter the neon, empty the streets, shut down the airport –

She knew they should have burned that notebook.

It was later, when she was in the bathroom, naked from the waist up, splashing cold water into her red eyes, that she heard from the television the name of Mamantov. And her first thought was, naïvely, that he had been arrested. After all, that was what Suvorin had promised her, wasn't it?

'We're going to find the man who did this terrible thing to your father, and we're going to lock him up.'

She grabbed a towel and darted back to the screen, hastily drying her face, and scrutinised him, and, oh yes, she knew it was him right enough, she could believe it of *him* – he looked a pitiless, cold bastard, with his wire-framed glasses and his thin, hard lips, and his Soviet-style hat and coat. He looked capable of anything.

He was saying something about 'the fascist usurper in the Kremlin' and it took her a minute to realise that actually he wasn't being arrested. On the contrary: he was being treated with respect. He was moving towards the train. He was boarding it. Nobody was stopping him. She could even see a couple of militia men, watching him. He turned on the step to the carriage and raised his hand. Lights flickered. He flashed his hangman's smile and disappeared inside.

Zinaida stared at the screen.

She searched through the pockets of her jacket until she found the telephone number Suvorin had given her.

It rang, unanswered.

She replaced the receiver calmly enough, wrapped the towel around her torso and unlocked her door.

Nobody was on the landing.

She went back into the flat and lifted the blind.

No sign of any militia car. Just the normal Saturday morning traffic beginning to build for the Izmaylovo market.

Afterwards, several witnesses came forward who claimed to have heard the sound of her cry, even above the noises of the busy street.

KELSO was overpowered with humiliating ease. He was pushed back on to the banquette, the satchel and the papers were taken from him, the door was wedged shut, and the young man in the black leather jacket took the seat opposite him, stretching one leg across the narrow aisle to prevent his prisoner from moving.

He unzipped the jacket just far enough to show Kelso a shoulder holster, and Kelso recognised him then: Mamantov's personal bodyguard from the Moscow apartment. He was a big, baby-faced lad, with a drooping left eyelid and a blubbery lower lip, and there was something about the way he let his boot rest against Kelso's thigh, cramming him against the window, that suggested hurting people might be his pleasure in life: that he needed violence as a swimmer requires water.

Kelso remembered Papu Rapava's slowly twisting body and began to sweat.

'It's Viktor, isn't it?'

No reply.

'How long am I supposed to stay here, Viktor?'

Again, no answer, and after a couple more half-hearted attempts to demand his release, Kelso gave up. He could hear the sound of boots in the corridor and he had the impression that the whole of the train was being secured.

After that, not much happened for several hours.

At 10.20 they stopped as scheduled at Danilov and more of Mamantov's people poured aboard.

Kelso asked if he could at least go to the lavatory.

No answer.

Later, outside the city of Yaroslavl, they passed a derelict factory with a rusting Order of Lenin pinned to its windowless side. On its roof, a line of youths was silhouetted, their arms raised high in a fascist salute.

Viktor looked at Kelso and smiled, and Kelso looked away.

IN Moscow, Zinaida Rapava's apartment was empty.

The Klims who lived in the flat beneath afterwards swore they had heard her go out soon after eleven. But old man Amosov, who was fixing his car in the street directly across from the block, insisted it was some time after that: more like noon, he thought. She went straight by him without uttering a word, which wasn't unusual for her – she had her head down, he said, and was wearing dark glasses, a leather jacket, jeans and boots – and she was heading in the direction of the Semyonovskaya metro station.

She didn't have her car: that was still parked outside her father's apartment.

The next authenticated sighting came an hour later, at one o'clock, when she turned up at the back of Robotnik. A cleaner, Vera Yanukova, recognised her and let her in and she went directly to the cloakroom where she retrieved a leather shoulder bag (she showed her ticket; there was no mistake). The cleaner opened up the front entrance for her to leave, but she preferred to go out the way she had come, thus avoiding the metal detectors which were switched on automatically whenever the door was unlocked.

According to the cleaner, she was nervous when she arrived, but once she had the bag she seemed in good spirits, calm and self-possessed.

Chapter Thirty-four

DID KELSO FALL asleep? He afterwards wondered if he might have done, for he had no real recollection of that long afternoon until he heard footsteps in the corridor and the sound of someone knocking softly on the door. And by then they were into the northern fringes of Moscow and the flat October light was already falling on the endless iron and concrete of the city.

Viktor idly swung his foot off the banquette and stood, hitching up his trousers. He removed his knife from the mechanism of the lock and slid back the door a fraction, then pulled it all the way, coming stiffly to attention, and suddenly Vladimir Mamantov was across the threshold and into the compartment, bringing with him that same odd odour of camphor and carbolic that Kelso remembered from his apartment. The same clump of dark bristles still nestled in the cleft of his chin.

He was all false smiles and apologies: so sorry if Kelso had been inconvenienced in any way, such a pity they had not been able to meet much earlier in the journey, but he had had other, more pressing matters to attend to. He was sure that Kelso understood.

His overcoat was unbuttoned. His face was sheened with sweat. He tossed his hat on to the banquette opposite Kelso and sat down next to it, grabbing the satchel, removing the documents, gesturing to Viktor to take the seat next to Kelso, calling to the second bodyguard he had left in the corridor to close the door and not to let anyone in.

This was not the Mamantov Kelso had met seven years ago

on his release from prison. This was not even the Mamantov from earlier in the week. This was Mamantov in his prime again. Mamantov rejuvenated. Mamantov *redux*.

Kelso watched him as his thick fingers checked through the notebook and the NKVD reports.

'Good,' he said, briskly, 'excellent. Everything is here, I think. Tell me: were you really were planning to destroy all this?'

'Yes.'

'All of it?'

'Yes.'

He looked at Kelso in wonderment and shook his head.

'And yet you are the one who is always bleating about the need to open every historical document for inspection!'

'Even so, I'd still have destroyed it. In the interests of stopping you.'

Kelso felt the increasing pressure of Viktor's elbow in his ribs, and he knew that the young man was longing for an opportunity to hurt him.

'Ah! So history is only to be permitted where it suits the subjective interests of those who hold the records?' Mamantov smiled again. 'Has the myth of so-called western "objectivity" ever been more completely exposed? I can see I shall have to take these documents back into my possession for safe-keeping.'

'Take them back?' said Kelso. He couldn't keep the incredulity out of his voice. 'You mean you had them before?'

Mamantov inclined his head graciously.

Indeed.

MAMANTOV had replaced the papers in the satchel and had fastened the straps. But he couldn't quite bring himself to leave. Not yet. After all, he had waited so long for this moment. He wanted Kelso know. It was fifteen years since Yepishev had first told him about this 'black oilskin notebook' and he had never lost faith that one day he would find it. And then, like a miracle, in the very darkest hours of the cause, who should turn up on the membership lists of Aurora but the very same Papu Rapava whose name had cropped up so often in the KGB's files? Mamantov had summoned him. And at long last – hesitantly, reluctantly at first, but eventually out of loyalty to his new chief – Rapava had told him the story of the night of Stalin's stroke.

Mamantov had been the first to hear it.

That had been a year ago.

It had taken him a whole nine months to get into the garden of Beria's mansion on Vspolnyi Street. And do you know what he had had to do? No? He had had to set up a property company – Moskprop – and *buy* the goddamn place off its owners, the former KGB, although that hadn't been too hard because Mamantov had plenty of friends at the Lubyanka who, in return for a percentage, were happy to sell state assets for a fraction of their true value. Some might call it corruption, or even robbery. He preferred the western term: privatisation.

The Tunisians had been kicked out, finally, under the terms of their lease, in August, and Rapava had led him to the exact spot in the garden. The toolbox had been retrieved. Mamantov had read the notebook, had flown to Archangel, had followed exactly the same trail as Kelso and O'Brian into the heart of the forest. And he had seen the potential at once. But he also had the sense – the genius, he would almost call it, but he would leave that judgement to others – the *wit*, let's say, to recognise what Kelso had just so aptly proved: that history, in the end, is a matter of subjectivity not objectivity.

'Suppose I had returned to Moscow with our mutual friend, convened a press conference and announced he was Stalin's son. What would have happened? I'll tell you. Nothing. I would have been ignored. Derided. Accused of forgery. And why?' He jabbed his finger at Kelso. 'Because the media is in the grip of cosmopolitan forces that loathe Vladimir Mamantov and all he stands for. Oh, but if Dr Kelso, the darling of the cosmopolitans – ah, yes, if *Kelso* says to the world, "Behold, I give you Stalin's son," then that is a different matter.'

So the son had been prevailed upon to wait a few weeks longer, until some other strangers would appear bearing the notebook.

(And that explained a lot, thought Kelso: the odd sense he had experienced in Archangel that people had been somehow waiting for them – the communist official, Vavara Safanova, the man himself. *'You are the ones, you are truly the ones; and I am the one you seek . . .'*)

'And why me?' he asked.

'Because I remembered you. Remembered you wheedling your way in to see me when I was fresh from Lefortovo after the coup – your fucking arrogance, your certainty that you and your kind had won and I was finished. The shit you wrote about me . . . What was it Stalin said? "To choose one's victims, to prepare one's plans minutely, to slake an implacable vengeance, and then to go to bed . . . there is nothing sweeter in the world." Sweet. That's it. Nothing sweeter in the world.'

ZINAIDA Rapava arrived at Moscow's Yaroslavl Station a few minutes after four o'clock. (What exactly she had been doing in the three hours since leaving Robotnik the authorities were never able to determine, although there were unconfirmed reports of a woman matching her description being seen at the Troekurovo cemetery, where her mother and brother were buried.)

At any rate, at five past four, she approached an employee of the Russian railway network. Afterwards he couldn't say why she stuck in his mind when so many others were milling around that day: perhaps it was the dark glasses she was wearing, despite the perpetual sunken gloom beneath the hooded arches of the railway terminus.

Like the rest, she wanted to know which platform the Archangel train would be arriving at.

The crowds were already beginning to build, and Aurora stewards were doing their best to keep them in order. A gangway had been roped off. A platform had been erected for the cameras. Flags were being distributed – the Tsarist eagle, the hammer and sickle, the Aurora emblem. Zinaida took a little red flag, and maybe it was that, or maybe it was the leather jacket that made her look like a typical Aurora activist, but whatever it was she secured a prime position, at the edge of the rope, and nobody bothered her.

She can be glimpsed, occasionally, on some of the videotape of the crowd, taken before the train arrived – cool, solitary, waiting.

THE train was trundling past the suburban stations. Curious Saturday afternoon shoppers looked to see what all the fuss was about. A man held up a child to wave but Mamantov was too busy talking to notice.

He was describing the way he had lured Kelso to Russia – and that, he said, was the touch he was proudest of: that was

416

a ruse worthy of Josef Vissarionovich himself.

He had arranged for a front company he owned in Switzerland – respectable, a family firm: it had been exploiting the workers for centuries – to contact Rosarkhiv and offer to sponsor a symposium on the opening up of the Soviet archives!

Mamantov slapped his own knee with mirth.

At first, Rosarkhiv hadn't wanted to invite Kelso – imagine that! they thought he was no longer of 'sufficient standing in the academic community' – but Mamantov, through the sponsors, had insisted, and two months later, sure enough, there he was, back in town, in his free hotel room, all expenses paid, like a pig in shit, come to wallow in *our* past, feeling superior to *us*, telling *us* to feel guilty, when all the time the only reason he was there was to bring the past back to life!

And Papu Rapava, asked Kelso, what had he thought of this plan?

For the first time, Mamantov's face darkened.

Rapava had claimed to like the plan. That was what he'd said. To spit in the capitalists' soup and then to watch them drink it? Oh yes please, comrade colonel: that had appealed to Rapava very much! He was supposed to tell Kelso his story overnight, then take him directly to Beria's old mansion, where they would retrieve the toolbox together. Mamantov had tipped off O'Brian who promised to turn up with his cameras at the Institute of Marxism–Leninism the next morning. The symposium was to provide the perfect launch pad. What a story! There would have been a feeding frenzy. Mamantov had the whole thing worked out.

But then: nothing. Kelso had called the following afternoon and that was when Mamantov had learned that

Rapava had failed in his mission: that he had told his story right enough, but then had run away.

'Why?' Mamantov frowned. 'You mentioned money to him, presumably?'

Kelso nodded. 'I offered him a share in the profits.'

A look of contempt spread across Mamantov's face. 'That *you* should seek to enrich yourself – that I'd expected: that was another reason I selected you. But that *he* should?' He shook his head in disgust. 'Human beings,' he murmured. 'They always let you down.'

'He might have felt the same about you,' said Kelso. 'Given what you did to him.'

Mamantov glanced at Viktor and something passed between the older man and the younger in that instant – a look of almost sexual intimacy – and Kelso knew at once that the pair of them had worked on Papu Rapava together. There must have been others but these two were at the centre of it: the craftsman and his apprentice.

He felt himself beginning to sweat again.

'But he never told you where he'd hidden it,' he said.

Mamantov frowned, as if trying to remember something. 'No,' he said, softly. 'No. He came of strong stock. I'll grant him that. Not that it matters. We followed you and the girl the next morning, saw you collect the material. In the end, Rapava's death changed nothing. I have it all now.'

Silence.

The train had slowed almost to walking pace. Beyond the flat roofs, Kelso could see the mast of the Television Tower.

'Time presses,' said Mamantov suddenly, 'and the world is waiting.'

He picked up the satchel and his hat. 'I've given some thought to you,' he said to Kelso, as he stood and began buttoning his coat. 'But really I can't see that you can harm us. You can withdraw your authentication of the papers, of course, but that won't make much difference now, except to make you look a fool – they're genuine: that will be established by independent experts in a day or two. You can also make certain wild allegations about the death of Papu Rapava, but no proof exists.' He bent to examine himself in the small mirror above Kelso's head, straightening the brim of his hat in readiness for the cameras. 'No. I think the best thing I can do is simply leave you to watch what happens next.'

'Nothing's going to happen next,' said Kelso. 'Don't forget I've talked to this creature of yours – the moment he opens his mouth, people will laugh.'

'You want to bet on it?' Mamantov offered his hand. 'No? You're wise. Lenin said: "The most important thing in any endeavour is to get involved in the fight, and in that way learn what to do next." And that's what we're going to do now. For the first time in nearly ten years we're going to be able to start a fight. And such a fight. Viktor.'

Reluctantly, and with a final, wistful glance at Kelso, the young man got to his feet.

The corridor was crowded with figures in black leather jackets.

'It was love,' said Kelso, when Mamantov was halfway out of the door.

'What?' Mamantov turned to stare at him.

'Rapava. That was the reason he didn't take me to the papers. You said he did it for the money, but I don't think he wanted the money for himself. He wanted it for his daughter. To make it up to her. It was love.'

'Love?' repeated Mamantov incredulously. He tested the

word in his mouth as if it was unfamiliar to him – the name of some sinister new weapon, perhaps, or a freshly discovered world capitalist–zionist conspiracy. 'Love?' No. It was no use. He shook his head and shrugged.

The door slid shut and Kelso collapsed back in his seat. A minute or two later he heard a noise like a high wind roaring through a forest and he pressed his face to the window. Up ahead, across an expanse of track, he could see a shifting mass of colour that gradually became more defined as they drew alongside the platform – faces, placards, waving flags, a podium, a red carpet, cameras, people waiting behind ropes, Zinaida –

SHE spotted him at the same instant and for a few long seconds their eyes locked. She saw him start to rise, mouthing something, gesturing at her, but then he was borne away and out of sight. The procession of dull green carriages, spattered with mud from the long journey, clanked slowly past then juddered to a halt, and the crowd, which had been festively noisy for the past half hour, was suddenly quiet.

Youths in leather jackets leapt from the train immediately in front of her. She saw the shadow of a marshal's cap move behind one of the windows.

The gun was out of her bag by now and hidden inside her jacket and she could feel the cold comfort of its shape against her palm. There was a ball of something very tight within her chest but it wasn't fear. It was a tension longing to be released.

In her mind she could see him very clearly, each mark upon his body a mark of his love for her.

'Who is your only friend, girl?'

There was a movement in the doorway of the carriage. The two men were coming out together.

'*Yourself, papa.*'

They stood together on the top step, waving, close enough for her to touch. People were cheering. The crowd surged at her back. She couldn't miss.

'*And who else?*'

She pulled out the gun very quickly and aimed.

'*You, papa. You –*'

FATHERLAND

ROBERT HARRIS

ACKNOWLEDGEMENTS

I thank the Librarian and staff of the Wiener Library in London for their help over several years.

I also wish to thank David Rosenthal and – especially – Robyn Sisman, without whom this book would never have been started, let alone finished.

Hitler's Berlin 1964

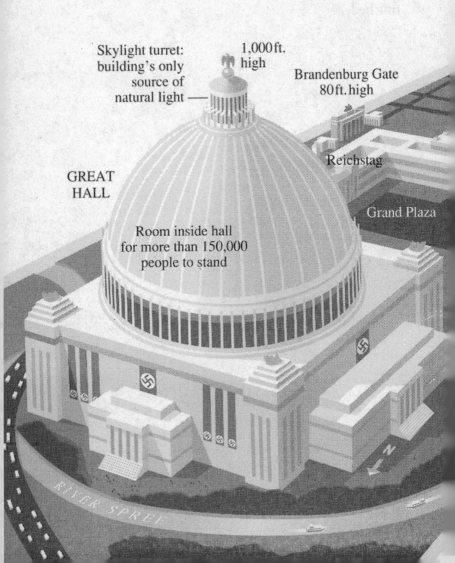

Skylight turret: building's only source of natural light

1,000 ft. high

Brandenburg Gate 80 ft. high

Reichstag

GREAT HALL

Grand Plaza

Room inside hall for more than 150,000 people to stand

RIVER SPREE

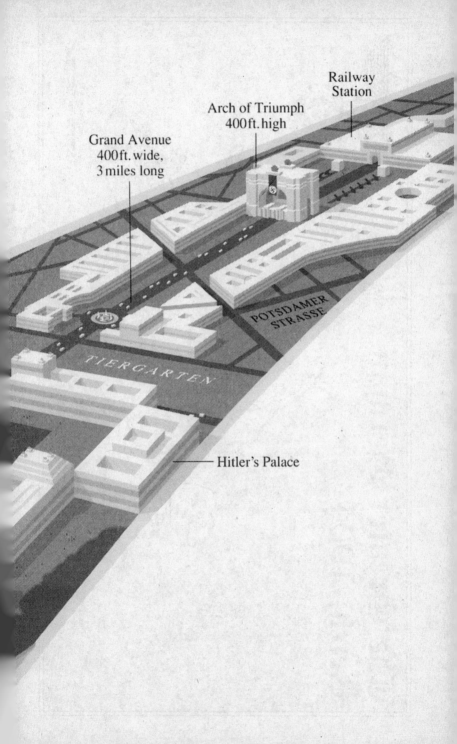

Railway
Station

Arch of Triumph
400 ft. high

Grand Avenue
400 ft. wide,
3 miles long

POTSDAMER
STRASSE

TIERGARTEN

——— Hitler's Palace

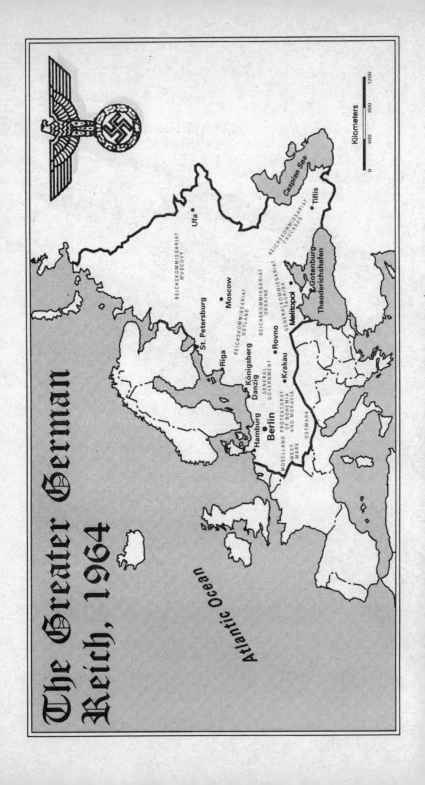

The hundred million self-confident German masters were to be brutally installed in Europe, and secured in power by a monopoly of technical civilisation and the slave-labour of a dwindling native population of neglected, diseased, illiterate cretins, in order that they might have leisure to buzz along infinite Autóbahnen, admire the Strength-Through-Joy Hostel, the Party headquarters, the Military Museum and the Planetarium which their Führer would have built in Linz (his new Hitleropolis), trot round local picture-galleries, and listen over their cream buns to endless recordings of *The Merry Widow*. This was to be the German Millennium, from which even the imagination was to have no means of escape.

HUGH TREVOR-ROPER
The Mind of Adolf Hitler

People sometimes say to me: 'Be careful! You will have twenty years of guerilla warfare on your hands!' I am delighted at the prospect . . . Germany will remain in a state of perpetual alertness.

ADOLF HITLER
29 August 1942

PART ONE

TUESDAY 14 APRIL 1964

I swear to Thee, Adolf Hitler,
As Führer and Chancellor of the German Reich,
Loyalty and Bravery.
I vow to Thee and to the superiors
Whom Thou shalt appoint
Obedience unto Death,
So help me God.

SS OATH

ONE

hick cloud had pressed down on Berlin all night, and now it was lingering into what passed for the morning. On the city's western outskirts, plumes of rain drifted across the surface of Lake Havel, like smoke.

Sky and water merged into a sheet of grey, broken only by the dark line of the opposite bank. Nothing stirred there. No lights showed.

Xavier March, homicide investigator with the Berlin Kriminalpolizei – the Kripo – climbed out of his Volkswagen and tilted his face to the rain. He was a connoisseur of this particular rain. He knew the taste of it, the smell of it. It was Baltic rain, from the north, cold and sea-scented, tangy with salt. For an instant he was back twenty years, in the conning tower of a U-boat, slipping out of Wilhelmshaven, lights doused, into the darkness.

He looked at his watch. It was just after seven in the morning.

Drawn up on the roadside before him were three other cars. The occupants of two were asleep in the drivers' seats. The third was a patrol car of the Ordnungspolizei – the Orpo, as every German called them. It was empty. Through its open window, sharp in the damp air, came the crackle of static, punctuated by jabbering bursts of speech. The revolving light on its roof lit up the forest beside the road: blue-black, blue-black, blue-black.

March looked around for the Orpo patrolmen, and saw them sheltering by the lake under a dripping birch tree. Something gleamed pale in the mud at their feet. On a nearby log sat a young man in a black tracksuit, SS insignia on his breast pocket. He was hunched forward, elbows

3

resting on his knees, hands pressed against the sides of his head – the image of misery.

March took a last draw on his cigarette and flicked it away. It fizzed and died on the wet road.

As he approached, one of the policemen raised his arm.

'Heil Hitler!'

March ignored him and slithered down the muddy bank to inspect the corpse.

It was an old man's body – cold, fat, hairless and shockingly white. From a distance, it could have been an alabaster statue dumped in the mud. Smeared with dirt, the corpse sprawled on its back half out of the water, arms flung wide, head tilted back. One eye was screwed shut, the other squinted balefully at the filthy sky.

'Your name, Unterwachtmeister?' March had a soft voice. Without taking his eyes off the body, he addressed the Orpo man who had saluted.

'Ratka, Herr Sturmbannführer.'

Sturmbannführer was an SS title, equivalent in Wehrmacht rank to major, and Ratka – dog-tired and skin-soaked though he was –seemed eager to show respect. March knew his type without even looking round: three applications to transfer to the Kripo, all turned down; a dutiful wife who had produced a football team of children for the Führer; an income of 200 Reichsmarks a month. A life lived in hope.

'Well, Ratka,' said March, in that soft voice again. 'What time was he discovered?'

'Just over an hour ago, sir. We were at the end of our shift, patrolling in Nikolassee. We took the call. Priority One. We were here in five minutes.'

'Who found him?'

Ratka jerked his thumb over his shoulder.

The young man in the tracksuit rose to his feet. He could not have been more than eighteen. His hair was cropped so close the pink scalp showed through the dusting of light brown hair. March noticed how he avoided looking at the body.

'Your name?'

'SS-Schütze Hermann Jost, sir.' He spoke with a Saxon accent – nervous, uncertain, anxious to please. 'From the Sepp Dietrich training academy at Schlachtensee.' March knew it: a monstrosity of concrete and asphalt built in the 1950s, just south of the Havel. 'I run here most mornings. It was still dark. At first, I thought it was a swan,' he added, helplessly.

Ratka snorted, contempt on his face. An SS cadet scared of one dead old man! No wonder the war in the Urals was dragging on forever.

'Did you see anyone else, Jost?' March spoke in a kindly tone, like an uncle.

'Nobody, sir. There's a telephone box in the picnic area, half a kilometre back. I called, then came here and waited until the police arrived. There wasn't a soul on the road.'

March looked again at the body. It was very fat. Maybe 110 kilos.

'Let's get him out of the water.' He turned towards the road. 'Time to raise our sleeping beauties.' Ratka, shifting from foot to foot in the downpour, grinned.

It was raining harder now, and the Kladow side of the lake had virtually disappeared. Water pattered on the leaves of the trees and drummed on the car roofs. There was a heavy rain-smell of corruption: rich earth and rotting vegetation. March's hair was plastered to his scalp, water trickled down the back of his neck. He did not notice. For March, every case, however routine, held – at the start, at least – the promise of adventure.

He was forty-two years old – slim, with grey hair and cool grey eyes that matched the sky. During the war, the Propaganda Ministry had invented a nickname for the men of the U-boats – the 'grey wolves' – and it would have been a good name for March, in one sense, for he was a determined detective. But he was not by nature a wolf, did not run with the pack, was more reliant on brain than muscle, so his colleagues called him 'the fox' instead.

U-boat weather!

He flung open the door of the white Skoda, and was hit by a gust of hot, stale air from the car heater.

'Morning, Spiedel!' He shook the police photographer's bony shoulder. 'Time to get wet.' Spiedel jerked awake. He gave March a glare.

The driver's window of the other Skoda was already being wound down as March approached it. 'All right, March. All right.' It was SS-Surgeon August Eisler, a Kripo pathologist, his voice a squeak of affronted dignity. 'Save your barrack-room humour for those who appreciate it.'

THEY gathered at the water's edge, all except Doctor Eisler, who stood apart, sheltering under an ancient black umbrella he did not offer to share. Spiedel screwed a flash bulb on to his camera and carefully planted his right foot on a lump of clay. He swore as the lake lapped over his shoe.

'Shit!'

The flash popped, freezing the scene for an instant: the white faces, the silver threads of rain, the darkness of the woods. A swan came scudding out of some nearby reeds to see what was happening, and began circling a few metres away.

'Protecting her nest,' said the young SS man.

'I want another here.' March pointed. 'And one here.'

Spiedel cursed again and pulled his dripping foot out of the mud. The camera flashed twice more.

March bent down and grasped the body under the armpits. The flesh was hard, like cold rubber, and slippery.

6

'Help me.'

The Orpo men each took an arm and together, grunting with the effort, they heaved, sliding the corpse out of the water, over the muddy bank and on to the sodden grass. As March straightened, he caught the look on Jost's face.

The old man had been wearing a pair of blue swimming trunks which had worked their way down to his knees. In the freezing water, the genitals had shrivelled to a tiny clutch of white eggs in a nest of black pubic hair.

The left foot was missing.

It had to be, thought March. This was a day when nothing would be simple. An adventure, indeed.

'Herr Doctor. Your opinion, please.'

With a sigh of irritation, Eisler daintily stepped forward, removing the glove from one hand. The corpse's leg ended at the bottom of the calf. Still holding the umbrella, Eisler bent stiffly and ran his fingers around the stump.

'A propeller?' asked March. He had seen bodies dragged out of busy waterways – from the Tegler See and the Spree in Berlin, from the Alster in Hamburg – which looked as if butchers had been at them.

'No.' Eisler withdrew his hand. 'An old amputation. Rather well done in fact.' He pressed hard on the chest with his fist. Muddy water gushed from the mouth and bubbled out of the nostrils. 'Rigor mortis fairly advanced. Dead twelve hours. Maybe less.' He pulled his glove back on.

A diesel engine rattled somewhere through the trees behind them.

'The ambulance,' said Ratka. 'They take their time.'

March gestured to Spiedel. 'Take another picture.'

Looking down at the corpse, March lit a cigarette. Then he squatted on his haunches and stared into the single open eye. He stayed that way a long while. The camera flashed again. The swan reared up, flapped her wings, and turned towards the centre of the lake in search of food.

ripo headquarters lie on the other side of Berlin, a twenty-five-minute drive from the Havel. March needed a statement from Jost, and offered to drop him back at his barracks to change, but Jost said no: he would sooner make his statement quickly. So once the body had been stowed aboard the ambulance and dispatched to the morgue, they set off in March's little four-door Volkswagen through the rush-hour traffic.

It was one of those dismal Berlin mornings, when the famous Berliner-luft seems not so much bracing as merely raw, the moisture stinging the face and hands like a thousand frozen needles. On the Potsdamer Chaussee, the spray from the wheels of the passing cars forced the few pedestrians close to the sides of the buildings. Watching them through the rain-flecked window, March imagined a city of blind men, feeling their way to work.

It was all so *normal*. Later, that was what would strike him most. It was like having an accident: before it, nothing out of the ordinary; then, the moment; and after it, a world that was changed forever. For there was nothing more routine than a body fished out of the Havel. It happened twice a month – derelicts and failed businessmen, reckless kids and lovelorn teenagers; accidents and suicides and murders; the desperate, the foolish, the sad.

The telephone had rung in his apartment in Ansbacher Strasse shortly after six-fifteen. The call had not woken him. He had been lying in the semi-darkness with his eyes open, listening to the rain. For the past few months he had slept badly.

'March? We've got a report of a body in the Havel.' It was Krause, the Kripo's Night Duty Officer. 'Go and take a look, there's a good fellow.'

March had said he was not interested.

'Your interest or lack of it is beside the point.'

'I am not interested,' said March, 'because I am not on duty. I was on duty last week, and the week before.' *And the week before that,* he might have added. 'This is my day off. Look again at your list.'

There had been a pause at the other end, then Krause had come back on the line, grudgingly apologetic. 'You are in luck, March. I was looking at last week's rota. You can go back to sleep. Or . . .' He had sniggered: 'Or whatever else it was you were doing.'

A gust of wind had slashed rain against the window, rattling the pane.

There was a standard procedure when a body was discovered: a pathologist, a police photographer and an investigator had to attend the scene at once. The investigators worked off a rota kept at Kripo headquarters in Werderscher Markt.

'Who is on today, as a matter of interest?'

'Max Jaeger.'

Jaeger. March shared an office with Jaeger. He had looked at his alarm clock and thought of the little house in Pankow where Max lived with his wife and four daughters: during the week, breakfast was just about the only time he saw them. March, on the other hand, was divorced and lived alone. He had set aside the afternoon to spend with his son. But the long hours of the morning stretched ahead, a blank. The way he felt it would be good to have something routine to distract him.

'Oh, leave him in peace,' he had said. 'I'm awake. I'll take it.'

That had been nearly two hours ago. March glanced at his passenger in the rear-view mirror. Jost had been silent ever since they left the Havel. He sat stiffly in the back seat, staring at the grey buildings slipping by.

At the Brandenburg Gate, a policeman on a motorcycle flagged them to a halt.

In the middle of Pariser Platz, an SA band in sodden brown uniforms wheeled and stamped in the puddles. Through the closed windows of the Volkswagen came the muffled thump of drums and trumpets, pounding out an old Party marching song. Several dozen people had gathered outside the Academy of Arts to watch them, shoulders hunched against the rain.

It was impossible to drive across Berlin at this time of year without encountering a similar rehearsal. In six days' time it would be Adolf Hitler's birthday – the Führertag, a public holiday – and every band in the Reich would be on parade. The windscreen wipers beat time like a metronome.

'Here we see the final proof,' murmured March, watching the crowd, 'that in the face of martial music, the German people are *mad*.'

He turned to Jost, who gave a thin smile.

A clash of cymbals ended the tune. There was a patter of damp applause. The bandmaster turned and bowed. Behind him, the SA men had already begun half-walking, half-running, back to their bus. The motorcycle cop waited until the Platz was clear, then blew a short blast on his whistle. With a white-gloved hand he waved them through the Gate.

The Unter den Linden gaped ahead of them. It had lost its lime trees in '36 – cut down in an act of official vandalism at the time of the Berlin Olympics. In their place, on either side of the boulevard, the city's Gauleiter, Josef Goebbels, had erected an avenue of ten-metre-high stone columns, on each of which perched a Party eagle, wings outstretched. Water dripped from their beaks and wingtips. It was like driving through a Red Indian burial ground.

March slowed for the lights at the Friedrich Strasse

intersection and turned right. Two minutes later they were parking in a space opposite the Kripo building in Werderscher Markt.

It was an ugly place – a heavy, soot-streaked, Wilhelmine monstrosity, six storeys high, on the south side of the Markt. March had been coming here, nearly seven days of the week, for ten years. As his ex-wife had frequently complained, it had become more familiar to him than home. Inside, beyond the SS sentries and the creaky revolving door, a board announced the current state of terrorist alert. There were four codes, in ascending order of seriousness: green, blue, black and red. Today, as always, the alert was red.

A pair of guards in a glass booth scrutinised them as they entered the foyer. March showed his identity card and signed in Jost.

The Markt was busier than usual. The workload always tripled in the week before the Führertag. Secretaries with boxes of files clattered on high heels across the marble floor. The air smelled thickly of wet overcoats and floor polish. Groups of officers in Orpo-green and Kripo-black stood whispering of crime. Above their heads, from opposite ends of the lobby, garlanded busts of the Führer and the Head of the Reich Main Security Office, Reinhard Heydrich, stared at one another with blank eyes.

March pulled back the metal grille of the elevator and ushered Jost inside.

The security forces which Heydrich controlled were divided into three. At the bottom of the pecking order were the Orpo, the ordinary cops. They picked up the drunks, cruised the Autobahnen, issued the speeding tickets, made the arrests, fought the fires, patrolled the railways and the airports, answered the emergency calls, fished the bodies out of the lakes.

At the top were the Sipo, the Security Police. The Sipo

embraced both the Gestapo and the Party's own security force, the SD. Their headquarters were in a grim complex around Prinz-Albrecht Strasse, a kilometre south-west of the Markt. They dealt with terrorism, subversion, counter-espionage and 'crimes against the state'. They had their ears in every factory and school, hospital and mess; in every town, in every village, in every street. A body in a lake would concern the Sipo only if it belonged to a terrorist or a traitor.

And somewhere between the other two, and blurring into both, came the Kripo – Department V of the Reich Main Security Office. They investigated straightforward crime, from burglary, through bank robbery, violent assault, rape and mixed marriage, all the way up to murder. Bodies in lakes – who they were and how they got there – they were Kripo business.

The elevator stopped at the second floor. The corridor was lit like an aquarium. Weak neon bounced off green linoleum and green-washed walls. There was the same smell of polish as in the lobby, but here it was spiced with lavatory disinfectant and stale cigarette smoke. Twenty doors of frosted glass lined the passage, some half open. These were the investigators' offices. From one came the sound of a solitary finger picking at a typewriter; in another, a telephone rang unanswered.

' "The nerve centre in the ceaseless war against the criminal enemies of National Socialism",' said March, quoting a recent headline in the Party newspaper, the *Völkischer Beobachter*. He paused, and when Jost continued to look blank he explained: 'A joke.'

'Sorry?'

'Forget it.'

He pushed open a door and switched on the light. His office was little more than a gloomy cupboard, a cell, its solitary window opening on to a courtyard of blackened brick. One wall was shelved: tattered, leather-bound volumes of statutes and decrees, a handbook on forensic science, a dictionary, an atlas, a Berlin street guide, telephone directories, box files with labels gummed to them – 'Braune', 'Hundt', 'Stark', 'Zadek' – every one a bureaucratic tombstone, memorialising some long-forgotten victim. Another side of the office was taken up by four filing cabinets. On top of one was a spider plant, placed there by a middle-aged secretary two years ago at the height of an unspoken and unrequited passion for Xavier March. It was now dead. That was all the furniture, apart from two wooden desks pushed together beneath the window. One was March's; the other belonged to Max Jaeger.

March hung his overcoat on a peg by the door. He preferred not to wear uniform when he could avoid it, and this morning he had used the rainstorm on the Havel as an excuse to dress in grey trousers and a thick blue sweater. He pushed Jaeger's chair towards Jost. 'Sit down. Coffee?'

'Please.'

There was a machine in the corridor. 'We've got fucking *photographs*. Can you believe it? Look at that.' Along the passage March could hear the voice of Fiebes of VB3 – the sexual crimes division – boasting of his latest success. 'Her maid took them. Look, you can see every *hair*. The girl should turn professional.'

What would this be? March thumped the side of the coffee machine and it ejected a plastic cup. Some officer's wife, he guessed, and a Polish labourer shipped in from the General Government to work in the garden. It was usually a Pole; a dreamy, soulful Pole, plucking at the heart of a wife whose husband was away at the front. It sounded as if they had been photographed *in flagrante* by some jealous girl from the Bund deutscher Mädel, anxious to please the authorities. This was a sexual crime, as defined in the 1935 Race Defilement Act.

He gave the machine another thump.

There would be a hearing in the People's Court, salaciously recorded in *Der Stürmer* as a warning to others. Two years in Ravensbrück for the wife. Demotion and disgrace for the husband. Twenty-five years for the Pole, if he was lucky; death if he was not.

'Fuck!' A male voice muttered something and Fiebes, a weaselly inspector in his mid-fifties whose wife had run off with an SS ski instructor ten years before, gave a shout of laughter. March, a cup of black coffee in either hand, retreated to his office and slammed the door behind him as loudly as he could with his foot.

Reichskriminalpolizei   *Werderscher Markt 5/6*
                                        Berlin

STATEMENT OF WITNESS

My name is Hermann Friedrich Jost. I was born on 23.2.45 in Dresden. I am a cadet at the Sepp Dietrich Academy, Berlin. At 05.30 this morning, I left for my regular training run. I prefer to run alone. My normal route takes me west through the Grunewald Forest to the Havel, north along the lakeshore to the Lindwerder Restaurant, then south to the barracks in Schlachtensee. Three hundred metres north of the Schwanenwerder causeway, I saw an object lying in the water at the edge of the lake. It was the body of a male. I ran to a telephone half a kilometre along the lake-path and informed the police. I returned to the body and waited for the arrival of the authorities. During all this time it was raining hard and I saw nobody.

I am making this statement of my own free will in the presence of Kripo investigator Xavier March.

       SS-Schütze H. F. Jost.
       08.24/14.4.64

March leaned back in his chair and studied the young man as he signed his statement. There were no hard lines to his face. It was as pink and soft as a baby's, with a clamour of acne around the mouth, a whisper of blond hair on the upper lip. March doubted if he shaved.

'Why do you run alone?'

Jost handed back his statement. 'It gives me a chance to think. It is good to be alone once in the day. One is not often alone in a barracks.'

'How long have you been a cadet?'

'Three months.'

'Do you enjoy it?'

'Enjoy it!' Jost turned his face to the window. 'I had just begun studying at the university at Göttingen when my call-up came through. Let us say, it was not the happiest day of my life.'

'What were you studying?'

'Literature.'

'German?'

'What other sort is there?' Jost gave one of his watery smiles. 'I hope to go back to the university when I have served my three years. I want to be a teacher; a writer. Not a soldier.'

March scanned his statement. 'If you are so anti-military, what are you doing in the SS?' He guessed the answer.

'My father. He was a founder member of the Leibstandarte Adolf Hitler. You know how it is: I am his only son; it was his dearest wish.'

'You must hate it.'

Jost shrugged. 'I survive. And I have been told – unofficially, naturally – that I will not have to go to the front. They need an assistant at the officer school in Bad Tolz to teach a course on the degeneracy of American literature. That sounds more my kind of thing: degeneracy.'

He risked another smile. 'Perhaps I shall become an expert in the field.'

March laughed and glanced again at the statement. Something was not right here, and now he saw it. 'No doubt you will.' He put the statement to one side and stood up. 'I wish you luck with your teaching.'

'Am I free to go?'

'Of course.'

With a look of relief, Jost got to his feet. March grasped the door handle. 'One thing.' He turned and stared into the SS cadet's eyes. 'Why are you lying to me?'

Jost jerked his head back. 'What. . . ?'

'You say you left the barracks at five-thirty. You call the cops at five past six. Schwanenwerder is three kilometres from the barracks. You are fit: you run every day. You do not dawdle: it is raining hard. Unless you suddenly developed a limp, you must have arrived at the lake quite some time before six. So there are – what? – twenty minutes out of thirty-five unaccounted for in your statement. What were you doing, Jost?'

The young man looked stricken. 'Maybe I left the barracks later. Or maybe I did a couple of circuits of the running track there first . . .'

' "Maybe, maybe . . ." ' March shook his head sadly. 'These are facts that can be checked, and I warn you: it will go hard for you if I have to find out the truth and bring it to you, rather than the other way round. You are a homosexual, yes?'

'Herr Sturmbannführer! For God's sake . . .'

March put his hands on Jost's shoulders. 'I don't care. Perhaps you run alone every morning so you can meet some fellow in the Grunewald for twenty minutes. That's your business. It's no crime in my book. All I'm interested in is the body. Did you see something? What did you really do?'

Jost shook his head. 'Nothing. I swear.' Tears were welling in his wide, pale eyes.

'Very well.' March released him. 'Wait downstairs. I'll arrange transport to take you back to Schlachtensee.' He opened the door. 'Remember what I said: better you tell me the truth now than I find it out for myself later.'

Jost hesitated, and for a moment March thought he might say something, but then he walked out into the corridor and was gone.

March rang down to the basement garage and ordered a car. He hung up and stared out of the grimy window at the wall opposite. The black brick glistened under the film of rainwater pouring down from the upper storeys. Had he been too hard on the boy? Probably. But sometimes the truth could only be ambushed, taken unguarded in a surprise attack. Was Jost lying? Certainly. But then if he was a homosexual, he could scarcely afford not to lie: anyone found guilty of 'anti-community acts' went straight to a labour camp. SS men arrested for homosexuality were attached to punishment battalions on the Eastern front; few returned.

March had seen a score of young men like Jost in the past year. There were more of them every day. Rebelling against their parents. Questioning the state. Listening to American radio stations. Circulating their crudely printed copies of proscribed books – Günter Grass and Graham Greene, George Orwell and J. D. Salinger. Chiefly, they protested against the war – the seemingly endless struggle against the American-backed Soviet guerillas, which had been grinding on east of the Urals for twenty years.

He felt suddenly ashamed of his treatment of Jost, and considered going down to apologise to him. But then he decided, as he always did, that his duty to the dead came first. His penance for his morning's bullying would be to put a name to the body in the lake.

*

THE Duty Room of the Berlin Kriminalpolizei occupies most of Werderscher Markt's third floor. March mounted the stairs two at a time. Outside the entrance, a guard armed with a machine gun demanded his pass. The door opened with a thud of electronic bolts.

An illuminated map of Berlin takes up half the far wall. A galaxy of stars, orange in the semi-darkness, marks the capital's one hundred and twenty-two police stations. To its left is a second map, even larger, depicting the entire Reich. Red lights pinpoint those towns big enough to warrant their own Kripo divisions. The centre of Europe glows crimson. Further east, the lights gradually thin until, beyond Moscow, there are only a few isolated sparks, winking like camp fires in the blackness. It is a planetarium of crime.

Krause, the Duty Officer for the Berlin Gau, sat on a raised platform beneath the display. He was on the telephone as March approached and raised his hand in greeting. Before him, a dozen women in starched white shirts sat in glass partitions, each wearing a headset with a microphone attached. What they must hear! A sergeant from a Panzer division comes home from a tour in the East. After a family supper, he takes out his pistol, shoots his wife and each of his three children in turn. Then he splatters his skull across the ceiling. An hysterical neighbour calls the cops. And the news comes here – is controlled, evaluated, reduced – before being passed downstairs to that corridor with cracked green linoleum, stale with cigarette smoke.

Behind the Duty Officer, a uniformed secretary with a sour face was making entries on the night incident board. There were four columns: crime (serious), crime (violent), incidents, fatalities. Each category was further quartered: time reported, source of information, detail of report, action taken. An average night of mayhem in the world's largest city, with its population of ten million, was reduced to hieroglyphics on a few square metres of white plastic.

There had been eighteen deaths since ten o'clock the previous night. The worst incident – *1H 2D 4K* – was three adults and four children killed in a car smash in Pankow just after 11. No action taken; that could be left to the Orpo. A family burned to death in a house-fire in Kreuzberg, a stabbing outside a bar in Wedding, a woman beaten to death in Spandau. The record of March's own disrupted morning was last on the list: *06:07 [O]* (that meant notification had come from the Orpo) *1H Havel/March*. The secretary stepped back and recapped her pen with a sharp click.

Krause had finished his telephone call and was looking defensive. 'I've already apologised, March.'

'Forget it. I want the missing list. Berlin area. Say: the last forty-eight hours.'

'No problem.' Krause looked relieved and swivelled round in his chair to the sour-faced woman. 'You heard the investigator, Helga. Check whether anything's come in in the last hour.' He spun back to face March, red-eyed with lack of sleep. 'I'd have left it an hour. But any trouble around that place – you know how it is.'

March looked up at the Berlin map. Most of it was a grey cobweb of streets. But over to the left were two splashes of colour: the green of the Grunewald Forest and, running alongside it, the blue ribbon of the Havel. Curling into the lake, in the shape of a foetus, was an island, linked to the shore by a thin umbilical causeway.

Schwanenwerder.

'Does Goebbels still have a place there?'

Krause nodded. 'And the rest.'

It was one of the most fashionable addresses in Berlin, practically a government compound. A few dozen large houses screened from the road. A sentry at the entrance to the causeway. A good place for privacy, for security, for forest views and private moorings; a bad place to discover a body. The corpse had been washed up fewer than three hundred metres away.

Krause said: 'The local Orpo call it "the pheasant run".'

March smiled: 'golden pheasants' was street slang for the Party leadership.

'It's not good to leave a mess for too long on *that* doorstep.'

Helga had returned. 'Persons reported missing since Sunday morning,' she announced, 'and still unaccounted for.' She gave a long roll of printed-out names to Krause, who glanced at it and passed it on to March. 'Plenty to keep you busy there.' He seemed to find this amusing. 'You should give it to that fat friend of yours, Jaeger. He's the one who should be looking after this business, remember?'

'Thanks. I'll make a start at least.'

Krause shook his head. 'You put in twice the hours of the others. You get no promotions. You're on shitty pay. Are you crazy or what?'

March had rolled the list of missing persons into a tube. He leaned forward and tapped Krause lightly on the chest with it. 'You forget yourself, comrade,' he said. 'Arbeit macht frei.' The slogan of the labour camps. Work Makes You Free.

He turned and made his way back through the ranks of telephonists. Behind him he could hear Krause appealing to Helga. 'See what I mean? What the hell kind of a joke is that?'

MARCH arrived back in his office just as Max Jaeger was hanging up his coat. 'Zavi!' Jaeger spread his arms wide. 'I got a message from the Duty Room. What can I say?' He wore the uniform of an SS Sturmbannführer. The black tunic still bore traces of his breakfast.

'Put it down to my soft old heart,' said March. 'And don't get too excited. There was nothing on the corpse to identify it and there are a hundred people missing in Berlin since Sunday. It'll take hours just to go through the list. And I've promised to take my boy out this afternoon, so you'll be on your own with it.'

He lit a cigarette and explained the details: the location, the missing foot, his suspicions about Jost. Jaeger took it in with a series of grunts. He was a shambling, untidy hulk of a man, two metres tall, with clumsy hands and feet. He was fifty, nearly ten years older than March, but they had shared an office since 1959 and sometimes worked as a team. Colleagues in Werderscher Markt joked about them behind their backs: the Fox and the Bear. And maybe there was something of the old married couple about them, in the way they bickered with and covered for each other.

'This is the "missing" list.' March sat down at his desk and unrolled the print-out: names, dates of birth, times of disappearance, addresses of informants. Jaeger leaned over his shoulder. He smoked stubby fat cigars and his uniform reeked of them. 'According to the good doctor Eisler, our man probably died some time after six last night, so the chances are nobody missed him until seven or eight at the earliest. They may even be waiting to see if he shows up this morning. So he may not be on the list. But we have to consider two other possibilities, do we not? One: he went missing some time *before* he died. Two – and we know from hard experience this is not impossible – Eisler has screwed up the time of death.'

'The guy isn't fit to be a vet,' said Jaeger.

March counted swiftly. 'One hundred and two names. I'd put the age of our man at sixty.'

21

'Better say fifty, to be safe. Twelve hours in the drink and nobody looks their best.'

'True. So we exclude everyone on the list born after 1914. That should bring it down to a dozen names. Identification couldn't be much easier: was grandpa missing a foot?' March folded the sheet, tore it in two, and handed one half to Jaeger. 'What are the Orpo stations around the Havel?'

'Nikolassee,' said Max. 'Wannsee. Kladow. Gatow. Pichelsdorf —but that's probably too far north.'

Over the next half hour, March called each of them in turn, including Pichelsdorf, to see if any clothing had been handed in, or if some local derelict matched the description of the man in the lake. Nothing. He turned his attention to his half of the list. By eleven-thirty he had exhausted every likely name. He stood up and stretched.

'Mister Nobody.'

Jaeger had finished calling ten minutes earlier and was staring out of the window, smoking. 'Popular fellow, isn't he? Makes even you looked loved.' He removed his cigar and picked some shreds of loose tobacco from his tongue. 'I'll see if the Duty Room have received any more names. Leave it to me. Have a good time with Pili.'

THE late morning service had just ended in the ugly church opposite Kripo headquarters. March stood on the other side of the street and watched the priest, a shabby raincoat over his vestments, locking the door. Religion was officially discouraged in Germany. How many worshippers, March wondered, had braved the Gestapo's spies to attend? Half-a-dozen? The priest slipped the heavy iron key into his pocket and turned round. He saw March looking at him, and immediately scuttled away, eyes cast down, like a man caught in the middle of an illegal transaction. March

buttoned his trenchcoat and followed him into the filthy
Berlin morning.

'onstruction of the Arch of Triumph was commenced in 1946 and work was completed in time for the Day of National Reawakening in 1950. The inspiration for the design came from the Führer and is based upon original drawings made by him during the Years of Struggle.'

The passengers on the tour bus – at least those who could understand – digested this information. They raised themselves out of their seats or leaned into the aisle to get a better view. Xavier March, half-way down the bus, lifted his son on to his lap. Their guide, a middle-aged woman clad in the dark green of the Reich Tourist Ministry, stood at the front, feet planted wide apart, back to the windscreen. Her voice over the address system was thick with cold.

'The Arch is constructed of granite and has a capacity of two million, three hundred and sixty-five thousand, six hundred and eighty-five cubic metres.' She sneezed. 'The Arc de Triomphe in Paris will fit into it forty-nine times.'

For a moment, the Arch loomed over them. Then, suddenly, they were passing through it – an immense, stone-ribbed tunnel, longer than a football pitch, higher than a fifteen-storey building, with the vaulted, shadowed roof of a cathedral. The headlights and tail-lights of eight lanes of traffic danced in the afternoon gloom.

'The Arch has a height of one hundred and eighteen metres. It is one hundred and sixty-eight metres wide and has a depth of one hundred and nineteen metres. On the inner walls are carved the names of the three million soldiers who fell in defence of the Fatherland in the wars of 1914 to 1918 and 1939 to 1946.'

She sneezed again. The passengers dutifully craned their

necks to peer at the Roll of the Fallen. They were a mixed party. A group of Japanese, draped with cameras; an American couple with a little girl Pili's age; some German settlers, from Ostland or the Ukraine, in Berlin for the Führertag. March looked away as they passed the Roll of the Fallen. Somewhere on it were the names of his father and both his grandfathers. He kept his eyes on the guide. When she thought no one was looking, she turned away and quickly wiped her nose on her sleeve. The coach re-emerged into the drizzle.

'Leaving the Arch we enter the central section of the Avenue of Victory. The Avenue was designed by Reich Minister Albert Speer and was completed in 1957. It is one hundred and twenty-three metres wide and five-point-six kilometres in length. It is both wider, and two and a half times longer, than the Champs Elysées in Paris.'

Higher, longer, bigger, wider, more expensive . . . Even in victory, thought March, Germany has a parvenu's inferiority complex. Nothing stands on its own. Everything has to be compared with what the foreigners have . . .

'The view from this point northwards along the Avenue of Victory is considered one of the wonders of the world.'

'One of the wonders of the world,' repeated Pili in a whisper.

And it was, even on a day like this. Dense with traffic, the Avenue stretched before them, flanked on either side by the glass and granite walls of Speer's new buildings: ministries, offices, big stores, cinemas, apartment blocks. At the far end of this river of light, rising as grey as a battleship through the spray, was the Great Hall of the Reich, its dome half hidden in the low cloud.

There were appreciative murmurs from the settlers. 'It's like a mountain,' said the woman sitting behind March. She was with her husband and four boys. They had probably been planning this trip all winter. A Tourist

Ministry brochure and a dream of April in Berlin: comforts to warm them in the snowbound, moonless nights of Minsk or Kiev, a thousand kilometres from home. How had they got here? A package tour organised by Strength-Through-Joy, perhaps: two hours in a Junkers jet with a stop-off in Warsaw. Or a three-day drive in the family Volkswagen on the Berlin-Moscow Autobahn.

Pili wriggled out of his father's grasp and walked unsteadily to the front of the coach. March pinched the bridge of his nose between thumb and forefinger, a nervous habit he had picked up – when? – in the U-boat service, he supposed, when the screws of the British warships sounded so close the hull shook and you never knew if their next depth charge would be your last. He had been invalided out of the navy in 1948 with suspected TB and spent a year convalescing. Then, for want of anything better to do, he had joined the Marine-Küstenpolizei, the Coastal Police, in Wilhelmshaven as a lieutenant. That year he had married Klara Eckart, a nurse he had met at the TB clinic. In 1952, he had joined the Hamburg Kripo. In 1954, with Klara pregnant and the marriage already failing, he had been promoted to Berlin. Paul – Pili – had been born exactly ten years and one month ago.

What had gone wrong? He did not blame Klara. She had not changed. She had always been a strong woman who wanted certain simple things from life: home, family, friends, acceptance. But March: he *had* changed. After ten years in the navy and twelve months in virtual isolation, he had stepped ashore into a world he barely recognised. As he went to work, watched television, ate with friends, even – God help him – slept beside his wife, he sometimes imagined himself aboard a U-boat still: cruising beneath the surface of everyday life; solitary, watchful.

He had picked Pili up at noon from Klara's place – a bungalow on a dreary post-war housing estate in

Lichtenrade, in the southern suburbs. Park in the street, sound the horn twice, watch for the twitch in the parlour curtain. This was the routine which had evolved, unspoken, since their divorce five years ago – a means of avoiding embarrassing encounters; a ritual to be endured one Sunday in four, work permitting, under the strict provisions of the Reich Marriages Act. It was rare for him to see his son on a Tuesday, but this was a school vacation: since 1959, children had been given a week off for the Führer's birthday, rather than for Easter.

The door had opened and Pili had appeared, like a shy child-actor being pushed out on stage against his will. Wearing his new Pimpf uniform – crisp black shirt and dark blue shorts – he had climbed wordlessly into the car. March had given him an awkward hug.

'You look smart. How's school?'

'All right.'

'And your mother?'

The boy shrugged.

'What would you like to do?'

He shrugged again.

They had lunch in Budapester Strasse, opposite the Zoo, in a modern place with vinyl seats and a plastic-topped table: father and son, one with beer and sausages, the other with apple juice and a hamburger. They talked about the Pimpf and Pili brightened. Until you were a Pimpf you were nothing, 'a non-uniformed creature who has never participated in a group meeting or a route march'. You were allowed to join when you were ten, and stayed until you were fourteen, when you passed into the full Hitler Youth.

'I was top in the initiation test.'

'Good lad.'

'You have to run sixty metres in twelve seconds,' said Pili. 'Do the long jump and the shot-put. There's a route march – a day and a half. Written stuff. Party philosophy. And you have to recite the *Horst Wessel Lied*.'

For a moment, March thought he was about to break into song. He cut in hurriedly: 'And your dagger?'

Pili fumbled in his pocket, a crease of concentration on his forehead. How like his mother he is, thought March. The same wide cheekbones and full mouth, the same serious brown eyes, set far apart. Pili laid the dagger carefully on the table before him. He picked it up. It reminded him of the day he got his own – when was it? '34? The excitement of a boy who believes he's been admitted to the company of men. He turned it over and the swastika on the hilt glinted in the light. He felt the weight of it in his hand, then gave it back.

'I'm proud of you,' he lied. 'What do you want to do? We can go to the cinema. Or the zoo.'

'I want to go on the bus.'

'But we did that last time. And the time before.'

'Don't care. I want to go on the bus.'

'THE Great Hall of the Reich is the largest building in the world. It rises to a height of more than a quarter of a kilometre, and on certain days – observe today – the top of its dome is lost from view. The dome itself is one hundred and forty metres in diameter and St Peter's in Rome will fit into it sixteen times.'

They had reached the top of the Avenue of Victory, and were entering Adolf Hitler Platz. To the left, the square was bounded by the headquarters of the Wehrmacht High Command, to the right by the new Reich Chancellery and Palace of the Führer. Ahead was the hall. Its greyness had dissolved as their distance from it had diminished. Now they could see what the guide was telling them: that the pillars supporting the frontage were of red granite, mined in

Sweden, flanked at either end by golden statues of Atlas and Tellus, bearing on their shoulders spheres depicting the heavens and the earth.

The building was as crystal-white as a wedding cake, its dome of beaten copper a dull green. Pili was still at the front of the coach.

'The Great Hall is used only for the most solemn ceremonies of the German Reich and has a capacity of one hundred and eighty thousand people. One interesting and unforeseen phenomenon: the breath from this number of humans rises into the cupola and forms clouds, which condense and fall as light rain. The Great Hall is the only building in the world which generates its own climate . . .'

March had heard it all before. He looked out of the window and saw the body in the mud. Swimming trunks! What had the old man been thinking of, swimming on Monday night? Berlin had been blanketed by black clouds from late afternoon. When the storm finally broke the rain had descended in steel rods, drilling the streets and roofs, drowning the thunder. Suicide, perhaps? Think of it. Wade into the cold lake, strike out for the centre, tread water in the darkness, watch the lightning over the trees, wait for tiredness to do the rest . . .

Pili had returned to his seat and was bouncing up and down in excitement.

'Are we going to see the Führer, papa?'

The vision evaporated and March felt guilty. This daydreaming was what Klara used to complain of: 'Even when you're here, you're not really here . . .'

He said: 'I don't think so.'

The guide again: 'On the right is the Reich Chancellery and Residence of the Führer. Its total façade measures exactly seven hundred metres, exceeding by one hundred metres the façade of Louis XIV's palace at Versailles.'

The Chancellery slowly uncoiled as the bus drove by:

29

marble pillars and red mosaics, bronze lions, gilded silhouettes, gothic script – a Chinese dragon of a building, asleep at the side of the square. A four-man SS honour guard stood at attention beneath a billowing swastika banner. There were no windows, but set into the wall, five storeys above the ground, was the balcony on which the Führer showed himself on those occasions when a million people gathered in the Platz. There were a few dozen sightseers even now, gazing up at the tightly drawn shutters, faces pale with expectation, hoping . . .

March glanced at his son. Pili was transfixed, his little dagger clutched tightly in his hand like a crucifix.

THE coach dropped them back at its pick-up point outside the Berlin-Gotenland railway station. It was after five as they descended from the bus, and the last vestiges of natural light were fading. The day was giving up on itself in disgust.

The entrance to the station was disgorging people – soldiers with kitbags walking with girlfriends and wives, foreign workers with cardboard suitcases and shabby bundles tied with string, settlers emerging after two days' travelling from the Steppes, staring in shock at the lights and the crowds. Uniforms were everywhere. Dark blue, green, brown, black, grey, khaki. It was like a factory at the end of a shift. There was a factory sound of shunting metal and shrill whistles, and a factory smell of heat and oil, stale air and steel-dust. Exclamation marks clamoured from the walls. 'Be vigilant at all times!' 'Attention! Report suspicious packages at once!' 'Terrorist alert!'

From here, trains as high as houses, with a gauge of four metres, left for the outposts of the German Empire – for Gotenland (formerly the Crimea) and Theoderichshafen (formerly Sevastopol); for the Generalkommissariat of Taurida and its capital, Melitopol; for Volhynia-Podolia,

Zhitomir, Kiev, Nikolaev, Dnepropetrovsk, Karkov, Rostov, Saratov . . . It was the terminus of a new world. Announcements of arrivals and departures punctuated the 'Coriolan Overture' on the public address system. March tried to take Pili's hand as they wove through the crowd, but the boy shook him away.

It took fifteen minutes to retrieve the car from the underground car park, and another fifteen to get clear of the clogged streets around the station. They drove in silence. It was not until they were almost back at Lichtenrade that Pili suddenly blurted out: 'You're an asocial, aren't you?'

It was such an odd word to hear on the lips of a ten-year-old, and so carefully pronounced, that March almost laughed out loud. An asocial: one step down from traitor in the Party's lexicon of crime. A non-contributor to Winter Relief. A non-joiner of the endless National Socialist associations. The NS Skiing Federation. The Association of NS Ramblers. The Greater German NS-Motoring Club. The NS Criminal Police Officers Society. He had even one afternoon come across a parade in the Lustgarten organised by the NS-League of Wearers of the Life-Saving Medal.

'That's nonsense.'

'Uncle Erich says it's true.'

Erich Helfferich. So he had become 'Uncle' Erich now, had he? A zealot of the worst sort, a full-time bureaucrat at the Party's Berlin headquarters. An officious, bespectacled scout master . . . March felt his hands tightening on the steering wheel. Helfferich had started seeing Klara a year ago.

'He says you don't give the Führer-salute and you make jokes about the Party.'

'And how does he know all this?'

'He says there's a file on you at Party Headquarters and it's only a matter of time before you're picked up.' The boy was almost in tears with the shame of it. 'I think he's right.'

'Pili!'

They were drawing up outside the house.

'I hate you.' This was delivered in a calm, flat voice. He got out of the car. March opened his door, ran round and followed him up the path. He could hear a dog barking inside the house.

'Pili!' he shouted once more.

The door opened. Klara stood there in the uniform of the NS-Frauenschaft. Lurking behind her, March glimpsed the brown-clad figure of Helfferich. The dog, a young German shepherd, came running out and leapt up at Pili, who pushed his way past his mother and disappeared into the house. March wanted to follow him, but Klara blocked his path.

'Leave the boy alone. Get out of here. Leave us all alone.'

She caught the dog and dragged it back by its collar. The door slammed on its yelping.

LATER, as he drove back towards the centre of Berlin, March kept thinking about that dog. It was the only living creature in the house, he realised, which was not wearing a uniform.

Had he not felt so miserable, he would have laughed.

'hat a pig of a day,' said Max Jaeger. It was seven-thirty in the evening and he was pulling on his coat in Werderscher Markt. 'No possessions handed in; no clothing. I've gone back on the missing list to Thursday. Nothing. So that's more than twenty-four hours since estimated time of death and not a soul has missed him. You sure he's not just some derelict?'

March gave a brief shake of the head. 'Too well-fed. And derelicts don't own swimming trunks. As a rule.'

'To cap it all,' Max took a last puff on his cigar and stubbed it out, 'I've got to go to a Party meeting tonight. "The German Mother: Warrior of the Volk on the Home Front".'

Like all Kripo investigators, including March, Jaeger had the SS rank of Sturmbannführer. Unlike March, he had joined the Party the previous year. Not that March blamed him. You had to be a Party member to gain promotion.

'Is Hannelore going?'

'Hannelore? Holder of the Honour Cross of the German Mother, Bronze Class? Naturally she's going.' Max looked at his watch. 'Just time for a beer. What do you say?'

'Not tonight, thanks. I'll walk down with you.'

They parted on the steps of the Kripo building. With a wave, Jaeger turned left towards the bar in Ob-wall Strasse, while March turned right, towards the river. He walked quickly. The rain had stopped, but the air was still damp and misty. The pre-war street lights gleamed on the black pavement. From the Spree came the low note of a foghorn, muffled by the buildings.

He turned a corner and walked alongside the river, enjoying the sensation of the cold night air against his face.

A barge was chugging upstream, a single light at its prow, a cauldron of dark water boiling at its stern. Apart from that, there was silence. There were no cars here; no people. The city might have vaporised in the darkness. He left the river with reluctance, crossing Spittel Markt to Seydel Strasse. A few minutes later he entered the Berlin city morgue.

Doctor Eisler had gone home. No surprise there. 'I love you,' breathed a woman's voice in the deserted reception, 'and I want to bear your children.' An attendant in a stained white tunic reluctantly turned away from his portable television and checked March's ID. He made a note in his register, picked up a bunch of keys, and gestured to the detective to follow him. Behind them, the theme tune of the Reichsrundfunk's nightly soap opera began to play.

Swing doors led on to a corridor identical to a dozen back in Werderscher Markt. Somewhere, thought March, there must be a Reichsdirektor for green linoleum. He followed the attendant into an elevator. The metal grille closed with a crash and they descended into the basement.

At the entrance to the storeroom, beneath a No Smoking sign, they both lit cigarettes – two professionals taking the same precaution, not against the smell of the bodies (the room was refrigerated: there was no stink of corruption) but to blot out the stinging fumes of the disinfectant.

'You want the old fellow? Came in just after eight?'

'Right,' said March.

The attendant pulled a large handle and swung open the heavy door. There was a whoosh of cold air as they stepped inside. Harsh neon strips lit a floor of white tiles, slightly sloping on either side down to a narrow gutter in the centre. Heavy metal drawers like filing cabinets were set into the walls. The attendant took a clipboard from a hook by the light-switch and walked along them, checking the numbers.

'This one.'

He tucked the clipboard under his arm and gave the

drawer a hard tug. It slid open. March stepped over and pulled back the white sheet.

'You can go now, if you like,' he said, without looking round. 'I'll call when I've finished.'

'Not allowed. Regulations.'

'In case I tamper with the evidence? Do me a favour.'

The body did not improve on second acquaintance. A hard, fleshy face, small eyes and a cruel mouth. The scalp was almost entirely bald, apart from the odd strand of white hair. The nose was sharp, with two deep indentations on either side of the bridge. He must have worn spectacles for years. The face itself was unmarked, but there were symmetrical bruises on either cheek. March inserted his fingers into the mouth and encountered only soft gum. At some point a complete set of false teeth must have been knocked loose.

March pulled the sheet right back. The shoulders were broad, the torso that of a powerful man, just beginning to run to fat. He folded the cloth neatly a few centimetres above the stump. He was always respectful of the dead. No society doctor on the Kurfürstendamm was more tender with his clients than Xavier March.

He breathed warmth on to his hands and reached into the inside pocket of his overcoat. He pulled out a small tin case, which he opened, and two white cards. The cigarette smoke tasted bitter in his mouth. He grasped the corpse's left wrist – so *cold*; it never ceased to shock him – and prised open the fingers. Carefully, he pressed each tip on to the pad of black ink in the tin. Then he put the tin down, picked up one of the cards, and pressed each finger on to that. When he was satisfied, he repeated the process on the old man's right hand. The attendant watched him, fascinated.

The smears of black on the white hands looked shocking; a desecration.

'Clean him up,' said March.

THE headquarters of the Reich Kripo are in Werderscher Markt, but the actual hardware of police business – the forensic laboratories, criminal records, armoury, workshops, detention cells – are in the Berlin Police Praesidium building in Alexander Platz. It was to this sprawling Prussian fortress, opposite the busiest U-bahn station in the city, that March went next. It took him fifteen minutes, walking briskly.

'You want *what*?'

The voice, edged high with incredulity, belonged to Otto Koth, deputy head of the fingerprint section.

'Priority,' repeated March. He took another draw on his cigarette. He knew Koth well. Two years ago they had trapped a gang of armed robbers who had killed a policeman in Lankwitz. Koth had got a promotion on the strength of it. 'I know you've got a backlog from here to the Führer's hundredth birthday. I know you've got the Sipo on your back for terrorists and God knows what. But do this for me.'

Koth leaned back in his chair. In the bookcase behind him, March could see Artur Nebe's book on criminology, published thirty years ago, but still the standard text. Nebe had been head of the Kripo since 1933.

'Let me see what you've got,' said Koth.

March handed over the cards. Koth glanced at them, nodding.

'Male,' said March. 'About sixty. Dead for a day.'

'I know how he feels.' Koth took off his glasses and rubbed his eyes. 'All right. They'll go to the top of the pile.'

'How long?'

'Should have an answer by morning.' Koth put his glasses back on. 'What I don't understand is how you know this man, whoever he was, had a criminal record.'

March did not know, but he was not going to hand Koth an excuse to wriggle out of his promise. 'Trust me,' he said.

MARCH arrived back at his flat at eleven. The ancient cage lift was out of order. The stairs, with their threadbare brown carpet, smelled of other people's old meals, of boiled cabbage and burned meat. As he passed the second floor he could hear the young couple who lived beneath him quarrelling.

'*How can you say that?*'

'*You've done nothing! Nothing!*'

A door slammed. A baby cried. Elsewhere, someone turned up the volume of their radio in response. The symphony of apartment life. This had been a fashionable block, once. Now, like many of its tenants, it had fallen on harder times. He continued on up to the next floor and let himself in.

The rooms were cold, the heating having failed to come on, as usual. He had five: a sitting room, with a good high ceiling, looking out on to Ansbacher Strasse; a bedroom with an iron bedstead; a small bathroom and an even smaller kitchen; a spare room was filled with salvage from his marriage, still packed in boxes five years later. Home. It was bigger than the forty-four square metres which was the standard size of a Volkswohnung – a People's Flat – but not much.

Before March had moved in it had been occupied by the widow of a Luftwaffe general. She had lived in it since the war and had let it go to ruin. On his second weekend, redecorating the bedroom, he had stripped off the mildewed wallpaper and found tucked behind it a photograph, folded up very small. A sepia portrait, all misty browns and creams, dated 1929, taken by a Berlin studio. A family stood before a painted backdrop of trees and fields. A dark-haired woman gazed at a baby in her arms. Her husband stood proud behind her, his hand resting on her shoulder. Next to him, a little boy. He had kept it on the mantelpiece ever since.

The boy was Pili's age, would be March's age today.

Who were these people? What had happened to the child? For years he had wondered, but hesitated – he always had plenty at the Markt to stretch his mind, without finding fresh mysteries to unravel. Then, just before last Christmas, for no reason he could properly define – a vague and growing uneasiness that happened to coincide with his birthday, no more than that – he had started to seek an answer.

The landlord's records showed that the apartment had been rented between 1928 and 1942 to one Weiss, Jakob. But there was no police file on any Jakob Weiss. He was not registered as having moved, or fallen sick, or died. Calls to the records bureaux of the Army, Navy and Luftwaffe confirmed he had not been conscripted to fight. The photographer's studio had become a television rental shop, its records lost. None of the young people in the landlord's office remembered the Weisses. They had vanished. *Weiss. White. A blank.* By now, in his heart, March knew the truth – perhaps had always known it – but he went round one evening with the photograph even so, like a policeman, seeking witnesses, and the other tenants in the house had looked at him as if he were crazy even for asking. Except one.

'They were Jews,' the crone in the attic had said as she closed the door in his face.

Of course. The Jews had all been evacuated to the east during the war. Everyone knew that. What had happened to them since was not a question anyone asked in public – or in private either, if they had any sense, not even an SS-Sturmbannführer.

And that, he could see now, was when his relationship with Pili had started to go bad; the time when he had started to wake up before it was light, and to volunteer for every case that came along.

MARCH stood for a few minutes without switching on the lights, looking down at the traffic heading south to Wittenberg Platz. Then he went into the kitchen and poured himself a large whisky. Monday's *Berliner Tageblatt* was lying by the sink. He carried it back with him into the sitting room.

March had a routine for reading the paper. He started at the back, with the truth. If Leipzig was said to have beaten Cologne four-nil at football, the chances were it was true: even the Party had yet to devise a means of rewriting the sports results. The sports news was a different matter. COUNTDOWN TO TOKYO OLYMPICS. US MAY COMPETE FOR FIRST TIME IN 28 YEARS. GERMAN ATHLETES STILL LEAD WORLD. Then the advertisements. GERMAN FAMILIES! PLEASURE BECKONS IN GOTENLAND, RIVIERA OF THE REICH! French perfume, Italian silks, Scandinavian furs, Dutch cigars, Belgian coffee, Russian caviar, British televisions — the cornucopia of Empire spilled across the pages. Births, marriages and deaths: TEBBE, Ernst and Ingrid; a son for the Führer. WENZEL, Hans, aged 71; a true National Socialist, sadly missed.

And the lonely hearts:

FIFTY years old. Pure Aryan doctor, veteran of the Battle of Moscow, who intends to settle on the land, desires male progeny through marriage with healthy, Aryan, virginal, young, unassuming, thrifty woman, adapted to hard work; broad-hipped, flat-heeled and earring-less essential.
WIDOWER aged sixty once again wishes to have Nordic

mate prepared to present him with children so that old family should not die out in male line.

Arts pages: Zarah Leander, still going strong, in *Woman of Odessa*, now showing at the Gloria-Palast: the epic story of the resettlement of the South Tyrolese. A piece by the music critic attacking the 'pernicious, Negroid wailings' of a group of young Englishmen from Liverpool, playing to packed audiences of German youth in Hamburg. Herbert von Karajan to conduct a special performance of Beethoven's Ninth Symphony – the European anthem – at the Royal Albert Hall in London on the Führer's birthday.

Editorial on the student anti-war demonstrations in Heidelberg: TRAITORS MUST BE SMASHED BY FORCE! The *Tageblatt* always took a firm line.

Obituary: some old Bonze from the Ministry of the Interior. 'A lifetime's service to the Reich . . .'

Reich news: SPRING THAW BRINGS FRESH FIGHTING ON SIBERIAN FRONT! GERMAN TROOPS SMASH IVAN TERROR GROUPS! In Rovno, capital of the Reichskommissariat Ukraine, five terrorist leaders had been executed for organising the massacre of a family of German settlers. There was a photograph of the Reich's latest nuclear submarine, the *Grossadmiral Dönitz*, at its new base in Trondheim.

World news: In London it had been announced that King Edward and Queen Wallis were to pay a state visit to the Reich in July 'further to strengthen the deep bonds of respect and affection between the peoples of Great Britain and the German Reich'. In Washington, it was believed that President Kennedy's latest victory in the US primaries had strengthened his chances of winning a second term . . .

The paper slipped from March's fingers and on to the floor.

Half an hour later, the telephone rang.

'So sorry to wake you.' Koth was sarcastic. 'I had the impression this was supposed to be priority. Shall I call back tomorrow?'

'No, no.' March was wide awake.

'This you will love. This is beautiful.' For the first time in his life, March heard Koth chuckle. 'Now, you are not playing a joke on me? This is not some little trick you and Jaeger have worked out between you?'

'Who is it?'

'The background first.' Koth was enjoying himself too much to be hurried. 'We had to go back a long way to get a match. A very long way. But we got one. Perfect. No mistake. Your man has a record all right. He was arrested just once in his life. By our colleagues in Munich, forty years ago. To be precise, on the ninth of November 1923.'

There was a silence. Five, six, seven seconds elapsed.

'Ah! I can tell that even you appreciate the significance of the date.'

'An alter Kämpfer.' March reached down beside his chair for his cigarettes. 'His name?'

'Indeed. An old comrade. Arrested with the Führer after the Bürgerbräukeller Putsch. You have fished out of the lake one of the glorious pioneers of the National Socialist Revolution.' Koth laughed again. 'A wiser man might have left him where he was.'

'*What is his name?*'

AFTER Koth had rung off, March paced around the apartment for five minutes, smoking furiously. Then he made three calls. The first was to Max Jaeger. The second was to the Duty Officer at Werderscher Markt. The third was to a Berlin number. A man's voice, slurred with sleep, answered just as March was about to give up.

'Rudi? It's Xavier March.'

'Zavi? Are you crazy? It's midnight.'

'Not quite.' March patrolled the faded carpet, the body of the telephone in one hand, the receiver tucked beneath his chin. 'I need your help.'

'For God's sake!'

'What can you tell me about a man named Josef Buhler?'

THAT night, March had a dream. He was at the lakeshore again in the rain and there was the body, face down in the mud. He pulled at the shoulder – pulled hard – but he could not move it. The body was grey-white lead. But when he turned to leave, it grabbed his leg, and began pulling him towards the surface of the lake. He scrabbled at the earth, trying to dig his fingers into the soft mud, but there was nothing to hold on to. The corpse's grip was immensely strong. And as they went under, its face became Pili's, contorted with rage, grotesque in its shame, screaming 'I hate you . . . I hate you . . . I hate you . . .'

PART TWO

WEDNESDAY 15 APRIL

détente, s.f. 1 (a) Relaxation, loosening, slackening (of something that is taut); relaxing (of muscles). (b) Easing (of political situation).

esterday's rain was a bad memory, already half-faded from the streets. The sun – the miraculous, impartial sun – bounced and glittered on the shopfronts and apartment windows.

In the bathroom, the rusted pipes clanked and groaned, the shower dangled a thread of cold water. March shaved with his father's old cut-throat razor. Through the open bathroom window, he could hear the sounds of the city waking up: the whine and clatter of the first tram; the distant hum of the traffic on Tauentzien Strasse; the footsteps of the early risers hurrying to the big Wittenberg Platz U-bahn station; the rattle of shutters going up in the bakery across the street. It was not quite seven and Berlin was alive with possibilities the day had yet to dull.

His uniform was laid out in the bedroom: the body-armour of authority.

Brown shirt, with black leather buttons. Black tie. Black breeches. Black jackboots (the rich smell of polished leather).

Black tunic: four silver buttons; three parallel silvered threads on the shoulder tabs; on the left sleeve, a red-white-and-black swastika armband; on the right, a diamond enclosing the gothic letter 'K', for Kriminalpolizei.

Black Sam Browne belt. Black cap with silver death's head and Party eagle. Black leather gloves.

March stared at himself in the mirror, and a Sturm-bannführer of the Waffen-SS stared back. He picked up his service pistol, a 9 mm Luger, from the dressing table, checked the action, and slotted it into his holster. Then he stepped out into the morning.

*

'SURE you have enough?'

Rudolf Halder grinned at March's sarcasm and unloaded his tray: cheese, ham, salami, three hard-boiled eggs, a pile of black bread, milk, a cup of steaming coffee. He arranged the dishes in a neat row on the white linen tablecloth.

'I understand that breakfasts provided by the Reich Main Security Office are not normally so lavish.'

They were in the dining room of the Prinz Friedrich Karl Hotel in Dorotheen Strasse, midway between Kripo headquarters and Halder's office in the Reichsarchiv. March used it regularly. The Friedrich Karl was a cheap stopover for tourists and salesmen, but it did a good breakfast. Dangling limply from a pole over the entrance was a European flag – the twelve gold stars of the European Community nations, on a dark-blue background. March guessed that the manager, Herr Brecker, had bought it second-hand and hung it there in an effort to drum up some foreign custom. It did not appear to have worked. A glance around the restaurant's shabby clientele and bored staff suggested little danger of being overheard.

As usual, people gave March's uniform a wide berth. Every few minutes, the walls shook as a train pulled into the Friedrich Strasse station.

'Is that all you're having?' asked Halder. 'Coffee?' He shook his head. 'Black coffee, cigarettes and whisky. As a diet: not good. Now I think of it, I haven't seen you eat a decent meal since you and Klara split.' He cracked one of his eggs and began removing pieces of shell.

March thought: of all of us, Halder has changed the least. Beneath the layer of fat, behind the slackened muscle of incipient middle age, there lurked still the ghost of the gangling recruit, straight from university, who had joined the U-174 more than twenty years before. He had been a wireless operator – a bad one, rushed through training and into service at the start of 1942, when losses were at their height, and Dönitz was ransacking Germany for replacements. Then as now, he wore wire-framed glasses and had thin ginger hair which stuck out at the back in a duck's tail. During a voyage, while the rest of the men grew beards, Halder sprouted orange tufts on his cheeks and chin, like a moulting cat. The fact that he was in the U-boat service at all was a ghastly mistake, a joke. He was clumsy, barely capable of changing a fuse. He had been designed by nature to be an academic, not a submariner, and he passed each voyage in a sweat of fear and sea-sickness.

Yet he was popular. U-boat crews were superstitious, and somehow the word got around that Rudi Halder brought good luck. So they looked after him, covering his mistakes, letting him have an extra half-hour to groan and thrash around on his bunk. He became a sort of mascot. When peace came, astonished to find that he had survived, Halder resumed his studies at the history faculty of Berlin University. In 1958 he had joined the team of academics working at the Reichsarchiv on the official history of the war. He had come full circle, spending his days hunched in a subterranean chamber in Berlin, piecing together the same grand strategy of which he had once been a tiny, frightened component. *The U-boat Service: Operations and Tactics, 1939–46* had been published in 1963. Now Halder was helping compile the third volume of the history of the German Army on the Eastern Front.

'It's like working at the Volkswagen works in Fallersleben,' said Halder. He took a bite out of his egg and chewed for a while. 'I do the wheels, Jaeckel does the doors, Schmidt drops in the engine.'

'How long is it going to take?'

'Oh, forever, I should think. Resources no object. This is the Arch of Triumph in words, remember? Every shot, every skirmish, every snowflake, every sneeze. Someone is even going to write the Official History of the Official Histories. Me, I'll do another five years.'

'And then?'

Halder brushed egg crumbs from his tie. 'A chair in a small university somewhere in the south. A house in the country with Ilse and the kids. A couple of books, respectfully reviewed. My ambitions are modest. If nothing else, this kind of work gives you a sense of perspective about your own mortality. Talking of which . . .' From his inside pocket he pulled a sheet of paper. 'With the compliments of the Reichsarchiv.'

It was a photocopy of a page from an old Party directory. Four passport-sized portraits of uniformed officials, each accompanied by a brief biography. Brün, Brunner. Buch. And Buhler.

Halder said: '*Guide to the Personalities of the NSDAP.* 1951 edition.'

'I know it well.'

'A pretty bunch, you'll agree.'

The body in the Havel was Buhler's, no question of it. He stared up at March through his rimless spectacles, prim and humourless, his lips pursed. It was a bureaucrat's face, a lawyer's face; a face you might see a thousand times and never be able to describe; sharp in the flesh, fudged in memory; the face of a machine-man.

'As you will see,' resumed Halder, 'a pillar of National Socialist respectability. Joined the Party in '22 – that's as respectable as they come. Worked as a lawyer with Hans Frank, the Führer's own attorney. Deputy President of the Academy of German Law.'

' "State Secretary, General Government, 1939," ' read March. ' "SS-Brigadeführer." ' Brigadeführer, by God. He took out a notebook and began to write.

'Honorary rank,' said Halder, his mouth full of food. 'I doubt if he ever fired a shot in anger. He was strictly a desk man. When Frank was sent out as Governor in '39 to run what was left of Poland, he must have taken his old legal partner, Buhler, with him, to be chief bureaucrat. You should try some of this ham. Very good.'

March was scribbling quickly. 'How long was Buhler in the East?'

'Twelve years, I guess. I checked the *Guide* for 1952. There's no entry for Buhler. So '51 must have been his last year.'

March stopped writing and tapped his teeth with his pen. 'Will you excuse me for a couple of minutes?'

There was a telephone booth in the foyer. He rang the Kripo switchboard and asked for his own extension. A voice growled: 'Jaeger.'

'Listen, Max.' March repeated what Halder had told him. 'The *Guide* mentions a wife.' He held up the sheet of paper to the booth's dim electric light and squinted at it. 'Edith Tulard. Can you find her? To get the body positively identified.'

'She's dead.'

'What?'

'She died more than ten years ago. I checked with the SS records bureau – even honorary ranks have to give next of kin. Buhler had no kids, but I've traced his sister. She's a widow, seventy-two years old, named Elizabeth Trinkl. Lives in Fürstenwalde.' March knew it: a small town about forty-five minutes' drive south-east of Berlin. 'The local cops are bringing her straight to the morgue.'

'I'll meet you there.'

'Another thing. Buhler had a house on Schwanenwerder.'

So that explained the location of the body. 'Good work, Max.' March rang off and made his way back to the dining room.

Halder had finished his breakfast. He threw down his

napkin as March returned and leaned back in his chair.
'Excellent. Now I can almost tolerate the prospect of sorting
through fifteen hundred signals from Kleist's First Panzer
Army.' He began picking his teeth. 'We should meet up
more often. Ilse is always saying: When are you going to
bring Zavi round?' He leaned forward. 'Listen: there's a
woman at the archives, working on the history of the Bund
deutscher Mädel in Bavaria, 1935 to 1950. A stunner.
Husband disappeared on the Eastern front last year, poor
devil. Anyway: you and she. What about it? We could have
you both round, say next week?'

March smiled. 'You're very kind.'

'That's not an answer.'

'True.' He tapped the photocopy. 'Can I keep this?'

Halder shrugged. 'Why not?'

'One last thing.'

'Go ahead.'

'State Secretary to the General Government. What
would he have done, exactly?'

Halder spread his hands. The backs were thick with freckles,
wisps of reddish-gold hair curled from his cuffs. 'He and Frank
had absolute authority. They did whatever they liked. At that
time, the main priority would have been resettlement.'

March wrote 'resettlement' in his notebook, and ringed
it. 'How did that happen?'

'What is this? A seminar?' Halder arranged a triangle of
plates in front of him – two smaller ones to the left, a larger
one to the right. He pushed them together so they touched.
'All this is Poland before the war. After '39, the western
provinces' – he tapped the small plates – 'were brought into
Germany. Reichsgau Danzig-West Prussia and Reichsgau
Wartheland.' He detached the large plate. 'And this became
the General Government. The rump state. The two western
provinces were Germanised. It's not my field, you understand, but I've seen some figures. In 1940, they set a target

density of one hundred Germans per square kilometre. And they managed it in the first three years. An incredible operation, considering the war was still on.'

'How many people were involved?'

'One million. The SS eugenics bureau found Germans in places you'd never have dreamed of – Rumania, Bulgaria, Serbia, Croatia. If your skull had the proper measurements and you came from the right village – you were just given a ticket.'

'And Buhler?'

'Ah. Well. To make room for a million Germans in the new Reichsgaue, they had to move out a million Poles.'

'And they went to the General Government?'

Halder turned his head and glanced around furtively, to make sure he was not overheard – 'the German look', people called it. 'They also had to cope with the Jews being expelled from Germany and the western territories – France, Holland, Belgium.'

'Jews?'

'Yes, yes. Keep your voice down.' Halder was speaking so quietly, March had to lean across the table to hear. 'You can imagine – it was chaos. Overcrowding. Starvation. Disease. From what one can gather, the place is still a shit-hole, despite what they say.'

Every week the newspapers and television carried appeals from the East Ministry for settlers willing to move to the General Government. 'Germans! Claim your birthright! A farmstead – free! Income guaranteed for the first five years.' The advertisements showed happy colonists living in luxury. But word of the real story had filtered back – an existence conditioned by poor soil, back-breaking work, and drab satellite towns to which the Germans had to return at dusk for fear of attack from local partisans. The General Government was worse than the Ukraine; worse than Ostland; worse, even, than Muscovy.

A waiter came over to offer more coffee. March waved him away. When the man was out of earshot, Halder continued in the same low tone: 'Frank ran everything from Wawel Castle in Krakau. That would have been where Buhler was based. I have a friend who works in the official archives there. God, he has some stories . . . Apparently, the luxury was incredible. Like something out of the Roman Empire. Paintings, tapestries, looted treasures from the church, jewellery. Bribes in cash and bribes in kind, if you know what I mean.' Halder's blue eyes shone at the thought, his eyebrows danced.

'And Buhler was involved in this?'

'Who knows? If not, he must have been about the only one who wasn't.'

'That would explain why he had a house on Schwanen-werder.'

Halder whistled softly. 'There you are then. We had the wrong sort of war, my friend. Cooped up in a stinking metal coffin two hundred metres under the Atlantic, when we could have been in a Silesian castle, sleeping on silk with a couple of Polish girls for company.'

There was more March would have liked to ask him but he had no time. As they were leaving, Halder said: 'So you'll come round to dinner with my BdM woman?'

'I'll think about it.'

'Maybe we can persuade her to wear her uniform.' Standing outside the hotel, with his hands thrust deep in his pockets and his long scarf wrapped twice around his neck, Halder looked even more like a student. Suddenly he struck his forehead with the flat of his hand. 'I clean forgot! I meant to tell you. My memory . . . A couple of Sipo guys were round at the Archiv last week asking about you.'

March felt his smile shrink. 'The Gestapo? What did they want?' He managed to keep his tone light, off-hand.

'Oh, the usual sort of stuff. "What was he like during the

52

war? Does he have any strong political views? Who are his friends?" What's going on, Zavi? You up for promotion or something?'

'I must be.' He told himself to relax. It was probably only a routine check. He must remember to ask Max if he had heard anything about a new screening.

'Well, when they've made you head of the Kripo, don't forget your old friends.'

March laughed. 'I won't.' They shook hands. As they parted, March said: 'I wonder if Buhler had any enemies.'

'Oh yes,' said Halder, 'of course.'

'Who were they then?'

Halder shrugged. 'Thirty million Poles, for a start.'

THE only person on the second floor at Werderscher Markt was a Polish cleaning woman. Her back was to March as he came out of the lift. All he could see was a large rump resting on the soles of a pair of black rubber boots, and the red scarf tied round her hair bobbing as she scrubbed the floor. She was singing softly to herself in her native language. As she heard him approach she stopped and turned her head to the wall. He squeezed past her and went into his office. When the door had closed he heard her begin singing again.

It was not yet nine. He hung his cap by the door and unbuttoned his tunic. There was a large brown envelope on his desk. He opened it and shook out the contents, the scene-of-crime photographs. Glossy colour pictures of Buhler's body, sprawled like a sunbather's at the side of the lake.

He lifted the ancient typewriter from the top of the filing cabinet and carried it across to his desk. From a wire basket he took two pieces of much-used carbon paper, two flimsy sheets and one standard report form, arranged them in order, and wound them into the machine. Then he lit a cigarette and stared at the dead plant for a few minutes.

He began to type.

To: Chief, VB3(a)
SUBJECT: Unidentified body (male)
FROM: X. March, SS-Sturmbannführer   15.4.64

I beg to report the following.

1.   At 06.28 yesterday, I was ordered to attend the recovery of a body from the Havel. The body had been discovered by SS-Schütze Hermann Jost at 06.02 and reported to the Ordnungspolizei (statement attached).

2.   No male of the correct description having been reported missing, I arranged for the fingerprints of the subject to be checked against records.

3.   This has enabled the subject to be identified as Doctor Josef Buhler, a Party member with the honorary rank of SS-Brigadeführer. The subject served as State Secretary in the General Government, 1939–51.

4.   A preliminary investigation at the scene by SS-Sturmbannführer Doctor August Eisler indicated the likely cause of death as drowning, and the likely time of death some time on the night of 13 April.

5.   The subject lived on Schwanenwerder, close to where the body was found.

6.   There were no obvious suspicious circumstances.

7.   A full autopsy examination will be carried out following formal identification of the subject by next-of-kin.

March pulled the report out of the typewriter, signed it, and left it with a messenger in the foyer on his way out.

THE old woman was sitting erect on a hard wooden bench in the Seydel Strasse mortuary. She wore a brown tweed suit, brown hat with a drooping feather, sturdy brown shoes and grey woollen stockings. She was staring straight ahead, a handbag clasped in her lap, oblivious to the medical orderlies, the policemen, the grieving relatives passing in the corridor. Max Jaeger sat beside her, arms folded, legs outstretched, looking bored. As March arrived, he took him to one side.

'Been here ten minutes. Hardly spoken.'

'In shock?'

'I suppose.'

'Let's get it over with.'

The old woman did not look up as March sat on the bench beside her. He said softly: 'Frau Trinkl, my name is March. I am an investigator with the Berlin Kriminalpolizei. We have to complete a report on your brother's death, and we need you to identify his body. Then we'll take you home. Do you understand?'

Frau Trinkl turned to face him. She had a thin face, thin nose (her brother's nose), thin lips. A cameo brooch gathered a blouse of frilly purple at her bony throat.

'Do you understand?' he repeated.

She gazed at him with clear grey eyes, unreddened by crying. Her voice was clipped and dry: 'Perfectly.'

They moved across the corridor into a small, windowless reception room. The floor was made of wood blocks. The walls were lime green. In an effort to lighten the gloom, someone had stuck up tourist posters given away by the Deutsche Reichsbahn Gesellschaft: a night-time view of the Great Hall, the Führer Museum at Linz, the

Starnberger See in Bavaria. The poster which had hung on the fourth wall had been torn down, leaving pockmarks in the plaster, like bullet holes.

A clatter outside signalled the arrival of the body. It was wheeled in, covered by a sheet, on a metal trolley. Two attendants in white tunics parked it in the centre of the floor – a buffet lunch awaiting its guests. They left and Jaeger closed the door.

'Are you ready?' asked March. She nodded. He turned back the sheet and Frau Trinkl stationed herself at his shoulder. As she leaned forward, a strong smell – of peppermint lozenges, of perfume mingled with camphor, an old lady's smell – washed across his face. She stared at the corpse for a long time, then opened her mouth as if to say something, but all that emerged was a sigh. Her eyes closed. March caught her as she fell.

'It's him,' she said. 'I haven't set eyes on him for ten years, and he's fatter, and I've never seen him before without his spectacles, not since he was a child. But it's him.' She was on a chair under the poster of Linz, leaning forward with her head between her knees. Her hat had fallen off. Thin strands of white hair hung down over her face. The body had been wheeled away.

The door opened and Jaeger returned carrying a glass of water, which he pressed into her skinny hand. 'Drink this.' She held it for a moment, then raised it to her lips and took a sip. 'I never faint,' she said. 'Never.' Behind her, Jaeger made a face.

'Of course,' said March. 'I need to ask some questions. Are you well enough? Stop me if I tire you.' He took out his notebook. 'Why had you not seen your brother for ten years?'

'After Edith died – his wife – we had nothing in

common. We were never close in any case. Even as children. I was eight years older than him.'

'His wife died some time ago?'

She thought for a moment. 'In '53, I think. Winter. She had cancer.'

'And in all the time since then you never heard from him? Were there any other brothers and sisters?'

'No. Just the two of us. He did write occasionally. I had a letter from him on my birthday two weeks ago.' She fumbled in her handbag and produced a single sheet of notepaper – good quality, creamy and thick, with an engraving of the Schwanenwerder house as a letterhead. The writing was copperplate, the message as formal as an official receipt: 'My dear sister! Heil Hitler! I send you greetings on your birthday. I earnestly hope that you are in good health, as I am. Josef.' March refolded it and handed it back. No wonder nobody missed him.

'In his other letters, did he ever mention anything worrying him?'

'What had he to be worried about?' She spat out the words. 'Edith inherited a fortune in the war. They had money. He lived in fine style, I can tell you.'

'There were no children?'

'He was sterile.' She said this without emphasis, as if describing his hair colour. 'Edith was so unhappy. I think that was what killed her. She sat alone in that big house – it was cancer of the soul. She used to love music – she played the piano beautifully. A Bechstein, I remember. And he – he was such a cold man.'

Jaeger grunted from the other side of the room: 'So you didn't think much of him?'

'No, I did not. Not many people did.' She turned back to March. 'I have been a widow for twenty-four years. My husband was a navigator in the Luftwaffe, shot down over France. I was not left destitute – nothing like that. But the pension . . . *very* small for one who was used to something a little better. Not once in all that time did Josef offer to help me.'

'What about his leg?' It was Jaeger again, his tone antagonistic. He had clearly decided to take Buhler's side in this family dispute. 'What happened to that?' His manner suggested he thought she might have stolen it.

The old lady ignored him and gave her answer to March. 'He would never speak of it himself, but Edith told me the story. It happened in 1951, when he was still in the General Government. He was travelling with an escort on the road from Krakau to Kattowitz when his car was ambushed by Polish partisans. A landmine, she said. His driver was killed. Josef was lucky only to lose a foot. After that, he retired from government service.'

'And yet he still swam?' March looked up from his notebook. 'You know that we discovered him wearing swimming trunks?'

She gave a tight smile. 'My brother was a fanatic about everything, Herr March, whether it was politics or health. He did not smoke, he never touched alcohol, and he took exercise every day, despite his . . . disability. So, no: I am not in the least surprised that he should have been swimming.' She set down her glass and picked up her hat. 'I would like to go home now, if I may.'

March stood up and held out his hand, helping her to her feet. 'What did Doctor Buhler do after 1951? He was only – what? – in his early fifties?'

'That is the strange thing.' She opened her handbag and took out a small mirror. She checked her hat was on straight, tucking stray hairs out of sight with nervous, jerky movements of her fingers. 'Before the war, he was so ambitious. He would work eighteen hours a day, every day of the week. But when he left Krakau, he gave up. He never even returned to the law. For more than ten years after poor

Edith died, he just sat alone in that big house all day and did nothing.'

Two floors below, in the basement of the morgue, SS Surgeon August Eisler of Kriminalpolizei Department VD2 (Pathology) was going about his business with his customary clumsy relish. Buhler's chest had been opened in the standard fashion: a Y incision, a cut from each shoulder to the pit of the stomach, a straight line down to the pubic bone. Now Eisler had his hands deep inside the stomach, green gloves sheened with red, twisting, cutting, pulling. March and Jaeger leaned against the wall by the open doorway, smoking a couple of Jaeger's cigars.

'Have you seen what your man had for lunch?' said Eisler. 'Show them, Eck.'

Eisler's assistant wiped his hands on his apron and held up a transparent plastic bag. There was something small and green in the bottom.

'Lettuce. Digests slowly. Stays in the intestinal tract for hours.'

March had worked with Eisler before. Two winters ago, with snow blocking the Unter den Linden and ice skating competitions on the Tegeler See, a barge master named Kempf had been pulled out of the Spree, almost dead with cold. He had expired in the ambulance on the way to hospital. Accident or murder? The time at which he had fallen into the water was crucial. Looking at the ice extending two metres out from the banks, March had estimated fifteen minutes as the maximum time he could have survived in the water. Eisler had said forty-five and his view had prevailed with the prosecutor. It was enough to destroy the alibi of the barge's second mate, and hang him.

Afterwards, the prosecutor – a decent, old-fashioned sort – had called March into his office and locked the door.

Then he'd shown him Eisler's 'evidence': copies of documents stamped geheime Reichssache – Top Secret State Document – and dated Dachau, 1942. It was a report of freezing experiments carried out on condemned prisoners, restricted to the department of the SS Surgeon-General. The men had been handcuffed and dumped in tanks of icy water, retrieved at intervals to have their temperatures taken, right up to the point at which they died. There were photographs of heads bobbing between floating chunks of ice, and charts showing heat-loss, projected and actual. The experiments had lasted two years and been conducted, among others, by a young Untersturmführer, August Eisler. That night, March and the prosecutor had gone to a bar in Kreuzberg and got blind drunk. Next day, neither of them mentioned what had happened. They never spoke to one another again.

'If you expect me to come out with some fancy theory, March, forget it.'

'I'd never expect that.'

Jaeger laughed. 'Nor would I.'

Eisler ignored their mirth. 'It was a drowning, no question about it. Lungs full of water, so he must have been breathing when he went into the lake.'

'No cuts?' asked March. 'Bruises?'

'Do you want to come over here and do this job? No? Then believe me: he drowned. There are no contusions to the head to indicate he was hit or held under.'

'A heart attack? Some kind of seizure?'

'Possible,' admitted Eisler. Eck handed him a scalpel. 'I won't know until I've completed a full examination of the internal organs.'

'How long will that take?'

'As long as it takes.'

Eisler positioned himself behind Buhler's head. Tenderly, he stroked the hair towards him, off the corpse's forehead, as if soothing a fever. Then he hunched down low and jabbed the scalpel through the left temple. He drew it in an arc across the top of the face, just below the hairline. There was a scrape of metal and bone. Eck grinned at them. March sucked a lungful of smoke from his cigar.

Eisler put the scalpel into a metal dish. Then he bent down once more and worked his forefingers into the deep cut. Gradually, he began peeling back the scalp. March turned his head away and closed his eyes. He prayed that no one he loved, or liked, or even vaguely knew, ever had to be desecrated by the butcher's work of an autopsy.

Jaeger said: 'So what do you think?'

Eisler had picked up a small, hand-sized circular saw. He switched it on. It whined like a dentist's drill.

March took a final puff on his cigar. 'I think we should get out of here.'

They made their way down the corridor. Behind them, from the autopsy room, they heard the saw's note deepen as it bit into the bone.

alf an hour later, Xavier March was at the wheel of one of the Kripo's Volkswagens, following the curving path of the Havelchaussee, high above the lake. Sometimes the view was hidden by trees. Then he would round a bend, or the forest would thin, and he would see the water again, sparkling in the April sun like a tray of diamonds. Two yachts skimmed the surface – children's cut-outs, white triangles brilliant against the blue.

He had the window wound down, his arm resting on the sill, the breeze plucking at his sleeve. On either side, the bare branches of the trees were flecked with the green of late spring. In another month, the road would be nose-to-tail with cars: Berliners escaping from the city to sail or swim, or picnic, or simply to lie in the sun on one of the big public beaches. But today there was still enough of a chill in the air, and winter was still close enough, for March to have the road to himself. He passed the red-brick sentinel of the Kaiser Wilhelm Tower and the road began to drop to lake level.

Within ten minutes he was at the spot where the body had been discovered. In the fine weather it looked utterly different. This was a tourist spot, a vantage-point known as the Grosse Fenster: the Picture Window. What had been a mass of grey yesterday was now a gloriously clear view, across eight kilometres of water, right up to Spandau.

He parked, and retraced the route Jost had been running when he discovered the body – down the woodland track, a sharp right turn, and along the side of the lake. He did it a second time; and a third. Satisfied, he got back into the car and drove over the low bridge on to Schwanenwerder. A red and white pole blocked the road. A sentry emerged from a small hut, a clipboard in his hand, a rifle slung across his shoulder.

'Your identification, please.'

March handed his Kripo ID through the open window. The sentry studied it and returned it. He saluted. 'That's fine, Herr Sturmbannführer.'

'What's the procedure here?'

'Stop every car. Check the papers and ask where they're going. If they look suspicious, we ring the house, see if they're expected. Sometimes we search the car. It depends whether the Reichsminister is in residence.'

'Do you keep a record?'

'Yes, sir.'

'Do me a favour. Look and see if Doctor Josef Buhler had any visitors on Monday night.'

The sentry hitched his rifle and went back into his hut. March could see him turning the pages of a ledger. When he returned he shook his head. 'Nobody for Doctor Buhler all day.'

'Did he leave the island at all?'

'We don't keep a record of residents, sir, only visitors. And we don't check people going, only coming.'

'Right.' March looked past the guard, across the lake. A scattering of seagulls swooped low over the water, crying. Some yachts were moored to a jetty. He could hear the clink of their masts in the wind.

'What about the shore. Is that watched at all?'

The guard nodded. 'The river police have a patrol every couple of hours. But most of those houses have enough sirens and dogs to guard a KZ. We just keep the sightseers away.'

KZ: pronounced *kat-set*. Less of a mouthful than Konzentrationslager. Concentration camp.

There was a sound of powerful engines gunning in the distance. The guard turned to look up the road behind him, towards the island.

'One moment, sir.'

Round the bend, at high speed, came a grey BMW with its headlights on, followed by a long black Mercedes limousine, and then another BMW. The sentry stepped back, pressed a switch, the barrier rose, and he saluted. As the convoy swept by, March had a glimpse of the Mercedes's passengers – a young woman, beautiful, an actress perhaps, or a model, with short blonde hair; and, next to her, staring straight ahead, a wizened old man, his rodent-like profile instantly recognisable. The cars roared off towards the city.

'Does he always travel that quickly?' asked March.

The sentry gave him a knowing look. 'The Reichsminister has been screen-testing, sir. Frau Goebbels is due back at lunchtime.'

'Ah. All is clear.' March turned the key in the ignition and the Volkswagen came to life. 'Did you know that Doctor Buhler was dead?'

'No, sir.' The sentry gave no sign of interest. 'When did that happen?'

'Monday night. He was washed up a few hundred metres from here.'

'I heard they'd found a body.'

'What was he like?'

'I hardly noticed him, sir. He didn't go out much. No visitors. Never spoke. But then, a lot of them end up like that out here.'

'Which was his house?'

'You can't miss it. It's on the east side of the island. Two large towers. It's one of the biggest.'

'Thanks.'

As he drove down the causeway, March checked in his mirror. The sentry stood looking after him for a few seconds, then hitched his rifle again, turned and walked slowly back to his hut.

Schwanenwerder was small, less than a kilometre long and half a kilometre wide, with a single loop of road running one-way, clockwise. To reach Buhler's property, March had to travel three-quarters of the way round the island. He drove cautiously, slowing almost to a halt each time he glimpsed one of the houses off to his left.

The place had been named after the famous colonies of swans which lived at the southern end of the Havel. It had become fashionable towards the end of the last century. Most of its buildings dated from then: large villas, steep-roofed and stone-fronted in the French style, with long drives and lawns, protected from prying eyes by high walls and trees. A piece of the ruined Tuileries Palace stood incongruously by the roadside – a pillar and a section of arch carted back from Paris by some long-dead Wilhelmine businessman. No one stirred. Occasionally, through the bars of a gate, he saw a guard dog, and – once – a gardener raking leaves. The owners were either at work in the city, or away, or lying low.

March knew the identities of a few of them: Party bosses; a motor industry tycoon, grown fat on the profits of slave labour immediately after the war; the managing director of Wertheim's, the great department store on Potsdamer Platz that had been confiscated from its Jewish owners more than thirty years before; an armaments manufacturer; the head of an engineering conglomerate building the great Auto-bahnen into the eastern territories. He wondered how Buhler could have afforded to keep such wealthy company, then he remembered Halder's description: luxury like the Roman Empire . . .

'KP17, this is KHQ. KP17, answer please!' A woman's urgent voice filled the car. March picked up the radio handset concealed under the dashboard.

'This is KP17. Go ahead.'

'KP17, I have Sturmbannführer Jaeger for you.'

He had arrived outside the gates to Buhler's villa. Through the metalwork, March could see a yellow curve of drive and the towers, exactly as the sentry had described.

'You said trouble,' boomed Jaeger, 'and we've got it.'

'Now what?'

'I hadn't been back here ten minutes when two of our esteemed colleagues from the Gestapo arrived. "In view of Party Comrade Buhler's prominent position, blah blah blah, the case has been redesignated a security matter." '

March thumped his hand against the steering wheel. 'Shit!'

' "All documents to be handed over to the Security Police forthwith, reports required from investigating officers on current status of inquiry, Kripo inquiry to be closed, effective immediately." '

'When did this happen?'

'It's happening now. They're sitting in our office.'

'Did you tell them where I am?'

'Of course not. I just left them to it and said I'd try and find you. I've come straight to the control room.' Jaeger's voice dropped. March could imagine him turning his back on the woman operator. 'Listen, Zavi, I wouldn't recommend any heroics. They mean serious business, believe me. The Gestapo will be swarming over Schwanenwerder any minute.'

March stared at the house. It was utterly still, deserted. Damn the Gestapo.

He made up his mind at that moment. He said: 'I can't hear you, Max. I'm sorry. The line is breaking up. I haven't been able to understand anything you've said. Request you report radio fault. Out.' He switched off the receiver.

About fifty metres before the house, on the right side of the road, March had passed a gated track leading into the woods that covered the centre of the island. Now he put the Volkswagen into reverse gear, rapidly backed up to it, and parked. He trotted back to Buhler's gates. He did not have much time.

They were locked. That was to be expected. The lock itself was a solid metal block a metre and a half off the ground. He wedged the toe of his boot into it and stepped up. There was a row of iron spikes, thirty centimetres apart, running along the top of the gate, just above his head. Gripping one in either hand, he hauled himself up until he was in a position to swing his left leg over. A hazardous business. For a moment he sat astride the gate, recovering his breath. Then he dropped down to the gravel driveway on the other side.

The house was large and of a curious design. It had three storeys capped by a steep roof of blue slate. To the left were the two stone towers the sentry had described. These were attached to the main body of the house, which had a balcony with a stone balustrade running the entire length of the first floor. The balcony was supported by pillars. Behind these, half-hidden in the shadows, was the main entrance. March started towards it. Beech trees and firs grew in untended profusion along the sides of the drive. The borders were neglected. Dead leaves, unswept since the winter, blew across the lawn.

He stepped between the pillars. The first surprise. The front door was unlocked.

March stood in the hall and looked round. There was an oak staircase to the right, two doors to the left, a gloomy passage straight ahead which he guessed led to the kitchen.

He tried the first door. Behind it was a panelled dining room. A long table and twelve high-backed carved chairs. Cold and musty from disuse.

The next door led to the drawing room. He continued his mental inventory. Rugs on a polished wooden floor. Heavy furniture upholstered in rich brocade. Tapestries on the wall – good ones, too, if March was any judge, which he wasn't. By the window was a grand piano on which stood two large photographs. March tilted one towards the light, which shone weakly through the dusty leaded panes. The frame was heavy silver, with a swastika motif. The picture showed Buhler and his wife on their wedding day, coming down a flight of steps between an honour guard of SA men holding oak boughs over the happy couple. Buhler was also in SA uniform. His wife had flowers woven into her hair and was – to use a favourite expression of Max Jaeger – as ugly as a box of frogs. Neither was smiling.

March picked up the other photograph, and immediately felt his stomach lurch. There was Buhler again, slightly bowing this time, and shaking hands. The man who was the object of this obeisance had his face half-turned to the camera, as if distracted in mid-greeting by something behind the photographer's shoulder. There was an inscription. March smeared his finger through the grime on the glass to decipher the crabbed writing. 'To Party Comrade Buhler,' it read. 'From Adolf Hitler. 17 May 1945.'

Suddenly, March heard a noise. A sound like a door being kicked, followed by a whimper. He replaced the photograph and went back into the hall. The noise was coming from the end of the passage.

He drew his pistol and edged down the corridor. As he had suspected, it gave on to the kitchen. The noise came again. A cry of terror and a drumming of feet. There was a smell, too – of something filthy.

At the far end of the kitchen was a door. He reached out and grasped the handle and then, with a jerk, pulled the door open. Something huge leapt out of the darkness. A dog, muzzled, eyes wide in terror, went crashing across the floor, down the passage, into the hall and out through the open front door. The larder floor was stinking-thick with faeces and urine and food which the dog had pulled down from the shelves but been unable to eat.

After that, March would have liked to have stopped for a few minutes to steady himself. But he had no time. He put the Luger away and quickly examined the kitchen. A few greasy plates in the sink. On the table, a bottle of vodka, nearly empty, with a glass next to it. There was a door to a cellar, but it was locked; he decided not to break it down. He went upstairs. Bedrooms, bathrooms – everywhere had the same atmosphere of shabby luxury; of a grand lifestyle gone to seed. And everywhere, he noticed, there were paintings – landscapes, religious allegories, portraits – most of them thick with dust. The place had not been properly cleaned for months, maybe years.

The room which must have been Buhler's study was on the top floor of one of the towers. Shelves of legal text books, case studies, decrees. A big desk with a swivel chair next to a window overlooking the back lawn of the house. A long sofa with blankets draped beside it, which appeared to have been regularly slept on. And more photographs. Buhler in his lawyer's robes. Buhler in his SS uniform. Buhler with a group of Nazi big-wigs, one of whom March vaguely recognised as Hans Frank, in the front row of what might have been a concert. All the pictures seemed to be at least twenty years old.

March sat at the desk and looked out of the window. The lawn led down to the Havel's edge. There was a small jetty with a cabin cruiser moored to it and, beyond that, a clear view of the lake, right across to the opposite shore. Far in the distance, the Kladow–Wannsee ferry chugged by.

He turned his attention to the desk itself. A blotter. A heavy brass inkstand. A telephone. He stretched his hand towards it.

It began to ring.

His hand hung motionless. One ring. Two. Three. The stillness of the house magnified the sound; the dusty air vibrated. Four. Five. He flexed his fingers over the receiver. Six. Seven. He picked it up.

'Buhler?' The voice of an old man more dead than alive; a whisper from another world. 'Buhler? Speak to me. Who is that?'

March said: 'A friend.'

Pause. *Click*.

Whoever it was had hung up. March replaced the receiver. Quickly, he began opening the desk drawers at random. A few pencils, some notepaper, a dictionary. He pulled the bottom drawers right out, one after the other, and put his hand into the space.

There was nothing.

There was something.

At the very back, his fingers brushed against an object small and smooth. He pulled it out. A small notebook bound in black leather, an eagle and swastika in gold lettering on the cover. He flicked through it. The Party diary for 1964. He slipped it into his pocket and replaced the drawers.

Outside, Buhler's dog was going crazy, running from side to side along the water's edge, staring across the Havel, whinnying like a horse. Every few seconds it would get down on its hind legs, before resuming its desperate patrol. He could see now that almost the whole of its right side was matted with dried blood. It paid no attention to March as he walked down to the lake.

The heels of his boots rang on the planks of the wooden jetty. Through the gaps between the rickety boards he could see the muddy water a metre below, lapping in the shallows. At the end of the jetty he stepped down into the boat. It rocked with his weight. There were several centimetres of rainwater on the aft deck, clogged with dirt and leaves, a rainbow of oil on the surface. The whole boat stank of fuel. There must be a leak. He stooped and tried the small door to the cabin. It was locked. Cupping his hands, he peered through the window, but it was too dark to see.

He jumped out of the boat and began retracing his steps. The wood of the jetty was weathered grey, except in one place, along the edge opposite the boat. Here there were orange splinters; a scrape of white paint. March was bending to examine the marks when his eye was caught by something pale gleaming in the water, close to the place where the jetty left the shore. He walked back and knelt, and by holding on with his left hand and stretching down as far as he could with his right, he was just able to retrieve it. Pink and chipped, like an ancient china doll, with leather straps and steel buckles, it was an artificial foot.

THE dog heard them first. It cocked its head, turned, and trotted up the lawn towards the house. At once, March dropped his discovery back into the water and ran after the wounded animal. Cursing his stupidity, he worked his way round the side of the house until he stood in the shadow of the towers and could see the gate. The dog was leaping up at the iron work, grunting through its muzzle. On the other side, March could make out two figures standing looking at the house. Then a third appeared with a large pair of bolt-cutters which he clamped on to the lock. After ten seconds of pressure, it gave way with a loud crack.

The dog backed away as the three men filed into the grounds. Like March, they wore the black uniforms of the SS. One seemed to take something from his pocket and walked towards the dog, hand outstretched, as if offering it a treat. The animal cringed. A single shot exploded the silence, echoing round the grounds, sending a flock of rooks cawing into the air above the woods. The man holstered his revolver and gestured at the corpse to one of his companions, who seized it by the hind legs and dragged it into the bushes.

All three men strode towards the house. March stayed

behind the pillar, slowly edging round it as they came up the drive, keeping himself out of sight. It occurred to him that he had no reason to hide. He could tell the Gestapo men he had been searching the property, that he had not received Jaeger's message. But something in their manner, in the casual ruthlessness with which they had disposed of the dog, warned him against it. *They had been here before*.

As they came closer, he could make out their ranks. Two Sturmbannführer and an Obergruppenführer – a brace of majors and a general. What matter of state security could demand the personal attention of a full Gestapo general? The Obergruppenführer was in his late fifties, built like an ox, with the battered face of an ex-boxer. March recognised him from the television, from newspaper photographs.

Who was he?

Then he remembered. Odilo Globocnik. Familiarly known throughout the SS as Globus. Years ago he had been Gauleiter of Vienna. It was Globus who had shot the dog.

'You – ground floor,' said Globus. 'You – check the back.'

They drew their guns and disappeared into the house. March waited half a minute, then set off for the gate. He skirted the perimeter of the garden, avoiding the drive, picking his way instead, almost bent double, through the tangled shrubbery. Five metres from the gate, he paused for breath. Built into the right-hand gatepost, so discreet it was scarcely noticeable, was a rusty metal container – a mail box – in which rested a large brown package.

This is madness, he thought. Absolute madness.

He did not run to the gate: nothing, he knew, attracts the human eye like sudden movement. Instead he made himself stroll from the bushes as if it were the most natural thing in the world, tugged the package from the mail box, and sauntered out of the open gate.

He expected to hear a shout from behind him, or a shot. But the only sound was the rustle of the wind in the trees. When he reached his car, he found his hands were shaking.

THREE

'**W**hy do we believe in Germany and the Führer?' 'Because we believe in God, we believe in Germany which He created in His world, and in the Führer, Adolf Hitler, whom He has sent us.'

'Whom must we primarily serve?'

'Our people and our Führer, Adolf Hitler.'

'Why do we obey?'

'From inner conviction, from belief in Germany, in the Führer, in the Movement and the SS, and from loyalty.'

'Good!' The instructor nodded. 'Good. Reassemble in thirty-five minutes on the south sports field. Jost: stay behind. The rest of you: dismissed!'

With their cropped hair and their loose-fitting light-grey drill uniforms, the class of SS cadets looked like convicts. They filed out noisily, with a scraping of chairs and a stamping of boots on the rough wooden floor. A large portrait of the late Heinrich Himmler smiled down on them, benevolently. Jost looked forlorn, standing to attention, alone in the centre of the classroom. Some of the other cadets gave him curious glances as they left. It had to be Jost, you could see them thinking. Jost: the queer, the loner, always the odd one out. He might well be due another beating in the barracks tonight.

The instructor nodded towards the back of the classroom. 'You have a visitor.'

March was leaning against a radiator, arms folded, watching. 'Hello again, Jost,' he said.

They walked across the vast parade ground. In one corner, a batch of new recruits was being harangued by an SS Hauptscharführer. In another, a hundred youths in black tracksuits stretched, twisted and touched their toes in perfect obedience to shouted commands. Meeting Jost here reminded March of visiting prisoners in jail. The same institutionalised smell, of polish and disinfectant and boiled food. The same ugly concrete blocks of buildings. The same high walls and patrols of guards. Like a KZ, the Sepp Dietrich Academy was both huge and claustrophobic; an entirely self-enclosed world.

'Can we go somewhere private?' asked March.

Jost gave him a contemptuous look. 'There is no privacy here. That's the point.' They took a few more paces. 'I suppose we could try the barracks. Everyone else is eating.'

They turned, and Jost led the way into a low, grey-painted building. Inside, it was gloomy, with a strong smell of male sweat. There must have been a hundred beds, laid out in four rows. Jost had guessed correctly: it was deserted. His bed was two-thirds of the way down, in the centre. March sat on the coarse brown blanket and offered Jost a cigarette.

'It's not allowed in here.'

March waved the packet at him. 'Go ahead. Say I ordered you.'

Jost took it, gratefully. He knelt, opened the metal locker beside the bed, and began searching for something to use as an ashtray. As the door hung open, March could see inside: a pile of paperbacks, magazines, a framed photograph.

'May I?'

Jost shrugged. 'Sure.'

March picked up the photograph. A family group, it reminded him of the picture of the Weisses. Father in an SS uniform. Shy-looking mother in a hat. Daughter: a pretty girl with blonde plaits; fourteen, maybe. And Jost himself: fat-cheeked and smiling, barely recognisable as the harrowed, cropped figure now kneeling on the stone barracks floor.

Jost said: 'Changed, haven't I?'

March was shocked, and tried to hide it. 'Your sister?' he asked.

'She's still at school.'

'And your father?'

'He runs an engineering business in Dresden now. He was one of the first into Russia in '41. Hence the uniform.'

March peered closely at the stern figure. 'Isn't he wearing the Knight's Cross?' It was the highest decoration for bravery.

'Oh yes,' said Jost. 'An authentic war hero.' He took the photograph and replaced it in the locker. 'What about your father?'

'He was in the Imperial Navy,' said March. 'He was wounded in the First War. Never properly recovered.'

'How old were you when he died?'

'Seven.'

'Do you still think about him?'

'Every day.'

'Did you go into the Navy?'

'Almost. I was in the U-boat service.'

Jost shook his head slowly. His pale face had flushed pink. 'We all follow our fathers, don't we?'

'Most of us, maybe. Not all.'

They smoked in silence for a while. Outside, March could hear the physical training session still in progress. 'One, two, three . . . One, two, three . . .'

'These people,' said Jost, and shook his head. 'There's a poem by Erich Kästner – "Marschliedchen".' He closed his eyes and recited:

'You love hatred and want to measure the world against it.
You throw food to the beast in man,
That it may grow, the beast deep within you!
Let the beast in man devour man.'

The young man's sudden passion made March uncomfortable. 'When was that written?'

'1932.'

'I don't know it.'

'You wouldn't. It's banned.'

There was a silence, then March said: 'We now know the identity of the body you discovered. Doctor Josef Buhler. An official of the General Government. An SS-Brigadeführer.'

'Oh God.' Jost rested his head in his hands.

'It has become a more serious matter, you see. Before coming to you, I checked with the sentries' office at the main gate. They have a record that you left the barracks at five-thirty yesterday morning, as usual. So the times in your statement make no sense.'

Jost kept his face covered. The cigarette was burning down between his fingers. March leaned forward, took it, and stubbed it out. He stood.

'Watch,' he said. Jost looked up and March began jogging on the spot.

'This is you, yesterday, right?' March made a show of exhaustion, puffing out his cheeks, wiping his brow with his forearms. Despite himself, Jost smiled. 'Good,' said March. He continued jogging. 'Now you're thinking about some book, or how awful your life is, when you come through the woods and on to the path by the lake. It's pissing with rain and the light's not good, but off to your left you see something . . .'

March turned his head. Jost was watching him intently.

'. . . Whatever it is, it's not the body . . .'

'But . . .'

March stopped and pointed at Jost. 'Don't dig yourself any deeper into the shit, is my advice. Two hours ago I went back and checked the place where the corpse was found – there's no way you could have seen it from the road.'

He resumed jogging. 'So: you see something, but you don't stop. You run past. But being a conscientious fellow, five minutes up the road you decide you had better go back for a second look. And then you discover the body. And only then do you call the cops.'

He grasped Jost's hands and pulled him to his feet. 'Run with me,' he commanded.

'I can't . . .'

'Run!'

Jost broke into an unwilling shuffle. Their feet clattered on the flagstones.

'Now describe what you can see. You're coming out of the woods and you're on the lake path . . .'

'Please . . .'

'Tell me!'

'I . . . I see . . . a car . . .' Jost's eyes were closed. '. . . Then three men . . . It's raining fast, they have coats, hoods – like monks . . . Their heads are down . . . Coming up the slope from the lake . . . I . . . I'm scared . . . I cross the road and run up into the trees so they don't see me . . .'

'Go on.'

'They get into the car and drive off . . . I wait, and then I come out of the woods and I find the body . . .'

'You've missed something.'

'No, I swear . . .'

'You see a face. When they get into the car, you see a face.'

'No . . .'

'Tell me whose face it is, Jost. You can see it. You know it. Tell me.'

'Globus!' shouted Jost. 'I see Globus.'

he package he had taken from Buhler's mailbox lay unopened on the front seat next to him. Perhaps it was a bomb, thought March, as he started the Volkswagen. There had been a blitz of parcel bombs over the past few months, blowing off the hands and faces of half a dozen government officials. He might just make page three of the *Tageblatt*: 'Investigator Dies in Mysterious Blast Outside Barracks'.

He drove around Schlachtensee until he found a delicatessen, where he bought a loaf of black bread, some Westphalian ham and a quarter-bottle of Scotch whisky. The sun still shone; the air was fresh. He pointed the car westwards, back towards the lakes. He was going to do something he had not done for years. He was going to have a picnic.

After Göring had been made Chief Reich Huntsman in 1934, there had been some attempt to lighten the Grunewald. Chestnut and linden, beech, birch and oak had all been planted. But the heart of it – as it had been a thousand years ago, when the plains of northern Europe were still forest – the heart remained the hilly woods of melancholy pine. From these forests, five centuries before Christ, the warring German tribes had emerged; and to these forests, twenty-five centuries later, mostly at weekends, in their campers and their trailers, the victorious German tribes returned. The Germans were a race of forest-dwellers. Make a clearing in your mind, if you liked; the trees just waited to reclaim it.

March parked and took his provisions and Buhler's mail bomb, or whatever it was, and walked carefully up a steep path into the forest. Five minutes' climbing brought him to a spot which commanded a clear view of the Havel and of the smoky blue slopes of trees, receding into the distance. The pines smelled strong and sweet in the warmth. Above his head, a large jet rumbled across the sky, making its approach to Berlin Airport. As it disappeared, the noise died, until at last the only sound was birdsong.

March did not want to open the parcel yet. It made him uneasy. So he sat on a large stone – no doubt casually deposited here by the municipal authorities for this very purpose – took a swig of whisky, and began to eat.

Of Odilo Globocnik—Globus—March knew little, and that only by reputation. His fortunes had swung like a weathercock over the past thirty years. An Austrian by birth, a builder by profession, he had become Party leader in Carinthia in the mid-1930s, and ruler of Vienna. Then there had been a period of disgrace, connected with illegal currency speculation, followed by a restoration, as a police chief in the General Government when the war started – he must have known Buhler there, thought March. At the end of the war, there had been a second fall to – where was it? – Trieste, he seemed to remember. But with Himmler's death Globus had come back to Berlin, and now he held some unspecified position within the Gestapo, working directly for Heydrich.

That smashed and brutal face was unmistakable, and, despite the rain and the poor light, Jost had recognised it at once. A portrait of Globus hung in the Academy's Hall of Fame, and Globus himself had delivered a lecture to the awestruck cadets – on the police structures of the Reich – only a few weeks earlier. No wonder Jost had been so frightened. He should have called the Orpo anonymously, and cleared out before they arrived. Better still, from his point of view, he should not have called them at all.

March finished his ham. He took the remains of the bread, broke it into pieces, and scattered the crumbs across the forest floor. Two blackbirds, which had watched him eat, emerged cautiously from the undergrowth and began pecking at them.

He took out the pocket diary. Standard issue to Party members, available in any stationers. Useful information at the beginning. The names of the Party hierarchy: government ministers, kommissariat bosses, gauleiters.

Public holidays: Day of National Reawakening, 30 January; Potsdam Day, 21 March; Führer's birthday, 20 April; National Festival of the German People, 1 May . . .

Map of the Empire with railway journey times: Berlin–Rovno, sixteen hours; Berlin–Tiflis, twenty-seven hours; Berlin–Ufa, four days . . .

The diary itself was a week to two pages, the entries so sparse that at first March thought it was blank. He went through it carefully. There was a tiny cross against 7 March. For 1 April, Buhler had written 'My sister's birthday'. There was another cross against 9 April. On 11 April, he had noted 'Stuckart/Luther, morning – 10'. Finally, on 13 April, the day before his death, Buhler had drawn another small cross. That was all.

March wrote down the dates in his notebook. He began a new page. The death of Josef Buhler. Solutions. One: the death was accidental, the Gestapo had learned of it some hours before the Kripo were informed, and Globus was merely inspecting the body when Jost passed by. Absurd.

Very well. Two: Buhler had been murdered by the Gestapo, and Globus had carried out the execution. Absurd again. The 'Night and Fog' order of 1941 was still in force. Buhler could have been bundled away quite legally to some secret death in a Gestapo cell, his property confiscated by the state. Who would have mourned him? Or questioned his disappearance?

And so, three: Buhler had been murdered by Globus, who had covered his tracks by declaring the death a matter of state security, and by taking over the investigation himself. But why had the Kripo been allowed to get involved at all? What was Globus's motive? Why was Buhler's body left in a public place?

March leaned back against the stone and closed his eyes. The sun on his face made the darkness blood red. A warm haze of whisky enveloped him.

He could not have been asleep more than half an hour, when he heard a rustle in the undergrowth beside him and felt something touch his sleeve. He was awake in an instant, in time to see the white tail and the hindquarters of a deer darting into the trees. A rural idyll, ten kilometres from the heart of the Reich! Either that, or the whisky. He shook his head and picked up the package.

Thick brown paper, neatly wrapped and taped. Indeed, *professionally* wrapped and taped. Crisp lines and sharp creases, an economy of materials used and effort expended. A paradigm of a parcel. No man March had ever met could have produced such an object – it must have been wrapped by a woman. Next, the postmark. Three Swiss stamps, showing tiny yellow flowers on a green background. Posted in Zürich at 1600 hours on 13.4.64. That was the day before yesterday.

He felt his palms begin to sweat as he unwrapped it with exaggerated care, first peeling off the tape and then slowly, centimetre by centimetre, folding back the paper. He lifted it fractionally. Inside was a box of chocolates.

Its lid showed flaxen-haired girls in red check dresses dancing around a maypole in a flowery meadow. Behind them, white-peaked against a fluorescent blue sky, rose the Alps. Overprinted in black gothic script was the legend: 'Birthday Greetings to Our Beloved Führer, 1964'. But there was something odd about it. The box was too heavy just to contain chocolates.

He took out a penknife and cut round the cellophane

cover. He set the box gently on the log. With his face turned away and his arm fully extended, he lifted the lid with the point of the blade. Inside, a mechanism began to whirr. Then this:

> Love unspoken
> Faith unbroken
> All life through
> Strings are playing
> Hear them saying
> 'I love you'
> Now the echo answers
> 'Say you'll want me too'
> All the world's in love with love
> And I love you

Only the tune, of course, not the words; but he knew them well enough. Standing alone on a hill in the Grunewald Forest, March listened as the box played the waltz-duet from Act Three of *The Merry Widow*.

he streets on the way back into central Berlin seemed unnaturally quiet and when March reached Werderscher Markt he discovered the reason. A large noticeboard in the foyer announced there would be a government statement at four-thirty. Personnel were to assemble in the staff canteen. Attendance: compulsory. He was just in time.

They had developed a new theory at the Propaganda Ministry, that the best time to make big announcements was at the end of the working day. News was thus received communally, in a comradely spirit: there was no opportunity for private scepticism or defeatism. Also, the broadcasts were always timed so that the workers went home slightly early – at four-fifty, say, rather than five – fostering a sense of contentment, subliminally associating the regime with good feelings. That was how it was these days. The snow-white Propaganda palace on Wilhelm Strasse employed more psychologists than journalists.

The Werderscher Markt staff were filing into the canteen: officers and clerks and typists and drivers, shoulder to shoulder in a living embodiment of the National Socialist ideal. The four television screens, one in each corner, were showing a map of the Reich with a swastika superimposed, accompanied by selections from Beethoven. Occasionally, a male announcer would break in excitedly: 'People of Germany, prepare yourselves for an important statement!' In the old days, on the radio, you got only the music. Progress again.

How many of these events could March remember? They stretched away behind him, islands in time. In '38, he had been called out of his classroom to hear that German troops were entering Vienna and that Austria had returned to the Fatherland. The headmaster, who had been gassed in the First War, had wept on the stage of the little gymnasium, watched by a gaggle of uncomprehending boys.

In '39, he had been at home with his mother in Hamburg. A Friday morning, 11 o'clock, the Führer's speech relayed live from the Reichstag: *'I am from now on just the first soldier of the German Reich. I have once more put on that uniform that was most sacred and dear to me. I will not take it off until victory is secured, or I will not survive the outcome.'* A thunder of applause. This time his mother had wept – a hum of misery as her body rocked backwards and forwards. March, seventeen, had looked away in shame, sought out the photograph of his father – splendid in the uniform of the Imperial German Navy – and he had thought: *Thank God. War at last. Maybe now I will be able to live up to what you wanted.*

He had been at sea for the next few broadcasts. Victory over Russia in the spring of '43 – a triumph for the Führer's strategic genius! The Wehrmacht summer offensive of the year before had cut Moscow off from the Caucasus, separating the Red armies from the Baku oilfields. Stalin's war machine had simply ground to a halt for want of fuel.

Peace with the British in '44 – a triumph for the Führer's counter-intelligence genius! March remembered how all U-boats had been recalled to their bases on the Atlantic coast to be equipped with a new cipher system: the treacherous British, they were told, had been reading the Fatherland's codes. Picking off merchant shipping had been easy after that. England was starved into submission. Churchill and his gang of war-mongers had fled to Canada.

Peace with the Americans in '46 – a triumph for the Führer's scientific genius! When America defeated Japan by detonating an atomic bomb, the Führer had sent a V-3 rocket to explode in the skies over New York to prove he could retaliate in kind if struck. After that, the war had dwindled to a series of bloody guerilla conflicts at the fringes of the new German Empire. A nuclear stalemate which the diplomats called the Cold War.

But still the broadcasts had gone on. When Goering had died in '51, there had been a whole day of solemn music before the announcement was made. Himmler had received similar treatment when he was killed in an aircraft explosion in '62. Deaths, victories, wars, exhortations for sacrifice and revenge, the dull struggle with the Reds on the Urals front with its unpronounceable battlefields and offensives – Oktyabr'skoye, Polunochnoye, Alapayevsk . . .

March looked at the faces around him. Forced humour, resignation, apprehension. People with brothers and sons and husbands in the East. They kept glancing at the screens.

'People of Germany, prepare yourselves for an important statement!'

What was coming now?

The canteen was almost full. March was pressed up against a pillar. He could see Max Jaeger a few metres away, joking with a bosomy secretary from VA(1), the legal department. Max spotted him over her shoulder and gave him a grin. There was a roll of drums. The room was still. A newsreader said: 'We are now going live to the Foreign Ministry in Berlin.'

A bronze relief glittered in the television lights. A Nazi eagle, clutching the globe, shot rays of illumination, like a child's drawing of a sunrise. Before it, with his thick black eyebrows and shaded jowls, stood the Foreign Ministry spokesman, Drexler. March suppressed a laugh: you would have thought that, in the whole of Germany, Goebbels could have found one spokesman who did not look like a convicted criminal.

'Ladies and gentlemen, I have a brief statement for you from the Reich Ministry for Foreign Affairs.' He was addressing an audience of journalists, who were off-camera. He put on a pair of glasses and began to read.

'In accordance with the long-standing and well-documented desire of the Führer and People of the Greater German Reich to live in peace and security with the countries of the world, and following extensive consultations with our allies in the European Community, the Reich Ministry for Foreign Affairs, on behalf of the Führer, has today issued an invitation to the President of the United States of America to visit the Greater German Reich for personal discussions aimed at promoting greater understanding between our two peoples. This invitation has been accepted. We understand that the American administration has indicated this morning that Herr Kennedy intends to meet the Führer in Berlin in September. Heil Hitler! Long live Germany!'

The picture faded to black and another drum roll signalled the start of the national anthem. The men and women in the canteen began to sing. March pictured them at that moment all over Germany – in shipyards and steelworks and offices and schools – the hard voices and the high merged together in one great bellow of acclamation rising to the heavens.

> Deutschland, Deutschland über Alles!
> Über Alles in der Welt!

His own lips moved in conformity with the rest, but no sound emerged.

'MORE fucking work for us,' said Jaeger. They were back in their office. He had his feet on the desk and was puffing at a

cigar. 'If you think the Führertag is a security nightmare –
forget it. Can you imagine what it will be like with Kennedy
in town as well?'

March smiled. 'I think, Max, you are missing the
historic dimension of the occasion.'

'Screw the historic dimension of the occasion. I'm
thinking about my sleep. The bombs are already going off
like fire crackers. Look at this.'

Jaeger swung his legs off the desk and rummaged through
a pile of folders. 'While you were playing around by the
Havel, some of us were having to do some work.'

He picked up an envelope and tipped out the contents. It
was a PPD file. Personal Possessions of the Deceased. From
a mound of papers he pulled out two passports and handed
them to March. One belonged to an SS officer, Paul Hahn;
the other to a young woman, Magda Voss.

Jaeger said: 'Pretty thing, isn't she? They'd just married.
Were leaving the reception in Spandau. On their way to
their honeymoon. He's driving. They turn into Nawener
Strasse. A lorry pulls out in front of them. Guy jumps out
the back with a gun. Our man panics. Goes into reverse.
Wham! Up the kerb, straight into a lamp-post. While he's
trying to get back into first gear – bang! – shot in the head.
End of groom. Little Magda gets out of the car, tries to
make a run for it. Bang! End of bride. End of honeymoon.
End of every fucking thing. Except it isn't, because the
families are still back at the reception toasting the newly-
weds and nobody bothers to tell them what's happened for
another two hours.'

Jaeger blew his nose on a grimy handkerchief. March
looked again at the girl's passport. She was pretty: blonde
and dark-eyed; now dead in the gutter at twenty-four.

'Who did it?' He handed the passports back.

Jaeger counted off on his fingers. 'Poles. Latvians.
Estonians. Ukrainians. Czechs. Croats. Caucasians.

Georgians. Reds. Anarchists. Who knows? Nowadays it could be anybody. The poor idiot stuck up an open invitation to the reception on his barracks noticeboard. The Gestapo reckon a cleaner, a cook, someone like that, saw it and passed on the word. Most of these barracks ancillaries are foreigners. They were all taken away this afternoon, poor bastards.'

He put the passports and identity cards back into the envelope and tossed it into a desk drawer.

'How did it go with you?'

'Have a chocolate.' March handed the box to Jaeger, who opened it. The tinny music filled the office.

'Very tasteful.'

'What do you know about it?'

'What? *The Merry Widow*? The Führer's favourite operetta. My mother was mad about it.'

'So was mine.'

Every German mother was mad about it. *The Merry Widow* by Franz Lehar. First performed in Vienna in 1905: as sugary as one of the city's cream cakes. Lehar had died in 1948, and Hitler had sent a personal representative to his funeral.

'What else is there to say?' Jaeger took a chocolate in one of his great paws and popped it into his mouth. 'Who are these from? A secret admirer?'

'I took them from Buhler's mailbox.' March bit into a chocolate and winced at the sickly taste of liquid cherry. 'Consider: you have no friends, yet someone sends you an expensive box of chocolates from Switzerland. With no message. A box that plays the Führer's favourite tune. Who would do that?' He swallowed the other half of the chocolate. 'A poisoner, perhaps?'

'Oh Christ!' Jaeger spat the contents of his mouth into his hand, pulled out his handkerchief and began wiping the brown smears of saliva from his fingers and lips. 'Sometimes I have my doubts about your sanity.'

'I am systematically destroying state evidence,' said March. He forced himself to eat another chocolate. 'No, worse than that: I am *consuming* state evidence, thereby committing a double offence. Tampering with justice while enriching myself.'

'Take some leave, man. I'm serious. You need a rest. My advice is to go down and dump those fucking chocolates in the trash as fast as possible. Then come home and have supper with me and Hannelore. You look as if you haven't had a decent meal in weeks. The Gestapo have taken the file. The autopsy report is going straight to Prinz-Albrecht Strasse. It's over. Done. Forget it.'

'Listen, Max.' March told him about Jost's confession, about how Jost had seen Globus with the body. He pulled out Buhler's diary. 'These names written here. Who are Stuckart and Luther?'

'I don't know.' Jaeger's face was suddenly drawn and hard. 'What's more, I don't want to know.'

A STEEP flight of stone steps led down to the semi-darkness. At the bottom, March hesitated, the chocolates in his hand. A doorway to the left led out to the cobbled centre courtyard, where the rubbish was collected from large, rusty bins. To the right, a dimly lit passage led to the Registry.

He tucked the chocolates under his arm and turned right.

The Kripo Registry was housed in what had once been a warren of rooms next to the boilerhouse. The closeness of the boilers and the web of hot water pipes criss-crossing the ceiling kept the place permanently hot. There was a reassuring smell of warm dust and dry paper, and in the poor light, between the pillars, the wire racks of files and reports seemed to stretch to infinity.

The Registrar, a fat woman in a greasy tunic who had once been a wardress at the prison in Plötzensee, demanded his ID. He handed it to her, as he had done more than once a week for the past ten years. She looked at it, as she always did, as if she had never seen it before, then at his face, then back, then returned it, and gave an upward tilt of her chin, something between an acknowledgement and a sneer. She wagged her finger. 'And no smoking,' she said, for the five-hundredth time.

From the shelf of reference books next to her desk he selected *Wer Ist's?*, the German *Who's Who* – a red-bound directory a thousand pages thick. He also took down the smaller, Party publication, *Guide to the Personalities of the NSDAP*, which included passport-sized photographs of each entrant. This was the book Halder had used to identify Buhler that morning. He lugged both volumes across to a table, and switched on the reading light. In the distance the boilers hummed. The Registry was deserted.

Of the two books, March preferred the Party's *Guide*. This had been published more or less annually since the mid-1930s. Often, during the dark, quiet afternoons of the winter, he had come down to the warmth to browse through old editions. It intrigued him to trace how the faces had changed. The early volumes were dominated by the grizzled ex-Freikorps red-baiters, men with necks wider than their foreheads. They stared into the camera, scrubbed and ill at ease, like nineteenth-century farmhands in their Sunday best. But by the 1950s, the beer-hall brawlers had given way to the smooth technocrats of the Speer type – well-groomed university men with bland smiles and hard eyes.

There was one Luther. Christian name: Martin. Now here, comrades, is an historic name to play with. But this Luther looked nothing like his famous namesake. He was pudding-faced with black hair and thick horn-rimmed glasses. March took out his notebook.

Born: 16 December 1895, Berlin. Served in the German Army transport division, 1914–18. Profession: furniture remover. Joined the NSDAP and the SA on 1 March 1933. Sat on the Berlin City Council for the Dahlem district. Entered the Foreign Office, 1936. Head of Abteilung Deutschland – the 'German Division' – of the Foreign Office until retirement in 1955. Promoted to Under State Secretary, July 1941.

The details were sparse, but clear enough for March to guess his type. Chippy and aggressive, a rough-and-tumble street politician. And an opportunist. Like thousands of others, Luther had rushed to join the Party a few weeks after Hitler had come to power.

He flicked through the pages to Stuckart, Wilhelm, Doctor of Law. The photograph was a professional studio portrait, the face cast in a film star's brooding half-shadow. A vain man, and a curious mixture: curly grey hair, intense eyes, straight jawline – yet a flabby, almost voluptuous mouth. He took more notes.

Born 16 November 1902, Wiesbaden. Studied law and economics at Munich and Frankfurt-am-Main universities. Graduated Magna Cum Laude, June 1928. Joined the Party in Munich in 1922. Various SA and SS positions. Mayor of Stettin, 1933. State Secretary, Ministry of the Interior, 1935–53. Publication: A *Commentary on the German Racial Laws* (1936). Promoted honorary SS-Obergruppenführer, 1944. Returned to private legal practice, 1953.

Here was a character quite different from Luther. An intellectual; an alter Kämpfer, like Buhler; a high-flyer. To be Mayor of Stettin, a port city of nearly 300,000, at the age of thirty-one . . . Suddenly, March realised he had read all this before, very recently. But where? He could not remember. He closed his eyes. *Come on.*

Wer Ist's? added nothing new, except that Stuckart was unmarried whereas Luther was on his third wife. He found a clean double-page in his notebook and drew three columns; headed them Buhler, Luther and Stuckart; and began making lists of dates. Compiling a chronology was a favourite tool of his, a method of finding a pattern in what seemed otherwise to be a fog of random facts.

They had all been born in roughly the same period. Buhler was sixty-four; Luther, sixty-eight; Stuckart, sixty-one. They had all become civil servants in the 1930s – Buhler in 1939, Luther in 1936, Stuckart in 1935. They had all held roughly similar ranks – Buhler and Stuckart had been state secretaries; Luther, an under state secretary. They had all retired in the 1950s – Buhler in 1951, Luther in 1955, Stuckart in 1953. They must all have known one another. They had all met at 10 am the previous Friday. Where was the pattern?

March tilted back in his chair and stared up at the tangle of pipes chasing one another like snakes across the ceiling.

And then he remembered.

He pitched himself forward, on to his feet.

Next to the entrance were loosely bound volumes of the *Berliner Tageblatt*, the *Völkischer Beobachter* and the SS paper, *Das Schwarzes Korps*. He wrenched back the pages of the *Tageblatt*, back to yesterday's issue, back to the obituaries. There it was. He had seen it last night.

Party Comrade Wilhelm Stuckart, formerly State Secretary of the Ministry of the Interior, who died suddenly of heart failure on Sunday, 13 April, will be remembered as a dedicated servant of the National Socialist cause . . .

The ground seemed to shift beneath his feet. He was aware of the Registrar staring at him.

'Are you ill, Herr Sturmbannführer?'

'No. I'm fine. Do me a favour, will you?' He picked up a file requisition slip and wrote out Stuckart's full name and date of birth. 'Will you see if there's a file on this person?'

She looked at the slip and held out a hand. 'ID.'

He gave her his identity card. She licked her pencil and entered the twelve digits of March's service number on to the requisition form. By this means a record was kept of which Kripo investigator had requested which file, and at what time. His interest would be there for the Gestapo to see, a full eight hours after he had been ordered off the Buhler case. Further evidence of his lack of National Socialist discipline. It could not be helped.

The Registrar had pulled out a long wooden drawer of index cards and was marching her square-tipped fingers along the tops of them. 'Stroop,' she murmured. 'Strunck. Struss. Stülpnagel . . .'

March said: 'You've gone past it.'

She grunted and pulled out a slip of pink paper. ' "Stuckart, Wilhelm." ' She looked at him. 'There is a file. It's out.'

'Who has it?'

'See for yourself.'

March leaned forwards. Stuckart's file was with Sturm-bannführer Fiebes of Kripo Department VB3. The sexual crimes division.

THE whisky and the dry air had given him a thirst. In the corridor outside the Registry was a water-cooler. He poured himself a drink and considered what to do.

What would a sensible man have done? That was easy. A sensible man would have done what Max Jaeger did every day. He would have put on his hat and coat and gone home to his wife and children. But for March that was not an option. The empty apartment in Ansbacher Strasse, the quarrelling neighbours and yesterday's newspaper, these held no attractions for him. He had narrowed his life to such a point, the only thing left was his work. If he betrayed that, what else was there?

And there was something else, the instinct that propelled him out of bed every morning into each unwelcoming day, and that was the desire to *know*. In police work, there was always another junction to reach, another corner to peer around. Who were the Weiss family, and what had happened to them? Whose was the body in the lake? What linked the deaths of Buhler and Stuckart? It kept him going, his blessing or his curse, this compulsion to *know*. And so, in the end, there was no choice.

He tossed the paper cup into the waste bin, and went upstairs.

alther Fiebes was in his office, drinking schnapps. Watching him from a table beneath the window was a row of five human heads – white plaster casts with hinged scalps, all raised like lavatory seats, displaying their brains in red and grey sections – the five strains which made up the German Empire.

Placards announced them from left to right, in descending order of acceptability to the authorities. Category One: Pure Nordic. Category Two: Predominantly Nordic or Phalic. Category Three: Harmonious Bastard with Slight Alpine Dinaric or Mediterranean Characteristics. These groups qualified for membership of the SS. The others could hold no public office and stared reproachfully at Fiebes. Category Four: Bastard of Predominantly East-Baltic or Alpine Origin. Category Five: Bastard of Extra-European Origin.

March was a One/Two; Fiebes, ironically, a borderline Three. But then, the racial fanatics were seldom the blue-eyed Aryan supermen – they, in the words of *Das Schwarzes Korps*, were 'too inclined to take their membership of the Volk for granted'. Instead, the swampy frontiers of the German race were patrolled by those less confident of their blood-worthiness. Insecurity breeds good border guards. The knock-kneed Franconian schoolmaster, ridiculous in his Lederhosen; the Bavarian shopkeeper with his pebble glasses; the red-haired Thuringian accountant with a nervous tic and a predilection for the younger members of the Hitler Youth; the lame and the ugly, the runts of the national litter – these were the loudest defenders of the Volk.

So it was with Fiebes – the myopic, stooping, buck-toothed, cuckolded Fiebes – whom the Reich had blessed with the one job he really wanted. Homosexuality and miscegenation had replaced rape and incest as capital offences. Abortion, 'an act of sabotage against Germany's racial future', was punishable by death. The permissive 1960s were showing a strong increase in such sex crimes. Fiebes, a sheet-sniffer by temperament, worked all the hours the Führer sent and was as happy, in Max Jaeger's words, as a pig in horseshit.

But not today. Now, he was drinking in the office, his eyes were moist, and his bat's-wing toupee hung slightly askew.

March said: 'According to the newspapers, Stuckart died of heart failure.'

Fiebes blinked.

'But according to the Registry, the file on Stuckart is out to you.'

'I cannot comment.'

'Of course you can. We are colleagues.' March sat down and lit a cigarette. 'I take it we are in the familiar business of "sparing the family embarrassment".'

Fiebes muttered: 'Not just the family.' He hesitated. 'Could I have one of those?'

'Sure.' March gave him a cigarette and flicked his lighter. Fiebes took an experimental draw, like a schoolboy.

'This affair has left me pretty well shaken, March, I don't mind admitting. The man was a hero to me.'

'You knew him?'

'By reputation, naturally. I never actually *met* him. Why? What is your interest?'

'State security. That is all I can say. You know how it is.'

'Ah. Now I understand.' Fiebes poured himself another large helping of schnapps. 'We're very much alike, March, you and I.'

'We are?'

'Sure. You're the only investigator who's in this place as often as I am. We've got rid of our wives, our children – all that shit. We live for the job. When it goes well, we're well. When it goes badly . . .' His head fell forward. Presently, he said: 'Do you know Stuckart's book?'

'Unfortunately, no.'

Fiebes opened a desk drawer and handed March a battered, leather-bound volume. *A Commentary on the German Racial Laws*. March leafed through it. There were chapters on each of the three Nuremberg Laws of 1935: the Reich Citizenship Law, the Law for the Protection of German Blood and German Honour, the Law for the Protection of the Genetic Health of the German People. Some passages were underlined in red ink, with exclamation marks beside them. 'For the avoidance of racial damage, it is necessary for couples to submit to medical examination before marriage.' 'Marriage between persons suffering from venereal disease, feeble-mindedness, epilepsy or "genetic infirmities" (see 1933 Sterilisation Law) will be permitted only after production of a sterilisation certificate.' There were charts: 'An Overview of the Admissibility of Marriage between Aryans and non-Aryans', 'The Prevalence of Mischling of the First Degree'.

It was all gobbledygook to Xavier March.

Fiebes said: 'Most of it is out of date now. A lot of it refers to Jews, and the Jews, as we know' – he gave a wink – 'have all gone east. But Stuckart is still the bible of my calling. This is the foundation stone.'

March handed him the book. Fiebes cradled it like a baby. 'Now what I really need to see', said March, 'is the file on Stuckart's death.'

He was braced for an argument. Instead, Fiebes merely made an expansive gesture with his bottle of schnapps. 'Go ahead.'

*

THE Kripo file was an ancient one. It went back more than a quarter of a century. In 1936, Stuckart had become a member of the Interior Ministry's 'Committee for the Protection of German Blood' – a tribunal of civil servants, lawyers and doctors who considered applications for marriage between Aryans and non-Aryans. Shortly afterwards, the police had started receiving anonymous allegations that Stuckart was providing marriage licences in exchange for cash bribes. He had also apparently demanded sexual favours from some of the women involved.

The first name complainant was a Dortmund tailor, a Herr Maser, who had protested to his local Party office that his fiancée had been assaulted. His statement had been passed to the Kripo. There was no record of any investigation. Instead, Maser and his girlfriend had been dispatched to concentration camps. Various other stories from informants, including one from Stuckart's wartime Blockwart, were included in the file. No action had ever been taken.

In 1953, Stuckart had begun a liaison with an eighteen-year-old Warsaw girl, Maria Dymarski. She had claimed German ancestry back to 1720 in order to marry a Wehrmacht captain. The conclusion of the Interior Ministry's experts was that the documents were forged. The following year, Dymarski had been given a permit to work as a domestic servant in Berlin. Her employer's name was listed as Wilhelm Stuckart.

March looked up. 'How did he get away with it for ten years?'

'He was an Obergruppenführer, March. You don't make complaints about a man like that. Remember what happened to Maser when he complained? Besides, nobody had any evidence – then.'

'And there is evidence now?'

'Look in the envelope.'

Inside the file, in a manila envelope, were a dozen colour photographs, of startlingly good quality, showing Stuckart and Dymarski in bed. White bodies against red satin sheets. The faces – contorted in some shots, relaxed in others – were easy to identify. They were all taken from the same position, alongside the bed. The girl's body, pale and undernourished, looked fragile beneath the man's. In one shot she sat astride him – thin white arms clasped behind her head, face tilted towards the camera. Her features were broad, Slavic. But with her shoulder-length hair dyed blonde she could have passed as a German.

'These weren't taken recently?'

'About ten years ago. He turned greyer. She put on a bit of weight. She looked more of a tart as she got older.'

'Do we have any idea where they are?' The background was a blur of colours. A brown wooden bedhead, red-and-white striped wallpaper, a lamp with a yellow shade; it could have been anywhere.

'It's not his apartment – at least, not the way it's decorated now. A hotel, maybe a whorehouse. The camera is behind a two-way mirror. See the way they sometimes seem to be staring into the camera? I've seen that look a hundred times. They're checking themselves in the mirror.'

March examined each of the pictures again. They were glossy and unscratched – new prints from old negatives. The sort of pictures a pimp might try and sell you in a back street in Kreuzberg.

'Where did you find them?'

'Next to the bodies.'

Stuckart had shot his mistress first. According to the autopsy report, she had lain, fully clothed, face down on the bed in Stuckart's apartment in Fritz Todt-Platz. He had put a bullet in the back of her head with his SS Luger (if that was so, thought March, it was probably the first time the old pen-pusher had ever used it). Traces of impacted cotton and down in the wound suggested he had fired the bullet through a pillow. Then he had sat on the edge of the bed and apparently shot himself through the roof of his mouth. In the scene-of-crime photographs neither body was recognisable. The pistol was still clutched in Stuckart's hand.

'He left a note,' said Fiebes, 'on the dining room table.'

'By this action I hope to spare embarrassment to my family, the Reich and the Führer. Heil Hitler! Long live Germany! Wilhelm Stuckart.'

'Blackmail?'

'Presumably.'

'Who found the bodies?'

'This is the best part.' Fiebes spat out each word as if it were poison: 'An American woman journalist.'

Her statement was in the file: Charlotte Maguire, aged 25, Berlin representative of an American news agency, World European Features.

'A real little bitch. Started shrieking about her rights the moment she was brought in. Rights!' Fiebes took another swig of schnapps. 'Shit, I suppose we have to be *nice* to the Americans now, do we?'

March made a note of her address. The only other witness questioned was the porter who worked in Stuckart's apartment block. The American woman claimed to have seen two men on the stairs immediately before the discovery of the bodies; but the porter insisted there had been no one.

March looked up suddenly. Fiebes jumped. 'What is it?'

'Nothing. A shadow at your door, perhaps.'

'My God, this place . . .' Fiebes flung open the frosted glass door and peered both ways along the corridor. While his back was turned, March detached the envelope pinned to the back of the file and slipped it into his pocket.

'Nobody.' He shut the door. 'You're losing your nerve, March.'

'An over-active imagination has always been my curse.' He closed the folder and stood up.

Fiebes swayed, squinting. 'Don't you want to take it with you? Aren't you working on this with the Gestapo?'

'No. A separate matter.'

'Oh.' He sat down heavily. 'When you said "state security", I assumed . . . Doesn't matter. Out of my hands. The Gestapo have taken it over, thank God. Obergruppenführer Globus has assumed responsibility. You must have heard of him? A thug, it is true, but he'll sort it out.'

THE information bureau at Alexander Platz had Luther's address. According to police records, he still lived in Dahlem. March lit another cigarette, then dialled the number. The telephone rang for a long time – a bleak, unfriendly echo, somewhere in the city. Just as he was about to hang up, a woman answered.

'Yes?'

'Frau Luther?'

'Yes.' She sounded younger than he had expected. Her voice was thick, as if she had been crying.

'My name is Xavier March. I am an investigator with the Berlin Kriminalpolizei. May I speak to your husband?'

'I'm sorry . . . I don't understand. If you're from the Polizei, surely you know . . .'

'Know? Know what?'

'That he is missing. He disappeared on Sunday.' She started to cry.

'I'm sorry to hear that.' March balanced his cigarette on the edge of the ashtray.

God in heaven, another one.

'He said he was going on a business trip to Munich and

would be back on Monday.' She blew her nose. 'But I have already explained all this. Surely you know that this matter is being dealt with at the *very highest* level. What. . . ?'

She broke off. March could hear a conversation at the other end. There was a man's voice in the background: harsh and questioning. She said something he could not hear, then came back on the line.

'Obergruppenführer Globocnik is with me now. He would like to talk to you. What did you say your name was?'

March replaced the receiver.

ON his way out, he thought of the call at Buhler's place that morning. An old man's voice:

'*Buhler? Speak to me. Who is that?*'

'*A friend.*'

Click.

ülow Strasse runs west to east for about a kilometre, through one of the busiest quarters of Berlin, close to the Gotenland railway station. The American woman's address proved to be an apartment block midway down.

It was seedier than March had expected: five storeys high, black with a century of traffic fumes, streaked with bird shit. A drunk sat on the pavement next to the entrance, turning his head to follow each passer-by. On the opposite side of the street was an elevated section of the U-bahn. As he parked, a train was pulling out of the Bülow Strasse station, its red and yellow carriages riding blue-white flashes of electricity, vivid in the gathering dark.

Her apartment was on the fourth floor. She was not in. 'Henry,' read a note written in English and pinned to her door, 'I'm in the bar on Potsdamer Strasse. Love, Charlie.'

March knew only a few words of English – but enough to grasp the sense of the message. Wearily, he descended the stairs. Potsdamer Strasse was a long street, with many bars.

'I'm looking for Fräulein Maguire,' he said to the concierge in the hall. 'Any idea where I might find her?'

It was like throwing a switch: 'She went out an hour ago, Sturmbannführer. You're the second man to ask. Fifteen minutes after she went out, a young chap came looking for her. Another foreigner – smartly dressed, short hair. She won't be back until after midnight, that much I can promise you.'

March wondered how many of her other tenants the old lady had informed on to the Gestapo.

'Is there a bar she goes to regularly?'

'Heini's, round the corner. That's where all the damned foreigners go.'

'Your powers of observation do you credit, madam.'

By the time he left her to her knitting five minutes later, March was laden with information about 'Charlie' Maguire. He knew she had dark hair, cut short; that she was small and slim; that she was wearing a raincoat of shiny blue plastic 'and high heels, like a tart'; that she had lived here six months; that she stayed out all hours and often got up at noon; that she was behind with the rent; that he should see the bottles of liquor the hussy threw out . . . No, thank you, madam, he had no desire to inspect them, that would not be necessary, you have been most helpful . . .

He turned right along Bülow Strasse. Another right took him to Potsdamer Strasse. Heini's was fifty metres up on the left. A painted sign showed a landlord with an apron and a handlebar moustache, carrying a foaming stein of beer. Beneath it, part of the red neon lettering had burnt out: Hei s.

The bar was quiet, except for one corner, where a group of six sat around a table, talking loudly in English accents. She was the only woman. She was laughing and ruffling an older man's hair. He was laughing, too. Then he saw March and said something and the laughter stopped. They watched him as he approached. He was conscious of his uniform, of the noise of his jackboots on the polished wooden floor.

'Fräulein Maguire, my name is Xavier March of the Berlin Kriminalpolizei.' He showed her his ID. 'I would like to speak with you, please.'

She had large dark eyes, glittering in the bar lights.

'Go ahead.'

'In private, please.'

'I've nothing more to say.' She turned to the man whose hair she had ruffled and murmured something March did not understand. They all laughed. March did not move.

Eventually, a younger man in a sports jacket and a button-down shirt stood up. He pulled a card from his breast pocket and held it out.

'Henry Nightingale. Second Secretary at the United States Embassy. I'm sorry, Herr March, but Miss Maguire has said all she has to say to your colleagues.'

March ignored the card.

The woman said: 'If you're not going to go, why don't you join us? This is Howard Thompson of the *New York Times*.' The older man raised his glass. 'This is Bruce Fallon of United Press. Peter Kent, CBS. Arthur Haines, Reuters. Henry, you've met. Me, you know, apparently. We're just having a little drink to celebrate the *great news*. Come on. The Americans and the SS – we're all friends now.'

'Careful, Charlie,' said the young man from the Embassy.

'Shut up, Henry. Oh, Christ, if this man doesn't move soon, I'll go and talk to him out of sheer boredom. Look –' There was a crumpled sheet of paper on the table in front of her. She tossed it to March. 'That's what I got for getting mixed up in this. My visa's withdrawn for "fraternising with a German citizen without official permission". I was supposed to leave today, but my friends here had a word with the Propaganda Ministry and got me a week's extension. Wouldn't have looked good, would it? Throwing me out on the day of the *great news*.'

March said: 'It's important.'

She stared at him, a cool look. The Embassy man put his hand on her arm. 'You don't have to go.'

That seemed to make up her mind. 'Will you shut up, Henry?' She shook herself free and pulled her coat over her shoulders. 'He looks respectable enough. For a Nazi. Thanks for the drink.' She downed the contents of her glass – whisky and water, by the look of it – and stood up. 'Let's go.'

The man called Thompson said something in English.
'I will, Howard. Don't worry.'

Outside, she said: 'Where are we going?'

'My car.'

'Then where?'

'Doctor Stuckart's apartment.'

'What fun.'

She *was* small. Even clattering on her high heels, she was several centimetres short of March's shoulder. He opened the door of the Volkswagen for her and, as she bent to get in, he smelled the whisky on her breath, and also cigarettes – French, not German – and perfume: something expensive, he thought.

The Volkswagen's 1300 cc engine rattled behind them. March drove carefully: west along Bülow Strasse, around the Berlin-Gotenland station, north up the Avenue of Victory. The captured artillery from the Barbarossa campaign lined the boulevard, barrels tilted towards the stars. Normally this section of the capital was quiet at night, Berliners preferring the noisy cafés behind the K-damm, or the jumbled streets of Kreuzberg. But on this evening, people were everywhere – standing in groups, admiring the guns and the floodlit buildings, strolling and window shopping.

'What kind of person wants to go out at night and look at guns?' She shook her head in wonderment.

'Tourists,' said March. 'By the twentieth, there'll be more than three million of them.'

It was risky, taking the American woman back to Stuckart's place, especially now Globus knew someone from the Kripo was looking for Luther. But he needed to see the apartment, to hear the woman's story. He had no plan, no real idea of what he might find. He recalled the Führer's words – 'I go the way that Providence dictates with the assurance of a sleepwalker' – and he smiled.

Ahead of them, searchlights picked out the eagle on top of the Great Hall. It seemed to hang in the sky, a golden bird of prey hovering over the capital.

She noticed his grin. 'What's funny?'

'Nothing.' He turned right at the European Parliament. The flags of the twelve member nations were lit by spots. The swastika which flew above them was twice the size of the other standards. 'Tell me about Stuckart. How well did you know him?'

'Hardly at all. I met him through my parents. My father was at the Embassy here before the war. He married a German, an actress. She's my mother. Monika Koch, did you ever hear of her?'

'No. I don't believe so.' Her German was flawless. She must have spoken it since childhood; her mother's doing, no doubt.

'She'd be sorry to hear that. She seems to think she was a big star over here. Anyway, they both knew Stuckart slightly. When I arrived in Berlin last year, they gave me a list of people to go and talk to – contacts. Half of them turned out to be dead, one way or another. Most of the rest didn't want to meet me. American journalists don't make healthy company, if you know what I mean. Do you mind if I smoke?'

'Go ahead. What was Stuckart like?'

'Awful.' Her lighter flared in the darkness; she inhaled deeply. 'He made a grab at me, even though this woman of his was in the apartment at the same time. That was just before Christmas. I kept away from him after that. Then, last week, I got a message from my office in New York. They wanted a piece for Hitler's seventy-fifth birthday, talking to some of the people who knew him from the old days.'

'So you rang Stuckart?'

'Right.'

'And arranged to meet him on Sunday, and when you got there, he was dead?'

'If you know it all,' she said irritably, 'why do you need to talk to me again?'

'I don't know it all, Fräulein. That's the point.'

After that, they drove in silence.

Fritz Todt-Platz was a couple of blocks from the Avenue of Victory. Laid out in the mid-1950s as part of Speer's redevelopment of the city, it was a square of expensive-looking apartment buildings, erected around a small memorial garden. In the centre stood an absurdly heroic statue of Todt, the creator of the Autobahnen, by Professor Thorak.

'Which one was Stuckart's?'

She pointed to a block on the other side of the square. March drove round and parked outside it.

'Which floor?'

'Fourth.'

He looked up. The fourth floor was in darkness. Good.

Todt's statue was floodlit. In the reflected light, her face was white. She looked as if she was about to be sick. Then he remembered the photographs Fiebes had shown him of the corpses – Stuckart's skull had been a crater, like a guttered candle – and he understood.

She said: 'I don't have to do this, do I?'

'No. But you will.'

'Why?'

'Because you want to know what happened as much as I do. That's why you've come this far.'

She stared at him again, then stubbed out her cigarette, twisting it and breaking it in the ashtray. 'Let's do it quickly. I want to get back to my friends.'

The keys to the building were still in the envelope which March had removed from Stuckart's file. There were five in all. He found the one that fitted the front door and let them into the foyer. It was vulgarly luxurious, in the new imperial style – white marble floor, crystal chandeliers, nineteenth-century gilt chairs with red plush upholstery, the air scented with dried flowers. No porter, thankfully: he must have gone off duty. Indeed, the entire building seemed deserted. Perhaps the tenants had left for their second homes in the country. Berlin could be unbearably crowded in the week before the Führertag. The smart set always fled the capital.

'Now what?'

'Just tell me what happened.'

'The porter was at the desk, here,' she said. 'I asked for Stuckart. He directed me to the fourth floor. I couldn't take the elevator, it was being repaired. There was a man working on it. So I walked.'

'What time was this?'

'Noon. Exactly.'

They climbed the stairs.

She went on: 'I had just reached the second floor when two men came running towards me.'

'Describe them, please.'

'It all happened too quickly for me to get a very good look. Both in their thirties. One had a brown suit, the other had a green anorak. Short hair. That's about it.'

'What did they do when they saw you?'

'They just pushed past me. The one in the anorak said something to the other, but I couldn't hear what it was. There was a lot of drilling going on from the elevator shaft. After that, I carried on up to Stuckart's apartment and rang the bell. There was no reply.'

'So what did you do?'

'I walked down to the porter and asked him to open Stuckart's door, to check he was okay.'

'Why?'

She hesitated. 'There was something about those two

men. I had a hunch. You know: that feeling when you knock on a door and nobody answers but you're sure someone's in.'

'And you persuaded the porter to open the door?'

'I told him I'd call the police if he didn't. I said he would have to answer to the authorities if anything had happened to Doctor Stuckart.'

Shrewd psychology, thought March. After thirty years of being told what to do, the average German was careful not to take final responsibility for anything, even for not opening a door. 'And then you found the bodies?'

She nodded. 'The porter saw them first. He screamed and I came running.'

'Did you mention the two men you'd seen on the stairs? What did the porter say?'

'He was too busy throwing up to talk at first. Then he just insisted he'd seen nobody. He said I must have imagined it.'

'Do you think he was lying?'

She considered this. 'No, I don't. I think he genuinely didn't see them. On the other hand, I don't see how he could have missed them.'

They were still on the second floor landing, at the point at which she said the men had passed her. March walked back down the flight of stairs. She waited for a moment, then followed him. At the foot of the steps a door led off to the first floor corridor.

He said, half to himself: 'They could have hidden along here, I suppose. Where else?'

They continued down to the ground floor. Here there were two more doors. One led to the foyer. March tried the other. It was unlocked. 'Or they could have got out down here.'

Bare concrete steps, neon-lit, led down to the basement. At the bottom was a long passage, with doors off it. March opened each in turn. A lavatory. A store-room. A generator room. A bomb shelter.

Under the 1948 Reich Civil Defence Law, every new building had to be equipped with a bomb shelter; those beneath offices and apartment blocks were also required to have their own generators and air-filtration systems. This one was particularly well-appointed: bunk beds, a storage cupboard, a separate cubicle with toilet facilities. March carried a metal chair across to the air vent, set into the wall two and a half metres above the ground. He grasped the metal cover. It came away easily in his hands. All the screws had been removed.

'The Ministry of Construction specifies an aperture with a diameter of half a metre,' said March. He unbuckled his belt and hung it and his pistol over the back of the chair. 'If only they appreciated the difficulties that gives us. Would you mind?'

He took off his jacket and handed it to the woman, then mounted the chair. Reaching into the shaft, he found something hard to hold on to, and pulled himself in. The filters and the fan had both been removed. By working his shoulders against the metal casing he was able to move slowly forwards. The darkness was complete. He choked on the dust. His hands, stretched out in front of him, touched metal, and he pushed. The outside cover yielded and crashed to the ground. The night air rushed in. For a moment, he felt an almost overpowering urge to crawl out into it, but instead he wriggled backwards and lowered himself into the basement shelter. He landed, dusty and grease-smeared.

The woman was pointing his pistol at him.

'Bang, bang,' she said. 'You're dead.' She smiled at his alarm: 'American joke.'

'Not funny.' He took the Luger and put it back in his holster.

'Okay,' she said, 'here's a better one. Two murderers are seen by a witness leaving a building and it takes the police four days to work out how they did it. I'd say that was funny, wouldn't you?'

'It depends on the circumstances.' He brushed the dust off his shirt. 'If the police found a note beside one of the victims in his own handwriting, saying it was suicide, I could understand why they wouldn't bother looking any further.'

'But then you come along and you do look further.'

'I'm the curious type.'

'Clearly.' She smiled again. 'So Stuckart was shot and the murderers tried to make it look like suicide?'

He hesitated. 'It's a possibility.'

He regretted the words the moment he uttered them. She had led him into disclosing more than was wise about Stuckart's death. Now a faint light of mockery played in her eyes. He cursed himself for underrating her. She had the cunning of a professional criminal. He considered taking her back to the bar and going on alone, but dismissed the idea. It was no good. To know what had happened, he needed to see it through her eyes.

He buttoned his tunic. 'Now we must inspect Party Comrade Stuckart's apartment.'

That, he was pleased to see, knocked the smile off her face. But she did not refuse to go with him. They climbed the stairs, and it struck him again that she was almost as anxious to see Stuckart's flat as he was.

They took the elevator to the fourth floor. As they stepped out, he heard, along the corridor to their left, a door being opened. He grabbed the American's arm and steered her round the corner, out of sight. When he looked back, he could see a middle-aged woman in a fur coat heading for the elevator. She was carrying a small dog.

'You're hurting my arm.'

'Sorry.'

He was hiding from shadows. The woman talked quietly

to the dog and disappeared into the lift. March wondered whether Globus had retrieved the file from Fiebes yet, whether he had discovered that the keys were missing. They would have to hurry.

The door to Stuckart's apartment had been sealed that day, close to the handle, with red wax. A note informed the curious that these premises were now under the jurisdiction of the Geheime Staatspolizei, the Gestapo, and that entry was forbidden. March pulled on a pair of thin leather gloves and broke the seal. The key turned easily in the lock.

He said: 'Don't touch anything.'

More luxury, to match the building: elaborate gilt mirrors, antique tables and chairs with fluted legs and ivory damask upholstery, a carpet of royal blue with Persian rugs. The spoils of war, the fruits of Empire.

'Now tell me again what happened.'

'The porter opened the door. We came into the hall.' Her voice had risen. She was trembling. 'He shouted and there was no reply, so we both came right in. I opened that door first.'

It was the sort of bathroom March had seen only in glossy magazines. White marble and brown smoky mirrors, a sunken bathtub, twin basins with gold taps . . . Here, he thought, was the hand of Maria Dymarski, leafing through German *Vogue* at the Ku-damm hairdressers, while her Polish roots were bleached Aryan white.

'Then, I came into the sitting room . . .'

March switched on the light. One wall consisted of tall windows, looking out over the square. The other three had large mirrors. Wherever he turned, he could see images of himself and the girl: the black uniform and the shiny blue coat incongruous among the antiques. Nymphs were the decorative conceit. Fashioned in gilt, they draped themselves around the mirrors; cast in bronze, they supported table lamps and clocks. There were paintings of nymphs and statues of nymphs; wood nymphs and water nymphs; Amphitrite and Thetis.

'I heard him scream. I went to help . . .'

March opened the door of the bedroom. She turned away. Blood in half-light looks black. Dark shapes, twisted and grotesque, leapt up the walls and across the ceiling, like the shadows of trees.

'They were on the bed, yes?'

She nodded.

'What did you do?'

'Rang the police.'

'Where was the porter?'

'In the bathroom.'

'Did you look at them again?'

'What do you think?' She brushed her sleeve angrily across her eyes.

'All right, Fräulein. It's enough. Wait in the sitting room.'

The human body contains six litres of blood: sufficient to paint a large apartment. March tried to avoid looking at the bed and the walls as he worked – opening the cupboard doors, feeling the lining of every item of clothing, skimming every pocket with his gloved hands. He moved on to the bedside cabinets. These had been unlocked and searched before. The contents of the drawers had been emptied out for inspection, then stuffed back haphazardly – a typical, clumsy Orpo job, destroying more clues than it uncovered.

Nothing, nothing. Had he risked everything for this?

He was on his knees, with his arm stretched beneath the bed, when he heard it. It took a second for the sound to register.

> Love unspoken
> Faith unbroken
> All life through . . .

115

'I'm sorry,' she said, when he rushed in. 'I shouldn't have touched it.'

He took the chocolate box from her, carefully, and closed the lid on its tune.

'Where was it?'

'On that table.'

Someone had collected Stuckart's mail for the past three days and had inspected it, neatly slicing open the envelopes, pulling out the letters. They were heaped up next to the telephone. He had not noticed them when he came in. How had he missed them? The chocolates, he could see, had been wrapped exactly as Buhler's had been, postmarked Zürich, 16.00 hours, Monday afternoon.

Then he saw she was holding a paper knife.

'I told you not to touch anything.'

'I said I'm sorry.'

'Do you think this is a game?' *She's crazier than I am.* 'You're going to have to leave.' He tried to grab her, but she twisted free.

'No way.' She backed away, pointing the knife at him. 'I reckon I have as much right to be here as you do. You try and throw me out and I'll scream so loudly I'll have every Gestapo man in Berlin hammering on that door.'

'You have a knife, but I have a gun.'

'Ah, but you daren't use it.'

March ran his hand through his hair. He thought: *You believed you were so clever, finding her, persuading her to come back. And all the time, she wanted to come. She's looking for something* . . . He had been an idiot.

He said: 'You've been lying to me.'

She said: 'You've been lying to me. That makes us even.'

'This is dangerous. I beg you, you have no idea . . .'

'What I do know is this: my career could have ended because of what happened in this apartment. I could be fired when I get back to New York. I'm being thrown out of this lousy country, and I want to find out why.'

'How do I know I can trust you?'

'How do I know I can trust *you*?'

They stood like that for perhaps half a minute: he with his hand to his hair, she with the silver paper knife still pointed at him. Outside, across the Platz, a clock began to chime. March looked at his watch. It was already ten.

'We have no time for this.' He spoke quickly. 'Here are the keys to the apartment. This one opens the door downstairs. This one is for the main door up here. This fits the bedside cabinet. That is a desk key. This one' – he held it up – 'this, I think, is the key to a safe. Where is it?'

'I don't know.' Seeing his look of disbelief, she added: 'I swear.'

They searched in silence for ten minutes, shifting furniture, pulling up rugs, looking behind paintings. Suddenly she said: 'This mirror is loose.'

It was a small antique looking glass, maybe thirty centimetres square, above the table on which she had opened the letters. March grasped the ormolu frame. It gave a little but would not come away from the wall.

'Try this.' She gave him the knife.

She was right. Two-thirds down the left-hand side, behind the lip of the frame, was a tiny lever. March pressed it with the tip of the paper knife, and felt something yield. The mirror was on a hinge. It swung open to reveal the safe.

He inspected it and swore. The key was not enough. There was also a combination lock.

'Too much for you?' she asked.

' "In adversity," ' quoted March, ' "the resourceful officer will always discover opportunity." ' He picked up the telephone.

EIGHT

cross a distance of five thousand kilometres, President Kennedy flashed his famous smile. He stood behind a cluster of microphones, addressing a crowd in a football stadium. Banners of red, white and blue streamed behind him – 'Re-elect Kennedy!' 'Four More in Sixty-Four!' He shouted something March did not understand and the crowd cheered back.

'What is he talking about?'

The television cast a blue glow in the darkness of Stuckart's apartment. The woman translated. ' "The Germans have their system and we have ours. But we are all citizens of one planet. And as long as our two nations remember that, I sincerely believe: we can have peace." Cue loud applause from dumb audience.'

She had kicked off her shoes and was lying full-length on her stomach in front of the set.

'Ah. Here's the serious bit.' She waited until he finished speaking, then translated again. 'He says he plans to raise human rights questions during his visit in the Fall.' She laughed and shook her head. 'God, Kennedy is so full of shit. The only thing he really wants to raise is his vote in November.'

' "Human rights"?'

'The thousands of dissidents you people lock up in camps. The millions of Jews who vanished in the war. The torture. The killing. Sorry to mention them, but we have this bourgeois notion that human beings have rights. Where have you been the last twenty years?'

The contempt in her voice jolted him. He had never properly spoken to an American before, had only encountered the occasional tourist – and those few had been chaperoned around the capital, shown only what the Propaganda Ministry wanted them to see, like Red Cross officials on a KZ inspection. Listening to her now it occurred to him she probably knew more about his country's recent history than he did. He felt he should make some sort of defence but did not know what to say.

'You talk like a politician,' was all he could manage. She did not even bother to reply.

He looked again at the figure on the screen. Kennedy projected an image of youthful vigour, despite his spectacles and balding head.

'Will he win?' he asked.

She was silent. For a moment, he thought she had decided not to speak to him. Then she said: 'He will now. He looks in good shape for a man of seventy-five, wouldn't you say?'

'Indeed.' March was standing a metre back from the window smoking a cigarette, alternately watching the television and watching the square. Traffic was sparse – mostly people returning from dinner or the cinema. A young couple held hands under the statue of Todt. They might be Gestapo; it was hard to tell.

The millions of Jews who vanished in the war . . . He was risking court martial simply by talking to her. Yet her mind must be a treasure house, full of ill-considered objects which meant nothing to her but would be gold to him. If he could somehow overcome her furious resentment, pick his way around the propaganda . . .

No. A ridiculous thought. He had problems enough as it was.

A solemn blonde newsreader filled the screen; behind her, a composite picture of Kennedy and the Führer and the single word 'Détente'.

Charlotte Maguire had helped herself to a glass of Scotch from Stuckart's drinks cabinet. Now she raised it to the television in mock salute. 'To Joseph P. Kennedy: President of the United States – appeaser, anti-Semite, gangster and sonofabitch. May you roast in hell.'

THE clock outside struck ten-thirty, ten forty-five, eleven.

She said: 'Maybe this friend of yours had second thoughts.'

March shook his head. 'He'll come.'

A few moments later, a battered blue Skoda entered the square. It made one slow circuit of the Platz, then came round again and parked opposite the apartment block. Max Jaeger emerged from the driver's side; from the other came a small man in a shabby sports jacket and trilby, carrying a doctor's bag. He squinted up at the fourth floor and backed away, but Jaeger took his arm and propelled him towards the entrance.

In the stillness of the apartment, a buzzer sounded.

'It would be best,' said March, 'if you didn't speak.'

She shrugged. 'As you like.'

He went into the hall and picked up the intercom.

'Hello, Max.'

He pressed a switch and unlocked the door. The corridor was empty. After a minute, a soft *ping* signalled the arrival of the elevator and the little man appeared. He scuttled down the passage and into Stuckart's hall without uttering a word. He was in his fifties and carried with him, like bad breath, the reek of the back-streets – of furtive deals and triple-entry accounting, of card-tables folded away at the sound of a tread on the stairs. Jaeger followed close behind.

When the man saw March was not alone, he shrank back into the corner.

'Who's the woman?' He appealed to Jaeger. 'You never said anything about a woman. Who's the woman?'

'Shut up, Willi,' said Max. He gave him a gentle push into the drawing room.

March said: 'Never mind her, Willi. Look at this.'

He switched on the lamp, angling it upwards.

Willi Stiefel took in the safe at a glance. 'English,' he said. 'Casing: one and a half centimetres, high-tensile steel. Fine mechanism. Eight-figure code. Six, if you're lucky.' He appealed to March: 'I beg you, Herr Sturmbannführer. It's the guillotine for me next time.'

'It'll be the guillotine for you this time,' said Jaeger, 'if you don't get on with it.'

'Fifteen minutes, Herr Sturmbannführer. Then I'm out of here. Agreed?'

March nodded. 'Agreed.'

Stiefel gave the woman a last, nervous look. Then he removed his hat and jacket, opened his case, and took out a pair of thin rubber gloves and a stethoscope.

March took Jaeger over to the window, and whispered: 'Did he take much persuading?'

'What do you think? But then I told him he was still covered by Forty-two. He saw the light.'

Paragraph Forty-two of the Reich Criminal Code stated that all 'habitual criminals and offenders against morality' could be arrested on suspicion that they *might* commit an offence. National Socialism taught that criminality was in the blood: something you were born with, like musical talent or blond hair. Thus the character of the criminal rather than his crime determined the sentence. A gangster stealing a few Marks after a fist-fight could be sentenced to death, on the grounds that he 'displayed an inclination towards criminality so deep-rooted that it precluded his ever becoming a useful member of the folk community'. But the next day, in the same court, a loyal Party member who had shot his wife for an insulting remark might merely be bound over to keep the peace.

Stiefel could not afford another arrest. He had recently served nine years in Spandau for a bank robbery. He had no choice but to co-operate with the Polizei, whatever they asked him to be – informant, *agent provocateur*, or safebreaker. These days, he ran a watch repair business in Wedding and swore he was going straight: a protestation of innocence it was hard to believe, watching him now. He had placed the stethoscope against the safe door and was twisting the dial a digit at a time. His eyes were closed as he listened for the click of the lock's tumblers falling into place.

Come on, Willi. March rubbed his hands. His fingers were numb with apprehension.

'Jesus Christ,' said Jaeger, under his breath. 'I hope you know what you're doing.'

'I'll explain later.'

'No thanks. I told you: I don't want to know.'

Stiefel straightened and let out a long sigh. 'One,' he said. One was the first digit of the combination.

Like Stiefel, Jaeger kept glancing at the woman. She was sitting demurely on one of the gilt chairs, her hands folded in her lap. 'A foreign *woman*, for God's sake!'

'Six.'

So it went on, one digit every few minutes, until, at 11.35, Stiefel said to March: 'The owner: when was he born?'

'Why?'

'It would save time. I think he's set this with the date of his birth. So far, I've got one-six-one-one-one-nine. The sixteenth of the eleventh, nineteen . . .'

March checked his notes from Stuckart's *Wer Ist's?* entry.

'Nineteen hundred and two.'

'Zero-two.' Stiefel tried the combination, then smiled. 'It's usually the owner's birthday,' he said, 'or the Führer's birthday, or the Day of National Reawakening.' He pulled open the door.

The safe was small: a fifteen-centimetre cube containing no bank notes or jewellery, just paper – old paper, most of it. March piled it on to the table and began rifling through it.

'I'd like to leave now, Herr Sturmbannführer.'

March ignored him. Tied up in red ribbon were the title deeds to a property in Wiesbaden – the family home, by the look of it. There were stock certificates. Hoesch, Siemens, Thyssen: the companies were standard, but the sums invested looked astronomical. Insurance papers. One human touch: a photograph of Maria Dymarski, in a 1950s cheesecake pose.

Suddenly, from the window, Jaeger gave a shout of warning: 'Here they come, you fucking, *fucking* fool!'

An unmarked grey BMW was driving round the square, fast, followed by an army truck. The vehicles swerved to a halt outside, blocking the street. A man in a belted leather coat leapt out of the car. The tailgate of the lorry was kicked down and SS troops carrying automatic rifles began jumping out.

'Move! Move!' yelled Jaeger. He began pushing Charlie and Stiefel towards the door.

With shaking fingers, March worked his way through the remaining papers. A blue envelope, unmarked. Something heavy in it. The flap of the envelope was open. He saw a letterhead in copperplate – Zaugg & Cie, Bankiers – and stuffed it into his pocket.

The buzzer from the door downstairs began sounding in long, urgent bursts.

'They must know we're up here!'

Jaeger said: 'Now what?' Stiefel had turned grey. The woman stood motionless. She did not seem to know what was going on.

'The basement,' shouted March. 'They might just miss us. Get the elevator.'

The other three ran out into the corridor. He began stuffing the papers back into the safe, slammed it shut, twirled the dial, pushed the mirror back into place. There was no time to do anything about the broken seal on the apartment door. They were holding the lift for him. He squeezed in and they began their descent.

Third floor, second floor . . .

March prayed it would not stop at the ground floor. It did not. It opened on to the empty basement. Above their heads they could hear the heels of the stormtroopers on the marble floor.

'This way!' He led them into the bomb shelter. The grating from the air vent was where he had left it, leaning against the wall.

Stiefel needed no telling. He ran to the air shaft, lifted his bag above his head and tossed it in. He grabbed at the brickwork, tried to haul himself after it, his feet scrabbling for a purchase on the smooth wall. He was yelling over his shoulder: 'Help me!' March and Jaeger seized his legs and heaved. The little man wriggled head first into the hole and was gone.

Coming closer – the ring and scrape of boots on concrete. The SS had found the entrance to the basement. A man was shouting.

March to Charlie: 'You next.'

'I'll tell you something,' she said, pointing at Jaeger. 'He'll never make it.'

Jaeger's hands went to his waist. It was true. He was too fat. 'I'll stay. I'll think of something. You two get out.'

'No.' This was turning into a farce. March took the envelope from his pocket and pressed it into Charlie's hand. 'Take this. We may be searched.'

'And you?' She had her stupid shoes in one hand, was

already mounting the chair.

'Wait until you hear from me. Tell nobody.' He grabbed her, locked his hands just below her knees, and threw. She was so light, he could have wept.

The SS were in the basement. Along the passage – the crash of doors flung open.

March swung the grating back into place and kicked away the chair.

PART THREE

THURSDAY 16 APRIL

When National Socialism has ruled long enough, it will no longer be possible to conceive of a form of life different from ours.

ADOLF HITLER,
11 July 1941

THURSDAY 16 APRIL

ONE

he grey BMW drove south down Saarland Strasse, past the slumbering hotels and deserted shops of central Berlin. At the dark mass of the Museum für Völkerkunde it turned left, into Prinz-Albrecht Strasse, towards the headquarters of the Gestapo.

There was a hierarchy in cars, as in everything. The Orpo were stuck with tinny Opels. The Kripo had Volkswagens – four-door versions of the original KdF-wagen, the round-backed workers' car which had been stamped out by the million at the Fallersleben works. But the Gestapo were smarter. They drove BMW 1800s – sinister boxes with growling, souped-up engines and dull grey bodywork.

Sitting in the back seat next to Max Jaeger, March kept his eyes on the man who had arrested them, the commander of the raid on Stuckart's apartment. When they had been led up from the basement into the foyer he had given them an immaculate Führer-salute. 'Sturmbannführer Karl Krebs, Gestapo!' That had meant nothing to March. It was only now, in the BMW, in profile, that he recognised him. Krebs was one of the two SS officers who had been with Globus at Buhler's villa.

He was about thirty years old with an angular, intelligent face, and without the uniform he could have been anything – a lawyer, a banker, a eugenicist, an executioner. That was how it was with young men of his age. They had come off an assembly line of Pimpf, Hitler Youth, National Service and Strength-Through-Joy. They had heard the same speeches, read the same slogans, eaten the same one-pot meals in aid of Winter Relief. They were the regime's workhorses, had known no authority but the Party, and were as reliable and commonplace as the Kripo's Volks-wagens.

The car drew up and almost at once Krebs was on the pavement, opening the door. 'This way, gentlemen. Please.'

March hauled himself out and looked down the street. Krebs might be as polite as a scoutmaster, but ten metres back, the doors of a second BMW were opening even before it stopped and armed plain-clothes men were emerging. That was how it had been since their discovery at Fritz-Todt Platz. No rifle-butts in the belly, no oaths, no handcuffs. Just a telephone call to headquarters, followed by a quiet request to 'discuss these matters further'. Krebs had also asked them to surrender their weapons. Polite, but behind the politeness, always, the threat.

Gestapo headquarters were in a grand, five-storey Wilhelmine construction that faced north and never saw the sun. Years ago, in the days of the Weimar Republic, the museum-like building had housed the Berlin School of Arts. When the secret police took over, the students had been forced to burn their modernist paintings in the courtyard. Tonight, the high windows were shielded by thick net curtains, a precaution against terrorist attack. Behind the gauze, as if in fog, chandeliers burned.

March had made it a policy in life never to cross the threshold, and until this night he had succeeded. Three stone steps ran up into an entrance hall. More steps, and then a large, vaulted foyer: a red carpet on a stone floor, the hollow resonance of a cathedral. It was busy. The early hours of the morning were always busy for the Gestapo. From the depths of the building came the muffled echo of bells ringing, footsteps, a whistle, a shout. A fat man in the uniform of an Obersturmführer picked his nose and regarded them without interest.

They walked on, down a corridor lined with swastikas

and marble busts of the Party leadership – Göring, Goebbels, Bormann, Frank, Ley and the rest – modelled after Roman senators. March could hear the plainclothes guards following. He glanced at Jaeger, but Max was staring fixedly ahead, jaw clenched.

More stairs, another passage. The carpet had given way to linoleum. The walls were dingy. March guessed they were somewhere near the back of the building, on the second floor.

'If you would wait here,' said Krebs. He opened a stout wooden door. Neon stuttered into life. He stood aside to allow them to file in. 'Coffee?'

'Thank you.'

And he was gone. As the door closed, March saw one of the guards, arms folded, take up station in the corridor outside. He half-expected to hear a key turn in the lock, but there was no sound.

They had been put in some sort of interview room. A rough wooden table stood in the centre of the floor, one chair either side of it, half a dozen others pushed up against the walls. There was a small window. Opposite it was a reproduction of Josef Vietze's portrait of Reinhard Heydrich in a cheap plastic frame. On the floor were small brown stains which looked to March like dried blood.

PRINZ-ALBRECHT STRASSE was Germany's black heart, as famous as the Avenue of Victory and the Great Hall, but without the tourist coaches. At number eight: the Gestapo. At number nine: Heydrich's personal headquarters. Around the corner: the Prinz-Albrecht Palace itself, headquarters of the SD, the Party's intelligence service. A complex of underground passages linked the three.

Jaeger muttered something and collapsed into a chair. March could think of nothing adequate to say so he looked out of the window. It commanded a clear view of the palace grounds running behind the Gestapo building – the dark clumps of the bushes, the ink-pool of the lawn, the skeletal branches of the limes raised in claws against the sky. Away to the right, lit up through the bare trees, was the concrete and glass cube of the Europa-Haus, built in the 1920s by the Jewish architect Mendelsohn. The Party had allowed it to stand as a monument to his 'pygmy imagination': dropped among Speer's granite monoliths, it was just a toy. March could remember a Sunday afternoon tea with Pili in its roof-garden restaurant. Ginger beer and Obsttorte mit Sahne, the little brass band playing – what else? –selections from *The Merry Widow*, the elderly women with their elaborate Sunday hats, their little fingers crooked over the bone china.

Most were careful not to look at the black buildings beyond the trees. For others, the proximity of Prinz-Albrecht Strasse seemed to provide a frisson of excitement, like picnicking next to a prison. Down in the cellar the Gestapo was licensed to practise what the Ministry of Justice called 'heightened interrogation'. The rules had been drawn up by civilised men in warm offices and they stipulated the presence of a doctor. There had been a conversation in Werderscher Markt a few weeks ago. Someone had heard a rumour about the torturers' latest trick: a thin glass catheter inserted into the suspect's penis, then snapped.

> Strings are playing
> Hear them saying
> 'I love you . . .'

He shook his head, pinched the bridge of his nose, tried to clear his mind.

Think.

He had left a paper-trail of clues, any one of which would

have been enough to lead the Gestapo to Stuckart's apartment. He had requested Stuckart's file. He had discussed the case with Fiebes. He had rung Luther's home. He had gone looking for Charlotte Maguire.

He worried about the American woman. Even if she had managed to get clear of Fritz-Todt Platz, the Gestapo could pull her in tomorrow. '*Routine questions, Fräulein . . . What is this envelope, please? . . . How did you come by it? . . . Describe the man who opened the safe . . .*' She was tough, with an actressy self-confidence, but in their hands she would not last five minutes.

March rested his forehead against the cold pane of glass. The window was bolted shut. There was a sheer drop of fifteen metres to the ground.

Behind him, the door opened. A swarthy man in shirt sleeves, stinking of sweat, came in and set two mugs of coffee on the table.

Jaeger, who had been sitting with his arms folded, looking at his boots, asked: 'How much longer?'

The man shrugged – *an hour? a night? a week?* – and left. Jaeger tasted the coffee and pulled a face. 'Pig's piss.' He lit a cigar, swilling the smoke around his mouth, before sending it billowing across the room.

He and March stared at one another. After a while, Max said: 'You know, you could have got out.'

'And left you to it? Hardly fair.' March tried the coffee. It was lukewarm. The neon light was flickering, fizzing, making his head throb. This was what they did to you. Left you until two or three in the morning, until your body was at its weakest, your defences at their most vulnerable. He knew this part of the game as well as they did.

He swallowed the filthy coffee and lit a cigarette. Anything to keep awake. Guilt about the woman, guilt about his friend.

'I'm a fool. I shouldn't have involved you. I'm sorry.'

'Forget it.' Jaeger waved away the smoke. He leaned forward and spoke softly. 'You have to let me carry my share of the blame, Zavi. Good Party Comrade Jaeger, here. Brownshirt. Blackshirt. Every goddamn shirt. Twenty years dedicated to the sacred cause of keeping my arse clean.' He grasped March's knee. 'I have favours to call in. I'm owed.'

His head was bent. He was whispering. 'They have you marked down, my friend. A loner. Divorced. They'll flay you alive. Me, on the other hand? The great conformer Jaeger. Married to a holder of the Cross of German Motherhood. Bronze Class, no less. Not so good at the job, maybe –'

'That's not true.'

' – but *safe*. Suppose I didn't tell you yesterday morning the Gestapo had taken over the Buhler case. Then when you got back *I* said let's check out Stuckart. They look at my record. They might buy that, coming from me.'

'It's good of you.'

'Christ, man – forget that.'

'But it won't work.'

'Why not?'

'Because this is beyond favours and clean sheets, don't you see? What about Buhler and Stuckart? They were in the Party before we were even born. And where were the favours when they needed them?'

'You really think the Gestapo killed them?' Jaeger looked scared.

March put his fingers to his lips and gestured to the picture. 'Say nothing to me you wouldn't say to Heydrich,' he whispered.

THE night dragged by in silence. At about three o'clock, Jaeger pushed some of the chairs together, lay down awkwardly, and closed his eyes. Within minutes, he was snoring. March returned to his post at the window.

He could feel Heydrich's eyes drilling into his back. He tried to ignore it, failed, and turned to confront the picture. A black uniform, a gaunt white face, silver hair – not a human countenance at all but a photographic negative of a skull; an X-ray. The only colour was in the centre of that death-mask face: those tiny pale blue eyes, like splinters of winter sky. March had never met Heydrich, or seen him; had only heard the stories. The press portrayed him as Nietzsche's Superman sprung to life. Heydrich in his pilot's uniform (he had flown combat missions on the Eastern front). Heydrich in his fencing gear (he had fenced for Germany in the Olympics). Heydrich with his violin (he could reduce audiences to tears by the pathos of his playing). When the aircraft carrying Heinrich Himmler had blown up in mid-air two years ago, Heydrich had taken over as Reichsführer-SS. Now he was said to be in line to succeed the Führer. The whisper around the Kripo was that the Reich's chief policeman liked beating up prostitutes.

March sat down. A numbing tiredness was seeping through him, a paralysis: the legs first, then the body, at last the mind. Despite himself, he drifted into a shallow sleep. Once, far away, he thought he heard a cry – human and forlorn – but it might have been a dream. Footsteps echoed in his mind. Keys turned. Cell doors clanged.

HE was jerked awake by a rough hand.

'Good morning, gentlemen. I hope you had some rest?'

It was Krebs.

March felt raw. His eyes were gritty in the sickly neon. Through the window the sky was pearl-grey with the approaching morning.

Jaeger grunted and swung his legs to the floor. 'Now what?'

'Now we talk,' said Krebs. 'Come.'

'Who is this kid,' grumbled Jaeger to March under his breath, 'to push us about?' But he was wary enough to keep his voice low.

They filed into the corridor and March wondered again what game was being played. Interrogation is a night-time art. Why leave it until the morning? Why give them a chance to regain their strength, to concoct a story?

Krebs had recently shaved. His skin was studded with pinpricks of blood. He said: 'Washroom on the right. You will wish to clean yourselves.' It was an instruction rather than a question.

In the mirror, red-eyed and unshaven, March looked more convict than policeman. He filled the basin, rolled up his sleeves and loosened his tie, splashed icy water on his face, his forearms, the nape of his neck, let it trickle down his back. The cold sting brought him back to life.

Jaeger stood alongside him. 'Remember what I said.'

March quickly turned the taps back on. 'Be careful.'

'You think they wire the toilet?'

'They wire everything.'

Krebs conducted them downstairs. The guards fell in behind them. *To the cellar?* They clattered across the vestibule – quieter now than when they had arrived – and out into the grudging light.

Not the cellar.

Waiting in the BMW was the driver who had brought them from Stuckart's apartment. The convoy moved off, north into the rush-hour traffic which was already building up around Potsdamer Platz. In the big shops, the windows piously displayed large, gilt-framed photographs of the Führer – the official portrait from the mid-1950s, by the English photographer, Beaton. Twigs and flowers garlanded the frames, the traditional decoration heralding the Führer's birthday. Four days to go, each of which would see a fresh sprouting of swastika banners. Soon the city would be a forest of red, white and black.

Jaeger was gripping the arm rest, looking sick. 'Come on, Krebs,' he said, in a wheedling voice. 'We're all the same rank. You can tell us where we're going.'

Krebs made no reply. The dome of the Great Hall loomed ahead. Ten minutes later, when the BMW turned left on to the East-West Axis, March guessed their destination.

IT was almost eight by the time they arrived. The iron gates of Buhler's villa had been swung wide open. The grounds were filled with vehicles, dotted with black uniforms. One SS trooper was sweeping the lawn with a proton-magnetometer. Behind him, jammed into the ground, was a trail of red flags. Three more soldiers were digging holes. Drawn up on the gravel were Gestapo BMWs, a lorry, and a large armoured security van of the sort used for transporting gold bullion.

March felt Jaeger nudge him. Parked in the shadows beside the house, its driver leaning against the bodywork, was a bulletproof Mercedes limousine. A metal pennant hung above the radiator grille: silver SS lightning flashes on a black background; in one corner, like a cabbalistic symbol, the gothic letter K.

he head of the Reich Kriminalpolizei was an old man. His name was Artur Nebe, and he was a legend.

Nebe had been head of the Berlin detective force even before the Party came to power. He had a small head and the sallow, scaly skin of a tortoise. In 1954, to mark his sixtieth birthday, the Reichstag had voted him a large estate, including four villages, near Minsk in the Ostland, but he had never even been to look at it. He lived alone with his bed-ridden wife in Charlottenburg, in a large house marked by the smell of disinfectant and the whisper of pure oxygen. It was sometimes said that Heydrich wanted to get rid of him, to put his own man in charge of the Kripo, but dared not. 'Onkel Artur' they called him in Werderscher Markt. Uncle Artur. He knew everything.

March had seen Nebe from a distance but never met him. Now he was sitting at Buhler's grand piano, picking out a high note with a single, yellowish claw. The instrument was untuned, the sound discordant in the dusty air.

At the window, his broad back to the room, stood Odilo Globus.

Krebs brought his heels together and saluted. 'Heil Hitler! Investigators March and Jaeger.'

Nebe continued to tap the piano key.

'Ah!' Globus turned round. 'The great detectives.'

Close up, he was a bull in uniform. His neck strained at his collar. His hands hung at his sides, bunched in angry red fists. There was a mass of scar tissue on his left cheek, mottled crimson. Violence crackled around him in the dry air, like static electricity. Every time Nebe struck a note, he winced. He wants to punch the old man, thought March, but he can't. Nebe outranked him.

'If the Herr Oberstgruppenführer has finished his recital,' said Globus, through his teeth, 'we can begin.'

Nebe's hand froze over the keyboard. 'Why would anyone have a Bechstein, and leave it untuned?' He looked at March. 'Why would he do that?'

'His wife was the musician, sir,' said March. 'She died eleven years ago.'

'And nobody played in all that time?' Nebe closed the lid quietly over the keys and drew his finger through the dust. 'Curious.'

Globus said: 'We have much to do. Early this morning I reported certain matters to the Reichsführer. As you know, Herr Oberstgruppenführer, it is on his orders that this meeting is taking place. Krebs will put the position of the Gestapo.'

March exchanged glances with Jaeger. It had gone up as far as Heydrich.

Krebs had a typed memorandum. In his precise, expressionless voice he began to read.

'Notification of Doctor Josef Buhler's death was received by teleprinter message at Gestapo Headquarters from the Night Duty Officer of the Berlin Kriminalpolizei at two-fifteen yesterday morning, April fifteenth.

'At eight-thirty, in view of Party Comrade Buhler's honorary SS rank of Brigadeführer, the Reichsführer was personally informed of his demise.'

March had his hands clasped behind his back, his nails digging into his palms. In Jaeger's cheek, a muscle fluttered.

'At the time of his death, the Gestapo was completing an investigation into the activities of Party Comrade Buhler. In view of this, and in view of the deceased's former position in the General Government, the case was redesignated a matter of state security, and operational control was passed to the Gestapo.

'However, due to an apparent breakdown in liaison procedures, this redesignation was not communicated to Kripo Investigator Xavier March, who effected an illegal entry to the deceased's home.'

The Gestapo was investigating Buhler? March struggled to keep his gaze fixed on Krebs, his expression impassive.

'Next: the death of Party Comrade Wilhelm Stuckart. Inquiries by the Gestapo indicated that the cases of Stuckart and Buhler were linked. Once again, the Reichsführer was informed. Once again, investigation of the matter was transferred to the Gestapo. And once again, Investigator March, this time accompanied by Investigator Max Jaeger, conducted his own inquiries at the home of the deceased.

'At zero-zero-twelve, sixteenth April, Investigators March and Jaeger were apprehended by myself at Party Comrade Stuckart's apartment block. They agreed to accompany me to Gestapo Headquarters, pending clarification of this matter at a higher level.

'Signed, Karl Krebs, Sturmbannführer.

'I have dated it and timed it at six this morning.'

Krebs folded the memorandum and handed it to the head of the Kripo. Outside, a spade rang on gravel.

Nebe slipped the paper into his inside pocket. 'So much for the record. Naturally, we shall prepare a minute of our own. Now, Globus: what is this really about? You are desperate to tell us, I know.'

'Heydrich wanted you to see for yourself.'

'See what?'

'What your man here missed on his little freelance excursion yesterday. Follow me, please.'

IT was in the cellar, although even if March had smashed

the padlock on the entrance and forced his way down, he doubted if he would have found it. Past the usual household rubbish – broken furniture, discarded tools, rolls of filthy carpet bound with rope – was a wood-panelled wall. One of the panels was false.

'We knew what we were looking for, you see.' Globus rubbed his hands. 'Gentlemen, I guarantee you will never have clapped eyes on the likes of this in your entire lives.'

Beyond the panel was a chamber. When Globus turned on the lights, it was indeed dazzling: a sacristy; a jewelbox. Angels and saints; clouds and temples; high-cheeked noblemen in white furs and red damask; sprawling pink flesh on perfumed yellow silk; flowers and sunrises and Venetian canals . . .

'Go in,' said Globus. 'The Reichsführer is anxious that you should see it properly.'

It was a small room – four metres square, March guessed – with a bank of spotlights built into the ceiling, directed on to the paintings which covered every wall. In the centre was an old-fashioned swivel chair, of the sort a nineteenth-century clerk might have had in a counting-house. Globus placed a gleaming jackboot on the arm and kicked, sending it spinning.

'Imagine him, sitting here. Door locked. Like a dirty old man in a brothel. We found it yesterday afternoon. Krebs?'

Krebs took the floor. 'An expert is on his way this morning from the Führermuseum in Linz. We had Professor Braun of the Kaiser Friedrich, here in Berlin, give us a preliminary assessment last night.'

He consulted his sheaf of notes.

'At the moment, we know we have *Portrait of a Young Man* by Raphael, *Portrait of a Young Man* by Rembrandt, *Christ Carrying the Cross* by Rubens, Guardi's *Venetian Palace, Krakau Suburbs* by Bellotto, eight Canalettos, at least thirty-five engravings by Dürer and Kulmbach, a

Gobelin. The rest he could only guess at.'

Krebs reeled them off as if they were dishes in a restaurant. He rested his pale fingers on an altar-piece of gorgeous colours, raised on planks at the end of the room.

'This is the work of the Nuremberg artist, Viet Stoss, commissioned by the King of Poland in 1477. It took ten years to complete. The centre of the triptych shows the Virgin asleep, surrounded by angels. The side panels show scenes from the lives of Jesus and Mary. The predella' – he pointed to the base of the altar-piece – 'shows the genealogy of Christ.'

Globus said: 'Sturmbannführer Krebs knows of these things. He is one of our brightest officers.'

'I'm sure,' said Nebe. 'Most interesting. And where did it all come from?'

Krebs began: 'The Viet Stoss was removed from the Church of Our Lady in Krakau in November 1939 – '

Globus interrupted: 'It came from the General Govern-ment. Warsaw, mainly, we think. Buhler recorded it as either lost or destroyed. God alone knows how much else the corrupt swine got away with. Think what he must have sold just to buy this place!'

Nebe reached out and touched one of the canvases: the martyred Saint Sebastian, bound to a Doric pillar, arrows jutting from his golden skin. The varnish was cracked, like a dried river bed, but the colours beneath – red, white, purple, blue – were bright still. The painting gave off a faint smell of must and incense – the scent of pre-war Poland, of a nation vanished from the map. Some of the panels, March saw, had powdery lumps of masonry attached to their edges – traces of the monastery and castle walls from which they had been wrenched.

Nebe was rapt before the saint. 'Something in his expression reminds me of you, March.' He traced the body's outline with his fingertips and gave a wheezing laugh. ' "The willing martyr." What do you say, Globus?'

Globus grunted. 'I don't believe in saints. Or martyrs.' He glared at March.

'Extraordinary,' murmured Nebe, 'to think of Buhler, of all people, with these . . .'

'You knew him?' March blurted out the question.

'Slightly, before the war. A committed National Socialist, and a dedicated lawyer. Quite a combination. A fanatic for detail. Like our Gestapo colleague here.'

Krebs gave a slight bow. 'The Herr Oberstgruppenführer is kind.'

'The point is this,' said Globus, irritably. 'We have known about Party Comrade Buhler for some time. Known about his activities in the General Government. Known about his associates. Unfortunately, at some point last week, the bastard found out we were on to him.'

'And killed himself?' Nebe asked. 'And Stuckart?'

'The same. Stuckart was a complete degenerate. He not only helped himself to beauty on canvas. He liked to taste it in the flesh. Buhler had the pick of what he wanted in the East. What were those figures, Krebs?'

'A secret inventory was compiled in 1940 by the Polish museum authorities. We now have it. Art treasures removed from Warsaw alone: two thousand seven hundred paintings of the European school; ten thousand seven hundred paintings by Polish artists; fourteen hundred sculptures.'

Globus again: 'We're digging up some of the sculptures in the garden right now. Most of this stuff went where it was intended: the Führermuseum, Reichsmarschall Göring's museum at Carinhall, galleries in Vienna, Berlin. But there's a big discrepancy between the Polish lists of what was taken and our lists of what we got. It worked like this. As State Secretary, Buhler had access to everything. He would ship the stuff under escort to Stuckart at the Interior

Ministry. Everything legal-looking. Stuckart would arrange for it to be stored, or smuggled out of the Reich to be exchanged for cash, jewels, gold – anything portable and non-traceable.'

March could see that Nebe was impressed, despite himself. His little eyes were drinking in the art. 'Was anyone else of high rank involved?'

'You are familiar with the former Under-Secretary of State at the Foreign Ministry, Martin Luther?'

'Of course.'

'He is the man we seek.'

'Seek? He is missing?'

'He failed to return from a business trip three days ago.'

'I take it you are certain of Luther's involvement in this affair?'

'During the war, Luther was head of the Foreign Ministry's German Department.'

'I remember. He was responsible for Foreign Ministry liaison with the SS, and with us at the Kripo.' Nebe turned to Krebs. 'Another fanatical National Socialist. You would have appreciated his – ah – enthusiasm. A rough fellow, though. Incidentally, at this point, I should like to state, for the record, my astonishment at his involvement in anything criminal.'

Krebs produced his pen. Globus went on: 'Buhler stole the art. Stuckart received it. Luther's position at the Foreign Ministry gave him the opportunity to travel freely abroad. We believe he smuggled certain items out of the Reich, and sold them.'

'Where?'

'Switzerland, mainly. Also Spain. Possibly Hungary.'

'And when Buhler came back from the General Government –when was that?'

He looked at March, and March said: 'In 1951.'

'In 1951, this became their treasure chamber.'

144

Nebe lowered himself into the swivel chair and spun round, slowly, inspecting each wall in turn. 'Extraordinary. This must have been one of the best collections of art in private hands anywhere in the world.'

'One of the best collections in *criminal* hands,' cut in Globus.

'Ach.' Nebe closed his eyes. 'So much perfection in one space deadens the senses. I need air. Give me your arm, March.'

As he stood, March could hear the ancient bones cracking. But the grip on his forearm was steel.

NEBE walked with a stick – *tap, tap, tap* – along the verandah at the back of the villa.

'Buhler drowned himself. Stuckart shot himself. Your case seems to be resolving itself rather conclusively, Globus, without requiring anything so embarrassing as a trial. Statistically, I should say Luther's chances of survival look rather poor.'

'As it happens, Herr Luther *does* have a heart condition. Brought on by nervous strain during the war, according to his wife.'

'You surprise me.'

'According to his wife, he needs rest, drugs, quiet – none of which will he be getting at the moment, wherever he is.'

'This business trip . . .'

'He was supposed to return from Munich on Monday. We've checked with Lufthansa. There was nobody called Luther on any Munich flights that day.'

'Maybe he's fled abroad.'

'Maybe. I doubt it. We'll hunt him down eventually, wherever he is.'

Tap, tap. March admired Nebe's nimbleness of mind. As Police Commissioner for Berlin in the 1930s, he had written a treatise on criminology. He remembered seeing it on Koth's shelves in the fingerprint section on Tuesday night. It was still a standard text.

'And you, March.' Nebe halted and swung round. 'What is your view of Buhler's death?'

Jaeger, who had been silent since their arrival at the villa, butted in anxiously: 'Sir, if I might say, we were merely collecting data – '

Nebe rapped the stone with his stick. 'The question was not addressed to you.'

March wanted a cigarette, badly. 'I have only preliminary observations,' he began. He ran his hand through his hair. He was out of his depth here; a long way out. It was not where to start, he thought, but where to end. Globus had folded his arms and was staring at him.

'Party Comrade Buhler,' he began, 'died some time between six o'clock on Monday evening and six o'clock the following morning. We await the autopsy report, but cause of death was almost certainly drowning – his lungs were full of fluid, indicating he was breathing when he entered the water. We also know, from the sentry on the causeway, that Buhler received no visitors during those crucial twelve hours.'

Globus nodded. 'Thus: suicide.'

'Not necessarily, Herr Obergruppenführer. Buhler received no visitors *by land*. But the woodwork on the jetty has been recently scraped, suggesting a boat may have moored there.'

'Buhler's boat,' said Globus.

'Buhler's boat has not been used for months; maybe, years.'

Now he held the attention of his small audience, March felt a rush of exhilaration; a sense of release. He was starting to talk quickly. Slow down, he told himself, be careful.

'When I inspected the villa yesterday morning, Buhler's

guard dog was locked in the pantry, muzzled. The whole of one side of its head was bleeding. I ask myself: why would a man intending to commit suicide do that to his dog?'

'Where is this animal now?' asked Nebe.

'My men had to shoot it,' said Globus. 'The creature was deranged.'

'Ah. Of course. Go on, March.'

'I think Buhler's assailants landed late at night, in darkness. If you recall, there was a storm on Monday night. The lake would have been choppy – that explains the damage to the jetty. I think the dog was alerted, and they clubbed it senseless, muzzled it, took Buhler unawares.'

'And threw him in the lake?'

'Not immediately. Despite his disability, according to his sister, Buhler was a strong swimmer. You could see that by the look of him: his shoulders were well-developed. But after he had been cleaned up, I inspected his body in the morgue. There was bruising here' – March touched his cheeks – 'and on the gums at the front of his mouth. On the kitchen table yesterday was a bottle of vodka, most of it gone. I think the autopsy report will show alcohol in Buhler's bloodstream. I think they forced him to drink, stripped him, took him out on their boat, and dumped him over the side.'

'Intellectual pigshit,' said Globus. 'Buhler probably drank the vodka to give him the guts to kill himself.'

'According to his sister, Party Comrade Buhler was a teetotaller.'

There was a long silence. March could hear Jaeger breathing heavily. Nebe was gazing out across the lake. Eventually, Globus muttered: 'What this fancy theory doesn't explain is why these mysterious killers didn't just put a bullet in Buhler's brain and have done with it.'

'I would have thought that was obvious,' said March. 'They wanted to make it look like suicide. But they bungled it.'

'Interesting,' murmured Nebe. 'If Buhler's suicide was faked, then it is logical to suppose that Stuckart's was, also.'

Because Nebe was still staring at the Havel, March did not realise at first that the remark was a question, addressed to him.

'That was my conclusion. That was why I visited Stuckart's apartment last night. Stuckart's murder, I think, was a three-man operation: two in the flat; one in the foyer, pretending to repair the elevator. The noise from his electric drill was supposed to mask the sound of the shot, giving the killers time to get away before the body was discovered.'

'And the suicide note?'

'Forged, perhaps. Or written under duress. Or . . .'

He stopped himself. He was thinking aloud, he realised – a potentially fatal activity. Krebs was staring at him.

'Is that it?' asked Globus. 'Are the Grimms' fairy stories over for the day? Excellent. Some of us have work to do. Luther is the key to this mystery, gentlemen. Once we have him, all will be explained.'

Nebe said: 'If his heart condition is as bad as you say, we need to move quickly. I shall arrange with the Propaganda Ministry for Luther's picture to be carried in the press and on television.'

'No, no. Absolutely not.' Globus sounded alarmed. 'The Reichsführer has expressly forbidden any publicity. The last thing we need is a scandal involving the Party leadership, especially now, with Kennedy coming. God in heaven, can you imagine what the foreign press would make of this? No. I assure you, we can catch him without alerting the media. What we need is a confidential flash to all Orpo patrols; a watch on the main railway stations, ports, airports, border crossings . . . Krebs can handle that.'

'Then I suggest he does so.'

'At once, Herr Oberstgruppenführer.' Krebs gave a slight

bow to Nebe and trotted off along the verandah, into the house.

'I have business to attend to in Berlin,' said Nebe. 'March here will act as Kripo liaison officer until Luther is caught.'

Globus sneered. 'That will not be necessary.'

'Oh, but it will. Use him wisely, Globus. He has a brain. Keep him informed. Jaeger: you can return to your normal duties.'

Jaeger looked relieved. Globus seemed about to say something, but thought better of it.

'Walk me to my car, March. Good day to you, Globus.'

WHEN they were round the corner, Nebe said: 'You are not telling the truth, are you? Or at least, not all of it. That is good. Get in the car. We need to talk.'

The driver saluted and opened the rear door. Nebe manoeuvred himself painfully into the back seat. March got in the other side.

'At six o'clock this morning, this arrived at my house by courier.' Nebe unlocked his briefcase and pulled out a file, a couple of centimetres thick. 'It's all about you, Sturmbannführer. Flattering, isn't it, to merit such attention?'

The windows of the Mercedes were tinted green. In the half-light, Nebe looked like a lizard in a reptile house.

'Born, Hamburg, 1922; father died of wounds, 1929; mother killed in a British air raid, 1942; joined the Navy, 1939; transferred to the U-boat service, 1940; decorated for bravery and promoted, 1943; given command of your own boat, 1946 – one of the youngest U-boat commanders in the Reich. A glittering career. And then it all starts going wrong.'

Nebe leafed through the file. March stared at the green lawn, the green sky.

'No police promotions for *ten years*. Divorced, 1957. And then the reports start. Blockwart: persistent refusal to contribute to Winter-Relief. Party officials at Werderscher Markt: persistent refusal to join the NSDAP. Overheard in the canteen making disparaging comments about Himmler. Overheard in bars, overheard in restaurants, overheard in corridors . . .'

Nebe was pulling pages out.

'Christmas 1963 – you start asking round about some Jews who used to live in your apartment. Jews! Are you mad? There is a complaint here from your ex-wife; one from your son . . .'

'My son? My son is ten years old . . .'

'Quite old enough to form a judgement, and be listened to – as you know.'

'May I ask what it is I am supposed to have done to him?'

' "Shown insufficient enthusiasm for his Party activities." The point is, Sturmbannführer, that this file has been ten years maturing in the Gestapo registry – a little here, a little there, year in, year out, growing like a tumour in the dark. And now you've made a powerful enemy, and he wants to use it.'

Nebe put the folder back in his briefcase.

'Globus?'

'Globus, yes. Who else? He asked to have you transferred to Colombia House last night, pending court martial from the SS.' Colombia House was the private SS prison in General-Pape Strasse. 'I have to tell you, March, there is easily enough here to send you to a KZ. After that, you're beyond help – from me or anybody else.'

'What stopped him?'

'To start court-martial proceedings against a serving Kripo officer, he first had to get permission from Heydrich. And Heydrich referred it to me. So what I said to our beloved Reichsführer was this. "This fellow Globus," I said, "is obviously terrified that March has got something on him, so he wants him done away with." "I see," says the Reichsführer, "so what do you suggest?" "Why not," say I, "give him until the Führertag to prove his case against Globus? That's four days." "All right," says Heydrich. "But if he's not come up with anything by then, Globus can have him." ' Nebe gave a smile of contentment. 'Thus are the affairs of the Reich arranged between colleagues of long standing.'

'I suppose I must thank the Herr Oberstgruppenführer.'

'Oh no, don't thank me.' Nebe was cheerful. 'Heydrich genuinely wonders if you do have something on Globus. He would like to know. So would I. Perhaps for a different reason.' He seized March's arm again – the same fierce grip – and hissed: 'These bastards are up to something, March. What is it? You find out. You tell me. Don't trust anyone. That's how your Uncle Artur has lasted as long as he has. Do you know why some of the old-timers call Globus "the submarine"?'

'No, sir.'

'Because he had a submarine engine hooked up to a Polish basement during the war, and used the exhaust fumes to kill people. Globus likes killing people. He'd like to kill you. You should remember that.' Nebe released March's arm. 'Now, we must say goodbye.'

He rapped on the glass partition with the top of his cane. The driver came round and opened March's door.

'I would offer you a lift into central Berlin, but I prefer travelling alone. Keep me informed. Find Luther, March. Find him before Globus gets to him.'

The door slammed. The engine whispered. As the limousine crunched across the gravel, March could barely make out Nebe – just a green silhouette behind the bullet-proof glass.

He turned to find Globus watching him.

The SS general started walking towards him, holding a Luger outstretched.

He is crazy, thought March. He is just about crazy enough to shoot me on the spot, like Buhler's dog.

But all Globus did was hand him the gun. 'Your pistol, Sturmbannführer. You will need it.' And then he came very close – close enough for March to smell the sour odour of garlic sausage on his hot breath. 'You have no witness,' was all he whispered. 'You have no witness. Not any more.'

MARCH ran.

He ran out of the grounds and across the causeway and off, up, into the woods – right the way through them, until he came to the autobahn which formed the Grunewald's eastern boundary.

There he stopped, his hands clutching his knees, his breath coming in sobs, as beneath him the traffic hurtled towards Berlin.

Then he was off again, despite the pain in his side, more of a trot now, over the bridge, past the Nikolassee S-bahn station, down Spanische Allee towards the barracks.

His Kripo ID got him past the sentries, his appearance – red-eyed, breathless, with more than a day's growth of beard – suggestive of some terrible emergency which brooked no discussion. He found the dormitory block. He found Jost's bed. The pillow was gone, the blankets had been stripped. All that remained was the ironwork and a hard, brown mattress. The locker was bare.

A solitary cadet, polishing his boots a few beds away, explained what had happened. They had come for Jost in the night. There were two of them. He was to be sent East, they said, for 'special training'. He had gone without a word – seemed to have been expecting it. The cadet shook his head in amazement: Jost of all people. The cadet was jealous. They all were. He would see some *real* fighting.

he telephone kiosk stank of urine and ancient cigarette smoke, a used condom had been trodden into the dirt.

'Come on, come on,' whispered March. He rapped a one-Reichsmark piece against the cloudy glass and listened to the electronic purr of her telephone ringing, unanswered. He let it ring for a long time before he hung up.

Across the street a grocery store was opening. He crossed and bought a bottle of milk and some warm bread which he gulped down beside the road, conscious all the time of the shop's owner watching him from the window. It occurred to him that he was living like a fugitive already – stopping to grab food only when he happened across it, devouring it in the open, always on the move. Milk trickled down his chin. He brushed it away with the back of his hand. His skin felt like sandpaper.

He checked again to see if he was being followed. On this side of the street, a uniformed nanny pushed a baby carriage. On the other, an old woman had gone into the telephone kiosk. A schoolboy hurried towards the Havel, clutching a toy yacht. Normal, normal . . .

March, the good citizen, dropped the milk bottle into a waste bin and set off down the suburban road.

'*You have no witness. Not any more . . .*'

He felt a great rage against Globus, the greater for being fuelled by guilt. The Gestapo must have seen Jost's statement in the file on Buhler's death. They would have checked with the SS academy and discovered that March had been back to re-interrogate him yesterday afternoon. That would have set them scurrying in Prinz-Albrecht Strasse. So his visit to the barracks had been Jost's death warrant. He had indulged his curiosity – and killed a man.

And now the American girl was not answering her telephone. What might they do to her? An army truck overtook him, the draught sucked at him, and a vision of Charlotte Maguire lying broken in the gutter bubbled in his mind. *'The Berlin authorities deeply regret this tragic accident . . . The driver of the vehicle concerned is still being sought . . .'* He felt like the carrier of a dangerous disease. He should carry a placard: keep clear of this man, he is contagious.

Circulating endlessly in his head, fragments of conversation –

Artur Nebe: *'Find Luther, March. Find him before Globus gets to him . . .'*

Rudi Halder: *'A couple of Sipo guys were round at the Archiv last week asking about you . . .'*

Nebe again: *'There is a complaint here from your ex-wife; one from your son . . .'*

He walked for half an hour along the blossoming streets, past the high hedges and picket fences of prosperous, suburban Berlin. When he reached Dahlem, he stopped a student to ask directions. At the sight of March's uniform, the young man bowed his head. Dahlem was a student quarter. The male undergraduates, like this one, let their hair grow a few centimetres over their collars; some of the women wore jeans – God only knew where they got them. White Rose, the student resistance movement which had flowered briefly in the 1940s until its leaders were executed, was suddenly alive again. 'Ihr Geist lebt weiter' said the graffiti: their spirit lives on. Members of White Rose grumbled about conscription, listened to banned music, circulated seditious magazines, were harassed by the Gestapo.

The student gestured vaguely in response to March's

question, his arms laden with books, and was glad to be on his way.

LUTHER'S house was close to the Botanischer Garten, set back from the road – a nineteenth-century country mansion at the end of a sickle of white gravel. Two men sat in an unmarked grey BMW, parked opposite the drive. The car and its colour branded them at once. There would be two more watching the back, and at least one cruising the neighbourhood streets. March walked past and saw one of the Gestapo watchers turn to the other and speak.

Somewhere, a motor mower was whining; the smell of freshly cut grass hung over the drive. The house and grounds must have cost a fortune – not as much as Buhler's villa, perhaps, but not far off it. The red box of a newly installed burglar alarm jutted beneath the eaves.

He rang the bell and felt himself come under inspection through the spy hole in the centre of the heavy door. After half a minute the door opened to reveal an English maid in a black and white uniform. He gave her his ID and she disappeared to check with her mistress, her feet flapping on the polished wooden floor. She returned to show March into the darkened drawing room. A sweet-smelling smog of eau de cologne lay over the scene. Frau Marthe Luther sat on a sofa, clutching a handkerchief. She looked up at him – glassy blue eyes cracked by minute veins.

'What news?'

'None, madam. I'm sorry to say. But you may be sure that no effort is being spared to find your husband.' *Truer than you know*, he thought.

She was a woman fast losing her attractiveness but gamely staging a fighting retreat. Her tactics, though, were ill-advised: unnaturally blonde hair, a tight skirt, a silk blouse undone just a button too far, to display fat, milky-white cleavage. She looked every centimetre a third wife. A romantic novel lay open, face down, on the embroidered cushion next to her. *The Kaiser's Ball* by Barbara Cartland.

She returned his identity card and blew her nose. 'Will you sit down? You look exhausted. Not even time to shave! Some coffee? Sherry, perhaps? No? Rose, bring coffee for the Herr Sturmbannführer. And perhaps I might fortify myself with just the *smallest* sherry.'

Perched uneasily on the edge of a deep, chintz-covered armchair, his notebook open on his knee, March listened to Frau Luther's woeful tale. Her husband? A very good man, short-tempered – yes, maybe, but that was his nerves, poor thing. Poor, poor thing – he had weepy eyes, did March know that?

She showed him a photograph: Luther at some Mediterranean resort, absurd in a pair of shorts, scowling, his eyes swollen behind the thick glasses.

On she went: a man of that age – he would be sixty-nine in December, they were going to Spain for his birthday. Martin was a friend of General Franco – a dear little man, had March ever met him?

No: a pleasure denied.

Ah, well. She couldn't bear to think what might have happened, always so careful about telling her where he was going, he had never done anything like this. It was such a help to talk, so sympathetic . . .

There was a sigh of silk as she crossed her legs, the skirt rising provocatively above a plump knee. The maid reappeared and set down coffee cup, cream jug and sugar bowl in front of March. Her mistress was provided with a glass of sherry, and a crystal decanter, three-quarters empty.

'Did you ever hear him mention the names Josef Buhler or Wilhelm Stuckart?'

A little crack of concentration appeared in the cake of makeup: 'No, I don't recall . . . No, definitely not.'

'Did he go out at all last Friday?'

'Last Friday? I think – yes. He went out early in the morning.' She sipped her sherry. March made a note.

'And when did he tell you he had to go away?'

'That afternoon. He returned about two, said something had happened, that he had to spend Monday in Munich. He flew on Sunday afternoon, so he could stay overnight and be up early.'

'And he didn't tell you what it was about?'

'He was old-fashioned about that sort of thing. His business was his business, if you see what I mean.'

'Before the trip, how did he seem?'

'Oh, irritable, as usual.' She laughed – a girlish giggle. 'Yes, perhaps he *was* a little more preoccupied than normal. The television news always depressed him – the terrorism, the fighting in the East. I told him to pay no attention – no good will come of worrying, I said – but things . . . yes, they preyed on his mind.' She lowered her voice. 'He had a breakdown during the war, poor thing. The strain . . .'

She was about to cry again. March cut in: 'What year was his breakdown?'

'I believe it was in '43. That was before I knew him, of course.'

'Of course.' March smiled and bowed his head. 'You must have been at school.'

'Perhaps not quite at *school* . . .' The skirt rose a little higher.

'When did you start to become alarmed for his safety?'

'When he didn't come home on Monday. I was awake all night.'

'So you reported him missing on Tuesday morning?'

'I was about to, when Obergruppenführer Globocnik arrived.'

March tried to keep the surprise out of his voice: 'He

arrived *before* you even told the Polizei? What time was that?'

'Soon after nine. He said he needed to speak to my husband. I told him the situation. The Obergruppenführer took it very seriously.'

'I'm sure he did. Did he tell you why he needed to speak to Herr Luther?'

'No. I assumed it was a Party matter. Why?' Suddenly, her voice had a harder edge. 'Are you suggesting my husband had done something wrong?'

'No, no . . .'

She straightened her skirt over her knees, smoothed it out with ring-encrusted fingers. There was a pause and then she said: 'Herr Sturmbannführer, what is the purpose of this conversation?'

'Did your husband ever visit Switzerland?'

'He used to, occasionally, some years ago. He had business there. Why?'

'Where is his passport?'

'It is not in his study. I checked. But I have been over this with the Obergruppenführer. Martin always carried his passport with him. He said he never knew when he might need it. That was his Foreign Ministry training. Really, there is nothing unusual about that, really . . .'

'Forgive me, madam.' He pressed on. 'The burglar alarm. I noticed it on my way in. It looks new.'

She glanced down at her lap. 'Martin had it installed last year. We had intruders.'

'Two men?'

She looked up at him with surprise. 'How did you know?'

That was a mistake. He said: 'I must have read the report in your husband's file.'

'Impossible.' Surprise had been replaced in her voice by suspicion. 'He never reported it.'

'Why not?'

159

She was on the point of making a blustering reply –
'What business is it of yours?' or something of the sort – but
then she saw the expression in March's eyes and changed
her mind. She said, in a resigned voice: 'I pleaded with
him, Herr Sturmbannführer. But he wouldn't. And he
wouldn't tell me why.'

'What happened?'

'It was last winter. We were planning to stay in for the
evening. Some friends called at the last minute and we
went out to dinner, at Horcher's. When we got back, there
were two men *in this room*.' She looked around as if they
might still be hiding somewhere. 'Thank God our friends
came in with us. If we'd been alone . . . When they saw
there were four of us, they jumped out of that window.' She
pointed behind March's shoulder.

'So he put in an alarm system. Did he take any other
precautions?'

'He hired a security guard. Four of them, in fact. They
worked shifts. He kept them on until after Christmas. Then
he decided he didn't trust them any more. He was so
frightened, Herr Sturmbannführer.'

'Of what?'

'He wouldn't tell me.'

Out came the handkerchief. Another helping of sherry
was sloshed from the decanter. Her lipstick had left thick
pink smears around the rim of her glass. She was sliding
towards the edge of tears again. March had misjudged her.
She was frightened for her husband, true. But she was
more frightened now that he might have been deceiving
her. The shadows were chasing one another across her
mind, and in her eyes they left their trails. Was it another
woman? A crime? A secret? Had he fled the country?
Gone for good? He felt sorry for her, and for a moment
considered warning her of the Gestapo's case against her
husband. But why add to her misery? She would know

soon enough. He hoped the state would not confiscate the house.

'Madam, I have intruded too long.' He closed his notebook and stood. She clutched his hand, peered up at him.

'I'm never going to see him again, am I?'

'Yes,' he said.

No, he thought.

IT was a relief to leave the dark and sickly room and escape into the fresh air. The Gestapo men were still sitting in the BMW. They watched him leave. He hesitated for a second, and then turned right, towards the Botanischer Garten railway station.

Four security guards!

He could begin to see it now. A meeting at Buhler's villa on Friday morning, attended by Buhler, Stuckart and Luther. A panicky meeting, old men in a sweat of fear – and with good reason. Perhaps they had each been given a separate task. At any rate, on Sunday, Luther had flown to Zürich. March was sure it was he who must have sent the chocolates from Zürich airport on Monday afternoon, maybe just as he was about to board another aircraft. What were they? Not a present: a signal. Was their arrival meant to be taken as a sign that his task had been completed successfully? Or that he had failed?

March checked over his shoulder. Yes, now he was being followed, he was almost certain. They would have had time to organise while he was in Luther's house. Which were their agents? The woman in the green coat? The student on his bicycle? Hopeless. The Gestapo were too good for him to spot. There would be three or four of them, at least. He lengthened his stride. He was nearing the station.

Question: did Luther return to Berlin from Zürich on

Monday afternoon, or did he stay out of the country? On balance, March inclined to the view that he had returned. That call to Buhler's villa yesterday morning – *'Buhler? Speak to me. Who is that?'* – that had been Luther, he was sure. So: assume Luther posted the packages just before he boarded his flight, say around five o'clock. He would have landed in Berlin about seven that evening. And disappeared.

The Botanischer Garten station was on the suburban electric line. March bought a one-Mark ticket and lingered around the barrier until the train approached. He boarded it and then, just as the doors sighed shut, jumped off, and sprinted over the metal foot-bridge to the other platform. Two minutes later he got on to the south-bound train, only to leap out at Lichterfelde, and re-cross the tracks. The station was deserted. He let the first north-bound train go by, caught the second, and settled into his seat. The only other occupant of the carriage was a pregnant woman. He gave her a smile; she looked away. Good.

Luther, Luther. March lit a cigarette. Nearing seventy with a nervous heart and rheumy eyes. Too paranoid to trust even your wife. They came for you six months earlier, and by luck you escaped. Why did you make a run for it from Berlin airport? Did you come through customs and decide to call your confederates? In Stuckart's apartment, the telephone would have rung unanswered, next to the silent, blood-washed bedroom. In Schwanenwerder, if Eisler's estimate of the time of death was accurate, Buhler must already have been surprised by his killers. Had they let the telephone ring? Or had one of them answered it, while the others held Buhler down?

Luther, Luther: something happened to make you run for your life – out into the freezing rain of that Monday night.

He got out at Gotenland station. It was yet another piece

of architectural fantasy come true – mosaic floors, polished stone, stained glass windows thirty metres high. The regime closed churches and compensated by building railway termini to look like cathedrals.

Gazing down from the overhead walkway on to the thousands of hurrying passengers, March almost gave in to despair. Myriad lives – each with its own secrets and plans and dreams, its individual luggage of guilt – criss-crossed beneath him, not one touching the other, separate and distinct. To think that he, alone, could possibly track down one old man among so many – for the first time, the idea struck him as fantastic, absurd.

But Globus could do it. Already, March could see, the police patrols had been increased in strength. That must have happened in the last half-hour. The Orpo men were scrutinising every male over sixty. A derelict without papers was being led away, complaining.

Globus! March turned away from the handrail and stepped on to the descending escalator, in search of the one person in Berlin who might be able to save his life.

FOUR

To travel on the central U-bahn line is, in the words of the Reich Ministry for Propaganda and Cultural Enlightenment, to take a trip through German history. Berlin-Gotenland, Bülow Strasse, Nollendorf Platz, Wittenberg Platz, Nürnberger Platz, Hohenzollern Platz – the stations succeed one another like pearls on a string.

The carriages which work this line are pre-war. Red cars for smokers, yellow for non-smokers. Hard wooden seats have been rubbed shiny by three decades of Berlin backsides. Most passengers stand, holding on to the worn leather hand-grips, swaying with the rhythm of the train. Signs urge them to turn informer. 'The fare-dodger's profit is the Berliner's loss! Notify the authorities of all wrong-doing!' 'Has he given up his seat to a woman or veteran? Penalty for failure: 25 Reichsmarks!'

March had bought a copy of the *Berliner Tageblatt* from a platform kiosk and was leaning next to the doors, skimming through it. Kennedy and the Führer, the Führer and Kennedy – that was all there was to read. The regime was clearly investing heavily in the success of the talks. That could only mean that things in the East were even worse than everyone thought. 'A permanent state of war on the Eastern front will help to form a sound race of men,' the Führer had once said, 'and will prevent us relapsing into the softness of a Europe thrown back upon itself.' But people *had* grown soft. What else was the point of victory? They had Poles to dig their gardens and Ukrainians to sweep their streets, French chefs to cook their food and English maids to serve it. Having tasted the comforts of peace they had lost their appetite for war.

Way down on an inside page, in type so small it was barely readable, was Buhler's obituary. He was reported as having died in a 'bathing accident'.

March stuffed the paper into his pocket and got out at Bülow Strasse. From the open platform he could see across to Charlotte Maguire's apartment. A shape moved against the curtain. She was at home. Or, rather, someone was at home.

The concierge was not in her chair, and when he knocked on the apartment door there was no reply. He knocked again, more loudly.

Nothing.

He walked away from the door and clattered down the first flight of steps. Then he stopped, counted to ten, and crept back up again, sideways, with his back pressed to the wall – one step, pause; another step, pause – wincing whenever he made a noise, until he stood once more outside the door. He drew his pistol.

Minutes passed. Dogs barked, cars and trains and planes went by, babies cried, birds sang: the cacophony of silence. And at one point, inside the apartment, loud above it all, a floorboard creaked.

The door opened a fraction.

March spun, rammed into it with his shoulder. Whoever was on the other side was knocked back by the force of the blow. And then March was in and on him, pushing him through the tiny hall and into the sitting room. A lamp toppled to the floor. He tried to bring up the gun, but the man had grabbed his arms. And now it was he who was being pushed backwards. The back of his legs made contact with a low table and he toppled over, cracking his head on something, the Luger skittering across the floor.

Well, now, this was quite funny, and in other circumstances March might have laughed. He had never been very good at this sort of thing, and now – having started with the advantage of surprise – he was on his back, unarmed, with his head in the fireplace and his legs still resting on top of the coffee table, in the position of a pregnant woman undergoing an internal examination.

His assailant fell on top of him, winding him. One gloved hand clawed at his face, the other seized his throat. March could neither see nor breathe. He twisted his head from side to side, chewed on the leather hand. He flailed at the other man's head with his fists, but could put no force behind his blows. What was on him was not human. It had the remorseless power of machinery. It was grinding him. Steel fingers had found that artery – the one March could never remember, let alone locate – and he felt himself surrendering to the force, the rushing blackness obliterating the pain. *So*, he thought, *I have walked the earth and come to this*.

A crash. The hands slackened, withdrew. March came swimming back into the fight, at least as a spectator. The man had been knocked sideways, hit on the head by a chair of tubular steel. Blood masked his face, pulsing from a cut above his eye. Crash. The chair again. With one arm, the man tried to ward off the blows, with the other he wiped frantically at his blinded eyes. He began shuffling on his knees for the door, a devil on his back – a hissing, spitting fury, claws scrabbling to find his eyes. Slowly, as if carrying an immense weight, he raised himself on one leg, then the other. All he wanted now was to get away. He blundered into the door frame, turned and hammered his tormentor against it – once, twice.

Only then did Charlie Maguire let him go.

CLUSTERS of pain, bursting like fireworks: his head, the backs of his legs, his ribs, his throat.

'Where did you learn to fight?'

He was in the tiny kitchen, bent over the sink. She was mopping blood from the cut on the back of his head.

'Try growing up as the only girl in a family with three brothers. You learn to fight. Hold still.'

'I pity the brothers. Ah.' March's head hurt the most. The bloody water dripping into the greasy plates a few centimetres from his face made him feel sick. 'In Hollywood, I think, it is traditional for the man to rescue the girl.'

'Hollywood is full of shit.' She applied a fresh cloth. 'This is quite deep. Are you sure you don't want to go to the hospital?'

'No time.'

'Will that man come back?'

'No. At least, not for a while. Supposedly, this is still a clandestine operation. Thank you.'

He held the cloth to the back of his head and straightened. As he did so, he discovered a new pain, at the base of his spine.

' "A clandestine operation"?' she repeated. 'You don't think he could have been an ordinary thief?'

'No. He was a professional. An authentic, Gestapo-trained professional.'

'And I beat him!' The adrenalin had given lustre to her skin; her eyes sparkled. Her only injury was a bruise on her shoulder. She was more attractive than he remembered. Delicate cheek bones, a strong nose, full lips, large brown eyes. She had brown hair, cut to the nape of her neck, which she wore swept back behind her ears.

'If his orders had been to kill you, he would have done so.'

'Really? Then why didn't he?' Suddenly she sounded angry.

'You're an American. A protected species, especially at the moment.' He inspected the cloth. The flow of blood had stopped. 'Don't underrate the enemy, Fräulein.'

'Don't underrate *me*. If I hadn't come home, he'd have killed you.'

He decided to say nothing. She clearly kept her temper on a hair-trigger.

The apartment had been thoroughly ransacked. Her clothes hung out of their drawers, papers had been spilled across the desk and on to the floor, suitcases had been up-ended. Not, he thought, that it could have been very neat before: the dirty dishes in the sink, the profusion of bottles (most of them empty) in the bathroom, the yellowing copies of the *New York Times* and *Time*, their pages sliced to ribbons by the German censors, stacked haphazardly around the walls. Searching it must have been a nightmare. Weak light filtered in through dirty net curtains. Every few minutes the walls shook as the trains passed.

'This is yours, I take it?' She pulled out the Luger from beneath a chair and held it up between finger and thumb.

'Yes. Thank you.' He took it. She had a gift for making him feel stupid. 'Is anything missing?'

'I doubt it.' She glanced around. 'I'm not sure I'd know if there was.'

'The item I gave you last night. . . ?'

'Oh that? It was here on the mantelpiece.' She ran her hand along it, frowning. 'It *was* here . . .'

He closed his eyes. When he opened them, she was grinning.

'Don't worry, Sturmbannführer. It's stayed close to my heart. Like a love-letter.'

She turned her back on him, unbuttoning her shirt. When she turned round, she had the envelope in her hand. He took it over to the window. It was warm to his touch.

It was long and slim, made of thick paper – a rich creamy-blue with brown specks of age, like liver spots. It was luxurious, hand-made, redolent of another age. There was no name or address.

Inside the envelope was a small brass key and a letter, on matching blue paper, as thick as cardboard. Printed in the top right-hand corner, in flowery copperplate, was: Zaugg & Cie, Bankiers, Bahnhof Strasse 44, Zürich. A single sentence, typed beneath, identified the bearer as a joint holder of account number 2402. The letter was dated 8 July 1942. It was signed Hermann Zaugg, Director.

March read it through again. He was not surprised Stuckart had kept it locked in his safe: it was illegal for a German citizen to possess a foreign bank account without the permission of the Reichsbank. The penalty for non-compliance was death.

He said: 'I was worried about you. I tried to call you a couple of hours ago, but there was no answer.'

'I was out, doing research.'

'Research?'

She grinned again.

AT March's suggestion, they went for a walk in the Tiergarten, the traditional rendezvous for Berliners with secrets to discuss. Even the Gestapo had yet to devise a means of bugging a park. Daffodils poked through the rough grass at the foot of the trees. Children fed the ducks on the Neuer See.

Getting out of Stuckart's apartment block had been easy, she said. The air shaft had emerged into the alley almost at ground level. There were no SS men. They were all round the front. So she had simply walked down the side of the building, to the street at the rear, and caught a taxi home. She had stayed up half the night waiting for him to call, re-reading the letter until she knew it off by heart. When, by nine o'clock, she had still heard nothing, she decided not to wait.

She wanted to know what had happened to him and

Jaeger. He told her only that they had been taken to Gestapo headquarters and released that morning.

'Are you in trouble?'

'Yes. Now tell me what you discovered.'

She had gone first to the public library in Nollendorf Platz – she had nothing better to do now her press accreditation had been withdrawn. In the library was a directory of European banks. Zaugg & Cie still existed. The bank's premises remained in Bahnhof Strasse. From the library she had gone to the US Embassy to see Henry Nightingale.

'Nightingale?'

'You met him last night.'

March remembered: the young man in the sports jacket and the button-down shirt, with his hand on her arm. 'You didn't tell him anything?'

'Of course not. Anyway, he's discreet. We can trust him.'

'I prefer to make my own judgements about whom I can trust.' He felt disappointed in her. 'Is he your lover?'

She stopped in her tracks. 'What kind of a question is that?'

'I have more at stake in this than you have, Fräulein. Much more. I have a right to know.'

'You have no right to know *at all*.' She was furious.

'All right.' He held up his hands. The woman was impossible. 'Your business.'

They resumed walking.

Nightingale, she explained, was an expert in Swiss commercial matters, having dealt with the affairs of several German refugees in the United States trying to extract their money from banks in Zürich and Geneva.

It was almost impossible.

In 1934, a Gestapo agent named Georg Hannes Thomae had been sent to Switzerland by Reinhard Heydrich to find out the names of as many German account-holders as possible. Thomae set up house in Zürich, began affairs with several lonely female cashiers, befriended minor bank officials. When the Gestapo had suspicions that a certain individual had an illegal account, Thomae would visit the bank posing as an intermediary and try to deposit money. The moment any cash was accepted, Heydrich knew an account existed. Its holder was arrested, tortured into revealing the details, and soon the bank would receive a detailed cable requesting, in proper form, the repatriation of all assets.

The Gestapo's war against the Swiss banks became increasingly sophisticated and extensive. Telephone calls, cables and letters between Germany and Switzerland were intercepted as a matter of routine. Clients were executed or sent to concentration camps. In Switzerland, there was an outcry. Finally, the Swiss National Assembly rushed through a new Banking Code making it illegal for banks to disclose any details of their clients' holdings, on pain of imprisonment. Georg Thomae was exposed and expelled.

Swiss banks came to regard doing business with German citizens as too dangerous and time-consuming to countenance. Communication with clients was virtually impossible. Hundreds of accounts had simply been abandoned by their terrified owners. In any case, respectable bankers had no desire to become involved in these life-and-death transactions. The publicity was damaging. By 1939 the once-lucrative German numbered-account business had collapsed.

'Then came the war,' said Charlie. They had reached the end of the Neuer See and were walking back. From beyond the trees came the hum of the traffic on the East-West Axis. The dome of the Great Hall rose above the trees. Berliners joked that the only way to avoid seeing it was to live inside it.

'After 1939, the demand for Swiss accounts increased dramatically, for obvious reasons. People were desperate to get their property out of Germany. So banks like Zaugg devised a new kind of deposit account. For a fee of 200 Francs, you received a box and a number, a key and a letter of authorisation.'

'Exactly like Stuckart.'

'Right. You simply needed to show up with the letter and the key, and it was all yours. No questions. Each account could have as many keys and letters of authorisation as the holder was prepared to pay for. The beauty of it was – the banks were no longer involved. One day, if she could get the travel permit, some little old lady might turn up with her life savings. Ten years later, her son could turn up with a letter and a key and walk off with his inheritance.'

'Or the Gestapo might turn up . . .'

'. . . and if they had the letter and the key, the bank could give them everything. No embarrassments. No publicity. No breaking the Banking Code.'

'These accounts – they still exist?'

'The Swiss Government banned them at the end of the war, under pressure from Berlin, and no new ones have been allowed since. But the old ones – they still exist, because the terms of the original agreement have to be honoured. They've become valuable in their own right. People sell them on to one another. According to Henry, Zaugg developed quite a speciality in them. God knows what he's got locked in those boxes.'

'Did you mention Stuckart's name to this Nightingale?'

'Of course not. I told him I was writing a piece for *Fortune* about "the lost legacies of the war".'

'Just as you told me you were going to interview Stuckart for an article about "the Führer's early years"?'

She hesitated, and said quietly: 'What's that supposed to mean?'

His head was throbbing, his ribs still ached. *What did he mean?* He lit a cigarette to give himself time to think.

'People who encounter violent death – they try to forget it, run away. Not you. Last night: your eagerness to go back to Stuckart's apartment, the way you opened his letters. This morning: turning up information about Swiss banks . . .'

He stopped speaking. An elderly couple passed on the footpath, staring at them. He realised they must look an odd pair: an SS Sturmbannführer, unshaven and slightly bashed around, and a woman who was clearly a foreigner. Her accent might be perfect, but there was something about her, in her expression, her clothes, her stance – something which betrayed that she was not German.

'Let's walk this way.' He led her off the path, towards the trees.

'Can I have one of those?'

In the shadows, as he lit her a cigarette, she cupped the flame. Reflections of the fire danced in her eyes.

'All right.' She took a pace back, hugging herself as if she were cold. 'It's true my parents knew Stuckart before the war. It's true I went to see him before Christmas. But I didn't call him. He called me.'

'When?'

'On Saturday. Late.'

'What did he say?'

She laughed. 'Oh no, Sturmbannführer. In my business information is a commodity, exchangeable on the open market. But I'm willing to trade.'

'What do you want to know?'

'Everything. Why you had to break into that apartment last night. Why you are keeping secrets from your own people. Why the Gestapo almost killed you an hour ago.'

'Oh *that* . . .' He smiled. He felt weary. He leaned his back against the rough bark of the tree and stared across the park. It seemed to him he had nothing to lose.

'Two days ago,' he began, 'I fished a body out of the Havel.'

He told her everything. He told her about Buhler's death and Luther's disappearance. He told her what Jost had seen, and what had happened to him. He told her about Nebe and Globus, about the art treasures and the Gestapo file. He even told her about Pili's statement. And – something he had noticed about criminals confessing, even those who knew that their confessions would one day hang them – when he finished, he felt better.

She was silent a long time. 'That's fair,' she said. 'I don't know how this helps, but this is what happened to me.'

SHE had gone to bed early on Saturday night. The weather had been foul – the start of that great bank of rain that had washed over the city for three days. She was not feeling sociable, had not for weeks. You know how it is. Berlin can get to you like that. Make you feel small and hopeless in the shade of those vast grey buildings; the endless uniforms; the unsmiling bureaucrats.

The phone went about eleven-thirty, just as she was drifting off to sleep. A man's voice. Taut. Precise. 'There is a telephone booth opposite your apartment. Go to it. I shall call you there in five minutes. If the booth is occupied, please wait.'

She had not recognised who it was, but something in the man's tone had told her it was not a joke. She had dressed, grabbed her coat, hobbled down the stairs, into the street, trying to pull on her shoes and walk at the same time. The rain had hit her like a slap across the face. Across the street, outside the station, was an old wooden telephone kiosk – empty, thank God.

It was while she was waiting for the call that she remembered where she had first heard the voice.

'Go back a bit,' said March. 'Your first meeting with Stuckart. Describe it.'

That was before Christmas. She had called him cold. Explained who she was. He seemed reluctant, but she had persisted, so he had invited her over for tea. He had a shock of white curly hair and one of those orangey tans, as if he had spent a long time in the sun, or under an ultra-violet lamp. The woman, Maria, was also in the apartment, but behaved like a maid. She served some tea then left them to it. Usual chat: how is your mother? Very well, thank you.

Ha, that was a joke.

She flicked ash from the end of her cigarette.

'My mother's career died when she left Berlin. My arrival buried it. As you can imagine, there wasn't a great demand for German actresses in Hollywood during the war.'

And then he had asked about her father, in a gritted-teeth kind of a way. And she had been able to take great pleasure in saying: very well, thank you. He had retired in 'sixty-one, when Kennedy took over. Deputy Under-Secretary of State Michael Maguire. God bless the United States of America. Stuckart had met him through Mom, had known him when he was at the Embassy here.

March interrupted: 'When was that?'

'Thirty-seven to 'thirty-nine.'

'Go on.'

Well, then he had wanted to know about the job and she had told him. World European Features: he had never heard of them. Not surprising, she said: nobody had. That sort of thing. Polite interest, you know. So when she left she gave him her card, and he had bent to kiss her hand, had lingered over it, made a meal of it, made her feel sick. He had patted her bottom on the way out. And that had been that, she was glad to say. Five months: nothing.

'Until Saturday night?'

Until Saturday night. She had been in the telephone kiosk no more than thirty seconds when he rang. Now all the arrogance was gone from his voice.

'Charlotte?' He had placed heavy emphasis on the second syllable. Shar-*lott*-e. 'Forgive this melodrama. Your telephone is tapped.'

'They say every foreigner's line is tapped.'

'This is true. When I was in the Ministry, I used to see transcripts. But public boxes are safe. I am in a public box now. I came on Thursday and took the number of the one you are in. It is serious, you see. I need to contact the authorities in your country.'

'Why not talk to the Embassy?'

'The Embassy is not safe.'

He had sounded terrified. And tight. Definitely, he had been drinking.

'Are you saying you want to defect?'

A long silence. Then there had been a noise behind her. A sound of metal tapping on glass. She had turned to discover, in the rain and the dark, a man, with his hands cupped round his eyes, peering into the kiosk, looking like a deep-sea diver. She must have let out a cry or something because Stuckart had got very frightened.

'What was that? What is it?'

'Nothing. Just someone wanting to use the phone.'

'We must be quick. I deal only with your father, not the Embassy.'

'What do you want me to do?'

'Come to me tomorrow and I will tell you everything. Shar-*lott*-e, I will make you the most famous reporter in the world.'

'Where? What time?'

'My apartment. Noon.'

'Is that safe?'

'Nowhere is safe.'

And then he had rung off. Those were the last words she had heard Stuckart speak.

She finished her cigarette, ground it under her foot.

The rest he knew, more or less. She had found the bodies, called the police. They had taken her to the big city station in Alexander Platz, where she had sat in a blank-walled room for more than three hours, going crazy. Then she had been driven to another building, to give a statement to some creepy SS man in a cheap wig, whose office had been more like that of a pathologist than a detective.

March smiled at the description of Fiebes.

She had already made up her mind not to tell the Polizei about Stuckart's call on Saturday night, for an obvious reason. If she had hinted that she had been preparing to help Stuckart defect, she would have been accused of 'activities incompatible with her status as a journalist', and arrested. As it was, they had decided to deport her anyway. So it goes.

THE authorities were planning a fireworks display in the Tiergarten, to commemorate the Führer's birthday. An area of the park had been fenced off, and pyrotechnicians in blue overalls were laying their surprises, watched by a curious crowd. Mortar tubes, sandbagged emplacements, dug-outs, kilometres of cable: these looked more like the preparations for an artillery bombardment than for a celebration. Nobody paid any attention to the SS-Sturmbannführer and the woman in the blue plastic coat.

He scribbled on a page of his notebook.

'These are my telephone numbers – office and home. Also, here are the numbers of a friend of mine called Max Jaeger. If you can't get hold of me, call him.' He tore out the page and gave it to her. 'If anything suspicious happens, anything worries you – it doesn't matter what the time is – call.'

'What about you? What are you going to do?'

'I'm going to try to get to Zürich tonight. Check out this bank account first thing tomorrow.'

He knew what she would say even before she opened her mouth.

'I'll come with you.'

'You will be much safer here.'

'But it's my story, too.'

She sounded like a spoilt child. 'It's not a story, for God's sake.' He bit back his anger. 'Look. A deal. Whatever I find out, I swear I'll tell you. You can have it all.'

'It's not as good as being there.'

'It's better than being dead.'

'They wouldn't do anything like that abroad.'

'On the contrary, that is exactly where they would do it. If something happens here, they are responsible. If something happens abroad . . .' He shrugged. 'Prove it.'

THEY parted in the centre of the Tiergarten. He strode briskly across the grass, towards the humming city. As he walked, he took the envelope out of his pocket, squeezed it to check the key was still in it and – on impulse – raised it to his nose. Her scent. He looked over his shoulder. She was walking through the trees with her back to him. She disappeared for a moment, then reappeared; disappeared, reappeared – a tiny birdlike figure – bright blue plumage against the dreary wood.

he door to March's apartment hung off its hinges like a broken jaw. He stood on the landing, listening, his pistol drawn. The place was silent, deserted.

Like Charlotte Maguire's, his apartment had been searched, but by hands of greater malevolence. Everything had been tipped into a heap in the centre of the sitting room – clothes and books, shoes and old letters, photographs and crockery and furniture – the detritus of a life. It was as if someone had intended to make a bonfire but had been distracted at the last minute, before they could apply the torch.

Wedged upright on top of the pyre was a wooden-framed photograph of March, aged twenty, shaking hands with the commander of the *U-Boot Waffe*, Admiral Dönitz. Why had it been left like that? What point was being made? He picked it up, carried it over to the window, blew dust off it. He had forgotten he even had it. Doenitz liked to come aboard every boat before it left Wilhelmshaven: an awesome figure, ramrod, iron-gripped, gruff. 'Good hunting,' he had barked at March. He growled the same to everyone. The picture showed five young crewmen lined up beneath the conning tower to meet him. Rudi Halder was to March's left. The other three had died later that year, trapped in the hull of U-175.

Good hunting.

He tossed the picture back on the pile.

It had taken time to do all this. Time, and anger, and the certainty of not being disturbed. It must have happened while he was under guard in Prinz-Albrecht Strasse. It could only have been the work of the Gestapo. He remembered a line of graffiti scrawled by White Rose on a wall near Werderscher Markt: 'A police state is a country run by criminals'.

They had opened his mail. A couple of bills, long overdue – they were welcome to *them* – and a letter from his ex-wife, dated Tuesday. He glanced through it. She had decided he was not to see Pili in future. It upset the boy too much. She hoped he would agree this was for the best. If necessary, she would be willing to swear a deposition before the Reich Family Court, giving her reasons. She trusted this would not be necessary, both for his sake and the boy's. It was signed 'Klara Eckart'. So she had gone back to her maiden name. He screwed it up and threw it next to the photograph, with the rest of the rubbish.

The bathroom at least had been left intact. He showered and shaved, inspecting himself in the mirror for damage. It felt worse than it looked: a large bruise developing nicely on his chest, more on the back of his legs and at the base of his spine; a livid mark at his throat. Nothing serious. What was it his father used to say – his paternal balm for all the batterings of childhood? 'You'll live, boy.' That was it. 'You'll live!'

Naked, he went back into the sitting room and searched through the wreckage, pulling out clean clothes, a pair of shoes, a suitcase, a leather hold-all. He feared they might have taken his passport but it was there, at the bottom of the mound. It had been issued in 1961, when March had gone to Italy to bring back a gangster being held in Milan. His younger self stared up at him, fatter-cheeked, half-smiling. *My God*, he thought, *I have aged ten years in three*.

He brushed down his uniform and put it back on, together with a clean shirt, and packed his suitcase. As he bent to snap it shut his eye was caught by something in the empty grate. The photograph of the Weiss family was lying face down. He hesitated, picked it up, folded it into a small square – exactly as he had found it five years earlier – and slipped it into his wallet. If he was stopped and searched, he would say they were his family.

Then he took a last look round and left, closing the broken door behind him as best he could.

At the main branch of the Deutschebank, in Wittenberg Platz, he asked how much he held in his account.

'Four thousand two hundred and seventy-seven Reichsmarks and thirty-eight pfennigs.'

'I'll take it.'

'All of it, Herr Sturmbannführer?' The teller blinked at him through wire-framed spectacles. 'You are closing the account?'

'All of it.'

March watched him count out forty-two one-hundred Mark notes, then stuffed them into his wallet, next to the photograph. Not much in the way of life savings.

This is what no promotions and seven years of alimony do to you.

The teller was staring at him. 'Did the Herr Sturmbannführer say something?'

He had given voice to his thoughts. He must be going mad. 'No. Sorry. Thank you.'

March picked up his suitcase, went out into the square and caught a taxi to Werderscher Markt.

Alone in his office, he did two things. He rang the headquarters of Lufthansa and asked the head of security – a former Kripo investigator he knew, called Friedman – to check if the airline had carried a passenger by the name of Martin Luther on any of its Berlin-Zürich flights on Sunday or Monday.

'Martin Luther, right?' Friedman was greatly amused. 'Anyone else you want, March? Emperor Charlemagne? Herr von Goethe?'

'It's important.'

'It's always important. Sure. I know.' Friedman promised to find out the information at once. 'Listen. When you get tired of chasing ambulances, there's always a job for you here if you want it.'

'Thanks. I may well.'

After he hung up, March took the dead plant down from the filing cabinet. He lifted the atrophied roots out of the pot, put in the brass key, replaced the plant, and returned the pot to its old position.

Five minutes later, Friedman called him back.

ARTUR NEBE'S suite of offices was on the fourth floor – all cream carpets and cream paintwork, recessed lighting and black leather sofas. On the walls were prints of Thorak's sculptures. Herculean figures with gargantuan torsos rolled boulders up steep hills, in celebration of the building of the Autobahnen; Valkyries fought the triple demons Ignorance, Bolshevism and Slav. The immensity of Thorak's statuary was a whispered joke. 'Thorax' they called him: 'The Herr Professor is not receiving visitors today – he is working in the left ear of the horse.'

Nebe's adjutant, Otto Beck, a smooth-faced graduate of Heidelberg and Oxford, looked up as March came into the outer office.

March said: 'I need to speak with the Oberstgruppen-führer.'

'He is seeing nobody.'

'He will see me.'

'He will not.'

March leaned very close to Beck's face, his fists on his desk. 'Ask.'

Behind him, he heard Nebe's secretary say: 'Shall I call security?'

'One moment, Ingrid.' It was fashionable among the graduates of the SS academy in Oxford to affect an English coolness. Beck flicked an invisible speck from the sleeve of his tunic. 'And what name is it?'

'March.'

'Ah. The famous *March*.' Beck picked up the telephone. 'Sturmbannführer March is demanding to see you, Herr Oberstgruppenführer.' He looked at March and nodded. 'Very well.'

Beck pressed a button concealed beneath the desk, releasing the electronic bolts. 'Five minutes, March. He has an appointment with the Reichsführer.'

The door to the inner office was solid oak, six centimetres thick. Inside, the blinds were tightly drawn against the day. Nebe was curled over his desk in a puddle of yellow light, studying a typed list through a magnifying glass. He turned one vast and blurry fish eye upon his visitor.

'What have we here. . . ?' He lowered the glass. 'Sturmbannführer March. Empty-handed, I assume?'

'Unfortunately.'

Nebe nodded. 'I learn from the duty office that the police stations of the Reich are even now being filled to overflowing with elderly beggars, ancient drunkards who have lost their papers, absconding geriatrics . . . Enough to keep Globus busy until Christmas.' He leaned back in his chair. 'If I know Luther, he is far too cunning to show himself yet. He will wait a few days. That must be your hope.'

'I have a favour to ask.'

'Proceed.'

'I wish to leave the country.'

Nebe let out a shout of laughter. He pounded the desk

with both hands. 'Your file is compendious, March, but nowhere does it mention your sense of humour. Excellent! Who knows? You may yet survive. Some KZ commandant may adopt you as a pet.'

'I wish to go to Switzerland.'

'Of course. The scenery is spectacular.'

'I have had a call from Lufthansa. Luther flew to Zürich on Sunday afternoon, and returned to Berlin on the last flight on Monday night. I believe he had access to a numbered bank account.'

Nebe's laughter had dwindled to an occasional snort. 'On what evidence?'

March placed the envelope on Nebe's desk. 'I removed this from Stuckart's apartment last night.'

Nebe opened it and inspected the letter through the magnifying glass. He glanced up. 'Should there not be a key with this?'

March was staring at the paintings behind Nebe's head – Schmutzler's 'Farm Girls Returning From the Fields', Padua's 'The Führer Speaks' – ghastly, orthodox muck.

'Ah. I see.' Nebe sat back again, stroking his cheek with the glass. 'If I don't allow you to go, I don't get the key. I could of course turn you over to the Gestapo, and they could persuade you to disgorge the key – probably quite quickly. But then it would be Globus and Heydrich who would learn the contents of the deposit box, rather than me.'

He was silent for a while. Then he dragged himself to his feet and hobbled across to the blinds. He opened the slats a fraction and peered out. March could see his eyes moving slowly from side to side.

At last he said: 'A tempting bargain. But why is it that I have this vision of myself, waving you off with a white handkerchief from the tarmac of Hermann Göring Airport, and of you never coming back?'

'I suppose giving you my word that I would return would be of no use?'

'The suggestion demeans our intelligence.'

Nebe went back to his desk and read the letter again. He pressed a switch on his desk. 'Beck.'

The adjutant appeared. 'March – give him your passport. Now, Beck, get that to the Interior Ministry and have them issue an immediate twenty-four-hour exit visa, starting at six tonight and expiring at six tomorrow.'

Beck glanced at March, then slid out of the office.

Nebe said: 'This is my offer. The Head of the Swiss Criminal Police, Herr Streuli, is a good friend of mine. From the moment you step off the aircraft until the moment you reboard it, his people will be watching you. Do not attempt to evade them. If you fail to return tomorrow, you will be arrested and deported. If you try to make a run to Bern, to enter a foreign embassy, you will be stopped. In any case, there is nowhere for you to go. After yesterday's happy announcement, the Americans will simply toss you back over the border to us. The British, French and Italians will do what we tell them. Australia and Canada will obey the Americans. There are the Chinese, I suppose, but if I were you I'd sooner take my chances in a KZ. And the moment you return to Berlin, you will tell me everything you have discovered. Good?'

March nodded.

'Good. The Führer calls the Swiss "a nation of hotel-keepers". I recommend the Baur au Lac on Tal Strasse, overlooking the See. Most luxurious. A fine place for a condemned man to spend a night.'

BACK in his office, a parody of a tourist, March booked his hotel room and reserved a plane seat. Within the hour, he had his passport back. The visa had been stamped inside:

the ubiquitous eagle and garlanded swastika, the blank spaces for the dates filled in by a crabbed and bureaucratic hand.

The duration of an exit visa was in direct ratio to the applicant's political reliability. Party bosses got ten years; Party members, five; citizens with unblemished records, one; the dregs of the camps naturally got nothing at all. March had been given a day-pass to the outside world. He was down there among the Untouchables of society – the grumblers, the parasites, the work-shy, the crypto-criminal.

He rang the Kripo's economic investigation division and asked for the resident Swiss expert. When he mentioned Zaugg's name and asked if the division had any information, the man at the other end laughed. 'How long do you have?'

'Start at the beginning.'

'Hold, please.' The man put down the phone and went to fetch the file.

Zaugg & Cie had been founded in 1877 by a Franco-German financier, Louis Zaugg. Hermann Zaugg, the signatory of Stuckart's letter, was the founder's grandson. He was still listed as the bank's chief director. Berlin had followed his activities for more than two decades. During the 1940s, Zaugg had dealt extensively with German nationals of dubious reliability. He was currently suspected of harbouring millions of Reichsmarks in cash, art, bullion, jewellery and precious stones – all of which rightfully should have been confiscated, but to none of which could the Finance Ministry gain access. They had been trying for years.

'What do we have on Zaugg personally?'

'Only the bare details. He's fifty-four, married, with one son. Has a mansion on the Zürichsee. Very respectable. Very private. Plenty of powerful friends in the Swiss government.'

March lit a cigarette and grabbed a scrap of paper. 'Give me that address again.'

MAX JAEGER arrived as March was writing him a note. He pushed open the door with his backside, came in carrying a stack of files, looking sweaty. Nearly two days' growth of beard gave him a menacing air.

'Zavi, thank Christ.' He peered over the top of the paperwork. 'I've been trying to reach you all day. Where have you been?'

'Around. What's this? Your memoirs?'

'The Spandau shootings. You heard Uncle Artur this morning.' He mimicked Nebe's reedy voice. ' "Jaeger, you can return to normal duties." '

He dropped the files on his desk. The window rattled. Dust shot across the office. 'Statements of witnesses and wedding guests. Autopsy report – they dug fifteen bullets out of that poor bastard.' He stretched, rubbed his eyes with his fists. 'I could sleep for a week. I tell you: I'm too old for scares like last night. My heart won't stand it.' He broke off. 'Now what the hell are you doing?'

March had lifted the dead plant from its pot and was retrieving the key to the safety deposit box.

'I have a plane to catch in two hours.'

Jaeger looked at his suitcase. 'Don't tell me – a holiday! A little balalaika music on the shores of the Black Sea . . .' He folded his arms and kicked out his legs in a dance, Russian-style.

March shook his head, smiling. 'Do you feel like a beer?'

'Do I feel like a beer?' Jaeger had danced out of the door before March could turn round.

THE little bar in Ob-wall Strasse was run by a retired Orpo

man called Fischer. It smelled of smoke and sweat, stale beer and fried onions. Most of its clientele were policemen. Green and black uniforms clustered around the bar, or lurked in the dimness of the wood-panelled booths.

The Fox and the Bear were greeted warmly.

'Taking a vacation, March?'

'Hey Jaeger! Stand a little closer to the razor next time!'

Jaeger insisted on buying the drinks. March took a booth in the corner, stowed his suitcase under the table, lit a cigarette. There were men here he had known for a decade. The drivers from Rahnsdorf with their poker schools and dirty stories. The heavy drinkers from Serious Crimes in Worth Strasse. He would not miss them. Walther Fiebes sat alone at the bar, moping over a bottle of schnapps.

Jaeger returned and raised his glass. 'Prost!'

'Prost.'

Max wiped the foam from his lips. 'Good sausages, good engines, good beer – Germany's three gifts to the world.' He always said this when they had a drink, and March always lacked the heart to point it out. 'So. What's this about a *plane*?' For Jaeger, the word seemed to conjure images of all that was exotic in the world. The furthest he had ever travelled from Berlin was to a family camp on the Black Sea – a holiday last summer near Gotenburg, organised by Strength-Through-Joy.

March turned his head slightly, glanced from side to side. The German look. The booths on either side were unoccupied. Shouts of laughter came from the bar.

'I have to go to Switzerland. Nebe's given me a twenty-four-hour visa. That key you saw just now in the office – I took it from Stuckart's safe last night. It opens a safety deposit box in Zürich.'

Jaeger's eyes opened wide. 'That must be where they keep the art stuff. Remember what Globus said this morning: they smuggled it out and sold it in Switzerland.'

'There's more to it than that. I've been speaking to the American girl again. It seems that Stuckart called her at home on Saturday night, wanting to defect.'

Defect. The unmentionable act. It hung in the air between them.

Jaeger said: 'But the Gestapo must know that already, Zavi. Surely her phone is tapped?'

March shook his head. 'Stuckart was too clever for that. He used the call box opposite her apartment.' He sipped his beer. 'You see how it goes, Max? I feel like a man descending stairs in the dark. First, the body in the lake turns out to be an alter Kämpfer. Then, his death is linked to Stuckart's. Last night, my one witness to Globus's involvement – the cadet, Jost – was taken away by the SS, on Globus's orders. Now it turns out that Stuckart wanted to defect. What comes next?'

'You'll fall down those stairs and break your neck, my friend. That's what comes next.'

'A fair prediction. And you don't know the worst of it.'

March told him about the Gestapo dossier. Jaeger looked stricken. 'Jesus Christ. What are you going to do?'

'I thought of trying to stay out of the Reich. I even withdrew all my money from the bank. But Nebe's right: no other country would touch me.' March finished his drink. 'Would you do something for me?'

'Name it.'

'The American woman's apartment was broken in to this morning. Could you ask the Orpo in Schöneberg to take a look occasionally –I've left the address on my desk. Also, I've given her your telephone number, in case of trouble.'

'No problem.'

'And can you look after this for Pili?' He handed Jaeger an envelope containing half the cash he had withdrawn from the bank. 'It's not much, but I may need the rest.

Hang on to it until he's old enough to know what to do with it.'

'Oh come on, man!' Max leaned across and clapped him on the shoulder. 'It's not as bad as that? Is it? Surely?'

March stared at him. After a second or two, Jaeger grunted and looked away. 'Yes. Well . . .' He tucked the envelope into his pocket. 'My God,' he said with sudden vehemence, 'if a lad of mine denounced me to the Gestapo, I'd be giving him something all right – and it wouldn't be money.'

'It's not the boy's fault, Max.'

Fault, thought March. *How could you fault a ten-year-old?* The boy needed a father-figure. That was what the Party provided –stability, companionship, something to believe in – all the things March should have given him and hadn't. Besides, the Pimpf *expected* the young to transfer their allegiance from their family to the state. No, he would not – could not – blame his son.

Gloom had settled over Jaeger. 'Another beer?'

'Sorry.' March stood. 'I have to go. I owe you.'

Jaeger lurched to his feet as well. 'When you get back, Zavi, come and stay with us for a couple of days. The younger girls are at a Bund deutscher Mädel camp for the week – you can have their room. We can work something out for the court martial.'

'Harbouring an asocial – that won't go down well with your local Party.'

'Fuck my local Party.'

This was said with feeling. Jaeger stuck out his hand, and March shook it – a great, calloused paw.

'Look after yourself, Zavi.'

'Look after yourself, Max.'

rawn up on the runways of the Flughafen Hermann Göring, shimmering through the haze of fuel, was the new generation of passenger jets: the blue and white Boeings of Pan-American, the red, white and black swastika-decked Junkers of Lufthansa.

Berlin has two airports. The old Tempelhof aerodrome near the city centre handles short-haul, internal flights. International traffic passes through Hermann Göring in the north-western suburbs. The new terminal buildings are long, low edifices of marble and glass, designed – of course – by Speer. Outside the arrivals hall stands a statue of Hanna Reitsch, Germany's leading aviatrix, made of melted-down Spitfires and Lancasters. She scans the sky for intruders. A sign behind her says WELCOME TO BERLIN, CAPITAL OF THE GREATER GERMAN REICH, in five languages.

March paid the taxi driver, tipped him, and walked up the ramp towards the automatic doors. The air here was cold and man-made: drenched with aviation fuel, torn by the screams of throttling engines. Then the doors opened, hissed shut behind him, and suddenly he was in the sound-proofed bubble of the departure terminal.

'*Lufthansa flight 401 to New York. Passengers are requested to make their way to gate number eight for boarding . . .*'

'*Final call for Lufthansa flight 014 to Theoderichshafen. Passengers . . .*'

March went first to the Lufthansa sales desk to pick up his ticket, then to the check-in where his passport was scrutinised carefully by a blonde with 'Gina' pinned to her left breast, a swastika badge in her lapel.

'Does the Herr Sturmbannführer wish to check in any luggage?'

'No thank you. I have only this.' He patted his small suitcase.

She returned his passport with his boarding card folded inside it. Accompanying this act was a smile as bright and cheerless as neon.

'Boarding in thirty minutes. Have a good flight, Herr Sturmbannführer.'

'Thank you, Gina.'

'You are welcome.'

'Thank you.'

They were bowing like a pair of Japanese businessmen. Air travel was a new world to March, a strange land with its own impenetrable rituals.

He followed the signs to the lavatory, selected the cubicle furthest from the wash-basins, locked the door, opened the suitcase, took out the leather hold-all. Then he sat down and tugged off his boots. White light gleamed on chrome and tile.

When he had stripped to his shorts, he put the boots and his uniform into the hold-all, stuffed his Luger into the middle of the bag, zipped it up and locked it.

Five minutes later he emerged from the cubicle transformed. In a light grey suit, white shirt, pale blue tie and soft brown shoes, the Aryan Superman had turned back into a normal citizen. He could see the transformation reflected in people's eyes. No more frightened glances. The attendant at the left-luggage area where he deposited the hold-all was surly. He handed March the ticket.

'Don't lose it. If you do, don't bother coming back.' He jerked his head to the sign behind him: 'Warning! Items returned on production of ticket only!'

At the passport control zone March lingered, noting the security. Barrier one: checking of boarding cards, unobtainable without the proper visa. Barrier two: re-checking of the visas themselves. Three members of the Zollgrenzschutz, the border protection police, were stationed on either side of the entrance, carrying sub-machine guns. The elderly man in front of March was scrutinised with particular care, the customs officer speaking to someone on the telephone before waving him through. They were still looking for Luther.

When March's turn came, he saw how his passport baffled the customs man. An SS-Sturmbannführer with only a twenty-four-hour visa? The normal signals of rank and privilege, usually so clear, were too confused to read. Curiosity and servility warred in the customs man's face. Servility, as usual, won.

'Enjoy your journey, Herr Sturmbannführer.'

On the other side of the barrier, March resumed his study of airport security. All luggage was scanned by X-ray. He was frisked, then asked to open his case. Each item was inspected – the sponge bag unzipped, the shaving foam uncapped and sniffed. The guards worked with the care of men who knew that, if an aircraft was lost to hijackers or to a terrorist bomb during their watch, they would spend the next five years in a KZ.

Finally he was clear of the checks. He patted his inside pocket to make sure Stuckart's letter was still there, turned the little brass key over in his other hand. Then he went to the bar and had a large whisky and a cigarette.

HE boarded the Junkers ten minutes before take-off.

It was the day's last flight from Berlin to Zürich and the cabin was full of businessmen and bankers in dark three-piece suits reading pink financial newspapers. March had a seat next to the window. The place beside his was empty. He stowed his suitcase in a compartment above his head, settled back and closed his eyes. Inside the plane, a Bach cantata was playing. Outside, the engines started. They climbed the scale, from hum to brittle whine, one coming in after another like a chorus. The aircraft jolted slightly and began to move.

For thirty-three hours out of the past thirty-six March had been awake. Now the music bathed him, the vibrations lulled him. He slept.

He missed the safety demonstration. The take-off barely penetrated his dreams. Nor did he notice the person slip into the seat beside him.

Not until they were cruising at 10,000 metres and the pilot was informing them that they were passing over Leipzig did he open his eyes. The stewardess was leaning towards him, asking him if he wanted a drink. He started to say 'A whisky', but was too distracted to finish his reply. Sitting next to him, pretending to read a magazine, was Charlotte Maguire.

THE Rhine slid beneath them, a wide curve of molten metal in the dying sun. March had never see it from the air. 'Dear Fatherland, no danger thine:/Firm stands thy watch along the Rhine.' Lines from his childhood, hammered out on an untuned piano in a draughty gymnasium. Who had written them? He could not remember.

Crossing the river was a signal that they had passed out of the Reich and into Switzerland. In the distance: mountains, grey-blue and misty; below: neat rectangular fields and dark clumps of pine forests; steep red roofs and little white churches.

When he woke she had laughed at the surprise on his face. You may be used to dealing with hardened criminals, she had said, and with the Gestapo and the SS. But you've never come up against the good old American press.

He had sworn, to which she had responded with a wide-eyed look, mock-innocent, like one of Max Jaeger's daughters. An act, deliberately done badly, which made it naturally an even better act, turning his anger against him, making him part of the play.

She had then insisted on explaining everything, whether he wanted to listen or not, gesturing with a plastic tumbler of whisky. It had been easy, she said. He had told her he was flying to Zürich that night. There was only one flight. At the airport she had informed the Lufthansa desk that she was supposed to be with Sturmbannführer March. She was late: could she please have the seat next to him? When they agreed, she knew he must be on board.

'And there you were, asleep,' she concluded, 'like a babe.'

'And if they had said they had no passenger called March?'

'I would have come anyway.' She was impatient with his anger. 'Listen, I already have most of the story. An art fraud. Two senior officials dead. A third on the run. An attempted defection. A secret Swiss bank account. At worst, alone, I'd have picked up some extra colour in Zürich. At best I might have charmed Herr Zaugg into giving me an interview.'

'I don't doubt it.'

'Don't look so worried, Sturmbannführer – I'll keep your name out of it.'

Zürich is only twenty kilometres south of the Rhine. They were descending quickly. March finished his Scotch and set the empty container on the stewardess's outstretched tray.

Charlotte Maguire drained her own glass in one and placed it next to his. 'We have whisky in common, Herr March, at least.' She smiled.

He turned to the window. This was her skill, he thought:

to make him look stupid, a Teutonic flat-foot. First, she had failed to tell him about Stuckart's telephone call. Then she had manoeuvred him into letting her join in his search of Stuckart's apartment. This morning, instead of waiting for him to contact her, she had talked to the American diplomat, Nightingale, about Swiss banks. Now this. It was like having a child forever at your heels – a persistent, intelligent, embarrassing, deceitful, dangerous child. Surreptitiously he felt his pockets again, to check he still had the letter and key. She was not beyond stealing them while he was asleep.

The Junkers was coming in to land. Like a film gradually speeding up, the Swiss countryside began rushing past: a tractor in a field, a road with a few headlights in the smoky dusk, and then – one bounce, two – they were touching down.

Zürich airport was not how he had imagined it. Beyond the aircraft and hangars were wooded hillsides, with no evidence of a city. For a moment, he wondered if Globus had discovered his mission and had arranged for the plane to be diverted. Perhaps they had been set down in some remote airbase in southern Germany? But then he saw ZÜRICH on the terminal building.

The instant the plane had taxied to a halt, the passengers – professional commuters, most of them – rose as one. She was on her feet, too, pulling down her case and that ridiculous blue coat. He reached past her.

'Excuse me.'

She shrugged on the coat. 'Where now?'

'I am going to my hotel, Fräulein. What you do is your concern.'

He managed to squeeze in front of a fat Swiss who was cramming documents into a leather attaché case. The manoeuvre left her trapped some way behind him. He did not look back as they shuffled down the aisle and off the aircraft.

He walked briskly through the arrivals hall to passport control, overtaking most of the other passengers to station himself near the head of the queue. Behind him, he heard a commotion as she tried to catch up.

The Swiss border official, a serious young man with a drooping moustache, leafed through his passport.

'Business or pleasure, Herr March?'

'Business.' Definitely business.

'One moment.'

The young man picked up the telephone, dialled three digits, turned away from March and whispered something into the receiver. He said: 'Yes. Yes. Of course.' Then he hung up and returned the passport to March.

THERE were two of them waiting for him by the baggage carousel. He spotted them from fifty metres away: bulky figures with close-cropped hair, wearing stout black shoes and belted fawn raincoats. Policemen – they were the same the world over. He walked past them without a glance and sensed rather than saw them falling in behind him.

He went unchallenged through the green customs channel and out into the main concourse. Taxis. Where were taxis?

Clip-clop, clip-clop. Coming up behind him.

The air outside was several degrees colder than in Berlin. *Clip-clop, clip-clop.* He wheeled round. There she was, in her coat, clutching her case, balanced on her high heels.

'Go away, Fräulein. Do you understand me? Do you need it in writing? Go back to America and publish your stupid story. I have business to attend to.'

Without waiting for her reply, he opened the rear door of the waiting taxi, threw in his case, climbed in after it. 'Baur au Lac,' he said to the driver.

They pulled out of the airport and on to the highway,

heading south towards the city. The day had almost gone. Craning his neck to look out of the back window, March could see a taxi tucked in ten metres behind them, with an unmarked white Mercedes following it. Christ, what a comedy this was turning into. Globus was chasing Luther, he was chasing Globus, Charlie Maguire was chasing him, and now the Swiss police were on the tails of both of them. He lit a cigarette.

'Can't you read?' said the driver. He pointed to a sign: THANK YOU FOR NOT SMOKING.

'Welcome to Switzerland,' muttered March. He wound down the window a few centimetres, and the cloud of blue smoke was plucked into the chilly air.

Zürich was more beautiful than he had expected. Its centre reminded him of Hamburg. Old buildings clustered around the edge of the wide lake. Trams in a livery of green and white rattled along the front, past well-lit shops and cafés. The driver was listening to the Voice of America. In Berlin it was a blur of static; here, it was clear. 'I wanna hold your hand,' sang a youthful English voice. 'I wanna hold your ha-a-and!' A thousand teenage girls screamed.

The Baur au Lac was a street's-width from the lake. March paid the taxi driver in Reichsmarks – every country on the continent accepted Reichsmarks, it was Europe's common currency – and went inside. It was as luxurious as Nebe had promised. His room cost him half a month's salary. 'A *fine place for a condemned man to spend a night*. . .' As he signed the register he glimpsed a flash of blue at the door, swiftly followed by the fawn raincoats. I am like a movie star, thought March, as he caught the elevator. Everywhere I go, I have two detectives and a brunette in tow.

HE spread a map of the city on the bed and sat down beside

it, sinking into the spongy mattress. He had so little time. The broad expanse of the Zürich See thrust up into the complex of streets, like a blue blade. According to his Kripo file, Hermann Zaugg had a place on See Strasse. March found it. See Strasse ran alongside the eastern shore of the lake, about four kilometres south of the hotel.

Someone tapped softly on the door. A man's voice called his name.

Now what? He strode across the room, flung open the door. A waiter was in the corridor, holding a tray. He looked startled.

'Sorry, sir. With the compliments of the lady in room 277, sir.'

'Yes. Of course.' March stood aside to let him through. The waiter came in hesitantly, as if he thought March might hit him. He set down the tray, lingered fractionally for a tip and then, when none was forthcoming, left. March locked the door behind him.

On the table was a bottle of Glenfiddich, with a one-word note. 'Détente?'

HE stood at the window, his tie loosened, sipping the malt whisky, looking out across the Zürich See. Traceries of yellow lanterns were strung around the black water; on the surface, pinpricks of red, green and white bobbed and winked. He lit yet another cigarette, his millionth of the week.

People were laughing in the drive beneath his window. A light moved across the lake. No Great Hall, no marching bands, no uniforms. For the first time in – what was it? – a year, at least – he was away from the iron and granite of Berlin. So. He held up his glass and studied the pale liquid. There *were* other lives, other cities.

He noticed, along with the bottle, that she had ordered two glasses.

He sat down on the edge of the bed and looked at the telephone. He drummed his fingers on the little table.

Madness.

She had a habit of thrusting her hands deep into her pockets and standing with her head on one side, half-smiling. On the plane, he remembered, she had been wearing a red wool dress with a leather belt. She had good legs, in black stockings. And when she was angry or amused, which was most of the time, she would flick at the hair behind her ear.

The laughter outside drifted away.

'*Where have you been the past twenty years?*' Her contemptuous question to him in Stuckart's apartment.

She knew so much. She danced around him.

'*The millions of Jews who vanished in the war . . .*'

He turned her note over in his fingers, poured himself another drink and lay back on the bed. Ten minutes later he lifted the receiver and spoke to the operator.

'Room 277.'

Madness, *madness*.

THEY met in the lobby, beneath the fronds of a luxuriant palm. In the opposite corner a string quartet scraped its way through a selection from *Die Fledermaus*.

March said: 'The Scotch is very good.'

'A peace offering.'

'Accepted. Thank you.' He glanced across at the elderly cellist. Her stout legs were held wide apart, as if she were milking a cow. 'God knows why I should trust you.'

'God knows why I should trust *you*.'

'Ground rules,' he said firmly. 'One: no more lies. Two: we do what I say, whether you want to or not. Three: you show me what you plan to print, and if I ask you not to write something, you take it out. Agreed?'

'It's a deal.' She smiled and offered him her hand. He took it. She had a cool, firm grip. For the first time he noticed she had a man's watch around her wrist.

'What changed your mind?' she asked.

He released her hand. 'Are you ready to go out?' She was still wearing the red dress.

'Yes.'

'Do you have a notebook?'

She tapped her coat pocket. 'Never travel without one.'

'Nor do I. Good. Let's go.'

SWITZERLAND was a cluster of lights in a great darkness, enemies all around it: Italy to the south, France to the west, Germany north and east. Its survival was a source of wonder: 'the Swiss miracle', they called it.

Luxembourg had become Moselland, Alsace-Lorraine was Westmark; Austria was Ostmark. As for Czechoslovakia – that bastard child of Versailles had dwindled to the Protectorate of Bohemia and Moravia. Poland, Latvia, Lithuania, Estonia – vanished from the map. In the East, the German Empire was carved four ways into the Reichskommissariats Ostland, Ukraine, Caucasus, Muscovy.

In the West, twelve nations – Portugal, Spain, France, Ireland, Great Britain, Belgium, Holland, Italy, Denmark, Norway, Sweden and Finland – had been corralled by Germany, under the Treaty of Rome, into a European trading bloc. German was the official second language in all schools. People drove German cars, listened to German radios, watched German televisions, worked in German-owned factories, moaned about the behaviour of German tourists in German-dominated holiday resorts, while

German teams won every international sporting competition except cricket, which only the English played.

In all this, Switzerland alone was neutral. That had not been the Führer's intention. But by the time the Wehrmacht's planners had designed a strategy to subdue the Swiss state the stalemate of the Cold War had begun. It remained a patch of no man's land, increasingly useful to both sides as the years went by, a place to meet and deal in secret.

'There are only three classes of citizen in Switzerland,' the Kripo's expert had told March. 'American spies, German spies, and Swiss bankers trying to get hold of their money.'

Over the past century those bankers had settled around the northern rim of the Zürich See like a rich crust; a tidemark of money. As on Schwanenwerder, their villas presented to the world a blank face of high walls and stout gates, backed by dense screens of trees.

March leaned forward and spoke to the driver. 'Slow down here.'

They were quite a cavalcade by now: March and Charlie in a taxi, followed by two cars, each occupied by a Swiss policeman. Bellerive Strasse turned into See Strasse. March counted off the numbers.

'Pull over here.'

The taxi swerved up on to the kerb. The police cars overtook them; a hundred metres down the road, their brake lights glowed.

Charlie looked around. 'Now what?'

'Now we take a look at the home of Doctor Hermann Zaugg.'

March paid the taxi driver, who promptly turned and set off back towards the city centre. The road was quiet.

All the villas were well-protected, but Zaugg's – the third they came to – was a fortress. The gates were solid metal, three metres high, flanked on either side by a stone wall. A security camera scanned the entrance. March took Charlie's arm and they strolled past, like lovers taking the air. They crossed the road and waited in a driveway on the other side. March looked at his watch. It was just after nine o'clock. Five minutes passed. He was about to suggest they leave when, with a clank and a hum of machinery, the gates began to swing open.

Charlie whispered: 'Someone's coming out.'

'No.' He nodded up the road. 'Coming in.'

The limousine was big and powerful: a British car, a Bentley, finished in black. It came from the direction of the city, travelling rapidly, swerved, and swung into the drive. A chauffeur and another man in the front; in the back, a flash of silver hair – Zaugg's, presumably. March just had time to notice how low the bodywork hung to the ground. Then, one after another, the tyres were absorbing the impact as the Bentley bounced over the kerb – *whump*, *whump, whump, whump* – and it was gone.

The gates started to close, then stopped halfway. Two men appeared from the direction of the house, walking fast.

'You!' one of them shouted. 'Both of you! Stay where you are!' He strode into the road. March seized Charlie by the elbow. At that instant, one of the police cars began reversing towards them, gearbox howling. The man glanced to his right, hesitated, and retreated.

The car skidded to a halt. The window was wound down. A weary voice said: 'For fuck's sake, get in.'

March opened the back door and ushered in Charlie, then slipped in after her. The Swiss policeman executed a rapid three-point turn, and accelerated away towards the city. Zaugg's bodyguards had already disappeared; the gates were banging shut behind them.

March twisted round to stare out of the rear window. 'Are all your bankers as well-protected as that?'

'Depends who they do business with.' The policeman adjusted his mirror to look at them. He was in his late forties, with bloodshot eyes. 'Are you planning any further adventures, Herr March? A brawl somewhere, perhaps? It would help if we had a little warning next time.'

'I thought you were supposed to be following us, not guarding us.'

' "Follow and protect as necessary": those are our orders. That's my partner in the car behind, by the way. It's been a fucking long day. Excuse my language, Fräulein – they never said there'd be a woman involved.'

'Can you drop us back at the hotel?' asked March.

The policeman grumbled. 'So now I am to add chauffeur to my list of duties?' He switched on his radio and spoke to his partner. 'Panic over. We're going back to the Baur au Lac.'

Charlie had her notebook open on her lap and was writing. 'Who are these people?'

March hesitated but then thought: what does it matter? 'This officer and his partner are members of the Swiss Polizei, here to ensure I don't attempt to defect while outside the borders of the Reich. And also to ensure I return in one piece.'

'Always a pleasure, assisting our German colleagues,' grunted a voice from the front.

Charlie said: 'There's a danger you might not?'

'Apparently.'

'Jesus.' She wrote something down. He looked away. Off to their left, a couple of kilometres across the See, the lights of Zürich formed a yellow ribbon on the dark water. His breath misted the window.

Zaugg must have been returning from his office. It was late, but the burghers of Zürich worked hard for their money – twelve or fourteen hours a day was common. The banker's house could only be reached by travelling this road, which ruled out the most effective security precaution: varying his route each night. And See Strasse, bounded on one side by the lake, and with several dozen streets leading off the other, was a security man's nightmare. That explained something.

'Did you notice his car?' he said to Charlie. 'How heavy it was, the noise its tyres made? You see those often in Berlin. That Bentley was armour-plated.' He ran his hand through his hair. 'Two bodyguards, a pair of prison gates, remote cameras and a bomb-proof car. What kind of banker is that?'

He could not see her face properly in the shadows, but he could feel her excitement beside him. She said: 'We've got the letter of authorisation, remember? Whatever kind of banker he is – he's *our* banker now.'

They ate at a restaurant in the old town – a place with thick linen napkins and heavy silver cutlery, where the waiters lined up behind them and whipped the covers from their plates like a troupe of conjurers performing a trick. If the hotel had cost him half a month's salary, this meal would cost him the other half, but March didn't care.

She was unlike any other woman he had met. She was not one of the homebodies of the Party's Women's League, all 'Kinder, Kirche und Kuche' – her husband's supper always ready on the table, his uniform freshly pressed, five children asleep upstairs. And while a good National Socialist girl abhorred cosmetics, nicotine and alcohol, Charlie Maguire made liberal use of all three. Her dark eyes soft in the candlelight, she talked almost without pause of New York, foreign reporting, her father's days in Berlin, the wickedness of Joseph Kennedy, politics, money, men, herself.

She had been born in Washington DC in the spring of 1939. ('The last spring of peace, my parents called it – in all senses.') Her father had recently returned from Berlin to work at the State Department. Her mother was trying to make a success as an actress, but after 1941 was lucky simply to escape internment. In the 1950s, after the war, Michael Maguire had gone to Omsk, capital of what was left of Russia, to serve in the US Embassy. It was considered too dangerous a place to take four children. *Charlotte* had been left behind to be educated at expensive schools in Virginia; *Charlie* had dropped out at seventeen – spitting and swearing and rebelling against everything in sight.

'I went to New York. Tried to be an actress. That didn't work. Tried to be a journalist. That suited me better. Enrolled at Columbia – to my father's great relief. And then – what do you know? – I start an affair with Teacher.' She shook her head. 'How stupid can you get?' She blew out a jet of cigarette smoke. 'Is there any more wine in there?'

He poured out the last of the bottle, ordered another. It seemed to be his turn to say something. 'Why Berlin?'

'A chance to get away from New York. My mother being German made it easier to get a visa. I have to admit: World European Features is not quite as grand as it sounds. Two men in an office on the wrong side of town with a telex machine. To be honest, they were happy to take anyone who could get a visa out of Berlin. Even me.' She looked at him with shining eyes. 'I didn't know he was married, you see. The teacher.' She snapped her fingers. 'Basic failure of research there, wouldn't you say?'

'When did it end?'

'Last year. I came to Europe to show them all I could do it. Him especially. That's why I felt so sick about being expelled. God, the thought of facing them all again . . .' She sipped her wine. 'Perhaps I've got a father-fixation. How old are you?'

'Forty-two.'

'Bang in my age range.' She smiled at him over the rim of her glass. 'You'd better watch out. Are you married?'

'Divorced.'

'Divorced! That's promising. Tell me about her.'

Her frankness kept catching him off-guard. 'She was,' he began, and corrected himself. 'She is . . .' He stopped. How did you summarise someone you were married to for nine years, divorced from for seven, who had just denounced you to the authorities? 'She is not like you,' was all he could think to say.

'Meaning?'

'She does not have ideas of her own. She is concerned about what people think. She has no curiosity. She is bitter.'

'About you?'

'Naturally.'

'Is she seeing anyone else?'

'Yes. A Party bureaucrat. Much more suitable than me.'

'And you? Do you have anyone?'

A klaxon sounded in March's mind. *Dive, dive, dive.* He had had two affairs since his divorce. A teacher who had lived in the apartment beneath his, and a young widow who taught history at the university – another friend of Rudi Halder's: he sometimes suspected Rudi had made it his mission in life to find him a new wife. The liaisons had drifted on for a few months, until both women had tired of the last-minute calls from Werderscher Markt: 'Something's come up, I'm sorry . . .'

Instead of answering her, March said: 'So many questions. You should have been a detective.'

She made a face at him. 'So few answers. *You* should have been a reporter.'

THE waiter poured more wine. After he had moved away, she said: 'You know, when I met you, I hated you on sight.'

'Ah. The uniform. It blots out the man.'

'That uniform does. When I looked for you on the plane this afternoon I barely recognised you.'

It occurred to March that here was another reason for his good mood: he had not caught a glimpse of his black silhouette in a mirror, had not seen people shrinking away at his approach.

'Tell me,' he said, 'what do they say of the SS in America?'

She rolled her eyes. 'Oh come on, March. Please. Don't let's ruin a good evening.'

'I mean it. I'd like to know.' He had to coax her into answering.

'Well, murderers,' she said eventually. 'Sadists. Evil personified. All that. You asked for it. Nothing personal intended, you understand? Any other questions?'

'A million. A lifetime's worth.'

'A lifetime! Well go ahead. I have nothing planned.'

He was momentarily dumbfounded, paralysed by choice. Where to start?

'The war in the East,' he said. 'In Berlin we hear only of victories. Yet the Wehrmacht has to ship the coffins home from the Urals front at night, on special trains, so nobody sees how many dead there are.'

'I read somewhere that the Pentagon estimates a hundred thousand Germans killed since 1960. The Luftwaffe is bombing the Russian towns flat day after day and still they keep coming back at you. You can't win because they've nowhere else to go. And you daren't use nuclear weapons in case we retaliate and the world blows up.'

'What else?' He tried to think of recent headlines. 'Goebbels says German space technology beats the Americans every time.'

'Actually, I think that's true. Peenemünde had satellites in orbit years ahead of ours.'

'Is Winston Churchill still alive?'

'Yes. He's an old man now. In Canada. He lives there. So does the Queen.' She noticed his puzzlement. 'Elizabeth claims the English throne from her uncle.'

'And the Jews?' said March. 'What do the Americans say we did to them?'

She was shaking her head. 'Why are you doing this?'

'Please. The truth.'

'The truth? How do I know what the truth is?' Suddenly she had raised her voice, was almost shouting. People at the next table were turning round. 'We're brought up to think of Germans as something from outer space. Truth doesn't enter into it.'

'Very well then. Give me the propaganda.'

She glanced away, exasperated, but then looked back with an intensity that made it difficult for him to meet her eyes. 'All right. They say you scoured Europe for every living Jew – men, women, children, babies. They say you shipped them to ghettos in the East where thousands died of malnutrition and disease. Then you forced the survivors farther East, and nobody knows what happened after that. A handful escaped over the Urals into Russia. I've seen them on TV. Funny old men, most of them; a bit crazy. They talk about execution pits, medical experiments, camps that people went into but never came out of. They talk about millions of dead. But then the German ambassador comes along in his smart suit and tells everyone it's all just communist propaganda. So nobody knows what's true and what isn't. And I'll tell you something else – most people don't care.' She sat back in her chair. 'Satisfied?'

'I'm sorry.'

'So am I.' She reached for her cigarettes, then stopped and looked at him again. 'That's why you changed your mind at the hotel about bringing me along, isn't it? Nothing to do with whisky. You wanted to pick my brains.' She started to laugh. 'And I thought *I* was using *you*.'

AFTER that, they got on better. Whatever poison there was between them had been drawn. He told her about his father and how he had followed him into the Navy, about how he had drifted into police work and found a taste for it – a vocation, even.

She said: 'I still don't understand how you can wear it.'

'What?'

'That uniform.'

He poured himself another glass of wine. 'Oh, there's a simple answer to that. In 1936, the Kriminalpolizei was merged into the SS; all officers had to accept honorary SS rank. So I have a choice: either I am an investigator in that uniform, and try to do a little good; or I am something else without that uniform, and do no good at all.'

And the way things are going, I shall soon not have that choice, he thought.

She tilted her head to one side and nodded. 'I can see that. That seems fair.'

He felt impatient, sick of himself. 'No it's not. It's bullshit, Charlie.' It was the first time he had called her that since she had insisted on it at the beginning of the dinner; using it sounded like a declaration. He hurried on: 'That's the answer I've given everybody, including myself, for the past ten years. Unfortunately, even I have stopped believing it.'

'But what happened – the worst of what happened – was during the war, and you weren't around. You told me: you were at sea.'

He looked down at his plate, silent. She went on: 'And anyway, wartime is different. All countries do wicked things in wartime. My country dropped an atom bomb on Japanese civilians – killed a quarter of a million people in an instant. And the Americans have been allies of the Russians for the past twenty years. Remember what the Russians did?'

There was truth in what she said. One by one, as they advanced eastwards, beginning with the bodies of 10,000 Polish officers in the Katyn forest, the Germans had discovered the mass graves of Stalin's victims. Millions had died in the famines, purges, deportations of the 1930s. Nobody knew the exact figure. The execution pits, the torture chambers, the gulags inside the Arctic Circle – all were now preserved by the Germans as memorials to the dead, museums of Bolshevik evil. Children were taken round them; ex-prisoners acted as guides. There was a whole school of historical studies devoted to investigating the crimes of communism. Television showed documentaries on Stalin's holocaust – bleached skulls and walking skeletons, bulldozed corpses and the earth-caked rags of women and children bound with wire and shot in the back of the neck.

She put her hand on his. 'The world is as it is. Even I see that.'

He spoke without looking at her. 'Yes. Fine. But everything you've said, I've already heard. "It was a long time ago." "That was war." "The Ivans were worst of all." "What can one man do?" I've listened to people whisper that for ten years. That's all they ever do, by the way. Whisper.'

She withdrew her hand and lit another cigarette, turning the little gold lighter over and over in her fingers. 'When I first came to Berlin, and my parents gave me that list of people they knew in the old days, there were lots of theatre people on it, artists – friends of my mother. I suppose quite of few them, in the way of things, must have been Jews, or homosexuals. And I went looking for them. All of them had gone, of course. That didn't surprise me. But they hadn't just vanished. *It was as if they'd never existed.*'

She tapped the lighter gently against the tablecloth. He noticed her fingers – slim, unmanicured, unadorned.

'Of course, there were people living in the places my mother's friends used to live in. Old people, often. They must have known, mustn't they? But they just looked blank. They were watching television, having tea, listening to music. There was nothing left *at all.*'

March said: 'Look at this.'

He pulled out his wallet, took out the photograph. It looked incongruous amid the plushness of the restaurant – a relic from someone's attic, rubbish from a flea market stall.

He gave it to her. She studied it. A strand of hair fell over her face and she brushed it away. 'Who are they?'

'When I moved into my apartment after Klara and I split, it hadn't been decorated for years. I found that tucked behind the wallpaper in the bedroom. I tell you, I took that place to pieces, but that was all there was. Their surname was Weiss. But who are they? Where are they now? What happened to them?'

He took the photograph, folded it into quarters, put it back in his wallet.

'What do you do,' he said, 'if you devote your life to discovering criminals, and it gradually occurs to you that the real criminals are the people you work for? What do you do when everyone tells you not to worry, you can't do anything about it, it was a long time ago?'

She was looking at him in a different way. 'I suppose you go crazy.'

'Or worse. Sane.'

SHE insisted, despite his protests, on paying half the bill. It was almost midnight by the time they left the restaurant. They walked in silence towards the hotel. Stars arched across the sky; at the bottom of the steep cobbled street, the lake waited.

She took his arm. 'You asked me if that man at the Embassy –Nightingale – if he was my lover.'

'That was rude of me. I'm sorry.'

'Would you have been disappointed if I'd said he was?'

He hesitated.

She went on: 'Well he isn't. He'd like to be. Sorry. That sounds like boasting.'

'It doesn't at all. I'm sure many would like to be.'

'I hadn't met anyone . . .'

Hadn't . . .

She stopped. 'I'm twenty-five. I go where I like. I do what I like. I choose whom I like.' She turned to him, touched him lightly on the cheek with a warm hand. 'God, I hate getting this sort of thing out of the way, don't you?'

She drew his head to hers.

*

How odd it is, thought March afterwards, *to live your life in ignorance of the past, of your world, yourself. Yet how easy to do it! You went along from day to day, down paths other people had prepared for you, never raising your head – enfolded in their logic, from swaddling clothes to shroud. It was a kind of fear.*

Well, goodbye to that. And good to leave it behind – whatever happened now.

His feet danced on the cobblestones. He slipped his arm around her. He had so many questions.

'Wait, wait,' she was laughing, holding on to him. 'Enough. Stop. I'm starting to worry you only want me for my *mind*.'

IN his hotel room, she unknotted his tie and reined him to her once more, her mouth soft on his. Still kissing him, she smoothed the jacket from his shoulders, unbuttoned his shirt, parted it. Her hands skimmed over his chest, around his back, across his stomach.

She knelt and tugged at his belt.

He closed his eyes and coiled his fingers in her hair.

After a few moments he pulled away gently, and knelt to face her, lifted her dress. Freed from it, she threw back her head and shook her hair. He wanted to know her completely. He kissed her throat, her breasts, her stomach; inhaled her scent, felt the firm flesh stretching smooth and taut beneath his hands, her soft skin on his tongue.

Later she guided him on to the bed and settled herself above him. The only light was cast by the lake. Rippling shadows all around them. When he opened his mouth to say something, she put a finger to his lips.

FRIDAY 17 APRIL

The Gestapo, the Kriminalpolizei and the security services are enveloped in the mysterious aura of the political detective story.

REINHARD HEYDRICH

ONE

The Berlin Börse had opened for trading thirty minutes earlier. In the window display of the Union des Banques Suisses on Zürich's Bahnhof Strasse, the numbers clicked like knitting needles. Bayer, Siemens, Thyssen, Daimler –up, up, up, up. The only stock falling on news of détente was Krupp.

A smart and well-dressed crowd had gathered anxiously, as they did every morning, to watch this monitor of the Reich's economic health. Prices on the Börse had been falling for six months and a mood close to panic had seized investors. But this week, thanks to old Joe Kennedy – he always knew a thing or two about markets, old Joe: made half a billion dollars on Wall Street in his day – yes, thanks to Joe, the slide had stopped. Berlin was happy. Everyone was happy. Nobody paid attention to the couple walking up the street from the lake, not holding hands but close enough for their bodies to touch occasionally, followed by a weary-looking pair of gentlemen in fawn raincoats.

March had been given a short briefing on the customs and practices of Swiss banking the afternoon he left Berlin.

'Bahnhof Strasse is the financial centre. It looks like the main shopping street, which it is. But it's the courtyards behind the shops and the offices above them that matter. That's where you'll find the banks. But you'll have to keep your eyes open. The Swiss say: the older the money, the harder to see it. In Zürich, the money's so old, it's invisible.'

Beneath the paving stones and tramlines of Bahnhof Strasse ran the catacomb of vaults in which three generations of Europe's rich had buried their wealth. March looked at the shoppers and tourists pouring along the street and wondered upon what ancient dreams and secrets, upon what bones they were treading.

These banks were small, family-run concerns: a dozen or two employees, a suite of offices, a small brass plate. Zaugg & Cie was typical. The entrance was in a side-street, behind a jewellers, scanned by a remote camera identical to the one outside Zaugg's villa. As March rang the bell beside the discreet door he felt Charlie brush his hand.

A woman's voice over the intercom demanded his name and business. He looked up at the camera.

'My name is March. This is Fräulein Maguire. We wish to see Herr Zaugg.'

'Do you have an appointment?'

'No.'

'The Herr Direktor sees no one without an appointment.'

'Tell him we have a letter of authorisation for account number 2402.'

'One moment, please.'

The policemen were lounging at the entrance to the side-street. March glanced at Charlie. It seemed to him her eyes were brighter, her skin more lustrous. He supposed he flattered himself. Everything looked heightened today – the trees greener, the blossom whiter, the sky bluer, as if washed with gloss.

She was carrying a leather shoulder bag, from which she now produced a camera, a Leica. 'I think a shot for the family album.'

'As you like. But leave me out of it.'

'Such modesty.'

She took a photograph of Zaugg's door and nameplate. The receptionist's voice snapped over the intercom. 'Please come to the second floor.' There was a buzz of bolts being released, and March pushed at the heavy door.

The building was an optical illusion. Small and

nondescript from the outside, inside a staircase of glass and tubular chrome led to a wide reception area, decorated with modern art. Hermann Zaugg was waiting to meet them. Behind him stood one of the bodyguards from last night.

'Herr March, is it?' Zaugg extended his hand. 'And Fräulein Maguire?' He shook her hand, too, and gave a slight bow. 'English?'

'American.'

'Ah. Good. Always a pleasure to meet our American friends.' He was like a little doll: silver hair, shiny pink face, tiny hands and feet. He wore a suit of immaculate black, a white shirt, a pearl-grey tie. 'I understand you have the necessary authorisation?'

March produced the letter. Zaugg held the paper swiftly to the light and studied the signature. 'Yes indeed. The hand of my youth. I fear my script has deteriorated since those years. Come.'

In his office, he directed them to a low sofa of white leather. He sat behind his desk. Now the advantage of height lay with him: the oldest trick.

March had decided to be frank. 'We passed your home last night. Your privacy is well protected.'

Zaugg had his hands folded on his desk. He made a non-committal gesture with his tiny thumbs, as if to say: *You know how it is.* 'I gather from my associates that you had protection of your own. Do I take it this visit is official, or private?'

'Both. That is to say, neither.'

'I am familiar with the situation. Next you will tell me it is "a delicate matter".'

'It is a delicate matter.'

'My speciality.' He adjusted his cuffs. 'Sometimes, it seems to me that the whole history of twentieth-century Europe has flowed through this office. In the 1930s, it was Jewish refugees who sat where you now sit – often pathetic creatures, clutching whatever they had managed to salvage. They were usually followed closely by gentlemen from the Gestapo. In the 1940s, it was German officials of – how shall we say? – recently-acquired wealth. Sometimes the very men who had once come to close the accounts of others now returned to open new ones on their own behalf. In the 1950s, we dealt with the descendants of those who had vanished during the 1940s. Now, in the 1960s, I anticipate an increase in American custom, as your two great countries come together once more. The 1970s I shall leave to my son.'

'This letter of authorisation,' said March, 'how much access does it give us?'

'You have the key?'

March nodded.

'Then you have total access.'

'We would like to begin with the account records.'

'Very well.' Zaugg studied the letter, then picked up his telephone. 'Fräulein Graf, bring in the file for 2402.'

She appeared a minute later, a middle-aged woman carrying a thin sheaf of papers in a manila binding. Zaugg took it. 'What do you wish to know?'

'When was the account opened?'

He looked through the papers. 'July 1942. The eighth day of that month.'

'And who opened it?'

Zaugg hesitated. He was like a miser with his store of precious information: parting with each fact was agony. But under the terms of his own rules he had no choice.

He said at last: 'Herr Martin Luther.'

March was making notes. 'And what were the arrangements for the account?'

'One box. Four keys.'

'*Four* keys?' March's eyebrows rose in surprise. That was Luther himself, and Buhler and Stuckart, presumably. But who held the fourth key? 'How were they distributed?'

'They were all issued to Herr Luther, along with four letters of authorisation. Naturally, what he chose to do with them is not our concern. You appreciate that this was a special form of account – an emergency, wartime account – designed to protect anonymity, and also to allow ease of access for any heirs or beneficiaries, should anything happen to the original account-holder.'

'How did he pay for the account.'

'In cash. Swiss francs. Thirty years' rental. In advance. Don't worry, Herr March – there is nothing to pay until 1972.'

Charlie said: 'Do you have a record of transactions relating to the account?'

Zaugg turned to her. 'Only the dates on which the box was opened.'

'What are they?'

'The eighth of July 1942. The seventeenth of December 1942. The ninth of August 1943. The thirteenth of April 1964.'

April the thirteenth! March barely suppressed a cry of triumph. His guess had been right. Luther *had* flown to Zürich at the start of the week. He scribbled the dates in his notebook. 'Only four times?' he asked.

'Correct.'

'And until last Monday, the box had not been opened for nearly twenty-one years?'

'That is what the dates indicate.' Zaugg closed the file with a flick of annoyance. 'I might add, there is nothing especially unusual about that. We have boxes here which have lain untouched for fifty years or more.'

'You set up the account originally?'

'I did.'

'Did Herr Luther say why he wanted to open it, or why he needed these particular arrangements?'

'Client privilege.'

'I'm sorry?'

'That is privileged information between client and banker.'

Charlie interrupted. 'But we are your clients.'

'No, Fräulein Maguire. You are beneficiaries of my client. An important distinction.'

'Did Herr Luther open the box personally on each occasion?' asked March.

'Client privilege.'

'Was it Luther who opened the box on Monday? What sort of mood was he in?'

'Client privilege, client privilege.' Zaugg held up his hands. 'We can go on all day, Herr March. Not only am I under no obligation to give you that information, it would be illegal under the Swiss Banking Code for me to do so. I have passed on all you are entitled to know. Is there anything else?'

'Yes.' March closed his notebook and looked at Charlie. 'We would like to inspect the box for ourselves.'

A SMALL elevator led down to the vault. There was just enough room for four passengers. March and Charlie, Zaugg and his bodyguard stood awkwardly pressed together. Close to, the banker reeked of eau de Cologne; his hair glistened beneath an oily pomade.

The vault was like a prison, or a mortuary: a white-tiled corridor which stretched ahead of them for thirty metres, with bars on either side. At the far end, next to the gate, a security guard sat at a desk. Zaugg pulled a heavy bunch of keys from his pocket, attached by a chain to his belt. He hummed as he searched for the right one.

The ceiling vibrated slightly as a tram passed overhead.

He let them into the cage. Steel walls gleamed in the neon light: banks of doors, each half a metre square. Zaugg moved in front of them, unlocked one at waist height and stood back. The security guard pulled out a long box, the size of a metal footlocker, and carried it over to a table.

Zaugg said: 'Your key fits the lock on that box. I shall wait outside.'

'There's no need.'

'Thank you, but I prefer to wait.'

Zaugg left the cage and stood outside, with his back to the bars. March looked at Charlie, and gave her the key.

'You do it.'

'I'm shaking . . .'

She inserted the key. It turned easily. The end of the box opened. She reached inside. There was a look of puzzlement on her face, then disappointment.

'It's empty, I think.' Her expression changed. 'No . . .'

She smiled and pulled out a flat cardboard box, about fifty centimetres square, five centimetres deep. The lid was sealed with red wax, with a typewritten label gummed on top: 'Property of the Reich Foreign Ministry Treaty Archive, Berlin.' And underneath, in Gothic lettering: 'Geheime Reichssache'. Top Secret State Document.

A *treaty?*

March broke the seal, using the key. He lifted the lid. The interior released a scent of mingled must and incense.

Another tram passed. Zaugg was still humming, jingling his keys.

Inside the cardboard box was an object wrapped in an oilcloth. March lifted it out and laid it flat on the desk. He drew back the cloth: a panel of wood, scratched and ancient; one of the corners was broken off. He turned it over.

Charlie was next to him. She murmured: 'It's beautiful.'

The edges of the panel were splintered, as if it had been wrenched from its setting. But the portrait itself was perfectly preserved. A young woman, exquisite, with pale brown eyes, was glancing to the right, a string of black beads looped twice around her neck. In her lap, in long, aristocratic fingers, she held a small animal with white fur. Not a dog, exactly; more like a weasel.

Charlie was right. It *was* beautiful. It seemed to suck in the light from the vault and radiate it back. The girl's pale skin glowed –luminous, like an angel's.

'What does it mean?' whispered Charlie.

'God knows.' March felt vaguely cheated. Was the deposit box no more than an extension of Buhler's treasure chamber? 'How much do you know about art?'

'Not much. But there is something familiar about it. May I?' She took it, held it at arm's length. 'It's Italian, I think. You see her costume – the way the neckline of her dress is cut square, the sleeves. I'd say Renaissance. Very old, and very genuine.'

'And very stolen. Put it back.'

'Do we have to?'

'Of course. Unless you can think of a good story for the Zollgrenzschutz at Berlin Airport.'

Another painting: that was all! Cursing under his breath, March ran the oilcloth through his hands, checked the cardboard container. He turned the safety deposit box on its end and shook it. Nothing. The empty metal mocked him. What had he hoped for? He did not know. But something to give him a better clue than this.

'We must leave,' he said.

'One minute.'

Charlie propped the panel up against the box. She crouched and took half-a-dozen photographs. Then she rewrapped the picture, replaced it in its container, and locked the box.

March called: 'We've finished here, Herr Zaugg. Thank you.'

Zaugg reappeared with the security guard – a fraction too

quickly, March thought. He guessed the banker had been straining to overhear them.

Zaugg rubbed his hands. 'All is to your satisfaction, I trust?'

'Perfectly.'

The guard slid the box back into the cavity, Zaugg locked the door, and the girl with the weasel was re-interred in darkness. *'We have boxes here which have lain untouched for fifty years or more . . .'* Was that how long it would be before she saw the light again?

They rode the elevator in silence. Zaugg shepherded them out at street-level. 'And so we say goodbye.' He shook hands with each of them in turn.

March felt he had to say something more, should try one final tactic. 'I feel I must warn you, Herr Zaugg, that two of the joint holders of this account have been murdered in the past week, and that Martin Luther himself has disappeared.'

Zaugg did not even blink. 'Dear me, dear me. Old clients pass away and new ones' – he gestured to them – 'take their place. And so the world turns. The only thing you can be sure of, Herr March, is that – whoever wins – still standing when the smoke of battle clears will be the banks of the cantons of Switzerland. Good day to you.'

They were out on the street and the door was closing when Charlie shouted: 'Herr Zaugg!'

His face appeared and before he could withdraw it, the camera clicked. His eyes were wide, his little mouth popped into a perfect O of outrage.

ZÜRICH'S lake was misty-blue, like a picture from a fairy-story – a landscape fit for sea-monsters and heroes to do battle in. If only the world had been as we were promised, thought March. Then castles with pointed turrets would have risen through that haze.

He was leaning against the damp stone balustrade outside the hotel, his suitcase at his feet, waiting for Charlie to settle her bill.

He wished he could have stayed longer – taken her out on the water, explored the city, the hills; had dinner in the old town; returned to his room each night, to make love, to the sound of the lake . . . A dream. Fifty metres to his left, sitting in their cars, his guardians from the Swiss Polizei yawned.

Many years ago, when March was a young detective in the Hamburg Kripo, he had been ordered to escort a prisoner serving a life-sentence for robbery, who had been given a special day-pass. The man's trial had been in the papers; his childhood sweetheart had seen the publicity and written to him; had visited him in gaol; agreed to marry him. The affair had touched that streak of sentimentality that runs so strong in the German psyche. There had been a public campaign to let the ceremony go ahead. The authorities had relented. So March took him to his wedding, stood handcuffed beside him throughout the service and even during the wedding pictures, like an unusually attentive best man.

The reception had been in a grim hall next to the church. Towards the end, the groom had whispered that there was a storeroom with a rug in it, that the priest had no objections . . . And March – young husband that he was – had checked the storeroom and seen there were no windows and had left the man and his wife alone for twenty minutes. The priest – who had worked as a chaplain in Hamburg's docks for thirty years, and seen most things – had given March a grave wink.

On the way back to prison, as the high walls came into view, March had expected the man to be depressed, to plead for extra time, maybe even dive for the door. Not at all. He had sat smiling, finishing his cigar. Standing by the

Zürich See, March realised how he had felt. It had been sufficient to know that the possibility of another life existed; one day of it had been enough.

He felt Charlie come up beside him. She kissed him lightly on the cheek.

A shop at Zürich airport was piled high with brightly coloured gifts – cuckoo clocks, toy skis, ashtrays glazed with pictures of the Matterhorn, and chocolates. March picked out one of the musical boxes with 'Birthday Greetings to Our Beloved Führer, 1964' written on the lid and took it to the counter where a plump middle-aged woman was waiting.

'Could you wrap this and send it for me?'

'No problem, sir. Write down where you want it to go.'

She gave him a form and a pencil and March wrote Hannelore Jaeger's name and address. Hannelore was even fatter than her husband, a lover of chocolates. He hoped Max would see the joke.

The assistant wrapped the box swiftly in brown paper, with skilled fingers.

'Do you sell many of these?'

'Hundreds. You Germans certainly love your Führer.'

'We do, it is true.' He was looking at the parcel. It was wrapped exactly like the one he had taken from Buhler's mailbox. 'You don't, I suppose, keep a record of the places to which you send these packages?'

'That would be impossible.' She addressed it, stuck on a stamp, and added it to the pile behind her.

'Of course. And you wouldn't remember serving an elderly German here, about four o'clock on Monday afternoon? He had thick glasses and runny eyes.'

Her face was suddenly hard with suspicion. 'What are you? A policeman?'

'It's of no importance.' He paid for the chocolates, and also for a mug with 'I LOVE ZÜRICH' printed on the side.

Luther would not have come all the way to Switzerland to *put* that painting in the bank vault, thought March. Even as a retired Foreign Ministry official, he could never have smuggled a package that size, stamped top secret, past the Zollgrenzschutz. He must have come here to *retrieve* something, to take it back to Germany. And as it was the first time he had visited the vault for twenty-one years, and as there were three other keys, and as he trusted nobody, he must have had doubts about whether *that other thing* would still be here.

He stood looking at the departure lounge and tried to imagine the elderly man hurrying into the terminal building, clutching his precious cargo, his weak heart beating sharply against his ribs. The chocolates must have been a message of success: so far, my old comrades, so good. What could he have been carrying? Not paintings or money, surely; they had plenty of both in Germany.

'*Paper.*'

'What?' Charlie, who had been waiting for him in the concourse, turned round in surprise.

'That must have been the link. Paper. They were all civil servants. They lived their lives by paper, on paper.'

He pictured them in wartime Berlin – sitting in their offices at night, circulating memos and minutes in a perpetual bureaucratic paper chase, building themselves a paper fortress. Millions of Germans had fought in the war: in the freezing mud of the Steppes, or in the Libyan desert, or in the clear skies over southern England, or – like March – at sea. But these old men had fought their war – had bled and expended their middle age – *on paper*.

Charlie was shaking her head. 'You're making no sense.'

'I know. To myself, perhaps. I bought you this.'

She unwrapped the mug and laughed, clasped it to her heart.

'I shall treasure it.'

THEY walked quickly through passport control. Beyond the barrier, March turned for a final look. The two Swiss policemen were watching from the ticket desk. One of them – the one who had rescued them outside Zaugg's villa – raised his hand. March waved in return.

Their flight number was being called for the last time: *'Passengers for Lufthansa flight 227 to Berlin must report immediately . . .'*

He let his arm fall back and turned towards the departure gate.

TWO

No whisky on this flight, but coffee – plenty of it, strong and black. Charlie tried to read a newspaper but fell asleep. March was too excited to rest.

He had torn a dozen blank pages from his notebook, had ripped them in half and half again. Now he had them spread out on the plastic table in front of him. On each he had written a name, a date, an incident. He reshuffled them endlessly – the front to the back, the back to the middle, the middle to the beginning – a cigarette dangling from his lips, smoke billowing, his head in the clouds. To the other passengers, a few of whom stole curious glances, he must have looked like a man playing a particularly demented form of patience.

JULY 1942. *On the Eastern Front, the Wehrmacht has launched Operation 'Blue': the offensive which will eventually win Germany the war. America is taking a hammering from the Japanese. The British are bombing the Ruhr, fighting in North Africa. In Prague, Reinhard Heydrich is recovering from an assassination attempt.*

So: good days for the Germans, especially those in the conquered territories. Elegant apartments, girlfriends, bribes – packing cases of plunder to send back home. Corruption from high to low; from corporal to Kommissar; from alcohol to altar-pieces. Buhler, Stuckart and Luther have an especially good racket in play. Buhler requisitions art treasures in the General Government, sends them under cover to Stuckart at the Interior Ministry – quite safe, for who would dare tamper with the mail of such powerful servants of the Reich? Luther smuggles the objects abroad to sell – safe again, for who would dare order the head of the Foreign Ministry's German Division to open his bags? All three retire in the 1950s, rich and honoured men.

And then, in 1964: catastrophe.

March shuffled his bits of paper, shuffled them again.

On Friday, 11 April, the three conspirators gather at Buhler's villa: the first piece of evidence which suggests a panic . . .

No. That was not right. He leafed back through his notes, to Charlie's account of her conversation with Stuckart. Of course.

On Thursday, 10 April, the day before the meeting, Stuckart stands in Bülow Strasse and notes the number of the telephone in the booth opposite Charlotte Maguire's apartment. Armed with that, he goes to Buhler's villa on Friday. Something so terrible threatens to overwhelm them that the three men contemplate the unthinkable: defection to the United States of America. Stuckart lays out the procedure. They cannot trust the Embassy, because Kennedy has stuffed it with appeasers. They need a direct link with Washington. Stuckart has it: Michael Maguire's daughter. It is agreed. On Saturday, Stuckart telephones the girl to arrange a meeting. On Sunday, Luther flies to Switzerland: not to fetch pictures or money, which they have in abundance in Berlin, but to collect something put there in the course of three visits, between the summer of 1942 and the spring of 1943.

But already it is too late. By the time Luther has made the withdrawal, sent the signal from Zürich, landed in Berlin, Buhler and Stuckart are dead. And so he decides to disappear, taking with him whatever he removed from the vault in Zürich.

March sat back and contemplated his half-finished puzzle. It was a version of events, as valid as any other.

Charlie sighed and stirred in her sleep, twisted to rest her head on his shoulder. He kissed her hair. Today was Friday. The Führertag was Monday. He had only the weekend left. 'Oh, my dear Fräulein Maguire,' he murmured. 'I fear we have been looking in the wrong place.'

'LADIES *and gentlemen, we shall shortly be beginning our descent to Flughafen Hermann Goering. Please return your seats to the upright position and fold away the tables in front of you . . .'*

Carefully, so as not to wake her, March withdrew his shoulder from beneath Charlie's head, gathered up his pieces of paper, and made his way, unsteadily, towards the back of the aircraft. A boy in the uniform of the Hitler Youth emerged from the lavatory and held the door open, politely. March nodded, went inside and locked it behind him. A dim light flickered.

The tiny compartment stank of stale air, endlessly recycled; of cheap soap; of faeces. He lifted the lid of the metal lavatory basin and dropped in the paper. The aircraft pitched and shook. A warning light pinged. ATTENTION! RETURN TO YOUR SEAT! The turbulence made his stomach lurch. Was this how Luther had felt, as the aircraft dropped towards Berlin? The metal was clammy to the touch. He pulled a lever and the lavatory flushed, his notes sucked from sight in a whirlpool of blue water.

Lufthansa had stocked the toilet not with towels but with moist little paper handkerchiefs, impregnated with some sickly liquid. March wiped his face. He could feel the heat of his skin through the slippery fabric. Another vibration, like a U-boat being depth-charged. They were falling fast. He pressed his burning forehead to the cool mirror. *Dive, dive, dive . . .*

*

SHE was awake, dragging a comb through her thick hair. 'I was beginning to think you had jumped.'

'It's true, the thought did enter my mind.' He fastened his seatbelt. 'But you may be my salvation.'

'You say the nicest things.'

'I said "may be".' He took her hand. 'Listen. Are you sure Stuckart told you he came on *Thursday* to check out that telephone opposite your apartment?'

She thought for a moment. 'Yes, I'm sure. I remember it made me realise: this man is serious, he's done his homework.'

'That's what I think. The question is, was Stuckart acting on his own – trying to set up his own private escape route – or was ringing you a course of action he had discussed with the others?'

'Does it matter?'

'Very much. Think about it. If he agreed it with the others on Friday, it means Luther may know who you are, and know the procedure for contacting you.'

She pulled her hand back in surprise. 'But that's crazy. He'd never trust me.'

'You're right, it's crazy.' They had dropped through one layer of cloud; beneath them was another. March could see the tip of the Great Hall poking through it, like the top of a helmet. 'But suppose Luther is still alive down there, what are his options? The airport is being watched. So are the docks, the railway stations, the border. He can't risk going direct to the American Embassy, not after what's happened about Kennedy's visit. He can't go home. What can he do?'

'I don't believe it. He could have called me Tuesday or Wednesday. Or Thursday morning. Why would he wait?'

But he could hear the doubt in her voice. He thought: You don't *want* to believe it. You thought you were clever, looking for your story in Zürich, but all the time your story might actually have been looking for you, in Berlin.

She had turned away from him, to stare through the window.

March felt suddenly deflated. In truth, he hardly knew her, despite everything. He said: 'The reason he would have waited is to try and find something better to do, something safer. Who knows? Maybe he's found it.'

She did not answer.

THEY landed in Berlin, in a thin drizzle, just before two o'clock. At the end of the runway, as the Junkers turned, the moisture scudded across the window, leaving threads of droplets. The swastika above the terminal building hung limp in the wet.

There were two queues at passport control: one for German and European Community nationals, one for the rest of the world.

'This is where we part,' said March. He had persuaded her, with some difficulty, to let him carry her case. Now he handed it back. 'What are you going to do?'

'Go back to my apartment, I guess, and wait for the telephone to ring. What about you?'

'I thought I would arrange myself a history lesson.' She looked at him, uncomprehending. He said: 'I'll call you later.'

'Be sure you do.'

A vestige of the old mistrust had returned. He could see it in her eyes, felt her searching it out in his. He wanted to say something, to reassure her. 'Don't worry. A deal is a deal.'

She nodded. An awkward silence. Then abruptly she stood on tiptoe and brushed her cheek against his. She was gone before he could think of a response.

*

THE line of returning Germans shuffled one at a time, in silence, into the Reich. March waited patiently with his hands clasped behind his back while his passport was scrutinised. In these last few days before the Führer's birthday, the border checks were always more stringent, the guards more jittery.

The eyes of the Zollgrenzschutz officer were hidden in the shade of his visor. 'The Herr Sturmbannführer is back with three hours to spare.' He drew a thick black line through the visa, scrawled 'void' across it, and handed the passport back. 'Welcome home.'

In the crowded customs hall March kept a look out for Charlie, but could not see her. Perhaps they had refused to let her back into the country. He almost hoped they had: it would be safer for her.

The Zollgrenzschutz were opening every bag. Never had he seen such security. It was chaos. The passengers milling and arguing around the mounds of clothes made the hall look like an Indian bazaar. He waited his turn.

It was after three by the time March reached the left-luggage area and retrieved his case. In the toilets he changed back into his uniform, folded his civilian clothes and packed them away. He checked his Luger and slipped it into his holster. As he left, he glanced at himself in the mirror. A familiar black figure.

Welcome home.

hen the sun shone the Party called it 'Führer weather'. They had no name for rain.

Nevertheless, it had been decreed, drizzle or not, that this afternoon was to be the start of the three-day holiday. And so, with dogged National Socialist determination, the people set about their celebrations.

March was in a taxi heading south through Wedding. This was workers' Berlin, a communist stronghold of the 1920s. The factory whistles, in a festive gesture, had sounded an hour earlier than usual. Now the streets were dense with damp revellers. The Blockwarts had been active. From every second or third building, a banner hung —mostly swastikas, but also the occasional slogan, strung between the iron balconies of the fortress-tenements. WORKERS OF BERLIN SALUTE THE FÜHRER ON HIS 75TH BIRTHDAY! LONG LIVE THE GLORIOUS NATIONAL SOCIALIST REVOLUTION! LONG LIVE OUR GUIDE AND FIRST COMRADE ADOLF HITLER! The back streets were in a delirium of colour, throbbing to the oohm-pah! of the local SA bands. And this was only Friday. March wondered what the Wedding authorities had planned for the day itself.

During the night, on the corner of Wolff Strasse, some rebellious spirit had added a piece of graffiti, in white paint: ANYONE FOUND NOT ENJOYING THEMSELVES WILL BE SHOT. A couple of anxious-looking brownshirts were trying to clean it off.

March took the taxi as far as Fritz-Todt Platz. His Volkswagen was still outside Stuckart's apartment, where he had parked it the night before last. He looked up at the fourth floor. Someone had drawn all the curtains.

At Werderscher Markt, he stowed his suitcase in his

office and rang the Duty Officer. Martin Luther had not been located.

Krause said: 'Between you and me, March, Globus is driving us all fucking mad. In here every half-hour, ranting and raving that someone will go to a KZ unless he gets results.'

'The Herr Obergruppenführer is a very dedicated officer.'

'Oh, he is, he is.' Krause's voice was suddenly panicky. 'I didn't mean to suggest – '

March hung up. That would give whoever was listening to his calls something to think about.

He lugged the typewriter across to his desk and inserted a single sheet of paper. He lit a cigarette.

To: Artur Nebe, SS-Oberstgruppenführer, Reich Kriminalpolizei
From: X. March, SS-Sturmbannführer   17.4.64

1.   I have the honour to inform you that at 10.00 this morning I attended the premises of Zaugg & Cie, Bankiers, Bahnhof Strasse, Zürich.

2.   The numbered account, whose existence we discussed yesterday, was opened by Foreign Ministry Under State Secretary Martin Luther on 8.7.42. Four keys were issued.

3.   The box was subsequently opened on three occasions: 17.12.42, 9.8.43, 13.4.64.

4.   On inspection by myself, the box was found to contain

March leaned back in his seat and blew a pair of neat smoke rings towards the ceiling. The thought of that painting in the hands of Nebe – dumped into his collection of bombastic, syrupy Schmutzlers and Kirchners – was repugnant, even sacrilegious. Better to leave her at peace in the darkness. He let his fingers rest on the typewriter keys for a moment, then tapped:

nothing.

He wound the paper out of the typewriter, signed it, and sealed it in an envelope. He called Nebe's office and was ordered to bring it up at once, personally. He hung up and stared out the window at the brickwork view.

Why not?

He stood and checked along the bookshelves until he found the Berlin area telephone directory. He took it down and looked up a number, which he dialled from the office next door, so as not to be overheard.

A man's voice answered: 'Reichsarchiv.'

TEN minutes later his boots were sinking into the soft mire of Artur Nebe's office carpet.

'Do you believe in coincidences, March?'

'No, sir.'

'No,' said Nebe. 'Good. Neither do I.' He put down his magnifying glass and pushed away March's report. 'I don't believe two retired public servants of the same age and rank *just happen* to choose to commit suicide rather than be exposed as corrupt. My God' – he gave a harsh little laugh – 'if every government official in Berlin took that approach, the streets would be piled high with the dead. Nor do they *just happen* to be murdered in the week an American president announces he will grace us with a visit.'

He pushed back his chair and hobbled across to a small bookcase lined with the sacred texts of National Socialism: *Mein Kampf*, Rosenberg's *Mythus der XX. Jahrhunderts*, Goebbels's *Tagebücher* . . . He pressed a switch and the front of the bookcase swung open to reveal a cocktail cabinet. The tomes, March saw now, were merely the spines of books, pasted on to the wood.

Nebe helped himself to a large vodka and returned to his desk. March continued to stand before him, neither fully at attention nor fully at ease.

'Globus works for Heydrich,' said Nebe. 'That's simple. Globus wouldn't wipe his own arse unless Heydrich told him it was time to do it.'

March said nothing.

'And Heydrich works for the Führer most of the time, and all of the time he works for himself . . .'

Nebe held the heavy tumbler to his lips. His lizard's tongue darted into the vodka, playing with it. He was silent for a while. Then he said: 'Do you know why we're greasing up to the Americans, March?'

'No, sir.'

'Because we're in the shit. Here is something you won't read in the little Doctor's newspapers. Twenty million settlers in the East by 1960, that was Himmler's plan. Ninety million by the end of the century. Fine. Well, we shipped them out all right. Trouble is, half of them want to come back. Consider that cosmic piece of irony, March: living space that no one wants to live in. Terrorism' – he gestured with his glass, the ice clinked – 'I don't need to tell an officer of the Kripo how serious terrorism has become. The Americans supply money, weapons, training. They've kept the Reds going for twenty years. As for us: the young don't want to fight and the old don't want to work.'

He shook his grey head at such follies, fished an ice cube out of his drink and sucked it noisily.

'Heydrich's mad for this American deal. He'd kill to keep it sweet. Is that what's happening here, March? Buhler, Stuckart, Luther – were they a threat to it somehow?'

Nebe's eyes searched his face. March stared straight ahead.

'You're an irony yourself, March, in a way. Did you ever consider that?'

'No, sir.'

' "No, sir." ' Nebe mimicked him. 'Well consider it now. We set out to breed a generation of supermen to rule an empire, yes? We trained them to apply hard logic – pitilessly, even cruelly. Remember what the Führer once said? "My greatest gift to the Germans is that I have taught them to think clearly." And what happens? A few of you – perhaps the best of you – begin to turn this pitiless clear thinking on to *us*. I tell you, I'm glad I'm an old man. I fear the future.' He was quiet for a minute, lost in his own thoughts.

At length, disappointed, the old man picked up the magnifying glass. 'Corruption it is, then.' He read through March's report once more, then tore it up and dropped it into his waste bin.

CLIO, the Muse of History, guarded the Reichsarchiv: an Amazonian nude designed by Adolf Ziegler, the 'Reich Master of the Pubic Hair'. She frowned across the Avenue of Victory towards the Soldiers' Hall, where a long queue of tourists waited to file past Frederick the Great's bones. Pigeons perched on the slopes of her immense bosom, like mountaineers on the face of a glacier. Behind her, a sign had been carved above the entrance to the archive, gold leaf inlaid on polished granite. A quotation from the Führer: FOR ANY NATION, THE RIGHT HISTORY IS WORTH 100 DIVISIONS.

Rudolf Halder led March inside, and up to the third floor. He pushed at the double-doors and stood aside to let him walk through. A corridor with stone walls and a stone floor seemed to stretch for ever.

'Impressive, yes?' In his place of work, Halder spoke in

the tone of a professional historian, conveying pride and sarcasm simultaneously. 'We call the style mock-Teutonic. This, you will not be surprised to hear, is the largest archive building in the world. Above us: two floors of administration. On this floor: researchers' offices and reading rooms. Beneath us: *six floors* of documents. You are treading, my friend, on the history of the Fatherland. For my part, I tend Clio's lamp in here.'

It was a monkish cell: small, windowless, the walls made of blocks of granite. Papers were stacked in piles half a metre high on the table; they spilled over on to the floor. Books were everywhere – several hundred of them – each sprouting a thicket of markers: multi-coloured bits of paper, tram tickets, pieces of cigarette carton, spent matches.

'The historian's mission. To bring out of chaos – more chaos.' Halder lifted a stack of old army signals off the solitary chair, knocked the dust off it, and gestured to March to sit.

'I need your help, Rudi – again.'

Halder perched on the edge of his desk. 'I don't hear from you for months, then suddenly it's twice in a week. I presume this also has to do with the Buhler business? I saw the obituary.'

March nodded. 'I should say now that you are talking to a pariah. You may be endangering yourself merely by meeting me.'

'That only makes it sound more fascinating.' Halder put his long fingers together and cracked the joints. 'Go on.'

'This is a real challenge for you.' March paused, took a breath. 'Three men: Buhler, Wilhelm Stuckart and Martin Luther. The first two dead; the last, a fugitive. All three senior civil servants, as you know. In the summer of 1942, they opened a bank account in Zürich. At first I assumed they put away a hoard of money or art treasures – as you suspected, Buhler was up to his armpits in corruption – but now I think it is more likely to have been documents.'

'What sort of documents?'

'Not sure.'

'Sensitive?'

'Presumably.'

'You've got one problem straight away. You're talking about three different ministries – Foreign, Interior and General Government, which isn't really a ministry at all. That's tons of documents. I mean it, Zavi, literally – tons.'

'Do you have their records here?'

'Foreign and Interior, yes. General Government is in Krakau.'

'Do you have access to them?'

'Officially – no. Unofficially . . .' He wobbled a bony hand. '. . . Perhaps, if I'm lucky. But, Zavi, it would take a lifetime simply to look through them. What are you suggesting we do?'

'There must be some clue in there: Perhaps there are papers missing.'

'But this is an impossible task.'

'I told you it was a challenge.'

'And how soon does this "clue" need to be discovered?'

'I need to find it tonight.'

Halder made an explosive sound, of mingled incredulity, anger, scorn. March said quietly: 'Rudi, in three days' time, they're threatening to put me in front of an SS Honour Court. You know what that means. *I have to find it now.*'

Halder looked at him for a moment, unwilling to believe what he was hearing, then turned away, muttering: 'Let me think . . .'

March said: 'Can I have a cigarette?'

'In the corridor. Not in here – this stuff is irreplaceable.'

As March smoked he could hear Halder, in his office,

pacing up and down. He looked at his watch. Six o'clock. The long corridor was deserted. Most of the staff must have gone home, to begin the holiday weekend. March tried a couple of office doors, but both were locked. The third was open. He picked up the telephone, listened to the tone, and dialled nine. The tone changed: an outside line. He rang Charlie's number. She answered at once.

'It's me. Are you all right?'

She said: 'I'm fine. I've discovered something – just a tiny thing.'

'Don't tell me over an open line. I'll talk to you later.' He tried to think of something else to say, but she had replaced the receiver.

Now Halder was on the telephone, his cheerful voice echoing down the flagstone corridor. 'Eberhard? Good evening to you . . . Indeed, no rest for some of us. A quick question, if I may. The Interior Ministry series . . . Oh, they have been? Good. On an office basis? . . . I see. Excellent. And all that is done? . . .'

March leaned against the wall with his eyes closed, trying not to think of the ocean of paper beneath his feet. Come on, Rudi. *Come on*.

He heard a bell tinkle as Halder hung up. A few seconds later Rudi appeared in the corridor, pulling on his jacket. A bunch of pen-tops jutted from his breast pocket. 'One small piece of luck. According to my colleague, the Interior Ministry files at least have been catalogued.' He set off down the passage at a rapid pace. March strode beside him.

'What does that mean?'

'It means there should be a central index, showing us which papers actually crossed Stuckart's desk, and when.' He hammered at the buttons beside the elevator. Nothing happened. 'Looks as if they've turned this thing off for the night. We'll have to walk.'

As they clattered down the wide spiral staircase, Halder

shouted: 'You appreciate this is completely against the rules? I'm cleared for Military, Eastern Front, not Administration, Internal. If we're stopped, you'll have to spin Security some yarn about Polizei business – something that'll take them a couple of hours to check. As for me, I'm just a poor sucker, doing you a favour, right?'

'I appreciate it. How much further?'

'All the way to the bottom.' Halder was shaking his head. 'An Honour Court! Dear God, Zavi, what's happened to you?'

Sixty metres beneath the ground the air circulated cool and dry, the lights were dimmed, to protect the archives. 'They say this place was built to withstand a direct hit from an American missile,' said Halder.

'What's behind there?'

March pointed to a steel door, covered with warning signs: 'ATTENTION! NO ADMITTANCE TO UNAUTHORISED PERSONS!' 'ENTRY FORBIDDEN!' 'PASSES MUST BE SHOWN'.

' "The right history is worth a hundred divisions", remember? That's the place where the wrong history goes. Shit. Look out.'

Halder pulled March into a doorway. A security guard was coming towards them, bent like a miner in an underground shaft, pushing a metal cart. March thought he was certain to see them, but he went straight past, grunting with effort. He stopped at the metal barrier and unlocked it. There was a glimpse of a furnace, a roar of flame, before the door clanged shut behind him.

'Let's go.'

As they walked, Halder explained the procedure. The archive worked on warehouse principles. Requisitions for files came down to a central handling area on each floor. Here, in ledgers a metre high and twenty centimetres thick, was kept the main index. Entered next to each file was a stack number. The stacks themselves were in fire-proof storerooms leading off from the handling area. The secret, said Halder, was to know your way round the index. He paraded in front of the crimson leather spines, tapping each with his finger until he found the one he wanted, then lugged it over to the floor manager's desk.

March had once been below-decks on the aircraft carrier, *Grossadmiral Raeder*. The depths of the Reichsarchiv reminded him of that: low ceilings strung with lights, the sense of something vast pressing down from above. Next to the desk: a photocopier – a rare sight in Germany, where their distribution was strictly controlled, to stop subversives producing illegal literature. A dozen empty carts were drawn up by the lift-shaft. He could see fifty metres in either direction. The place was deserted.

Halder gave a cry of triumph. 'State Secretary: Office Files, 1939 to 1950. Oh Christ: four hundred boxes. What years do you want to look at?'

'The Swiss bank account was opened in July '42, so let's say the first seven months of that year.'

Halder turned the page, talking to himself. 'Yes. I see what they've done. They've arranged the papers in four series: office correspondence, minutes and memoranda, statutes and decrees, ministry personnel . . .'

'What I'm looking for is something that connects Stuckart with Buhler and Luther.'

'In that case, we'd better start with office correspondence. That should give us a feel for what was going on at the time.' Halder was scribbling notes. 'D/15/M/28–34. Okay. Here we go.'

Storeroom D was twenty metres down on the left. Stack fifteen, section M was in the dead centre of the room. Halder said: 'Only six boxes, thank God. You take January to April, I'll do May to August.'

The boxes were made of cardboard, each the size of a large desk drawer. There was no table, so they sat on the floor. With his back pressed against the metal shelving, March opened the first box, pulled out a handful of papers, and began to read.

You need a little luck in this life.

The first document was a letter dated 2 January, from the under state secretary at the Air Ministry, regarding the distribution of gas masks to the Reichsluftschutzbund, the Air Raid Protection organisation. The second, dated 4 January, was from the Office of the Four-Year Plan and concerned the alleged unauthorised use of gasoline by senior government officials.

The third was from Reinhard Heydrich.

March saw the signature first – an angular, spidery scrawl. Then his eyes travelled to the letterhead – the Reich Main Security Office, Berlin SW 11, Prinz-Albrecht Strasse 8 – then to the date: 6 January 1942. And only then to the text:

> This is to confirm that the inter-agency discussion followed by luncheon originally scheduled for 9 December 1941 has now been postponed to 20 January 1942 in the office of the International Criminal Police Commission, Berlin, Am grossen Wannsee, Nr. 56/58.

March leafed through the other letters in the box: carbon flimsies and creamy originals; imposing letterheads – Reichschancellery, Economics Ministry, Organisation-Todt; invitations to luncheons and meetings; pleas, demands, circulars. But there was nothing else from Heydrich.

March passed the letter to Halder. 'What do you make of this?'

Halder frowned. 'Unusual, I would say, for the Main

Security Office to convene a meeting of government agencies.'

'Can we find out what they discussed?'

'Should be able to. We can cross-reference it to the minutes and memoranda series. Let's see: 20 January . . .'

Halder looked at his notes, pulled himself to his feet and walked along the stack. He dragged out another box, returned with it and sat, cross-legged. March watched him flick through the contents. Suddenly, he stopped. He said slowly: 'My God . . .'

'What is it?'

Halder handed him a single sheet of paper, on which was typed: 'In the interests of state security, the minutes of the inter-agency meeting of 20 January 1942 have been removed at the request of the Reichsführer-SS.'

Halder said: 'Look at the date.'

March looked. It was 6 April 1964. The minutes had been extracted by Heydrich eleven days earlier.

'Can he do that – legally, I mean?'

'The Gestapo can weed out whatever it wants on the grounds of security. They usually transfer the papers to the vaults in Prinz-Albrecht Strasse.'

There was a noise in the corridor outside. Halder held up a warning finger. Both men were silent, motionless, as the guard clattered past, wheeling the empty cart back from the furnace room. They listened as the sounds faded towards the other end of the building.

March whispered: 'Now what do we do?'

Halder scratched his head. 'An inter-agency meeting at the level of state-secretary . . .'

March saw what he was thinking. 'Buhler and Luther would have been invited, as well?'

'It would seem logical. At that rank, they get fussy about protocol. You wouldn't have a state secretary from one ministry attending, and only a junior civil servant from another. What time is it?'

'Eight o'clock.'

'They're an hour ahead in Krakau.' Halder chewed his lip for a moment, then reached a decision. He stood. 'I'll telephone my friend who works at the archives in the General Government and ask if the SS have been sniffing around there in the past couple of weeks. If they haven't, maybe I can persuade him to go in tomorrow and see if the minutes are still in Buhler's papers.'

'Couldn't we just check here, in the Foreign Ministry archives? In Luther's papers?'

'No. Too vast. It could take us weeks. This is the best way, believe me.'

'Be careful what you say to him, Rudi.'

'Don't worry. I'm aware of the dangers.' Halder paused at the door. 'And no smoking while I'm gone, for Christ's sake. This is the most inflammable building in the Reich.'

True enough, thought March. He waited until Halder had gone and then began walking up and down between the stacks of boxes. He wanted a cigarette, badly. His hands were trembling. He thrust them into his pockets.

What a monument to German bureaucracy this place was. Herr A, wishing to do something, asked permission of Doctor B. Doctor B covered himself by referring it upwards to Ministerialdirektor C. Ministerialdirektor C shuffled it to Reichsminister D, who said he would leave it to the judgement of Herr A, who naturally went back to Doctor B . . . The alliances and rivalries, traps and intrigues of three decades of Party rule wove in and out of these metal stacks; ten thousand webs, spun from paper threads, suspended in the cool air.

Halder was back within ten minutes. 'The SS were in Krakau two weeks ago all right.' He was rubbing his hands uneasily. 'Their memory is still vivid. A distinguished visitor. Obergruppenführer Globocnik himself.'

'Everywhere I turn,' said March. 'Globocnik!'

'He flew in on a Gestapo jet from Berlin, with special authorisation from Heydrich, personally signed. He gave them all the shits, apparently. Shouting and swearing. Knew exactly what he was looking for: one file removed. He was out of there by lunchtime.'

Globus, Heydrich, Nebe. March put his hand to his head. It was dizzying. 'So here it ends?'

'Here it ends. Unless you think there might be something else in Stuckart's papers.'

March looked down at the boxes. The contents seemed to him as dead as dust; dead men's bones. The thought of sifting through them any more was repugnant to him. He needed to breathe some fresh air. 'Forget it, Rudi. Thanks.'

Halder stooped to pick up Heydrich's note. 'Interesting that the conference was postponed, from December the ninth to January the twentieth.'

'What's the significance of that?'

Halder gave him a pitying look. 'Were you really so completely cooped-up in that fucking tin can we had to live in? Did the outside world never penetrate? On December the seventh, 1941, you blockhead, the forces of His Imperial Majesty, Emperor Hirohito of Japan, attacked the US Pacific fleet at Pearl Harbor. On December the eleventh, Germany declared war on the United States. Good reasons to postpone a conference, wouldn't you say?' Halder was grinning, but slowly the grin faded, to be replaced by a more thoughtful expression. 'I wonder . . .'

'What?'

He tapped the paper. 'There must have been an original invitation, before this one.'

'So what?'

'It depends. Sometimes our friends from the Gestapo are not quite as efficient at weeding out embarrassing details as they like to think, especially if they're in a hurry . . .'

March was already standing in front of the stack of boxes, glancing up and down, his depression lifted. 'Which one? Where do we start?'

'For a conference at that level, Heydrich would have had to have given the participants at least two weeks' notice.' Halder looked at his notes. 'That would mean Stuckart's office correspondence file for November 1941. Let me see. That should be box twenty-six, I think.'

He joined March in front of the shelves and counted off the boxes until he found the one he wanted. He pulled it down, cradled it. 'Don't snatch, Zavi. All in good time. History teaches us patience.'

He knelt, placed the box in front of him, opened it, pulled out an armful of papers. He glanced at each in turn, placing them in a pile to his left. 'Invitation to a reception given by the Italian ambassador: boring. Conference organised by Walther Darre at the Agriculture Ministry: *very* boring . . .'

He went on like that for perhaps two minutes, with March standing, watching, nervously grinding his fist into his palm. Then suddenly Halder froze. 'Oh shit.' He read it through again and looked up. 'Invitation from Heydrich. Not boring at all, I'm afraid. Not boring at all.'

he heavens were in chaos. Nebulae exploded. Comets and meteors rushed across the sky, disappeared for an instant, then detonated against green oceans of cloud.

Above the Tiergarten, the firework display was nearing its climax. Parachute flares lit up Berlin like an air raid.

As March waited in his car to turn left on to Unter den Linden, a gang of SA men lurched out in front of him. Two of them, their arms draped around one another, performed a drunken can-can in the beam of the headlights. The others banged on the Volkswagen's body work, or pressed their faces against the windows – eyes bulging, tongues lolling; grotesque apes. March put the engine into first gear and skidded away. There was a thud as one of the dancers was sent spinning.

He drove back to Werderscher Markt. All police leave had been cancelled. Every window was ablaze with electric light. In the foyer, someone hailed him, but March ignored them. He clattered down the stairs to the basement.

Bank vaults and basements and underground store rooms . . . I am turning into a troglodyte, thought March; a cave-dweller, a recluse; a robber of paper tombs.

The Gorgon of the Registry was still sitting in her lair. Did she never sleep? He showed her his ID. There were a couple of other detectives at the central desk, leafing in a languid manner through the ubiquitous manila files. March took a seat in the farthest corner of the room. He switched on an angle-poise lamp, bent its shade low over the table. From inside his tunic he drew the three sheets of paper he had taken from the Reichsarchiv.

They were poor-quality photostats. The machine had been set too faint, the originals had been thrust into it, hastily and skewed. He did not blame Rudi for that. Rudi had not wanted to make the copies at all. Rudi had been terrified. All his schoolboy bravado had vanished when he read Heydrich's invitation. March had been obliged virtually to drag him to the photocopier. The moment the historian had finished, he had darted back into the storeroom, shovelled the papers back into the boxes, put the boxes back on to the shelves. At his insistence, they had left the archive building by a rear entrance.

'I think, Zavi, we should not see one another for a long time now.'

'Of course.'

'You know how it is . . .'

Halder had stood, miserable and helpless, while above their heads the fireworks had whooshed and banged. March had embraced him –'Don't feel bad; I know: your family come first' – and quickly walked away.

Document One. Heydrich's original invitation, dated 19 November 1941:

On 31.7.1941, the Reichsmarschall of the Greater German Reich charged me, in co-operation with all the other relevant central agencies, to make all the necessary preparations with regard to organisational, technical and material measures for a complete solution of the Jewish question in Europe and to present him shortly with a complete draft proposal on this matter. I enclose a photocopy of this commission.

In view of the extraordinary importance which must be accorded to these questions, and in the interest of securing a uniform view among the relevant central agencies of the further tasks concerned with the remaining work on this final solution, I propose to make these problems the subject of a general discussion. This is particularly necessary since from 10 October onwards the Jews have been evacuated from Reich territory, including the Protectorate, to the East in a continuous series of transports.

I therefore invite you to join me and others, whose names I enclose, at a discussion followed by luncheon on 9 December 1941 at 12.00 in the office of the International Criminal Police Commission, Berlin, Am grossen Wannsee, Nr. 56/58.

Document Two. A photostat of a photostat, almost illegible in places, the words rubbed away like an ancient inscription on a tomb. Hermann Goering's directive to Heydrich, dated 31 July 1941:

To supplement the task that was assigned to you on 24 January 1939, which dealt with the solution of the Jewish problem by emigration and evacuation in the most suitable way, I hereby charge you with making all necessary preparations with regard to organisational, technical and material matters for bringing about a complete solution of the Jewish question within the German sphere of influence in Europe.

Wherever other governmental agencies are involved, these are to co-operate with you.

I request you further to send me, in the near future, an overall plan covering the organisational, technical and material measures necessary for the accomplishment of the final solution of the Jewish question which we desire.

Document Three. A list of the fourteen people Heydrich had invited to the conference. Stuckart was third on the list; Buhler, sixth; Luther, seventh. March recognised a couple of the others.

He ripped a sheet from his notebook, wrote down eleven names and took it to the issuing desk. The two detectives had gone. The Registrar was nowhere to be seen. He rapped on the counter and shouted: 'Shop!' From behind a row of filing cabinets came a guilty clink of glass on bottle. So that was her secret. She must have forgotten he was there. A moment later, she waddled into view.

'What do we have on these eleven men?'

He tried to hand her the list. She folded a pair of plump arms across a greasy tunic. 'No more than three files at any one time, without special authorisation.'

'Never mind that.'

'It is not permitted.'

'It is not permitted to drink alcohol on duty, either, yet you stink of it. Now get me these files.'

To every man and woman, a number; to every number, a file. Not all files were held at Werderscher Markt. Only those whose lives had come into contact with the Reich Kriminalpolizei, for whatever reason, had left their spoor here. But by using the information bureau at Alexander Platz, and the obituaries of the *Völkischer Beobachter* (published annually as *The Roll Call of the Fallen*) March was able to fill in the gaps. He tracked down every name. It took him two hours.

The first man on the list was Doctor Alfred Meyer of the East Ministry. According to his Kripo file, Meyer had committed suicide in 1960 after undergoing treatment for various mental illnesses.

The second name: Doctor Georg Leibrandt, also of the East Ministry. He had died in an automobile accident in 1959, his car crushed by a truck on the autobahn between Stuttgart and Augsburg. The driver of the truck had never been found.

Erich Neumann, State Secretary in the Office of the Four Year Plan, had shot himself in 1957.

Doctor Roland Freisler, State Secretary from the Justice Ministry: hacked to death by a maniac with a knife on the steps of the Berlin People's Court in the winter of 1954. An investigation into how his security guards had managed to let a criminal lunatic come so close had concluded that nobody was to blame. The assassin had been shot seconds after the attack on Freisler.

At this point, March had gone into the corridor for a cigarette. He drew the smoke deep into his lungs, tilted back his head and let it out slowly, as if taking a cure.

He returned to find a fresh heap of files on his desk.

SS-Oberführer Gerhard Klopfer, deputy head of the Party Chancellery, had been reported missing by his wife in May 1963; his body had been found by building-site workers in southern Berlin, stuffed into a cement mixer.

Friedrich Kritzinger. That name was familiar. Of course. March remembered the scenes from the television news: the familiar taped-off street, the wrecked car, the widow supported by her sons. Kritzinger, the former Ministerialdirektor from the Reich Chancellery, had been blown up outside his home in Munich just over a month ago, on 7 March. No terrorist group had yet claimed responsibility.

Two men were recorded by the *Völkischer Beobachter* as having died of natural causes. SS-Standartenführer Adolf Eichmann of the Reich Main Security Office had succumbed to a heart attack in 1961. SS-Sturmbannführer Doctor Rudolf Lange of KdS Latvia had died of a brain tumour in 1955.

Heinrich Müller. Here was another name March knew. The Bavarian policeman Müller, the former head of the Gestapo, had been on board Himmler's plane when it crashed in 1962, killing everyone on board.

SS-Oberführer Doctor Karl Schöngarth, representing the security services of the General Government, had fallen beneath the wheels of a U-bahn train pulling into Zoo Station on 9 April 1964 – barely more than a week ago. There were no witnesses.

SS-Obergruppenführer Otto Hoffmann of the Reich Security Office had been found hanging from a length of clothesline in his Spandau apartment on Boxing Day 1963.

That was all. Of the fourteen men who had attended the conference at Heydrich's invitation, thirteen were dead. The fourteenth – Luther – was missing.

As part of its campaign to raise public awareness about terrorism, the Propaganda Ministry had produced a series of children's cartoons. Someone had pinned one up on the noticeboard on the second floor. A little girl receives a parcel and begins opening it. In each succeeding picture she removes more layers of wrapping paper, until she is left holding an alarm clock with two sticks of dynamite attached to it. The last picture is an explosion, with the caption: 'Warning! Do not open a parcel unless you know its contents!'

A good joke. A maxim for every German policeman. Do not open a parcel unless you know its contents. Do not ask a question unless you know the answer.

Endlösung: final solution. *Endlösung*. *Endlösung*. The word tolled in March's head as he half-walked, half-ran along the corridor and into his office.

Endlösung.

He wrenched open the drawers of Max Jaeger's desk and searched through the clutter. Max was notoriously inefficient about administrative matters, had often been reprimanded for his laxity. March prayed he had not taken the warnings to heart.

He had not.

Bless you, Max, you dumbhead.

He slammed the drawers shut.

Only then did he notice it. Someone had attached a

yellow message slip to March's telephone: 'Urgent. Contact the Duty Office immediately.'

$\mathfrak{I}$n the marshalling yards of the Gotenland railway station, they had set up arc lights around the body. From a distance the scene looked oddly glamorous, like a film set.

March stumbled towards it, up and down, across the wooden sleepers and metal tracks, over the diesel-soaked stone.

Before it had been renamed Gotenland, this had been the Anhalter Bahnhof: the Reich's main eastern railway terminus. It was from here that the Führer had set out in his armoured train, *Amerika*, for his wartime headquarters in East Prussia; from here, too, that Berlin's Jews – the Weisses among them – must have embarked on their journey east.

'. . . *from 10 October onwards the Jews have been evacuated from Reich territory to the East in a continuous series of transports* . . .'

In the air behind him, growing fainter: the platform announcements; somewhere ahead, the clank of wheels and couplings, a bleak whistle. The yard was vast – a dreamscape in the orange sodium lighting – at its centre, the one patch of brilliant white. As March neared it, he could make out a dozen figures standing in front of a high-sided goods train: a couple of Orpo men, Krebs, Doctor Eisler, a photographer, a group of anxious officials of the Deutsche Reichsbahn, and Globus.

Globus saw him first, and slowly clapped his gloved hands in muffled and mocking applause. 'Gentlemen, we can relax. The heroic forces of the Kriminalpolizei have arrived to give us their theories.'

One of the Orpo men sniggered.

The body, or what was left of it, was under a rough woollen blanket spread across the tracks, and also in a green plastic sack.

'May I see the corpse?'

'Of course. We haven't touched him yet. We've been waiting for you, the great detective.' Globus nodded to Krebs, who pulled away the blanket.

A man's torso, neatly cropped at either end, along the lines of the rails. He was belly down, slanted across the tracks. One hand had been severed, the head was crushed. Both legs had also been run over, but the bloodied shards of clothing made it difficult to gauge the precise point of amputation. There was a strong smell of alcohol.

'And now you must look in here.' Globus was holding the plastic sack up to the light. He opened it and brought it close to March's face. 'The Gestapo does not wish to be accused of concealing evidence.'

The stumps of feet, one of them still shod; a hand ending in ragged white bone and the gold band of a wristwatch. March did not close his eyes, which seemed to disappoint Globus. 'Ach, well.' He dropped the sack. 'They're worse when they stink, when the rats have been at them. Check his pockets, Krebs.'

In his flapping leather coat, Krebs squatted over the body like carrion. He reached beneath the corpse, feeling for the inside of the jacket. Over his shoulder, Krebs said: 'We were informed two hours ago by the Reichsbahn Polizei that a man answering Luther's description had been seen here. But by the time we got here . . .'

'He had already suffered a fatal accident.' March smiled bitterly. 'How unexpected.'

'Here we are, Herr Obergruppenführer.' Krebs had retrieved a passport and wallet. He straightened, and handed them to Globus.

'This is his passport, no question,' said Globus, flicking

through it. 'And here are several thousand Reichsmarks in cash. Money enough for silk sheets at the Hotel Adlon. But, of course, the bastard couldn't show his face in civilised company. He had no choice but to sleep rough out here.'

This thought appeared to give him satisfaction. He showed March the passport: Luther's ponderous face peered out from above his calloused thumb. 'Look at it, Sturmbannführer, then run along and tell Nebe it is all over. The Gestapo will handle everything from now on. You can clear off and get some rest.' And enjoy it, his eyes said, while you can.

'The Herr Obergruppenführer is kind.'

'You'll discover how kind I am, March, that much I promise you.' He turned to Eisler. 'Where's that fucking ambulance?'

The pathologist stood to attention. 'On its way, Herr Obergruppenführer. Most definitely.'

March gathered he had been dismissed. He moved towards the railway workers, standing in a forlorn group about ten metres away. 'Which of you discovered the body?'

'I did, Herr Sturmbannführer.' The man who stepped forward wore the dark blue tunic and soft cap of a locomotive driver. His eyes were red, his voice raw. Was that because of the body, wondered March, or was it fear at the unexpected presence of an SS general?

'Cigarette?'

'God, yes, sir. Thanks.'

The driver took one, giving a furtive glance towards Globus, who was now talking to Krebs.

March offered him a light. 'Relax. Take your time. Has this happened to you before?'

'Once.' The man exhaled and looked gratefully at the cigarette. 'It happens here every three or four months. The derelicts sleep under the wagons, to keep out of the rain, poor devils. Then, when the engines start, instead of staying where they are, they try to get out of the way.' He put his hand to his eyes. 'I must have reversed over him, but I never heard a thing. When I looked back up the track, there he was – just a heap of rags.'

'Do you get many derelicts in this yard?'

'Always a couple of dozen. The Reichsbahn Polizei try to keep them away, but the place is too big to patrol properly. Look over there. Some of them are making a run for it.'

He pointed across the tracks. At first, March could make out nothing, except a line of cattle-trucks. Then, almost invisible in the shadow of the train, he spotted a movement – a shape, running jerkily, like a marionette; then another; then more. They ran along the sides of the wagons, darted into the gaps between the trucks, waited, then scampered out again towards the next patch of cover.

Globus had his back to them. Oblivious to their presence, he was still talking to Krebs, smacking his right fist into the palm of his left hand.

March watched as the stick-figures worked their way to safety –then suddenly the rails were vibrating, there was a rush of wind, and the view was cut off by the sleeper train to Rovno, accelerating out of Berlin. The wall of double-decker dining cars and sleeping compartments took half a minute to pass and by the time it had cleared the little colony of drifters had vanished into the orangey dark.

SATURDAY 18 APRIL

Most of you know what it means when one hundred corpses are lying side by side. Or five hundred. Or one thousand. To have stuck it out and at the same time – apart from some exceptions caused by human weakness – to have remained decent fellows, that is what has made us hard. This is a page of glory in our history which has never to be written and is never to be written.

HEINRICH HIMMLER
secret speech to senior SS officers,
Poznan, 4 October 1943

SATURDAY 18 APRIL

𝔄 crack of light showed beneath her door. Inside her apartment a radio was playing. Lovers' music – soft strings and low crooning, appropriate for the night. A party? Was this how Americans behaved in the presence of danger? He stood alone on the tiny landing and looked at his watch. It was almost two. He knocked and after a few moments the volume was turned down. He heard her voice.

'Who is it?'

'The police.'

A second or two elapsed, then there was a clatter of bolts and chains, and the door opened. She said: 'You're very funny,' but her smile was a false one, pasted on for his benefit. In her dark eyes exhaustion showed, and also – was it? – fear? He bent to kiss her, his hands resting lightly on her waist, and immediately felt a pricking of desire. *My God*, he thought, *she's turning me into a sixteen-year-old* . . .

Somewhere in the apartment: a footstep. He looked up. Over her shoulder, a man loomed in the doorway of the bathroom. He was a couple of years younger than March: brown brogues, sports jacket, a bow tie, a white jersey pulled on casually over a business shirt. Charlie stiffened in March's embrace and gently broke free of him. 'You remember Henry Nightingale?'

He straightened, feeling awkward. 'Of course. The bar in Potsdamer Strasse.'

Neither man made a move towards the other. The American's face was a mask.

March stared at Nightingale and said softly: 'What's going on here, Charlie?'

She stood on tiptoe and whispered in his ear. 'Don't say anything. Not here. Something's happened.' Then, loudly: 'Isn't this interesting, the three of us?' She took March's arm and guided him towards the bathroom. 'I think you should come into my parlour.'

IN the bathroom, Nightingale assumed a proprietorial air. He turned on the cold water taps above the basin and the bath, increased the volume of the radio. The programme had changed. Now the clapboard walls vibrated to the strains of 'German jazz' – a watery syncopation, officially approved, from which all traces of 'Negroid influences' had been erased. When he had arranged everything to his satisfaction, Nightingale perched on the edge of the bath. March sat next to him. Charlie squatted on the floor.

She opened the meeting: 'I told Henry about my visitor the other morning. The one you had the fight with. He thinks the Gestapo may have planted a bug.'

Nightingale gave an amiable grin. 'Afraid that's the way your country works, Herr Sturmbannführer.'

Your country . . .

'I'm sure – a wise precaution.'

Perhaps he isn't younger than me, thought March. The American had thick blond hair, blond eyelashes, a ski-tan. His teeth were absurdly regular – strips of enamel, gleaming white. Not many one-pot meals in *his* childhood, no watery potato soups or sawdust sausages in *that* complexion. His boyish looks embraced all ages from twenty-five to fifty.

For a few moments nobody spoke. Euro-pap filled the silence. Charlie said to March: 'I know you told me not to speak to anyone. But I had to. Now you have to trust Henry and Henry has to trust you. Believe me, there's no other way.'

'And, naturally, we *both* have to trust you.'

'Oh come on . . .'

'All right.' He held up his hands in a gesture of surrender.

Next to her, balanced on top of the lavatory, was the latest in American portable tape recorders. Trailing from one of its sockets was a cable, at the end of which, instead of a microphone, was a small suction cup.

'Listen,' she said. 'You'll understand.' She leaned across and pressed a switch. The spools of tape began to revolve.

'*Fräulein Maguire?*'

'*Yes?*'

'*The same procedure as before, Fräulein, if you please.*'

There was a click, followed by a buzz.

She pressed another switch, stopping the tape. 'That was the first call. You said he'd ring. I was waiting for him.' She was triumphant. 'It's Martin Luther.'

THIS was a crazy business, the craziest he had ever known, like picking your way through a haunted house in the Tiergarten fun fair. No sooner did you plant your feet on solid ground than the floorboards gave way beneath you. You rounded a corner and a madman rushed out. Then you stepped back and found that all the time you had been looking at yourself in a distorting mirror.

Luther.

March said: 'What time was that?'

'Eleven forty-five.'

Eleven forty-five: forty minutes after the discovery of the body on the railway tracks. He thought of the exultant look on Globus's face, and he smiled.

Nightingale said: 'What's so funny?'

'Nothing. I'll explain. What happened next?'

'Exactly as before. I went over to the telephone box and five minutes later he rang again.'

March raised his hand to his brow. 'Don't tell me you dragged that machine all the way across the street?'

'Damn it, I needed some proof!' She glared at him. 'I knew what I was doing. Look.' She stood to demonstrate. 'The deck hangs from this shoulder strap. The whole thing fits under my coat. The wire runs down my sleeve. I attach the suction cup to the receiver, like this. Easy. It was dark. Nobody could have seen a thing.'

Nightingale, the professional diplomat, cut in smoothly: 'Never mind how you got the tape, Charlie, or whether you should have got it.' He said to March: 'May I suggest we simply let her play it?'

Charlie pushed a button. There was a fumbling noise, greatly magnified – the sound of her attaching the microphone to the telephone – and then:

'We have not much time. I am a friend of Stuckart.'

An elderly voice, but not frail. A voice with the sarcastic, sing-song quality of the native Berliner. He spoke exactly as March had expected. Then Charlie's voice, in her good German:

'Tell me what you want.'

'Stuckart is dead.'

'I know. I found him.'

A long pause. On the tape, in the background, March could hear a station announcement. Luther must have used the distraction caused by the discovery of the body to make a phone call from the Gotenland platform.

Charlie whispered: 'He went so quiet, I thought I'd frightened him away.'

March shook his head. 'I told you. You're his only hope.'

The conversation on the tape resumed.

'You know who I am?'

'Yes.'

Wearily: *'You say: What do I want? What do you think I want? Asylum in your country.'*

'Tell me where you are.'

'I can pay.'

'That won't –'

'I have information. Certain facts.'

'Tell me where you are. I'll come and fetch you. We'll go to the Embassy.'

'Too soon. Not yet.'

'When?'

'Tomorrow morning. Listen to me. Nine o'clock. The Great Hall. Central steps. Have you got that?'

'Right.'

'Bring someone from the Embassy. But you must be there as well.'

'How do we recognise you?'

A laugh. 'No. I shall recognise you, show myself when I am satisfied.' Pause. 'Stuckart said you were young and pretty.' Pause. 'That was Stuckart all over.' Pause. 'Wear something that stands out.'

'I have a coat. Bright blue.'

'Pretty girl in blue. It is good. Until the morning, Fräulein.'

Click.

Purr.

The clatter of the tape machine being switched off.

'Play it again,' said March.

She rewound the tape, stopped it, pressed PLAY. March looked away, watched the rusty water swirling down the plughole, as Luther's voice mingled with the reedy sound of a single clarinet. 'Pretty girl in blue . . .' When they had heard it through for the second time, Charlie reached over and turned off the machine.

'After he hung up, I came over here and dropped off the tape. Then I went back to the telephone box and tried to call you. You weren't there. So I called Henry. What else could I do? He says he wants someone from the Embassy.'

'Got me out of bed,' said Nightingale. He yawned and stretched, revealing an expanse of pale, hairless leg. 'What I don't understand is why he didn't just let Charlie pick him up and bring him straight to the Embassy tonight.'

'You heard him,' said March. 'Tonight is too soon. He daren't show himself. He has to wait until the morning. By then the Gestapo's search for him will probably have been called off.'

Charlie frowned. 'I don't understand . . .'

'The reason you couldn't reach me two hours ago was because I was on my way to the Gotenland marshalling yards, where the Gestapo were hugging themselves with joy that they had finally discovered Luther's body.'

'That can't be.'

'No. It can't.' March pinched the bridge of his nose and shook his head. It was hard to keep his mind clear. 'My guess is Luther's been hiding in the rail yard for the past four days, ever since he got back from Switzerland, trying to work out some way of contacting you.'

'But how did he survive all that time?'

March shrugged. 'He had money, remember. Perhaps he picked out some drifter he thought he could trust, paid him to bring him food and drink; warm clothes, maybe. Until he had his plan.'

Nightingale said: 'And what was his plan, Sturmbann-führer?'

'He needed someone to take his place, to convince the Gestapo he was dead.' Was he talking too loudly? The Americans' paranoia was contagious. He leaned forward and said softly: 'Yesterday, when it was dark, he must have killed a man. A man of roughly his age and build. Got him drunk, knocked him out – I don't know how he did it – dressed him in his clothes, gave him his wallet, his passport, his watch. Then he put him under a goods train, with his hands and head on the rails. Stayed with him to make sure he didn't move until the wheels went over him. He's trying to buy himself some time. He's gambling that by nine o'clock this morning, the Berlin Polizei will have stopped looking for him. A fair bet, I would say.'

'Jesus Christ.' Nightingale looked from March to Charlie and back again. 'And this is the man I'm supposed to take in to the Embassy?'

'Oh, it gets better than that.' From the inside pocket of his tunic, March produced the documents from the archive. 'On the twentieth of January 1942, Martin Luther was one of fourteen men summoned to attend a special conference at the headquarters of Interpol in Wannsee. Since the end of the war, six of those men have been murdered, four have committed suicide, one has died in an accident, two have supposedly died of natural causes. Today only Luther is left alive. A freak of statistics, you would agree?' He handed Nightingale the papers. 'As you will see, the conference was called by Reinhard Heydrich to discuss the final solution of the Jewish question in Europe. My guess is Luther wants to make you an offer: a new life in America in exchange for documentary proof of what happened to the Jews.'

The water ran. The music ended. An announcer's silky voice whispered in the bathroom: 'And now, for you night-lovers everywhere, Peter Kreuder and his orchestra with their version of *I'm in Heaven . . .*'

Without looking at him, Charlie held out her hand. March took it. She laced her fingers into his and squeezed, hard. Good, he thought, she should be afraid. Her grip tightened. Their hands were linked like parachutists in free fall. Nightingale had his head hunched over the documents and was murmuring 'Jesus Christ, Jesus Christ' over and over again.

*

'WE have a problem here,' said Nightingale. 'I'll be frank with you both. Charlie, this is off the record.' He was talking so quietly they had to strain to hear. 'Three days ago, the President of the United States, for whatever reason, announced he was going to visit this Godforsaken country. At which point, twenty years of American foreign policy was turned upside down. Now this guy Luther, in theory – if what you say is true – could turn it upside down again, all in the space of seventy-two hours.'

Charlie said: 'Then at least it would end the week the right way up.'

'That's a cheap crack.'

He said this in English. March stared at him. 'What are you saying, Mister Nightingale?'

'I'm saying, Sturmbannführer, that I'm going to have to talk to Ambassador Lindbergh and Ambassador Lindbergh is going to have to talk to Washington. And my hunch is they're both going to want a lot more proof than this – ' he tossed the photocopies on to the floor ' – before they open the Embassy gates to a man you say is probably a common murderer.'

'But Luther is offering you the proof.'

'So *you* say. But I don't think Washington will want to risk all the progress that's been made on détente this week just because of your . . . theories.'

Now Charlie was on her feet. 'This is insane. If Luther doesn't go straight with you to the Embassy, he'll be captured and killed.'

'Sorry, Charlie. I can't do that.' He appealed to her. 'Come on! I can't take in every old Nazi who wants to defect. Not without authorisation. Especially not with things as they are.'

'I don't believe what I'm hearing.' She had her hands on her hips and was staring at the floor, shaking her head.

'Just think it through for a minute.' He was almost

pleading. 'This Luther character seeks asylum. The Germans say: hand him over, he's just killed a man. We say: no, because he's going to tell us what you bastards did to the Jews in the war. What will that do for the summit? No – Charlie – don't just look away. *Think*. Kennedy put on ten points in the polls *overnight* on Wednesday. How's the White House going to react if we drop this on them?' For a second time, Nightingale glimpsed the implications; for a second time he shuddered. 'Jesus Christ, Charlie, what have you got yourself mixed up in here?'

THE Americans argued back and forth for another ten minutes, then March said quietly: 'Aren't you overlooking something, Mister Nightingale?'

Nightingale switched his attention reluctantly from Charlie. 'Probably. You're the policeman. You tell me.'

'It seems to me that all of us – you, me, the Gestapo – we all keep underestimating good Party Comrade Luther. Remember what he said to Charlie about the nine o'clock meeting: "*you must be there as well*".'

'So what?'

'He knew this would be your reaction. Don't forget he had worked at the Foreign Ministry. With a summit coming, he guessed the Americans might want to throw him straight back to the Gestapo. Otherwise, why did he not simply take a taxi from the airport to the Embassy on Monday night? That's why he wanted to involve a journalist. As a witness.' March stooped and picked up the documents. 'Forgive me, as a mere *policeman* I do not understand the workings of the American press. But Charlie has her story now, does she not? She has Stuckart's death, the Swiss bank account, these papers, her tape-recording of Luther . . .' He turned to her. 'The fact that the American government chooses not to give Luther asylum, but abandons him to the Gestapo – won't that just make it even more attractive to the degenerate US media?'

Charlie said: 'You bet.'

Nightingale had started to look desperate again. 'Hey. Come on, Charlie. All that was off the record. I never said I agreed with any of it. There are plenty of us at the Embassy who don't think Kennedy should come here. At all. Period.' He fiddled with his bow-tie. 'But this situation – it's as tricky as hell.'

EVENTUALLY they reached an agreement. Nightingale would meet Charlie on the steps of the Great Hall at five minutes to nine. Assuming Luther turned up, they would hustle him quickly into a car which March would drive. Nightingale would listen to Luther's story and decide on the basis of what he heard whether to take him to the Embassy. He would not tell the Ambassador, Washington, or anyone else what he was planning to do. Once they were inside the Embassy compound, it would be up to what he called 'higher authorities' to decide Luther's fate – but they would have to act in the knowledge that Charlie had the whole story, and would print it. Charlie was confident the State Department would not dare turn Luther away.

Exactly how they would smuggle him out of Germany was another matter.

'We have methods,' said Nightingale. 'We *have* handled defectors before. But I'm not discussing it. Not in front of an SS officer. However trustworthy.' It was Charlie, he said, whom he was most worried about. 'You're going to come under a lot of pressure to keep your mouth shut.'

'I can handle it.'

'Don't be so sure. Kennedy's people – they fight dirty. All right. Let's suppose Luther *has* got something. Let's say it stirs everybody up – speeches in Congress, demonstrations, editorials – this is election year, remember? So suddenly the White House is in trouble over the summit. What do you think they're going to do?'

'I can handle it.'

'They're going to tip a truckful of shit over your head, Charlie, and over this old Nazi of yours. They'll say: what's he got that's new? The same old story we've heard for twenty years, plus a few documents, probably forged by the communists. Kennedy'll go on TV and he'll say: "My fellow Americans, ask yourselves: why has all this come up now? In whose interest is it to disrupt the summit?" ' Nightingale leaned close to her, his face a few centimetres from hers. 'First off, they'll put Hoover and the FBI on to it. Know any left-wingers, Charlie? Any Jewish militants? Slept with any? Because, sure as hell, they'll find a few who say you have, whether you've ever met them or not.'

'Screw you, Nightingale.' She shoved him away with her fist. 'Screw *you*.'

NIGHTINGALE really was in love with her, thought March. Lost in love, hopeless in love. And she knew it, and she played on it. He remembered that first night he saw them together in the bar: how she had shrugged off his restraining hand. Tonight: how he had looked at March when he saw him kissing her; how he had absorbed her temper, watching her with his moony eyes. In Zürich, her whisper: *'You asked if he was my lover . . . He'd like to be . . .'*

And now, on her doorstep, in his raincoat: hovering, uncertain, reluctant to leave them behind together, then finally disappearing into the night.

He would be there to meet Luther tomorrow, thought March, if only to make sure she was safe.

*

AFTER the American had gone they lay side by side on her narrow bed. For a long time neither spoke. The street lights cast long shadows, the window frame slanted across the ceiling like cell bars. In the slight breeze the curtains trembled. Once, there were the sounds of shouts and car doors slamming – revellers returning from watching the fireworks.

They listened to the voices fade along the street, then March whispered: 'Last night on the telephone – you said you had found something.'

She touched his hand, climbed off the bed. In the sitting room he could hear her rummaging among the heaps of paper. She returned half a minute later carrying a large coffee-table book. 'I bought this on the way back from the airport.' She sat on the edge of the bed, switched on the lamp, turned the pages. 'There.' She handed March the open book.

It was a reproduction, in black and white, of the painting in the Swiss bank vault. The monochrome did not do it justice. He marked the page with his finger and closed the book to read its title. *The Art of Leonardo da Vinci*, by Professor Arno Braun of the Kaiser Friedrich Museum, Berlin.

'My God.'

'I know. I thought I recognised it. Read it.'

The Lady with the Ermine, the scholars called it. 'One of the most mysterious of all Leonardo's works.' It was believed to have been painted *circa* 1483–6, and 'believed to show Cecilia Gallerani, the young mistress of Lodovico Sforza, ruler of Milan'. There were two published references to it: one in a poem by Bernardino Bellincioni (died 1492); the other, an ambiguous remark about an 'immature' portrait, written by Cecilia Gallerani herself in a letter dated 1498. 'But sadly for the student of Leonardo, the real mystery today is the painting's whereabouts. It is known to have entered the collection of the Polish Prince Adam Czartoryski in the late eighteenth century, and was photographed in Krakau in 1932. Since then it has disappeared into what Karl von Clausewitz so eloquently called "the fog of war". All efforts by the Reich authorities to locate it have so far failed, and it must now be feared that this priceless flowering of the Italian Renaissance is lost to mankind forever.'

He closed the book. 'I think, another story for you.'

'And a good one. There are only nine undisputed Leonardos in the world.' She smiled. 'If I ever get out of here to write it.'

'Don't worry. We'll get you out.' He lay back and closed his eyes. After a few moments he heard her put down the book, then she joined him on the bed, wriggling close to him.

'And you?' she breathed in his ear. 'Will you come out with me?'

'We can't talk now. Not here.'

'Sorry. I forgot.' Her tongue tip touched his ear.

A jolt, like electricity.

Her hand rested lightly on his leg. With her fingers, she traced the inside of his thigh. He started to murmur something, but again, as in Zürich, she placed a finger to his lips.

'The object of the game is: not to make a sound.'

LATER, unable to sleep himself, he listened to her: the sigh of her breath, the occasional mutter – far away and indistinct. In her dreams, she turned towards him, groaning. Her arm was flung across the pillow, shielding her face. She seemed to be fighting some private battle. He stroked the tangle of her hair, waiting until whatever demon it was had released her, then he slipped out from beneath the sheets.

The kitchen floor was cold to his naked feet. He opened a couple of cupboards. Dusty crockery and a few half-empty packets of food. The refrigerator was ancient, might have been borrowed from some institute of biology, its contents blue-furred and mottled with exotic moulds. Self-catering, it was clear, was not a priority around here. He boiled a kettle, rinsed a mug and heaped in three spoonfuls of instant coffee.

He wandered through the apartment sipping the bitter drink. In the sitting room he stood beside the window and pulled back the curtain a fraction. Bülow Strasse was deserted. He could see the telephone box, dimly illuminated, and the shadows of the station entrance behind it. He let the curtain fall back.

America. The prospect had never occurred to him before. When he thought of it, his brain reached automatically for the images Doctor Goebbels had thoughtfully planted there. Jews and Negroes. Top-hatted capitalists and smokestack factories. Beggars on the streets. Striptease bars. Gangsters shooting at one another from vast automobiles. Smouldering tenements and modern jazz bands, wailing across the ghettos like police sirens. Kennedy's toothy smile. Charlie's dark eyes and white limbs. *America*.

He went into the bathroom. The walls were stained by steam clouds and splashes of soap. Bottles everywhere, and tubes, and small pots. Mysterious feminine objects of glass and plastic. It was a long time since he had seen a woman's bathroom. It made him feel clumsy and foreign – the heavy-footed ambassador of some other species. He picked up a few things and sniffed at them, squeezed a drop of white cream on to his finger and rubbed at it with his thumb. This smell of her mingled with the others already on his hands.

He wrapped himself in a large towel and sat down on the floor to think. Three or four times before dawn he heard her shout out in her sleep – cries of real fear. Memory or prophecy? He wished he knew.

TWO

Just before seven he went down into Bülow Strasse. His Volkswagen was parked a hundred metres up the street, on the left, outside a butcher's shop. The owner was hanging plump carcasses in the window. A heaped tray of blood-red sausages at his feet reminded March of something.

Globus's fingers, that's what it was – those immense raw fists.

He bent over the back seat of the Volkswagen, tugging his suitcase towards him. As he straightened, he glanced quickly in either direction. There was nothing special to see – just the usual signs of an early Saturday morning. Most shops would open as normal but then close at lunchtime in honour of the holiday.

Back in the apartment he made more coffee, set a mug on the bedside table beside Charlie, and went into the bathroom to shave. After a couple of minutes he heard her come in behind him. She clasped her arms around his chest and squeezed, her breasts pressing into his bare back. Without turning round he kissed her hand and wrote in the steam on the mirror: PACK. NO RETURN. As he wiped away the message, he saw her clearly for the first time – hair tangled, eyes half-closed, the lines of her face still soft with sleep. She nodded and ambled back into the bedroom.

He dressed in his civilian clothes as he had for Zürich, but with one difference. He slipped his Luger into the right-hand pocket of his trench coat. The coat – old surplus Wehrmacht-issue, picked up cheaply long ago – was baggy enough for the weapon not to show. He could even hold the pistol and aim it surreptitiously through the material of the pocket, gangster-style: 'Okay, buddy, let's go.' He smiled to himself. America, again.

The possible presence of a microphone cast a shadow over their preparations. They moved quietly around the apartment without speaking. At ten past eight she was ready. March collected the radio from the bathroom, placed it on the table in the sitting room, and turned up the volume. '*From the pictures sent in for exhibition it is clear that the eye of some men shows them things other than as they are – that there really are men who on principle feel meadows to be blue, the heavens green, the clouds sulphur-yellow . . .*' It was the custom at this time to rebroadcast the Führer's most historic speeches. They replayed this one every year – the attack on modern painters, delivered at the inauguration of the House of German Art in 1937.

Ignoring her silent protests, March picked up her suitcase as well as his own. She donned her blue coat. From one shoulder she hung a leather bag. Her camera dangled from the other. On the threshold, she turned for a final look.

'*Either these "artists" do really see things in this way and believe in that which they represent – then one has but to ask how the defect in vision arose, and if it is hereditary the Minister of the Interior will have to see to it that so ghastly a defect shall not be allowed to perpetuate itself – or, if they do not believe in the reality of such impressions but seek on other grounds to impose them upon the nation, then it is a matter for a criminal court.*'

They closed the door on a storm of laughter and applause.

As they went downstairs, Charlie whispered: 'How long does this go on?'

'All weekend.'

'That will please the neighbours.'

'Ah, but will anyone dare ask you to turn it down?'

At the foot of the stairs, as still as a sentry, stood the concierge – a bottle of milk in one hand, a copy of the *Völkischer Beobachter* tucked under her arm. She spoke to Charlie but stared at March: 'Good morning, Fräulein.'

'Good morning, Frau Schustermann. This is my cousin, from Aachen. We are going to record the images of spontaneous celebration on the streets.' She patted her camera. 'Come on, Harald, or we'll miss the start.'

The old woman continued to scowl at March and he wondered if she recognised him from the other night. He doubted it: she would only remember the uniform. After a few moments she grunted and waddled back into her apartment.

'You lie very plausibly,' said March, when they were out on the street.

'A journalist's training.' They walked quickly towards the Volkswagen. 'It was lucky you weren't wearing your uniform. Then she really would have had some questions.'

'There is no possibility of Luther getting into a car driven by a man in the uniform of an SS-Sturmbannführer. Tell me: do I look like an Embassy chauffeur?'

'Only a very distinguished one.'

He stowed the suitcases in the trunk of the car. When he was settled in the front seat, before he switched on the engine, he said: 'You can never go back, you realise that? Whether this works or not. Assisting a defector – they'll think you're a spy. It won't be a question of deporting you. It's much more serious than that.'

She waved her hand dismissively. 'I never cared for that place anyway.'

He turned the key in the ignition and they pulled out into the morning traffic.

DRIVING carefully, checking every thirty seconds to make

sure they were not being followed, they reached Adolf Hitler Platz at twenty to nine. March executed one circuit of the square. Reich Chancellery, Great Hall, Wehrmacht High Command building – all seemed as it should be: masonry gleamed, guards marched; everything was as crazily out of scale as ever.

A dozen tour buses were already disgorging their awed cargoes. A crocodile file of children made its way up the snowy steps of the Great Hall, towards the red granite pillars, like a line of ants. In the centre of the Platz, beneath the great fountains, were piles of crush barriers, ready to be put into position on Monday morning, when the Führer was due to drive from the Chancellery to the Hall for the annual ceremony of thanksgiving. Afterwards he would return to his residence to appear on the balcony. German television had erected a scaffolding tower directly opposite. Live broadcast vans clustered around its base.

March pulled into a parking space close to the tourist coaches. From here he had a clear view across the lanes of traffic to the centre of the Hall.

'Walk up the steps,' he said, 'go inside, buy a guide book, look as natural as you can. When Nightingale appears, bump into him: you're old friends, isn't it marvellous, you stop and talk for a while.'

'What about you?'

'When I see you've made contact with Luther, I'll drive across and pick you up. The rear doors are unlocked. Keep to the lower steps, close to the road. And don't let him drag you into a long conversation – we need to get out of here fast.'

She was gone before he could wish her luck.

Luther had chosen his ground well. There were vantage points all around the Platz: the old man would be able to watch the steps without showing himself. Nobody would pay any attention to three strangers meeting. And if something did go wrong, the throngs of visitors offered the ideal cover for escape.

March lit a cigarette. Twelve minutes to go. He watched as Charlie climbed the long flight of steps. She paused at the top for breath, then turned and disappeared inside.

Everywhere: activity. White taxis and the long, green Mercedes of the Wehrmacht High Command circled the Platz. The television technicians checked their camera angles and shouted instructions at one another. Stallholders arranged their wares – coffee, sausages, postcards, newspapers, ice cream. A squadron of pigeons wheeled overhead in tight formation and fluttered in to land beside one of the fountains. A couple of young boys in Pimpf uniforms ran towards them, flapping their arms, and March thought of Pili – a stab – and closed his eyes for an instant, confining his guilt to the dark.

At five to nine exactly she came out of the shadows and began descending the steps. A man in a fawn raincoat strode towards her. Nightingale.

Don't make it too obvious, idiot . . .

She stopped and threw her arms wide – a perfect mime of surprise. They began talking.

Two minutes to nine.

Would Luther come? If so, from which direction? From the Chancellery to the east? The High Command building to the west? Or directly north, from the centre of the Platz?

Suddenly, at the window beside him, a gloved hand appeared. Attached to it: the body of an Orpo traffic cop in leather uniform.

March wound down the window.

The cop said: 'Parking here suspended.'

'Understood. Two minutes and I'm out of here.'

'Not two minutes. Now.' The man was a gorilla, escaped from Berlin Zoo.

March tried to keep his eyes on the steps, maintain a

conversation with the Orpo man, while pulling his Kripo ID out of his inside pocket.

'You are screwing up badly, friend,' he hissed. 'You are in the middle of a Sipo surveillance operation and, I have to tell you, you are blending into the background as well as a prick in a nunnery.'

The cop grabbed the ID and held it close to his eyes. 'Nobody told me about any operation, Sturmbannführer. What operation? Who's being watched?'

'Communists. Freemasons. Students. Slavs.'

'Nobody told me about it. I'll have to check.'

March clutched the steering wheel to steady his shaking hands. 'We are observing radio silence. You break it and Heydrich personally will have your balls for cufflinks, I guarantee you. Now: my ID.'

Doubt clouded the Orpo man's face. For an instant he almost looked ready to drag March out of the car, but then he slowly returned the ID. 'I don't know . . .'

'Thank you for your co-operation, Unterwachtmeister.' March wound up his window, ending the discussion.

One minute past nine. Charlie and Nightingale were still talking. He glanced in his mirror. The cop had walked a few paces, had stopped, and was staring back at the car. He looked thoughtful, then made up his mind, went over to his bike and picked up his radio.

March swore. He had two minutes, at the outside.

Of Luther: no sign.

AND then he saw him.

A man with thick-framed glasses, wearing a shabby overcoat, had emerged from the Great Hall. He stood, peering around him, his hand touching one of the granite pillars as if afraid to let go. Then, hesitantly, he began to make his way down the steps.

March switched on the engine.

Charlie and Nightingale still had their backs to him. He was heading towards them.

Come on. Come on. Look round at him, for God's sake.

At that moment Charlie did turn. She saw the old man and recognised him. Luther's arm came up, like an exhausted swimmer reaching for the shore.

Something is going to go wrong, thought March suddenly. *Something is not right. Something I haven't thought of* . . .

Luther had barely five metres to go when his head disappeared. It vanished in a puff of moist red sawdust and then his body was pitching forward, rolling down the steps, and Charlie was putting up her hand to shield her face from the sunburst of blood and brain.

A beat. A beat and a half. Then the crack of a high-velocity rifle howled around the Platz, scooping up the pigeons, scattering them like grey litter across the square.

PEOPLE started to scream.

March threw the car into gear, flashed his indicator and cut sharply into the traffic, ignoring the outraged hooting – across one lane, and then another. He drove like a man who believed himself invulnerable, as if faith and will-power alone would protect him from collision. He could see a little group had formed around the body which was leaking blood and tissue down the steps. He could hear police whistles. Figures in black uniforms were converging from all directions – Globus and Krebs among them.

Nightingale had Charlie by the arm and was propelling her away from the scene, towards the road, where March was braking to a halt. The diplomat wrenched open the door and threw her into the back seat, crammed himself in after her. The door slammed. The Volkswagen accelerated away.

WE *were betrayed.*

Fourteen men summoned; now fourteen dead.

He saw Luther's hand outstretched, the fountain bursting from his neck, his trunk exploded toppling forwards. Globus and Krebs running. Secrets scattered in that shower of tissue; salvation gone . . .

Betrayed . . .

HE drove to an underground parking lot just off Rosen Strasse, close to the Börse, where the Synagogue used to stand – a favourite spot of his for meeting informers. Was there anywhere more lonely? He took a ticket from the machine and pointed the car down the steep ramp. The tyres cried against the concrete; the headlights picked out ancient stains of oil and carbon on the floors and walls, like cave paintings.

Level two was empty – on Saturdays, the financial sector of Berlin was a desert. March parked in a central bay. When the engine died the silence was complete.

Nobody said anything. Charlie was dabbing at her coat with a paper handkerchief. Nightingale was leaning back with his eyes closed. Suddenly, March slammed his fists down on the top of the steering wheel.

'Whom did you tell?'

Nightingale opened his eyes. 'Nobody.'

'The Ambassador? Washington? The resident spy-master?'

'I told you: nobody.' There was anger in his voice.

'This is no help,' said Charlie.

'It's also insulting and absurd. Christ, you two . . .'

'Consider the possibilities.' March counted them off on his fingers. 'Luther betrayed *himself* to somebody – ridiculous. The telephone box in Bülow Strasse was tapped – impossible: even the Gestapo does not have the resources to bug every public telephone in Berlin. Very well. So was our discussion last night overheard? Unlikely, as we could hardly hear it ourselves!'

'Why does it have to be this big conspiracy? Maybe Luther was just followed.'

'Then why not pick him up? Why shoot him in public, at the very moment of contact?'

'He was looking straight at me . . .' Charlie covered her face with her hands.

'It needn't have been me,' said Nightingale. 'The leak could have come from one of you two.'

'How? We were together all night.'

'I'm sure you were.' He spat out the words and fumbled for the door. 'I don't have to take this sort of shit from you. Charlie – you'd better come back to the Embassy with me. Now. We'll get you on a flight out of Berlin tonight and just hope to Christ no one connects you with any of this.' He waited. 'Come on.'

She shook her head.

'If not for your sake, then think of your father.'

She was incredulous. 'What's my father got to do with it?'

Nightingale hauled himself out of the Volkswagen. 'I should never have let myself be talked into this insanity. You're a fool. As for him' – he nodded towards March – 'he's a dead man.'

He walked away from the car, his footsteps ricocheting around the deserted lot – loud at first, but fast becoming fainter. There was the clang of a metal door banging shut, and he was gone.

March looked at Charlie in the mirror. She seemed very small, huddled up in the back seat.

Far away: another noise. The barrier at the top of the ramp was being raised. A car was coming. March felt suddenly panicky, claustrophic. Their refuge could serve equally well as a trap.

'We can't stay here,' he said. He switched on the engine. 'We have to keep moving.'

'In that case I want to take more pictures.'

'Do you have to?'

'You assemble your evidence, Sturmbannführer, and I'll assemble mine.'

He glanced at her again. She had put aside her handkerchief and was staring at him with a fragile defiance. He took his foot off the brake. Crossing the city was risky, no question, but what else were they to do? Lie behind a locked door waiting to be caught?

He swung the car round in a circle and headed towards the exit as headlights flashed in the gloom behind them.

hey parked beside the Havel and walked to the shore. March pointed to the spot where Buhler's body had been found. Her camera clicked as Spiedel's had four days before, but there was little left to record. A few footprints were just visible in the mud. The grass was flattened slightly where the corpse had been dragged from the water. But in a day or two these signs would disappear. She turned away from the water and drew her coat around her, shivering.

It was too dangerous to drive to Buhler's villa so he stopped at the end of the causeway with the engine running. She leaned out to take a picture of the road leading to the island. The red and white pole was down. No sign of the sentry.

'Is that it?' she asked. '*Life* won't pay much for these.'

He thought for a moment. 'Perhaps there is another place.'

NUMBERS fifty-six to fifty-eight Am grossen Wannsee turned out to be a large nineteenth-century mansion with a pillared façade. It no longer housed the German headquarters of Interpol. At some point in the years since the war it had become a girls' school. March looked this way and that, up and down the leafy street where the blossom was in full pink bloom, and tried the gate. It was unlocked. He gestured to Charlie to join him.

'We are Herr and Frau March,' he said, as he pushed open the gate. 'We have a daughter . . .'

Charlie nodded. 'Yes, of course, Heidi. She is seven. With plaits . . .'

'She is unhappy at her present school. This one was recommended. We wanted to look around . . .' They stepped into the grounds. March closed the gates behind them.

She said: 'Naturally, if we are trespassing, we apologise . . .'

'But surely Frau March does not look old enough to have a sevenyear-old daughter?'

'She was seduced at an impressionable age by a handsome investigator . . .'

'A likely story.'

The gravel drive looped around a circular flower bed. March tried to picture it as it might have looked in January 1942. A dusting of snow on the ground, perhaps, or frost. Bare trees. A couple of guards shivering by the entrance. The government cars, one after the other, crunching over the icy gravel. An adjutant saluting and stepping forward to open the doors. Stuckart: handsome and elegant. Buhler: his lawyer's notes carefully arranged in his briefcase. Luther: blinking behind his thick spectacles. Did their breath hang in the air after them? And Heydrich. Would he have arrived first, as host? Or last, to demonstrate his power? Did the cold impart colour even to those pale cheeks?

The house was barred and deserted. While Charlie took a picture of the entrance, March picked his way through a small shrubbery to peer through a window. Rows of dwarf-sized desks with dwarf-sized chairs up-ended and stacked on top. A pair of blackboards from which the pupils were being taught the Party's special grace. On one:

BEFORE MEALS —
Führer, my Führer, bequeathed to me by the Lord,
Protect and preserve me as long as I live!
Thou hast rescued Germany from deepest distress,

I thank thee today for my daily bread.
Abideth thou long with me, forsaketh me not,
Führer, my Führer, my faith and my light!
Heil, mein Führer!

On the other:

AFTER MEALS –
Thank thee for this bountiful meal,
Protector of youth and friend of the aged!
I know thou hast cares, but worry not,
I am with thee by day and by night.
Lie thy head in my lap,
Be assured, my Führer, that thou art great.
Heil, mein Führer!

Childish paintings decorated the walls – blue meadows, green skies, clouds of sulphur-yellow. Children's art was perilously close to degenerate art; such perversity would have to be knocked out of them . . . March could smell the school-smell even from here: the familiar compound of chalk dust, wooden floors and stale, institutional food. He turned away.

Someone in a neighbouring garden had lit a bonfire. Pungent white smoke – wet wood and dead leaves – drifted across the lawn at the back of the house. A wide flight of steps flanked by stone lions with frozen snarls led down to the lawn. Beyond the grass, through the trees, lay the dull, glassy surface of the Havel. They were facing south. Schwanenwerder, less than half a kilometre away, would be just visible from the upstairs windows. When Buhler bought his villa in the early 1950s, had the proximity of the two sites been a motive –was he the villain being drawn back to the scene of his crime? If so, what crime was it exactly?

March bent and dug up a handful of soil, sniffed at it, let it run through his fingers. The trail had gone cold years ago.

AT the bottom of the garden were a couple of wooden barrels, green with age, used by the gardener to collect rainwater. March and Charlie sat on them side by side, legs dangling, looking across the lake. He was in no hurry to move on. Nobody would look for them here. There was something indescribably melancholy about it all – the silence, the dead leaves blowing across the lawn, the smell of the smoke – something that was the opposite of spring. It spoke of autumn, of the end of things.

He said: 'Did I tell you that before I went away to sea, there were Jews in our town? When I got back, they were all gone. I asked about it. People said they had been evacuated to the East. For resettlement.'

'Did they believe that?'

'In public, of course. Even in private it was wiser not to speculate. And easier. To pretend it was true.'

'Did *you* believe it?'

'I didn't think about it.

'Who cares?' he said suddenly. 'Suppose everyone knew all the details. Who would care? Would it really make any difference?'

'Someone thinks so,' she reminded him. 'That's why everyone who attended Heydrich's conference is dead. Except Heydrich.'

He looked back at the house. His mother, a firm believer in ghosts, used to tell him that brickwork and plaster soaked up history, stored what they had witnessed, like a sponge. Since then March had seen his share of places in which evil had been done and he did not believe it. There was nothing especially wicked about Am grossen Wannsee 56/58. It was just a large, businessman's mansion, now converted into a girls' school. So what were the walls absorbing now? Teenage crushes? Geometry lessons? Exam nerves?

He pulled out Heydrich's invitation. 'A discussion followed by luncheon.' Starting at noon. Ending at – what? – three or four in the afternoon. It would have been growing dark by the time they left. Yellow lamps in the windows; mist from the lake. Fourteen men. Well-fed; maybe some of them tipsy on the Gestapo's wine. Cars to take them back to central Berlin. Chauffeurs who had waited a long time outside, with cold feet and noses like icicles . . .

And then, less than five months later, in Zürich in the heat of midsummer, Martin Luther had marched into the offices of Hermann Zaugg, banker to the rich and frightened, and opened an account with four keys.

'I wonder why he was empty-handed.'

'What?' She was distracted. He had interrupted her thoughts.

'I always imagined Luther carrying a small suitcase of some sort. Yet when he came down the steps to meet you, he was empty-handed.'

'Perhaps he had stuffed everything into his pockets.'

'Perhaps.' The Havel looked solid; a lake of mercury. 'But he must have landed from Zürich with luggage of some sort. He had spent the night out of the country. And he had collected something from the bank.'

The wind stirred in the trees. March looked round. 'He was a suspicious old bastard after all. It would have been in his character to have kept back the really valuable material. He wouldn't have risked giving the Americans everything at once – otherwise how could he have bargained?'

A jet passed low overhead, dropping towards the airport, the pitch of its engines descending with it. Now *that* was a sound which did not exist in 1942 . . .

Suddenly he was on his feet, lifting her down to join him, and then he was striding up the lawn towards the house and she was following – stumbling, laughing, shouting at him to slow down.

HE parked the Volkswagen beside the road in Schlachtensee and sprinted into the telephone kiosk. Max Jaeger was not replying, neither at Werderscher Markt nor at his home. The lonely purr of the unanswered phone made March want to reach someone, anyone.

He tried Rudi Halder's number. Perhaps he could apologise, somehow hint it had been worth the risk. Nobody was in. He looked at the receiver. What about Pili? Even the boy's hostility would be contact of a sort. But in the bungalow in Lichtenrade there was no response either.

The city had shut down on him.

He was halfway out of the kiosk when, on impulse, he turned back and dialled the number of his own apartment. On the second ring, a man answered.

'Yes?' It was the Gestapo: Krebs's voice. 'March? I know it's you! Don't hang up!'

He dropped the receiver as if it had bitten him.

HALF an hour later he was pushing through the scuffed wooden doors into the Berlin city morgue. Without his uniform he felt naked. A woman cried softly in one corner, a female police auxiliary sitting stiffly beside her, embarrassed at this display of emotion in an official place. He showed the attendant his ID and asked after Martin Luther. The man consulted a set of dog-eared notes.

'Male, mid-sixties, identified as Luther, Martin. Brought in just after midnight. Railway accident.'

'What about the shooting this morning, the one in the Platz?'

The attendant sighed, licked a nicotined forefinger and

turned a page. 'Male, mid-sixties, identified as Stark, Alfred. Came in an hour ago.'

'That's the one. How was he identified?'

'ID in his pocket.'

'Right.' March moved decisively towards the elevator, forestalling any objection. 'I'll make my own way down.'

It was his misfortune, when the elevator doors opened, to find himself confronted by Doctor August Eisler.

'March!' Eisler looked shocked and took a pace backwards. 'The word is, you've been arrested.'

'The word is wrong. I'm working under cover.'

Eisler was staring at his civilian suit. 'What as? A pimp?' This amused the SS surgeon so much he had to take off his spectacles and wipe his eyes. March joined in his laughter.

'No, as a pathologist. I'm told the pay is good and the hours are non-existent.'

Eisler stopped smiling. '*You* can say that. *I've* been here since midnight.' He dropped his voice. 'A very senior man. Gestapo operation. Hush hush.' He tapped the side of his long nose. 'I can say nothing.'

'Relax, Eisler. I am aware of the case. Did Frau Luther identify the remains?'

Eisler looked disappointed. 'No,' he muttered. 'We spared her that.'

'And Stark?'

'My, my, March – you are well-informed. I'm on my way to deal with him now. Would you care to join me?'

In his mind March saw again the exploding head, the thick spurt of blood and brain. 'No. Thank you.'

'I thought not. What was he shot with? A Panzerfaust?'

'Have they caught the killer?'

'You're the investigator. You tell me. "Don't probe too deeply" was what I heard.'

'Stark's effects. Where are they?'

'Bagged and ready to go. In the property room.'

'Where's that?'

'Follow the corridor. Fourth door on the left.'

March set off. Eisler shouted after him: 'Hey March! Save me a couple of your best whores!' The pathologist's high-pitched laughter pursued him down the passage.

The fourth door on the left was unlocked. He checked to make sure he was unobserved, then let himself in.

It was a small storeroom, three metres wide, with just enough room for one person to walk down the centre. On either side of the gangway were racks of dusty metal shelving heaped with bundles of clothing wrapped in thick polythene. There were suitcases, handbags, umbrellas, artificial legs, a pushchair – grotesquely twisted – hats . . . From the morgue the deceased's belongings were usually collected by the next-of-kin. If the circumstances were suspicious, they would be taken away by the investigators, or sent direct to the forensic laboratories in Schönweld. March began inspecting the plastic tags, each of which recorded the time and place of death and the name of the victim. Some of the stuff here went back years – pathetic bundles of rags and trinkets, the final bequests of corpses nobody cared about, not even the police.

How typical of Globus not to admit to his mistake. The infallibility of the Gestapo must be preserved at all costs! Thus Stark's body continued to be treated as Luther's, while Luther would go to a pauper's grave as the drifter, Stark.

March tugged at the bundle closest to the door, turned the label to the light. *18.4.64. Adolf Hitler Pl. Stark, Alfred*.

So Luther had left the world like the lowest inmate of a KZ – violently, half-starved, in someone else's filthy clothes, his body unhonoured, with a stranger picking over his belongings after his death. Poetic justice – about the only sort of justice to be found.

He pulled out his pocket knife and slit the bulging plastic. The contents spilled over the floor like guts.

He did not care about Luther. All he cared about was how, in the hours between midnight and nine that morning, Globus had discovered Luther was still alive.

Americans!

He tore away the last of the polythene.

The clothes stank of shit and piss, of vomit and sweat – of every odour the human body nurtures. God only knew what parasites the fabric harboured. He went through the pockets. They were empty. His hands itched. *Don't give up hope. A left-luggage ticket is a small thing – tightly rolled, no bigger than a matchstick; an incision in a coat collar would conceal it.* With his knife he hacked at the lining of the long brown overcoat, matted with congealing blood, his fingers turning brown and slippery . . .

Nothing. All the usual scraps that in his experience tramps will carry – the bits of string and paper, the buttons, the cigarette-ends –had been removed already. The Gestapo had searched Luther's clothes with care. Naturally they had. He had been a fool to think they wouldn't. Furious, he slashed at the material – right to left, left to right, right to left . . .

He stood back from the heap of rags panting like an assassin. Then he picked up a piece of rag and wiped his knife and hands.

'You know what I think?' said Charlie when he returned to the car empty-handed. 'I think he never brought anything here from Zürich at all.'

She was still in the back seat of the Volkswagen. March turned to look at her. 'Yes he did. Of course he did.' He tried to hide his impatience; it was not her fault. 'But he was too scared to keep it with him. So he stored it, received a ticket for it – either at the airport or the station – and planned on collecting it later. I'm sure that's it. Now Globus has it, or it's lost for good.'

'No. Listen. I was thinking. Yesterday, when I was coming through the airport, I thanked God you stopped me trying to bring the painting back with us to Berlin. Remember the queues? They searched every bag. How could Luther have got *anything* past the Zollgrenzschutz?'

March considered this, massaging his temples. 'A good question,' he said eventually. 'Maybe,' he added a minute later, 'the best question I ever heard.'

AT the Flughafen Hermann Göring the statue of Hanna Reitsch was steadily oxidising in the rain. She stared across the concourse outside the departure terminal with rust-pitted eyes.

'You'd better stay with the car,' said March. 'Do you drive?'

She nodded. He dropped the keys in her lap. 'If the Flughafen Polizei try to move you on, don't argue with them. Drive off and come round again. Keep circling. Give me twenty minutes.'

'Then what?'

'I don't know.' His hand fluttered in the air. 'Improvise.'

He strode into the airport terminal. The big digital clock above the passport control zone flicked over: 13:22. He glanced behind him. He could measure his freedom probably in minutes. Less than that, if Globus had issued a general alert, for nowhere in the Reich was more heavily patrolled than the airport.

He kept thinking of Krebs in his apartment, and Eisler: *'The word is, you've been arrested.'*

A man with a souvenir bag from the Soldiers' Hall looked familiar. A Gestapo watcher? March abruptly changed direction and headed into the toilets. He stood at the urinal, pissing air, his eyes fixed on the entrance. Nobody came in. When he emerged, the man had gone.

'*Last call for Lufthansa flight two-zero-seven to Tiflis . . .*'

He went to the central Lufthansa desk and showed his ID to one of the guards. 'I need to speak to your head of security. Urgently.'

'He may not be here, Sturmbannführer.'

'Look for him.'

The guard was gone a long time. 13:27 said the clock. 13:28. Perhaps he was calling the Gestapo. 13:29. March put his hand in his pocket and felt the cold metal of the Luger. Better to make a stand here than crawl around the stone floor in Prinz-Albrecht Strasse spitting teeth into your hand.

13:30.

The guard returned. 'This way, Herr Sturmbannführer. If you please.'

FRIEDMAN had joined the Berlin Kripo at the same time as March. He had left it five years later, one step ahead of a corruption investigation. Now he wore hand-made English suits, smoked duty-free Swiss cigars, and made five times his official salary by methods long suspected but never proved. He was a merchant prince, the airport his corrupt little kingdom.

When he realised March had come not to investigate him but to beg a favour he was almost ecstatic. His excellent mood persisted as he led March along a passage away from the terminal building. 'And how is Jaeger? Spreading chaos I suppose? And Fiebes? Still jerking-off over pictures of Aryan maidens and Ukrainian window-cleaners? Oh, how

I miss you all, I don't think! Here we are.' Friedman transferred his cigar from his hand to his mouth and tugged at a large door. 'Behold the cave of Aladdin!'

The metal slid open with a crash to reveal a small hangar stuffed with lost and abandoned property. 'The things people leave behind,' said Friedman. 'You would not believe it. We even had a leopard once.'

'A leopard? A cat?'

'It died. Some idle bastard forgot to feed it. It made a good coat.' He laughed and snapped his fingers and from the shadows an elderly, stoop-shouldered man appeared – a Slav, with wide-set, fearful eyes.

'Stand up straight, man. Show respect.' Friedman gave him a shove that sent him staggering backwards. 'The Sturmbannführer here is a good friend of mine. He's looking for something. Tell him, March.'

'A case, perhaps a bag,' said March. 'The last flight from Zürich on Monday night, the thirteenth. Either left on the aircraft, or in the baggage reclaim area.'

'Got that? Right?' The Slav nodded. 'Well go on then!' He shuffled away and Friedman gestured to his mouth. 'Dumb. Had his tongue cut out in the war. The ideal worker!' He laughed and clapped March on the shoulder. 'So. How goes it?'

'Well enough.'

'Civilian clothes. Working the weekend. Must be something big.'

'It may be.'

'This is the Martin Luther character, right?' March made no reply. 'So you're dumb, too. I see.' Friedman flicked cigar ash on the clean floor. 'Fair enough by me. A brown-pants job. Possibly?'

'A what?'

'Zollgrenzschutz expression. Someone plans to bring in something they shouldn't. They get to the customs shed, see the security, start shitting themselves. Drop whatever it is and run.'

'But this is special, yes? You don't open every case every day?'

'Just in the week before the Führertag.'

'What about the lost property, do you open that?'

'Only if it looks valuable!' Friedman laughed again. 'No. A jest. We haven't the manpower. Anyway, it's been X-rayed, remember –no guns, no explosives. So we just leave it here, wait for someone to claim it. If no one's turned up in a year, then we open it, see what we've got.'

'Pays for a few suits, I suppose.'

'What?' Friedman plucked at his immaculate sleeve. 'These poor rags?' There was a sound and he turned round. 'Looks like you're in luck, March.'

The Slav was returning, carrying something. Friedman took it from him and weighed it in his hand. 'Quite light. Can't be gold. What do you think it is, March? Drugs? Dollars? Contraband silk from the East? A treasure map?'

'Are you going to open it?' March touched the gun in his pocket. He would use it if he had to.

Friedman appeared shocked. 'This is a favour. One friend to another. Your business.' He handed the case to March. 'You'll remember that, Sturmbannführer, won't you? A favour? One day you'll do the same for me, comrade to comrade?'

THE case was of the sort that doctors carry, with brass-reinforced corners and a stout brass lock, dull with age. The brown leather was scratched and faded, the heavy stitching dark, the hand-grip worn smooth like a brown pebble by years of carrying, until it felt like an extension of the hand. It proclaimed reliability and reassurance; professionalism; quiet wealth. It was certainly pre-war, maybe even pre-

Great War – built to last a generation or two. Solid. Worth a lot.

All this March absorbed on the walk back to the Volkswagen. The route avoided the Zollgrenzschutz – another favour from Friedman.

Charlie fell upon it like a child upon a birthday present and swore with disappointment when she found it locked. As March drove out of the airport perimeter she fished in her own bag and retrieved a pair of nail scissors. She picked desperately at the lock, the blades making ineffective scrabblings on the brass.

March said: 'You're wasting your time. I'll have to break it open. Wait till we get there.'

She shook the bag with frustration. 'Get where?'

He ran a hand through his hair.

A good question.

EVERY room in the city was booked. The Eden with its roof-garden café, the Bristol on Unter den Linden, the Kaiserhof in Mohren Strasse – all had stopped taking reservations months ago. The monster hotels with a thousand bedrooms and the little rooming houses dotted around the railway termini were filled with uniforms. Not just the SA and the SS, the Luftwaffe and the Wehrmacht, the Hitler Youth and the League of German Girls, but all the others besides: the National Socialist Empire War Association, the German Falconry Order, the National Socialist Leadership Schools . . .

Outside the most famous and luxurious of all Berlin's hotels – the Adlon, on the corner of Pariser Platz and Wilhelm Strasse – the crowds were straining at the metal barriers for a glimpse of celebrity: a film star, a footballer, a Party satrap in town for the Führertag. As March and Charlie passed it, a Mercedes was drawing up, its black-uniformed passengers bathed in the light of a score of flashguns.

March drove straight over the Platz into Unter den Linden, turned left and then right into Dorotheen Strasse. He parked among the dustbins at the back of the Prinz Friedrich Karl Hotel. It was here, over breakfast with Rudi Halder, that this business had really begun. When was that? He could not remember.

The manager of the Friedrich Karl was habitually clad in an old-fashioned black jacket and a pair of striped pants and he bore a striking resemblance to the late President Hindenburg. He came bustling out to the front desk, smoothing a large pair of white whiskers as if they were pets.

'Sturmbannführer March, what a pleasure! What a pleasure indeed! And dressed for relaxation!'

'Good afternoon, Herr Brecker. A difficult request. I must have a room.'

Brecker threw up his hands in distress. 'It is impossible! Even for as distinguished a customer as yourself.'

'Come, Herr Brecker. You must have something. An attic would do, a broom cupboard. You would be rendering the Reichskriminalpolizei the greatest assistance . . .'

Brecker's elderly eye travelled over the luggage and came to rest on Charlie, at which point a gleam entered it. 'And this is Frau March?'

'Unfortunately, no.' March put his hand on Brecker's sleeve and guided him into a corner, where they were watched with suspicion by the elderly receptionist. 'This young lady has information of a crucial character, but we wish to interrogate her . . . how shall I put it?'

'In an informal setting?' suggested the old man.

'Precisely!' March pulled out what was left of his life savings and began peeling off notes. 'For this "informal setting" the Kriminalpolizei naturally would wish to reimburse you handsomely.'

'I see.' Brecker looked at the money and licked his lips. 'And since this is a matter of security, no doubt you would prefer it if certain formalities – registration, for example – were dispensed with?'

March stopped counting, pressed the entire roll of notes into the manager's moist hands and closed his fingers around it.

IN return for bankrupting himself March was given a kitchen maid's room in the roof, reached from the third floor by a rickety back staircase. They had to wait in the reception for five minutes while the girl was turned out of her home and fresh linen was put on the bed. Herr Brecker's repeated offers to help with their luggage were turned down by March, who also ignored the lascivious looks which the old man kept giving Charlie. He did, however, ask for some food – some bread, cheese, ham, fruit, a flask of black coffee – which the manager promised to bring up personally. March told him to leave it in the corridor.

'It's not the Adlon,' said March when he and Charlie were alone. The little room was stifling. All the heat in the hotel seemed to have risen and become trapped beneath the tiles. He climbed on a chair to tug open the attic window and jumped down in a shower of dust.

'Who cares about the Adlon?' She flung her arms around him, kissed him hard on the mouth.

THE manager set down the tray of food as instructed outside the door. Climbing the stairs had almost done for him. Through three centimetres of wood, March listened to his ragged breathing, and then to his footsteps retreating along the passage. He waited until he was sure the old man had gone before retrieving the tray and setting it on the flimsy dressing table. There was no lock on the bedroom door, so he wedged a chair under the handle.

MARCH laid Luther's case on the hard wooden bed and took out his pocket knife.

The lock had been fashioned to withstand exactly this sort of assault. It took five minutes of hacking and twisting, during which he snapped one short blade, before the fastener broke free. He pulled the bag open.

That papery smell again – the odour of a long-sealed filing cabinet or desk drawer, a whiff of typewriter oil. And behind that, something else: something antiseptic, medicinal . . .

Charlie was at his shoulder. He could feel her warm breath on his cheek. 'Don't tell me. It's empty.'

'No. It's not empty. It's full.'

He pulled out his handkerchief and wiped the sweat from his hands. Then he turned the case upside down and shook the contents out on to the counterpane.

FOUR

Affidavit sworn by Wilhelm Stuckart, State Secretary, Interior Ministry:

[4 pages; typewritten]

On Sunday 21 December 1941, the Interior Ministry's Adviser on Jewish Affairs, Dr Bernhard Losener, made an urgent request to see me in private. Dr Losener arrived at my home in a state of extreme agitation. He informed me that his subordinate, the Assistant Adviser on Racial Affairs, Dr Werner Feldscher, had heard 'from a fully reliable source, a friend' that the one thousand Jews recently evacuated from Berlin had been massacred in the Rumbuli Forest in Poland. He further informed me that his feelings of outrage were sufficient to prevent him from continuing his present employment in the Ministry, and he therefore requested to be transferred to other duties. I replied that I would seek clarification on this matter.

The following day, at my request, I visited Obergruppenführer Reinhard Heydrich in his office in Prinz-Albrecht Strasse. The Obergruppenführer confirmed that Dr Feldscher's information was correct, and pressed me to discover its source, as such breaches of security could not be tolerated. He then dismissed his adjutant from the room and said that he wished to speak to me on a private basis.

He informed me that in July he had been summoned to the Führer's headquarters in East Prussia. The Führer had spoken to him frankly in the following terms: He had decided to resolve the Jewish Question once and for all. The hour had arrived. He could not rely upon his successors having the necessary will or the military power which he now commanded. He was not afraid of the consequences. People presently revered the French Revolution, but who now remembered the thousands of innocents who died? Revolutionary times were governed by their own laws. When Germany had won the war, nobody would ask afterwards how we did it. Should Germany lose the mortal struggle, at least those who had hoped to profit from the defeat of National Socialism would be wiped out. It was necessary to remove the biological bases of Judaism once and for all. Otherwise the problem would erupt to plague future generations. That was the lesson of history.

Obergruppenführer Heydrich stated further that the necessary powers to enable him to implement this Führer Order had been granted to him by Reichsmarschall Goering on 31.7.41. These matters would be discussed at the forthcoming inter-departmental conference. In the meantime, he urged me to use whatever means I considered necessary to discover the identity of Dr Feldscher's source. This was a matter of the highest security classification.

I thereupon suggested that, in view of the grave issues involved, it would be appropriate, from a legal point of view, to have the Führer Order placed in writing. Obergruppenführer Heydrich stated that such a course was impossible, due to political considerations, but that if I had any reservations I should take them up with the Führer personally. Obergruppenführer Heydrich concluded our meeting by remarking in a jocular manner that we should have no cause for concern on legalistic grounds, considering that I was the Reich's chief legal draftsman and he was the Reich's chief policeman.

I hereby swear that this is a true record of our conversation, based upon notes taken by myself that same evening.

> SIGNED, Wilhelm Stuckart (attorney)
> DATED 4 June 1942, Berlin
> WITNESSED, Josef Buhler (attorney)

FIVE

𝔄 cross the city the day died. The sun dropped behind the dome of the Great Hall, gilding it like the cupola of a giant mosque. With a hum, the floodlights cut in along the Avenue of Victory and the East-West Axis. The afternoon crowds melted, dissolved, re-formed as night-time queues outside the cinemas and restaurants, while above the Tiergarten, lost in the gloom, an airship droned.

REICH MINISTRY FOR FOREIGN AFFAIRS SECRET STATE DOCUMENT

DISPATCH FROM GERMAN AMBASSADOR IN LONDON,
HERBERT VON DIRKSEN

*Account of conversations with Ambassador Joseph P. Kennedy,
United States Ambassador to Great Britain*

[Extracts; two pages, printed]

Received Berlin, 13 June 1938

Although he did not know Germany, [Ambassador Kennedy] had learned from the most varied sources that the present Government had done great things for Germany and that the Germans were satisfied and enjoyed good living conditions.

The Ambassador then touched upon the Jewish question and stated that it was naturally of great importance to German–American relations. In this connection it was not so much the fact that we wanted to get rid of the Jews that was harmful to us, but rather the loud clamour with which we accompanied this purpose. He himself understood our Jewish policy completely; he was from Boston and there, in one golf club, and in other clubs, no Jews had been admitted for the past fifty years.

Received Berlin, 18 October 1938
Today, too, as during former conversations, Kennedy mentioned that very strong anti-Semitic tendencies existed in the United States and that a large portion of the population had an understanding of the German attitude toward the Jews . . . From his whole personality I believe he would get on very well with the Führer.

'WE can't do this alone.'
'We must.'
'Please. Let me take them to the Embassy. They could smuggle them out through the diplomatic bag.'
'No!'
'You can't be certain he betrayed us . . .'
'Who else could it be? And look at this. Do you really think American diplomats would want to touch it?'
'But if we're caught with it . . . It's a death warrant.'
'I have a plan.'
'A good one?'
'It had better be.'

CENTRAL CONSTRUCTION OFFICE, AUSCHWITZ, TO GERMAN EQUIPMENT
WORKS, AUSCHWITZ, 31 MARCH 1943

Your letter of 24 March 1943

[Excerpt]

In reply to your letter, the three airtight towers are to be built in accordance with the order of 18 January 1943, for Bw 30B and 3c, in the same dimensions and in the same manner as the towers already delivered.

We take this occasion to refer to another order of 6 March 1943, for the delivery of a gas door 100/192 for

corpse cellar I of crematory III, Bw 30a, which is to be built
in the manner and according to the same measure as the
cellar door of the opposite crematory II, with peep-hole of
double 8 millimetre glass encased in rubber. This order is
to be viewed as especially urgent . . .

NOT far from the hotel, north of Unter den Linden, was an
all-night pharmacy. It was owned, as all businesses were, by
Germans, but it was run by Rumanians – the only people
poor enough and willing enough to work such hours. It was
stocked like a bazaar with cooking pans, paraffin heaters,
stockings, baby food, greeting cards, stationery, toys, film
. . . Among Berlin's swollen population of guest workers it
did a brisk trade.

They entered separately. At one counter, Charlie spoke
to the elderly woman assistant who promptly disappeared
into a back room and returned with an assortment of
bottles. At another, March bought a school exercise book,
two sheets of thick brown paper, two sheets of gift wrap
paper and a roll of clear tape.

They left and walked two blocks to the Friedrich Strasse
station where they caught the south-bound U-bahn train.
The carriage was packed with the usual Saturday night
crowd – lovers holding hands, families off to the illumina-
tions, young men on a drinking spree – and nobody, as far
as March could tell, paid them the slightest attention.
Nevertheless, he waited until the doors were about to slide
shut before he dragged her out on to the platform of the
Tempelhof station. A ten-minute journey on a number
thirty-five tram brought them to the airport.

Throughout all this they sat in silence.

KRAKAU

18.7.43

[Handwritten]

My dear Kritzinger,
Here is the list.

Auschwitz	50.02N	19.11E
Kulmhof	53.20N	18.25E
Blezec	50.12N	23.28E
Treblinka	52.48N	22.20E
Majdanek	51.18N	22.31E
Sobibor	51.33N	23.31E

Heil Hitler!

[Signed]

Buhler [?]

TEMPELHOF was older than the Flughafen Hermann Goering – shabbier, more primitive. The departures terminal had been built before the war and was decorated with pictures of the pioneering days of passenger flight – old Lufthansa Junkers with corrugated fuselages, dashing pilots with goggles and scarves, intrepid women travellers with stout ankles and cloche hats. Innocent days! March took up a position by the entrance to the terminal and pretended to study the photographs as Charlie approached the car rentals desk.

Suddenly, she was smiling, making apologetic gestures with her hands – playing to perfection the lady in distress. She had missed the flight, her family was waiting . . . The rental agent was charmed, and consulted a typed sheet. For a moment, the issue hung in the balance – and then, yes, as it happened, Fräulein, he *did* have something. Something for someone with eyes as pretty as yours, of course . . . Your driving licence, please . . .

She handed it over. It had been issued the previous year in the name of Voss, Magda, aged twenty-four, of Mariendorf, Berlin. It was the licence of the girl murdered on her wedding day five days ago – the licence Max Jaeger had left in his desk, along with all the other papers from the Spandau shootings.

March looked away, forcing himself to study an old aerial photograph of the Tempelhof airfield. BERLIN was painted in huge white letters along the runway. When he glanced back, the agent was entering details of the licence on the rental form, laughing at some witticism of his own.

As a strategy it was not without risk. In the morning, a copy of the rental agreement would be forwarded automatically to the Polizei, and even the Orpo would wonder why a murdered woman was hiring a car. But tomorrow was Sunday, Monday was the Führertag, and by Tuesday – the earliest the Orpo were likely to pull their fingers out of their backsides – March reckoned he and Charlie would either be safe or arrested, or dead.

Ten minutes later, with a final exchange of smiles, she was given the keys to a four-door black Opel, with ten thousand kilometres on the clock. Five minutes after that, March joined her in the parking lot. He navigated while she drove. It was the first time he had seen her behind the wheel: another side of her. In the busy traffic she displayed an exaggerated caution which he felt did not come naturally.

Sketch of Installation by Martin Luther

[Dated 15 July 1943; handwritten; 1 page]

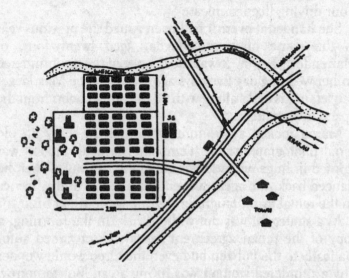

THE lobby of the Prince Friedrich Karl was deserted: the guests were out for the night. As they passed through it towards the stairs the receptionist kept her head down. They were just another of Herr Brecker's little scams – best not to know too much.

Their room had not been searched. The cotton threads hung where March had wedged them, between door and frame. Inside, when he pulled Luther's case out from beneath the bed, the single strand of hair was still laced through the lock.

CHARLIE stepped out of her dress and wrapped a towel around her shoulders.

In the bathroom at the end of the passage, a naked

bulb lit a grimy sink. A bath stood on tiptoe, on iron claws.

MARCH walked back to the bedroom, shut himself in, and once more propped the chair up against the door. He piled the contents of the case on the dressing table – the map, the various envelopes, the minutes and memoranda, the reports, including the one with the rows of statistics, typed on the machine with the extra-large letters. Some of the paper crackled with age. He remembered how he and Charlie had sat during the sunlit afternoon, with the rumble of traffic outside; how they had passed the evidence backwards and forwards to one another – at first with excitement, then stunned, disbelieving, silent, until at last they came to the pouch with the photographs.

Now he needed to be more systematic. He pulled up a chair, cleared a space, and opened the exercise book. He tore out thirty pages. At the top of each sheet he wrote the year and the month, beginning with July 1941 and ending in January 1944. He took off his jacket and draped it over the back of the chair. Then he began to work his way through the heap of papers, making notes in his clear script.

A RAILWAY timetable – badly printed on yellowing wartime paper:

Date	Train no	From	Departs	To	Arrives
26.1	Da 105	Theresienstadt		Auschwitz	
27.1	Lp 106	Auschwitz		Theresienstadt	
29.1	Da 13	Berlin	17.20	Auschwitz	10.48
	Da 107	Theresienstadt		Auschwitz	
30.1	Lp 108	Auschwitz		Theresienstadt	

315

31.1	Lp 14	Auschwitz		Zamocz	
1.2	Da 109	Theresienstadt		Auschwitz	
2.2	Da 15	Berlin	17.20	Auschwitz	10.48
	Lp 110	Auschwitz		Myslowitz	
3.2	Po 65	Zamocz	11.00	Auschwitz	
4.2	Lp 16	Auschwitz		Litzmannstadt	

. . . and so on, until, in the second week of February, a new destination appeared. Now almost all the times had been worked out to the minute:

11.2	Pj 131	Bialystok	9.00	Treblinka	12.10
	Lp 132	Treblinka	21.18	Bialystok	1.30
12.2	Pj 133	Bialystok	9.00	Treblinka	12.10
	Lp 134	Treblinka	21.18	Grodno	
13.2	Pj 135	Bialystok	9.00	Treblinka	12.10
	Lp 136	Treblinka	21.18	Bialystok	1.30
14.2	Pj 163	Grodno	5.40	Treblinka	12.10
	Lp 164	Treblinka		Scharfenwiese	

. . . and so on again, until the end of the month.

A rusty paper clip had mottled the edge of the timetable. Attached to it was a telegraphic letter from the General Management, Directorate East, of the German Reich Railways, dated Berlin, 13 January 1943. First, a list of recipients:

> Reich Railway Directorates
> Berlin, Breslau, Dresden, Erfurt, Frankfurt, Halle (S), Karlsruhe, Königsberg (Pr), Linz, Mainz, Oppeln, East in Frankfurt (O), Posen, Vienna
> General Directorate of East Railway in Krakau
> Reichsprotektor, Group Railways in Prague
> General Traffic Directorate Warsaw
> Reich Traffic Directorate Minsk

Then, the main text:

Subject: Special trains for resettlers during the period from 20 January to 28 February 1943.
We enclose a compilation of the special trains (Vd, Rm, Po, Pj and Da) agreed upon in Berlin on 15 January 1943 for the period from 20 January 1943 to 28 February 1943 and a circulatory plan for cars to be used in these trains.

Train formation is noted for each recirculation and attention is to be paid to these instructions. After each full trip cars are to be well cleaned, if necessary fumigated, and upon completion of the programme prepared for further use. Number and kinds of cars are to be determined upon dispatch of the last train and are to be reported to me by telephone with confirmation on service cards.

[Signed] Dr Jacobi
33 Bfp 5 Bfsv   Minsk 9 Feb. 1943

March flicked back to the timetable and read it through again. Theresienstadt/Auschwitz, Auschwitz/Theresienstadt, Bialystok/ Treblinka, Treblinka/Bialystok: the syllables drummed in his tired brain like the rhythm of wheels on a railway track.

He ran his finger down the columns of figures, trying to decipher the message behind them. So: a train would be loaded in the Polish town of Bialystok at breakfast time. By lunchtime, it would be at this hell, Treblinka. (Not all the journeys were so brief – he shuddered at the thought of the *seventeen hours* from Berlin to Auschwitz.) In the afternoon, the cars would be unloaded at Treblinka and fumigated. At nine o'clock that evening they would return to Bialystok, arriving in the early hours, ready to be loaded up again at breakfast.

On 12 February, the pattern breaks. Instead of going back to Bialystok, the empty train is sent to Grodno. Two days in the sidings there, and then – in the dark, long before dawn – the train is once more heading back, fully laden, to Treblinka. It arrives at lunchtime. Is unloaded. And that night begins rattling back westwards again, this time to Scharfenweise.

What else could an investigator of the Berlin Kriminal-polizei deduce from this document?

Well, he could deduce numbers. Say: sixty persons per car, an average of sixty cars per train. Deduction: three thousand six hundred persons per transport.

By February, the transports were running at the rate of one per day. Deduction: twenty-five thousand persons per week; one hundred thousand persons per month; one and a quarter million persons per year. And this was the average achieved in the depths of the Central European winter, when the points froze and drifts of snow blocked the tracks and the partisans materialised from the woods like ghosts to plant their bombs.

Deduction: the numbers would be even greater in the spring and summer.

HE stood at the bathroom door. Charlie, in a black slip, had her back to him and was bending over the wash basin. With her hair wet she looked smaller; almost fragile. The muscles in her pale shoulders flexed as she massaged her scalp. She rinsed her hair a final time and stretched a hand out blindly behind her. He gave her a towel.

Along the edge of the bath she had set out various objects – a pair of green rubber gloves, a brush, a dish, a spoon, two bottles. March picked up the bottles and studied their labels. One contained a mixture of magnesium carbonate and sodium acetate, the other a twenty-volume solution of hydrogen peroxide. Next to the mirror above the basin she had propped open the girl's passport. Magda Voss regarded March with wide and untroubled eyes.

'Are you sure this is going to work?'

Charlie wound the towel around her head into a turban.

'First I go red. Then orange. Then white-blonde.' She took the bottles from him. 'I was a fifteen-year-old schoolgirl with a crush on Jean Harlow. My mother went crazy. Trust me.'

She squeezed her hands into the rubber gloves and measured the chemicals into the dish. With the spoon she began to mix them into a thick blue paste.

SECRET REICH MATTER. CONFERENCE MINUTES. 30 COPIES. COPY NUMBER . . .

(The figure had been scratched out.)

The following participated in the conference of 20 January 1942, in Berlin, Am grossen Wannsee 56/58, on the final solution of the Jewish question . . .

March had read the minutes twice that afternoon. Nevertheless, he forced himself to wade through the pages again. 'Around 11 million Jews are involved in this final solution of the Jewish problem . . .' Not just German Jews. The minutes listed more than thirty European nationalities, including French Jews (865,000), Dutch Jews (160,000), Polish Jews (2,284,000), Ukrainian Jews (2,994,684); there were English, Spanish, Irish, Swedish and Finnish Jews; the conference even found room for the Albanian Jews (all 200 of them).

In the course of the final solution, the Jews should be brought under appropriate direction in a suitable manner to the east for labour utilisation. Separated by sex, the Jews capable of work will be led into these areas in large labour columns to build roads, whereby doubtless a large part will fall away through natural reduction.

The inevitable final remainder which doubtless constitutes the toughest element will have to be dealt with appropriately, since it represents a natural selection which upon liberation is to be regarded as a germ cell of a new Jewish development. (See the lesson of history.)

In the course of the practical implementation of the final solution, Europe will be combed from west to east.'

'*Brought under appropriate direction in a suitable manner . . . the toughest element will have to be dealt with appropriately . . .*' 'Appropriate, appropriately'. The favourite words in the bureaucrat's lexicon – the grease for sliding round unpleasantness, the funk-hole for avoiding specifics.

March unfolded a set of rough photostats. These appeared to be copies of the original draft minutes of the Wannsee conference, compiled by SS-Standartenführer Eichmann of the Reich Main Security Office. It was a typewritten document, full of amendments and angry crossings-out in a neat hand which March had come to recognise as belonging to Reinhard Heydrich.

For example, Eichmann had written:

Finally, Obergruppenführer Heydrich was asked about the practical difficulties involved in the processing of such large numbers. The Obergruppenführer stated that various methods had been employed. Shooting was to be regarded as an inadequate solution for various reasons. The work was slow. Security was poor, with the consequent risk of panic among those awaiting special treatment. Also, this method had been observed to have a deleterious effect upon our men. He invited Sturmbannführer Dr Rudolf Lange (KdS Latvia) to give an eyewitness report.

Sturmbannführer Lange stated that three methods had been undertaken recently, providing an opportunity for comparison. On 30 November, one thousand Berlin Jews had been shot in the forest near Riga. On 8 December, his men had organised a special treatment at Kulmhof with gas lorries. In the meantime, commencing in October, experiments had been conducted at the Auschwitz camp on Russian prisoners and Polish Jews using Zyklon B. Results here were especially promising from the point of view of both capacity and security.

Against this, in the margin, Heyrich had written 'No!' March checked in the final version of the minutes. This entire section of the conference had been reduced to a single phrase:

Finally, there was a discussion of the various types of solution possibilities.

Thus sanitised, the minutes were fit for the archives.

March scribbled more notes: October, November, December 1941. Slowly the blank sheets were being filled. In the dim light of the attic room, a picture was developing: connections, strategies, causes and effects . . . He looked up the contributions of Luther, Stuckart and Buhler to the Wannsee conference. Luther foresaw problems in 'the nordic states' but 'no major difficulties in south-eastern and western Europe'. Stuckart, when asked about persons with one Jewish grandparent, 'proposed to proceed with compulsory sterilisation'. Buhler, characteristically, toadied to Heydrich: 'He had only one favour to ask – that the Jewish question in the General Government be solved as rapidly as possible.'

HE broke off for five minutes to smoke a cigarette, pacing the corridor, shuffling his papers, an actor learning his lines. From the bathroom: the sound of running water. From the rest of the hotel: nothing except creaks in the darkness, like a galleon at anchor.

SIX

NOTES ON A VISIT TO AUSCHWITZ-BIRKENAU BY MARTIN
LUTHER, UNDER STATE SECRETARY, REICHS MINISTRY FOR
FOREIGN AFFAIRS

[Handwritten; 11 pages]

14 July 1943

At last, after almost a year of repeated requests, I am given
permission to undertake a full tour of inspection of the
Auschwitz-Birkenau camp, on behalf of the Foreign
Ministry.

I land at Krakau airfield from Berlin shortly before sunset
and spend the night with Governor-General Hans Frank,
State Secretary Josef Buhler and their staff at Wawel Castle.
Tomorrow morning at dawn I am to be picked up from the
castle and driven to the camp (journey time: approximately
one hour) where I am to be received by the Commandant,
Rudolf Hoess.

15 July 1943

The camp. My first impression is of the sheer scale of the
installation, which measures, according to Hoess, almost 2
km. × 4 km. The earth is of yellowish clay, similar to that
of Eastern Silesia – a desert-like landscape broken
occasionally by green thickets of trees. Inside the camp,
stretching far beyond the limits of my vision, are hundreds
of wooden barracks, their roofs covered with green tar-
paper. In the distance, moving between them, I see small
groups of prisoners in blue-and-white striped clothing –
some carrying planks, others shovels and picks; a few are
loading large crates on to the backs of trucks. A smell hangs
over the place.

I thank Hoess for receiving me. He explains the
administrative set-up. This camp is under the jurisdiction

of the SS Economic Administration Main Office. The others, in the Lublin district, fall under the control of SS-Obergruppenführer Odilo Globocnik. Unfortunately, the pressure of his work prevents Hoess from conducting me around the camp personally, and he therefore entrusts me into the care of a young Untersturmführer, Weidemann. He orders Weidemann to ensure I am shown everything, and that all my questions are answered fully. We begin with breakfast in the SS barracks.

After breakfast: we drive into the southern sector of the camp. Here: a railway siding, approx 1.5 km. in length. On either side: wire fencing supported from concrete pylons, and also wooden observation towers with machine-gun nests. It is already hot. The smell is bad here, a million flies buzz. To the west, rising above trees: a square, red-brick factory chimney, belching smoke.

7.40 am: the area around the railway track begins to fill with SS troops, some with dogs, and also with special prisoners delegated to assist them. In the distance we hear the whistle of a train. A few minutes later: the locomotive pulls slowly through the entrance, its exhalations of steam throw up clouds of yellow dust. It draws to a halt in front of us. The gates close behind it. Weidemann: 'This is a transport of Jews from France.'

I reckon the length of the train to be some 60 freight cars, with high wooden sides. The troops and special prisoners crowd round. The doors are unbolted and slid open. All along the train the same words are shouted: 'Everyone get out! Bring your hand-baggage with you! Leave all heavy baggage in the cars!' The men come out first, dazed by the light, and jump to the ground – 1.5 metres – then turn to help their women and children and the elderly, and to receive their luggage.

The deportees' state: pitiful – filthy, dusty, holding out bowls and cups, gesturing to their mouths, crying with thirst. Behind them in the trucks lie the dead and those too sick to move – Weidemann says their journey began four nights ago. SS guards force those able to walk into two lines. As families separate, they shout to one another. With many gestures and calls the columns march off in different directions. The able-bodied men go towards the work camp. The rest head towards the screen of trees, with Weidemann and myself following. As I look back, I see the prisoners in their striped clothing clambering into the freight cars, dragging out the baggage and the bodies.

8.30 am: Weidemann puts the size of the column at nearly 2,000: women carrying babies, children at their skirts; old men and women; adolescents; sick people; mad people. They walk five abreast down a cinder path for 300 metres, through a courtyard, along another path, at the end of which twelve concrete steps lead down to an immense underground chamber, 100 metres long. A sign proclaims in several languages (German, French, Greek, Hungarian): 'Baths and Disinfecting Room'. It is well-lit, with scores of benches, hundreds of numbered pegs.

The guards shout: 'Everyone undress! You have 10 minutes!' People hesitate, look at one another. The order is repeated, more harshly, & this time, hesitantly but calmly, they comply. 'Remember your peg number, so you can recover your clothes!' The camp trusties move among them, whispering encouragement, helping the feeble-bodied and the feeble-minded to strip. Some mothers try to hide their babies in the piles of discarded clothing, but the infants are quickly discovered.

9.05 am: Naked, the crowd shuffles through large oak doors flanked by troops into a second room, as large as the first, but utterly bare, apart from four thick, square columns supporting the ceiling at twenty-metre intervals. At the bottom of each column is a metal grille. The chamber fills, the doors swing shut. Weidemann gestures. I follow him out through the empty changing room, up the concrete steps, into the air. I can hear the sound of an automobile engine.

Across the grass which covers the roof of the installation bounces a small van with Red Cross markings. It stops. An SS officer & a doctor emerge wearing gas masks & carrying four metal canisters. Four squat concrete pipes jut from the grass, twenty metres apart. The doctor & SS man lift the lids of the pipes & pour in a mauve granulated substance. They remove the masks, light cigarettes in sunshine.

9.09 am: Weidemann conducts me back downstairs. Only sound is a muffled drumming coming from the far end of the room, from beyond the suitcases & the piles of still-warm clothes. A small glass panel is set into the oak doors. I put my eye to it. A man's palm beats against the aperture & I jerk my head away.

Says one guard: 'The water in the shower rooms must be very hot today, since they shout so loudly.'

Outside, Weidemann says: now we must wait twenty minutes. Would I care to visit Canada? I say: What? He laughs: 'Canada' – a section of the camp. Why Canada? He shrugs: nobody knows.

Canada. 1 km. north of gas chamber. Huge rectangular yard, watchtower in each corner & surrounded by barbed wire. Mountains of belongings – trunks, rucksacks, cases, kitbags, parcels; blankets; prams, wheelchairs, false limbs; brushes, combs. Weidemann: figures prepared for RF-SS on property recently sent to Reich – men's shirts: 132,000, women's coats: 155,000, women's hair: 3,000 kg. ('a freight car'), boys' jackets: 15,000, girls' dresses: 9,000, handkerchiefs: 135,000. I get doctor's bag, beautifully made, as souvenir – Weidemann insists.

9.31 am: Return underground installation. Loud electric humming fills the air – the patented 'Exhator' system, for evacuation of gas. Doors open. The bodies are piled up at one end *[Illegible]* legs smeared excrement, menstrual blood; bite & claw marks. Jewish *Sonderkommando* detachment enters to hose down corpses, wearing rubber boots, aprons, gas masks (according to W., pockets of gas remain trapped at floor level for up to 2 hours). Corpses slippery. Straps around wrists used to haul them to four double-doored elevators. Capacity of each: 25 *[Illegible]* bell rings, ascend one floor to . . .

10.02 am: Incineration room. Stifling heat: 15 ovens

operating full-blast. Loud noise: diesel motors ventilating flames. Corpses from elevator loaded on to conveyor belt (metal rollers). Blood etc into concrete gutter. Barbers either side shave heads. Hair collected in sacks. Rings, necklaces, bracelets, etc dropped into metal box. Last: dental team – 8 men with crowbars & pliers – removal gold (teeth, bridgework, fillings). W. gives me tin of gold to test weight: very heavy. Corpses tipped into furnaces from metal pushcarts.

Weidemann: four such gas chamber/crematorium installations in camp. Total capacity of each: 2,000 bodies per day = 8,000 overall. Operated by Jewish labour, changed every 2–3 months. The operation thus self-supporting; the secret self-sealing. Biggest security headache – stink from chimneys & flames at night, visible over many kilometres, especially to troop trains heading east on main line.

MARCH checked dates. Luther had visited Auschwitz on 15 July. On 17 July Buhler had forwarded the map locations of the six camps to Kritzinger of the Reich Chancellery. On 9 August the last deposit had been made in Switzerland. That same year, according to his wife, Luther had suffered a breakdown.

He made a note. Kritzinger was the fourth man. His name was everywhere. He checked with Buhler's pocket diary. Those dates tallied also. Another mystery solved.

His pen moved across the paper. He was almost finished.

A SMALL thing, it had passed unnoticed during the afternoon; one of a dozen or so scraps of paper stuffed at random into a torn folder. It was a circular from SS-Gruppenführer Richard Glücks, Chief of *Amtsgruppe* D in the SS Economic Administration Main Office. It was dated 6 August 1942.

> Re: the utilisation of cut hair.
>
> In response to a report, the Chief of the SS Economic Administration Main Office, SS-Obergruppenführer Pohl, has ordered that all human hair cut off in concentration camps should be utilised. Human hair will be processed for industrial felt and spun into thread. Female hair which has been cut and combed out will be used as thread to make socks for U-boat crews and felt stockings for the railways.
>
> You are instructed, therefore, to store the hair of female prisoners after it has been disinfected. Cut hair from male prisoners can only be utilised if it is at least 20 mm. in length.
>
> The amounts of hair collected each month, separated into female and male hair, must be reported on the 5th of each month to this office, beginning with the 5th September 1942.

He read it again: '*U-boat crews . . .*'

'ONE. Two. Three. Four. Five . . .' March was underwater, holding his breath, counting. He listened to the muffled noises, saw patterns like strings of algae float past him in the dark. 'Fourteen. Fifteen. Sixteen . . .' With a roar he rose above the surface, sucking in air, streaming water. He filled his lungs a few more times, took an immense gulp of oxygen, then went down again. This time he made it to twenty-five before his breath exploded and he burst upwards, slopping water on to the bathroom floor.

Would he ever be clean again?

Afterwards, he lay with his arms dangling over the sides of the tub, his head tilted back, staring at the ceiling, like a drowned man.

PART SIX

SUNDAY 19 APRIL

However this war may end, we have won the war against you; none of you will be left to bear witness, but even if someone were to survive, the world would not believe him. There will perhaps be suspicions, discussions, research by historians, but there will be no certainties, because we will destroy the evidence together with you. And even if some proof should remain and some of you survive, people will say that the events you describe are too monstrous to be believed: they will say that they are the exaggerations of Allied propaganda and will believe us, who will deny everything, and not you. We will be the ones to dictate the history of the Lagers.

SS officer, quoted in *The Drowned and the Saved*
by Primo Levi

ONE

In July 1953, when Xavier March had not long turned thirty and his work as yet consisted of little more than the arresting of whores and pimps around the docks of Hamburg, he and Klara had taken a holiday. They had started in Freiburg, in the foothills of the Black Forest, had driven south to the Rhine, then eastwards in his battered KdF-wagen towards the Bodensee, and in one of the little riverside hotels, during a showery afternoon, with a rainbow cast across the sky, they had planted the seed that grew into Pili.

He could see the place still: the wrought-iron balcony, the Rhine valley beyond, the barges moving lazily in the wide water; the stone walls of the old town, the cool church; Klara's skirt, waist to ankle, sunflower yellow.

And there was something else he could still see: a kilometre down-river, spanning the gulf between Germany and Switzerland – the glint of a steel bridge.

Forget about trying to escape through the main air or sea ports: they were watched and guarded as tightly as the Reich Chancellery. Forget about crossing the border to France, Belgium, Holland, Denmark, Hungary, Yugoslavia, Italy – that was to scale the wall of one prison merely to drop into the exercise yard of another. Forget about mailing the documents out of the Reich: too many packages were routinely opened by the postal service for that to be safe. Forget about giving the material to any of the other correspondents in Berlin: they would only face the same obstacles and were, in any case, according to Charlie, as trustworthy as rattlesnakes.

The Swiss border offered the best hope; the bridge beckoned.

*

Now hide it. Hide it all.

He knelt on the threadbare carpet and spread out a single sheet of brown paper. He made a neat stack of the documents, squaring off the edges. From his wallet he took the photograph of the Weiss family. He stared at it for a moment, then added it to the pile. He wrapped the entire collection tightly in the paper, binding the clear sticky tape around and around it until the package felt as solid as a block of wood.

He was left with an oblong parcel, ten centimetres thick, unyielding to the touch, anonymous to the eye.

He let out a breath. That was better.

He added another layer, this time of gift paper. Golden letters spelled GOOD LUCK! and HAPPINESS!, the words curling like streamers amid balloons and champagne corks behind a smiling bride and groom.

BY autobahn from Berlin to Nuremberg: five hundred kilometres. By autobahn from Nuremberg to Stuttgart: one hundred and fifty kilometres. From Stuttgart the road then wound through the valleys and forests of Wurttemberg to Waldshut on the Rhine: a hundred and fifty kilometres again. Eight hundred kilometres in all.

'What's that in miles?'

'Five hundred. Do you think you can manage it?'

'Of course. Twelve hours, maybe less.' She was perched on the edge of the bed, leaning forward, attentive. She wore two towels —one wrapped around her body, the other in a turban around her head.

'No need to rush it – you've got twenty-four. When you reckon you've put a safe distance between yourself and Berlin, telephone the Hotel Bellevue in Waldshut and reserve a room – it's out of season, there should be no difficulty.'

'Hotel Bellevue. Waldshut.' She nodded slowly as she memorised it. 'And you?'

'I'll be following a couple of hours behind. I'll aim to join you at the hotel around midnight.'

He could see she did not believe him. He hurried on: 'If you're willing to take the risk, I think you should carry the papers, and also this . . .' From his pocket he drew out the other stolen passport. Paul Hahn, SS-Sturmbannführer, born Cologne, 16 August 1925. Three years younger than March, and looked it.

'She said: Why don't you keep it?'

'If I'm arrested and searched, they'll find it. Then they'll know whose identity you're using.'

'You've no intention of coming.'

'I've every intention of coming.'

'You think you're finished.'

'Not true. But my chances of travelling eight hundred kilometres without being stopped are less than yours. You must see that. That's why we go separately.'

She was shaking her head. He came and sat beside her, stroked her cheek, turned her face to his, her eyes to his. 'Listen. You're to wait for me – listen! – wait for me at the hotel until eight-thirty tomorrow morning. If I haven't arrived, you drive across without me. Don't wait any longer, because it won't be safe.'

'Why eight-thirty?'

'You should aim to cross the border as close to nine as you can.' Her cheeks were wet. He kissed them. He kept on talking. She had to understand. 'Nine is the hour when the beloved Father of the German People leaves the Reich Chancellery to travel to the Great Hall. It's months since he's been seen – their way of building excitement. You may be sure the guards will have a radio in the customs post, and be listening to it. If ever there's a time when they're more likely just to wave you through, that's it.'

SHE stood and unwrapped the turban. In the weak light of the attic room, her hair gleamed white.

She let the second towel drop.

Pale skin, white hair, dark eyes. A ghost. He needed to know that she was real, that they were both alive. He stretched out a hand and touched her.

THEY lay entwined on the little wooden cot and she whispered their future to him. Their flight would land at New York's Idlewild airport early tomorrow evening. They would go straight to the *New York Times* building. There was an editor there she knew. The first thing was to make a copy – a dozen copies – and then to get as much printed as possible, as soon as possible. The *Times* was ideal for that.

'What if they won't print it?' This idea of people printing whatever they wanted was hard for him to grasp.

'They'll print it. God, if they won't, I'll stand on Fifth Avenue like one of those mad people who can't get their novels published and hand out copies to passers-by. But don't worry – they'll print it, and we'll change history.'

'But will anyone believe it?' That doubt had grown within him ever since the suitcase had been opened. 'Isn't it unbelievable?'

No, she said, with great certainty, because now they had facts, and facts changed everything. Without them, you had nothing, a void. But produce facts – provide names, dates, orders, numbers, times, locations, map references, schedules, photographs, diagrams, descriptions – and suddenly that void had geometry, was susceptible to measurement, had become a solid thing. Of course, this

334

solid thing could be denied, or challenged, or simply ignored. But each of these reactions was, by definition, a *reaction*, a response to some thing which existed.

'Some people won't believe it – they wouldn't believe it no matter how much evidence we had. But there's enough here, I think, to stop Kennedy in his tracks. No summit. No re-election. No détente. And five years from now, or fifty years, this society will fall apart. You can't build on a mass grave. Human beings are better than that – they have to be better than that – I do believe it – don't you?'

He did not reply.

HE was awake to see another dawn in the Berlin sky. A familiar grey face at the attic window, an old opponent.

'Your name is?'

'Magda Voss.'

'Born?'

'Twenty-fifth October 1939.'

'Where?'

'Berlin.'

'Your occupation?'

'I live at home with my parents, in Berlin.'

'Where are you going?'

'To Waldshut, on the Rhine. To meet my fiancé.'

'Name?'

'Paul Hahn.'

'What is the purpose of your visit to Switzerland?'

'A friend's wedding.'

'Where?'

'In Zürich.'

'What is this?'

'A wedding present. A photograph album. Or a Bible? Or a book? Or a chopping board?' She was testing the answers on him.

'Chopping board – very good. Exactly the sort of gift a girl like Magda *would* drive eight hundred kilometres to give.' March had been pacing the room. Now he stopped and pointed at the package in Charlie's lap. 'Open it, please, Fräulein.'

She thought for a moment. 'What do I say to that?'

'There's nothing you can say.'

'Terrific.' She took out a cigarette and lit it. 'Well, would you look at that? My hands are trembling.'

It was almost seven. 'Time to go.'

THE hotel was beginning to wake. As they passed the lines of flimsy doors they heard water splashing, a radio, children laughing. Somewhere on the second floor, a man snored on regardless.

They had handled the package with care, at arm's length, as if it were uranium. She had hidden it in the centre of her suitcase, buried in her clothes. March carried it down the stairs, across the empty lobby and out the narrow fire exit at the rear of the hotel. She was wearing a dark blue suit, her hair hidden by a scarf. The hired Opel stood next to his Volkswagen. From the kitchens came shouts, the smell of fresh coffee, the hiss of frying food.

'When you leave the Bellevue, turn right. The road follows the line of the valley. You can't miss the bridge.'

'You've told me this already.'

'Try and see what level of security they're operating, before you commit yourself. If it looks as if they're searching everything, turn round and try and hide it somewhere. Woods, ditch, barn – somewhere you can remember, a place where someone can go back and retrieve it. Then get out. Promise me.'

'I promise you.'

'There's a daily Swissair flight from Zürich to New York. It leaves at two.'

'At two. I know. You've told me twice.'

He took a step towards her, to hold her, but she fended him away. 'I'm not saying goodbye. Not here. I shall see you tonight. *I shall see you.*'

There was a moment of anti-climax when the Opel refused to start. She pulled out the choke and tried again, and this time the engine fired. She reversed out of the parking space, still refusing to look at him. He had one last glimpse of her profile – and then she was gone, leaving a trail of blue-white vapour hanging in the chilly morning air.

MARCH sat alone in the empty room, on the edge of the bed, holding her pillow. He waited until an hour had passed before putting on his uniform. He stood in front of the dressing-table mirror, buttoning his black tunic. It would be the last time he wore it, one way or the other.

'*We'll change history . . .*'

He donned his cap, adjusted it. Then he took his thirty sheets of paper, his notebook and Buhler's pocket diary, folded them together, wrapped them in the remaining sheet of brown paper, and slipped them into his inside pocket.

Was history changed so easily? he wondered. Certainly, it was his experience that secrets were an acid – once spilled, they could eat their way through anything: if a marriage, why not a presidency, why not a state? But talk of history – he shook his head at his own reflection – history was beyond him. Investigators turned suspicion into evidence. He had done that. History he would leave to her.

HE carried Luther's bag into the bathroom and shovelled

into it all the rubbish that Charlie had left behind – the discarded bottles, the rubber gloves, the dish and spoon, the brushes. He did the same in the bedroom. It was strange how much she had filled these places, how empty they seemed without her. He looked at his watch. It was eight-thirty. She should be well clear of Berlin by now, perhaps as far south as Wittenberg.

In the reception, the manager hovered.

'Good day, Herr Sturmbannführer. Is the interrogation finished?'

'It is indeed, Herr Brecker. Thank you for your patriotic assistance.'

'A pleasure.' Brecker gave a short bow. He was twisting his fat white hands together as if rubbing in oil. 'And if ever the Sturmbannführer feels the desire to do a little more interrogation . . .' His bushy eyebrows danced. 'Perhaps I might even be able to supply him with a suspect or two. . . ?'

March smiled. 'Good day to you, Herr Brecker.'

'Good day to *you*, Herr Sturmbannführer.'

HE sat in the front passenger seat of the Volkswagen and thought for a moment. Inside the spare tyre would be the ideal place, but he had no time for that. The plastic door panels were securely fastened. He reached under the dashboard until his fingers encountered a smooth surface. It would serve his purpose. He tore off two lengths of sticky tape and attached the package to the cold metal.

Then he dropped the roll of tape into Luther's case and dumped the bag in one of the rubbish bins outside the kitchens. The brown leather looked too incongruous lying on the surface. He found a broken length of broom-handle and dug a grave for it, burying it at last beneath the coffee dregs, the stinking fish-heads, the lumps of grease and maggoty pork.

ellow signs bearing the single word *Fernverkehr* – long-distance traffic – pointed the way out of Berlin, towards the race-track autobahn that girdled the city. March had the southbound carriageway almost to himself – the few cars and buses about this early on a Sunday morning were heading the other way. He passed the perimeter wire of the Tempelhof aerodrome and abruptly he was into the suburbs, the wide road pushing through dreary streets of red-brick shops and houses, lined by sickly trees with blackened trunks.

To his left, a hospital; to his right, a disused church, shuttered and daubed with Party slogans. 'Marienfelde,' said the signs. 'Bückow.' 'Lichtenrade.'

At a set of traffic lights he stopped. The road to the south lay open – to the Rhine, to Zürich, to America . . . Behind him someone hooted. The lights had changed. He flicked the indicator, turned off the main road and was quickly lost in the gridiron streets of the housing estate.

IN the early 'fifties, in the glow of victory, the roads had been named for generals: Student Strasse, Reichenau Strasse, Manteuffel Allee. March was always confused. Was it right off Model into Dietrich? Or was it left into Paulus, and *then* Dietrich? He drove slowly along the rows of identical bungalows until at last he recognised it.

He pulled over in the familiar place and almost sounded the horn until he remembered that this was the third Sunday in the month, not the first – and therefore not his – and that in any case his access had been revoked. A frontal assault would be needed, an action in the spirit of Hasso Manteuffel himself.

There was no litter of toys along the concrete drive and when he rang the bell, no dog barked. He cursed silently. It seemed to be his fate this week to stand outside deserted houses. He backed away from the porch, his eyes fixed on the window beside it. The net curtain flickered.

'Pili! Are you there?'

The corner of the curtain was abruptly parted, as if some hidden dignitary had pulled a cord unveiling a portrait, and there it was – his son's white face staring at him.

'Can I come in? I want to talk!'

The face was expressionless. The curtain dropped back.

A good sign or bad? March was uncertain. He waved to the blank window and pointed to the garden. 'I'll wait for you here!'

He walked back to the little wooden gate and checked the street. Bungalows on either side, bungalows opposite. They extended in every direction, like the huts of an army camp. Old folks lived in most of them: veterans of the First War, survivors of all that followed – inflation, unemployment, the Party, the Second War. Even ten years ago, they were grey and bowed. They had seen enough, endured enough. Now they stayed at home, and shouted at Pili for making too much noise, and watched television all day.

March prowled around the tiny handkerchief of lawn. Not much of a life for the boy. Cars passed. Two doors down an old man was repairing a bicycle, inflating the tyres with a squeaky pump. Elsewhere, the noise of a lawnmower . . . No sign of Pili. He was wondering if he would have to get down on his hands and knees and shout his message through the letter box when he heard the door being opened.

'Good lad. How are you? Where's your mother? Where's Helfferich?' He could not bring himself to say 'Uncle Erich'.

341

Pili had opened the door just enough to enable him to peer around it. 'They're out. I'm finishing my picture.'

'Out where?'

'Rehearsing for the parade. I'm in charge. They said so.'

'I bet. Can I come in and talk to you?'

He had expected resistance. Instead, the boy stood aside without a word and March found himself crossing the threshold of his ex-wife's house for the first time since their divorce. He took in the furniture –cheap, but good-looking; the bunch of fresh daffodils on the mantelpiece; the neatness; the spotless surfaces. She had done it as well as she could, without much to spend. He would have expected that. Even the picture of the Führer above the telephone – a photograph of the old man hugging a child – was tasteful: Klara's deity always was a benign god, New Testament rather than Old. He took off his cap. He felt like a burglar.

He stood on the nylon rug and began his speech. 'I have to go away, Pili. Maybe for a long time. And people, perhaps, are going to say some things to you about me. Horrible things, that aren't true. And I wanted to tell you . . .' His words petered out. *Tell you what?* He ran his hand through his hair. Pili was standing with his arms folded, gazing at him. He tried again. 'It's hard not having a father around. My father died when I was very little – younger even than you are now. And sometimes, I hated him for that . . .'

Those cool eyes . . .

'. . . But that passed, and then – I missed him. And if I could talk to him now – ask him . . . I'd give anything . . .'

'. . . *all human hair cut off in concentration camps should be utilised. Human hair will be processed for industrial felt and spun into thread . . .*'

He was not sure how long he stood there, not speaking, his head bowed. Eventually he said: 'I have to go now.'

And then Pili was coming towards him and tugging at his

hand. 'It's all right, papa. Please don't go yet. Please. Come and look at my picture.'

THE boy's bedroom was like a command centre. Model Luftwaffe jets assembled from plastic kits swooped and fought, suspended from the ceiling by invisible lengths of fishing-line. On one wall, a map of the Eastern front, with coloured pins to show the positions of the armies. On another, a group photograph of Pili's Pimpf unit – bare knees and solemn faces, photographed against a concrete wall.

As he drew, Pili kept up a running commentary, with sound effects. 'These are our jets – rrroowww! – and these are the Reds' AA-guns. Pow! Pow!' Lines of yellow crayon streaked skywards. 'Now we let them have it. Fire!' Little black ants' eggs rained down, creating jagged red crowns of fire. 'The commies call up their own fighters, but they're no match for ours . . .' It went on for another five minutes, action piled on action.

Abruptly, bored by his own creation, Pili dropped the crayons and dived under the bed. He pulled out a stack of wartime picture magazines.

'Where did you get those?'

'Uncle Erich gave them to me. He collected them.'

Pili flung himself on the bed and began to turn the pages. 'What do the captions say, papa?' He gave March the magazine and sat close to him, holding on to his arm.

' "The sapper has worked his way right up to the wire obstacles protecting the machine gun position," ' read March. ' "A few spurts of flame and the deadly stream of burning oil has put the enemy out of action. The flame throwers must be fearless men with nerves of steel." '

'And that one?'

This was not the farewell March had envisaged, but if it

was what the boy wanted . . . He ploughed on: ' "I want to fight for the new Europe: so say three brothers from Copenhagen with their company leader in the SS training camp in Upper Alsace. They have fulfilled all the conditions relating to questions of race and health and are now enjoying the manly open-air life in the camp in the woods." '

'What about these?'

He was smiling. 'Come on, Pili. You're ten years old. You can read these easily.'

'But I want you to read them. Here's a picture of a U-boat, like yours. What does it say?'

He stopped smiling and put down the magazine. There was something wrong here. What was it? He realised: the silence. For several minutes now, nothing had happened in the street outside —not a car, not a footstep, not a voice. Even the lawnmower had stopped. He saw Pili's eyes flick to the window, and he understood.

Somewhere in the house: a tinkle of glass. March scrambled for the door, but the boy was too quick for him – rolling off the bed, grabbing his legs, curling himself around his father's feet in a foetal ball, a parody of childish entreaty. *'Please don't go, papa,'* he was saying, *'please . . .'* March's fingers grasped the door-handle but he couldn't move. He was anchored, mired. *I have dreamed this before*, he thought. The window imploded behind them, showering their backs with glass – now real uniforms with real guns were filling the bedroom – and suddenly March was on his back gazing up at the little plastic warplanes bobbing and spinning crazily at the ends of their invisible wires.

He could hear Pili's voice: 'It's going to be all right, papa. They're going to help you. They'll make you better. Then you can come and live with us. They promised . . .'

is hands were cuffed tight behind his back, wrists outwards. Two SS men propped him against the wall, against the map of the Eastern front, and Globus stood before him. Pili had been hustled away, thank God. 'I have waited for this moment,' said Globus, 'as a bridegroom waits for his bride', and he punched March in the stomach, hard. March folded, dropped to his knees, dragging the map and all its little pins down with him, thinking he would never breathe again. Then Globus had him by the hair and was pulling him up, and his body was trying to retch and suck in oxygen at the same time and Globus hit him again and he went down again. This process was repeated several times. Finally, while he was lying on the carpet with his knees drawn up, Globus planted his boot on the side of his head and ground his toe into his ear. 'Look,' he said, 'I've put my foot on shit' and from a long way away, March heard the sound of men laughing.

'WHERE'S the girl?'

'What girl?'

Globus slowly extended his stubby fingers in front of March's face, then brought his hand arcing down in a karate blow to the kidneys.

This was much worse than anything else – a blinding white flash of pain that shot straight through him and put him on the floor again, retching bile. And the worst was to know that he was merely in the foothills of a long climb. The stages of torture stretched before him, ascending as notes on a scale, from the dull bass of a blow in the belly, through the middle register of kidney-punches, onwards and upwards to some pitch beyond the range of the human ear, a pinnacle of crystal.

'Where's the girl?'

'What . . . girl. . . ?'

THEY disarmed him, searched him, then they half-pushed, half-dragged him out of the bungalow. A little crowd had gathered in the road. Klara's elderly neighbours watched as he was bundled, head bowed, into the back of the BMW. He glimpsed briefly along the street four or five cars with revolving lights, a lorry, troops. What had they been expecting? A small war? Still no sign of Pili. The handcuffs forced him to sit hunched forward. Two Gestapo men were jammed on the back seat, one on either side of him. As the car pulled away, he could see some of the old folks already shuffling back into their houses, back to the reassuring glow of their television sets.

HE was driven north through the holiday traffic, up into Saarland Strasse, east into Prinz-Albrecht Strasse. Fifty metres past the main entrance to Gestapo headquarters, the convoy swung right, through a pair of high prison gates, into a brick courtyard at the back of the building.

He was pulled out of the car and through a low entrance, down steep concrete steps. Then his heels were scraping along the floor of an arched passage. A door, a cell, and silence.

THEY left him alone, to allow his imagination to go to work – standard procedure. Very well. He crawled into a corner and rested his head against the damp brick. Every minute which passed was another minute's travelling time for her. He thought of Pili, of all the lies, and clenched his fists.

The cell was lit by a weak bulb above the door, imprisoned in its own rusty metal cage. He glanced at his wrist, a useless reflex, for they had taken away his watch. Surely she could not be far from Nuremberg by now? He tried to fill his mind with images of the Gothic spires – St Lorenz, St Sebaldus, St Jakob . . .

Every limb – every part of him to which he could put a name – ached, yet they could not have worked him over for more than five minutes, and still they had managed not to leave a mark on his face. Truly, he had fallen into the hands of experts. He almost laughed, but that hurt his ribs, so he stopped.

HE was taken along the passage to an interview room: whitewashed walls, a heavy oak table with a chair on each side; in the corner, an iron stove. Globus had disappeared, Krebs was in command. The handcuffs were removed. Standard procedure again – first the hard cop, then the soft. Krebs even attempted a joke: 'Normally, we would arrest your son and threaten him as well, to encourage your co-operation. But in your case, we know that such a course would be counter-productive.' Secret policeman's humour! He leaned back in his chair, smiling, and pointed his pencil. 'Nevertheless. A remarkable boy.'

' "Remarkable" – your word.' At some point during his beating, March had bitten his tongue. He talked now as if he had spent a week in a dentist's chair.

'Your ex-wife was given a telephone number last night,' said Krebs, 'in case you attempted contact. The boy memorised it. The instant he saw you, he called. He's inherited your brains, March. Your initiative. You should feel some pride.'

'At this moment, my feelings towards my son are indeed strong.'

Good, he thought, *let's keep this up. Another minute, another kilometre.*

But Krebs was already down to business, turning the pages of a thick folder. 'There are two issues here, March. One: your general political reliability, going back over many years. That does not concern us today – at least, not directly. Two: your conduct over the past week – specifically, your involvement in the attempts of the late Party Comrade Luther to defect to the United States.'

'I have no such involvement.'

'You were questioned by an officer of the Ordnungspolizei in Adolf Hitler Platz yesterday morning – at the exact time the traitor Luther was planning to meet the American journalist, Maguire, together with an official of the United States Embassy.'

How did they know that? 'Absurd.'

'Do you deny you were in the Platz?'

'No. Of course not.'

'Then why were you there?'

'I was following the American woman.'

Krebs was making notes. 'Why?'

'She was the person who discovered the body of Party Comrade Stuckart. I was also naturally suspicious of her, in her role as an agent of the bourgeois democratic press.'

'Don't piss me about, March.'

'All right. I had insinuated myself into her company. I thought: if she can stumble across the corpse of one retired state secretary, she might stumble across another.'

'A fair point.' Krebs rubbed his chin and thought for a moment, then opened a fresh pack of cigarettes and gave one to March, lighting it for him from an unused box of matches. March filled his lungs with smoke. Krebs had not taken one for himself, he noticed – they were merely a part of his act, an interrogator's props.

The Gestapo man was leafing through his notes again, frowning. 'We believe that the traitor Luther was planning to disclose certain information to the journalist Maguire. What was the nature of this information?'

'I have no idea. The art fraud, perhaps?'

'On Thursday, you visited Zürich. Why?'

'It was the place Luther went before he vanished. I wanted to see if there was any clue there which might explain why he disappeared.'

'And was there?'

'No. But my visit was authorised. I submitted a full report to Oberstgruppenführer Nebe. Have you not seen it?'

'Of course not.' Krebs made a note. 'The Oberstgruppenführer shows his hand to no one, not even us. Where is Maguire?'

'How should I know?'

'You should know because you picked her up from Adolf Hitler Platz after the shooting yesterday.'

'Not me, Krebs.'

'Yes you, March. Afterwards, you went to the morgue and searched through the traitor Luther's personal effects – this we know absolutely from Doctor Eisler.'

'I was not aware that the effects *were* Luther's,' said March. 'I understood they belonged to a man named Stark who was three metres away from Maguire when he was shot. Naturally, I was interested to see what he was carrying, because I was interested in Maguire. Besides, if you recall, *you* showed me what you said was Luther's body on Friday night. Who did shoot Luther, as a matter of interest?'

'Never mind that. What did you expect to pick up at the morgue?'

'Plenty.'

'What? Be exact!'

'Fleas. Lice. A skin rash from his shitty clothes.'

Krebs threw down his pencil. He folded his arms. 'You're a brainy fellow, March. Take comfort from the fact we credit you with that, at least. Do you think we'd give a shit if you were just some dumb fat fuck, like your friend Max Jaeger? I bet you could keep this up for hours. But we don't have hours, and we're less stupid than you think.' He shuffled through his papers, smirked, and then he played his ace.

'What was in the suitcase you took from the airport?'

March looked straight back at him. *They had known all along.* 'What suitcase?'

'The suitcase that looks like a doctor's bag. The suitcase that doesn't weigh very much, but might contain paper. The suitcase Friedman gave you thirty minutes before he called us. He got back to find a telex, you see, March, from Prinz-Albrecht Strasse – an alert to stop you leaving the country. When he saw that, he decided – as a patriotic citizen – he'd better inform us of your visit.'

'Friedman!' said March. 'A "patriotic citizen"? He's fooling you, Krebs. He's hiding some scheme of his own.'

Krebs sighed. He got to his feet and came round to stand behind March, his hands resting on the back of March's chair. 'When this is over, I'd like to get to know you. Really. Assuming there's anything left of you to get to know. Why did someone like you go bad? I'm interested. From a technical point of view. To try to stop it happening in the future.'

'Your passion for self-improvement is laudable.'

'There you go again, you see? A problem of attitude. Things are changing in Germany, March – from within – and you could have been a part of it. The Reichsführer himself takes a personal interest in the new generation – listens to us, promotes us. He believes in restructuring, greater openness, talking to the Americans. The day of men like Odilo Globocnik is passing.' He stooped and whispered in March's ear: 'Do you know why Globus doesn't like you?'

'Enlighten me.'

'Because you make him feel stupid. In Globus's book, that's a capital offence. Help me, and I can shield you from him.' Krebs straightened and resumed, in his normal voice: 'Where is the woman? What was the information Luther wanted to give her? Where is Luther's suitcase?'

Those three questions, again and again.

INTERROGATIONS have this irony, at least: they can enlighten those being questioned as much – or more – than those who are doing the questioning.

From what Krebs asked, March could measure the extent of his knowledge. This was, on certain matters, very good: he knew March had visited the morgue, for example, and that he had retrieved the suitcase from the airport. But there was a significant gap. Unless Krebs was playing a fiendishly devious game, it seemed he had no idea of the *nature* of the information Luther was promising the Americans. Upon this one, narrow ground rested March's only hope.

After an inconclusive half-hour, the door opened and Globus appeared, swinging a long truncheon of polished wood. Behind him stood two thick-set men in black uniforms.

Krebs leapt to attention.

Globus said: 'Has he made a full confession?'

'No, Herr Obergruppenführer.'

'What a surprise. My turn then, I think.'

'Of course.' Krebs stooped and collected his papers.

Was it March's imagination, or did he see on that long, impassive face a flicker of regret, even of distaste?

*

AFTER Krebs had gone, Globus prowled around, humming an old Party marching song, dragging the length of wood over the stone floor.

'Do you know what this is, March?' He waited. 'No? No answer? It's an American invention. A baseball bat. A pal of mine at the Washington Embassy brought it back for me.' He swung it around his head a couple of times. 'I'm thinking of raising an SS team. We could play the US Army. What do you think? Goebbels is keen. He thinks the American masses would respond well to the pictures.'

He leant the bat against the heavy wooden table and began unbuttoning his tunic.

'If you want my opinion, the original mistake was in 'thirty-six, when Himmler said every Kripo flat-foot in the Reich had to wear SS uniform. That's when we were landed with scum like you, and shrivelled-up old cunts like Artur Nebe.'

He handed his jacket to one of the two guards and began rolling up his sleeves. Suddenly he was shouting.

'My God, we used to know how to deal with people like you. But we've gone soft. It's not "Has he got guts?" any more, it's "Has he got a doctorate?" We didn't need doctorates in the East, in 'forty-one, when there was fifty degrees of frost and your piss froze in mid-air. You should have heard Krebs, March. You'd've loved it. Fuck it, I think he's one of your lot.' He adopted a mincing voice. ' "With permission, Herr Obergruppenführer, I would like to question the suspect first. I feel he may respond to a more subtle approach." Subtle, my arse. What's the point of you? If you were my dog, I'd feed you poison.'

'If I were your dog, I'd eat it.'

Globus grinned at one of the guards. 'Listen to the big man!' He spat on his hands and picked up the baseball bat. He turned to March. 'I've been looking at your file. I see you're a great one for writing. Forever taking notes, compiling lists. Quite the frustrated author. Tell me: are you left-handed or right-handed?'

'Left-handed.'

'Another lie. Put your right arm on the table.'

March felt as if iron bands had been fastened around his chest. He could barely breathe. 'Go screw yourself.'

Globus glanced at the guards and powerful hands seized March from behind. The chair toppled and he was being bent head first over the table. One of the SS men twisted his left arm high up his back, wrenched it, and March was roaring with the pain of that as the other man grabbed his free hand. The man half-climbed on to the table and planted his knee just below March's right elbow, pinning his forearm, palm down, to the wooden planks.

In seconds, everything was locked in place except his fingers, which were just able to flutter slightly, like a trapped bird.

Globus stood a metre from the table, brushing the tip of the bat lightly across March's knuckles. Then he lifted it, swung it in a great arc, like an axe, through three hundred degrees, and with all his force brought it smashing down.

HE did not faint, not at first. The guards let him go and he slid to his knees, a thread of spit dribbling from the corner of his mouth, leaving a snail's trail across the table. His arm was still stretched out. He stayed like that for a while, until he raised his head and saw the remains of his hand – some alien pile of blood and gristle on a butcher's slab – and then he fainted.

FOOTSTEPS in the darkness. Voices.

'Where is the woman?'

Kick.

'What was the information?'

Kick.

'What did you steal?'

Kick. Kick.

A jackboot stamped on his fingers, twisted, ground them into the stone.

WHEN he came to again he was lying in the corner, his broken hand resting on the floor next to him, like a still-born baby left beside its mother. A man – Krebs perhaps – was squatting in front of him, saying something. He tried to focus.

'What is this?' Krebs's mouth was saying. 'What does it mean?'

The Gestapo man was breathless, as if he had been running up and down stairs. With one hand he grasped March's chin, twisting his face to the light. In the other he held a sheaf of papers.

'What does it mean, March? They were hidden in the front of your car. Taped underneath the dashboard. What does it mean?'

March pulled his head away and turned his face to the darkening wall.

Tap, tap, tap. In his dreams. *Tap, tap, tap.*

SOME time later – he could not be more accurate than that, for time was beyond measurement, now speeding, now slowing to an infinitesimal crawl – a white jacket appeared above him. A flash of steel. A thin blade poised vertically before his eyes. March tried to back away but fingers locked around his wrist, the needle was jabbed into a vein. At first, when his hand was touched, he howled, but then he felt the fluid spreading through his veins and the agony subsided.

THE torture doctor was old and hunch-backed and it seemed to March, who brimmed with gratitude towards him, that he must have lived in the basement for many years. The grime had settled in his pores, the darkness hung in pouches beneath his eyes. He did not speak. He cleaned the wound, painted it with a clear liquid that smelled of hospitals and morgues, and bound it tightly in a white crepe bandage. Then, still without speaking, he and Krebs helped March to his feet. They put him back in his chair. An enamel mug of sweet, milky coffee was set on the table before him. A cigarette was slipped into his good hand.

FOUR

In his mind March had built a wall. Behind it he placed Charlie in her speeding car. It was a high wall, made of everything his imagination could collect – boulders, concrete blocks, burnt-out iron bedsteads, overturned tramcars, suitcases, prams – and it stretched in either direction across the sunlit German countryside like a postcard of the Great Wall of China. In front of it, he patrolled the ground. *He would not let them beyond the wall.* Everything else, they could have.

Krebs was reading March's notes. He sat with both elbows on the table, his chin resting on his knuckles. Occasionally he removed a hand to turn a page, replaced it, went on reading. March watched him. After his coffee and his cigarette and with the pain dulled he felt almost euphoric.

Krebs finished and momentarily closed his eyes. His complexion was white, as always. Then he straightened the pages and laid them in front of him, alongside March's notebook and Buhler's diary. He adjusted them by millimetres, into a line of parade-ground precision. Perhaps it was the effect of the drug, but suddenly March was seeing everything so clearly – how the ink on the cheap fibre pages had spread slightly, each letter sprouting minute hairs; how badly Krebs had shaved: that clump of black stubble in the fold of skin below his nose. In the silence he actually believed he could hear the dust falling, pattering across the table.

'Have you killed me, March?'

'Killed you?'

'With these.' Krebs's hand hovered a centimetre above the notes.

'It depends who knows you have them.'

'Only some cretin of an Unterscharführer who works in the garage. He found them when we brought in your car. He gave them directly to me. Globus doesn't know a thing – yet.'

'Then that is your answer.'

Krebs started rubbing his face vigorously, as if drying himself. He stopped, his hands pressed to his cheeks, and stared at March through his spread fingers. 'What is happening here?'

'You can read.'

'I can read, but I don't understand.' Krebs snatched up the pages and leafed through them. 'Here, for example – what is "Zyklon B"?'

'Crystallised hydrogen cyanide. Before that, they used carbon monoxide. Before that, bullets.'

'And here – "Auschwitz/Birkenau". "Kulmhof". "Belzec". "Treblinka". "Majdanek". "Sobibor".'

'The killing grounds.'

'These figures: eight thousand a day . . .'

'That's the total they could destroy at Auschwitz/ Birkenau using the four gas chambers and crematoria.'

'And this "eleven million"?'

'Eleven million is the total number of European Jews they were after. Maybe they succeeded. Who knows? I don't see many around, do you?'

'Here: the name "Globocnik" . . .'

'Globus was SS and Police Leader in Lublin. He built the killing centres.'

'I didn't know.' Krebs dropped the notes on the table as if they were contagious. 'I didn't know any of this.'

'Of course you knew! You knew every time someone made a joke about "going East", every time you heard a mother tell her child to behave or they'd go up the chimney. We knew when we moved into their houses,

357

when we took over their property, their jobs. We knew but we didn't have the facts.' He pointed to the notes with his left hand. 'Those put flesh on the bones. Put bones where there was just clear air.'

'I meant: I didn't know that Buhler, Stuckart and Luther were involved in this. I didn't know about Globus . . .'

'Sure. You just thought you were investigating an art robbery.'

'It's true! It's true,' repeated Krebs. 'Wednesday morning – can you remember back that far? – I was investigating corruption at the Deutsche Arbeitsfront: the sale of labour permits. Then, out of the blue, I am summoned to see the Reichsführer, one-to-one. He tells me retired civil servants have been discovered in a colossal art fraud. The potential embarrassment for the Party is huge. Obergruppenführer Globocnik is in charge. I am to go at once to Schwanenwerder and take my orders from him.'

'Why you?'

'Why not? The Reichsführer knows of my interest in art. We have spoken of these matters. My job was simply to catalogue the treasures.'

'But you must have realised that Globus killed Buhler and Stuckart?'

'Of course. I'm not an idiot. I know Globus's reputation as well as you. But Globus was acting on Heydrich's orders, and if Heydrich had decided to let him loose, to spare the Party a public scandal – who was I to object?'

'Who were you to object?' repeated March.

'Let's be clear, March. Are you saying their deaths had nothing to do with the fraud?'

'Nothing. The fraud was a coincidence that became a useful cover story, that's all.'

'But it made sense. It explained why Globus was acting as state executioner, and why he was desperate to head off an investigation by the Kripo. On Wednesday night I was still cataloguing the pictures on Schwanenwerder when he called in a rage – about you. Said you'd been officially taken off the case, but you'd broken in to Stuckart's apartment. I was to go and bring you in, which I did. And I tell you: if Globus had had his way, that would have been the end of you right there, but Nebe wouldn't have it. Then, on Friday night, we found what we thought was Luther's body in the railway yard, and that seemed to be the end of it.'

'When did you discover the corpse wasn't Luther's?'

'Around six on Saturday morning. Globus telephoned me at home. He said he had information Luther was still alive and was planning to meet the American journalist at nine.'

'He knew this,' asserted March, 'because of a tip-off from the American Embassy.'

Krebs snorted. 'What sort of crap is that? He knew because of a wire-tap.'

'That cannot be . . .'

'Why can't it be? See for yourself.' Krebs opened one of his folders and extracted a single sheet of flimsy brown paper. 'It was rushed over from the wire-tappers in Charlottenburg in the middle of the night.'

March read:

Forschungsamt   *Geheime Reichssache*
G745,275
23:51

MALE:	You say: What do I want? What do you think I want? Asylum in your country.
FEMALE:	Tell me where you are.
MALE:	I can pay.
FEMALE:	[Interrupts]
MALE:	I have information. Certain facts.
FEMALE:	Tell me where you are. I'll come and fetch you. We'll go to the Embassy.
MALE:	Too soon. Not yet.

FEMALE: When?
MALE: Tomorrow morning. Listen to me. Nine
            o'clock. The Great Hall. Central Steps. Have
            you got that?

Once more he could hear her voice; smell her; touch her.
In a recess of his mind, something stirred.

He slid the paper back across the table to Krebs, who returned it to the folder and resumed: 'What happened next, you know. Globus had Luther shot the instant he appeared – and, let me be honest, that shocked me. To do such a thing in a public place . . . I thought: this man is mad. Of course, I didn't know then quite why he was so anxious Luther shouldn't be taken alive.' He stopped abruptly, as if he had forgotten where he was, the role he was supposed to be playing. He finished quickly: 'We searched the body and found nothing. Then we came after you.'

March's hand had started to throb again. He looked down and saw crimson spots soaking through the white bandage.

'What time is it?'

'Five forty-seven.'

She had been gone almost eleven hours.

God, his hand . . . The specks of red were spreading, touching; forming archipelagos of blood.

'THERE were four of them in it altogether,' said March. 'Buhler, Stuckart, Luther and Kritzinger.'

'Kritzinger?' Krebs made a note.

'Friedrich Kritzinger, Ministerialdirektor of the Reich Chancellery. I wouldn't write any of this down if I were you.'

Krebs laid aside his pencil.

'What concerned them wasn't the extermination programme itself – these were senior Party men, remember – it was the lack of a proper Führer Order. Nothing was written down. All they had were verbal assurances from Heydrich and Himmler that this was what the Führer wanted. Could I have another cigarette?'

After Krebs had given him one, and he had taken a few sweet draughts, he went on: 'This is conjecture, you understand?' His interrogator nodded. 'I assume they asked themselves: why is there no direct written link between the Führer and this policy? And I assume their answer was: because it is so monstrous, the Head of State cannot be seen to be involved. So where did this leave them? It left them in the shit. Because if Germany lost the war, they could be tried as war criminals, and if Germany won it, they might one day be made the scapegoats for the greatest act of mass-murder in history.'

Krebs murmured: 'I am not sure I want to know this.'

'So they took out an insurance policy. They swore affidavits – that was easy: three of them were lawyers – and they removed documents whenever they could. And gradually they put together a documentary record. Either outcome was covered. If Germany won and action was taken against them, they could threaten to expose what they knew. If the Allies won, they could say: look, we opposed this policy and even risked our lives to collect information about it. Luther also added a touch of blackmail – embarrassing documents about the American Ambassador to London, Kennedy. Give me those.'

He nodded to his notebook and to Buhler's diary. Krebs hesitated, then slid them across the table.

It was difficult to open the notebook with only one hand. The bandage was sodden. He was smearing the pages.

'The camps were organised to make sure there were no witnesses. Special prisoners ran the gas chambers, the crematoria. Eventually, those special prisoners were themselves destroyed, replaced by others, who were also destroyed. And so on. If that could happen at the lowest level, why not the highest? Look. Fourteen people at the Wannsee conference. The first one dies in 'fifty-four. Another in 'fifty-five. Then one a year in 'fifty-seven, 'fifty-nine, 'sixty, 'sixty-one, 'sixty-two. Intruders probably planned to kill Luther in 'sixty-three, and he hired security guards. But time passed and nothing happened, so he assumed it was just a coincidence.'

'That's enough, March.'

'By 'sixty-three, it had started to accelerate. In May, Klopfer dies. In December, Hoffmann hangs himself. In March this year, Kritzinger is blown up by a car bomb. Now, Buhler is really frightened. Kritzinger is the trigger. He's the first of the group to die.'

March picked up the pocket diary.

'Here – you see – he marks the date of Kritzinger's death with a cross. But after that the days go by; nothing happens; perhaps they are safe. Then, on April the ninth – another cross! Buhler's old colleague from the General Government, Schöngarth, has slipped beneath the wheels of a U-bahn train in Zoo Station. Panic on Schwanenwerder! But by then it's too late . . .'

'I said: that's enough!'

'One question puzzled me: why were there eight deaths in the first nine years, followed by six deaths in just the last six months? Why the rush? Why this terrible risk, after the exercise of so much patience? But then, we policemen seldom lift our eyes from the mud to look at the broader picture, do we? Everything was supposed to be completed by last Tuesday, ready for the visit of our good new friends, the Americans. And that raises a further question –'

'Give me those!' Krebs pulled the diary and the notebook from March's grasp. Outside in the passage: Globus's voice . . .

' – Would Heydrich have done all this on his own initiative, or was he acting on orders from a higher level? Orders, perhaps, from the same person who would not put his signature to any document. . . ?'

Krebs had the stove open and was stuffing in the papers. For a moment they lay smouldering on the coals, then ignited into yellow flame as the key turned in the cell door.

FIVE

'Kulmhof!' he shouted at Globus when the pain became too bad. 'Belzec! Treblinka!'

'Now we're getting somewhere.' Globus grinned at his two assistants.

'Majdanek! Sobibor! Auschwitz/Birkenau!' He held up the names like a shield to ward off the blows.

'What am I supposed to do? Shrivel up and die?' Globus squatted on his haunches and grabbed March by the ears, twisting his face towards him. 'They're just names, March. There's nothing there any more, not even a brick. Nobody will ever believe it. And shall I tell you something? *Part of you can't believe it either.*' Globus spat in his face – a gobbet of greyish-yellow phlegm. 'That's how much the world will care.' He thrust him away, bouncing his head against the stone floor.

'Now. Again. Where's the girl?'

ime crawled on all fours, broken-backed. He was shivering. His teeth chattered like a clockwork toy. Other prisoners had been here years before him. In lieu of tombstones they had scratched on the cell's walls with splintered fingernails. 'J.F.G. 22.2.57'. 'Katja'. 'H.K. May 44'. Someone had got no further than half the letter 'E' before strength or time or will had run out on them. Yet still this urge to write . . .

None of the marks, he noticed, was more than a metre above the floor.

The pain in his hand was making him feverish. He had hallucinations. A dog ground his fingers between its jaws. He closed his eyes and wondered what time was doing now. When he had last asked Krebs it had been – what? – almost six. Then they had talked for perhaps another half-hour. After that there had been his second session with Globus – infinite. Now this stretch alone in his cell, slithering in and out of the light, tugged one way by exhaustion, the other by the dog.

The floor was warm to his cheek, the smooth stone dissolved.

HE dreamed of his father – his childhood dream – the stiff figure in the photograph come to life, waving from the deck of the ship as it pulled out of harbour, waving until he had dwindled to a stick-figure, until he disappeared. He dreamed of Jost, running on the spot, intoning his poetry in his solemn voice: 'You throw food to the beast in man/That it may grow . . .' He dreamed of Charlie.

But most often he dreamed he was back in Pili's bedroom

at that dreadful instant when he understood what the boy had done out of kindness – *kindness!* – when his arms were reaching for the door but his legs were trapped – and the window was exploding and rough hands were dragging at his shoulders . . .

THE jailer shook him awake.

'On your feet!'

He was curled up tight on his left side, foetus-like – his body raw, his joints welded. The guard's push awoke the dog and he was sick. There was nothing in him to bring up, but his stomach convulsed anyway, for old time's sake. The cell retreated a long way and came rushing back. He was pulled upright. The jailer swung a pair of handcuffs. Next to him stood Krebs, thank God, not Globus.

Krebs looked at him with distaste and said to the guard: 'You'd better put them on at the front.'

His wrists were locked before him, his cap was stuffed on his head, and he was marched, hunched forward, along the passage, up the steps, into the fresh air.

A cold night, and clear. The stars sprayed across the sky above the courtyard. The buildings and the cars were silver-edged in the moonlight. Krebs pushed him into the back seat of a Mercedes and climbed in after him. He nodded to the driver: 'Columbia House. Lock the doors.'

As the bolts slid home in the door beside him, March felt a flicker of relief.

'Don't raise your hopes,' said Krebs. 'The Obergruppen-führer is still waiting for you. We have more modern technology at Columbia, that's all.'

They pulled out through the gates, looking to any who saw them like two SS officers and their chauffeur. A guard saluted.

Columbia House was three kilometres south of Prinz-

Albrecht Strasse. The darkened government buildings quickly yielded to shabby office blocks and boarded-up warehouses. The area close to the prison had been scheduled for redevelopment in the nineteen-fifties, and here and there Speer's bulldozers had made destructive forays. But the money had run out before anything could be built to replace what they had knocked down. Now, overgrown patches of derelict land gleamed in the bluish light like the corners of old battlefields. In the dark side-streets between them dwelt the teeming colonies of East European gastarbeiter.

March was sitting stretched out, his head resting on the back of the leather seat, when Krebs suddenly leaned towards him and shouted: 'Oh, for fuck's sake!' He turned to the driver: 'He's pissing himself. Pull over here.'

The driver swore, and braked hard.

'Open the doors!'

Krebs got out, came round to March's side, and yanked him out. 'Quickly! We haven't got all night!' To the driver: 'One minute. Keep the engine running.'

Then March was being pushed – stumbling across rough stones, down an alley, into the doorway of a disused church, and Krebs was unlocking the handcuffs.

'You're a lucky man, March.'

'I don't understand . . .'

Krebs said: 'You've got a favourite uncle.'

Tap, tap, tap. From the darkness of the church. *Tap, tap, tap.*

'YOU should have come to me at once, my boy,' said Artur Nebe. 'You would have spared yourself such agony.' He brushed March's cheek with his fingertips. In the heavy shadows, March could not make out the detail of his face, only a pale blur.

'Take my pistol.' Krebs pressed the Luger into March's left hand. 'Take it! You tricked me. Got hold of my gun. Understand?'

He was dreaming, surely? But the pistol felt solid enough . . .

Nebe was still talking – a low, urgent voice. 'Oh March, March. Krebs came to me this evening – shocked! so shocked! – told me what you had. We all suspected it, of course, but never had the proof. Now you've got to get it out. For all our sakes. You've got to stop these bastards . . .'

Krebs interrupted: 'Forgive me, sir, our time is almost gone.' He pointed. 'Down there, March. Can you see? A car.'

Parked under a broken street lamp at the far end of the alley March could just see a low shape, could hear a motor running.

'What is this?' He looked from one man to the other.

'Walk to the car and get in. We've no more time. I count to ten, then I yell.'

'Don't fail us, March.' Nebe squeezed his cheek. 'Your uncle is an old man, but he hopes to live long enough to see those bastards hang. Go on. Get the papers out. Get them published. We're risking everything, giving you a chance. Take it. Go.'

Krebs said: 'I'm counting: one, two, three . . .'

March hesitated, started to walk, then broke into a loping run. The car door was opening. He looked back. Nebe had already disappeared into the dark. Krebs had cupped his hands to his mouth and was starting to shout.

March turned and struggled towards the waiting car where a familiar voice was calling: 'Zavi! Zavi!'

PART SEVEN

FÜHRERTAG

The railway to Krakau continues north-east past Auschwitz (348 kilometres from Vienna), an industrial town of 12,000 inhabitants, the former capital of the Piast Duchies of Auschwitz and Zator (Hotel Zator 20 bedrooms), whence a secondary railway runs via Skawina to Krakau (69 kilometres in three hours) . . .

Baedeker's *General Government*, 1943

idnight peals of bells rang out to welcome the day. Drivers whipped past, flashing their headlights, hammering their horns, leaving a smear of sound hanging over the road behind them. Factory hooters called to one another across Berlin, like stationary trains.

'My dear old friend, what have they done to you?'

Max Jaeger was trying to concentrate on driving, but every few seconds his head would swivel to the right, in horrified fascination, to the passenger seat beside him.

He kept repeating it: 'What have they done to you?'

March was in a daze, uncertain what was dream and what reality. He had his back half-turned and was staring out of the rear window. 'Where are we going, Max?'

'God alone knows. Where do you want to go?'

The road behind was clear. March carefully pulled himself round to look at Jaeger. 'Didn't Nebe tell you?'

'Nebe said *you'd* tell me.'

March looked away, at the buildings sliding by. He did not see them. He was thinking of Charlie in the hotel room in Waldshut. Awake, alone, waiting for him. There were still more than eight hours to go. He and Max would have the Autobahnen almost to themselves. They could probably make it.

'I was at the Markt,' Jaeger was saying. 'This was about nine. The telephone rings. It's Uncle Artur. "Sturmbannführer! How good a friend is Xavier March?" "There's nothing I wouldn't do," I said – by this time, the word was out about where you were. He said, very quietly: "All right, Sturmbannführer, we'll see how good a friend you are. Kreuzberg. Corner of Axmann-weg, north of the abandoned church. Wait from quarter to midnight to quarter past. And not a word to anyone or you'll be in a KZ by morning." That was it. He hung up.'

There was a sheen of sweat on Jaeger's forehead. He glanced from the road to March and back again. 'Fuck it, Zavi. I don't know what I'm doing. I'm scared. I'm heading south. Is that okay?'

'You're doing fine.'

'Aren't you glad to see me?' asked Jaeger.

'Very glad.'

March felt faint again. He twisted his body and wound down the window with his left hand. Above the sound of the wind and the tyres: a noise. What was it? He put his head out and looked up. He could not see it, but he could hear it overhead. The clatter of a helicopter. He closed the window.

He remembered the telephone transcript. *'What do I want? What do you think I want? Asylum in your country . . .'*

The car's dials and gauges shone a soft green in the darkness. The upholstery smelled of fresh leather.

He said: 'Where did you get the car, Max?' It was a Mercedes he saw: the latest model.

'From the pool at Werderscher Markt. A beauty, yes? She's got a full tank. We can go anywhere you want. Anywhere at all.'

March began to laugh then. Not very hard and not for very long because his aching ribs soon forced him to stop. 'Oh Max, Max,' he said, 'Nebe and Krebs are such good liars, and you're so lousy, I almost feel sorry for them, having to have you on their team.'

Jaeger stared ahead. 'They've pumped you full of drugs, Zavi. They've hurt you. You're confused, believe me.'

'If they'd picked any other driver but you, I might almost have fallen for it. But you . . . Tell me, Max: why is the road behind so empty? I suppose, if you're following a shiny new car that's packed with electronics and transmitting a signal, you needn't come closer than a kilometre. Especially if you can use a helicopter.'

'I risk my life,' whined Jaeger, 'and this is my reward.'

March had Krebs's Luger in his hand – his left hand, it was awkward to hold. Nevertheless he managed a convincing enough show of digging the barrel into the thick folds of Jaeger's neck. 'Krebs gave me his gun. To add that essential touch of authenticity. Not loaded, I'm sure. But do you want to take that risk? I think not. Keep your left hand on the wheel, Max, and your eyes on the road, and with your right hand give me your Luger. Very slowly.'

'You've gone mad.'

March increased the pressure. The barrel slid up the sweaty skin and came to rest just behind Jaeger's ear.

'All right, all right . . .'

Jaeger gave him the gun.

'Excellent. Now, I'm going to sit with this pointed at your fat belly, and if you try anything, Max – anything – I'll put a bullet in it. And if you have any doubts about that, just sit there and work it out. And you'll conclude I've got nothing to lose.'

'Zavi . . .'

'Shut up. Just keep driving on this road until we reach the outer Autobahn.'

He hoped Max could not see his hand trembling. He rested the gun in his lap. It was good, he reassured himself. Really good. It proved they had not picked her up. Nor had they discovered where she was. Because if they had managed either, they would never have resorted to this.

TWENTY-FIVE kilometres south of the city, the lights of the Autobahn looped across the darkness like a necklace.

Great slabs of yellow thrust out of the ground bearing in black the names of the Imperial cities: clockwise from Stettin, through Danzig, Königsberg, Minsk, Posen, Krakau, Kiev, Rostov, Odessa, Vienna; then up through Munich, Nuremberg, Stuttgart, Strasbourg, Frankfurt and Hanover to Hamburg.

At March's direction, they turned anti-clockwise. Twenty kilometres later, at the Friedersdorf intersection, they forked right.

Another sign: Liegnitz, Breslau, Kattowitz . . .

The stars arched. Little flecks of luminous cloud shone above the trees.

THE Mercedes flew down the slip road and joined the moonlit Autobahn. The road gleamed like a wide river. Behind them, sweeping round to follow, he pictured a dragon's tail of lights and guns.

He was the head. He was pulling them after him – away from her, along the empty highway towards the east.

ain and exhaustion stalked him. To keep awake he talked.

'I suppose,' he said, 'we have Krause to thank for this.'

Neither of them had spoken for almost an hour. The only sounds were the hum of the engine and the drumming of the wheels on the concrete road. Jaeger jumped at March's voice. 'Krause?'

'Krause mixed up the rotas, ordered me to Schwanenwerder instead of you.'

'Krause!' Jaeger scowled. His face was a stage demon's, painted green by the glow of the instrument panel. All the troubles in his life could be traced back to Krause!

'The Gestapo fixed it so you'd be on duty on Monday night, didn't they? What did they tell you? "There'll be a body in the Havel, Sturmbannführer. No hurry about identifying it. Lose the file for a few days . . ." '

Jaeger muttered: 'Something like that.'

'And then you overslept, and by the time you got to the Markt on Tuesday I'd taken over the case. Poor Max. Never could get up in the mornings. The Gestapo must have loved you. Whom were you dealing with?'

'Globocnik.'

'Globus himself!' March whistled. 'I bet you thought it was Christmas! What did he promise you, Max? Promotion? Transfer to the Sipo?'

'Fuck you, March.'

'So then you kept him informed of everything I was doing. When I told you Jost had seen Globus with the body at the lakeside, you passed it along and Jost disappeared. When I called you from Stuckart's apartment, you warned them where we were and we were arrested. They searched the woman's apartment the next morning because you told them she had something from Stuckart's safe. They left us together in Prinz-Albrecht Strasse so you could do their interrogation for them – '

Jaeger's right hand flashed across from the steering wheel and grabbed the gun barrel, twisting it up and away, but March's fingers were caught around the trigger and squeezed it.

The explosion in the enclosed space tore their eardrums. The car swerved across the Autobahn and up on to the grass strip separating the two carriageways and they were bouncing along the rough track. For an instant, March thought he had been hit, then he thought that Jaeger had been hit. But Jaeger had both hands on the wheel and was fighting to control the Mercedes and March still had the gun. Cold air was rushing into the car through a jagged hole in the roof.

Jaeger was laughing like a madman and saying something but March was still deaf from the shot. The car skidded off the grass and rejoined the Autobahn.

IN the shock of the blast, March had been thrown against his shattered hand and had almost blacked-out, but the stream of freezing air pummelled him back into consciousness. He had a frantic desire to finish his story – *I only knew for certain you'd betrayed me when Krebs showed me the wire-tap: I knew because you were the only person I'd told about the telephone kiosk in Bülow Strasse, how Stuckart called the girl* – but the wind whipped away his words. In any case, what did it matter?

In all this, the irony was Nightingale. The American had been an honest man; his closest friend, the traitor.

Jaeger was still grinning like a lunatic, talking to himself as he drove, the tears glistening on his plump cheeks.

*

JUST after five they pulled off the autobahn into an all-night filling station. Jaeger stayed in the car and told the attendant through the open window to fill the tank. March kept the Luger pressed to Jaeger's ribs, but the fight seemed to have gone out of him. He had dwindled. He was just a sack of flesh in a uniform.

The young man who operated the pumps looked at the hole in the roof and looked at them – two SS-Sturmbannführer in a brand-new Mercedes – bit his lip, and said nothing.

Through the line of trees separating the service area from the autobahn, March could see the occasional passing headlight. But of the cavalcade he knew was following them: no sign. He guessed they must have halted a kilometre back, to wait and see what he planned to do next.

WHEN they were back on the road, Jaeger said: 'I never meant any harm to come to you, Zavi.'

March, who had been thinking of Charlie, grunted.

'Globocnik is a police general, for God's sake. If he tells you: "Jaeger! Look the other way!" – you look the other way, right? I mean, that's the law, isn't it? We're police-men. We have to obey the law!'

Jaeger took his eyes off the road long enough to glance at March, who said nothing. He returned his attention to the Autobahn.

'Then, when he ordered me to tell him what you'd found out – what was I supposed to do?'

'You could have warned me.'

'Yes? And what would you have done? I know you: you'd have carried on anyway. And where would that have left me – me, and Hannelore and the kids? We're not all made to be heroes, Zavi. There have to be people like me, so people like you can look so clever.'

They were driving towards the dawn. Over the low wooded hills ahead of them was a pale glow, as if a distant city was on fire.

'Now I suppose they'll kill me, for allowing you to pull the gun on me. They'll say I let you do it. They'll shoot me. Jesus, it's a joke, isn't it?' He looked at March with wet eyes. 'It's a joke!'

'It's a joke,' said March.

IT was light by the time they crossed the Oder. The grey river stretched either side of the high steel bridge. A pair of barges crossed in the centre of the slow-moving water, and hooted a loud good morning to one another.

The Oder: Germany's natural frontier with Poland. Except there was no longer any frontier; there was no Poland.

March stared straight ahead. This was the road down which the Wehrmacht's Tenth Army had rolled in September 1939. In his mind, he saw again the old newsreels: the horse-drawn artillery, the Panzers, the marching troops . . . Victory had seemed so easy. How they had cheered!

There was an exit sign to Gleiwitz, the town where the war had started.

Jaeger was moaning. 'I'm shattered, Zavi. I can't drive much longer.'

March said, 'Not far now.'

HE thought of Globus. *'There's nothing there any more, not even a brick. Nobody will ever believe it. And shall I tell you something? Part of you can't believe it either.'* That had been his worst moment, because it was true.

A TOTENBURG – a Citadel of the Dead – stood on a bare hilltop not far from the road: four granite towers, fifty metres high, set in a square, enclosing a bronze obelisk. For a moment as they passed, the weak sun glinted on the metal, like a reflecting mirror. There were dozens of such tumuli between here and the Urals – imperishable memorials to the Germans who had died – were dying, would die – for the conquest of the East. Beyond Silesia, across the Steppes, the Autobahnen were built on ridges to keep them clear of the winter's snows – deserted highways ceaselessly swept by the wind . . .

THEY drove for another twenty kilometres, past the belching factory chimneys of Kattowitz, and then March told Jaeger to leave the Autobahn.

HE can see her in his mind.

She is checking out of the hotel. She says to the receptionist: 'You're sure there've been no messages?' The receptionist smiles. 'None, Fräulein.' She has asked a dozen times. A porter offers to help her with her luggage, but she refuses. She sits in the car overlooking the river, reading again the letter she found hidden in her case. 'Here is the key to the vault, my darling. Make sure she sees the light one day . . .' A minute passes. Another. Another. She keeps looking north, towards the direction from which he should come.

At last she checks her watch. Then she nods slowly, switches on the engine and turns right into the quiet road.

*

Now they were passing through industrialised countryside: brown fields bordered by straggling hedgerows; whitish grass; black slopes of coal waste; the wooden towers of old mineshafts with ghostly spinning wheels, like the skeletons of windmills.

'What a shit-hole,' said Jaeger. 'What happens here?'

The road ran beside a railway track, then crossed a river. Rafts of rubbery scum drifted along the banks. They were directly downwind of Kattowitz. The air stank of chemicals and coaldust. The sky here really was a sulphur-yellow, the sun an orange disc in the smog.

They dipped, went through a blackened railway bridge, then over a rail crossing. Close, now . . . March tried to remember Luther's crude sketch map.

They reached a junction. He hesitated.

'Turn right.'

Past corrugated iron sheds, scraps of trees, rattling over more steel tracks . . .

He recognised a disused rail line. 'Stop!'

Jaeger braked.

'This is it. You can turn off the engine.'

Such silence. Not even a birdcall.

Jaeger looked around with distaste at the narrow road, the barren fields, the distant trees. A wasteland. 'But we're in the middle of nowhere!'

'What time is it?'

'Just after nine.'

'Turn on the radio.'

'What is this? You want a little music? *The Merry Widow*?'

'Just turn it on.'

'Which channel?'

'The channel doesn't matter. If it's nine they'll all sound the same.'

Jaeger pressed a switch, turned a dial. A noise like an ocean breaking on a rocky shore. As he scanned the frequencies the noise was lost, came back, was lost and then came back at full strength: not the ocean, but a million human voices raised in acclamation.

'Take out your handcuffs, Max. That's it. Give me the key. Now attach yourself to the wheel. I'm sorry, Max.'

'Oh, Zavi . . .'

'*Here he comes!*' shouted the commentator. '*I can see him! Here he comes!*'

HE had been walking for a little over five minutes and had almost reached the birch woods when he heard the helicopter. He looked back a kilometre, past the waving grass, along the overgrown tracks. The Mercedes had been joined on the road by a dozen other cars. A line of black figures was starting towards him.

He turned and carried on walking.

SHE is pulling up at the border crossing – now. The swastika flag flaps over the customs post. The guard takes her passport. 'For what purpose are you leaving Germany, Fräulein?' 'To attend a friend's wedding. In Zürich.' He looks from the passport photograph to her face and back again, checks the dates on the visa. 'You are travelling alone?' 'My fiancé was supposed to be with me, but he's been delayed in Berlin. Doing his duty, officer. You know how it is.' Smiling, natural . . . That's it, my darling. Nobody can do this better than you.

HE had his eyes on the ground. There must be something.

*

ONE *guard questions her, another circles the car. 'What luggage are you carrying, please?' 'Just overnight clothes. And a wedding present.' She puts on a puzzled expression: 'Why? Is there a problem? Would you like me to unpack?' She starts to open the door . . . Oh, Charlie, don't overplay it. The guards exchange looks . . .*

AND then he saw it. Almost buried at the base of a sapling: a streak of red. He bent and picked it up, turned it over in his hand. The brick was pitted with yellow lichen, scorched by explosive, crumbling at the corners. But it was solid enough. It existed. He scraped at the lichen with his thumb and the carmine dust crusted beneath his fingernail like dried blood. As he stooped to replace it, he saw others, half-hidden in the pale grass – ten, twenty, a hundred . . .

A PRETTY *girl, a blonde, a fine day, a holiday . . . The guard checks the sheet again. It says here only that Berlin is anxious to trace an American, a brunette. 'No, Fräulein –' he gives her back her passport and winks at the other guard ' – a search will not be necessary.' The barrier lifts. 'Heil Hitler!' he says. 'Heil Hitler,' she replies.*

Go on, Charlie. Go on . . .

It is as if she hears him. She turns her head towards the East, towards him, to where the sun is fresh in the sky, and as the car moves forward she seems to dip her head in acknowledgement. Across the bridge: the white cross of Switzerland. The morning light glints on the Rhine . . .

SHE had got away. He looked up at the sun and he knew it – knew it for an absolute, certain fact.

'Stay where you are!'

The black shape of the helicopter flapped above him. Behind him, shouts – much closer now – metallic, robot-like commands: 'Drop your weapon!'

'Stay where you are!'

'Stay where you are!'

He took off his cap and threw it, sent it skimming across the grass the way his father used to skim flat stones across the sea. Then he tugged the gun from his waistband, checked to make sure it was loaded, and moved towards the silent trees.

AUTHOR'S NOTE

Many of the characters whose names are used in this novel actually existed. Their biographical details are correct up to 1942. Their subsequent fates, of course, were different.

Josef Buhler, State Secretary in the General Government, was condemned to death in Poland and executed in 1948.

Wilhelm Stuckart was arrested at the end of the war and spent four years in detention. He was released in 1949 and lived in West Berlin. In December 1953 he was killed in a car 'accident' near Hanover: the 'accident' was probably arranged by a vengeance squad hunting down those Nazi war criminals still at large.

Martin Luther attempted to oust the German Foreign Minister, Joachim von Ribbentrop, in a power struggle in 1943. He failed and was sent to Sachsenhausen concentration camp where he attempted suicide. He was released in 1945, shortly before the end of the war, and died in a local hospital of heart failure in May 1945.

Odilo Globocnik was captured by a British patrol at Weissensee, Carinthia, on 31 May 1945. He committed suicide by swallowing a cyanide capsule.

Reinhard Heydrich was assassinated in Prague by Czech agents in the summer of 1942.

Artur Nebe's fate, typically, is more mysterious. He is believed to have been involved in the July 1944 plot against Hitler, to have gone into hiding on an island in the Wannsee, and to have been betrayed by a rejected mistress. Officially, he was executed in Berlin on 21 March 1945. However, he is said subsequently to have been sighted in Italy and Ireland.

Those named as having attended the Wannsee Conference all did so. Alfred Meyer committed suicide in 1945. Roland Freisler was killed in an air raid in 1945. Friedrich Kritzinger died at liberty after a severe illness. Adolf Eichmann was executed by the Israelis in 1962. Karl Schöngarth was condemned to death by a British court in 1946. Otto Hoffmann was sentenced to 15 years' imprisonment by a US military court. Heinrich Müller went missing at the end of the war. The others continued to live, either in Germany or South America.

The following documents quoted in the text are authentic: Heydrich's invitation to the Wannsee Conference; Goering's order to Heydrich of 31 July 1941; the dispatches of the German Ambassador describing the comments of Joseph P. Kennedy; the order from the Auschwitz Central Construction Office; the railway timetable (abridged); the extracts from the Wannsee Conference Minutes; the memorandum on the use of prisoners' hair.

Where I have created documents, I have tried to do so on the basis of fact – for example, the Wannsee Conference *was* postponed, its minutes *were* written up in a much fuller form by Eichmann and subsequently edited by Heydrich; Hitler did – notoriously – avoid putting his name to anything like a direct order for the Final Solution, but almost certainly issued a verbal instruction in the summer of 1941.

The Berlin of this book is the Berlin that Albert Speer planned to build.

Leonardo da Vinci's portrait of Cecilia Gallerani was recovered from Germany at the end of the war and returned to Poland.